BLOOD SONG

The blade was a sliver of light in the shadows, a half crescent of steel, wielded with speed and skill, it should have taken his head off at the shoulders. He ducked it, going into a roll, feeling the wind rush as the sword bit the air above him, coming to his feet, forming the parry stance in the same movement, the sword blade clashing with his own. He whirled, going down on one knee, sword arm fully extended, his arm jarring as his blade met flesh, drawing a stifled shout of pain and brief rainfall spatter of blood on floor tiles. His attacker wore cotton garments of black, a mask over his face, soot smeared on the brows and eyelids. His eyes glared up at Vaelin from the floor as he clutched at the deep gash in his thigh, not in anger but in shocked surprise.

Vaelin killed him with a slash to the neck, left him writhing in a welter of arterial blood as he ran on, the fire in his chest now an inferno of pain, his vision blurring, losing focus, fixing on the Aspect's door, no more than a few feet away now. He stumbled, colliding with the wall, pushing himself onwards with an angry grunt of self reproach.

SAVE HER!

By Anthony Ryan

Raven's Shadow

Blood Song
Tower Lord
Queen of Fire

BLOOD SONG

A RAVEN'S SHADOW NOVEL

ANTHONY RYAN

www.orbitbooks.net

ORBIT

First published in Great Britain in 2013 by Orbit
This paperback edition published in 2014 by Orbit

5 7 9 11 12 10 8 6

Copyright © 2011 by Anthony Ryan

Maps by Anthony Ryan

Excerpt from *A Dance of Cloaks* by David Dalglish
Copyright © 2013 by David Dalglish

The moral right of the author has been asserted.

A CIP catalogue record for this book
is available from the British Library.

ISBN 978-0-356-50248-9

Printed and bound by CPI Group (UK) Ltd, Croydon, CR0 4YY

Papers used by Orbit are from well-managed forests
and other responsible sources.

MIX
Paper from
responsible sources
FSC® C104740

Orbit
An imprint of
Little, Brown Book Group
100 Victoria Embankment
London EC4Y 0DY

An Hachette UK Company
www.hachette.co.uk

www.orbitbooks.net

For Dad, who never let me give up

PACK ICE

NORTHERN REACHES

UNIFIED REALM

GREAT NORTHERN FOREST

LINNAR DOMINION

VELLAN PASS

FALLEN CITY

NORTH TOWERS

CARDURIN

RENFAEL

NILSAEL

ANDURIN

URLISH FOREST

FROSTPORT

THE GREYPEAKS

BRINEWASH RIVER

VARINSHOLD

MEANSHALL

HIGH KEEP

ASRAEL

WARNSCLAVE

MARTISHE FOREST

LAKE IHIL

CUMBRAEL

ALLTOR

SOUTH TOWER

MAELINSCOVE

MELDENEAN ISLANDS

ERINEAN SEA

LINESH

UNTESH

LEHLUN OASIS

THE BLOODY HILL

MARBELLIS

ALPIRAN EMPIRE

PART I

Raven's shadow
Sweeps across my heart,
Freezes the torrent of my tears.

—SEORDAH POEM, AUTHOR UNKNOWN

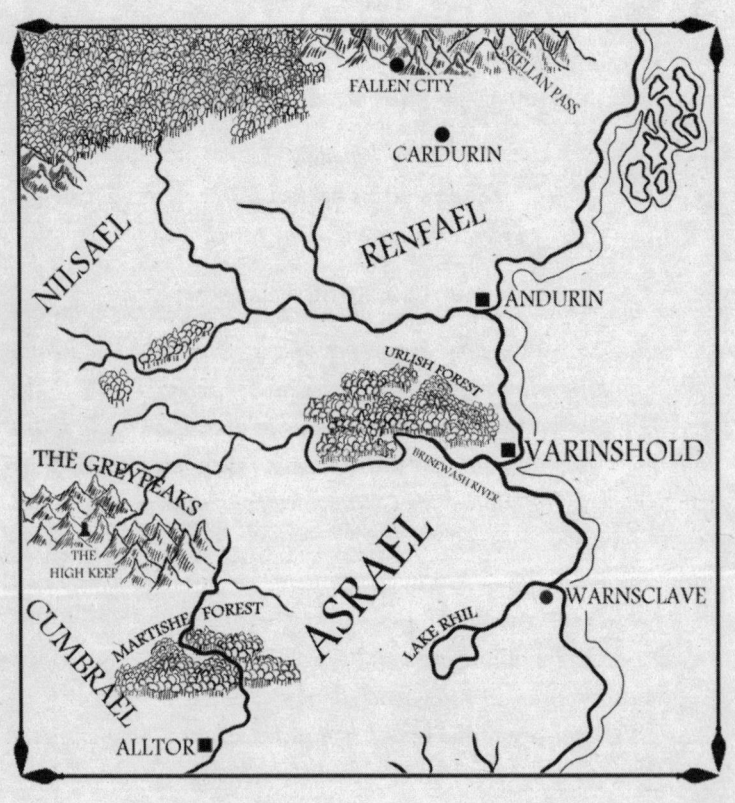

Verniers' Account

He had many names. Although yet to reach his thirtieth year, history had seen fit to bestow upon him titles aplenty: Sword of the Realm to the mad king who sent him to plague us, the Young Hawk to the men who followed him through the trials of war, Darkblade to his Cumbraelin enemies and, as I was to learn much later, Beral Shak Ur to the enigmatic tribes of the Great Northern Forest – the Shadow of the Raven.

But my people knew him by only one name and it was this that sang in my head continually the morning they brought him to the docks: Hope Killer. Soon you will die and I will see it. Hope Killer.

Although he was certainly taller than most men, I was surprised to find that, contrary to the tales I had heard, he was no giant, and whilst his features were strong they could hardly be called handsome. His frame was muscular but not possessed of the massive thews described so vividly by the storytellers. The only aspect of his appearance to match his legend was his eyes: black as jet and piercing as a hawk's. They said his eyes could strip a man's soul bare, that no secret could be hidden if he met your gaze. I had never believed it but seeing him now, I could see why others would.

The prisoner was accompanied by a full company of the Imperial

Guard, riding in close escort, lances ready, hard eyes scanning the watching crowd for trouble. The crowd, however, were silent. They stopped to stare at him as he rode through, but there were no shouts, no insults or missiles hurled. I recalled that they knew this man, for a brief time he had ruled their city and commanded a foreign army within its walls, yet I saw no hate in their faces, no desire for vengeance. Mostly they seemed curious. Why was he here? Why was he alive at all?

The company reined in on the wharf, the prisoner dismounting to be led to the waiting vessel. I put my notes away and rose from my resting place atop a spice barrel, nodding at the captain. 'Honour to you, sir.'

The captain, a veteran Guards officer with a pale scar running along his jawline and the ebony skin of the southern Empire, returned the nod with practised formality. 'Lord Verniers.'

'I trust you had an untroubled journey?'

The captain shrugged. 'A few threats here and there. Had to crack a few heads in Jesseria, the locals wanted to hang the Hope Killer's carcass from their temple spire.'

I bridled at the disloyalty. The Emperor's Edict had been read in all towns through which the prisoner would travel, its meaning plain: no harm will come to the Hope Killer. 'The Emperor will hear of it,' I said.

'As you wish, but it was a small matter.' He turned to the prisoner. 'Lord Verniers, I present the Imperial prisoner Vaelin Al Sorna.'

I nodded formally to the tall man, the name a steady refrain in my head. Hope Killer, Hope Killer . . . 'Honour to you, sir,' I forced the greeting out.

His black eyes met mine for a second, piercing, enquiring. For a moment I wondered if the more outlandish stories were true, if there was magic in the gaze of this savage. Could he truly strip the truth from a man's soul? Since the war, stories had abounded of the

Hope Killer's mysterious powers. He could talk to animals, command the Nameless and shape the weather to his will. His steel was tempered with the blood of fallen enemies and would never break in battle. And worst of all, he and his people worshipped the dead, communing with the shades of their forebears to conjure forth all manner of foulness. I gave little credence to such folly, reasoning that if the Northmen's magics were so powerful, how had they contrived to suffer such a crushing defeat at our hands?

'My lord.' Vaelin Al Sorna's voice was harsh and thickly accented, his Alpiran had been learned in a dungeon and his tones were no doubt coarsened by years of shouting above the clash of weapons and screams of the fallen to win victory in a hundred battles, one of which had cost me my closest friend and the future of this Empire.

I turned to the captain. 'Why is he shackled? The Emperor ordered he be treated with respect.'

'The people didn't like seeing him riding unfettered,' the captain explained. 'The prisoner suggested we shackle him to avoid trouble.' He moved to Al Sorna and unlocked the restraints. The big man massaged his wrists with scarred hands.

'My lord!' A shout from the crowd. I turned to see a portly man in a white robe hurrying towards us, face wet with unaccustomed exertion. 'A moment, please!'

The captain's hand inched closer to his sabre but Al Sorna was unconcerned, smiling as the portly man approached. 'Governor Aruan.'

The portly man halted, wiping sweat from his face with a lace scarf. In his left hand he carried a long bundle wrapped in cloth. He nodded at the captain and myself but addressed himself to the prisoner. 'My lord. I never thought to see you again. Are you well?'

'I am, Governor. And you?'

The portly man spread his right hand, lace scarf dangling from his thumb, jewelled rings on every finger. 'Governor no longer. Merely *a poor merchant these days. Trade is not what it was, but we make our way.'*

'Lord Verniers.' Vaelin Al Sorna gestured at me. 'This is Holus Nester Aruan, former Governor of the City of Linesh.'

'Honoured Sir.' Aruan greeted me with a short bow.

'Honoured Sir,' I replied formally. So this was the man from whom the Hope Killer had seized the city. Aruan's failure to take his own life in dishonour had been widely remarked upon in the aftermath of the war but the Emperor (Gods preserve him in his wisdom and mercy) had granted clemency in light of the extraordinary circumstances of the Hope Killer's occupation. Clemency, however, had not extended to a continuance of his Governorship.

Aruan turned back to Al Sorna. 'It pleases me to find you well. I wrote to the Emperor begging mercy.'

'I know, your letter was read at my trial.'

I knew from the trial records that Aruan's letter, written at no small risk to his life, had formed part of the evidence describing curiously uncharacteristic acts of generosity and mercy by the Hope Killer during the war. The Emperor had listened patiently to it all before ruling that the prisoner was on trial for his crimes, not his virtues.

'Your daughter is well?' the prisoner asked Aruan.

'Very, she weds this summer. A feckless son of a shipbuilder, but what can a poor father do? Thanks to you, at least she is alive to break my heart.'

'I am glad. About the wedding, not your broken heart. I can offer no gift except my best wishes.'

'Actually, my lord, I come with a gift of my own.'

Aruan lifted the long, cloth-covered bundle in both hands, presenting it to the Hope Killer with a strangely grave expression. 'I hear you will have need of this again soon.'

There was a definite hesitation in the Northman's demeanour

before he reached out to take the bundle, undoing the ties with his scarred hands. The cloth came away to reveal a sword of unfamiliar design, the scabbard-clad blade was a yard or so in the length and straight, unlike the curved sabres favoured by Alpiran soldiery. A single tine arched around the hilt to form a guard and the only ornamentation to the weapon was a plain steel pommel. The hilt and the scabbard bore many small nicks and scratches that spoke of years of hard use. This was no ceremonial weapon and I realised with a sickening rush that it was his sword. The sword he had carried to our shores. The sword that made him the Hope Killer.

'You kept that?' I sputtered at Aruan, appalled.

The portly man's expression grew cold as he turned to me. 'My honour demanded no less, my lord.'

'My thanks,' Al Sorna said, before any further outrage could spill from my lips. He hefted the sword and I saw the Guard Captain stiffen as Al Sorna drew the blade an inch or so from the scabbard, testing the edge with his thumb. 'Still sharp.'

'It's been well cared for. Oiled and sharpened regularly. I also have another small token.' Aruan extended his hand. In his palm sat a single ruby, a well-cut stone of medium weight, no doubt one of the more valued gems in the family collection. I knew the story behind Aruan's gratitude, but his evident regard for this savage and the sickening presence of the sword still irked me greatly.

Al Sorna seemed at a loss, shaking his head. 'Governor, I cannot . . .'

I moved closer, speaking softly. 'He does you a greater honour than you deserve, Northman. Refusing will insult him and dishonour you.'

He flicked his black eyes over me briefly before smiling at Aruan, 'I cannot refuse such generosity.' He took the gem. 'I'll keep it always.'

'I hope not,' Aruan responded with a laugh. 'A man only keeps a jewel when he has no need to sell it.'

'You there!' A voice came from the vessel moored a short distance along the quay, a sizeable Meldenean galley, the number of oars and the width of the hull showing it to be a freighter rather than one of their fabled warships. A stocky man with an extensive black beard, marked as the captain by the red scarf on his head, was waving from the bow. 'Bring the Hope Killer aboard, you Alpiran dogs!' he shouted with customary Meldenean civility. 'Any more dithering and we'll miss the tide.'

'Our passage to the Islands awaits,' I told the prisoner, gathering my possessions. 'We'd best avoid the ire of our captain.'

'So it's true then,' Aruan said. 'You go to the Islands to fight for the lady?' I found myself disliking the tone in his voice, it sounded uncomfortably like awe.

'It's true.' He clasped hands briefly with Aruan and nodded at the captain of his guard before turning to me. 'My lord. Shall we?'

'You may be one of the first in line to lick your Emperor's feet, scribbler' – the ship's captain stabbed a finger into my chest – 'but this ship is my kingdom. You berth here or you can spend the voyage roped to the mainmast.'

He had shown us to our quarters, a curtained-off section of the hold near the prow of the ship. The hold stank of brine, bilge water and the intermingled odour of the cargo, a sickly, cloying mélange of fruit, dried fish and the myriad spices for which the Empire was famous. It was all I could do to keep from gagging.

'I am Lord Verniers Alishe Someren, Imperial Chronicler, First of the Learned and honoured servant of the Emperor,' I responded, the handkerchief over my mouth muffling my words somewhat. 'I am emissary to the Ship Lords and official escort to the Imperial prisoner. You will treat me with respect, pirate, or I'll have twenty guardsmen aboard in a trice to flog you in front of your crew.'

The captain leaned closer; incredibly his breath smelt worse than the hold. 'Then I'll have twenty-one bodies to feed to the orcas when we leave the harbour, scribbler.'

Al Sorna prodded one of the bedrolls on the deck with his foot and glanced around briefly. 'This'll do. We'll need food and water.'

I bristled. 'You seriously suggest we sleep in this rat-hole? It's disgusting.'

'You should try a dungeon. Plenty of rats there too.' He turned to the captain. 'The water barrel is on the foredeck?'

The captain ran a stubby finger through the mass of his beard, contemplating the tall man, no doubt wondering if he was being mocked and calculating if he could kill him if he had to. They have a saying on the northern Alpiran coast: turn your back on a cobra but never a Meldenean. 'So you're the one who's going to cross swords with the Shield? They're offering twenty to one against you in Ildera. Think I should risk a copper on you? The Shield is the keenest blade in the Islands, can slice a fly in half with a sabre.'

'Such renown does him credit.' Vaelin Al Sorna smiled. 'The water barrel?'

'It's there. You can have one gourd a day each, no more. My crew won't go short for the likes of you two. You can get food from the galley, if you don't mind eating with scum like us.'

'No doubt I've eaten with worse. If you need an extra man at the oars, I am at your disposal.'

'Rowed before have you?'

'Once.'

The captain grunted, 'We'll manage.' He turned to go, muttering over his shoulder, 'We sail within the hour, stay out of the way until we clear the harbour.'

'Island savage!' I fumed, unpacking my belongings, laying out my quills and ink. I checked there were no rats lurking under my bedroll before sitting down to compose a letter to the Emperor. I intended to let him know the full extent of this insult. 'He'll find no berth in an Alpiran harbour again, mark you.'

Vaelin Al Sorna sat down, resting his back against the hull. 'You speak my language?' he asked, slipping into the Northern tongue.

'I study languages,' I replied in kind. 'I can speak the seven major tongues of the Empire fluently and communicate in five more.'

'Impressive. Do you know the Seordah language?'

I looked up from my parchment. 'Seordah?'

'The Seordah Sil of the Great Northern Forest. You've heard of them?'

'My knowledge of northern savages is far from comprehensive. As yet I see little reason to complete it.'

'For a learned man you seem happy with your ignorance.'

'I feel I speak for my entire nation when I say I wish we had all remained in ignorance of you.'

He tilted his head, studying me. 'That's hate in your voice.'

I ignored him, my quill moving rapidly over the parchment, setting out the formal opening for Imperial correspondence.

'You knew him, didn't you?' Vaelin Al Sorna went on.

My quill stopped. I refused to meet his eye.

'You knew the Hope.'

I put my quill aside and rose. Suddenly the stench of the hold and the proximity of this savage were unbearable. 'Yes, I knew him,' I grated. 'I knew him to be the best of us. I knew he would be the greatest Emperor this land has ever seen. But that's not the reason for my hate, Northman. I hate you because I knew the Hope as my friend, and you killed him.'

I stalked away, climbing the steps to the main deck, wishing for the first time in my life that I could be a warrior, that my arms were thick with muscle and my heart hard as stone, that I could wield a sword and take bloody vengeance. But such things were beyond me. My body was trim but not strong, my wits quick but not ruthless. I was no warrior. So there would be no vengeance for me. All I could do for my friend was witness the death of his killer and write the formal end to his story for the pleasure of my Emperor and the eternal truth of our archive.

I stayed on the deck for hours, leaning on the rail, watching the green-tinged waters of the north Alpiran coast deepen into the blue of the inner Erinean Sea as the ship's bosun beat the drum for the oarsmen and our journey began. Once clear of the coast the captain ordered the mainsail unfurled and our speed increased, the sharp prow of the vessel cutting through the gentle swell, the figurehead, a traditional Meldenean carving of the winged serpent, one of their innumerable sea gods, dipping its many-toothed head amidst a haze of spume. The oarsmen rowed for two hours before the bosun called a rest and they shipped oars, trooping off to their meal. The day watch stayed on deck, running the rigging and undertaking the never-ending chores of ship life. A few favoured me with a customary glare or two, but none attempted to converse, a mercy for which I was grateful.

We were several leagues from the harbour when they came into view, black fins knifing through the swell, heralded by a cheerful shout from the crow's nest. 'Orcas!'

I couldn't tell how many there were, they moved too fast and too fluidly through the sea, occasionally breaking the surface to spout a cloud of steam before diving below. It was only when they came closer that I fully realised their size, over twenty feet from nose to tail. I had seen dolphins before in the southern seas, silvery, playful creatures that could be taught simple tricks. These were different, their size and the dark, flickering shadows they traced through the water seemed ominous to me, threatening shades of nature's indifferent cruelty. My shipmates clearly felt differently, yelling greetings from the rigging as if hailing old friends. Even the captain's habitual scowl seemed to have softened somewhat.

One of the orcas broke the surface in a spectacular display of foam, twisting in midair before crashing into the sea with a boom that shook the ship. The Meldeneans roared their appreciation. Oh Seliesen, I thought. The poem you would have written to honour such a sight.

'They think of them as sacred.' I turned to find that the Hope Killer had joined me at the rail. 'They say when a Meldenean dies at sea the orcas will carry his spirit to the endless ocean beyond the edge of the world.'

'Superstition,' I sniffed.

'Your people have their gods, do they not?'

'My people do, I do not. Gods are a myth, a comforting story for children.'

'Such words would make you welcome in my homeland.'

'We are not in your homeland, Northman. Nor would I ever wish to be.'

Another orca rose from the sea, rising fully ten feet into the air before plunging back down. 'It's strange,' Al Sorna mused. 'When our ships came across this sea the orcas ignored them and made only for the Meldeneans. Perhaps they share the same belief.'

'Perhaps,' I said. 'Or perhaps they appreciate a free meal.' I nodded at the prow, where the captain was throwing salmon into the sea, the orcas swooping on them faster than I could follow.

'Why are you here, Lord Verniers?' Al Sorna asked. 'Why did the Emperor send you? You're no gaoler.'

'The Emperor graciously consented to my request to witness your upcoming duel. And to accompany the Lady Emeren home of course.'

'You came to see me die.'

'I came to write an account of this event for the Imperial Archive. I am the Imperial Chronicler after all.'

'So they told me. Gerish, my gaoler, was a great admirer of your history of the war with my people, considered it the finest work in

Alpiran literature. He knew a lot for a man who spends his life in a dungeon. He would sit outside my cell for hours reading out page after page, especially the battles, he liked those.'

'Accurate research is the key to the historian's art.'

'Then it's a pity you got it so wrong.'

Once again I found myself wishing for a warrior's strength. 'Wrong?'

'Very.'

'I see. Perhaps if you work your savage's brain, you could tell me which sections were so very wrong.'

'Oh, you got the small things right, mostly. Except you said my command was the Legion of the Wolf. In fact it was the Thirty-fifth Regiment of Foot, known amongst the Realm Guard as the Wolfrunners.'

'I'll be sure to rush out a revised edition on my return to the capital,' I said dryly.

He closed his eyes, remembering. '"King Janus's invasion of the northern coast was but the first step in pursuance of his greater ambition, the annexation of the entire Empire."'

It was a verbatim recitation. I was impressed by his memory, but was damned if I'd say so. 'A simple statement of fact. You came here to steal the Empire. Janus was a madman to think such a scheme could succeed.'

Al Sorna shook his head. 'We came for the northern coastal ports. Janus wanted the trade routes through the Erinean. And he was no madman. He was old and desperate, but not mad.'

I was surprised at the sympathy evident in his voice; Janus was the great betrayer after all, it was part of the Hope Killer's legend. 'And how do you know the man's mind so well?'

'He told me.'

'Told you?' I laughed. 'I wrote a thousand letters of enquiry to every ambassador and Realm official I could think of. The few who

bothered to reply all agreed on one thing: Janus never confided his plans to anyone, not even his family.'

'And yet you claim he wanted to conquer your whole Empire.'

'A reasonable deduction based on the available evidence.'

'Reasonable, maybe, but wrong. Janus had a king's heart, hard and cold when he needed it to be. But he wasn't greedy and he was no dreamer. He knew the Realm could never muster the men and treasure needed to conquer your Empire. We came for the ports. He said it was the only way we could secure our future.'

'Why would he confide such intelligence to you?'

'We had . . . an arrangement. He told me many things he would tell no other. Some of his commands required an explanation before I would obey them. But sometimes I think he just needed to talk to someone. Even kings get lonely.'

I felt a curious sense of seduction; the Northman knew I hungered for the information he could give me. My respect for him grew, as did my dislike. He was using me, he wanted me to write the story he had to tell. Quite why I had no idea. I knew it was something to do with Janus and the duel he would fight in the Islands. Perhaps he needed to unburden himself before his end, leave a legacy of truth so he would be known to history as more than just the Hope Killer. A final attempt to redeem both his spirit and that of his dead king.

I let the silence string out, watching the orcas until they had eaten their fill of free fish and departed to the east. Finally, as the sun began to dip towards the horizon and the shadows grew long, I said, 'So tell me.'

Chapter One

T he mist sat thick on the ground the morning Vaelin's father took him to the House of the Sixth Order. He rode in front, his hands grasping the saddle's pommel, enjoying the treat. His father rarely took him riding.

'Where do we go, my lord?' he had asked as his father led him to the stable.

The tall man said nothing but there was the briefest pause before he hoisted the saddle onto one of his chargers. Accustomed to his father's failure to respond to most questions, Vaelin thought nothing of it.

They rode away from the house, the charger's iron shoes clattering on the cobbles. After a while they passed through the north gate, where the bodies hung in cages from the gibbet and stained the air with the sick stench of decay. He had learned not to ask what they had done to earn such punishment, it was one of the few questions his father had always been willing to answer and the stories he told would leave Vaelin sweating and tearful in the night, whimpering at every noise beyond the window, wondering if the thieves or rebels or Dark-afflicted Deniers were coming for him.

The cobbles soon gave way to the turf beyond the walls, his father spurring the charger to a canter then a gallop, Vaelin laughing with excitement. He felt a momentary shame at his enjoyment. His mother had passed just two months previously and his father's sorrow was a black cloud that sat over the whole household, making servants fearful and callers rare. But Vaelin was only ten years old and had a child's view of death: he missed his mother but her passing was a mystery, the ultimate secret of the adult world, and although he cried, he didn't know why, and he still stole pastries from the cook and played with his wooden swords in the yard.

They galloped for several minutes before his father reined in, although to Vaelin it was all too brief, he wanted to gallop forever. They had stopped before a large, iron gate. The railings were tall, taller than three men set end to end, each topped with a wicked spike. At the apex of the gate's arch stood a figure made of iron, a warrior, sword held in front of his chest, pointing downwards, the face a withered skull. The walls on either side were almost as tall as the gate. To the left a brass bell hung from a wooden crossbeam.

Vaelin's father dismounted then lifted him from the saddle.

'What is this place, my lord?' he asked. His voice felt as loud as a shout although he spoke in a whisper. The silence and the mist made him uneasy, he didn't like the gate and the figure that sat atop it. He knew with a child's certainty that the blank eye sockets were a lie, a trick. It was watching them, waiting.

His father didn't reply. Walking over to the bell, he took his dagger from his belt and struck it with the pommel. The noise seemed like an outrage in the silence. Vaelin put his hands over his ears until it died away. When he looked up his father was standing over him.

'Vaelin,' he said in his coarse, warrior's voice. 'Do you remember the motto I taught you? Our family creed.'

'Yes, my lord.'

'Tell me.'

'"Loyalty is our strength."'

'Yes. Loyalty is our strength. Remember it. Remember that you are my son and that I want you to stay here. In this place you will learn many things, you will become a brother of the Sixth Order. But you will always be my son, and you will honour my wishes.'

There was a scrape of gravel beyond the gate and Vaelin started, seeing a tall, cloaked figure standing behind the railings. He had been waiting for them. His face was hidden by the mist but Vaelin squirmed in the knowledge of being studied, appraised. He looked up at his father, seeing a large, strong-featured man with a greying beard and deep lines in his face and forehead. There was something new in his expression, something Vaelin had never seen before and couldn't name. In later years he would see it in the faces of a thousand men and know it as an old friend: fear. It struck him that his father's eyes were unusually dark, much darker than his mother's. This was how he would remember him throughout his life. To others he was the Battle Lord, First Sword of the Realm, the hero of Beltrian, King's saviour and father of a famous son. To Vaelin he would always be a fearful man abandoning his son at the gate to the House of the Sixth Order.

He felt his father's large hand pressing against his back. 'Go now Vaelin. Go to him. He will not hurt you.'

Liar! Vaelin thought fiercely, his feet dragging on the soil as he was pushed towards the gate. The cloaked figure's face became clearer as they neared, long and narrow with thin lips and pale blue eyes. Vaelin found himself staring into them. The long-faced man stared back, ignoring his father.

'What is your name, boy?' The voice was soft, a sigh in the mist.

Why his voice didn't tremble Vaelin never knew. 'Vaelin, my lord. Vaelin Al Sorna.'

The thin lips formed a smile. 'I am not a lord, boy. I am Gainyl Arlyn, Aspect of the Sixth Order.'

Vaelin recalled his mother's many lessons in etiquette. 'My apologies, Aspect.'

There was a snort behind him. Vaelin turned to see his father riding away, the charger quickly swallowed by the mist, hooves drumming on the soft earth, fading to silence.

'He will not be coming back, Vaelin,' said the long-faced man, the Aspect, his smile gone. 'You know why he brought you here?'

'To learn many things and be a brother of the Sixth Order.'

'Yes. But no-one may enter except by his own choice, be he man or boy.'

A sudden desire to run, to escape into the mist. He would run away. He would find a band of outlaws to take him in, he would live in the forest, have many grand adventures and pretend himself an orphan . . . *Loyalty is our strength.*

The Aspect's gaze was impassive but Vaelin knew he could read every thought in his boy's head. He wondered later how many boys, dragged or tricked there by treacherous fathers, did run away, and if so, if they ever regretted it.

Loyalty is our strength.

'I wish to come in, please,' he told the Aspect. There were tears in his eyes but he blinked them away. 'I wish to learn many things.'

The Aspect reached out to unlock the gate. Vaelin noticed his hands bore many scars. He beckoned Vaelin inside as the gate swung open. 'Come, little Hawk. You are our brother now.'

Vaelin quickly realised that the House of the Sixth Order was not truly a house, it was a fortress. Granite walls rose like cliffs above him as the Aspect led him to the main gate. Dark figures patrolled the battlements, strongbows in hand, glancing down at him with blank, mist-shrouded eyes. The entrance was an arched doorway, portcullis raised to allow them entry, the two spearmen on guard, both senior students of seventeen, bowed in profound respect as the Aspect passed through. He barely acknowledged them, leading Vaelin through the courtyard, where other students swept straw from the cobbles and the ring of hammer on metal came from the blacksmith's shop. Vaelin had seen castles before, his father and mother had taken him to the King's palace once, trussed into his best clothes and wriggling in boredom as the Aspect of the First Order droned on about the greatness of the King's heart. But the King's palace was a brightly lit maze of statues and tapestries and clean, polished marble and soldiers with breastplates you could see your face in. The King's palace didn't smell of dung and smoke and have a hundred shadowed doorways, all no doubt harbouring dark secrets a boy shouldn't know.

'Tell me what you know of this Order, Vaelin,' the Aspect instructed, leading him on towards the main keep.

Vaelin recited from his mother's lessons: 'The Sixth Order wields the sword of justice and smites the enemies of the Faith and the Realm.'

'Very good.' The Aspect sounded surprised. 'You are well taught. But what is it that we do that the other Orders do not?'

Vaelin struggled for an answer until they passed into the keep and saw two boys, both about twelve, fighting with wooden swords, ash cracking together in a rapid exchange of thrust, parry and slash. The boys fought within a circle of white chalk; every time their struggle brought them close to the edge of the circle the instructor, a skeletal shaven-headed man, would lash them with a cane. They barely flinched from the blows, intent on their contest. One boy overextended a lunge and took a blow to the head. He reeled back, blood streaming from the wound, falling heavily across the circle to draw another blow from the instructor's cane.

'You fight,' Vaelin told the Aspect, the violence and the blood making his heart hammer in his chest.

'Yes.' The Aspect halted and looked down at him. 'We fight. We kill. We storm castle walls braving arrows and fire. We stand against the charge of horse and lance. We cut our way through the hedge of pike and spear to claim the standard of our enemy. The Sixth Order fights, but what does it fight for?'

'For the Realm.'

The Aspect crouched until their faces were level. 'Yes, the Realm, but what is more than the Realm?'

'The Faith?'

'You sound uncertain, little Hawk. Perhaps you are not as well taught as I believed.'

Behind him the instructor dragged the fallen boy to his feet amidst a shower of abuse. 'Clumsy, slack-witted, shit-eating oaf! Get back in there. Fall again and I'll make sure you never get up.'

'"The Faith is the sum of our history and our spirit,"' Vaelin recited. '"When we pass into the Beyond our essence joins with the souls of the Departed to lend us their guidance in this life. In return we give them honour and faith."'

The Aspect raised an eyebrow. 'You know the catechism well.'

'Yes, sir. My mother tutored me often.'

The Aspect's face clouded. 'Your mother . . .' He stopped, his expression switching back to the same emotionless mask. 'Your mother should not be mentioned again. Nor your father, or any other member of your family. You have no family now save the Order. You belong to the Order. You understand?'

The boy with the cut on his head had fallen again and was being beaten by the master, the cane rising and falling in regular, even strokes, the master's skull-like face betraying scant emotion. Vaelin had seen the same expression on his father's face when he took the strap to one of his hounds.

You belong to the Order. To his surprise his heart had slowed, and he felt no quaver in his voice when he answered the Aspect, 'I understand.'

The master's name was Sollis. He had lean, weathered features and the eyes of a goat: grey, cold and staring. He took one look at Vaelin, and asked, 'Do you know what carrion is?'

'No, sir.'

Master Sollis stepped closer, looming over him. Vaelin's heart still refused to beat any faster. The image of the skull-faced master swinging his cane at the boy on the floor of the keep had replaced his fear with a simmering anger.

'It's dead meat, boy,' Master Sollis told him. 'It's the flesh left on the battlefield to be eaten by crows and gnawed by rats. That's what awaits you, boy. Dead flesh.'

Vaelin said nothing. Sollis's goat eyes tried to bore into him but he knew they saw no fear. The master made him angry, not afraid.

There were ten other boys allocated to the same room, an attic in the north tower. They were all his age or close to it, some sniffling in loneliness and abandonment, others smiling continually with the novelty of parental separation. Sollis made them line up, lashing his cane at a beefy boy who was too slow. 'Move smartly, dung head.'

He eyed them individually, stepping closer to insult a few. 'Name?' he asked a tall, blond-haired boy.

'Nortah Al Sendahl, sir.'

'It's master not sir, shit-wit.' He moved down the line. 'Name?'

'Barkus Jeshua, Master,' the beefy boy he had caned replied.

'I see they still breed carthorses in Nilsael.'

And so on until he had insulted them all. Finally he stepped back to make a short speech: 'No doubt your families sent you here for their own reasons,' Sollis told them. 'They wanted you to be heroes, they wanted you to honour their name, they wanted to boast about you between swilling ale or whoring about town, or maybe they just wanted to be rid of a squalling brat. Well, forget them. If they wanted you, you wouldn't be here. You're ours now, you belong to the Order. You will learn to fight, you will kill the enemies of the Realm and the Faith until the day you die. Nothing else matters. Nothing else concerns you. You have no family, you have no dreams, you have no ambitions beyond the Order.'

He made them take the rough cotton sacks from their beds and run down the tower's numerous steps and across the courtyard to the stable, where they filled them with straw amidst a flurry of cane strokes. Vaelin was sure the cane fell on his back more than the others and suspected Sollis of forcing him towards the older, damper patches of straw. When the sacks were full he whipped them back up to the tower, where they placed them on the wooden frames that would serve as their beds. Then it was another run down to the vaults beneath the keep. He made them line up, breath steaming in the chill air, gasps echoing loudly. The vaults seemed vast, brick archways disappearing into the darkness on every side. Vaelin's fear began to rekindle as he stared into the shadows, bottomless and pregnant with menace.

'Eyes forward!' Sollis's cane left a welt on his arm and he choked down a pain-filled sob.

'New crop, Master Sollis?' a cheerful voice enquired. A very large man had appeared from the darkness, oil lamp flickering in his ham-sized fist. He was the first man Vaelin had seen who seemed broader than he was long. His girth was confined within a voluminous cloak, dark blue like the other masters', but with a single red rose embroidered on the breast. Master Sollis's cloak was bare of any decoration.

'Another sweeping of shit, Master Grealin,' he told the large man with an air of resignation.

Grealin's fleshy face formed a brief smile. 'How fortunate they are to have your guidance.'

There was a moment's silence and Vaelin sensed the tension between the two men, finding it noteworthy that Sollis spoke first. 'They need gear.'

'Of course.' Grealin moved closer to inspect them, he seemed strangely light of foot for such an enormous man, appearing to glide across the flagstones. 'Little warriors must be armed for the battles to come.' He still smiled but Vaelin noticed that his eyes showed no mirth as he scanned them. Once again he thought of his father, of the way he looked when they visited the horse traders' fair and one of the breeders tried to interest him in a charger. His father would walk around the animal, telling Vaelin how to spot the signs of a good warhorse, the thickness of muscle that indicated whether it would be strong in the melee but too slow in the charge, how the best mounts needed some spirit left after breaking. 'The eyes, Vaelin,' he told him. 'Look for a horse with a spark of fire in its eyes.'

Was that what Master Grealin was looking for now, fire in their eyes? Something to gauge who would last, how they would do in the charge or the melee.

Grealin paused next to a slightly built boy named Caenis, who had endured some of Sollis's worst insults. Grealin looked down at him intently, the boy shifting uncomfortably under the scrutiny. 'What's your name, little warrior?' Grealin asked him.

Caenis had to swallow before he could answer. 'Caenis Al Nysa, Master.'

'Al Nysa.' Grealin looked thoughtful. 'A noble family of some wealth, if memory serves. Lands in the south, allied by marriage to the House of Hurnish. You are a long way from home.'

'Yes, Master.'

'Well, fret not. You have a new home in the Order.' He patted Caenis on the shoulder three times, making the boy flinch a little. Sollis's cane had no doubt left him fearing even the gentlest touch. Grealin moved along the line, asking various questions of the boys, offering reassurances, all the while Master Sollis beat his cane against his booted calf, the *tack, tack, tack* of stick on leather echoing through the vaults.

'I think I know your name already, little warrior.' Grealin's bulk towered over Vaelin. 'Al Sorna. Your father and I fought together in the Meldenean war. A great man. You have his look.'

Vaelin saw the trap and didn't hesitate. 'I have no family, Master. Only the Order.'

'Ah, but the Order is a family, little warrior.' Grealin gave a short chuckle as he moved away. 'And Master Sollis and I are your uncles.' This made him laugh even more. Vaelin glanced at Sollis, now glaring at Grealin with undisguised hatred.

'Follow me, gallant little men!' Grealin called, his lamp raised above his head as he moved deeper into the vaults. 'Don't wander off, the rats don't like visitors, and some of them are bigger than you.' He chuckled again. Beside Vaelin, Caenis let out a short whimper, wide eyes staring into the fathomless blackness.

'Ignore him,' Vaelin whispered. 'There're no rats down here. The place is too clean, there's nothing for them to eat.' He wasn't at all sure it was true but it sounded vaguely encouraging.

'Shut your mouth, Sorna!' Sollis's cane snapped the air above his head. 'Get moving.'

They followed Master Grealin's lamp into the black emptiness of the vaults, footsteps and the fat man's laughter mingling to form a surreal echo punctuated by the occasional snap of Sollis's cane. Caenis's eyes darted about constantly, no doubt searching for giant rats. It seemed an age before they came to a solid oak door set into the rough brickwork. Grealin bade them wait as he unclasped his keys from his belt and unlocked the door.

'Now, little men,' he said, swinging the door open wide. 'Let us arm you for the battles to come.'

The room beyond the door seemed cavernous. Endless racks of swords, spears, bows, lances and a hundred other weapons glittered in the torchlight and barrel after barrel lined the walls along with uncountable sacks of flour and grain. 'My little domain,' Grealin told them. 'I am the Master of the Vaults and the keeper of the armoury. There is not a bean or an arrowhead in this store that I have not counted, twice. If you need anything, it is provided by me. And you answer to me if you lose it.' Vaelin noted that his smile had disappeared.

They lined up outside the storeroom as Grealin fetched their bundles, ten grey muslin sacks bulging with various items. 'These are the Order's gifts, little men,' Grealin told them brightly, moving along the line to deposit a sack at each boy's feet. 'Each of you will find the following in your bundle: one wooden sword of the Asraelin pattern, one hunting knife twelve inches in length, one pair of boots, two pairs of trews, two shirts of cotton, one cloak, one clasp, one purse, empty of course, and one of these . . .' Master Grealin held something up to the lantern, it shone in the glow, twisting gently on its chain. It was a medallion, a circle of silver inset with a figure Vaelin recognised as the skull-headed warrior that sat atop the gate outside the Order House. 'This is the sigil of our Order,' Master Grealin went on. 'It represents Saltroth Al Jenrial, first Aspect of the Order. Wear it always, when you sleep, when you wash, always. I'm sure Master Sollis has many punishments in mind for boys who forget to keep it on.'

Sollis kept quiet, the cane still tapping his boot said it all.

'My other gift is but a few words of advice,' Master Grealin continued. 'Life in the Order is harsh and often short. Many of you will be expelled before your final test, perhaps all of you, and those who win the right to stay with us will spend your lives patrolling distant frontiers, fighting endless wars against savages, outlaws or heretics during which you will most likely die if you are lucky or be maimed if you are not. Those few left alive after fifteen years' service will be given their own commands or return here to teach those who will replace you. This is the life to which your families have given you. It may not seem so, but it is an honour, cherish it, listen to your masters, learn what we can teach you and always hold true to the Faith. Remember these words and you will live long in the Order.' He smiled again, spreading his plump hands. 'That is all I can tell you, little warriors. Run along now, no doubt I'll see you all soon when you lose your precious gifts.' He chuckled again, disappearing into the storeroom, the echo of his laughter following them as Sollis's cane hounded them from the vaults.

The post was six feet tall and painted red at its top, blue in the middle and green at the base. There were about twenty of them, dotted around the practice field, silent witnesses to their torment. Sollis made them stand in front of a post and strike at the colours with their wooden swords as he called them out.

'Green! Red! Green! Blue! Red! Blue! Red! Green! Green . . .'

Vaelin's arm began to ache after the first few minutes but he kept swinging the wooden sword as hard as he could. Barkus had momentarily dropped his arm after a few swings, earning a salvo of cane strokes, robbing him of his habitual smile and leaving his forehead bloody.

'Red! Red! Blue! Green! Red! Blue! Blue . . .'

Vaelin found that the blow would jar his arm unless he angled the sword at the last instant, letting the blade slash across the post rather than thump into it. Sollis came to stand behind him, making his back itch in expectation of the cane. But Sollis just watched for a moment and grunted before moving off to punish Nortah for striking at the blue instead of the red. 'Open your ears, you foppish clown!' Nortah took the blow on his neck and blinked away tears as he continued to fight the post.

He kept them at it for hours, his cane a sharp counterpoint to the solid thwack of their swords against the posts. After a while he made them switch hands. 'A brother of the Order fights with both hands,' he told them. 'Losing a limb is no excuse for cowardice.'

After another interminable hour or more he told them to stop, making them line up as he swapped his cane for a wooden sword. Like theirs it was of the Asraelin pattern: a straight blade with a hand-and-a-half-long hilt and pommel and a thin, metal tine curving around the hilt to protect the fingers of the wielder. Vaelin knew about swords, his father had many hanging above the fire-place in the dining hall, tempting his boy's hands although he never dared touch them. Of course they were larger than these wooden toys, the blades a yard or more in length and worn with use, kept sharp but showing the irregular edge that came from the smith's stone grinding away the many nicks and dents a sword would accumulate on the battlefield. There was one sword that always drew his eye more than the others, hung high on the wall well out of his reach, its blade pointed down straight at his nose. It was a simple enough blade, Asraelin like most of the others, and lacking the finely wrought craftsmanship of some, but unlike them its blade was unrepaired, it was highly polished but every nick, scratch and dent had been left to disfigure the steel. Vaelin dared not ask his father about it so approached his mother but with only marginally less trepidation; he knew she hated his father's swords. He found her in the drawing room, reading as she often did. It was in the early days of her illness and her face had taken on a gauntness that Vaelin couldn't help but stare at. She smiled as he crept in, patted the seat next to her. She liked to show him her books, he would look at the pictures as she told him stories about the Faith and the Kingdom. He sat listening patiently to the tale of Kerlis the Faithless, cursed to the ever-death for denying the guidance of the Departed, until she paused long enough for him to ask: 'Mother, why does Father not repair his sword?'

She stopped in midpage, not looking at him. The silence stretched out and he wondered if she was going to adopt his father's practice of simply ignoring him. He was about to apologise and ask permission to leave when she said, 'It was the sword your father was given when he joined the King's army. He fought with it for many years during the birth of the Realm and when the war was done the King made him a Sword of the Realm, which is why you are called Vaelin Al Sorna and not just plain Vaelin Sorna. The marks on its blade are a history of how your father came to be who he is. And so he leaves it that way.'

'Wake up, Sorna!' Sollis's bark brought him back to the present with a start. 'You can be first, rat-face,' Sollis told Caenis, gesturing for the slight boy to stand a few feet in front of him. 'I will attack, you defend. We will be at this until one of you parries a blow.'

It seemed that he blurred then, moving too fast to follow, his sword extended in a lunge that caught Caenis squarely on the chest before he could raise his sword, sending him sprawling.

'Pathetic, Nysa,' Sollis told him curtly. 'You next, what's your name, Dentos.'

Dentos was a sharp-faced boy with lank hair and gangling limbs. He spoke with a thick west-Renfaelin brogue that Sollis found less than endearing. 'You fight as well as you speak,' he commented after the ash blade of his sword had cracked against

Dentos's ribs, leaving him winded on the ground. 'Jeshua, you're next.'

Barkus managed to dodge the first lightning lunge but his riposte failed to connect with the master's sword and he went down to a blow that swept his legs from under him.

The next two boys went down in quick succession as did Nortah, although he came close to side-stepping the thrust, which did nothing to impress Sollis. 'Have to do better than that.' He turned to Vaelin. 'Let's get it over with, Sorna.'

Vaelin took his position in front of Sollis and waited. Sollis's gaze met his, a cold stare that commanded his attention, the pale eyes *fixing* him . . . Vaelin didn't think, he simply acted, stepping to the side and bringing his sword up, the blade deflecting Sollis's lunge with a sharp crack.

Vaelin stepped back, sword ready for another blow. Trying to ignore the frozen silence of the others, concentrating on Master Sollis's next likely avenue of attack, an attack no doubt fuelled with the fury of humiliation. But no attack came. Master Sollis simply packed up his wooden sword and told them to gather their things and follow him to the dining hall. Vaelin watched him carefully as they walked across the practice ground and into the courtyard, searching for a sudden tension that could signal another swipe of the cane, but Sollis's dour demeanour remained unchanged. Vaelin found it hard to believe he would swallow the insult and vowed not to be taken unawares when the inevitable punishment came.

Mealtime proved to be something of a surprise. The hall was crowded with boys and the tumult of voices engaging in the habitual ridicule and gossip of youth. The tables were arranged according to age, the youngest boys near the doors, where they would enjoy the strongest draught, and the oldest at the far end next to the masters' table. There seemed to be about thirty masters altogether, hard-eyed, mostly silent men, many scarred, a few showing livid burns. One man, sitting at the end of the table quietly eating a plate of bread and cheese, appeared to have had his entire scalp seared away. Only Master Grealin seemed cheerful, laughing heartily, a drumstick gripped in his meaty fist. The other masters either ignored him or nodded politely at whatever witticism he had chosen to share.

Master Sollis led them to the table closest to the door and told them to sit down. There were other groups of boys about their own age already at table. They had arrived a few weeks earlier and been in training longer under other masters. Vaelin noted the sneering superiority some exhibited, the nudges and smirks, finding that he didn't like it at all.

'You may talk freely,' Sollis told them. 'Eat the food, don't throw it. You have an hour.' He leaned down, speaking softly to Vaelin. 'If you fight, don't break any bones.' With that he left to join the other masters.

The table was crammed with plates of roasted chicken, pies, fruit, bread, cheese, even cakes. The feast was a sharp contrast with the stark austerity Vaelin had seen so far. Only once before had he seen so much food in one place, at the King's palace, and then he had hardly been allowed to eat anything. They sat in silence for a moment, partly in awe at the amount of food on the table but mostly out of simple awkwardness; they were strangers after all.

'How did you do it?'

Vaelin looked up to find Barkus, the hefty Nilsaelin boy, addressing him over the mound of pastries between them. 'What?'

'How did you parry the blow?'

The other boys were looking at him intently, Nortah dabbing a napkin at the bloody lip Sollis had given him. He couldn't tell if they were jealous or resentful. 'His eyes,' he said, reaching for the water jug and pouring a measure into the plain tin goblet next to his plate.

'What about his eyes?' Dentos asked, he had taken a bread roll and was cramming pieces into his mouth, crumbs fountaining from his lips as he spoke. 'Ye tellin' us it was the Dark?'

Nortah laughed, so did Barkus, but the rest of the boys seemed chilled by the suggestion, except Caenis, who was concentrating on a modest portion of chicken and potatoes, apparently indifferent to the conversation.

Vaelin shifted in his seat, disliking the attention. 'He fixes you with his eyes,' he explained. 'He stares, you stare back, you're fixed, then he attacks while you're still wondering what he's planning. Don't look at his eyes, look at his feet and his sword.'

Barkus took a bite from an apple and grunted. 'He's right you know. I thought he was trying to hypnotise me.'

'What's hypnotise?' asked Dentos.

'It's looks like magic but really it's just a trick,' Barkus replied. 'At last year's Summertide Fair there was a man who could make people think they were pigs. He'd get them to root in the ground and oink and roll in shit.'

'How?'

'I don't know, some kind of trick. He'd wave a bauble in front of their eyes and talk quietly to them for a while, then they'd do whatever he said.'

'Do you think Master Sollis can do such things?' asked Jennis, the boy Sollis said looked like a donkey.

'Faith, who knows? I've heard the masters of the Orders know many Dark things, especially in the Sixth Order.' Barkus held up a drumstick appreciatively before taking a large bite. 'It seems that they know cookery as well. They make us sleep on straw and beat us every hour of the day, but they want to feed us well.'

'Yeh,' Dentos agreed. 'Like my Uncle Sim's dog.'

There was a puzzled silence. 'Your Uncle Sim's dog?' Nortah enquired.

Dentos nodded, chewing busily on a mouthful of pie. 'Growler. Best fightin' hound in the western counties. Ten victories 'fore he 'ad 'is throat torn out last winter. Uncle Sim loved that dog, 'ad four kids of 'is own, to three diff'rent women mind, but he loved that dog better'n any of 'em, feed Growler 'fore the kids he would. Best of stuff too, mind. Give the kids gruel and the dog beefsteak.' He chuckled wryly. 'Rotten old bastard.'

Nortah was unenlightened. 'What does it matter what some Renfaelin peasant feeds his dog?'

'So it would fight better,' Vaelin said. 'Good food builds strong muscles. That's why warhorses are fed best corn and oats and not set to grazing pasture.' He nodded at the food on the table. 'The better they feed us, the better we'll fight.' He met Nortah's eyes. 'And I don't think you should call him a peasant. We're all peasants here.'

Nortah stared back coldly. 'You have no right to lead, Al Sorna. You may be the Battle Lord's son . . .'

'I'm no-one's son and neither are you.' Vaelin took a bread roll, his stomach was growling. 'Not any more.'

They lapsed into silence, concentrating on the meal. After a while a fight broke out at one of the other tables, plates and food scattering amidst a flurry of fists and kicks. Some boys joined in right away, others stood by shouting encouragement, most simply stayed at their tables, some not even glancing up. The fight raged for a few minutes before one of the masters, the large man with the seared scalp, came over to break it up, swinging a hefty stick with grim efficiency. The boys who had been in the thick of the fight were checked for serious injury, blood mopped from noses and lips, and sent back to the table. One had been knocked unconscious and two boys were ordered to carry him to the infirmary. Before long the din of conversation returned to the hall as if nothing had happened.

'I wonder how many battles we'll be in,' Barkus said.

'Lots and lots,' Dentos responded. 'You 'eard what the fat master said.'

'They say war in the Realm is a thing of the past,' said Caenis. It was the first time he had spoken and he seemed wary of offering an opinion. 'Maybe there won't be any battles for us to fight.'

'There's always another war,' Vaelin said. It was something he had heard his mother say, actually she shouted it at his father during one of their arguments. It was before the last time his father went away, before she got sick. The King's Messenger had arrived in the morning with a sealed letter. After reading it, his father began to pack his weapons and ordered the groom to saddle his best charger. Vaelin's mother had cried and they went into her drawing room to argue out of Vaelin's sight. He couldn't hear his father's words, he spoke softly, soothingly. His mother would have none of it. 'Do not come to my bed when you return!' she spat. 'Your stench of blood sickens me.'

His father said something else, still maintaining the same soothing tone.

'You said that last time. And the time before that,' his mother replied. 'And you'll say it again. There's always another war.'

After a while she began to cry again and there was silence in the house before his father emerged, patted Vaelin briefly on the head and went out to mount his waiting horse. After his return, four long months later, Vaelin noted that his parents slept in separate rooms.

After the meal it was time for observance. The plates were cleared away and they sat in silence as the Aspect recited the articles of the Faith in a clear, ringing voice that filled the hall. Despite his dark mood, Vaelin found the Aspect's words oddly uplifting, making him think of his mother and the strength of her belief, which had never wavered throughout her long illness. He wondered briefly if he would have been sent here if she were still alive, and knew with absolute certainty she would never have allowed it.

When the Aspect had finished his recitation he told them to take a moment for private contemplation and offer thanks for their blessings to the Departed. Vaelin sent his love to his mother and asked her guidance for the trials to come, fighting tears as he did so.

The first rule of the Order seemed to be that the youngest boys got the worst chores. Accordingly, after observance Sollis trooped them to the stables, where they spent several foul hours mucking out the stalls. They then had to cart the dung over to the manure mounds in Master Smentil's gardens. He was a very tall man who seemed incapable of speech, directing them with frantic gestures of his earth-darkened hands and strange, guttural grunts, the varying pitch of which would indicate if they were doing something right or not. His communication with Sollis was different, consisting of intricate hand gestures that the master seemed to understand instantly. The gardens were large, covering at least two acres of the land outside the walls, comprising long, orderly rows of cabbages, turnips and other vegetables. He also kept a small orchard surrounded by a stone wall. It being late winter he was busily engaged in pruning and one of their chores was gathering up the pruned branches for use as kindling.

It was as they carried the baskets of kindling back to the main keep that Vaelin dared ask a question of Master Sollis. 'Why can't Master Smentil speak, Master?'

He was prepared for a caning but Sollis confined his rebuke

to a sharp glance. They trudged on in silence for a few moments before Sollis muttered, 'The Lonak cut his tongue out.'

Vaelin shivered involuntarily. He had heard of the Lonak, everyone had. At least one of the swords in his father's collection had been carried through a campaign against the Lonak. They were wild men of the mountains to the far north who loved to raid the farms and villages of Renfael, raping, stealing and killing with gleeful savagery. Some called them wolfmen because it was said they grew fur and teeth and ate the flesh of their enemies.

'How come he's still livin', Master?' Dentos enquired. 'My Uncle Tam fought agin the Lonak an' said they never let a man live once they got him captured.'

Sollis's glance at Dentos was markedly sharper than the one he had turned on Vaelin. 'He escaped. He is a brave and resourceful man and a credit to the Order. We've talked of this enough.' He lashed his cane against Nortah's legs. 'Pick your feet up, Sendahl.'

After chores it was more sword practice. This time Sollis would perform a series of moves they had to copy. If any of them got it wrong, he made them run full pelt around the practice ground. At first they seemed to make a mistake at every attempt and they did a lot of running, but eventually they got it right more than they got it wrong.

Sollis called an end when the sky began to darken and they returned to the dining hall for an evening meal of bread and milk. There was little talk; they were too tired. Barkus made a few jokes and Dentos told a story about another of his uncles but there was little interest. Following the meal Sollis forced them to run up the stairs to their room, then lined them up, panting, drained, exhausted.

'Your first day in the Order is over,' he told them. 'It is a rule of the Order that you can leave in the morning if you wish. It will only get harder from now on so think carefully.'

He left them there, panting in the candlelight, thinking of the morning.

'Do ye think they'll give us eggs for breakfast?' Dentos wondered.

Later, as Vaelin squirmed in his bed of straw, he found he couldn't sleep despite his exhaustion. Barkus was snoring but it wasn't this that kept him awake. His head was full of the enormity of the change in his life over the course of a single day. His father had given him away, pushed him into this place of beatings and lessons in death. It was clear his father hated him, he was a reminder of his dead wife best kept out of sight. Well he could hate too, hate was easy, hate would fuel him if his mother's love could not. *Loyalty is our strength.* He snorted a silent laugh of derision. *Let loyalty be your strength, Father. My hate for you will be mine.*

Someone was crying in the dark, shedding tears on his straw pillow. Was it Nortah? Dentos? Caenis? There was no way to tell. The sobs were a forlorn, deeply lonely counterpoint to the regular woodsaw rhythm of Barkus's snoring. Vaelin wanted to cry too, wanted to shed tears and wallow in self-pity, but the tears wouldn't come. He lay awake, restless, heart thumping so hard with alternating hatred and anger that he wondered if it would burst through his ribs. Panic made it beat even faster, sweat beaded his forehead and bathed his chest. It was terrible, unbearable, he had to get out, get away from this place . . .

'*Vaelin.*'

A voice. A word spoken in darkness. Clear and real and true. His racing heart slowed instantly as he sat up, eyes searching the shadowed room. There was no fear for he knew the voice. The voice of his mother. Her shade had come to him, come to offer comfort, come to save him.

She didn't come again, although he strained his ears for another hour, no further words were spoken. But he knew he had heard it. She had come.

He settled back into the needle discomfort of the mattress, tiredness finally overtaking him. The sobs had ceased and even Barkus's snores seemed softer. He drifted into a dreamless, untroubled sleep.

CHAPTER TWO

It was a year into his time in the Order when Vaelin first killed a man. A year of hard lessons imparted by hard masters, a year of punishing, unending routine. They woke at the fifth hour and began with the sword, hours of swinging their wooden blades at the posts on the practice ground, trying to fend off Master Sollis's attacks and copying the increasingly complicated sword scales he taught them. Vaelin continued to be most adept at parrying Sollis's blows but the master frequently found a way past his guard to send him bruised and frustrated to the dirt. The lesson of not allowing oneself to be fixed by his eyes had been well learned but Sollis knew many other tricks.

Feldrian was given over entirely to sword work but Ildrian was the day of the bow, when Master Checkrin, a muscular, softly spoken Nilsaelin, had them loosing arrows at the butts with their boy-sized strongbows. 'Rhythm, boys, it's all in the rhythm,' he told them. 'Notch, draw, loose . . . Notch, draw, loose . . .'

Vaelin found the bow a hard skill to master. The weapon was tough to draw and difficult to aim, leaving his fingertips raw from the bowstring and his arms aching with growing muscle. His arrows often sank into the edge of the target or missed altogether. He came to dread the day he would face the Test of the Bow, four arrows sunk into the bull's-eye at twenty paces in the time it took a dropped scarf to fall to the ground. It seemed an impossible feat.

Dentos quickly proved himself the best archer, his shafts rarely failing to find the bull's-eye. 'Done this before, eh boy?' Master Checkrin asked him.

'Aye, Master. My Uncle Drelt taught me, he used to poach the Fief Lord's deer till they cut his fingers off.'

To Vaelin's annoyance Nortah was second best, his arrows finding the bull with grating regularity. The tension between them had grown since the first meal, unleavened by the blond boy's arrogance. He sneered at the failings of the other boys, usually behind their backs, and spoke constantly of his family though none of the others did. Nortah spoke of his family's lands, their many houses, the days he had spent hunting and riding with his father, who he claimed was First Minister to the King. It was his father who had taught him the bow, a longbow of yew like the Cumbraelins used, not the composite horn and ash of their strongbows. Nortah thought the longbow a superior weapon, all things considered, his father swore by it. Nortah's father seemed to be a man of many opinions.

Oprian was the day of the staff, taught them by Master Haunlin, the burnt man Vaelin had first seen in the dining hall. They sparred with wooden staffs of about four feet in length, later they would be replaced with the five-foot pole-axe used by the Order when they fought en masse. Haunlin was a cheerful man, with a quick smile and a liking for song. He would often sing or chant as they practised, soldier's songs mostly and a few love ballads, sung with a strange precision and clarity that reminded Vaelin of the minstrel he had once seen in the King's palace.

He took to the staff quickly, liking the way it whistled when he swung it, the feel of it in his hands. At times he even preferred it to the sword, it was easier to handle and more solid somehow. His appreciation for the staff deepened when it became clear Nortah had no ability with it at all. His staff was often snapped out of his hands by an opponent's blow and he was ever sucking numbed fingers.

Kigrian was a day they quickly came to dread, as it meant service in the stables, hours spent shovelling dung, dodging iron-shod hooves and sharp teeth then cleaning the myriad pieces of tack that hung on the walls. Master Rensial was ruler of the stable and his liking for the cane made Master Sollis seem positively restrained. 'I said clean it, don't tickle it, lackwit!' he spat at Caenis, his cane leaving red wheals on the boy's neck as he tried to work polish into a stirrup. Whatever his harshness to the boys Rensial was all tenderness to his horses, speaking to them in soft whispers and lovingly brushing their hides. Vaelin's dislike of the man was tempered by the blankness he saw in his eyes. Master Rensial preferred horses to people, his hands twitched constantly and he often stopped in mid-tirade, wandering off mumbling under his breath. The eyes said it all: Master Rensial was mad.

Retrian was a favourite with most of the boys, the day when Master Hutril would teach them the ways of the wild. They were led on long treks through the woods and hills, learning which plants were safe to eat and which could be used as a poison to be smeared on arrowheads. They were taught to light fires without flint and trap rabbits and hares. They would lie for hours in the undergrowth, trying to remain hidden as Hutril hunted them down, usually within a few minutes. Vaelin was often second last to be found with Caenis remaining hidden longest. Of all the boys, even those who had grown up amongst woodland and fields, he proved the most adept in the outdoors, particularly in tracking. Sometimes they would stay in the forest overnight and it was always Caenis who brought in the first meal.

Master Hutril was one of the few masters who never used the cane but his punishments could be severe, once making Nortah and Vaelin run bare-arsed through a copse of nettles for bickering over how best to place a snare. He spoke with a quiet confidence and rarely used more words than he had to, seeming to prefer the sign language some of the masters used. It was similar to that used by tongueless Master Smentil when he communicated with Sollis, but less complex, designed for use when enemies or prey were near. Vaelin learned quickly, as did Barkus, but Caenis seemed to absorb it instantly, his slender fingers forming the intricate shapes with uncanny accuracy.

Despite his aptitude, Master Hutril seemed oddly distant from Caenis, his praise restrained, if expressed at all. Sometimes, during one of the overnight treks, Vaelin would catch Hutril staring at Caenis from across the camp, his expression unreadable in the firelight.

Heldrian was the hardest of days, hours of running around the practice ground with a heavy stone in each hand, freezing swims across the river, and hard lessons in unarmed combat under Master Intris, a compact but lightning-fast man with a broken nose and several missing teeth. He taught them the secrets of the kick and the punch, how to twist the fist at the last instant, how to raise the knee first then to extend the leg into a kick, how to block a blow, trip an opponent or throw one over your shoulder. Few boys enjoyed Heldrian, it left them too bruised and exhausted to appreciate the evening meal. Only Barkus liked it, his large frame best suited to soaking up the punishment, he seemed impervious to pain and none relished being partnered with him for the sparring.

Eltrian was supposedly a day of rest and observance but for the youngest boys it meant a round of tedious drudgery in the laundry or the kitchen. If they were lucky, they would be chosen to help Master Smentil in the gardens, which at least provided the chance at a stolen apple or two. In the evening there would be extra observance and catechism, this being the Faith's day, and a solid hour of silent contemplation, where they would sit, heads bowed, each lost in his own thoughts or succumbing to the over-powering need for sleep, which could be dangerous as any boy caught sleeping would earn the harshest beating and a night walking the walls with no cloak.

Vaelin's favourite part of each day was the hour before lights out. All the discipline would evaporate in a round of raucous banter and horseplay. Dentos would tell another story about his uncles, Barkus would make them laugh with a joke or an uncanny imitation of one of the masters, Caenis, normally given to silence, would tell one of the thousand or more old stories he knew whilst they practised their sign language or sword strokes. He found himself spending more time with Caenis than the others, the slight boy's reticence and intelligence a faint echo of his mother. For his part Caenis seemed surprised but gratified by the companionship. Vaelin suspected his life before the Order had been somewhat lonely as Caenis was clearly so unused to being with other boys, although neither of them talked of their lives before, unlike Nortah, who had never been able to shake the habit, despite angry responses from the others and the occasional beating from the masters. *You have no family but the Order.* Vaelin knew the truth of the Aspect's words now; they were becoming family, they had no-one but each other.

Their first test came in the month of Sunterin, nearly a year since Vaelin had been left at the gate: the Test of the Run. They had been told little about what it entailed except that each year this test saw more expulsions than any other. They were trooped out into the courtyard along with the other boys of similar age, about two hundred in all. They had been told to bring their bows, one quiver of arrows, hunting knife, water flask and nothing else.

The Aspect led them in a brief recitation of the Catechism of Faith before informing them of what to expect: 'The Test of the Run is where we discover who among you is truly fit to serve the Order. You have had the privilege of a year in service to the Faith, but in the Sixth Order privileges must be earned. You will be taken upriver by boat and left at different places on the bank. You must be back here by midnight tomorrow. Any who do not arrive in time will be allowed to keep their weapons and will be given three gold crowns.'

He nodded to the masters and left. Vaelin felt the fear and uncertainty about him but did not share it. He would pass the test, he had to, there was nowhere for him to go.

'To the riverbank at the run!' Sollis barked. 'No slacking. Pick your feet up, Sendahl, this isn't a shitting dance floor.'

Waiting at the riverside wharf were three barges, large, shallow-draught boats with black-painted hulls and red canvas sails. They were a common sight on the Corvien River estuary, running coal along the coast from the mines in the south to feed the myriad chimneys of Varinshold. Bargemen were a distinct group, wearing black scarves around their necks and a band of silver in their left ear, notorious drinkers and brawlers when not plying their trade. Many an Asraelin mother would warn a wayward daughter: 'Be a good girl or you'll wed no better than a bargeman.'

Sollis exchanged a few words with the master of their barge, a wiry man who glared suspiciously at the silent assembly of boys, handing him a purse of coin and barking at them to get aboard and muster in the centre of the deck. 'And don't touch anything, lack-brains!'

'I've never been to sea before,' Dentos commented as they sat down on the hard planks of the deck.

'This isn't the sea,' Nortah informed him. 'It's the river.'

'My Uncle Jimnos went to sea,' Dentos continued, ignoring Nortah as most of them did. 'Never came back. Me mam said he got eaten by a whale.'

'What's a whale?' asked Mikehl, a plump Renfaelin boy who had contrived to retain his excess weight despite months of hard exercise.

'It's a big animal that lives in the sea,' Caenis replied, he tended to know the answer to most questions. He gave Dentos a nudge. 'And it doesn't eat people. Your uncle was probably eaten by a shark, some of them grow as big as a whale.'

'How would you know?' Nortah sneered, as he usually did whenever Caenis offered an opinion. 'Ever seen one?'

'Yes.'

Nortah flushed and fell silent, scratching at a loose splinter on the deck with his hunting knife.

'When, Caenis?' Vaelin prompted his friend. 'When did you see the shark?'

Caenis smiled a little, something he did rarely. 'A year or so ago, in the Erinean. My . . . I was taken to sea once. There are many creatures that live in the sea, seals and orcas and more fish than you can count. And sharks, one of them came up to our ship. It was over thirty feet from tip to tail, one of the sailors said they feed on orcas and whales, people too if you're unlucky enough to be in the water when they're around. There are stories of them ramming ships to sink them and feed on the crew.'

Nortah snorted in derision but the others were clearly fascinated.

'Did you see pirates?' Dentos asked eagerly. 'They say the Erinean is thick with 'em.'

Caenis shook his head. 'No pirates. They don't bother Realm ships since the war.'

'Which war?' Barkus said.

'The Meldenean, the one Master Grealin talks about all the time. The King sent a fleet to burn the Meldeneans' biggest city, all the pirates in the Erinean are Meldeneans, so they learned to leave us alone.'

'Wouldn't it make more sense to burn their fleet?' Barkus wondered. 'That way there wouldn't be any pirates at all.'

'They can always build more ships,' Vaelin said. 'Burning a city leaves a memory, passed from parent to child. Makes sure they won't forget us.'

'Could've just killed them all,' Nortah suggested sullenly. 'No pirates, no piracy.'

Master Sollis's cane swept down from nowhere, catching him on the hand and making him release his knife, still embedded in the deck. 'I said don't touch anything, Sendahl.' His gaze swivelled to Caenis. 'Voyager are you, Nysa?'

Caenis bowed his head. 'Only once, Master.'

'Really? Where did you go on this adventure?'

'To the Wensel Isle. My – erm, one of the passengers had business there.'

Sollis grunted, bent down to prise Nortah's knife from the deck and tossed it to him. 'Sheath it, fop. You'll need a sharp blade before long.'

'Were you there, Master?' Vaelin asked him. He was the only one who dared ask Sollis anything, braving the risk of a caning. Sollis could be fierce or he could be informative. It was impossible to tell which until you asked the question. 'Were you there when the Meldenean city burned?'

Sollis's gaze flicked to him, pale eyes meeting his. There was a question in them, an inquisitiveness. For the first time Vaelin

realised Sollis thought he knew more than he did, thought his
father had told him stories of his many battles, that there was
an insult concealed in his questions.

'No,' Sollis replied. 'I was on the northern border then. I'm
sure Master Grealin will answer any questions you have about that
war.' He moved away to thrash another boy whose hand had
strayed too close to a coil of rope.

The barges sailed north, following the long arc of the river and
dashing any thought Vaelin had of simply following the riverbank
back to the Order House; it was too long a journey. If he wanted
to be back in time, it meant a trek through the forest. He eyed
the dark mass of trees warily. Although the lessons with Master
Hutril had made them familiar with the forest, the thought of a
blind journey through the woods was not pleasant. He knew how
easily a boy could be lost in amongst the trees, wandering in circles
for hours.

'Head south,' Caenis, whispering next to his ear. 'Away from
the North Star. Head south until you meet the riverbank, then
follow it until you come to the wharf. Then you have to swim the
river.'

Vaelin glanced at him and saw that Caenis was gazing blithely
up at the sky as if he hadn't spoken. Looking around at the bored
faces of his companions it was clear to Vaelin they hadn't heard the
advice. Caenis was helping him but not the others.

They began to drop the boys off after about three hours' sailing.
There was little ceremony to it, Sollis simply chose a boy at random
and told him to jump over the side and swim for shore. Dentos
was the first from their group to go.

'See you back at the House, Dentos,' Vaelin encouraged him.

Dentos, silent for once, smiled back weakly before hitching
his strongbow over his shoulder and vaulting over the rail into

the river. He swam to the bank quickly and paused to shake off the river water then disappeared into the trees with a brief wave. Barkus was next, theatrically balancing atop the rail before performing a backflip into the river. A few boys clapped appreciatively. Mikehl went next but not without some trepidation. 'I'm not sure I can swim that far, Master,' he stammered, staring down at the dark waters of the river.

'Then try to drown quietly,' Sollis said, tipping him over the rail. Mikehl made a loud splash and seemed to remain underwater for an age, it was with some relief they saw him surface a short distance away, sputtering and flailing before he regained his composure and began to swim towards the bank.

Caenis was next, accepting Vaelin's wish of good luck with a nod before jumping wordlessly over the rail. Nortah followed him shortly after. Controlling his evident fear with some effort, he said to Sollis, 'Master, if I don't return, I would like my father to know . . .'

'You don't have a father, Sendahl. Get in there.'

Nortah bit back an angry retort and hauled himself onto the rail, diving in after a second's hesitation.

'Sorna, your turn.'

Vaelin wondered if it was significant that he was last to go and would therefore have the longest distance to travel. He went to the rail, his bowstring tight against his chest, pulling the strap on his quiver taut so it wouldn't come adrift in the water. He put both hands on the rail and prepared to vault over.

'The others are not to be helped, Sorna,' Sollis told him. He had said nothing like this to the other boys. 'Get yourself back, let them worry about themselves.'

Vaelin frowned, 'Master?'

'You heard me. Whatever happens, it's their fate, not yours.' He jerked his head at the river. 'On your way.'

It was clear he would say nothing more so Vaelin took a firm grip of the rail and swung himself over, falling feetfirst into the water, enveloped instantly in the shocking coldness of it. He fought a moment's panic as his head went under then kicked for the surface. Breaking into the air, he dragged it into his lungs and struck out for the shore, which suddenly seemed a lot further away. By the time he struggled to his feet on the shingle bank the barges had passed him by and were well upstream. He thought he saw Master Sollis still at the rail, staring after him, but couldn't be sure.

He unhitched his bow and ran the string through his forefinger and thumb to wring the water out. Master Checkrin said a damp bowstring was as much use as a legless dog. He checked his arrows, making sure the water hadn't penetrated the waxed-leather seal on the quiver and made sure his knife was still at his side. He shook water from his hair as he scanned the trees, seeing only a mass of shadow and foliage. He knew he was facing south but would soon wander off course when night came. If he was to follow Caenis's advice, he would have to climb a tree or two to find the North Star, not something easily attempted in the dark.

Although grateful that the test took place in summer, he was starting to chill from the swim. Master Hutril had taught them that the best way to dry off without benefit of a fire was to run, the heat of the body would turn the water to steam. He set off at a steady run, trying not to sprint, knowing he would need his energy in the hours to come. He was soon embraced by the cool dark of the forest and found himself instinctively scanning the shadows, a habit he had acquired during the many hours of hunting and hiding. Master Hutril's words came back to him: *A smart enemy seeks the shadow and stays quiet.* Vaelin suppressed a shiver and ran on.

He ran for a solid hour, keeping a steady pace and ignoring

the growing ache in his legs. The river water was quickly replaced by sweat and his chill receded. He checked his direction with occasional glances at the sun and tried to fight the sensation of time passing quicker than it should. The thought of being pushed out of the gates with a handful of coins and nowhere to go was both terrifying and incomprehensible. He had a brief and equally nightmarish vision of turning up on his father's doorstep, pathetically clutching his coins and begging to be let in. He forced the image away and kept running.

He took a break after covering about five miles, perching on a log to drink from his flask and catch a breath. He wondered how his companions were faring, were they running like him or stumbling lost amongst the trees? *The others are not to be helped.* Was it a warning, or a threat? Certainly there were dangers in the forest but nothing to pose a serious threat to the boys of the Order, toughened by months of training.

He pondered for a short while, finding no answers, before stoppering his flask and rising, still scanning the shadows . . . He froze.

The wolf sat on its haunches ten short yards away, bright green eyes regarding him with silent curiosity. Its pelt was grey and silver, and it was very large. Vaelin had never been this close to a wolf before, his only glimpses vague loping shadows seen through the mists of the morning, a rare sight so close to the city. He was struck by the size of the animal, the power evident in the muscle beneath its fur. The wolf tilted its head as Vaelin returned his gaze. He felt no fear, Master Hutril had told them that stories of wolves stealing babies and savaging shepherd boys were myths. *Wolf'll leave you be if you leave him be,* he'd said. But still, the wolf was big, and its eyes . . .

The wolf sat, silent, still, a faint breeze ruffling the silver-grey mass of its fur, and Vaelin felt something new stir in his boy's heart. 'You're beautiful,' he told the wolf in a whisper.

It was gone in an instant, turning and leaping into the foliage quicker than he could follow. It barely made a sound.

He felt a rare smile on his lips and stored the memory of the wolf firmly in his head, knowing he would never forget it.

The forest was called the Urlish, a twenty-mile-thick and seventy-mile-long band of trees stretching from the northern walls of Varinshold to the foothills of the Renfaelin border. Some said the King had a love for the forest, that it had captured his soul somehow. It was forbidden to take a tree from the Urlish without a King's Command and only those families who had lived within its confines for three generations were allowed to remain. From his meagre knowledge of the Realm's history Vaelin knew war had come here once, a great battle between the Renfaelins and Asraelins raging amongst the trees for a day and a night. The Asraelins won and the Lord of Renfael had to bow the knee to King Janus, which was why his heirs were now called Fief Lords and had to give money and soldiers to the King whenever he wanted them. It was a story his mother told him when she had succumbed to his pestering for more information on his father's exploits. It was here that he had won the King's regard and been raised to Sword of the Realm. His mother was vague on the details, saying simply that his father was a great warrior and had been very brave.

He found himself sweeping his gaze across the forest floor as he ran, eyes searching for the glitter of metal, hoping to find some token from the battle, an arrowhead or perhaps a dagger or even a sword. He wondered if Sollis would let him keep any souvenirs and, thinking it unlikely, began to ponder the best hiding places on offer in the House . . .

Snap!

He ducked, rolled, came up on his feet, crouched behind the trunk of an oak, the whisper of the arrow's flight hissing through the ferns. The sound of a bowstring was an unmistakable warning for a boy like him. He calmed his pounding heart with effort and strained to listen for further signals.

Was it a hunter? Perhaps he had been mistaken for a deer. He discounted the thought instantly. He was no deer and any hunter could tell the difference. Someone had tried to kill him. He realised he had unhitched his bow and notched an arrow, all done instinctively. He rested his back against the trunk and waited, listening to the forest, letting it tell him who was coming for him. *Nature has a voice,* Hutril's words. *Learn to hear it and you'll never be lost and no man will ever take you unawares.*

He opened his ears to the voice of the forest, the sigh of the wind, the rustle of the leaves and the creak of the branches. No birdsong. It meant a predator was close. It could be one man, could be more. He waited for the telltale crack of a branch underfoot or the scrape of boot leather on soil but nothing came. If his enemy was on the move, he knew how to mask the sound. But he had other senses and the forest could tell him many things. He closed his eyes and inhaled softly through his nose. *Don't suck the air in like a pig at a trough,* Hutril had cautioned him once. *Give your nose time to sort the scent. Be patient.*

He let his nose do the work, tasting the mingled perfume of bluebells in bloom, rotting vegetation, animal droppings . . . and sweat. Man's sweat. The wind was coming from his left, carrying the scent. It was impossible to tell whether the bowman was waiting or moving.

It was the faintest sound, little more than a rustle of cloth, but to Vaelin it was a shout. He darted from behind the oak in a crouch, drawing and loosing the shaft in a single motion, before scooting back into cover, rewarded with a short grunt of pained surprise.

He lingered for the briefest second. *Stay or flee?* The

compulsion to run was strong, the dark embrace of the forest suddenly a welcome refuge. But he knew he couldn't. *The Order doesn't run*, Sollis had said.

He peered out from behind his oak, taking a second before he saw it, the gull-fletched shaft of his arrow sticking upright from the carpet of ferns about fifteen yards away. He notched another arrow and approached in a low crouch, eyes scanning constantly for other enemies, ears alive with the voice of the forest, nose twitching.

The man was dressed in dirty green trews and tunic, he had an ash bow clutched in his hand with a crow-feathered shaft notched in the string, a sword strapped across his back, a knife in his boot and Vaelin's arrow in his throat. He was quite dead. Stepping closer Vaelin saw the growing patch of blood spreading out from the neck wound, a lot of blood. *Caught the big vein*, Vaelin realised. *And I thought I was a poor archer*.

He laughed, high and shrill, then convulsed and vomited, collapsing to all fours and retching uncontrollably.

It was a few moments before the shock and nausea receded enough for him to think clearly. This man, this dead man, had tried to kill him. *Why?* He had never seen him before. Was he an outlaw? Some homeless footpad thinking he had found an easy victim in a lone boy?

He forced himself to look at the dead man again, noting the quality of his boots and the stitching on his clothes. He hesitated then lifted the dead man's right hand, lying slack on the bowstring. It was a bowman's hand: rough palms with calluses on the tips of the first two fingers. This man had made his living with the bow. Vaelin doubted any outlaw would be so practised, or so well dressed.

A sudden, sickening thought popped into his head: *Is it part of the test?*

For a moment he was almost convinced. What better way to weed out the chaff? Seed the forest with assassins and see who survived. *Think of all the gold coins they'd save.* But somehow he couldn't bring himself to believe it. The Order was brutal but not murderous.

Then why?

He shook his head. It was a mystery he wouldn't solve by staying here. Where there was one there could be more. He would get back to the Order House and ask Master Sollis for guidance . . . If he lived that long. He got shakily to his feet, spitting the last dregs of gorge from his mouth, taking a final look at the dead man and debating whether to take his sword or his knife but deciding it would be a mistake. For some reason he suspected it might be necessary to deny knowledge of the killing, which led him to briefly consider retrieving the arrow from the man's neck but he couldn't face the prospect of drawing the shaft from the flesh. Instead he contented himself with snipping off the fletching with his hunting knife, the gull feathers were a clear signal that the man had been killed by a member of the Order. He fought a fresh bout of nausea at the grinding sensation of the arrow as he grasped it and the wet, sucking sound it made as he sawed at the shaft. It was done quickly but seemed to take an age.

He pocketed the fletching and backed away from the corpse, scraping his boots on the soil to erase any tracks, before turning and resuming his run. His legs felt leaden and he stumbled several times before his body remembered the smooth, loping stride learned through months of training on the practice ground. The slack, lifeless features of the dead man flashed through his mind continually but he shook the image away, suppressing it ruthlessly. *He tried to kill me. I won't grieve for a man who would seek to murder a boy.* But he found he couldn't deafen himself to the words his mother had once shouted at his father: *Your stench of blood sickens me.*

Night seemed to fall in an instant, probably because he dreaded it. He found himself seeing bowmen lurking in every shadow, more than once he leapt for shelter from assassins which turned out to be bushes or tree stumps when he looked closer. He had rested only once since killing the assassin, a brief, feverish sip of water behind the broad trunk of a beech, his eyes darting about constantly for enemies. It felt safer to run, a moving target was harder to hit. But this vague sense of security evaporated when the darkness came, it was like running in a void where every step brought the threat of a painful fall. He had tripped twice, sprawling in a tangle of weapons and fear, before accepting that he would have to walk from now on.

The bearings he took from the North Star by finding the odd clearing or hauling himself up a tree trunk told him he was holding a steady course southward but how far he had come or the distance he still had to cover he couldn't tell. He peered ahead with increasing desperation, all the time hoping to glimpse the silver sheen of the river through the trees. It was when he had stopped to get another bearing that he saw the fire. A single flickering blob of orange in the black-blue mass of the forest.

Keep running. He almost followed the instinctive command, turning away and taking another stride towards the south, but stopped. None of the boys from the Order would light a fire during the test, they just didn't have time. It could be a coincidence, just some of the King's Foresters camped out for the night. But something made him doubt it, a murmur of wrongness in the back of his mind. It was a strange sensation, almost musical.

He turned around, unslinging his bow and notching an arrow, before beginning a cautious advance. He knew he was taking a risk, both in investigating the fire and indulging in a delay when his deadline for getting back to the House could not be far away. But he had to know.

The blob grew into a fire slowly, flickering red and gold in the infinite blackness. He stopped, opening himself to the song of the forest again, hunting through the nocturnal resonance until he caught them: voices. Male. Adult. Two men. Quarrelling.

He crept closer, using the hunter's walk taught by Master Hutril, lifting his foot a hair's breadth from the ground and sliding it forward and to the side before laying it down softly after tentatively checking the soil for any branches or twigs that could give him away in an instant. The voices became clearer as he closed on the camp, confirming his suspicions. Two men, engaged in bitter argument.

'. . . 'asn't stopped bleedin'!' a self-pitying whine, its owner as yet invisible. 'Look, it's gushing like a slit hog . . .'

'Stop fiddling with it then, shit brain!' an exasperated hiss. Vaelin could see this one, a stocky man seated to the right of the fire, the sight of the sword on his back and the bow propped close to his hand provoking an icy shiver. *No coincidence.* He had a sack open on the floor between his booted feet, studying its contents intently in between casting tired insults at his companion.

'Little bastard!' the unseen whiner continued, deaf to the admonishments of his stocky companion. 'Playing dead, vicious, sneaky little bastard.'

'You were warned they were tough,' the stocky man said. 'Should've put another iron-head in him to make sure before you got so close.'

'Got him square in the neck, didn't I? Should've been enough. I've seen grown men go down like a sack of spuds from a wound like that. Not that little shit though. Wish we'd kept him breathing a little longer . . .'

'You disgusting animal.' There was little venom in the stocky man's words. He was increasingly preoccupied with the contents of the sack, a frown creasing his broad forehead. 'Y'know, I'm still not sure it's him.'

Vaelin, fighting to keep his heart steady, shifted his gaze to the sack, noting the roundness of its contents and the dark wet stain on the lower half. A sudden, overpowering chill of realisation gripped him, fearing he would faint as the forest swayed around him and he fought down a gasp of horror, the sound undoubtedly an invite for a quick death.

'Lemme see,' the whiner said, moving into view for the first time. He was short, wiry with pointed features and a wispy beard on his bony chin. His left arm was cradled in his right, a bloodied bandage leaking continually through his spidery fingers. 'Gotta be him. Has to be.' He sounded desperate. 'You 'eard what the other one said.'

Other one? Vaelin strained to hear more, still sickened but his heart steadied by a growing anger.

'He gave me the shivers, he did,' the stocky man responded with a shudder. 'Wouldn't've trusted him if he'd told me the sky was blue.' He squinted at the sack again then reached inside, extracting the contents, holding it up by the hair, dripping, turning it to examine the slack, distorted features. Vaelin would have vomited again if there was anything left in his stomach. *Mikehl! They killed Mikehl.*

'Could be him,' the stocky man mused. 'Death'll change a face for sure. Just don't see much of a family resemblance.'

'Brak would know. Said he'd seen the boy before.' The whiner moved out of the firelight again. 'Where is he anyway? Should've been here by now.'

'Yeh,' the stocky man agreed, returning his trophy to the sack. 'Don't think he's gonna.'

Whiner was silent for a moment before muttering, 'Little Order shits.'

Brak . . . So he had a name. Vaelin wondered briefly if anyone would wear a mourning locket for Brak, if his widow or mother or brother would offer thanks for his life and the goodness and wisdom he had left behind. But as Brak was an assassin, a killer waiting in the woods to murder children, he doubted it. No-one would weep for Brak . . . as no-one would weep for these two. His fist tightened on the bow, bringing it up to draw a bead on the stocky man's throat. He would kill this one and wound the other, an arrow in the leg or the stomach would do it, then he would make him talk, then he would kill him too. *For Mikehl.*

Something growled in the forest, something hidden, something deadly.

Vaelin whirled, drawing the bow – too late, knocked flat by a hard mass of muscle, his bow gone from his hand. He scrabbled for his knife, instinctively kicking out as he did so, hitting nothing. There were screams as he surged to his feet, screams of pain and terror, something wet lashed across his face, stinging his eyes. He staggered, tasting the iron sting of blood, wiping frantically at his eyes, blearily focusing on the now-silent camp, seeing two yellow eyes gleaming in the firelight above a red-stained muzzle. The eyes met his, blinked once and the wolf was gone.

Random thoughts tumbled through his mind. *It tracked me . . . You're beautiful . . . Followed me here to kill these men . . . Beautiful wolf . . . They killed Mikehl . . . No family resemblance . . .*

STOP THAT!

He forced discipline on the torrent of thought, dragging air into his lungs, calming down enough to move closer to the camp. The stocky man lay on his back, hands reaching towards a throat that was no longer there, his face frozen in fear. The whiner had managed to run a few strides before being cut down. His head was twisted at a sharp angle to his shoulders. From the stench staining the air around him it was clear his fear had mastered him at the end. There was no sign of the wolf, just the whisper of undergrowth moving in the wind.

Reluctantly he turned to the sack still lying at the stocky man's feet. *What do I do for Mikehl?*

'Mikehl's dead,' Vaelin told Master Sollis, water dripping from his face. It had started to rain a few miles back and he was drenched as he laboured up the hill towards the gate, exhaustion and the shock of the events in the forest combining to leave him numb and incapable of more than the most basic words. 'Assassins in the forest.'

Sollis reached out to steady him as he swayed, his legs suddenly feeling too weak to keep him upright. 'How many?'

'Three. That I saw. Dead too.' He handed Sollis the fletching he had cut from his arrow.

Sollis asked Master Hutril to watch the gate and led Vaelin inside. Instead of taking him to the boys' room in the north tower he led him to his own quarters, a small room in the south-wall bastion. He built up the fire and told Vaelin to strip off his wet clothes, giving him a blanket to warm himself while fire began to lick at the logs in the hearth.

'Now,' he said, handing Vaelin a mug of warmed milk. 'Tell me what happened. Everything you can remember. Leave nothing out.'

So he told him of the wolf and the man he had killed and the whiner and the stocky man . . . and Mikehl.

'Where is it?'

'Master?'

'Mikehl's . . . remains.'

'I buried it.' Vaelin suppressed a violent shudder and drank more milk, the warmth burning his insides. 'Scraped the soil up with my knife. Couldn't think of anything else to do with it.'

Master Sollis nodded and stared at the fletching in his hand, his pale eyes unreadable. Vaelin glanced around the room, finding it less bare than he expected. Several weapons were set on the wall: a pole-axe, a long, iron-bladed spear, some kind of stone-headed club plus several daggers and knives of different patterns. Several books stood on the shelves, the lack of dust indicating Master Sollis hadn't placed them there for decoration. On the far wall there was some kind of tapestry fashioned from a goatskin stretched on a wooden frame, the hide adorned with a bizarre mix of stick figures and unfamiliar symbols.

'Lonak war banner,' Sollis said. Vaelin looked away, feeling like a spy. To his surprise Sollis went on. 'Lonak boy children become part of a war band from an early age. Each band has its own banner and every member swears a blood oath to die defending it.'

Vaelin rubbed a bead of water from his nose. 'What do the symbols mean, Master?'

'They list the band's battles, the heads they have taken, the honours granted them by their High Priestess. The Lonak have a passion for history. Children are punished if they cannot recite the saga of their clan. It's said they have one of the largest libraries in the world, although no outsider has ever seen it. They love their stories and will sit for hours around the campfire listening to the shamans. They especially like the heroic tales, stories of outnumbered war bands winning victory against the odds, brave lone warriors questing for lost talismans in the bowels of the earth . . . boys killing assassins in the forest with the aid of a wolf.'

Vaelin looked at him sharply. 'It's no story, Master.'

Sollis tossed another log on the fire, scattering sparks over the hearth. He prodded the logs with a poker, not looking at Vaelin as he spoke. 'The Lonak have no word for secret. Did you know that? To them everything is important, to be written down, recorded, told over and over. The Order has no such belief. We have fought battles that left more than a hundred corpses on the ground and not a word of it has ever been set down. The Order fights, but often it fights in shadow, without glory or reward. We have no banners.' He tossed Vaelin's fletching into the fire, the damp feathers hissed in the flame then curled and withered to nothing. 'Mikehl was taken by a bear, a rare sight in the Urlish but some still prowl the depths of the woods. You found the remains and reported it to me. Tomorrow Master Hutril will retrieve them and we will give our fallen brother to the fire and thank him for the gift of his life.'

Vaelin felt no shock, no surprise. It was obvious there was more here than he could know. 'Why did you warn me not to help the others, Master?'

Sollis stared into the fire for a while and Vaelin had decided he wasn't going to answer when he said, 'We sever our ties with our blood when we give ourselves to the Order. We understand this, outsiders do not. Sometimes the Order is no protection against the feuds that rage beyond our walls. We cannot always protect you. The others were not likely to be hunted.' His fist was white on the poker as he prodded the fire, his cheek muscles bulged with suppressed rage. 'I was wrong. Mikehl paid the price of my mistake.'

My father, Vaelin thought. *They sought my death to wound him. Whoever they are they know him not.*

'Master, what of the wolf? Why would a wolf seek to aid me?'

Master Sollis put the poker aside and rubbed his chin thoughtfully. 'That's a thing I don't understand. I've been many places and seen many things but a wolf killing men is not one of them, and killing without feeding.' He shook his head. 'Wolves don't do that. There is something else at work here. Something that touches the Dark.'

Vaelin's shivers intensified momentarily. *The Dark.* The servants in his father's house had used the phrase sometimes, usually in hushed tones when they thought no-one else could hear. It was something people said when things happened that shouldn't happen: children being born with the blood-sign discolouring their faces, dogs giving birth to cats and ships found adrift at sea with no crew. *Dark.*

'Two of your brothers made it back before you did,' Sollis said. 'You'd better go and tell them about Mikehl.'

This interview was clearly over. Sollis would tell him nothing else. It was obvious, and sad. Master Sollis was a man of many stories and much wisdom, he knew much more than the correct grip on a sword or the right angle to slash a blade at a man's eyes, but Vaelin suspected little of it was ever heard. He wanted to hear more of the Lonak and their war bands and their High Priestess, he wanted to know of the Dark, but Sollis's eyes were fixed on the fire, lost in thought, the way his father had looked so many times. So he got to his feet and said, 'Yes, Master.' He drained the rest of his warm milk and gathered the blanket around him, clutching his damp clothes as he moved to the door.

'Tell no-one, Sorna.' There was a note of command in Sollis's voice, the tone he used before he swung his cane. 'Confide in no-one. This is a secret that could mean your death.'

'Yes, Master,' Vaelin repeated. He went out into the chilled hallway and made his way to the north tower, huddled and shivering, the cold so intense he wondered if he would collapse before he made it up the steps, but the milk Master Sollis had given him left just enough warmth and sustenance to fuel his journey.

He found Dentos and Barkus in the room when he staggered

through the door, both slumped on their bunks, fatigue evident in their faces. Strangely they seemed enlivened by his arrival, both rising to greet him with backslaps and forced jokes.

'Can't find your way in the dark, eh?' Barkus laughed. 'Would've beaten this one back easily if I hadn't been caught by the current.'

'Current?' Vaelin asked, bemused by the warmth of their welcome.

'Crossed too early,' Barkus explained. 'Up near the narrows. I thought I was done I can tell you. Got washed up right opposite the gate but Dentos was already there.'

Vaelin dumped his clothes on his bunk and moved to the fire, bathing in the warmth. 'You were first, Dentos?'

'Aye. Was sure it would be Caenis but we've not seen him yet.'

Vaelin was surprised too; Caenis's woodcraft left them all to shame. Still he lacked Barkus's strength and Dentos's speed.

'At least we beat the other companies,' Barkus said, referring to the boys in other groups. 'None of them have turned up yet. Lazy bastards.'

'Yeh,' Dentos agreed. 'Passed a few of them on the way. Lost as a virgin in a brothel they were.'

Vaelin frowned. 'What's a brothel?'

The other two exchanged an amused glance and Barkus changed the subject. 'We smuggled some apples from the kitchen.' He pulled back his bedcovers to reveal his prizes. 'Pies too. We'll have us a feast when the others get here.' He lifted an apple to his mouth for a hearty bite. They had all become enthusiastic thieves, it was a universal habit, anything of the meanest value could be expected to disappear in short order if not securely hidden. The straw in their mattresses had long since been replaced with any stray piece of fabric or soft hide they could lay their hands on. Punishment for theft was often severe but bereft of any lectures on immorality or dishonesty and soon they came to realise that they were not being punished for stealing but for getting caught.

Barkus was their most prolific thief, especially when it came to food, closely followed by Mikehl, who specialised in clothing . . . *Mikehl*.

Vaelin stared into the fire, biting his lip, deciding how to phrase the lie. *It's a bad thing,* he decided. *It's a hard thing to lie to your friends.* 'Mikehl's dead,' he said finally. He couldn't think of a kinder way to say it and winced at the sudden silence. 'He . . . was taken by a bear. I – I found what was left.' Behind him he heard Barkus spit out his mouthful of apple. There was a rustle as Dentos sank heavily onto his bunk. Vaelin gritted his teeth and went on, 'Master Hutril will bring the body back tomorrow so we can give him to the fire.' A log cracked in the fireplace. The chill was almost gone and the heat was starting to make his skin itch. 'So we can give thanks for his life.'

Nothing was said. He thought Dentos might be crying but didn't have the heart to turn and see for sure. After a while he moved away from the fire and went to his bunk, laying his clothes out to dry, unstringing his bow and stowing his quiver.

The door opened and Nortah entered, rain-soaked but triumphant. 'Fourth!' he exulted. 'I was sure I'd be last.' Vaelin hadn't seen him cheerful before, it was disconcerting. As was Nortah's ignorance of their evident grief.

'I even got lost twice.' He laughed, dumping his gear on his bunk. 'Saw a wolf too.' He went to the fire, hands splayed to soak up the heat. 'So scared I couldn't move.'

'You saw a wolf?' Vaelin asked.

'Oh yes. Big bastard. Think he'd already fed though. There was blood on his snout.'

'What kind of bear?' Dentos asked.

'What?'

'Was it a black or a brown? Browns are bigger and nastier. Blacks don't come near men mostly.'

'Wasn't a bear,' Nortah said, puzzled. 'A wolf I said.'

'I don't know,' Vaelin told Dentos. 'I didn't see it.'

'Then how d'y'know it was a bear?'

'Mikehl got taken by a bear,' Barkus told Nortah.

'Claw marks,' Vaelin said, realising deceit was more difficult than he had imagined. 'He was . . . in bits.'

'Bits!' Nortah exclaimed in disgust. 'Mikehl was in bits?!'

''Cos my uncle said y'don't get browns in the Urlish,' Dentos said dully. 'Only get 'em in the north.'

'I bet it was that wolf I saw,' Nortah whispered in shock. 'The wolf I saw ate Mikehl. It would've eaten me if it hadn't been full.'

'Wolves don't eat people,' Dentos said.

'Maybe it was rabid.' He sank onto his bunk in shock. 'I was nearly eaten by a rabid wolf!'

And so it went, the other boys arrived one by one, tired and wet but relieved at having passed the test, their smiles fading when they heard the news. Dentos and Nortah argued over wolves and bears and Barkus shared out his meagre spoils to be eaten in numb silence. Vaelin wrapped himself in his blanket and tried to forget the sight of Mikehl's slack, lifeless features and the feel of dead flesh through the fabric of the sack as he scraped a shallow grave in the dirt . . .

He woke shuddering with cold a few hours later. The last vestiges of a dream fled from his mind as his eyes grew accustomed to the dark. He was grateful the dream had slipped away, the few images lingering in his mind told him it was best forgotten. The other boys were asleep, Barkus snoring, softly for once, the logs in the fireplace blackened and smouldering. He stumbled out of bed to relight the fire, the darkness of the room suddenly scared him more than the gloom of the forest.

'There are no more logs, brother.'

He turned to find Caenis sitting on his bunk. He was still

dressed, his clothes glistening with damp in the dim moonlight seeping through the shutters. His face was hidden in shadow.

'When did you get in?' Vaelin asked, rubbing feeling back into his hands. He never knew a body could get so cold.

'A while ago.' Caenis's voice was a vacant drone, drained of emotion.

'You heard about Mikehl?' Vaelin began to pace about, hoping to walk some warmth back into his muscles.

'Yes,' Caenis replied. 'Nortah said it was a wolf. Dentos said a bear.'

Vaelin frowned, detecting a note of humour in his brother's voice. He shrugged it off. They all reacted differently. Jennis, Mikehl's closest friend, had actually laughed when they told him, a full hearty laugh that went on and on, in fact he laughed so much Barkus had to slap him before he stopped.

'A bear,' Vaelin said.

'Really?' Vaelin was sure Caenis hadn't moved, but he fancied there was a quizzical incline to his head. 'Dentos said you found him. That must have been bad.'

Mikehl's blood was thick, clotting in the sack, seeping through the weave to stain his hands . . . 'I thought you'd be here when I got in.' Vaelin wrapped his blanket more firmly around his shoulders. 'I bet Barkus an afternoon in the garden you'd beat us all back.'

'Oh, I would have. But I was distracted. I happened across a mystery in the forest. Perhaps you could help me puzzle it out. Tell me, what do you make of a dead man with an arrow in his throat? An arrow with no fletching?'

Vaelin's shudders became almost uncontrollable, his flesh trembling so much his blanket slipped to the floor. 'The woods are thick with outlaws, I hear,' he stammered.

'Indeed. So thick I found two more. Not killed with arrows

though, mayhap they were taken by a bear, like Mikehl. Perhaps even the same bear.'

'P-perhaps.' *What is this?* Vaelin held up his hand, staring at the twitching fingers. *This is not cold. This is more . . .* He had a sudden, almost irresistible impulse to tell Caenis everything, unburden himself, seek solace in confidence. Caenis was his friend after all. His best friend. Who better to tell? With assassins hunting him he would need a friend to watch his back. They would fight them together . . .

Confide in no-one . . . This is a secret that could mean your death. Sollis's words stilled his tongue, firming his resolve. Caenis was his friend it was true, but he couldn't tell him the truth. It was too big, too important for a whispered secret between boys.

He found his shivers receding as his resolve grew. It really wasn't that cold. The fear and horror of his night in the forest had left a mark on him, a mark that might never fade, but he would face it and overcome it. There was no other choice.

He retrieved his blanket from the floor and climbed back into his bunk. 'Truly the Urlish is a dangerous place,' he said. 'You better get those clothes off, brother. Master Sollis'll whip you raw if you're too chilled to train tomorrow.'

Caenis sat in unmoving silence, a thin sigh escaping his lips in a slow hiss. After a second he rose to undress, laying out his garments with his habitual neatness, carefully stowing his weapons before slipping into bed.

Vaelin lay back and prayed for sleep to take him, dreams and all. He longed for this night to be over, to feel the warmth of the dawn's light, searing away all the blood and fear that crowded his soul. *Is this a warrior's lot?* he wondered. *A life lived shivering in the shadows?*

Caenis's voice was barely a whisper but Vaelin heard him clearly.

'I'm glad you're alive, brother. I'm glad you made it through the forest.'

Comradeship, he realised. *Also a warrior's lot. You share your life with those who would die for you.* It didn't make the fear and the sick, hard feeling in his guts disappear, but it did take the edge off his sorrow. 'I'm glad you made it too, Caenis,' he whispered back. 'Sorry I couldn't help with your mystery. You should talk to Master Sollis.'

He never knew if it was a laugh or a sigh that came from Caenis then. Many years later he would think how much pain he would have saved himself and so many others if only he had heard it clearly, if he had known one way or the other. At the time he took it for a sigh and the words that followed a simple statement of obvious fact, 'Oh, I think there'll be mysteries aplenty in our future.'

They built the pyre on the practice ground, cutting logs from the forest and piling them up under Master Sollis's direction. They had been excused training for the day but the work was hard enough, Vaelin found his muscles aching after hours of heaving freshly cut timber onto the wagon for transport back to the House but resisted the temptation to voice a complaint. Mikehl deserved a day's work at least. Master Hutril returned early in the afternoon, leading a pony laden with a tightly bound burden. As he passed by on his way to the gate they paused in their labour, staring at the cloth-wrapped body.

This will happen again, Vaelin realised. *Mikehl is just the first. Who'll be next? Dentos? Caenis? Me?*

'We should've asked him,' Nortah said, after Master Hutril disappeared through the gate.

'Asked him what?' said Dentos.

'If it was a wolf or a be—' He ducked, narrowly avoiding the log Barkus threw at him.

The masters laid the body on the pyre as the boys paraded onto the practice ground in the early evening, over four hundred in all, standing silently in their companies. After Sollis and Hutril stepped down the Aspect came forward, a flaming torch held aloft in his bony, scarred hand. He stood next to the pyre and scanned the assembled students, his face was as lacking in expression as ever. 'We come to witness the end of the vessel that carried our fallen brother through his life,' he said, again displaying the uncanny ability to project his somnolent tones for the whole crowd to hear.

'We come to give thanks for his deeds of kindness and courage, and forgiveness for his moments of weakness. He was our brother and fell in service to the Order, an honour that comes to us all in the end. He is with the Departed now, his spirit will join with them to guide us in our service to the Faith. Think of him now, offer your own thanks and forgiveness, remember him, now and always.'

He lowered the torch to the pyre, touching the flames to the apple-wood kindling they had worked into the gaps between the logs. Soon the fire began to build, flames and smoke rising, the sweet apple scent lost amidst the stench of burning flesh.

Watching the flames, Vaelin tried to remember Mikehl's deeds of kindness and courage, hoping for a memory of nobility or compassion he could carry through his life, but instead found himself stuck on the time Mikehl had conspired with Barkus to put pepper into one of the feed bags in the stable. Master Rensial had fitted it over the muzzle of a newly acquired stallion and narrowly escaped being kicked to death amidst a shower of horse snot. Was that courage? Certainly the punishment had been severe, although both Mikehl and Barkus swore the beatings were worth it and Master Rensial's confused mind had soon let the incident slip into the cloudy morass of his memory.

He watched the flames rise and consume the mutilated flesh and bone that had once been his friend and thought: *I'm sorry, Mikehl. I'm sorry you died because of me. I'm sorry I wasn't there to save you. If I can, one day I will find who sent those men into the forest and they will pay for your life. My thanks go with you.*

He looked around to see that most of the other boys had drifted away, gone to the evening meal, but his group was still there, even Nortah, although he looked more bored than sorrowful. Jennis was crying softly, hugging himself, tears streaming down his face.

Caenis laid a hand on Vaelin's shoulder. 'We should eat. Our brother is gone.'

Vaelin nodded. 'I was thinking about the time in the stables. Remember? The feed bag.'

Caenis grinned a little. 'I remember. I was jealous I hadn't thought of it.' They walked back to the dining hall, Jennis being dragged along by Barkus, still crying, the others exchanging memories about Mikehl as the fire burned on behind them, taking his body away. In the morning they found that the remnants had been cleared, leaving only a circle of black ash to scar the grass. In the months and years that followed even that would fade.

CHAPTER THREE

The days came and went, they trained, they fought, they learned. Summer became autumn and then winter descended with driving rain and biting winds that soon gave way to the blizzards common to Asrael in the month of Ollanasur. After the pyre, Mikehl's name was rarely mentioned, they never forgot him but they didn't talk about him, he was gone. Watching a new batch of recruits march through the gates in early winter, they had the odd sensation of no longer being the youngest, suddenly the worst chores would be someone else's burden. Looking at the newcomers, Vaelin wondered if he had ever looked so young and alone. He wasn't a child any more, he knew this, none of them were. They were different, changed. They were not like other boys. And his difference ran deeper than the others, he was a killer.

Ever since the forest his sleep had been troubled and he was often left sweating and shivering in the dark by dreams in which Mikehl's slack, lifeless face came to ask why he hadn't saved him. Sometimes it was the wolf that came, silent, staring, licking blood from its muzzle, its eyes holding a question Vaelin couldn't fathom. Even the faces of the assassins, bloodied and torn, would come to spit hate-filled accusations that would rend him from sleep shouting unrepentant defiance: 'Murderers! Scum! I hope you rot!'

'Vaelin?' It was usually Caenis he woke, some of the others too, but usually Caenis.

Vaelin would lie, say it was a dream of his mother, fighting the guilt of using her memory to hide the truth. They would talk for a while until Vaelin felt the tug of fatigue pulling him to sleep. Caenis proved a mine of many stories, he knew all the tales of the Faithful by heart and many others besides, especially the tale of the King.

'King Janus is a great man,' he said continually. 'He built our Kingdom with the sword and the Faith.' He never tired of hearing how Vaelin had once met King Janus, how the tall, red-haired man had laid a hand on his head to ruffle his hair and say, 'Hope you have your father's arm, boy,' with a deep chuckle. In fact, Vaelin barely remembered the King, he had only eight years when his father nudged him forward at the palace reception. But he did recall the opulence of the palace and the rich clothing of the assembled nobles. King Janus had a son and a daughter, a serious-looking boy of about seventeen and a girl of Vaelin's own age who scowled at him from behind her father's long, ermine-rimmed cloak. The King had no queen by then, she had died the previous summer, they said his heart was broken and he would never take another bride. Vaelin recalled that the girl, his mother called her a princess, had lingered when the King moved on to greet another guest. She looked him up and down coldly. 'I'm not marrying you,' she sneered. 'You're dirty.' With that she scampered after her father without looking back. Vaelin's father had voiced one of his rare laughs, saying, 'Don't worry, boy. I'd not curse you with her.'

'What did he look like?' Caenis asked eagerly. 'Was he six feet tall like they say?'

Vaelin shrugged. 'He was tall. Couldn't say how tall. And he had funny red marks on his neck, like he'd been burnt.'

'When he was seven he was struck down by the Red Hand,' Caenis told him, dropping into his storyteller voice. 'For ten days he suffered the agonies and blood sweats that would have killed a grown man before his fever broke and he grew strong again. Even the Red Hand, which had brought death to every family in the land, couldn't take Janus. Though but a child, his spirit was too strong to break.'

Vaelin surmised that Caenis would know many stories about his father, his time in the Order having taught him the true extent of the Battle Lord's fame, but never asked to hear any. To Caenis, Vaelin's father was a legend, a hero who stood at the King's side throughout the Wars of Unification. To Vaelin he was a rider disappearing into the fog two years ago.

'What are his children called?' Vaelin asked. For some reason his parents had never told him much about the court.

'The King's son and heir to the throne is Prince Malcius, said to be a studious and dutiful young man. His daughter is Princess Lyrna, who many think will grow to outshine even her mother's beauty.'

Sometimes Vaelin was disturbed by the light that shone in Caenis's eyes when he talked about the King and his family. It was the only time his thoughtful frown disappeared, as if he wasn't thinking at all. Vaelin had seen similar expressions on people's faces when they offered thanks to the Departed, as if their normal self had stepped out for a moment leaving only the Faith behind.

As winter deepened and snow covered the land, preparation began for the Test of the Wild. Their treks with Master Hutril became longer, his lessons more detailed and urgent, he made them run through the snow until they ached and handed out severe punishments for laxness and inattention. But they knew the importance of learning all they could. By now they had been in the Order long enough for the older boys to favour them with the occasional word of advice, normally consisting of a lurid warning of future dangers, the Test of the Wild featuring large among them: *They thought he had disappeared for good but they found his body the next year, frozen to a tree . . . He tried to eat fire berries and spewed his liver up . . . Wandered into a wild cat's den and came out carrying his guts in his arms . . .* The stories were no doubt exaggerated but concealed an essential truth: boys died in every Test of the Wild.

When the time came they were taken out in small groups over the course of a month to lessen the chance they might meet up and help each other through the ordeal. This was a trial each boy had to face alone. There was a short barge trip upriver then a long cart journey over a featureless, snow-covered road winding into the lightly forested hill country beyond the Urlish. At intervals of five miles Master Hutril would stop the cart and take one of the boys into the trees, returning sometime later to take up the reins again. When Vaelin's turn came he was led along a small stream running into a sheltered gully.

'You have your flint?' Master Hutril asked.

'Yes, Master.'

'Twine, fresh bowstring, extra blanket?'

'Yes, Master.'

Hutril nodded, pausing, his breath steaming in the chilled air. 'The Aspect has given me a message for you,' he said after a moment. Vaelin found it odd that Hutril was avoiding his gaze. 'He says, as you are likely to be hunted whenever you leave the shelter of the House, you may return with me and be given a pass on this test.'

Vaelin was speechless. The shock of the Aspect's offer coupled with the fact that this was the first time any of the Masters had referred to his ordeal in the forest left him dumfounded. The tests were not just arbitrary torments, dreamt up over the years by sadistic masters. They were part of the Order, set down by its founder four hundred years ago and never changed since. They were more than a legacy, they were an article of the Faith. He couldn't help feeling that to avoid a test and still continue in the Order would be more than just dishonest, not to say disrespectful to his friends, it would be blasphemy. Pondering further, another thought came to him: *What if this is another test? What if the Aspect wants to see if I will avoid an ordeal my brothers cannot?* But as he looked into Master Hutril's guarded gaze, he saw something that told him the offer was genuine: shame. Hutril thought the offer an insult.

'I fear to contradict the opinion of the Aspect, Master,' he said. 'But I think it unlikely an assassin would brave these hills in winter.'

Hutril nodded again, a soft sigh of relief escaping him, a rare, very slight smile on his lips. 'Do not range far, listen to the voice of the hills, follow only the freshest tracks.' With that he shouldered his bow and began his long trek back to the cart.

Vaelin watched him go, feeling very hungry despite the hearty breakfast they had all eaten that morning. He was glad he had taken the opportunity to steal some bread from the kitchen before they left.

In accordance with Hutril's lessons Vaelin began building a shelter immediately. Finding a useful nook between two large rocks to serve as walls, he set about gathering wood for a roof. There were some fallen branches about that he could use but soon had to resort to cutting extra covering from the surrounding trees. He walled off one side by piling up snow, rolling it into thick blocks as he had been taught. His work complete he rewarded himself with a bread roll, forcing himself not to bolt it, despite his hunger, taking small bites and chewing thoroughly before swallowing.

Next he had to light a fire, arranging some small rocks in a circle next to the shelter's entrance, clearing the snow from the centre and filling it with twigs and small branches he had prepared by stripping away the snow-damp bark to reveal the dry timber beneath. A few sparks from his flint and soon he was warming his hands above a respectably lively fire. *Food, shelter and heat,* Master Hutril always told them. *That's what keeps a man alive. Everything else is luxury.*

His first night in the shelter was restless, beset by howling winds and biting cold against which the blanket he had draped over the entrance was scant protection. He resolved to fashion a more sturdy covering the next day and passed the hours trying to hear voices in the winds. It was said that the winds would carry into the Beyond and the Departed used them to send messages back to the Faithful, some of whom would stand for hours on hillsides straining for words of wisdom or comfort from lost loved ones. Vaelin had never heard a voice on the wind and wondered who it would be if he did. His mother perhaps, although she hadn't come to him again since his first night in the Order. Mikehl maybe, or the assassins, spitting their hatred into the wind. But tonight there were no voices to hear and he drifted into a fitful, chilled slumber.

The next day saw him gathering thin branches to weave into a door for his shelter. The work was long and tricky, leaving his already numb fingers aching from the effort. He spent the rest of the day on the hunt, arrow notched into his bowstring as he scanned the snow for tracks. He fancied there had been a deer through the gully in the night but the tracks were too faint to follow successfully. He did find fresh goat tracks but they led to a steep rise he had little hope of climbing before nightfall. In the end he had to content himself with bringing down a couple of crows that had mistakenly perched too close to his shelter and setting a few snares for any unwary rabbits that felt the need to venture into the snow.

He plucked the crows and kept the feathers for kindling, spitting the birds and roasting them over his fire. The meat was dry and tough, making him appreciate why crow was not considered a delicacy. As night came there was little to do but huddle near his fire until it burned down then settle into his shelter. The door he had made was more use than the blanket but still the cold seemed to settle into his bones. His stomach growled but the wind howled ever louder, and still he heard no voices.

He had better luck in the morning, bringing down a snow hare. He was proud of the kill, the arrow catching the animal as it scampered for its hole. He had it skinned and cleaned within an hour and took a great amount of pleasure in roasting it over the fire, staring with wide eyes at the grease running over the blistering skin. *They should call this the Test of Hunger,* he decided as his stomach gave voice to another obscenely loud growl. He ate half the meat and stashed the other half in a tree hole he had chosen for a good hiding place. It was a good distance off the ground, he had to climb to reach it, and the tree was too slender to support the weight of a scavenging bear. It was a real effort to resist the urge to gobble all the meat at once but he knew if he did, he might have to face the next day without a meal.

The rest of the day was spent hunting without success, his snares remained frustratingly empty and he had to content himself digging for roots from under the snow. The roots he found were hardly filling, and took a lot of boiling before they were edible, but sufficed to take the edge off his hunger. His one stroke of luck was finding a yallin root, inedible but possessed of a particularly foul-smelling juice that would be useful in protecting his food store and shelter from prowling wolves or bears.

He was trudging back to his shelter after another fruitless hunt when it began to snow in earnest, the wind soon whipping the flakes into a blizzard. He made it back before the snow became too thick for him to see his way and wedged his door of woven branches firmly into the entrance, warming his ice-cold hands in the hare's pelt he had chosen to use as a muffler. He couldn't light a fire in the middle of a snowstorm and had no choice but to sit it out, shivering, flexing his hands in the fur to stop the numbness setting in.

The wind was louder than ever, still howling, leaving its voices in the Beyond . . . *What was that?* He sat up, holding his breath, ears straining. A voice, a voice on the wind. Faint, plaintive. He sat still and quiet, waiting for it to come again. The shriek of the wind was continuous and infuriating, every change in tone seemed to herald another call of the mystery voice. He waited, breathing softly, but nothing came.

Shaking his head, he lay down again, huddling beneath the blanket, trying to make himself as small as possible . . .

'. . . curse you . . .'

He jerked upright, instantly awake. There was no mistaking it. There was a voice on the wind. It came again, quickly this time, the wind allowing only a few words to reach him. '. . . you hear me? I curse you! . . . regret nothing! I . . . nothing . . .'

The voice was faint but he could hear the rage in it clearly, this soul had sent a message of hate back across the void. Was it for him? He felt cold dread grip him like a giant fist. *The assassins, Brak and the other two.* His shivers deepened but not through cold.

'. . . nothing!' the voice raged. 'Nothing . . . have done has . . . anything! You hear me?'

Vaelin thought he knew fear, he thought the ordeal in the forest had hardened him, made him in some ways immune to terror.

He was wrong. Some of the masters had talked of men pissing themselves when fear overcame them. He had never believed it until now.

'. . . I'll carry my hate into the Beyond! If you cursed my life, you'll curse my death a thousand times . . .'

Vaelin's shivers stopped momentarily. *Death? What kind of Departed soul speaks of dying?* A very obvious thought occurred to him in a rush of embarrassment he was glad no-one was there to see: *someone is outside in the storm whilst I sit here cowering.*

He had to dig his way out, the blizzard had piled a drift against his door fully three feet high. After a few moments' effort, he scrambled out into the fury of the storm. The wind was like a knife cutting through his cloak as if it were made of paper, snow pelted his face like nails, he could see almost nothing.

'Ho there!' he called, feeling the words vanish into the gale as soon as they escaped his lips. He dragged air into his lungs, swallowing snow, and tried again, 'HO! WHO'S THERE?'

Something shifted in the blizzard, a vague shape in the wall of white. Gone before he could make sense of it. Drawing another breath, he began to fight his way towards where he thought the shape had been, heaving his legs out of the freezing drifts. He stumbled several times before he found them, two shapes, huddled together, partially covered by the blizzard, one large, one small.

'Get up!' Vaelin shouted, prodding the largest shape. It groaned, rolling over, snow falling away from a frost-encrusted face, two pale blue eyes staring out from the mask of ice. Vaelin drew back slightly. He had never seen a gaze so intense. Not even Master Sollis's stare could pierce a soul like this. Unconsciously his hand closed over the knife beneath his cloak. 'If you stay here, you'll freeze to death in minutes,' he shouted.

'I have shelter.' He waved back the way he had come. 'Can you walk?'

The eyes kept staring, the frost face immobile. *My luck holds true,* Vaelin thought ruefully. *Only I could find a madman in the middle of a snowstorm.*

'I can walk.' The man's voice was a growl. He jerked his head at the smaller shape next to him. 'I'll need help with this one.'

Vaelin moved to the small shape, dragging it to its feet, drawing a pained gasp. As he pulled the figure upright a hood fell away to reveal a pale, elfin face and a shock of auburn hair. The girl remained standing for only an instant before collapsing against him.

'Here,' the man grunted, taking one of her arms and laying it across his shoulders. Vaelin took the other arm and together they struggled back to the shelter. It seemed to take an age; incredibly the storm was growing in intensity and Vaelin knew that if they stopped for even a second, death would follow soon after. Reaching the shelter, he scraped the already regrown drift away from the entrance and pushed the girl in first, gesturing for the man to follow. He shook his head. 'You first, boy.'

Vaelin noted the adamant tone in his growl and knew lingering to argue would be pointless, and possibly deadly. He crawled into the shelter, pushing the girl's body deeper as he did so, cramming them both in as tightly as he could. The man followed them in quickly, his bulk leaving little remaining space, and jammed Vaelin's door into the entrance.

They lay together, mingled breath clouding the confines of the shelter, Vaelin's lungs burned from the effort of struggling through the snow and his hands trembled uncontrollably. He put them inside his cloak, hoping to stave off frostbite. An irresistible tiredness began to creep over him, clouding his vision as he slid towards unconsciousness. He had a final glimpse of the man next to him, peering out at the storm through a gap in the door. Before exhaustion overtook him completely Vaelin heard the man mutter, 'A little longer then. Just a little longer.'

He surfaced with a splitting headache, a thin beam of sunlight lancing through the roof directly into his eye provoking a painful yelp. Next to him the girl shifted in her sleep, one of her boots leaving a bruise on his shin. The man wasn't in the shelter and a strong, distinctly appetising aroma was wafting through the entrance. Vaelin decided he would rather be outside.

He found the man cooking oat cakes over his campfire on an iron skillet, the smell provoking an excruciating surge of hunger. Free of the mask of ice, his features were lean though deeply lined. The rage that had clouded his eyes in the storm was gone, replaced with a bright friendliness Vaelin found disconcerting. He put the man's age in the mid-thirties but it was difficult to tell for sure, there was a depth to the face, a gravity in his stare that spoke of a wide breadth of experience. Vaelin kept his distance, worried he would grab at the cakes if he got too close.

'Went back for our gear,' the man said, nodding at the two snow-dusted packs nearby. 'We had to drop them last night a few miles back. Too much weight.' He took the cakes off the heat and offered the skillet to Vaelin.

Vaelin, mouth flooded with drool, shook his head. 'I can't.'

'Order boy, eh?'

Vaelin nodded, dumb with longing.

'Why else would a boy be living out here?' He shook his head sadly. 'Still, if you weren't, Sella and I would be lying under the snow.' He got up, approaching to offer his hand. 'My thanks, young sir.'

Vaelin took the hand, feeling the hard callus that covered the palm. *A warrior?* Looking the man over, Vaelin doubted it.

The masters all had a certain way of moving and talking that marked them out. This man was different. He had the strength but not the look.

'Erlin Ilnis,' the man introduced himself.

'Vaelin Al Sorna.'

The man raised an eyebrow. 'The name of the Battle Lord's family.'

'Yes, I've heard.'

Erlin Ilnis nodded and let the subject drop. 'How many days to go?'

'Four. If I don't starve before then.'

'Then accept my apologies for intruding on your test. I hope it won't spoil your chances of passing.'

'As long as you don't help me it shouldn't matter.'

The man squatted down to eat his breakfast, cutting the cakes into portions with a thin-bladed knife and lifting them to his mouth. Unable to bear it any longer Vaelin rushed off to collect his stash of hare meat from the tree hole. He had to dig through a thick covering of snow but was soon back at the camp with his prize.

'Haven't seen a storm like that for many a year,' Erlin commented softly as Vaelin began roasting his meat. 'Used to think it an omen when the weather turned bad. Always seemed like a war or a plague would follow soon after. Now I just think it means the weather turned bad.'

Vaelin felt compelled to talk, it took his mind off the endless growl of his stomach. 'Plague? The Red Hand you mean. You couldn't be old enough to have seen it.'

The man gave a faint smile. 'I am . . . widely travelled. Plague comes to many lands, in many forms.'

'How many?' Vaelin pressed. 'How many lands have you seen?'

Erlin stroked his stubble-grey chin as he pondered the

question. 'I honestly couldn't say. I've seen the glories of the Alpiran Empire and the ruins of the Leandren temples. I've walked the dark paths of the Great Northern Forest and trod the endless steppes where the Eorhil Sil hunt the great elk. I've seen cities and islands and mountains aplenty. But always, without fail, everywhere I go, I find myself in a storm.'

'You are not from the Realm?' Vaelin was puzzled. The man's accent was odd, possessed of vowels that jarred on the ear, but still clearly Asraelin.

'Oh, I was born here. There's a village a few miles south of Varinshold, so small it doesn't even have a name. You'll find my kin there.'

'Why did you leave? Why travel to so many places?'

The man shrugged. 'I had a lot of time on my hands and I couldn't think of anything else to do.'

'Why were you so angry?'

Erlin turned to him sharply. 'What?'

'I heard you. I thought it was a voice on the wind, one of the Departed. You were angry, I could hear it. It's how I found you.'

Erlin's face took on an expression of deep, almost frightening sadness. Such was the depth of his sorrow that Vaelin wondered again if he hadn't rescued a madman.

'When a man faces death he says many foolish things,' Erlin said. 'When they make you a full brother I'm sure you'll hear dying men say the most ridiculous nonsense.'

The girl emerged from the shelter, blinking dazedly in the sunlight, a shawl clutched about her shoulders. Seeing her clearly for the first time, Vaelin found it hard not to stare. Her face was a flawless pale oval framed by light auburn curls. She was older than he by a couple of years and an inch or two taller. He realised he hadn't even seen a girl for a long time and felt uncomfortably out of his depth.

'Sella,' Erlin greeted her. 'More cakes in my pack if you're hungry.'

She smiled tightly, casting a wary glance at Vaelin.

'This is Vaelin Al Sorna,' Erlin told her. 'A novice brother of the Sixth Order. We owe him our thanks.'

She hid it well but Vaelin saw her tense when Erlin mentioned the Order. She turned to Vaelin and moved her hands in a series of intricate, fluid movements, an empty smile fixed on her face. *Mute,* he realised.

'She said we are fortunate to find such a brave soul in the midst of the wilderness,' Erlin related.

In fact she had said: *Tell him I said thank you, and let's go.* Vaelin decided it would be better if he kept his knowledge of sign language to himself. 'You're welcome,' he said. She inclined her head and moved to the packs.

Vaelin began to eat, shovelling the food down with dirty fingers and not caring that Master Hutril would have been appalled at such a spectacle. Erlin and Sella conversed in sign language whilst he ate. The shapes they made were practised and formed with a fluency which shamed his own clumsy attempts to mimic Master Smentil. But despite the fluency of their communication Vaelin marked the sharp, nervous movements of her hands and the more restrained, calming shapes made by Erlin.

Does he know who we are? she asked him.

No, Erlin replied. *He is a child. Brave and clever, but a child. They are taught to fight. The Order tells them nothing of other faiths.*

She cast a brief, guarded glance in Vaelin's direction. He grinned back, licking grease from his fingers.

Will he kill us if he knows? she asked Erlin.

He saved us, don't forget. Erlin paused and Vaelin got the impression he was trying not to look at him. *And he's different,* his hands said. *Other brothers of the Sixth Order are not like him.*

Different how?

There is more in him, more feeling. Can't you sense it?

She shook her head. *I sense only danger. It's all I've felt for days.* She paused for a moment, a frown creasing her smooth brow. *He has the Battle Lord's name.*

Yes. I think this is his son. I heard he gave him to the Order after his wife died.

Her movements became frantic, insistent. *We have to leave* now!

Erlin forced a smile in Vaelin's direction. *Calm down or you'll make him suspicious.*

Vaelin got up and went to the stream to wash the grease from his hands. *Fugitives,* he thought. *But from what? And what was this talk of other faiths?* Not for the first time he wished one of the masters were here to guide him. Sollis or Hutril would know what to do. He wondered if he should try to hold them here somehow. Overpower them and tie them up. He wasn't sure he could do it. The girl didn't present a problem but Erlin was a grown man, and strong. And Vaelin suspected he knew how to fight even if he wasn't a warrior by trade. All he could do was keep watching their conversation to learn more.

He caught it by chance, the wind shifted and brought it to him, faint but unmistakable: horse sweat. *Must be close if I can smell it. More than one. Coming from the south.*

He hurriedly climbed the south side of the gully, scanning the southern hills. He spotted them quickly, a dark knot of riders a half a mile or so to the southeast. Five or six of them, plus a trio of hunting dogs. They had halted, it was difficult to make out what they were doing from this distance but Vaelin surmised they were waiting for the dogs to pick up a scent.

He forced himself to stroll slowly back to the camp, finding the girl sullenly prodding the fire with a stick and Erlin retying one of the straps on his pack.

'We'll be on our way soon,' Erlin assured him. 'We've put you to enough trouble.'

'Heading north?' Vaelin asked.

'Yes. The Renfaelin coast. Sella has family there.'

'You're not her family?'

'Just a friend and travelling companion.'

Vaelin went to the shelter and fetched his bow, feeling the girl's mounting tension as he strung the bowstring and slung the quiver over his shoulder. 'I have to hunt.'

'Of course. I wish we could give you some of our food.'

'It's not permitted to take aid from others during this test. Besides I'm sure you can't spare any.'

The girl's hands moved irritably: *True.*

'I suppose we should take our leave now,' Erlin said, coming over to offer his hand. 'Once again, my thanks, young sir. It's unusual to meet such a generous soul. Trust me, I know . . .'

Vaelin moved his hands, the shapes he made clumsy compared to theirs but the meaning was clear enough: *Riders to the south. With dogs. Why?*

Sella's hand went to her mouth, her pale face nearly white with fear. Erlin's hand inched closer to the curve-bladed knife at his belt.

'Don't do that,' Vaelin instructed him. 'Just tell me why you're running. And who's hunting you.'

Erlin and the girl exchanged frantic glances. Her hands fidgeted as she fought the impulse to communicate. Erlin took her hand, Vaelin wasn't sure if he was trying to calm or silence her.

'So they teach you the signs,' he said, his tone neutral.

'They teach us many things.'

'Did they teach you about Deniers?'

Vaelin frowned, remembering one of his father's infrequent explanations. It had been the first time he saw the city gate and the bodies rotting in the cages that hung from the wall. 'Deniers are blasphemers and heretics. Those who deny the truth of the Faith.'

'And do you know what happens to Deniers, Vaelin?'

'They are killed and hung from the city walls in cages.'

'They are hung from the walls whilst still alive and left to starve to death. Their tongues are cut out so their screams will not disturb passersby. This is done purely because they follow a different faith.'

'There is no different Faith.'

'Yes there is, Vaelin!' Erlin's tone was fierce, implacable. 'I told you I had been all over this world. There are countless faiths, countless gods. There are more ways to honour the divine than there are stars in the sky.'

Vaelin shook his head, finding the argument irrelevant. 'And that's what you are? Deniers?'

'No. I follow the same Faith as you.' He gave a short bitter laugh. 'I've little choice after all. But Sella has a different path. Her belief is different, but just as true as yours and mine. But if she's taken by the men hunting us, they will torture and kill her. Do you think that's right? Do you think all Deniers deserve such a fate?'

Vaelin studied Sella. Fear dominated her face, her lips trembling, but her eyes were untouched by her terror. They stared into his, unblinking, magnetic, questing, making him think of Master Sollis during that first sword lesson. 'You can't trick me,' he told her.

She took a deep breath, gently disentangled her hands from Erlin's and signed: *I am not trying to trick you. I'm looking for something.*

'And what's that?'

Something I didn't see before. She turned to Erlin. *He will help us.*

Vaelin opened his mouth to retort but found the words dying on his lips. She was right: he would help them. There was no complexity to the decision. It was right, he knew it. He would help them because Erlin was honest and brave and Sella was pretty and had seen something in him. He would help them because he knew they didn't deserve to die.

He went into the shelter and returned with the yallin root. 'Here.' He tossed it to Erlin. 'Cut it in half and smear the juice on your feet and hands. Whose scent do they have?'

Erlin sniffed the root uncertainly. 'What is this?'

'It'll mask your scent. Which of you do they follow?'

Sella patted her chest. Vaelin noted the silk scarf around her neck. He pointed at it, motioning for her to hand it over.

My mother's, she protested.

'Then she'll be glad it saved your life.'

After a moment's hesitation she undid the scarf and gave it to him. He tied it around his wrist.

'This is disgusting!' Erlin complained, smearing the yallin juice on his boots, face contorted at the pungent stench.

'Dogs think so too,' Vaelin told him.

After Sella had anointed her own boots and hands he led them into the densest part of the surrounding woodland. There was a hollow a few hundred yards from the camp, deep enough to hide two people but offering little protection against expert eyes. Vaelin was hoping whoever hunted them wouldn't get close enough to see it. When they had settled into the hollow he took the yallin root from Sella and smeared as much juice as he could squeeze from it on the surrounding ground and foliage.

'Stay here, keep quiet. If you hear the dogs, lie still, don't run. If I don't return in an hour, head south for two days then circle west, follow the coast road north, stay out of the towns.'

He made to leave when Sella reached out to him, her hand

hovering close to his. She seemed wary of touching him. Her eyes met his again, not questing this time, just bright with gratitude. He smiled back briefly and was gone, running full pelt towards the hunters. The sparse woods blurred around him, his body aching from the effort. He pushed his pains away and ran on, the scarf on his wrist trailing in the wind.

It took five long minutes of hard running before he heard the dogs, distant, high-pitched yelps growing into sharp, threatening barks as they drew closer. Vaelin chose a defensible position atop a fallen birch trunk and quickly took the scarf from his wrist, tying it around his neck and tucking it out of sight. He waited, arrow notched tight to his bowstring, breath steaming as he dragged air into his lungs and fought the tremble from his limbs.

The dogs were on him quicker than he expected, three dark forms bursting from the undergrowth twenty yards away, snarling, yellow teeth flashing, churning snow as they sped towards him. Vaelin was momentarily shocked by the sight of them, they were an unfamiliar breed. Larger, faster and more thickly muscled than any other hunting dog he had seen. Even the Renfaelin hounds in the Order's kennels seemed like pets in comparison. The worst thing was their eyes, glaring yellow, filled with hate, they seemed to glow with it as they closed on him, drool trailing from snarling maws.

His arrow took the first one in the throat, sending it tumbling into the snow with a surprised, piteous whine. He tried for another arrow but the second dog was on him before the shaft was clear of the quiver. It leapt, sharp-nailed paws scrabbling at his chest, head angled to fix the flashing teeth on his neck. He rolled with the force of the lunge, letting his bow slip away, his right hand pulling the knife free from his belt to stab upwards as his back connected with the ground, the dog's momentum helping bury the blade in its chest, punching through ribs and cartilage to find the heart, blood gouting from the mouth in a thick black spray. Fighting nausea, Vaelin put his boots under the twitching body and heaved it away, rolling upright, knife levelled at the third dog, ready for the charge.

It didn't come.

The dog sat, ears flattened, head lowered near the ground, eyes averted. Whining, it raised its muscular form to edge closer then sat again, glancing at him with a strange, fearful but expectant expression.

'You better be rich, boy,' a gruff, deeply angry voice said. 'You owe me for three dogs.'

Vaelin whirled, knife ready, finding a ragged, stocky man emerging from the bushes, his heaving chest indicating the hardship of running in the wake of the dogs. A sword of the Asraelin pattern was strapped across his back and he wore a soiled, dark blue cloak.

'Two dogs,' Vaelin said.

The man glowered and spat on the ground, reaching back to draw his sword in a practised, easy movement. 'These are Volarian slave-hounds, you little shit. The third's no good to me now.' He came closer, his feet moving over the snow in a familiar dancing motion, sword point low, arm slightly bent.

The dog growled, a low, menacing rumble. Vaelin risked a glance at it, expecting to find it advancing on him once again, but instead its yellow, hate-filled gaze was fixed on the man with the sword, lips trembling over bared teeth.

'You see!' the man shouted at Vaelin. 'See what you've done? Four years to train these bastards in the shitter.'

It came to Vaelin then, a rush of recognition he should have felt as soon as the man appeared. He raised his left hand slowly, showing it to be empty, and reached inside his shirt to pull out his medallion, holding it up for the man to see. 'My apologies, brother.'

Momentary confusion played over the man's face, Vaelin realised he wasn't puzzled at the sight of the medallion, he was calculating if he was still permitted to kill him even though he was of the Order. In the event the decision was made for him.

'Sheathe your sword, Makril,' said a strident, cultured voice. Vaelin turned as a horse and rider emerged from the trees. The sharp-faced man on the horse nodded at him cordially as he guided his mount closer. It was a grey Asraelin hunter from the southlands, a long-legged breed renowned for stamina rather than aggression. The man reined in a few feet away, looking down at Vaelin with what might have been genuine goodwill. Vaelin noted the colour of his cloak, black: the Fourth Order.

'Good day to you, little brother,' the sharp-faced man greeted him.

Vaelin nodded back, sheathing his knife. 'And you, Master.'

'Master?' He smiled faintly. 'I think not.' He glanced at the remaining dog, now growling at him. 'I fear we may have provided you an unwelcome companion, little brother.'

'Companion?'

'Volarian slave-hounds are an unusual breed. Savage beyond belief at times but possessed of a rigid hierarchical code. You killed this animal's pack leader and the one who would have replaced him. Now he sees you as the pack leader. He's too young to challenge you so instead will provide you with unswerving loyalty, for now.'

Vaelin looked at the dog, seeing a snarling, drooling mass of muscle and teeth with an intricate web of scars on its snout and fur matted with mingled dirt and shit. 'I don't want it,' he said.

'Too late for that, you little sod,' Makril muttered behind him.

'Oh stop being so tiresome, Makril,' the sharp-faced man admonished him. 'You lost some dogs, we'll get some more.' He

BLOOD SONG · 91

bent down to offer Vaelin his hand. 'Tendris Al Forne, brother of the Fourth Order and servant of the Council for Heretical Transgressions.'

'Vaelin Al Sorna.' Vaelin shook the hand. 'Novice brother of the Sixth Order, awaiting confirmation.'

'Yes, of course.' Tendris sat back in his saddle. 'Test of the Wild, is it?'

'Yes, brother.'

'I certainly don't envy your Order's tests.' Tendris offered a sympathetic smile. 'Remember your tests, brother?' he asked Makril.

'Only in my nightmares.' Makril was circling the clearing, eyes fixed on the ground, occasionally crouching to peer closely at a mark in the snow. Vaelin had seen Master Hutril do the same thing, but with considerably more grace. Hutril gave off an aura of calm reflection when he looked for tracks. Makril was a sharp contrast, constantly on the move, agitated, restless.

The crunch of hooves on snow heralded the arrival of three more brothers from the Fourth Order, all mounted on Asraelin hunters like Tendris, and possessing the hardy, weathered look of men who spent most of their lives on the hunt. They each greeted Vaelin with a brief wave when Tendris introduced him, before going off to scour the surrounding area. 'They may have tracked through here,' Tendris told them. 'The dogs must have scented something beyond a likely meal in our young brother here.'

'May I ask what you're searching for, brother?' Vaelin enquired.

'The bane of our realm and our Faith, Vaelin,' Tendris replied sadly. 'The Unfaithful. It is a task charged to me and the brothers with whom I ride. We hunt those who would deny the Faith. It may be a surprise to you that such folk exist, but believe me they do.'

'There's nothing here,' Makril said. 'No tracks, nothing for the dogs to scent.' He made his way through a heavy snowdrift to stand in front of Vaelin. 'Except you, brother.'

Vaelin frowned. 'Why would your dogs track me?'

'Have you met anyone during your test?' Tendris asked. 'A man and a girl perhaps?'

'Erlin and Sella?'

Makril and Tendris exchanged a glance. 'When?' Makril demanded.

'Two nights ago.' Vaelin was proud of the smoothness of the lie, he was becoming more adept at dishonesty. 'The snow was heavy, they needed shelter. I offered them mine.' He looked at Tendris. 'Was I wrong to do so, brother?'

'Kindness and generosity are never wrong, Vaelin.' Tendris smiled. Vaelin was disturbed by the fact that the smile seemed genuine. 'Are they still at your camp?'

'No, they left the next morning. They said little, in fact the girl said nothing.'

Makril snorted a mirthless laugh. 'She can't speak, boy.'

'She did give me this.' Vaelin pulled Sella's silk scarf from under his shirt. 'By way of thanks the man said. I saw no harm in taking it. It offers no warmth. If you're hunting them, perhaps your dogs scented this.'

Makril leaned closer, sniffing the scarf, nostrils flared, his eyes locked on Vaelin's. *He doesn't believe a word of it,* Vaelin realised.

'Did the man tell you where they were going?' Tendris asked.

'North, to Renfael. He said the girl had family there.'

'He lied,' Makril said. 'She has no family anywhere.' Next to Vaelin the dog's growls deepened. Makril moved back slowly, making Vaelin wonder what kind of dog could provoke fear in its own master.

'Vaelin, this is very important,' Tendris said, leaning forward in his saddle, studying Vaelin intently. 'Did the girl touch you at all?'

'Touch me, brother?'

'Yes. Even the slightest touch?'

Vaelin remembered the hesitancy as Sella reached to him and realised she hadn't touched him at all, although the depth of her gaze when she found something in him had felt almost like being touched, touched on the inside. 'No. No she didn't.'

Tendris settled back into the saddle, nodding in satisfaction. 'Then you were indeed fortunate.'

'Fortunate?'

'The girl's a Denier witch, boy,' Makril said. He had perched on the birch trunk and was chewing a sugar cane that had appeared in his weathered fist. 'She can twist your heart with a touch of that dainty hand of hers.'

'What our brother means,' Tendris explained, 'is that this girl has a power, an ability that comes from the Dark. The heresy of the Unfaithful sometimes manifests itself in strange ways.'

'She has a power?'

'It's better we don't burden you with the details.' He tugged his horse's reins, guiding it to the edge of the clearing, looking around for tracks. 'They left yesterday morning, you say?'

'Yes, brother.' Vaelin tried not to look at Makril, knowing the stocky tracker was subjecting him to an intense, dubious scrutiny. 'Heading north.'

'Mmm.' Tendris glanced at Makril. 'Can we still track them without the dogs?'

Makril shrugged. 'Maybe, won't be easy after last night's storm.' He took another bite from his sugar cane and tossed it away. 'I'll do some scouting north of the hills. Best if you take the others and check towards the west and east. They may have tried to double back to throw us off their trail.' He gave Vaelin a final, hostile glare before disappearing into the trees at a dead run.

'It's time for me to take my leave, brother,' Tendris said. 'I'm sure I'll see you again when you've passed all your tests. Who knows, perhaps there'll be a place in my company for a young brother with a brave heart and a quick eye.'

Vaelin looked at the bodies of the two dogs, streaks of blood staining the white blanket of snow. *They would have killed me. That's what they're bred for. Not just tracking. If they'd found Sella and Erlin . . .* 'Who knows down what paths the Faith leads us, brother,' he told Tendris, not having the stomach to force more than a neutral tone into his voice.

'Indeed.' Tendris nodded, accepting the wisdom. 'Well, luck go with you.'

Vaelin was so surprised that his plan had worked that he let Tendris guide his horse to the edge of the clearing before he remembered to ask a vital question.

'Brother! What do I do with this dog?'

Tendris looked over his shoulder as he rode away, spurring his mount to a canter. 'Kill it if you're smart. Keep it if you're brave.' He laughed, raising a hand as his horse accelerated into a gallop, snow rising into a thick cloud that shimmered in the winter sun.

Vaelin looked down at the dog. It gazed up at him with adoring eyes, long pink tongue lolling from a mouth wet with drool. Again he noted the numerous scars on its snout. Although still young, this animal clearly had endured a hard life. 'Scratch,' he told it. 'I'll call you Scratch.'

Dog flesh proved a tough, sinewy meat but Vaelin was long past being choosy over his food. Scratch had whined continually as Vaelin butchered one of the carcasses back at the clearing, slicing a rear haunch off the largest dog. He had kept his distance as

Vaelin carried the prize back to the camp and cut strips of meat to roast over his fire. Only when the meat had been eaten and Vaelin had hidden the remainder in his tree hole did the dog venture closer, snuffling at Vaelin's feet in search of reassurance. Whatever the savage traits of Volarian slave-hounds, it appeared cannibalism was not among them.

'Don't know what I'm going to feed you if you won't eat your own kind,' Vaelin mused, patting Scratch awkwardly on the head. The dog was clearly unused to being petted and shrank warily when Vaelin first tried it.

He had been back at the camp for over an hour, cooking, building the fire, clearing snow from his shelter and resisting the temptation to go and see if Erlin and Sella were still hiding in the hollow. He had felt a sense of wrongness ever since Tendris had ridden away, a suspicion that the man had accepted his word a little too easily. He could be wrong, of course. Tendris had struck him as the kind of brother whose Faith was absolute and unshake-able. If so, then the concept of a fellow brother lying, lying to protect a Denier at that, simply wouldn't occur to him. On the other hand, could a man who spent his life hunting the Realm for heretics remain so free of cynicism?

Without answers to these questions Vaelin couldn't risk checking on the fugitives. There was nothing on the wind to warn him otherwise, no change in the song of the wild threatening ambush but still he stayed in his camp, ate dog flesh and puzzled over what to do with his gift.

Scratch seemed an oddly cheerful animal considering he had been bred to hunt and kill people. He scampered about the camp, playing with sticks or bones he dug out of the snow, bringing them to Vaelin who quickly learned trying to wrestle them away was a pointlessly tiring task. He wasn't remotely sure he would be allowed to keep the dog when he returned to the

Order. Master Chekril, the keeper of the kennels, was unlikely to want such a beast near his beloved hounds. More likely they would pull a dagger across its throat as soon as he appeared at the gates.

They went hunting in the afternoon, Vaelin expecting another fruitless search, but it wasn't long before Scratch picked up a trail. With a brief yelp he was off, bounding through the snow, Vaelin struggling in his wake. It wasn't long before he found the source of the trail: the frozen carcass of a small deer no doubt caught in the storm the night before. Oddly it was untouched, Scratch sat patiently beside the corpse, eyeing Vaelin warily as he approached. Vaelin gutted the carcass, tossing the entrails to Scratch, whose ecstatic reaction took him by surprise. He yelped happily, gulping the meat down in a frenzy of teeth and snapping jaws. Vaelin dragged the deer back to camp, pondering the odd change in his circumstances. He had gone from near starvation to an abundance of food in less than a day, more food in fact than he could eat before Master Hutril returned to take him back to the Order House.

Darkness came swiftly, a cloudless, moonlit night turning the snow into folds of blue silver and laying out a vast panorama of stars above him. If Caenis had been here, he could have named all the constellations but Vaelin could pick out only a few of the more obvious ones: the Sword, the Stag, the Maiden. Caenis had told him of a legend that claimed the first souls of the Departed had cast the stars into the sky from the Beyond as a gift for the generations to come, making patterns to guide the living through the path of life. Many claimed to be able to read the message written in the sky, most of them seemed to congregate in marketplaces and fairs, offering guidance for a palmful of copper.

He was wondering at the meaning of the Sword pointing towards the south when his sense of wrongness hardened into cold certainty. Scratch tensed, lifting his head slightly. There was no scent, no sound, no warning at all, but something wasn't right.

Vaelin turned, glancing over his shoulder at the unmoving foliage behind him. *So silent,* he wondered, a little awed. *No assassin could be that skilful.*

'If you're hungry, brother,' he called. 'I have plenty of meat to spare.' He turned back to the fire, adding some logs to keep the flames high. After a short interval there was a crunch of boots on snow as Makril stepped past him to crouch opposite, spreading his hands to the fire. He didn't look at Vaelin but glowered at Scratch.

'Should've killed that bloody thing,' he grumbled.

Vaelin ducked into his shelter to fetch a portion of meat. 'Deer.' He tossed it to Makril.

The stocky man speared the meat with his knife and arranged a small mound of rocks to secure it over the fire before spreading his bedroll on the ground to sit down.

'A fine night, brother,' Vaelin said.

Makril grunted, undoing his boots to massage his feet. The smell was enough to make Scratch get up and slink away.

'I am sorry Brother Tendris did not find my word trustworthy,' Vaelin continued.

'He believed you.' Makril picked something from between his toes and tossed it into the fire, where it popped and hissed. 'He's a true man of the Faith. Whereas I am a suspicious, gutter-born bastard. That's why he keeps me with him. Don't get me wrong, he's a man of many abilities, finest horseman I ever saw and he can extract information from a Denier quicker than you could blow your nose. But in some ways he's an innocent. He trusts the Faithful. For him all the Faithful have the same belief, his belief.'

'But not yours?'

Makril placed his boots near the fire to dry. 'I hunt. Tracks, signs, spoor, a scent on the wind, the rush of blood that comes from a kill. That's my Faith. What's yours, boy?'

Vaelin shrugged. He suspected a trap in Makril's openness, luring him into an admission best kept silent. 'I follow the Faith,' he replied, forcing certainty into his words. 'I am a brother of the Sixth Order.'

'The Order has many brothers, all different, all finding their own path in the Faith. Don't kid yourself that the Order is filled with virtuous men who spend every spare moment grovelling to the Departed. We're soldiers, boy. Soldier's life is hard, short on pleasure and long on pain.'

'The Aspect says there's a difference between a soldier and a warrior. A soldier fights for pay or loyalty. We fight for the Faith, war is our way of honouring the Departed.'

Makril's face took on a sombre cast, a craggy, hairy mask in the yellow firelight, his eyes distant, focused on unhappy memories. 'War? War is blood and shit and men maddened with pain calling for their mothers as they bleed to death. There's no honour in it, boy.' His eyes shifted, meeting Vaelin's. 'You'll see it, you poor little bastard. You'll see it all.'

Suddenly uncomfortable, Vaelin added another log to the fire. 'Why were you hunting that girl?'

'She's a Denier. A Denier most foul, for she has power to twist the hearts of virtuous men.' He gave a short, ironic laugh. 'So I think I'd be safe if she ever met me.'

'What is it? This power?'

Makril tested the meat with his fingers and began to eat, biting off small mouthfuls, chewing thoroughly then swallowing. It was the practised, unconscious action of a man who did not savour food but merely took it into himself as fuel. 'It's a dark tale, boy,' he said, between mouthfuls. 'Might give you nightmares.'

'I've got those already.'

Makril raised a bushy eyebrow but didn't comment. Instead he finished his meat and fished in his pack for a small, leather flask. 'Brother's Friend,' he explained, taking a swig. 'Cumbraelin brandy mixed with redflower. Keeps the fire in a man's belly when he's walking a wall on the northern frontier waiting for Lonak savages to cut his throat.' He offered the flask to Vaelin, who shook his head. Liquor wasn't forbidden in the Order, but it was frowned upon by the more Faithful masters. Some said anything that dulled the senses was a barrier to the Faith, the less a man remembered of his life the less he had to take with him to the Beyond. Clearly, Brother Makril didn't share this view.

'So you want to know about the witch.' He relaxed, resting his back against a rock, intermittently sipping from his flask. 'Well, the story goes she was arrested on Council orders following reports of Unfaithful practices. Allegations are usually a load of nonsense; people claiming to have heard voices from the Beyond that don't come from the Departed, healing the sick, communing with beasts and so on. Mostly it's just frightened peasants blaming each other for their misfortunes, but every once in a while you get one like her.

'There'd been trouble in her village. She and her father were outsiders, from Renfael. Kept to themselves, he made a living as a scribe. A local landowner wanted him to forge some deeds, something to do with a dispute over the inheritance of some pasture. The scribe refused and ended up with an axe in his back a few days later. The landowner was a cousin of the local magistrate so nothing was done. Two days later he walked into the local tavern, confessed his crime and cut his own throat from ear to ear.'

'And they blamed her for that?'

'It seems they had been seen together earlier in the day, which was odd because there was said to be hatred between them even before the bastard killed her father. They said she touched him, a short pat on the arm. Didn't help that she was mute, and an outsider. Being a little too pretty and a little too smart didn't do her any favours either. They always said there was something about her, she wasn't *right*. But they always say that.'

'So you arrested her?'

'Oh no. Tendris and me, we only hunt the ones that run. Brothers from the Second Order searched her house and found evidence of Denier activity. Forbidden books, images of gods, herbs and candles, the usual stuff. Turned out she and her father were followers of the Sun and the Moon, a minor sect. They're pretty harmless mostly since they don't try to convert others to their heresy, but a Denier's a Denier. She was taken to the Blackhold. The next night she escaped.'

'She escaped the Blackhold?' Vaelin was unsure if Makril was mocking him. The Blackhold was a squat, ugly fortress in the centre of the capital, its stones stained with soot from the nearby foundries, famed as a place where people were taken and didn't come out again unless it was to walk the path to the gallows or the gibbet. If a man went missing and his neighbours heard he was taken to the Blackhold, they stopped asking when he would return, in fact they didn't mention him at all. And no-one ever escaped.

'How is such a thing possible?' Vaelin wondered.

Makril took a long pull from his flask before continuing. 'Did you ever hear of Brother Shasta?'

Vaelin recalled some of the more lurid battle stories told by the older boys. 'Shasta the Axe?'

'That's him. A legend in the Order, a great brute of a man, arms like tree trunks, fists like hams, they said he'd killed over a hundred men before they sent him to the Blackhold. Truly he was a hero . . . and quite the stupidest shithead I ever met. Mean with it too, 'specially when he'd had a drink. He was her gaoler.'

'I had heard he was a great warrior who did the Order much service,' Vaelin said.

Makril snorted. 'The Blackhold is where the Order puts its relics, boy. The ones that survive their fifteen years who're too stupid or too mad to be masters or commanders, they get sent to the Blackhold to live out their time locking up heretics, even if they're no bloody good at it. I've seen plenty of Shastas, big, ugly, brutish idiots with no thought in their heads but the next battle or the next tankard of ale. Usually they don't last long enough to be a problem but if they're big and strong enough, they linger, like a bad smell. Shasta lingered long enough to be sent to the Blackhold, Faith help us.'

'So,' Vaelin ventured carefully, 'this oaf left her cell open and she walked out?'

Makril laughed, a hard, unpleasant sound. 'Not quite. He gave her the keys to the front gate, took his axe down from the wall of his quarters and started killing the other brothers on watch. Cut down ten men before one of the archers put enough shafts in him to slow him down. Even then he killed two more before they gutted him. Weird thing, he died with a smile on his face, and before he died he said something: "She touched me."'

Vaelin realised his fingers were playing on the subtle weave of Sella's scarf. 'She touched him?' he asked, auburn curls and elfin features looming large in his head.

Makril took another long gulp from his flask. 'So they say. Didn't know the nature of her Dark affliction, see? If she touches you, you're hers forever.'

Vaelin was feverishly engaged in recalling his every encounter with Sella. *I pushed her into the shelter, did I touch her then? No, she was well clothed . . . She reached to me though . . . I felt her, in my head. Was that how she touched me? Is that why I helped her?* He felt an urge to ask Makril for more information but knew it would be folly. The tracker was suspicious enough already. Drunk as he was it would be unwise to question him further.

'Tendris and me've been hunting her ever since,' Makril continued. 'Four weeks now. This is the closest we've got. It's that bastard she's with, swear I'm gonna make him squeal good and long before I kill him.' He cackled and drank some more.

Vaelin found his hand inching closer to his knife. He was forming a deep dislike of Brother Makril, he reminded him too much of the assassins in the forest. And who knew what conclusions he had drawn. 'He told me his name was Erlin,' he said.

'Erlin, Rellis, Hetril, he's got a hundred names.'

'So who is he really?'

Makril gave an extravagant shrug. 'Who knows? He helps Deniers. Helps them hide, helps them run. Did he tell you about his travels? From the Alpiran Empire to the Leandren Temples.'

The knife hilt was tight in Vaelin's grasp. 'He told me.'

'Impressed were you?' Makril belched, a long rumble of escaping gas. 'I've travelled, y'know. I've bloody travelled. Meldenean Islands, Cumbrael, Renfael. Killed rebels, heretics and outlaws all over this great land, I have. Men, women, children . . .'

Vaelin's knife was halfway out of its sheath. *He's drunk, won't be too difficult.*

'One time, me and Tendris found a whole sect, families, bowing to one of their gods in a barn in the Martishe. Tendris got angry, it's best not to argue with him when he gets like that. He ordered us to lock the doors and douse the place in lamp oil, then he struck a flint . . . Wouldn't have thought children could scream so loud.'

The knife was almost clear of its sheath when Vaelin saw something that made him stop: beads of silver were shining in Makril's beard. He was crying.

'They screamed for such a long time.' He lifted his flask to his mouth but found it was empty. 'Shit!' Grumbling, he got unsteadily to his feet and stumbled off into the darkness, a short while later came the distinctive sound of piss hissing into snow.

Vaelin knew if he was going to do it, now was the time. *Slit the bastard's throat when he's having a piss.* A fitting end for such a vile man. *How many more children will he kill if I let him live?* But the tears were troubling, tears that told him Makril was a man who hated what he did. And he was a brother of the Order. It seemed wrong to kill a man whose fate he might be sharing in years to come. A sudden conviction rose in him then, fierce and implacable: *I'll fight but I won't murder. I'll kill men who face me in battle but I won't take the sword to innocents. I won't kill children.*

'Is Hutril still there?' Makril slurred, stumbling back to collapse onto his bedroll. 'Still teaching you little shits how to track?'

'He's still there. We are grateful for his wisdom.'

'Fuck his wisdom. Was supposed to be my job, y'know. Commander Lilden said I was the finest tracker in the Order. Said when he got made Aspect he'd bring me back to the House to be master of the wild. Then the silly bastard got a Meldenean sabre through his guts and Arlyn was chosen. Never liked me, the sanctimonious shit. Chose Hutril, legendary silent hunter of the Martishe forest. Sent me off to hunt heretics with Tendris.' He slumped onto his back, his eyes half-lidded, his voice softening to a whisper. 'Never asked for this. I just wanted to learn how to track . . . Like my old man could . . . Just wanted to track . . .'

Vaelin watched him pass out and added more wood to the fire. Scratch crept back to camp and settled next to him after a few wary glances at Makril. Vaelin scratched his ears, reluctant to go to bed, knowing his dreams would be full of burning barns and screaming children. Although his urge to kill Makril had evaporated, he still didn't feel comfortable sharing a camp with the man.

He spent another hour studying the stars with Scratch beside him. On the other side of the fire Makril slept his drunken sleep in silence. It was odd that the tracker made so little noise, not a snore or a grunt, even his breathing was soft. Vaelin wondered if this was a skill that could be learned, or was it an instinct all brothers gained after years of service; no doubt the ability to sleep in silence could prolong a man's life. He took to the shelter when tiredness made his eyelids droop, settling into his blanket with Scratch between him and the entrance. He had decided Makril hadn't come to kill him but it was best to be safe and it seemed highly unlikely the man would attempt an attack if he had to get past the dog.

Vaelin huddled close to the animal, drawing warmth and feeling glad he had kept him. A boy could do worse than have a slave-hound for a friend . . .

In the morning Makril was gone. Vaelin searched thoroughly but found no sign the tracker had ever been close by. As expected the hollow where he had hidden Sella and Erlin was empty. He took Sella's scarf from his neck, studying the intricate pattern woven into the silk, gold threads describing various sigils. Some were clearly recognisable, a crescent moon, the sun, a bird, others unfamiliar. Probably icons of her Denier beliefs. If so, he should discard it, any Master finding it would mete out severe punishment, maybe more than a beating. But it was such a well-made thing, so finely woven, the gold thread glittered like new. He knew Sella would grieve its loss terribly, it had been her mother's after all.

Sighing, he tucked the scarf into his sleeve and sent a silent plea to the Departed to see the pair safely to wherever they were going. He made his way back to the camp, lost in thought. He had to decide what to tell Master Hutril and needed time to consider his lies carefully. Scratch scampered ahead of him, snapping at the snow joyfully.

It was a silent ride back with Master Hutril, Vaelin was the only boy in the cart. He asked about the others and received only a grunted response: 'Bad year, the storm.' Vaelin shivered, suppressing panicked thoughts about his comrades, and climbed onto the cart. Hutril started off with Scratch scampering after in the deep ruts left in the snow. Hutril had listened to Vaelin's story in silence, staring expressionlessly at Scratch as Vaelin stumbled through his partially invented account. He stuck mostly to the same story he had told Tendris but left out Makril's visit the night before. Hutril's only reaction had come when Vaelin mentioned the tracker's name; a raised eyebrow. Otherwise he said nothing, letting the silence drag out when Vaelin had finished talking.

'Erm, I suggest we take the dog back to the House, Master,' Vaelin said. 'Master Jeklin may find a use for him.'

'The Aspect will decide that,' Hutril said. 'Get in.'

At first it seemed the Aspect would have even less to say than Master Hutril, sitting behind his large oak-wood desk, staring wordlessly at Vaelin over steepled fingers as he repeated his tale, desperately hoping he remembered it correctly. The presence of Master Sollis, seated in the corner, did little to alleviate his discomfort. Vaelin had been to the Aspect's rooms only once before, on an errand to deliver parchment, and found the piles of books and papers that littered the place had grown since. There must have been hundreds of books crammed in here, stacks stretching from floor to ceiling, with countless scrolls and ribbon-bound sheaves of documents occupying the remaining space. It was a collection that made his mother's library seem paltry in comparison.

Vaelin had been surprised at the lack of interest in Scratch. The Masters seemed preoccupied, besides which they were difficult men to impress at the best of times. Sollis had met him in the courtyard as he got down from the cart. Favouring Scratch with a brief look of incurious disgust, he said, 'Nysa and Dentos made it back so far, the others are due in tomorrow. Leave your gear here and follow me to the Aspect's chambers. He wants to see you.'

Vaelin assumed the Aspect wanted an explanation as to why he had returned with a large and savage animal in tow and repeated his story when the Aspect asked for a report on his test.

'You seem well fed,' the Aspect observed. 'Usually boys return thinner and weaker.'

'I was fortunate, Aspect. Scr – the dog helped by scenting a stag killed in a storm. I didn't think it would breach the conditions of the test as we are permitted to use whatever tools we find in the wild.'

'Yes.' The Aspect clasped his long fingers together, resting them on the desk. 'Very resourceful. Pity you couldn't help Brother Tendris in his search. He is one of the Faith's most valued servants.'

Vaelin thought of burning children and forced an earnest nod. 'Indeed, Aspect. I was impressed with his devotion.'

Vaelin heard Sollis make a small noise behind him and couldn't decide if it was a laugh or a snort of derision.

The Aspect smiled, an odd sight on such a thin face, but it was a smile of regret. 'There have been . . . events beyond our walls since your test began,' he said. 'That is why I called you here. The Battle Lord has resigned from the King's service. This has caused disharmony in the Realm, the Battle Lord was popular with the common folk. That being the case, and in recognition of his service, the King has granted him a boon. Do you know what that is?'

'A gift, Aspect.'

'Yes, a king's gift. Anything which it is in the King's power to give. The Battle Lord has chosen his boon and the King looks to us to fulfil it. Except our Order cannot be commanded by the King, we defend the Realm but we serve the Faith and the Faith is above the Realm. But still, he looks to us, and it is not an easy thing to refuse a king.'

Vaelin stirred uncomfortably. The Aspect seemed to be expecting something from him but he had no idea what it could be. Eventually, finding the silence unbearable he said, 'I see, Aspect.'

The Aspect exchanged a brief glance with Master Sollis. 'You understand Vaelin? You know what this means?'

I am the Battle Lord's son no longer, Vaelin thought. He wasn't sure how to feel about that, in fact he wasn't sure he felt anything at all about it. 'I am a brother of the Order, Aspect,' he said. 'Events outside these walls do not concern me until I pass the Test of the Sword and am sent forth to defend the Faith.'

'Your presence here was a symbol of the Battle Lord's devotion to the Faith and the Realm,' the Aspect explained. 'But he is Battle Lord no longer and wishes his son returned to him.'

Vaelin wondered at the absence of joy or surprise, no leap of the heart or stomach-churning surge of excitement. Just numb puzzlement. *The Battle Lord wishes his son returned to him.* He remembered the drumbeat thud of hooves on damp sod fading into morning fog, the stern command in his father's words, *Loyalty is our strength.*

He forced himself to meet the Aspect's eye. 'You would send me away, Aspect?'

'My wishes are not at issue here. Neither are Master Sollis's, although rest assured he has made them plain. No, this decision falls to you, Vaelin. As the King cannot command us, and it is a cherished maxim of our Order that no student is forced to leave unless he fails a test or transgresses the Faith, the King has given the choice to you.'

Vaelin suppressed a bitter laugh. *Choice? My father made a choice once. Now so will I.* 'The Battle Lord has no son,' he told the Aspect. 'And I have no father. I am a brother of the Sixth Order. My place is here.'

The Aspect looked down at his desk, suddenly seeming older than Vaelin had seen him before. *How old is he?* It was difficult to tell. He had the same fluid movements of the other masters, but his long features were lean and worn with outdoor living, his eyes aged and heavy with experience. There was a sadness too, a regret as he pondered Vaelin's words.

'Aspect,' Master Sollis said. 'The boy needs rest.'

The Aspect looked up, meeting Vaelin's gaze with his old, tired eyes. 'If that is your final word.'

'It is, Aspect.'

The Aspect smiled, Vaelin could tell it was forced. 'You gladden my heart, young brother. Take your dog to Master Chekril, I think he'll prove more welcoming than you might expect.'

'Thank you, Aspect.'

'Thank you, Vaelin, you may go.'

'A Volarian slave-hound.' Master Chekril breathed in awe as Scratch stared up at him, his scarred head angled in puzzlement. 'Haven't seen one in twenty years or more.'

Master Chekril was a cheerful, wiry man in early middle age, his movements more jerky and less measured than the other masters, mirroring the hounds he cared for with such dedication. His robe was dirtier than any Vaelin had seen, stained with earth, hay and a mixture of urine and dog muck. The odour he emitted was truly spectacular but he didn't seem to mind, or pay the slightest heed to any offence it might cause anyone else.

'You killed its pack brothers, you say?' he asked Vaelin.

'Yes, Master. Brother Makril said it saw me as pack leader now.'

'Oh yes. He's right about that. Dogs are wolves, Vaelin, they live in packs, but their instincts are dulled, the packs they run in are temporary, they quickly forget who is leader and who is not. But slave-hounds are different, got enough of the wolf left in them to keep the pack order but they're more vicious than any wolf, bred that way centuries ago. Only the nastier pups got bred, some say there was a touch of the Dark in their breeding. They were changed somehow, made more than a dog but less than a wolf, and different to both. When you killed the pack leader it adopted you, saw you as stronger, a worthy leader. Doesn't happen every time though. You've certainly got a measure of luck, young man.'

Master Chekril took a small piece of dried beef from the pouch at his belt and crouched lower to offer it to Scratch, Vaelin noting the hesitant, wary movements of the man. *He's scared,* he realised, appalled. *He's frightened of Scratch.*

Scratch sniffed the meat cautiously, glancing uncertainly at Vaelin.

'See?' Chekril said. 'He won't take it from me. Here.' He tossed the morsel to Vaelin. 'You try.'

Vaelin held the meat out to Scratch, who snapped it up and wolfed it down in an instant.

'Why's he called a slave-hound, Master?' Vaelin asked.

'Volarians keep slaves, lots of them. When one of them runs they bring him back and cut the small fingers off his hands. If he runs again, they send the slave-hounds after him. They don't bring him back, except in their bellies. It's not an easy thing for a dog to kill a man. Men are stronger than you think, and more cunning than any fox. For a dog to kill a man it must be strong and swift but also cunning, and vicious, very vicious.'

Scratch lay down at Vaelin's feet and rested his head on his boots, tail thumping slowly on the stone floor. 'He seems friendly enough.'

'He is, to you. But never forget, he's a killer. It's what he's bred for.' Master Chekril went to the rear of the large, stone storeroom that served as his kennels and opened a pen. 'I'll put him in here,' he said over his shoulder. 'You better lead him in, he won't stay otherwise.'

Scratch obediently followed Vaelin to the pen and went inside, briefly circling a patch of straw before lying down.

'You'll have to feed him too,' Chekril said. 'Muck him out and so on. Twice a day.'

'Of course, Master.'

'He'll need exercise, plenty of it. Can't take him out with the other hounds, he'd kill them.'

'I'll attend to it, Master.' He went into the pen and patted Scratch on the head, provoking a slobbering attack of licks that knocked him off his feet. Vaelin laughed and wiped the drool away. 'I had wondered if you would be happy to see him, Master,' he told Chekril. 'I thought you might want him killed.'

'Killed? Faith no! Would a blacksmith throw away a finely made sword? He'll be the start of a new blood line, he'll sire many puppies and hopefully they'll be just as strong as him but easier to manage.'

He stayed in the kennels for another hour, feeding Scratch and making sure he was comfortable in his new surroundings. When it came time to leave, Scratch's whines were heart-rending but Master Chekril told him he had to get the dog used to being left so he didn't turn around after he closed the pen door. Scratch started howling when he went out of his sight.

The evening was subdued, an unspoken tension reigning in the room. He exchanged stories of hardship and hunger with the others.

Caenis, like Vaelin, looking better fed than when he left, had taken shelter in the hollow trunk of an ancient oak only to find himself attacked by an angry eagle owl. Dentos, never fleshy at the best of times but now distinctly gaunt, had spent a miserable week fighting starvation with roots and the few birds and squirrels he managed to catch. Like the masters, neither seemed all that impressed with Vaelin's story. It was as if hardship bred indifference.

'What's a slave-hound?' Caenis asked dully.

'Volarian beast,' Dentos muttered. 'Nasty buggers. Can't use 'em for fighting, they turn on the handlers.' He turned to Vaelin, his gaze suddenly interested. 'Did you bring any food back with you?'

They spent the night in a sort of exhausted trance, Caenis honing the edge on his hunting knife with a whetstone and Dentos nibbling at the dried venison Vaelin had hidden in his cloak, with the small bites they knew best when you had an empty stomach; bolting would only make you sick.

'Never thought it was gonna end,' Dentos said eventually. 'Really thought I'd die out there.'

'None of the brothers I went out with came back,' Vaelin commented. 'Master Hutril said it was the storm.'

'Starting to see why there are so few brothers in the Order.'

The next day was probably the least punishing they had endured so far. Vaelin had expected a return to the harsh routine but instead Master Sollis filled the morning with a sign-language lesson, Vaelin found his meagre ability had improved after his brief exposure to Sella and Erlin's fluid signs although not by much and he still lagged behind Caenis. The afternoon was taken up with sword practice, Master Sollis introducing a new exercise, throwing rotten fruit and vegetables at them with blinding speed as they tried to fend off the putrid projectiles with their wooden swords. It was smelly but strangely enjoyable, more like a game than most of their exercises, which normally left them sporting a few bruises or a bloody nose.

Afterwards they ate their evening meal in uncomfortable silence, the dining hall was much quieter than usual, the many empty places seemed to stall attempts at conversation. The older boys gave them a few looks of sympathy or grim amusement but no-one commented on the absences. It was like the aftermath of Mikehl's death only on a grander scale. Some boys were already lost and wouldn't be coming back, others were yet to return and the tension of worrying over their possible nonappearance was palpable. Vaelin and the others exchanged some grunted comments about stinking like compost from the afternoon practice but there was little real humour in it. They concealed a few apples and bread rolls in their cloaks and returned to the tower.

It grew dark and still no-one returned. Vaelin began to feel a sinking certainty that they were the only boys left in their group. No more Barkus to make them laugh, no Nortah to bore them with another of his father's axioms. It was a truly chilling prospect.

They were climbing into bed when the sound of footsteps on the stone staircase outside caused them to freeze in wary anticipation.

'Two apples says it's Barkus,' Dentos said.

'Taken,' Caenis accepted.

'Ho there!' Nortah greeted them brightly, coming in to dump his gear on his bed. He was thinner than Caenis and Vaelin but didn't quite match Dentos's haggard emaciation, and his eyes were red with exhaustion. Despite it all, he seemed cheerful, even triumphant.

'Barkus here yet?' he asked, stripping his clothes away.

'No,' Caenis said, smiling at Dentos, who curled a disgusted lip.

Vaelin noticed something new about Nortah as he pulled his

shirt over his head, a necklace of what looked like elongated beads around his neck. 'Did you find that?' he asked, gesturing at the necklace.

There was a flash of smug satisfaction on Nortah's face, a mingled expression of victory and anticipation. 'Bear claws,' he said. Vaelin admired his offhanded manner and imagined the hours of rehearsal it must have taken. He decided to keep quiet and force Nortah to tell the tale of his own volition, but Dentos spoiled it.

'You found a bear-claw necklace,' he said. 'So what? Took it off some poor fool caught in the storm, eh?'

'No, I made it from the claws of a bear I killed.'

He continued to undress, affecting disinterest in their reaction, but Vaelin saw clearly how much he was enjoying the moment.

'Killed a bear my arse!' Dentos sneered.

Nortah shrugged. 'Believe me or not, it's of no matter.'

They lapsed into silence, Dentos and Caenis refusing to ask the inevitable question despite their obvious curiosity. The moment stretched and Vaelin decided he was too tired to let the tension endure.

'Please, brother,' he said. 'Tell us how you killed a bear.'

'I put an arrow in its eye. It took a fancy to a deer I'd brought down. Couldn't have that. Anyone who tells you bears sleep through the winter is a liar.'

'Master Hutril says they only wake up when they're forced. You must have found a very unusual bear, brother.'

Nortah fixed him with an odd look, coldly superior, which was usual, but also knowing, which was not. 'I must say I'm surprised to find you here, brother. I met a trapper in the wilds, a rough fellow to be sure, and a drunkard if I'm any judge. He had a lot of news to share about events in the wider world.'

Vaelin said nothing. He had decided not to tell the others about the King's boon to his father but it seemed Nortah would leave him little choice.

'The Battle Lord left the King's service,' Caenis said. 'Yes, we heard.'

'Some say he asked a boon of the King to return his son from the Order,' Dentos put in. 'But since the Battle Lord don't have a son, how could he be returned?'

They knew, Vaelin realised. *They knew ever since I arrived. That's why they've been so quiet. They were wondering when I was going to leave. Master Sollis must have told them I was staying today.* He wondered if it was truly possible to keep a secret in the Order.

'Perhaps,' Nortah was saying. 'The Battle Lord's son, if he had one, would be grateful for an opportunity to escape this place and return to the comfort of his family. It's not a chance any of the rest of us will ever get.'

Silence reigned. Dentos and Nortah glaring at each other fiercely and Caenis fidgeting in uncomfortable embarrassment. Finally, Vaelin said, 'It must have been a fine piece of bow work, brother. Putting an arrow in a bear's eye. Was it charging?'

Nortah gritted his teeth, controlling his anger. 'Yes.'

'Then it's to your credit that you held your nerve.'

'Thank you, brother. Do you have any stories to share?'

'I met a pair of fugitive heretics, one with the power to twist men's minds, killed two Volarian slave-hounds and kept another. Oh, and I met Brother Tendris and Brother Makril, they hunt Deniers.'

Nortah threw his shirt onto his bed, standing with his muscular arms on his hips, face set in a neutral frown. His self-control was admirable, the disappointment he felt barely showing but Vaelin saw it. This was to be his moment of triumph, he had killed a bear and Vaelin was leaving. It should have been one of the sweetest moments of his young life. Instead, Vaelin had refused the chance of escape, a chance Nortah hungered for, and his adventures made Nortah's look paltry in comparison. Watching him, Vaelin was struck by Nortah's physique. Although still only thirteen, the shape of the man he would become was clear; sculpted muscle and lean, handsome features. A son to make his King's Minister father proud. If he had lived his life outside the Order, it would have been a tale of romance and adventure played out under the admiring gaze of the court. Instead, he was doomed to a life of war, squalor and hardship in service to the Faith. A life he hadn't chosen.

'Did you take its pelt?' Vaelin asked.

Nortah frowned in irritated puzzlement. 'What?'

'The bear, did you skin it?'

'No. The storm was brewing, and I couldn't drag it back to my shelter so I hacked its paw off to take the claws.'

'A wise move, brother. And an impressive achievement.'

'I dunno,' Dentos said. 'I thought Caenis's eagle-owl thing was pretty good too.'

'An owl?' Vaelin said. '*I* brought back a slave-hound.'

They bickered good-naturedly for a while, even Nortah joined in with caustic observations of Dentos's thinness, they were family once more, but still incomplete. They went to bed later than usual, nervous of not greeting the next arrival, but tiredness overtook them. Vaelin's sleep was dreamless for once and when he woke it was with a startled shout, hands instinctively scrabbling for his hunting knife. He stopped when his eyes fixed on the bulky shape on the next bunk.

'Barkus?' he asked groggily.

There was a soft grunt, the shape immobile in the gloom.

'When did you get in?'

No answer. Barkus sat still, his silence disconcerting. Vaelin sat up, fighting the deep-seated desire to snuggle back into his blankets. 'Are you all right?' he asked.

More silence, stretching until Vaelin wondered if he should fetch Master Sollis, but Barkus said, 'Jennis is dead.' His voice was chilling in its complete lack of emotion. Barkus was the sort of boy who always felt something, joy or anger or surprise, it was always there, writ large in his face and his voice. But now there was nothing, just cold fact. 'I found him frozen to a tree. He didn't have his cloak on. I think he wanted it to happen. He hadn't been the same since Mikehl died.'

Mikehl, Jennis . . . How many more? Would any of them be left by the end? *I should be angry,* he thought. *We are just boys and these tests kill us.* But there was no anger, just fatigue and sorrow. *Why can't I hate them? Why don't I hate the Order?*

'Go to bed, Barkus,' he told his friend. 'In the morning we'll offer thanks for our brother's life.'

Barkus shivered, hugging himself closely. 'I'm scared of what I'll see when I sleep.'

'As am I. But we are of the Order and therefore of the Faith. The Departed do not want us to suffer. They send us dreams to guide us, not to hurt us.'

'I was hungry, Vaelin.' Tears glittered in Barkus's eyes. 'I was hungry and I didn't think about poor Jennis being dead or how we'd miss him or anything. I just looked through his clothes for food. He didn't have any so I cursed him, I cursed my dead brother.'

At a loss, Vaelin sat and watched Barkus crying in the darkness. *The Test of the Wild,* he thought. *More a test of the heart and the soul. Hunger tests us in so many ways.* 'You didn't kill Jennis,' he said eventually. 'You can't curse a soul that's joined the Departed. Even if our brother heard you, he would understand the weight of the test.'

It took a lot of persuading but Barkus went to bed about an hour later, his tiredness now too acute to be denied. Vaelin settled back into his own bed, knowing sleep would evade him now and the next day would be spent in a fug of clumsiness and confusion. *Master Sollis will start caning us again tomorrow,* he realised. He lay awake and thought about his test and his dead friend and Sella and Erlin and Makril crying like Barkus had cried. Was there a place for such thoughts in the Order? A sudden, unbidden thought, loud and bright in his mind, shocking him: *Go back to your father and you could think what you like.*

He squirmed in his bed. Where had that come from? *Go back to my father?* 'I have no father.' He didn't realise he had spoken aloud until Barkus groaned, turning over restlessly. On the other side of the room Caenis too had been disturbed, sighing heavily and pulling his blankets over his head.

Vaelin sank deeper into his bed, seeking comfort, willing himself to sleep, clinging to the thought: *I have no father.*

CHAPTER FOUR

S pring saw the snow-covered practice field darken into deep
  green as they laboured under Master Sollis's tutelage, their
  skills growing with every day, as did their bruises. A new
element was introduced late in the month of Onasur; studies for
the Test of Knowledge under the guidance of Master Grealin.

Every day they were trooped down into the cavernous cellars
and made to sit and listen to his tales of the history of the Order.
He spoke well, a natural storyteller conjuring images of great
deeds, heroism and justice that had most of them rapt in attentive silence. Vaelin liked the stories too but his interest was
dampened by the fact that they all related to daring exploits or
great battles and never featured Deniers being hunted through
the countryside or imprisoned in the Blackhold. At the end of
every lesson Grealin would ask them questions on what they
had heard. Boys who answered correctly were given sweets,
those who couldn't answer were favoured with a sad shake
of the head and a sorrowful comment or two. Master Grealin
was the least harsh of all the masters, he never caned them, his
punishments were words or gestures, and he never cursed or
swore, something all the other masters did, even mute Master

Smentil, whose hands could shape profanity with remarkable accuracy.

'Vaelin,' Grealin said after relating the tale of the siege of Baslen Castle during the first War of Unification. 'Who held the bridge so his brothers could close the gate behind him?'

'Brother Nolnen, Master.'

'Very good Vaelin, have a barley sugar.'

Vaelin also noticed that every time Master Grealin gave them sweets he rewarded himself too. 'Now then,' he said, his considerable jowls quivering as he worked the barley sugar around his teeth. 'What was the name of the commander of the Cumbraelin forces?' He scanned them for a moment, seeking a victim. 'Dentos?'

'Erm, Verlig, Master.'

'Oh dear.' Master Grealin held up a toffee and shook his large head sadly. 'No reward for Dentos. In fact, remind me, little brother, how many rewards have you received this week?'

'None,' Dentos muttered.

'I beg your pardon, Dentos, what was that?'

'None, Master,' Dentos said loudly, his voice echoing in the caverns.

'None. Yes. None. I seemed to recall you received no rewards last week either. Isn't that right?'

Dentos looked as if he'd rather be suffering under Master Sollis's cane. 'Yes, Master.'

'Mmmm.' Grealin popped the toffee into his mouth, chins bobbing as he chewed with gusto. 'Pity. These toffees are quite superlative. Caenis, perhaps you can enlighten us.'

'Verulin commanded the Cumbraelin forces at the siege of Baslen Castle, Master.' Caenis's replies were always prompt and correct. Vaelin suspected sometimes his knowledge of the Order's history was equal if not superior to Master Grealin's.

'Quite so. Have a sugared walnut.'

'Bastard!' Dentos fumed later in the main hall as they ate their evening meal. 'Fat, smart-arsed bastard. Who cares if we know what some bugger did two hundred years ago? What's it gotta do with anythin'?'

'The lessons of the past guide us in the present,' Caenis quoted. 'Our Faith is strengthened by the knowledge of those who have gone before us.'

Dentos glowered at him over the table. 'Oh piss off. Just because the big mound of blubber loves you so much. "Yes, Master Grealin"' – he dropped into a surprisingly accurate impression of Caenis's soft tones – '"the battle of shithouse bend lasted two days and thousands of poor sods like us died in it. Let me have a sugar cane and I'll wipe your arse too."'

Next to Dentos, Nortah chuckled nastily.

'Watch your mouth, Dentos,' Caenis warned.

'Or what? You'll bore me to death with another bloody story about the King and his brats . . .'

Caenis was a blur, leaping across the table in a perfectly executed display of gymnastics, his boots connecting with Dentos's face, blood erupting as his head snapped back and they tumbled to the floor. The fight was short but bloody, their hard-won skills made fights dangerous affairs they usually tried to avoid even during the most fractious arguments, and Caenis was sporting a broken tooth and dislocated finger by the time they pulled them apart. Dentos wasn't much better, his nose broken and ribs severely bruised.

They took them both to Master Henthal, the Order's healer, who patched them up as they stared sullenly at each other from opposite bunks.

'What happened?' Master Sollis demanded of Vaelin as they waited outside.

'A disagreement between brothers, Master,' Nortah told him, it was the standard response in situations like this.

'I wasn't asking you, Sendahl,' Sollis snapped. 'Get back to the hall. You as well, Jeshua.'

Barkus and Nortah left quickly after giving Vaelin a puzzled glance. It was unusual for the masters to take a close interest in disagreements between the boys. Boys were boys after all, and boys would fight.

'Well?' Sollis said when they had gone.

Vaelin had a momentary impulse to lie but the hard fury in Master Sollis's gaze told him it would be a very bad idea. 'It's the test, Master. Caenis is sure to pass, Dentos isn't.'

'So, what are you going to do about it?'

'Me, Master?'

'We all have different roles to play in the Order. Most of us fight, some track heretics across the kingdom, others slip into the shadows to do their work in secret, a few will teach, and a few, a very few, lead.'

'You . . . want me to lead?'

'The Aspect seems to think it's your role, and he is rarely mistaken.' He glanced over his shoulder at Master Henthal's room. 'Leadership is not learned by watching your brothers beat each other bloody. Nor is it learned by letting them fail their tests. Fix this.'

He turned and left without another word. Vaelin rested his head against the stone wall and sighed heavily. *Leadership. Don't I have burdens enough?*

'You lot are getting meaner by the year,' Master Henthal told him brightly as Vaelin entered. 'Time was boys in their third year could only manage to bruise each other. Clearly we're teaching you too well.'

'We are grateful for your wisdom, Master,' Vaelin assured him. 'May I speak with my brothers?'

'As you wish.' He pressed a ball of cotton to Dentos's nose. 'Hold that until the bleeding stops. Don't swallow the blood, keep spitting it out. And use a bowl. Get any on my floor, and you'll wish your brother had killed you.' He left them alone in strained silence.

'How is it?' Vaelin asked Dentos.

Dentos could speak only in a wet rasp. 'Id bokken.'

Vaelin turned to Caenis, cradling his bandaged hand. 'And you?'

Caenis glanced down at his bandaged fingers. 'Master Henthal popped it back into place. Said it'll be sore for a while. Won't be able to hold a sword for about a week.' He paused, hawking and spitting a thick wad of blood into a bowl next to his bunk. 'Had to pull what was left of my tooth. Packed it with cotton and gave me redflower for the pain.'

'Does it work?'

Caenis winced a little. 'Not really.'

'Good. You deserve it.'

Caenis's face flashed with anger. 'You heard what he said . . .'

'I heard what he said. I heard what you said before that. You know he's having trouble with this but you decide to give him a lecture.' He turned to Dentos. 'And you should know better than to provoke him. We get enough chances to hurt each other on the practice field. Do it there if you have to.'

''E pisshes me od,' Dentos sputtered. 'Bein' shmart alla time.'

'Then maybe you should learn from him. He has knowledge, you need it, who better to ask?' He sat down next to Dentos. 'You know if you don't pass this test, you'll have to leave. Is that what you want? Go back to Nilsael and help your uncle fight his dogs and tell all the drunkards in the tavern how you nearly got to be in the Sixth Order? I bet they'll be impressed.'

'Shod off, Vaelin.' Dentos leaned over to let a large glob of blood fall from his nose into the bowl at his feet.

'You both know I didn't have to stay here,' Vaelin said. 'Do you know why I did?'

'You hate your father,' Caenis said, forgetting the usual convention.

Vaelin, unaware his feelings were so obvious, bit back a retort. 'I couldn't just leave. I couldn't go and live outside the Order always waiting to hear one day about what happened to the rest of you, wondering maybe if I'd been there, it wouldn't have happened. We lost Mikehl, we lost Jennis. We can't lose anyone else.' He got up and moved to the door. 'We're not boys any more. I can't make you do anything. It's up to you.'

'I'm sorry,' Caenis said, stopping him. 'What I said about your father.'

'I don't have a father,' Vaelin reminded him.

Caenis laughed, blood seeping thick and fast from his lip. 'No, neither do I.' He turned and threw his bloodied cloth at Dentos. 'How about you, brother? Got a father?'

Dentos laughed, long and hard, his face streaked with crimson. 'Wouldn't know the bugger if he gave me a pound of gold!'

They laughed together, for a long time. Pain receded and was forgotten. They laughed and never spoke about how much it hurt.

They took it on themselves to teach Dentos. He continued to learn next to nothing from Master Grealin so every night after practice they would relate a story of the Order's past and make him repeat it back, over and over again until he knew it by heart. It was tedious and exhausting work, undertaken following hours of exercise when all they wanted to do was sleep, but they stuck to their task with grim determination. As the most knowledgeable, much of the burden fell on Caenis, who proved a diligent if impatient mentor. His normally placid nature was tested to extremes by the stubborn refusal of Dentos's memory to store more than a few facts at a time. Barkus, who had a sound but not exhaustive knowledge of Order lore, tended to stick to the most humorous tales, like the legend of Brother Yelna who, bereft of weapons, had caused an enemy to faint with the remarkably noxious nature of his flatulence.

'They're not going to ask him about the farting brother,' Caenis said in disgust.

'They might,' Barkus replied. 'It's still history, isn't it?'

Surprisingly, Nortah proved the most able teacher, his story-telling technique straightforward but effective. He seemed to have an uncanny ability to make Dentos remember more. Instead of simply telling the tale and expecting Dentos to repeat it word for word, he would pause to ask questions, encouraging Dentos to think about the meaning of the story. His usual taste for ridicule was also put aside and he ignored numerous opportunities to laugh at the ignorance of his pupil. Vaelin normally found much to criticise in Nortah but he had to admit he was as determined as the rest of them to ensure the continuance of their group; life in the Order was hard enough, without his friends he might find it unbearable. Although his methods bore fruit, Nortah's choice of tale was fairly narrow; whilst Barkus favoured humour and Caenis liked parables illustrating the virtues of the Faith, Nortah had a taste for tragedy. He related the Order's defeats with relish, the fall of the citadel of Ulnar, the death of great Lesander, considered by many the finest warrior ever to serve in the Order, fatally flawed by his forbidden love for a woman who betrayed him to his enemies. Nortah's tales of woe seemed endless, some of them were new to Vaelin and he occasionally wondered if the blond brother wasn't just making them up.

Vaelin, with his added duties of seeing to Scratch in the kennels every evening, took on the task of testing Dentos's acquired knowledge at the end of each week, firing questions at him with increasing rapidity. It was often frustrating. Dentos's knowledge was growing, but he was fighting years of happy ignorance with a few weeks' effort. Nevertheless he did manage to earn some rewards from Master Grealin, who confined his surprise to a raised eyebrow.

With the month of Prensur the remaining time narrowed to a few days and Master Grealin informed them their lessons were over.

'Knowledge is what shapes us, little brothers,' he told them, for once his smile was absent, his tone entirely serious. 'It makes us who we are. What we know informs everything we do and every decision we make. In the next few days think hard on what you have learned here, not just the names and the dates, think on the reasons, think on the meaning. All I have told you is the sum of our Order, what it means, what it does. The test of knowledge is the hardest many of you will face, no other test bares a boy's soul.' He smiled again, gravely this time, then brightened into his habitual humour. 'Now then, final rewards for my little warriors.' He produced a large bag of sweets, moving down the line and dropping a selection into their upturned hands. 'Enjoy, little men. Sweetness is a rare thing in a brother's life.' Sighing heavily, he turned and waddled slowly back to the storeroom, closing the door softly behind him.

'What was that about?' Nortah wondered.

'Brother Grealin is a very strange man,' Caenis said with a shrug. 'Swap you a honey-drop for a sugar bean.'

Nortah snorted. 'A sugar bean is worth three honey-drops at least . . .'

Vaelin resisted the temptation to barter his sweets and took them to the kennels, where Scratch rolled and yelped with delight as he tossed the treats into the air for him to catch. He didn't miss a single one.

The test began on a Feldrian morning, two days before Summertide. Those boys who passed would be rewarded not only with the right to stay in the Order but also a pass for the great Summertide Fair at Varinshold, the first time they would be allowed out of the Order's care since the day of their joining. Those who failed would be given their gold coins and told to leave. For once the older boys had no dire warnings or ridicule to offer. Vaelin noted that mention of the Test of Knowledge around their peers provoked only sullen looks and vicious cuffs. He wondered what made them so angry, it was only a few questions after all.

'The only brother to journey through the Great Northern Forest,' he demanded of Dentos as they made their way to the dining hall.

'Lesander,' Dentos replied smugly. 'That was too easy by half.'

'Third Aspect of the Order?'

Dentos paused, brow furrowed as he searched his memory for the answer. 'Kinlial?'

'Are you asking or telling?'

'Telling.'

'Good. You're right.' Vaelin clapped him on the back as they continued across the courtyard. 'Dentos, my brother, I think you may pass this test today.'

They were called to the test in the afternoon, lining up outside a chamber in the south wall. Master Sollis gave them a stern warning to behave themselves and told Barkus he was first. Barkus seemed about to make a joke but the gravity on Sollis's face stopped him and he gave them only a brief bow before entering the chamber. Sollis closed the door behind him.

'Wait here,' he ordered. 'When you're done get to the dining hall.' He stalked off, leaving them staring at the solid oak door to the chamber.

'I thought he'd be doing this,' Dentos said, a little weakly.

'Doesn't look like it, does it?' Nortah said. He went to the door, leaning down to put his ear to the wood.

'Hear anything?' Dentos whispered.

Nortah shook his head, straightening. 'Just mumbles, the door's too thick.' He reached inside his cloak and came out with a board of pinewood about a foot square with numerous scars on its surface and an inch-wide circle of black paint in the centre. 'Knives anyone?'

Knives had become their principal game in recent months, a simple enough contest of skill where they would take turns trying to get their throwing knives as close to the centre of the board as possible. The winner would keep all the other knives in the board. There were variations on the basic game, where a board was propped against a convenient wall, sometimes it would be suspended from a rope tied to a roof beam and the object was to hit it as it swung back and forth, in other games it would be thrown in the air, occasionally set spinning end over end. Throwing knives were a kind of surrogate currency in the Order, they could be swapped for treats or favours and a brother's popularity was invariably enhanced if he managed to amass a large stock. The weapons themselves were plain, cheaply made items, triangular six-inch blades with a stubby handle, little larger than an arrowhead. Master Grealin had begun to hand them out at the start of their third year, ten for each boy, the supply to be renewed every six months. There was no formal instruction in how to use them, they simply watched the older boys and learned as they played. Predictably the best archers turned out to be the most successful players, Dentos and Nortah had the largest knife collection with Caenis a close third. Vaelin won only one game in ten but knew he was consistently improving, unlike Barkus, who seemed incapable of winning a single match, making him guard his knives jealously, although he became skilled at bartering for more with the spoils of his many thieving expeditions.

'Shitting, stupid, sodding thing!' Dentos fumed as his knife struck sparks on the wall behind the board. Evidently his nerves were throwing off his aim.

'You're out,' Nortah informed him. If a player missed the board, he was out of the game and his knife was forfeit.

Vaelin went next, sinking the knife into the outer edge of the circle, a better throw than he usually managed. Caenis's knife was a little further in but Nortah took the game with a blade only a finger width from the centre.

'I'm just too good at this,' he commented, retrieving his knives. 'I really should stop playing, it's not fair on everyone else.'

'Piss off!' Dentos spat. 'I've beaten you tons of times.'

'Only when I let you,' Nortah replied mildly. 'If I didn't, you wouldn't keep coming back for more.'

'Right.' Dentos snatched a knife from his belt and let fly at the target in a single smooth movement. It was probably the best throw Vaelin had seen, the knife buried dead in the centre of the board up to the hilt. 'Beat that, rich boy,' Dentos told Nortah.

Nortah raised an eyebrow. 'Luck smiles on you today, brother.'

'Luck my arse. You gonna throw or not?'

Nortah shrugged, taking a knife and eyeing the board carefully. He slowly drew back his arm and then snapped it forward so fast his hand blurred, the knife a brief glitter of silver as it spun towards the target. There was the high ping of metal on metal as it rebounded from Dentos's knife hilt and landed a few feet away.

'Oh well.' Nortah went to retrieve his knife, its blade bent at the tip. 'Yours I believe,' he said, offering it to Dentos.

'We should call it a draw. You would've hit centre if my knife wasn't in the way.'

'But it was, brother. And I didn't.' He continued to hold the knife out until Dentos took it.

'I won't trade this one,' he said. 'This'll be my charm, for luck y'know? Like that silk scarf Vaelin thinks we haven't noticed.'

Vaelin snorted in disgust. 'Can't I keep anything from you buggers?'

They passed the remaining time playing toss board, hurling knives at the board as Vaelin tossed it into the air. It was Caenis's best game and he was up five more knives by the time Barkus emerged.

'Thought you'd be in there forever,' Dentos said.

Barkus seemed subdued, responding only with a brief, guarded smile before turning and walking quickly away.

'Shit,' Dentos breathed, his rebuilt confidence faltering visibly.

'Bear up, brother.' Vaelin clapped him on the shoulder. 'Soon be over.' His tone hid a real unease. Barkus's demeanour worried him, reminding him of the older boys' sullen silence when the subject of this test came up. Master Grealin's words coming back to him as he puzzled over why this test inspired such grim reticence. *No other test bares a boy's soul.*

He steeled himself as he approached the door, a hundred and one likely questions flitting through his head. *Remember,* he told himself emphatically, *Carlist was the third Aspect in the Order's history not the second. It's a common mistake due to the assassination of the previous incumbent only two days after inauguration.* He took a breath, forcing the tremble from his hand as he turned the heavy brass door handle and went inside.

The chamber was small, an unremarkable space with a low, arched ceiling and a single narrow window. Candles had been placed around the room but did little to alleviate the oppressive gloom. Three people sat behind a solid oak table, three people who wore robes a different colour to his own dark blue, three people who were not of the Sixth Order. Vaelin's trepidation took another leap and he couldn't suppress a visible start. *What kind of test is this?*

'Vaelin.' One of the strangers addressed him, a blonde woman in a grey robe. She smiled warmly, gesturing at the empty chair facing the table. 'Please sit down.'

He steadied himself and moved to the chair. The three strangers studied him in silence, giving him the chance to return the scrutiny. The man in the green robe was fat and bald, with a thin beard tracing the line of this jaw and mouth, although his corpulence didn't compare to Master Grealin's, he had none of the brother's innate strength, his pink, fleshy face shining with sweat, his jowls wobbling as he chewed. A bowl of cherries sat on the table next to his left hand, his lips a telltale red of continual indulgence. He regarded Vaelin with a mixture of curiosity and obvious disdain. By contrast the man in the black robe was thin to the point of emaciation, although he was equally bald. His expression was more troubling than the fat man's, it was the same fierce mask of blind devotion he had seen on brother Tendris's face.

But it was the woman in grey who commanded most of his attention. She seemed to be in her thirties, her angular face framed by gold-blonde hair that hung down over her shoulders, was comely and vaguely familiar. But it was her eyes that intrigued him, bright with warmth and compassion. He was reminded of Sella's pale face, and the kindness he had seen in her when she stopped herself touching him. But Sella had been full of fear, whereas he found it hard to imagine this woman's ever being so vulnerable. There was a strength in her. The same strength he saw in the Aspect and Master Sollis. He found it hard not to stare.

'Vaelin,' she said. 'Do you know who we are?'

He saw little point in trying to guess. 'No, my lady.'

The fat man grunted and popped a cherry into his mouth. 'Another ignorant whelp,' he said, chewing noisily. 'Don't they teach you little savages anything but the arts of slaughter?'

'They teach us to defend the Faithful and the Realm, sir.'

The fat man stopped chewing, his contempt suddenly replaced by anger. 'We'll see what you know of the Faith, young man,' he said evenly.

'I am Elera Al Mendah,' the blonde woman said. 'Aspect of the Fifth Order. These are my brother Aspects, Dendrish Hendril of the Third Order' – she gestured to the fat man in green – 'and Corlin Al Sentis of the Fourth Order.' The thin man in black nodded gravely.

Vaelin was taken aback to be in such august company. Three Aspects, all in the same room, all talking to him. He knew he should feel honoured but instead there was only a chilling uncertainty. What could three Aspects from other Orders ask him about the history of his own?

'You're wondering about all your hard-earned facts on the fascinating history of the Sixth Order and its innumerable bloodbaths.' Dendrish Hendril, the fat man, spat a cherry stone into a delicately embroidered handkerchief. 'Your masters have been misleading you, boy. We have no questions on long-dead heroes or best-forgotten battles. That's not the strain of knowledge we seek.'

Elera Al Mendah turned her smile on her fellow Aspect. 'I think we should explain the test in greater detail, dearest brother.'

Dendrish Hendril's eyes narrowed slightly but he gave no reply, reaching instead for another cherry.

'The Test of Knowledge,' Elera went on, turning back to Vaelin, 'is unique in that all brothers and sisters in training in each of the Orders must pass it. It is not a test of strength, skill or memory. It is a test of knowledge, self-knowledge. To serve your Order you must have more than skill with arms, just as servants of my order must know more than the arts of healing. It is your soul that makes you who you are, your soul that guides your service to the Faith. This test will tell us, and you, if you know the nature of your soul.'

'And don't bother lying,' Dendrish Hendril instructed. 'You can't lie in here and you'll fail the test if you try.'

Vaelin's uncertainty deepened further. The lies he told kept him safe. Lying had become a necessary act of survival. Erlin and Sella, the wolf in the forest and the assassin he had killed. All secrets shrouded in lies. Fighting panic, he forced himself to nod and say, 'I understand, Aspect.'

'No you don't, boy. You're shitting your pants. I can almost smell it.'

Aspect Elera's smile faltered slightly but she kept her attention on Vaelin. 'Are you afraid, Vaelin?'

'Is this the test, Aspect?'

'The test started the moment you entered the room. Please, answer me.'

You can't lie. 'I am . . . worried. I don't know what to expect. I don't want to leave the Order.'

Dendrish Hendril snorted. 'Scared of facing your father more like. Think he'll be happy to see you?'

'I don't know,' Vaelin replied honestly.

'Your father wanted you returned to him,' Elera said. 'Doesn't that tell you he cares about you?'

Vaelin squirmed in discomfort. He had avoided or suppressed memories of his father for so long this kind of scrutiny was hard to endure. 'I don't know what it means. I . . . barely knew him before I came here. He was often away, fighting the King's wars, and when he was home he said little to me.'

'So you hate him?' Dendrish Hendril enquired. 'I can certainly understand that.'

'I don't hate him. I don't know him. He is not my family. My family is here.'

The thin man, Corlin Al Sentis, spoke for the first time. His voice was harsh, rasping. 'You killed a man during the Test of the Run,' he said, his fierce eyes locked onto Vaelin's. 'Did you enjoy it?'

Vaelin was stunned. *They know! How much more do they know?*

'Aspects share information, boy,' Dendrish Hendril told him. 'It's how our Faith endures. Unity of purpose, unity of trust. Our Realm was named for it. Something you'd do well to remember. And don't worry, your sordid secrets are safe with us. Answer Aspect Sentis's question.'

Vaelin took a deep breath, trying to still the heavy thump in his chest. He thought back to the Test of the Run, the snap of the bowstring that had saved him from the assassin's arrow, the slack, inanimate mask of the man's face, his gorge rising as he sawed at the fletching with his knife . . . 'No. No I didn't enjoy it.'

'Do you regret it?' Corlin Al Sentis persisted.

'The man was trying to kill me. I had no choice. I cannot regret staying alive.'

'So that's all you care about?' Dendrish Hendril asked. 'Staying alive?'

'I care about my brothers, I care about the Faith and the Realm . . .' *I care about Sella the Denier witch and Erlin who helped her run. But I can't say I care much for you, Aspect.*

He tensed, waiting for rebuke or punishment, but the three Aspects said nothing, exchanging unreadable glances. *They can hear lies,* he realised. *But not thoughts.* He could hide things, he didn't have to lie. Silence could be his shield.

It was Aspect Elera who spoke next, her question the worst yet. 'Do you remember your mother?'

Vaelin's discomfort was abruptly replaced by anger. 'We leave our family ties behind when we enter this house . . .'

'Don't be impertinent, boy!' Aspect Hendril snapped. 'We ask, you answer. That's how this works.'

Vaelin's jaw ached with the effort of biting back a furious retort.

Fighting to control his anger, he grated, 'Of course I remember my mother.'

'I remember her too,' Aspect Elera said. 'She was a good woman who sacrificed much to marry your father and bring you into this world. Like you she had chosen a life in the service of the Faith. She was once a sister in the Fifth Order, highly respected for her knowledge of healing; she was to be a Mistress in our House. She may even have become Aspect in time. At the King's command she travelled with his army when it moved against the first Cumbraelin revolt. She met your father when he was wounded after the Battle of the Hallows. As she tended his wounds love grew between them and she left the Order to marry. Did you know that?'

Vaelin, numb with shock, could only shake his head. His memories of childhood outside the Order were dimmed with time and deliberate suppression but he recalled occasional suspicions of his parents' dissimilar origins; their voices were different, his father's lack of grammar and clipped vowels a contrast to the even, precise tones of his mother. His father also knew little of table manners, often ignoring the knife and fork next to his plate and reaching for the food with his hands, seeming genuinely bemused when his mother sighed a gentle rebuke, 'Please dear. This is not a barracks.' But he had never dreamt she too once served the Faith.

'If she were still alive' – Aspect Elera's voice snapped him back to the present – 'would she let you give your life to the Order?'

The temptation to lie was almost overwhelming. He knew what his mother would have said, how she would have felt to see him in this robe, his hands and face bruised and raw from practice, how it would have hurt her. But if he said it, it became real, he couldn't hide from it any longer. But he knew it was a trap. *They want me to lie*, he realised. *They want me to fail.*

'No,' he said. 'She hated war.' So it was out. He was living a life his mother would never have wanted, he was dishonouring her memory.

'She told you that?'

'No, she told my father. She didn't want him to leave for the war against the Meldeneans. She said the stench of blood sickened her. She wouldn't have wanted this life for me.'

'How does that make you feel?' Elera persisted.

He found himself speaking without thinking, 'Guilty.'

'And yet you stayed, when you had the chance to leave.'

'I felt that I needed to be here. I needed to stay with my brothers. I needed to learn what the Order could teach me.'

'Why?'

'I . . . think it's what I'm supposed to do. It's what the Faith requires of me. I know the sword and the staff as a blacksmith knows his hammer and anvil. I have strength and speed and cunning and . . .' He hesitated, knowing he had to force the words out, hating them even so. 'And I can kill,' he said, meeting her eyes. 'I can kill without hesitating. I was meant to be a warrior.'

There was silence in the room save for the soft wet sound of Dendrish Hendril chewing another cherry. Vaelin stared at each of them in turn, appalled by the fact that none of them wanted to return his gaze. Elera Al Mendah's reaction was almost shocking, looking down at her hands clasped in front her, she looked as if she was about to cry.

Finally, Dendrish Hendril broke the silence, 'That'll do, boy. You can go. Don't talk to your friends on the way out.'

Vaelin rose uncertainly. 'The test is over, Aspect?'

'Yes. You passed. Congratulations. I am sure you'll be a credit to the Sixth Order.' His acid tone spoke clearly that he did not consider this a compliment.

Vaelin moved to the door, glad for the release; the atmosphere in the room was oppressive, the scrutiny of the Aspects difficult to bear.

'Brother Vaelin,' Corlin Al Sentis's cold rasp stopped him as he reached for the door handle.

Vaelin swallowed a sigh of exasperation and forced himself to turn. Corlin Al Sentis was giving him the full benefit of his fanatical gaze. Aspect Elera didn't look up and Dendrish Al Hendril gave him a brief, disinterested glance.

'Yes, Aspect?'

'Did she touch you?'

Vaelin knew whom he meant, of course. It was foolish of him to think he could escape without facing this question. 'You mean Sella, Aspect?'

'Yes, Sella the murderer, Denier and student of the Dark. You helped her and the traitor in the wild, did you not?'

'I didn't know who they were until later, Aspect.' The truth, hiding a lie. He felt himself start to sweat and prayed it didn't show on his face. 'They were strangers lost in a storm. The Catechism of Charity tells us to treat a stranger as a brother.'

Corlin Al Sentis raised his head slightly, his unwavering glare taking on a calculating cast. 'I didn't know the Catechism of Charity was taught here.'

'It isn't, Aspect. My . . . mother taught me all the catechisms.'

'Yes. She was a lady of considerable charity. You haven't answered my question.'

He didn't have to lie. 'She didn't touch me, Aspect.'

'You know the power of her touch? What it does to men's souls?'

'Brother Makril told me. Truly I was fortunate to escape such a fate.'

'Truly.' The Aspect's gaze softened, but only slightly. 'You may feel that this test has been harsh but you realise what awaits you will be harder still. Life in your Order is never easy. Many of your brothers will succumb to madness or maiming before they are called to the Departed. You know this?'

Vaelin nodded. 'I do, Aspect.'

'It does you credit that you decided to stay, when you could have left with no stain on your character. Your devotion to the Faith will be remembered.'

For no apparent reason Vaelin felt these words to be a threat, a threat the Aspect didn't even know he was making. But he forced himself to say, 'Thank you, Aspect.'

Outside, he closed the door softly behind him, resting his back to it, exhaling explosively in relief. He didn't notice the others staring for a few seconds. They looked worried, especially Dentos.

'Faith help me,' Dentos breathed softly, clearly appalled at Vaelin's countenance.

Vaelin straightened, fixed what he knew to be a weak smile on his face and walked away, trying not to hurry.

With the exception of Dentos, the Test of Knowledge left a cloud of depression over them all. Caenis was silent, Barkus monosyllabic, Nortah aggressively truculent and Vaelin so preoccupied with memories of his mother that he found himself wandering through the rest of the day in a miserable daze, tossing scraps to Scratch and fending off his attempts at play, before joining the others for a desultory game of knives on the practice field.

'What a piece of piss that was,' Dentos said, the only one of them to retain any semblance of good humour, sending a knife skyward to connect with the board Barkus had tossed into the air. His cheerfulness was made more annoying by his apparent ignorance of the mood of his companions. 'I mean they didn't ask me anything about the Order, just kept going on about my mum and where I grew up. The lady Aspect, Elera whatsername, asked if I was homesick. Homesick? Like I'd *want* to go back to that shit pit.'

He retrieved the board, working his knife loose and casting it upwards for Nortah's throw. The knife went wide, in fact it went so wide it nearly caught Dentos on the head.

'Watch it!'

'Stop talking about the test,' Nortah said in a tone heavy with dark promise.

'What's the problem?' Dentos laughed, genuinely puzzled. 'I mean we all passed didn't we? We're all still here, and we get to go to the Summertide Fair.'

Vaelin wondered why it hadn't occurred to him before that they had all passed the test. *Because it doesn't feel like a success,* he realised.

'We just don't want to talk about it, Dentos,' he said. 'We didn't find it as easy as you did. Best if we don't mention it again.'

Altogether six boys from other groups failed the test and had to leave. They watched them go the next morning, dark, huddled shapes in the mist, walking silently through the gate bearing their meagre possessions in the packs they had been allowed to keep. Sobbing could be heard echoing through the courtyard. It was impossible to tell which of the boys was crying, whether it was one or all. It seemed to go on for a long time, even after they had faded from view.

'I wouldn't be shedding any tears, that's for sure,' Nortah said. They were on the wall, wrapped tightly in their cloaks, waiting for the sun to burn the mist away and breakfast to appear in the dining hall.

'Wonder where they'll go,' Barkus said. 'Wonder if they've got anywhere *to* go.'

'The Realm Guard,' Nortah replied. 'It's full of rejects from the Order. May be why they hate us so much.'

'Sod that,' Dentos grunted. 'I know where I'd be headed. Straight for the docks. Get me a berth on one of them big trader ships that go west. Uncle Fantis went to the Far West on a ship, came back rich as stink. Silks and medicines. The only rich man in our village's history. Didn't do him any good, dropped dead a year after coming back, a black pox he picked up from some harbour doxy.'

'Life on a ship's no life, what I hear,' Barkus said. 'Bad food, floggings, work from morn to night. Like being in the Order I s'pose, except for the food. Reckon I'd take to the woods, make myself a famous outlaw. I'd have my own band of cut-throats, but we wouldn't cut anyone's throat. We'd just steal their gold and jewels, only rich folk though. Poor folk've got nothing worth stealing.'

'Clearly, you've put a lot of thought into it, brother,' Nortah commented dryly.

'Man needs a plan in this life. What about you? Where'd you go?'

Nortah turned back to the gate, still shrouded in the morning mist, his face drawn in a depth of longing Vaelin hadn't seen before. 'Home,' he said softly. 'I'd just go home.'

CHAPTER FIVE

A week or so after the Test of Knowledge Master Sollis took them to a cavernous chamber off the courtyard, thick with heat and the stench of smoke and metal. Waiting inside was Master Jestin, the Order's rarely seen principal blacksmith. He was a large man, emanating strength and confidence, brawny arms crossed in front of his chest, his hairy body marked with numerous pink scars where splashes of molten metal had escaped the forge. Struck by the evident power of the man, Vaelin wondered if he had even felt it.

'Master Jestin will forge your swords,' Sollis informed them. 'For the next two weeks you will work under his guidance and assist in the forging. By the time you leave the smithy you will each have a sword you will carry for the rest of your time in the Order. You should remember that Master Jestin does not share my generous and forgiving nature, mind him well.'

Alone with the blacksmith they stood in silence as he surveyed them, his bright blue eyes scanning each in turn.

'You.' He pointed a thick, blackened finger at Barkus, who was looking at a stack of freshly made pole-axes. 'You've been in a smithy before.'

Barkus hesitated. 'My f – . . . I grew up near a smithy in Nilsael, Master.'

Vaelin raised an eyebrow at Caenis. Given that Barkus adhered strictly to the rules and said little or nothing about his upbringing, it was a surprise to find that his father had been a craftsman. Boys with fathers in trade tended not to end up in the Order, a boy with a future had no need to seek a life elsewhere.

'Ever see a sword forged?' Master Jestin asked him.

'No, Master. Knives, plough blades, many horseshoes, a weather vane or two.' He laughed a little. Master Jestin didn't.

'Weather vane's a difficult thing to forge,' he said. 'Not all smiths can do it. Only master smiths are allowed to forge such a thing. It's a rule of the guild, shaping metal to read the song of the wind is a rare skill. Know that, did you?'

Barkus looked away and Vaelin realised he was chastened, shamed somehow. Something had passed between them, he knew, something the rest of them couldn't understand. It had to do with this place and the art practised here, but he knew Barkus wouldn't talk of it. In his own way he had as many secrets as the rest of them. 'No, Master,' was all he said.

'This place,' Master Jestin said, spreading his arms, encompassing the smithy. 'This place is of the Order but it belongs to me. I am King, Aspect, Commander, Lord and Master of this place. This is not a place for games. It is not a place for japes. It is a place for work and learning. The Order requires that you know the art of working metal. To truly wield a weapon with skill it is necessary that you understand the nature of its fashioning, to be part of the craft that brought it into being. The swords you will make here will keep you alive and defend the Faith in the years to come. Work well, and you will have a sword to rely on, a blade of strength with an edge keen enough to cut steel plate. Work poorly, and your swords will break in your first battle and you will die.'

Once more he turned his gaze on Barkus, his cold stare seeming to contain a question. 'The Faith is the source of all our strength, but our service to the Faith requires steel. Steel is the instrument by which we honour the Faith. Steel and blood is the whole of your future. Do you understand?'

They all murmured their agreement, but Vaelin knew Barkus was the only one to whom the question had been addressed.

The rest of the day was spent shovelling coke into the furnace and lifting stacks of iron rods into the smithy from a heavily laden cart in the courtyard. Master Jestin spent his time at the anvil, his hammer a constant, singing rhythm of metal on metal, glancing up occasionally to issue instructions amidst a fountain of sparks. Vaelin found it grim, monotonous work, his throat raw with smoke and his ears dulled from the endless din of the hammer.

'I can see why you didn't relish a life in the smithy, Barkus,' he commented as they trudged wearily back to their room at the end of the day.

'I'll say,' Dentos agreed, massaging his aching arm. 'Give me a day of bow practice anytime.'

Barkus said nothing, staying silent for the rest of the night amidst their tired grumbling. Vaelin knew he barely heard them, his mind was still fixed on Master Jestin's questions, the one in his words and the one in his eyes.

The next day saw them back at the smithy, once more lifting and carrying, lugging sacks of coke into the large chamber that served as a fuel store. Master Jestin said little, concentrating on inspecting every one of the iron rods they had carried inside the day before, holding each one up to the light, running his fingers along them and either grunting in satisfaction and setting it back on the pile or tutting in annoyance and adding it to a small but growing stack of rejects.

'What's he looking for?' Vaelin wondered, groaning with effort as he heaved another sack into the storeroom. 'One piece of iron's the same as another, isn't it?'

'Impurities,' Barkus answered, glancing over at Master Jestin. 'The rods have been forged by another smith before they get here, most likely by less skilled hands than our Master's. He's checking to see if the smith who made them put too much poor iron in the mix.'

'How can he tell?'

'Touch mostly. The rods are made of many layers of iron hammered together then twisted and flattened. The forging leaves a pattern on the metal. A good smith can tell quality rods from bad by the pattern. I've heard tales of some that could even smell quality.'

'Could you do it? The touching thing I mean, not the smelling.'

Barkus laughed, Vaelin sensing a note of bitterness in the sound. 'Not in a thousand years.'

At noon Master Sollis appeared and ordered them onto the practice field for sword work, saying they needed to keep their skills sharp. They were sluggish from the hard labour in the smithy and his cane fell more frequently than usual, although Vaelin found it didn't sting as much as it once did. He wondered briefly if Master Sollis was lightening his blows and dismissed the idea immediately. Master Sollis wasn't going soft, they were growing hard. *He's beaten us into shape,* he realised. *He's our smith.*

'It's time to fire the forge,' Master Jestin told them when they returned to the smithy after a hastily consumed afternoon meal. 'There is only one thing to remember about the forge.' He held his arms up displaying the numerous scars that marked the thickly muscled flesh. 'It's hot.'

He had them empty several sacks of coke into the brick circle that formed the forge then told Caenis to fire it, a task that involved crawling underneath and setting light to the oak wood tinder in the gap beneath. Vaelin would have balked at it but Caenis scrambled to it without any hesitation, flaming taper in hand. He emerged a few moments later, blackened but undamaged. 'Seems well alight, Master,' he reported.

Master Jestin ignored him and crouched to inspect the growing blaze. 'You.' He nodded at Vaelin, he never called them by name, seemingly recalling names was a pointless distraction. 'On the bellows. You too.' He flicked a finger at Nortah. Barkus, Dentos and Caenis were told to stand and wait for instructions.

Hefting his heavy, blunt-headed hammer, Master Jestin lifted one of the iron rods from the stack next to the anvil. 'A sword blade of the Asraelin pattern is fashioned from three rods,' he told them. 'A thick central rod and two thinner rods for the edge. This' – he held up the rod in his hand – 'is one of the edge rods. It must be shaped before it is melded with the others. The edge is the hardest part of the sword to forge, it must be fine but strong, it must cut but also withstand a blow from another blade. Look at the metal, look closely.' He held the rod out to each of them in turn, his rough, uneven voice oddly hypnotic. 'See the flecks of black there?'

Vaelin peered at the rod, picking out the small black fragments amidst the dark grey of the iron.

'It's called star silver because it glows brighter than the heavens when it's put to the flame,' Jestin went on. 'But it's not silver, it's a form of iron, rare iron that comes from the earth like all metals, there's nothing Dark about it. But it's this that makes swords of the Order stronger than others. With this, your blades will withstand blows that would shatter others and, if wielded with skill, will cut through mail and armour. This is our secret. Guard it well.'

He motioned for Vaelin and Nortah to begin pumping the

bellows and watched as their efforts were rewarded by the gradual appearance of a deep red-orange glow in the mass of coke. 'Now,' he said, hefting his hammer. 'Watch closely, try and learn.'

Vaelin and Nortah started to sweat profusely as they heaved at the heavy wooden handle of the bellows, the heat in the smithy rising with every flush of air they forced into the forge. The atmosphere seemed to thicken with it, drawing a breath becoming an effort in itself.

Get on with it for Faith's sake, Vaelin groaned inwardly, his sweat-slicked arms aching, as Master Jestin waited . . . and waited.

Finally satisfied, the smith took hold of the rod with a pair of iron tongs and plunged it into the forge, waiting until the red-orange glow flowed into the metal and along its length before taking it out and placing it on the anvil. The first blow was light, little more than a tap, scattering a small cloud of sparks. Then he began to work in earnest, the hammer rising and falling with drumbeat precision, sparks fountaining around him, the hammer sometimes blurring with the speed of his swing. Oddly, there seemed to be scant change in the glowing rod at first, although it may have gotten a little longer by the time Master Jestin plunged it into the forge again, gesturing irritably for Vaelin and Nortah to pump harder.

It wore on for what seemed like an hour but could only have been about ten minutes, Master Jestin hammering at the rod, returning it to the forge, hammering again. Vaelin found himself longing for the bruising comforts of the practice field, hand-to-hand combat on icy ground was better than this. When Master Jestin signalled them to stop they both staggered away from the bellows and leaned their heads out of the door, heaving great gulps of sweet-tasting air into their lungs.

'The bastard's trying to kill us,' Nortah gasped.

'Get back here,' Master Jestin growled and they hurried inside. 'You need to get used to real work. Look here.' He held up the rod, its original rounded shape had changed to a three-sided strip of metal about a yard long. 'This is an edge. It seems rough now, but melded with its brothers, it will be keen and bright with purpose.'

Dentos and Caenis were told to take over the bellows and Master Jestin started on the other edge, the toll of the hammer a ringing counterpoint to the rasp of their breath as they worked. When the second edge was complete he began on the thick central rod, his blows becoming harder and more rapid, extending the rod's length to match the edges then tempering the blade to form a raised spine along the middle. By the time he was finished Caenis and Dentos were ready to drop and Barkus partnered Vaelin at the bellows. The smith took a bracket to bind the three rods together at the base and made ready to meld them.

'The melding is the test of a sword smith,' he informed them. 'It is the hardest skill to learn. Too hard a blow will spoil the blade, too light and the rods won't meld.' He glanced over at Vaelin and Barkus. 'Heave hard, keep the fire hot. No slacking.'

As they worked, Vaelin praying for an end, he noticed Barkus's gaze was fixed on Master Jestin, his arms rising and falling without pause, seeming oblivious to the pain, his whole attention riveted on the process unfolding on the anvil. At first Vaelin wondered what was so interesting, it was a man hitting a piece of metal with a hammer. He saw no spectacle in it, no mystery. But as he followed Barkus's gaze he found himself increasingly absorbed by the sight of the blade taking shape, the three rods fusing together under the force of the hammer. Occasionally the flecks of star silver in the edge rods would flare as Master Jestin took the blade from the forge, glowing so brightly he had to look away. He believed what the smith had said about the star silver being just another metal but still it was unnerving.

'You.' Master Jestin nodded at Nortah as he finished shaping the point. 'Fetch the bucket closer.'

Nortah obediently dragged the heavy wooden bucket closer to the anvil, it was nearly full to the brim and water sloshed over his feet as he heaved it into place. 'This is salt water,' Jestin told them. 'A blade quenched in brine will always be stronger than one quenched in fresh water. Stand back, it'll boil.'

He took a firm grip on the tang at the base of the blade and plunged it into the bucket, making it steam and roil as the heat seeped into the water. He held it there until the boil subsided then withdrew the steaming blade, holding it up for inspection. It was black, the metal stained with soot, but Master Jestin seemed content with it. The edges were straight and the point perfectly symmetrical.

'Now,' he said. 'The real work begins. You.' He turned to Caenis. 'Since you lit the forge, you can have this one.'

'Um,' Caenis said, clearly wondering if this was an honour or a curse. 'Thank you, Master.'

Jestin carried the blade to the far end of the smithy, laying it on a bench next to a large, pedal-driven grindstone. 'A new-forged blade is only half-born,' he informed them. 'It must be sharpened, polished, honed.' He had Caenis stand at the grindstone and set it turning with the pedal, demonstrating how to get a good rhythm going by counting 'one two, one two' before telling him to increase the speed and hold the blade to the stone. The instant fountain of sparks made Caenis step back in alarm but Jestin ordered him to keep at it, guiding his hands to get the correct angle then showing him how to move the blade across the stone so that its whole length was honed. 'That's it,' he grunted after a while when Caenis grew confident enough to move the blade on his own. 'Ten minutes for each edge then show me what you've done. The rest of you back to the forge. You and you on the bellows . . .'

And so they worked and sweated in the forge, seven long days of heaving bellows, grinding edges and working polish into the blades so that the soot disappeared and they gleamed like silver. None of them escaped unscathed, Vaelin bore a livid scar on the back of his hand where a speck of molten metal landed, the pain and the smell of his own skin burning was uniquely sickening. The others suffered similar injury, Dentos coming off worst with a scattering of sparks into his eyes during a careless moment on the grinder. The sparks left a cluster of blackened scars around his left eye but luckily there was no damage to his vision.

Despite the exhaustion, the risk of disfiguring injury and the tedium of the work, Vaelin couldn't resist a certain fascination with the process. There was a beauty to it: the gradual birth of the blades under Master Jestin's hammer, the feel of the edge against the grindstone, the pattern that emerged in the blade as he polished it, dark swirls in the blue-grey of the steel, as if the flames of the forge had been frozen in the metal somehow.

'It comes from the merging of the rods,' Barkus explained. 'Different kinds of metal coming together leaves a mark. I guess the star silver makes it more noticeable in Order blades.'

'I like it,' Vaelin said, lifting the half-polished blade up to the light. 'It's . . . interesting.'

'It's just metal.' Barkus sighed, turning back to the stone, where he was putting an edge on his own sword. 'Heat it, beat it, shape it. There's no mystery there.'

Vaelin watched his friend work at the wheel, the way his hands moved expertly, honing the edge with perfect precision. When Barkus's turn came Master Jestin hadn't even bothered to show him, just handed him the blade and walked away. Somehow Barkus's skill was obvious to the smith, they said little, barely exchanging more than a few grunts or mumbled agreements, as if they had been working together for many years. But Barkus showed no joy in his work, no satisfaction. He stuck to it readily enough, the skills he displayed putting them all to shame, but his face was an uncharacteristic mask of grim endurance whenever they were in the smithy, only brightening when they escaped to the practice field or dining hall.

The next day saw the fitting of the hilts. These were ready-made, almost identical, Master Jestin fitting them to the blades and securing them with three iron nails hammered through the tang, which extended into the hilt. They were then set to work filing down the nail-heads so they were flush with the oak handles.

'You are done here,' Jestin told them at the end of the day. 'The swords are yours. Use them well.' It was the closest he had come to sounding like the other masters. He turned back to the forge without another word. They stood around uncertainly, holding their swords and wondering if they were supposed to say anything in return.

'Erm,' Caenis said. 'Thank you for your wisdom, Master.'

Jestin lifted an unfinished spear-head onto his anvil and began to work the bellows.

'Our time here was very . . .' Caenis began but Vaelin nudged him and gestured at the door.

As they were leaving Jestin spoke again. 'Barkus Jeshua.'

They stopped, Barkus turning, his expression guarded. 'Master.'

'The door's always open to you,' Jestin said without turning. 'I could use the help.'

'I'm sorry, Master,' Barkus said tonelessly. 'I'm afraid my training leaves me little time as it is.'

Jestin released the bellows and lifted the spear-head into the forge. 'I'll be here, so will the forge, when you get tired of the blood and the shit. We'll be here.'

Barkus missed the evening meal, something none of them could remember happening before. Vaelin found him on the wall after paying his nightly visit to Scratch's kennel. 'Brought you some left-overs.' Vaelin handed him a sack containing a pie and a few apples.

Barkus nodded his thanks, his attention fixed on the river, where a barge was making its way upstream to Varinshold.

'You want to know,' he said after a while. His voice held none of his usual humour or irony but Vaelin was chilled to detect a faint trace of fear.

'If you want to tell me,' he said. 'We all have our secrets, brother.'

'Like why you keep that scarf.' He gestured at Sella's scarf around Vaelin's neck. Vaelin tucked it out of sight and patted him on the shoulder before turning to go.

'It first happened when I was ten,' Barkus said.

Vaelin paused, waiting for him to continue. In his own way Barkus could be as closed as the rest of them, he would talk or he wouldn't, prompting or persuasion would be useless.

'My father had me working in the smithy since I was little,' Barkus continued after a moment. 'I loved it, loved watching him shape the metal, loved the way it glowed in the forge. Some say the ways of the smith are mysterious. For me it was all so obvious, so easy. I understood it all. My father hardly had to teach me anything, I just knew what to do. I could see the shape the metal would take before the hammer fell, could tell if a plough blade would cut through soil or get stuck or if a shoe would fall from a hoof after only a few days. My father was proud, I knew it. He wasn't much for talk, not like me, I get that from my mother, but I knew he was proud. I wanted to make him even more proud. I had shapes in my head, shapes of knives, swords, axes, all waiting to be forged. I knew exactly how to make them, exactly the right mix of metals to use. So I snuck into the smithy one night to make one. A hunting knife, a small thing, I thought. A Winterfall present for my father.'

He paused, staring out into the night as the barge moved further downstream, the shapes of the bargemen on the deck vague and ghostlike in the dim light from the bow lantern.

'So you made the knife,' Vaelin prompted. 'But your father was . . . angry?'

'Oh, he wasn't angry.' Barkus sounded bitter. 'He was scared. The blade folded over and over to strengthen it, the edge keen enough to cut silk or pierce armour, so polished you could use it as a mirror.' The small smile forming on his lips faded. 'He threw it in the river and told me never to speak of it to anyone, ever.'

Vaelin was puzzled. 'He should have been proud. A knife like that made by his son. Why would it scare him?'

'My father had seen a lot in his life. He'd travelled with the Lord's host, served on a merchant ship in the eastern seas, but he'd never seen a knife forged in a smithy where the forge was cold.'

Vaelin's puzzlement deepened. 'Then how did you . . . ?' Something in Barkus's face made him stop.

'Nilsaelins are a great people in many ways,' Barkus went on. 'Hardy, kind, hospitable. But they fear the Dark above all things. In my village there was once an old woman who could heal with a touch, or so they said. She was respected for the work she did but always feared. When the Red Hand came she could do nothing to stop it, dozens died, every family in the village lost someone, but she never caught it. They locked her in her house and set it on fire. The ruin's still there, no-one ever had the courage to build on it.'

'How did you make that knife, Barkus?'

'I'm still not sure. I remember shaping the metal at the anvil, the hammer in my hand. I remember fitting the handle, but for the life of me I can't remember lighting the forge. It was as if when I started to work I lost myself, as if I was just a tool, like the hammer . . . like something was working through me.' He shook his head, clearly disturbed by the memory. 'My father wouldn't let me in the smithy after that. Took me to old man Kalus, the horse breeder, told him he'd tried his best to teach me but I just wasn't going to make a smith. Paid him five coppers a month to teach me the horse trade.'

'He was trying to protect you,' Vaelin said.

'I know. But that's not how it felt to a boy. It felt like . . . like he was frightened by what I'd done, worried that I'd shame him somehow. I even thought he might be jealous. So I decided to show him, show him what I could really do. I waited until he was away hawking wares at the Summertide Fair and went back to the smithy. There wasn't much to work with, some old horseshoes and nails. He'd taken most of his stock to sell at the fair. But I took what he'd left and I made something . . . something special.'

'What was it?' Vaelin asked, envisioning mighty swords and gleaming axes.

'A sun vane.'

Vaelin frowned. 'A what?'

'Like a wind vane except instead of pointing at the direction of the wind it pointed at the sun. Wherever it was in the sky you always knew what time of day it was, even when the sky was clouded over. When the sun went down it'd point at the ground and track it through the earth. I made it pretty too, had flames coming out of the shaft and everything.'

Vaelin could only guess at the value of such an item, and the stir it would cause in a village terrified of the Dark. 'What happened to it?'

'I don't know. I suppose my father melted it down. When he came back from the fair I was standing there, showing him what I'd made, I felt very smug. He told me to pack. My mother was away at my aunt's so he didn't have to explain it to her. Faith knows what he told her when she came back and found me gone. We spent three days on the road then took ship to Varinshold then came here. He spoke to the Aspect for a while then left me at the gate. Said if I ever told anyone what I could do, they would certainly kill me. Said I'd be safe here.' He laughed shortly. 'Hard to believe he thought he was doing me a favour. Sometimes I think he got lost on the way to the House of the Fifth Order.'

Vaelin shook away the memory of hoofbeats and, remembering Sella's tale, said, 'He was right, Barkus. You shouldn't tell anyone. You probably shouldn't have told me.'

'Why, going to kill me are you?'

Vaelin smiled grimly. 'Well, not today.'

They stood at the wall in companionable silence, watching the barge until it turned the bend in the river and disappeared.

'I think he knew, y'know,' Barkus said. 'Master Jestin. I think he could sense it, what I can do.'

'How could he know such a thing?'

'Because I could sense the same thing in him.'

CHAPTER SIX

The next day saw the first practice with their new swords. It seemed to Vaelin that half the lesson was taken up with the correct method of strapping it across the back so it could be drawn by reaching over the shoulder.

'Tighter, Nysa.' Sollis tugged hard at Caenis's belt strap, drawing a pained grunt. 'This thing gets loose in a battle, you'll know about it soon enough. Can't kill an enemy if you're tripping over your own sword belt.'

They then spent over an hour learning the correct method of drawing the sword in a smooth, swift motion. It was harder than Master Sollis made it look. The leather strap holding the sword firmly in the scabbard had to be thumbed aside and the blade pulled clear without snagging or cutting its owner. Their first attempts were so clumsy Sollis ran them twice around the field at full speed, the unfamiliar weight of the swords making them sluggish.

'Faster, Sorna!' Sollis lashed at him as he stumbled. 'You too, Sendahl, pick your feet up.'

He ordered them to try again. 'Do it right. The faster you can get your sword in your hand and ready to use the less likely some bastard is going to spill your guts out in front of you.'

There were more runs and several canings before he was satisfied they were making progress. For some reason Vaelin and Nortah were attracting most of his ire today, the cane falling on them more than the others. Vaelin surmised it was punishment for some forgotten infraction. Sollis was like that sometimes, often remembering past misdemeanours after an interval of weeks or months.

As the lesson ended, he lined them up to make an announcement. 'Tomorrow you little buggers are to be let loose on the Summertide Fair. Some boys from the city may try to fight you to prove themselves. Try not to kill any. Some of the local girls may also see you as a different kind of challenge. Avoid them. Sendahl, Sorna, you're staying here. I'll teach you to slack off.'

Vaelin, crushed by disappointment and injustice, could only gape in shock. Nortah, however, was fully capable of voicing his feelings.

'You must be bloody joking!' he shouted. 'The others were just as bad as us. How come we have to stay?'

Later, as he sat on his bed nursing a bruised and aching jaw, his anger was no less fierce. 'That bastard's always hated me more than the rest of you.'

'He hates everyone,' Barkus said. 'You and Vaelin were just unlucky today.'

'No, it's because my father's the King's First Minister. I'm sure of it.'

'If your old man's such a biggy big, how come he can't get you out of the Order?' Dentos asked. 'I mean you hate being here.'

'How should I know?' Nortah exploded. 'I didn't ask him to send me to this pit. I didn't ask to be frozen, nearly killed ten times over, beaten every day, live in this hovel with peasants . . .' He trailed off miserably, huddling on his bunk, head buried in his pillow. 'I thought they would let me leave at the Test of Knowledge,' he said, more to himself than them, his voice muffled. 'When they saw my heart. But that dammed woman said I was where the Faith needed me to be. I even started lying about everything but they wouldn't let me go. That pig Hendril said the Sixth Order would benefit from having one of my breeding in its ranks.'

He fell silent, still hiding his face. Barkus moved to pat him on the shoulder but Vaelin stopped him with a shake of the head. He pulled the small oak chest from under his bed, his most valued possession next to Sella's scarf, stolen from the back of a merchant's cart carelessly left near the front gate. He unlocked it and retrieved a leather pouch containing all the coins he had found, won or stolen over the years. He tossed it to Caenis. 'Bring me back some toffees. And a new pair of soft leather boots if you find any that'll fit me.'

The morning dawned thick with mist, a heavy, soft blue haze hanging over the surrounding fields, waiting for the summer sun to burn it away. Vaelin and Nortah sat in miserable silence through the morning meal as the others tried not to appear too eager to leave for the fair.

'Think they'll be any bears?' Dentos asked casually.

'I suppose,' Caenis said. 'Always bears at the Summertide Fair. Drunkards wrestle them for money. Plenty of other things too. When I went, there was a magician from the Alpiran Empire who could play a flute and make a snake dance.'

Vaelin had been taken to the fair every year before his father gave him to the Order and he retained vivid memories of dancers, jugglers, hawkers, acrobats and a thousand other marvels amidst the mass of sound and smell. He hadn't realised before just how badly he had wanted to see it again, to touch something from his childhood and see if it matched the whirlwind of colour and joy he remembered.

'The King will be there,' he said to Caenis, recalling a distant view of the royal pavilion, where Janus and his family looked down on the many contests played out on the tourney field. There were horse races, wrestling, fistfights, archery, the victors receiving a red ribbon from the hand of the King. It had seemed a poor reward for so much effort but the winners all seemed happy enough.

'Maybe you'll get close enough to let him use you as a foot scraper,' Nortah said. 'You'd like that wouldn't you?'

Caenis seemed unperturbed. 'It's not my fault you're not allowed to go, brother,' he responded mildly.

Nortah looked as if he was about to voice another insult but instead just pushed his plate away and got up from the table, stalking from the hall, his face set in a mask of anger.

'He's really not taking this well,' Barkus observed.

After the meal, Vaelin bade them farewell in the courtyard, gratified by the effort they put into their façade of reluctance.

'I'll . . .' Caenis began with an effort, 'stay if you want me to.'

Vaelin was touched by the offer, he knew how badly Caenis wanted to see the King. 'If you don't go, how am I going to get my boots?' He clasped hands with each of them and waved as they walked to the main gate.

He went to see Scratch and found to his surprise that the slave-hound had made a new friend, an Asraelin wolf-hound bitch almost as tall at the shoulder as he was, although nowhere near as muscular.

'She got into his pen a few nights ago,' Master Jeklin told him. 'Faith knows how. Surprised he didn't kill her outright. Think he wanted the company. Reckon I'll leave 'em be, maybe have us a litter in a few months.'

Scratch was his usual happy, bouncing self at seeing Vaelin, the bitch cautious but reassured by Scratch's welcome. Vaelin tossed scraps to them, noting how the bitch wouldn't eat until Scratch had.

'She's afraid of him,' he commented.

'With good reason,' Master Jeklin said cheerfully. 'Can't keep away though. Bitches are like that sometimes, choose a mate and won't let go whatever he does. Typical women, eh?' He laughed. Vaelin, having no idea what he meant, laughed along politely.

'Not at the fair then?' Jeklin continued, moving away to toss some food to the three Nilsaelin terriers he kept at the far end of the kennels. They were deceptively pretty animals with short, pointed snouts and big brown eyes, but would nip viciously at any hand that came too close. Master Jeklin kept them for hunting hares and rabbits, an activity at which they excelled.

'Master Sollis felt I was slacking at sword practice,' Vaelin explained.

Jeklin tutted in disapproval. 'Never make a brother if you don't try hard. Course in my day they'd flog you with a horsewhip for slacking off. Ten strokes for a first offence, ten more for each offence after that. Used to lose ten or twelve brothers a year through flogging.' His sigh was heavy with nostalgia. 'Pity you'll miss the fair though. They have some fine dogs for sale there. Be off myself when I've finished up here. It'll be terrible crowded though, what with the execution and all. Here you go, you little monsters.' He threw some meat into the terriers' cage, provoking an explosion of yelps and growls as they fought each other for the food. Master Jeklin chuckled at the sight.

'Execution, Master?' Vaelin asked.

'What? Oh, the King's having his First Minister hung. Treason and corruption, usual thing. S'why there'll be such a crowd. Everyone in the Realm hates the bastard. Taxes y'see.'

Vaelin felt his mouth go dry and his heart sink into his gut. *Nortah's father. They're going to kill Nortah's father. That's why Sollis kept us here. Made me stay too so it didn't look suspicious . . . So I would be here when the news arrived.* He found himself taking a closer look at Master Jeklin.

'Did Master Sollis visit here this morning?' he asked

Jeklin didn't look at him, still smiling down at his dogs. 'Master Sollis is very wise. You should appreciate him more.'

'*I* have to tell him?' Vaelin grated.

Jeklin said nothing, dangling some ham through the bars of the cage, grunting a laugh every time the terriers jumped for it.

'Erm,' Vaelin stumbled over the words, clearing his throat, backing towards the door. 'If you'll excuse me, Master.'

Jeklin waved a hand, not turning, laughing affectionately at the squabbling terriers. 'Little monsters.'

Crossing the courtyard, Vaelin felt that the weight of responsibility might force him to the cobbles. Suddenly he hated Sollis and the Aspect. *Leadership?* he thought bitterly. *You can keep it.*

But there was another thought, a growing suspicion as he reluctantly ascended the winding steps to the tower room, a lingering image of Nortah's face as he stalked from the dining hall. Vaelin had seen only anger at the time but now realised there had been something more, a sense of determination, a decision . . .

He stopped as realisation hit him. *Oh please, Faith no!*

He took the remaining steps at a run, bursting into the room, panic making him shout, 'NORTAH!'

Empty. *Maybe he's at the stables. He likes the horses . . .*

Then he saw it, the open window, the absence of sheets and blankets on their beds. Leaning out of the window he saw the knotted linen dangling a good twenty feet below, which left another fifteen-foot drop to the roof of the north gatehouse and ten more from there to the ground. For Nortah, like the rest of them, it was hardly a challenging prospect. The lingering morning mist would enable him to slip away under the noses of the brothers on the

wall, most of whom would have been preoccupied with the anticipation of breakfast.

For the briefest moment Vaelin considered finding Master
Sollis or the Aspect but discounted it. Nortah's punishment would
be severe and he already had at least a half-hour start. Besides,
Vaelin didn't even know if Sollis or the Aspect were in the House,
they may well have been at the fair too. And there was another
possibility, ringing loud and terribly clear in his head: *What if he
makes it there first? What if he sees?*

Vaelin quickly gathered a water bottle and a couple of knives
then strapped his sword across his back. He went to the window,
took a firm grip on Nortah's rope and began to descend. As
expected it was an easy climb, taking barely a moment to reach
the ground. With the mist all but gone he had to be wary of being
seen, standing flat against the wall until the brother on the battlements above, a bored-looking boy of about seventeen, wandered
away, then sprinting full tilt for the trees. The run would have
seemed short on the practice field, scarcely two hundred yards to
the forest, but it felt like a mile or more with the wall at his back,
expecting every second to hear a shout of alarm or even the thrum
of an arrow. At this range few brothers would miss. So it was with
relief that he entered the cool shadow of the trees and dropped
his speed to a half sprint, still faster than he would have liked for
comfort but he couldn't afford to waste any time. He stayed in the
trees for half a mile or so then turned onto the road.

It was busier than he had ever seen it, packed with farmers
driving carts laden with produce for sale at the fair, families making
the once-a-year journey to see the contests and the many spectacles
on offer, this year no doubt the promise of a First Minister's execution added a certain spice to the occasion. None of the travellers
seemed daunted by the prospect. Vaelin saw cheerful, laughing
faces everywhere, he even passed a cart full of what he took to be

woodsmen from their collection of axes, all singing a raucous doggerel about the impending event:

His name was Artis Sendahl
He was a greedy old goat
King Janus came to count his purse
And stretched his greedy throat.

'Don't run so fast, Order boy!' one of the woodsmen called to him as he passed, swaying as he raised a stoneware bottle. 'They can't choke the bastard till we get there. Some bugger has to cut the wood for the fire.' The rest of the woodsmen roared with laughter as Vaelin ran on, resisting the urge to see how well a drunkard could cut wood with his fingers broken.

He heard it before he saw it, a dull roar beyond the next hill, the sound of thousands of voices speaking at once. As a child he had thought it a monster and snuggled into his mother's embrace in fear. 'Hush now,' she said, stroking his hair, turning his head gently as they crested the rise. 'Look Vaelin. Look at all the people.'

To his boy's eyes it had seemed every subject in the Realm had come to the expansive plain before the walls of Varinshold to share in the blessings of summer, a vast throng covering several acres. Now he found he was amazed to see the crowd was even larger than he remembered, stretching the whole length of the city's western wall, a haze of mingled exhalation and woodsmoke hanging over the mass, tents and brightly coloured marquees rising from the carpet of bodies. For a youth who had spent much of the last four years in the cramped fortress of the Order House it was almost overwhelming.

How can I track him in this? he wondered. Behind him came the song of the drunken woodsmen again as their cart caught up, still rejoicing in the death of the King's Minister. *Don't look for him,* he realised. *Look for the gallows. He'll be there.*

Entering the crowd was an odd experience, mingling exhilaration with trepidation, the throng enveloping him in a mass of moving bodies and unfamiliar odours. Hawkers were everywhere, their shouts barely audible above the noise, selling everything from sweetmeats to earthenware. Here and there a knot of spectators had gathered around players and performers, jugglers, acrobats and magicians, drawing either cheers and applause or jeers of derision. Vaelin tried not to be distracted but found himself stopping at the more spectacular sights. There was a hugely muscled man who could breathe fire and a dark-skinned man in silk robes who pulled trinkets from the ears of people in the crowd. Vaelin would linger for a few seconds before remembering his mission and shamefacedly moving on. It was as he stopped, amazed at the sight of a half-naked female tumbler, that he felt a hand inside his cloak. It was deft, almost unnoticeable, searching. He caught the intruder's wrist with his left hand and dragged the owner forward, tripping him over his left ankle. The pickpocket went down heavily, grunting painfully with the impact. It was a boy, small, skinny, dressed in rags. He looked up at Vaelin and snarled, lashing out with his free hand and desperately trying to pull away.

'Ha, thief!' A man in the crowd laughed nastily. 'Should know better than to try it on with the Order.'

At the mention of the Order, the boy's efforts to free himself redoubled, scratching and biting at Vaelin's hand.

'Kill him, brother,' another passerby suggested. 'One less thief in the city's always a good thing.'

Vaelin ignored the voice and lifted the pickpocket off his feet; it wasn't difficult, the boy was little more than skin and bone. 'You need practice,' he told him.

'Fuck you,' the boy spat, squirming frantically. 'You're not a real brother. You're one of them boy brothers. You're no better'n me.'

'Needs a beatin' this one,' a man said, emerging from the crowd to aim a cuff at the boy's head.

'Go away,' Vaelin instructed. The man, a plump fellow with a large ale-soaked beard and eyes showing the unfocused gaze of the newly drunk, gave Vaelin a brief appraisal and quickly moved away. At fourteen Vaelin was already taller than most men, the Order's regime making him both broad and lean. He stared in turn at the several other spectators who had paused to watch the small drama. They all moved on rapidly. *It's not just me,* Vaelin surmised. *They fear the Order.*

'Lemme go, y'bastard,' the boy said, fear and fury colouring his voice in equal measure. He had exhausted himself struggling and dangled in Vaelin's grasp, face set in a soot-stained mask of impotent rage. 'I got friends, y'know, people you don't want to cross . . .'

'I have friends too,' Vaelin said. 'I'm looking for one. Where are the gallows?'

The boy's face constricted in a puzzled frown. 'Wassat?'

'The gallows where they're going to hang the King's Minister. Where are they?'

The boy's creased brows formed into an arch of calculation. 'Wossit worth?'

Vaelin tightened his grip. 'A broken wrist.'

'Miserable Order bastard,' the boy muttered sullenly. 'Break me wrist if you want. Break me bloody arm. What odds does it make anyway?'

Vaelin met his eyes, seeing fear and anger but something more, something that made him relax his grip: defiance. The boy had pride enough not to be a victim to his fear. Vaelin saw how truly ragged and threadbare the boy's clothes were and the mud covering his bare feet. *Maybe pride is all he has.*

'I'm going to put you down,' he told the boy. 'If you run, I'll catch you.' He pulled the boy closer until they were face-to-face. 'Do you believe me?'

The boy shrank back a little, head bobbing. 'Uh-huh.'

Vaelin set him down and released his wrist. He saw the boy fight the instinctive impulse to run, rubbing his wrist and edging back a little. 'What's your name?' Vaelin asked him.

'Frentis,' the boy replied cautiously. 'What's yours?'

'Vaelin Al Sorna.' There was a flicker of recognition in the boy's gaze. Even he, at the bottom of the pile in the city's hierarchy, had heard of the Battle Lord. 'Here.' Vaelin fished a throwing knife from his pocket and tossed it to the boy. 'It's all I have to trade. You get another two when you show me the gallows.'

The boy peered at the knife curiously. 'Whassis?'

'A knife, you throw it.'

'Couldja kill someone with it?'

'Only after a lot of practice.'

The boy touched the tip of the knife, tutting painfully and licking his bloodied finger when he discovered it was sharper than it looked. 'You teach me,' he mumbled around his fingers. 'Teach me how to throw it and I'll show ya the gallows.'

'After,' Vaelin said. Seeing the boy's distrust, he added, 'My word on it.'

The word of the Order seemed to carry some weight with Frentis and his suspicion receded, but not completely. 'This way,' he said, turning and moving into the crowd. 'Stay close.'

Vaelin followed the boy through the mass of people, sometimes losing him amidst the crush only to find him a few steps on, standing impatiently and muttering for him to keep up.

'Don't they teach ya how to follow folk then?' he asked as they struggled through a particularly thick knot of spectators at a dancing-bear show.

'They teach us how to fight,' Vaelin replied. 'I'm . . . unused to so many people. I haven't been to the city for four years.'

'Lucky bastard. I'd give me right nut to never see this dump again.'

'You've never been anywhere else?'

Frentis gave him a look that told him he was very stupid. 'Oh yeah, got me own river barge I 'ave. Go anywhere I please.'

It seemed to take an age of struggling through the crowd before Frentis halted, pointing at a wooden frame rising above the throng about a hundred yards away. 'There y'go. That's where they'll stretch the poor sod's neck. What they killin' 'im for anyway?'

'I don't know,' Vaelin replied honestly. He handed the boy the two knives he had promised. 'Come to the Order House on Eltrian evening and I'll teach you how to use them. Wait by the north gate, I'll find you.'

Frentis nodded, the knives quickly disappearing into his rags. 'You gonna watch it then? The hanging.'

Vaelin moved away from him, eyes scanning the crowd. 'I hope not.'

He searched for a good quarter hour, checking every face, watching for any sign of Nortah, finding nothing. He shouldn't have been surprised; they all knew ways of avoiding searching eyes, subtle ways of making oneself unrecognisable and just another body in the crowd. He paused by a puppet show, feeling a mounting knot of panic building in his gut. *Where is he?*

'Oh, blessed souls of the Departed,' the puppeteer was saying in a mock-tragic tone, his expert hands working the strings, moulding the wooden doll on the stage into a pose of despair. 'Ever have I been Faithless, but even a wretch such as I deserves not this fate.'

Kerlis the Faithless. Vaelin knew the story, it was one of his mother's favourites. Kerlis denied the Faith and was cursed to live forever until the Departed consented to allow him entry to the Beyond. It was said he still wandered the land, seeking his Faith but never finding it.

'You have made your fate, Faithless one,' intoned the puppeteer, bobbing the collection of wooden heads that represented the Departed. 'We do not judge you. You judge yourself. Find your Faith and we will welcome you . . .'

Vaelin, momentarily distracted by the puppeteer's skill and the craftsmanship evident in the dolls, forced himself to turn back to the crowd. *Look,* he told himself. *Concentrate. He's here. He has to be.*

His survey stopped when a face in the audience caught his attention, a man in his thirties with lean, strong features and a sad gaze. A familiar gaze. *Erlin!* Vaelin stared in astonishment. *He came back here. Is he mad?*

Erlin seemed completely rapt by the puppet show, his sad gaze utterly absorbed. Vaelin puzzled over what to do. Speak to him? Ignore him? . . . Kill him? Dark thoughts flickered through his head, driven by panic. *I helped him and the girl. If they catch him* . . . It was the image of the girl's face and the feel of her scarf around his neck that forced sanity back into his thoughts. *Walk away,* he decided. *Safer if you never saw him . . .*

Erlin looked up then, his eyes meeting Vaelin's, widening into alarmed recognition. He glanced once back at the puppet show, his expression an unreadable confusion of emotion, then turned and disappeared into the crowd. Vaelin was seized by a compulsion to follow him, find out if Sella was well, but as he started forward a shout erupted behind him followed by the sound of clashing blades. It was fifty yards away, near the gallows.

A crowd was knotted around the scene of the disturbance and he had to force his way through, drawing grunts of pain and insults as his desperation made him less than gentle.

'What was he doing?' someone in the crowd was saying.

'Trying to get through the cordon,' another voice said. 'Oddest thing. Not what you expect from a brother.'

'Think they'll hang him too?'

Finally he was through the throng and drew up short at the scene before him. There were five of them, soldiers of the Twenty-seventh Cavalry judging by the black tail feathers in their tunics that gave them their informal name: the Blackhawks. Reputedly a favourite with the King because of their service during the Wars of Unification, the Blackhawks were often given the honour of policing public events or ceremonials. One of them, the largest, had Nortah by the throat, a beefy arm wrapped around his neck as two of his comrades attempted to restrain him. A fourth man stood back a little, his sword raised, poised for a strike. 'Hold the bastard still, Faith's sake!' he shouted. They all bore bruises or cuts, showing Nortah had not been easily captured. A fifth man was kneeling nearby, clutching at a bloody wound on his arm, his face grey with pain and tense with fury. 'Kill the fucker!' he snarled. 'He's bloody crippled me!'

Seeing the man with the sword draw his arm back further, Vaelin acted without thought. His one remaining throwing knife left his hand before he knew he had drawn it. It was the finest throw he had ever managed, the blade catching the swordsman just below the wrist. The sword dropped to the ground instantly, its owner gaping in shock at the shiny piece of metal impaling his limb.

Vaelin was already moving, his sword hissing from the scabbard on his back. As Vaelin charged, one of the men holding Nortah's arms released him, scrabbling at his belt for his own sword. Nortah saw the opportunity and brought his elbow round to smash into the soldier's face, making him stagger into Vaelin's flying kick. The soldier stumbled a few more paces, blood streaming thickly from his nose and mouth, before collapsing heavily to the earth.

Nortah snatched a throwing knife from his belt and stabbed backwards, sinking the blade deep into the thigh of the man choking his neck, forcing him to release his hold. Vaelin moved in and dropped him with a blow to the temple from his sword hilt. The remaining Blackhawk had released his hold on Nortah and was backing away, sword drawn, the trembling point flicking between them.

'You're . . .' he stammered. 'You're breaking the King's peace. You're under arr—'

Nortah moved with blinding speed, ducking under the sword and smashing his fist into the man's face. Two more punches and he was down.

'Hawks?' Nortah spat on the unconscious soldier. 'More like sheep.' He turned to Vaelin, a hysterical desperation shining in his eyes. 'Thank you, brother. Come.' He turned away wildly. 'We have to rescue my fa—'

Vaelin's blow took him under the ear, a technique they had learned after much painful tutelage under Master Intris. It rendered the victim unconscious but without lasting damage.

Vaelin knelt next to his friend, checking the pulse in his neck. 'I'm sorry, brother,' he whispered before sheathing his sword and gathering him up, hoisting his inert form over his shoulder with difficulty. Vaelin was bigger than Nortah but still his brother's weight was a substantial burden as he moved towards the cordon of stunned spectators. Not one of them said a word as he gestured for them to make way.

'Hold there!' A shouted command breaking the silence like glass, the crowd's shock giving way to sudden babble of incomprehension and amazement.

'Beat five Blackhawks, just the two of them . . .'

'Never seen the like . . .'

'It's treason to strike a soldier. King's Edict said so . . .'

'HOLD!' The voice again, cutting through the noise. Looking round, Vaelin saw a mounted figure kicking his horse forward through the crush, occasionally laying about himself with a riding crop to speed progress. 'Make way!' he commanded. 'King's business. Make way!'

Emerging from the throng, he drew his mount up and Vaelin saw him clearly. A tall man on a black warhorse, a thoroughbred of Renfaelin stock. He wore a ceremonial uniform with a black feather in his tunic and the short-plumed helmet of an officer on his head. Beneath the visor the rider's lean, clean-shaven face was hard with fury. The single four-pointed star on his breastplate depicted his rank: Lord Marshal of the Realm Guard. Behind the mounted man a troop of Blackhawks on foot emerged and fanned out, swords drawn, pushing the crowd back with the aid of a few kicks and punches. Some of them tended to their fallen comrades, casting vengeful glances at Vaelin as they did so. The man with Vaelin's knife through his wrist was weeping openly in pain.

Seeing no avenue of escape, Vaelin gently laid Nortah on the earth and stepped away, careful to keep himself between his friend and the man on the horse.

'What is this?' the marshal demanded.

'I answer to the Order,' Vaelin replied.

'You'll answer to me, Order whelp, or I'll string you from the nearest tree by your guts.'

Vaelin resisted the impulse to draw his sword as some of the Blackhawks moved closer. He knew he couldn't fight them all, not without killing a few, which was unlikely to help Nortah.

'Might I know your name, my lord?' he enquired, desperately playing for time and hoping his voice didn't tremble.

'I'll know your name first, whelp.'

'Vaelin Al Sorna. Brother of the Sixth Order, awaiting confirmation.'

The name ran through the crowd like a wave. 'Sorna . . .'

'Battle Lord's boy . . .'

'Should've known, spitting image . . .'

The rider's eyes narrowed at the name but his furious expression remained firmly in place. 'Lakrhil Al Hestian,' he said. 'Lord Marshal of the Twenty-seventh Regiment of Horse and Sword of the Realm.' He nudged his mount closer, peering down at Nortah's inert form. 'And him?'

'Brother Nortah,' Vaelin said.

'I'm told he tried to rescue the traitor. Why would a brother of the Order do such a thing, I wonder?'

He knows, Vaelin realised. *He knows who Nortah is.* 'I couldn't say, Lord Marshal,' he replied. 'I saw my brother about to be murdered and prevented it.'

'Murdered my arse!' one of the Blackhawks spat, face flushed with anger. 'He was resisting lawful arrest.'

'He is of the Order.' Vaelin spoke to Al Hestian. 'Like me. We answer to the Order. If you believe we have transgressed, you must take the matter to our Aspect.'

'All are subject to King's Law, boy,' Al Hestian replied evenly. 'Brothers, soldiers and Battle Lords.' He stared hard into Vaelin's eyes. 'And you and your brother will answer to it.' He motioned his men forward. 'Keep you hands clear of your weapons, boy, or you'll be answering to the Departed.'

Vaelin reached back to grasp his sword hilt as the Blackhawks advanced. Perhaps if he wounded a few, he could create enough confusion to escape into the crowd with Nortah. There could be no return to the Order after this, no welcome for those that fought the Realm Guard. *Life as an outlaw,* Vaelin pondered. *Can't be that bad.*

'Easy now, lad,' one of the Blackhawks warned, a veteran sergeant with a weather-beaten face. He advanced slowly, his sword held low, a dagger in his left hand. Seeing the way his feet moved and the easy balance of his stance, Vaelin judged him to be the most dangerous of his opponents. 'Leave the sword where it is,' the sergeant continued. 'No need for any more blood here. You let us take you in, and it'll all get sorted out, nice and civilised.'

Seeing the wary fury in the faces of the other Blackhawks, Vaelin judged that the treatment he and Nortah would receive would be anything but civilised.

'I've no wish to spill any blood,' he told the sergeant, drawing his sword. 'But I will if you make me.'

'The hour drags ever onwards, Sergeant,' Al Hestian drawled, leaning forward in his saddle. 'End this . . .'

'Well here's a pretty picture!' a voiced boomed from the crowd, the throng parting amidst shouts of protest as three figures forced their way through.

Vaelin felt a tug at his heart. It was Barkus, flanked by Caenis and Dentos. Barkus was smiling at the Hawks, a picture of affability. By contrast Caenis and Dentos stared at them with the flat concentrated aggression they had learned through years of hard training. They all had their swords drawn.

'A pretty picture indeed!' Barkus went on as the three of them fell in beside Vaelin. 'A brace of Hawks all lined up for plucking.'

'Get out of here, boy!' Al Hestian spat at Barkus. 'This is not your concern.'

'Heard the commotion,' Barkus told Vaelin, ignoring Al Hestian. He glanced back at Nortah's inert form. 'Snuck out, did he?'

'Yes. They're going to execute his father.'

'We heard,' Caenis said. 'Bad business. They say he was a good man. Still, the King is just and must have his reasons.'

'Tell that to Nortah,' Dentos said. 'Poor bastard. Did they do that to him?'

'No,' Vaelin said. 'Couldn't think of another way to stop him.'

'Master Sollis is going to beat us for week,' Dentos grumbled.

They fell silent, watching the Blackhawks, who stared back, faces full of malevolent anger but making no move to advance.

'They're afraid,' Caenis observed.

'They should be,' Barkus said.

Vaelin risked a glance at Al Hestian. Clearly not a man used to being balked, the marshal was visibly shaking with fury. 'You!' He stabbed a finger at one of the cavalrymen. 'Find Captain Hintil. Tell him to bring his company.'

'A whole company!' Barkus sounded cheerful at the prospect. 'You do us much honour, my lord!'

A few people in the crowd laughed, making Al Hestian's rage even more palpable. 'You'll all be flayed for this!' he shouted, his voice nearly a scream. 'Don't imagine the King will grant you an easy death!'

'Speaking for my father again, Lord Marshal?'

A tall, red-haired young man had emerged from the mass of onlookers. His clothes were modest but finely made, and there was something strange about the way the crowd parted before him, each citizen's eyes averted, heads bowed, a few even dropping to one knee. Vaelin was shocked when he turned back and found Caenis and the Hawks all doing the same.

'Kneel, brothers!' Caenis hissed. 'Honour the prince.'

Prince? Looking at the tall man again Vaelin recalled the serious youth he had seen at the King's palace so many years before. Prince Malcius had grown almost as tall and broad as his father. Vaelin looked for soldiers of the Royal Guard but saw no-one accompanying the prince. *A prince who walks alone amongst his people,* he thought, puzzled.

'Vaelin!' Caenis whispered insistently.

As he made to kneel, the prince waved his hand. 'No need, brother. Please rise, all of you.' He smiled at the kneeling multitude.

'The ground is muddy. Now then, my lord.' He turned to Al Hestian. 'What manner of disturbance is this?'

'A traitorous outrage, Highness,' Al Hestian said forcefully, rising from a bow, his left knee caked in mud. 'These boys attacked my men in an effort to rescue the prisoner.'

'You bloody liar!' Barkus exploded. 'We came to help our brothers when they had been attacked . . .' He fell silent as the prince held up his hand. Malcius paused and surveyed the scene, taking in the wounded Blackhawks and Nortah's unconscious form.

'You, brother,' he said to Vaelin. 'Are you a traitor as the Lord Marshal claims?' Vaelin noted his eyes barely left Nortah.

'I am no traitor, Highness,' Vaelin replied, trying to keep any trace of fear or anger from his voice. 'Neither are my brothers. They are here only in my defence. If an answer must be given for what has happened here, then it is mine alone to make.'

'And your fallen brother.' Prince Malcius moved closer, staring down at Nortah with an odd intensity. 'Should he make an answer too?'

'His . . . actions were driven by grief,' Vaelin faltered. 'He will answer to our Aspect.'

'Is he badly hurt?'

'A blow to the head, Highness. He should wake in an hour or so.'

The prince continued to stare down at Nortah for a moment longer before turning away, saying softly, 'When he wakes tell him I grieve too.'

He moved away and addressed Al Hestian. 'This is a very serious business, Lord Marshal. Very serious.'

'Indeed, Highness.'

'So serious that full resolution will take so much time as to delay the execution, something I should hate to explain to the King. Unless you wish to do so.'

Al Hestian's eyes briefly met the prince's, the light of mutual enmity shining clearly. 'I should hate to intrude on the King's time needlessly,' he grated through clenched teeth.

'I am grateful for your consideration.' Prince Malcius turned to the Hawks. 'Take these wounded men to the royal pavilion, they will have the care of the King's physician. Lord Marshal, I hear there are some riotous drunkards near the west gate in need of your attentions. Do not let me detain you further.'

Al Hestian bowed and remounted, guiding his horse past Vaelin and the others with the promise of retribution writ large in his face. 'Out of the way!' he shouted, his riding crop lashing at the crowd as he forced his way through.

'Take your brother back to the Order,' Prince Malcius told Vaelin. 'Make sure you tell your Aspect what occurred here, lest he hear it from other lips first.'

'We will, Highness,' Vaelin assured him, bowing as low as he could.

A hundred yards away a steady, monotonous drumbeat was sounding, the crowd falling silent as the beat increased in volume. Vaelin could see a row of spear-points rising above the throng, moving in time with the drum, drawing ever closer to the dark silhouette of the gallows.

'Take him away!' the prince commanded. 'Senseless or not, he should not be here.'

It was as they made their way through the silent crowd, Vaelin and Caenis carrying Nortah, Dentos and Barkus forcing a passage, that the drumbeat stopped. There was a silence so thick Vaelin could feel the anticipation like a weight pressing him into the earth. There was a distant clatter then an eruption of cheering, thousands of fists raised in the air in triumph, manic joy on every face.

Caenis surveyed the celebrating crowd with naked disgust.

Vaelin couldn't hear the word he mouthed but the shape of his lips carried the meaning clearly enough: 'Scum.'

Nortah disappeared into the care of the masters as soon as they were within the walls of the Order House. It was obvious from the guarded looks of the other boys and the glares of the masters that word of their adventure had sped ahead of their return.

'We'll see to him,' Master Checkrin said, relieving them of Nortah's burden, lifting him easily in his muscle-thick arms. 'You lot get to your room. Do not come out until ordered. Do not talk to anyone until ordered.'

To ensure the instruction was followed, Master Haunlin accompanied them to the north tower, the burnt man's usual passion for song evidently quelled by the circumstances. When the door slammed behind them, Vaelin was sure the master was waiting outside. *Are we prisoners now?* he wondered.

In the room they set aside their gear and waited.

'Did you get my boots?' Vaelin asked Caenis.

'I didn't get the chance. Sorry.'

Vaelin shrugged. The silence stretched.

'Barkus nearly shagged a tart behind the ale tent,' Dentos blurted. He always found silence particularly oppressive. 'Right saucy bint she was too. Tits like melons. Right, brother?'

Barkus stared balefully at his brother from across the room. 'Shut up,' he said flatly.

More silence.

'You know they'll give you your coins if you get caught?' Vaelin said to Barkus. Occasionally, girls from Varinshold and surrounding villages turned up at the gate with swollen bellies or squalling infants in tow. The guilty brother would be forced into a hasty joining ceremony conducted by the Aspect and given his coins plus an extra two, one for the girl and one for the child. Oddly,

176 · Anthony Ryan

a few boys actually seemed happy to be leaving under such circumstances although others would protest their innocence, but a truth test by the Second Order would soon prove the matter one way or the other.

'I didn't bloody do anything,' Barkus sputtered.

'You had your tongue down her throat,' Dentos laughed.

'I'd had a few ales. Besides, it was Caenis getting all the attention.'

Vaelin turned to Caenis, seeing a slow flush creeping up his friend's cheeks. 'Really?'

'Not half. All over him they were. "Ooh, isn't he pretty?"'

Vaelin suppressed a laugh as Caenis began to blush furiously. 'I'm sure he resisted manfully.'

'I dunno,' Dentos mused. 'A few more minutes I reckon we'd've had a whole troop of pretty bastards at the gates in nine months' time. Lucky some drunk came in and started shouting about a fight between the Hawks and the Order.'

Mention of the fight brought the silence again. It was Barkus who finally said it: 'You don't think they'll kill him, do you?'

The room was growing dark before the door opened and Master Sollis strode in, a mountainous anger dominating his expression. 'Sorna,' he grated. 'Come with me. The rest of you get a meal from the kitchens then go to bed.'

The urge to ask about Nortah was overwhelming but Sollis's thunderous visage was enough to keep them silent. Vaelin followed him down the stairs and across the courtyard to the west wall, all the time watching for any sign of his cane. He expected to be led to the Aspect's chambers but instead they made their way to the infirmary, finding Master Henthal tending Nortah. He was laid in bed, his face slack, half-lidded eyes unfocused and dimmed. Vaelin knew the look; sometimes boys with grievous injuries had need of strong medicine, which took the pain away but left them out of touch with the world.

'Redflower and Shade Bloom,' Master Henthal explained as Vaelin and Sollis entered. 'He was raving when he came round. Gave the Aspect a nasty whack before we got him under control.'

Vaelin moved to the bed, heart heavy with the sight of his brother. *He looks so weak . . .*

'Will he be all right, Master?' he asked.

'Seen it before, raving and thrashing about. Usually happens to men who've seen a battle too many. He'll sleep soon. When he wakes he'll be shaky but himself again.'

Vaelin turned to Sollis. 'Has the Aspect made judgement, Master?'

Sollis glanced at Master Henthal, who nodded and left the room. 'Judgement is not warranted,' Sollis replied.

'We wounded the King's soldiers . . .'

'Yes. If you had been more attentive to my teaching, you might have killed them.'

'The Lord Marshal . . .'

'Does not command here. Nortah disobeyed instruction, for which punishment should be levied. However, the Aspect feels punishment has been levied already. As for you, your disobedience was in defence of your brother. Judgement is not required.'

Master Sollis moved to the far side of the bed and placed a hand against Nortah's brow. 'His fever should fade when the redflower wears off. He'll feel it though, feel the pain like a knife, sticking in his guts, twisting. Pain like that can either make a boy into a man or a monster. It is my opinion that the Order has seen enough of monsters.'

Vaelin understood it then; Sollis's anger. *It's not us,* he realised. *It's what the King did to Nortah's father, what that did to Nortah.*

We're his swords, he beats us into shape. The King has spoiled one of his blades.

'My brothers and I will guide him,' Vaelin said. 'His pain will be ours. We will help him bear it.'

'See that you do.' Sollis looked up, his gaze more intense than usual. 'When a brother goes to the bad there is but one way of dealing with him, and brother should not kill brother.'

Nortah came round in the morning, his groan waking Vaelin, who had stayed beside him through the night.

'What?' Nortah gazed around with bleary eyes. 'What's this . . . ?' Seeing Vaelin, he fell silent, the light of memory returning to his eyes as his hand went to the lump on the back of his head. 'You hit me,' he said. Vaelin watched the dreadful knowledge flood back, draining Nortah's face of colour and making him slump under the weight of his sorrow.

'I'm sorry, Nortah,' Vaelin said. It was all he could think to say.

'Why did you stop me?' Nortah whispered through tears.

'They would have killed you.'

'Then they would have done me a service.'

'Don't talk like that. I doubt your father's soul would have dwelt happily in the Beyond knowing that you had followed him there so soon.'

Nortah wept silently for a while and Vaelin watched him, a hundred empty condolences dying on his lips. *I don't have the words,* he realised. *There are no words for this.*

'Did you see it?' Nortah asked finally. 'Did he suffer?'

Vaelin thought of the clatter of the trap and the exultation of the crowd. *A fearful knowledge to take into the Beyond that so many rejoiced at your death.* 'It was quick.'

'They said he stole from the King. My father would never do that, he cherished the King and served him well.'

Vaelin seized on the only comfort he could offer. 'Prince Malcius said to tell you that he grieves also.'

'Malcius? He was there?'

'He helped us, made the Hawks let us go. I thought that he recognised you.'

Nortah's expression softened a little, becoming distant. 'When I was a boy we would ride together. Malcius was my father's student and often came to our home. My father taught many boys of the noble houses. His wisdom in statecraft and diplomacy was famed.' Nortah fumbled for the cloth on the table nearby and wiped the tears from his face. 'What is the Aspect's judgement?'

'He feels you have been punished enough.'

'Then I am not even granted the mercy of release from this place.'

'We were both sent here at the behest of our fathers. I have respected my father's wishes by staying here although I do not know why he gave me to the Order. Your father also would have had good reason for sending you here. It was his wish in life, it will remain his wish now he is with the Departed. Perhaps you should respect it.'

'So I should languish here while my father's lands are forfeit and my family left destitute?'

'Will your family be any less destitute with you at their side? Do you have riches that will help them? Think what kind of life you would have outside the Order. You will be the son of a traitor, marked by the King's soldiers for vengeance. Your family will have burdens enough without you at their side. The Order is no longer your prison, it's your protection.'

Nortah sank back into the bed, staring at the ceiling in mixed exhaustion and grief. 'Please, brother, I must be alone for a time.'

Vaelin rose and went to the door. 'Remember you are not alone in this. Your brothers will not allow you to fall victim to grief.'

Outside, he lingered at the door, listening to Nortah's hard, pain-filled sobs. *So much pain.* He wondered if his own father had been on the gallows if he would have fought so hard to save him. *Would I have even cried?*

That night he collected Scratch from the kennels and took him to the north gate, where they played fetch the ball and waited for the boy Frentis to arrive for his knife-throwing lesson. Scratch seemed to be growing stronger and faster with each passing day. Master Jeklin's dog feed, a hash of minced beef, bone marrow and pulped fruit, had put even more meat on his frame and his constant exercise with Vaelin left his physique both lean and powerful. Despite his fierce appearance and unnerving size, Scratch retained the same happy, face-licking spirit of an overgrown puppy.

'Don't you normally take him to the woods?' It was Caenis, slipping from the shadows cast by the gatehouse. Vaelin was a little annoyed at himself for not sensing his brother's presence but Caenis was unusually skilled at remaining hidden and took a perverse delight in appearing apparently from nowhere.

'Do you have to do that?' Vaelin asked.

'I'm practising.'

Scratch came scampering up with the ball in his mouth, dropping it at Vaelin's feet and greeting Caenis with a sniff of his boots. Caenis patted him uncertainly on the head. Like the other brothers he had never lost his basic fear of the animal.

'Nortah still sleeping?' Caenis asked.

Vaelin shook his head. He didn't want to talk about Nortah; his brother's tears had left a hard knot in his chest that was taking a long time to fade.

'The coming months will be hard,' Caenis went on with a sigh.

'Aren't they always?' Vaelin hurled the ball towards the river,

Scratch hurtling after it with a joyful yelp. 'Sorry you didn't get to see the King.'

'No, but I saw the prince. That was enough. What a great man he'll be.'

Vaelin gave Caenis a sidelong glance, seeing the familiar glint in his eye. He had never been comfortable with his friend's blind devotion to the King. 'He . . . was a very impressive man. I'm sure he'll be a fine king one day.'

'Yes, he'll lead us to glory.'

'Glory, brother?'

'Of course. The King has ambitions, he wishes to make the Realm even greater, perhaps as great as the Alpiran Empire. There will be battles, Vaelin. Mighty, glorious battles, and we will see them, fight them.'

War is blood and shit . . . There's no honour in it, Makril's words. Vaelin knew they would mean nothing to Caenis. He was knowledgeable and often frighteningly intelligent but he was also a dreamer. He had a mental library of a thousand stories and seemed to believe them all. Heroes, villains, princesses in need of rescue, monsters and magical swords. It all lived in his head, as vital and real as his own memories.

'I think we have different notions of glory, brother,' Vaelin said as Scratch came bounding back with the ball in his jaws.

They waited for another hour but the boy didn't come.

'He probably sold the knives,' Caenis said, after Vaelin had told him the story. 'He'll have tanked up on grog in a gutter somewhere, or gambled it away. Likely you'll never see him again.'

They walked back to the stables, Vaelin tossing the ball into the air for Scratch to catch. 'I'd rather believe he spent the money on shoes,' he said glancing back at the gate.

PART II

What is the body?

The body is a shell, the cradle of the soul.

What is the body without the soul?

Corrupted flesh, nothing more. Mark the passing of loved ones by giving their shell to the fire.

What is death?

Death is but a gateway to the Beyond and union with the Departed. It is both ending and beginning. Fear it and welcome it.

—THE CATECHISM OF FAITH

VERNIERS' ACCOUNT

'It was Blood Rose, wasn't it?' I asked. 'The Lord Marshal at the Summertide Fair.'

'Al Hestian? Yes,' the Hope Killer replied. 'Though he didn't earn that name until the war.'

I drew a line under the passage I had just set down, finding myself nearly out of ink. 'A moment,' I said, rising to open my chest and extract another bottle and some more parchment. I had filled several pages already and worried that I might exhaust my supply. I hesitated before opening the chest, finding his hateful sword propped against it. Seeing my discomfort, he reached for the weapon and rested it on his knees.

'The Lonak have a superstition that imbues their weapons with the souls of the enemies they kill,' he said. 'They give names to their war clubs and knives, imagining them possessed of the Dark. My people have no such illusions. A sword is just a sword. It's the man who kills, not the blade.'

Why was he telling me this? Did he want me to hate him even more? Seeing his scarred, powerful hand resting on the sword hilt, I recalled how Seliesen, after the Emperor formally named him as the Hope, had submitted himself to months of harsh tutelage under the Imperial Guard, becoming proficient, even skilled, with sabre and lance. 'The Hope must be a warrior,' he told me. 'The Gods and the people expect it.' The Imperial Guard had taken him in like one of their own and he had ridden with them against the Volarians the summer before Janus sent his armies to our shores, winning plaudits for his courage in the melee. It had availed him nothing against the Hope Killer. I knew the moment would come when the Northman would relate what had happened on that terrible day, and, even though I had heard many accounts of the event, the prospect of hearing it from Al Sorna himself was both dreadful and irresistible.

I sat down again and opened the ink bottle, dipped the quill and smoothed a fresh sheet of parchment on the deck. 'The Dark,' I said. 'What's that?'

'Your people call it magic, I believe.'

'They might, I call it superstition. You believe in such things?'

There was a moment's pause and I formed the impression he was considering his next words carefully. 'There are many unknown facets of this world.'

'There are stories told of the war, stories that ascribe great and powerful magic to the Northmen, and to you in particular. Some claim it was with magic that you clouded our soldiers' minds at the Bloody Hill, and that you stole through the walls of Linesh with sorcery.'

His mouth twitched in faint amusement. 'There was no magic at the Bloody Hill, just men possessed of a mindless anger hurling themselves at certain death. As for Linesh, a shit-stinking sewer in the harbour hardly counts as sorcery. Besides, any Realm Guard officer who even suggested use of the Dark would most likely find himself hanged from the nearest tree by his own men. The Dark is believed to be integral to those forms of worship that deny the Faith.'

He paused again, looking down at the sword resting in his lap.

'There's a story, if you'd like to hear it. A story we tell our children to warn them against the dangers of the Dark.'

He glanced up at me, eyebrows raised. Although I consider myself a historian and not a compiler of myths and fables, such tales often shed some light on the truth of events, if only to illustrate the delusions that many mistake for reason. 'Tell me,' I said with a shrug.

When he spoke again his voice had taken on a new tone, grave but engaging, a storyteller's voice. 'Gather close and listen well to the tale of the Witch's Bastard. This is not a story for the faint of heart or the weak of bladder. This is the most terrible and frightful of tales and when I am done you may curse my name for ever having given it voice.

'In the darkest part of the darkest woods in old Renfael, long before the time of the Realm, there stood a village. And in this village there dwelt a witch, comely to the eye but with a heart blacker than the blackest night. Sweet and kind was the face she offered to the village, but mean and jealous was the soul behind it. For it was lust that drove this woman, lust for flesh, lust for gold and lust for death. The Dark had taken her at an early age and she had surrendered to its vileness with willing abandon, denying the Faith and winning power in return, the power to possess men, inflame their desires and have them commit dreadful acts in her name.

'First to fall under her spell was the village Factor, a good and kind man, grown wealthy through thrift and hard work, grown wealthy enough to arouse the witch's lust. Every day she would wander past his place of business, flaunting herself in subtle ways, stoking the flames of his passion until they became a raging fire, burning away his reason, making him prey for her Dark-whispered plan: kill your wife and take me in her place. And so, one fateful night, he sprinkled the poison known as Hunter's Arrow into his wife's supper and, come the morn, she breathed no more.

'Being a woman of middle years with a history of illness, the *passing of the Factor's wife was taken as simply an act of nature by the village. But of course the witch knew better, hiding her delight with tears when they gave the poor murdered woman to the fire, all the time calling to the Factor with her Dark power: "Lavish gifts on me, and I will be yours." And gifts he gave her, a fine horse, jewels and gold and silver, but the witch was clever and refused it all, making a great show of outrage at the impropriety of a man pressing his suit on so young a woman, and so soon after his wife's passing at that. How she tormented him, calling to him and then rebuffing his every advance, it wasn't long before her cruelty unhinged his reason and, seeking escape from the Dark enslavement of her lust, he stole away into the forest and stretched his neck from the high branch of a tall oak, leaving writ word of his ill deed and naming the witch as the cause of his madness.*

'Of course the villagers wouldn't believe it, so sweet she was, so kind. The Factor was clearly driven mad by his own delusion of love for a younger woman. They gave him to the fire and endeavoured to forget this dread episode. But, of course, the witch was not done, for her eye had alighted on the village blacksmith, a great, handsome fellow, strong of arm and strong of heart, but even his heart could be twisted by her Dark power.

'She had taken to living apart from the villagers, all the better to practise her vile arts away from prying eyes. As she could turn a man's heart this witch could also turn the wind, and as the blacksmith burned charcoal in the forest, she called a northern gale to whip snow down from the mountains, forcing him to seek shelter under her roof, and there, although he resisted with all his mighty strength, she forced him to lie with her, a black, evil union from which her dread bastard would be born.

'It was shame that broke her spell, shame of a good man forced to betray his wife, shame that made him deaf to her sweet entice- ments the next morn, and deaf to the threats she screamed as he

fled back to the village, where, foolishly, he told no-one of what had transpired.

'*And the witch, she waited. As the black seed grew in her belly, she waited. As winter gave way to spring and the crops grew tall, she waited. And then, when the scythes were sharpened for harvest and her foul creation clawed from between her legs, she acted.*

'*It was a storm unlike any seen before or since, heralded by ashen clouds that covered the whole sky from north to south, east to west, bringing wind and rain in terrible abundance. For three weeks the rain fell and the wind blew and the villagers huddled in fearful misery until, when at last it was over, they ventured into the fields to find every acre a wasted ruin. The only crop they would reap that year would be hunger.*

'*They looked to the forest, seeking game to fill their bellies, but finding all the beasts driven off by some Dark whisper of the witch. The children cried to be so hungry, the old people sickened and, one by one, began to pass into the Beyond, and all the time the witch kept to her small cottage in the woods, for she and her bastard always had plenty to eat, unwitting beasts could be easily snared by one so well versed in the Dark.*

'*It was the death of the blacksmith's beloved mother that finally drove the truth from him. Confess he did to the gathered villagers, telling them all of the witch's designs and how he had fallen under her spell to sire the well-fed bastard she carried through the forest, mocking their starving young with his happy laughter. The villagers voted and none disagreed: the witch must be driven out.*

'*At first she tried to use her power to assuage them, casting lies at the blacksmith, accusing him of the most terrible of crimes: rape. But her power had no effect now they could see the truth, now they could hear the venom that coloured every lie she told, the evil glint in her eye showing the vileness hidden behind her pretty face. And so with torches flaming, they drove her forth, her cottage burned by* their righteous anger as she fled into the forest, clutching her vile whelp to her breast, all pretence gone as she cursed them . . . and promised revenge.

'And so, while the villagers returned to their homes and tried best they could to survive the coming winter, the witch sought out a hiding place in the dark reaches of the forest, a place where no foot had stepped before, and began to teach her spawn the ways of the Dark.

'Years passed, the village buried its dead and refused to die. Years went by and the witch became but a memory then a story told on cold nights to frighten children. The crops grew, the seasons passed and all seemed right with the world once more. How blind they were, how naked before the coming storm. For the witch had made a monster of her bastard, seemingly but a scrawny, ragged boy gone wild in the woods, but in truth possessed of all the Dark she could pour into him, first with the tainted milk of her breast then the whispered tutelage in their stinking refuge and finally with her own blood. For she had sacrificed herself, this witch, this hate-filled woman, when he had grown old enough she took a knife to her wrists and bade him drink. And drink he did, hard and deep until the witch was but a husk, gone to the nothingness that awaits the Unfaithful but succoured by the knowledge of her impending vengeance.

'He started with their animals, beloved pets taken in the dead of night and found tormented to death on the morn. Then heifers or pigs were taken, their severed heads impaled on fence posts at each corner of the village. Fearful, ignorant of the true danger that assailed them, the villagers set watches, lit torches, kept weapons close to hand when darkness came. It availed them nothing.

'After the beasts he came for the children, tottering infants and babes still in their cribs, any he could take he took, and gruesome was their fate. Enraged, maddened, they scoured the forest, hunters sought tracks, every known hiding place checked, traps set to ensnare this unseen monster. They found nothing, and on it went, through the autumn and into winter, the nightly toll of torture and death continued. And then, as winter's chill gripped them, he finally made himself known, simply walking into the village at noon. By now their fear was so great no hand was lifted against him, and they begged. They begged for their children and their lives, they offered all they had if he would just leave them in peace.

'And the Witch's Bastard laughed. It was not a laugh any normal child could make, nor a laugh that could have come from any human throat. And with that laugh, they knew they were doomed.

'He called forth the lightning and the village burned. The people fled to the river but he swelled it with rain until the banks burst and carried them away. Still his vengeance was not sated and he brought down a blast of wind from the far north to encase them in ice. And when the ice had set, he walked across it until he found the face of his father the blacksmith, frozen in terror for all time.

'No-one knows what became of him, although some say on the coldest nights, in a place where it's said a village once stood, you can hear laughter echoing through the woods, for that is how it is with those who give themselves over to the Dark so completely, release from life is denied them, and the Beyond closed to them forevermore.'

Al Sorna fell silent, his expression thoughtful as he returned his gaze to the sword in his lap. I had a sense that he attached some importance to this lurid tale, something in the gravity with which he had related the story spoke of a significance I couldn't discern. 'You believe this story?' I asked.

'They say all myths have some kernel of truth at their heart. Perhaps in time, a learned fellow like you could find the truth in this one.'

'Folklore is not my field.' I set aside the parchment upon which

I had set down the tale of the Witch's Bastard. It would be several years before I read it again, by which time I had good cause to bitterly regret not following his suggestion.

I reached for fresh pages, looking at him expectantly.

He smiled. 'Let me tell you how I first came to meet King Janus.'

CHAPTER ONE

They began riding late in the month of Prensur. Their horses were all stallions, no more than two years old, youthful mounts for youthful riders. The pairing was done under Master Rensial's supervision, his more extreme behaviour thankfully in check today, although he muttered constantly to himself as he led each of them to their mount.

'Yes, tall, yes,' he mused, surveying Barkus. 'Need strength.' He tugged Barkus by the sleeve and led him to the largest of the horses, a hefty chestnut stallion standing at least seventeen hands. 'Brush his coat, check his shoes.'

Caenis was led to a fleet-looking dark brown stallion and Dentos a sturdy, dappled grey. Nortah's mount was almost completely black, with a blaze of white on his forehead. 'Fast,' Master Rensial muttered. 'Fast rider, fast horse.' Nortah regarded his horse in silence, his reaction to most things since his return from the infirmary. Their constant attempts to engage him in conversation were met with shrugs or blank indifference. The only time he seemed to come alive was on the practice field, displaying a new-found ferocity with sword and pole-axe that left them all bruised or cut.

Vaelin's own mount turned out to be a sturdy, russet-coloured stallion with a cluster of scars on his flanks. 'Broken,' Master Rensial told him. 'Not bred. Wild horse from the north lands. Still got some spirit left, needs guidance.'

Vaelin's horse bared its teeth at him and whinnied loudly, the shower of spit making him step back. He hadn't ridden a horse since leaving his father's house and found the prospect oddly daunting.

'Care for them today, ride them tomorrow,' Master Rensial was saying. 'Win their trust and they will carry you through war, without their trust you will die.' He stopped talking and, seeing his eyes take on the unfocused cast that signified another onset of rambling or violence, they quickly led their mounts to the stables for grooming.

They began to ride the next morning and did little else for the next four weeks. Nortah, having ridden from an early age, was by far the best horseman, beating them all in every race and traversing the most difficult course Master Rensial could devise with relative ease. Only Dentos could compete with him, taking to the saddle like a natural. 'Used to go to the races every month in summertime,' he explained. 'Me mum would make a packet betting on me. Said I could get a race out of a carthorse.'

Caenis and Vaelin proved adequate if not expert riders and Barkus learned quickly although it was clear he didn't relish the lessons. 'My arse feels like it's been hit with a thousand hammers,' he groaned one night, lowering himself to his bed facedown.

The others soon became bonded to their horses, naming them and getting to know their ways. Vaelin called his horse Spit, since that was all the animal ever seemed to do when he attempted to win his trust. He was perennially bad-tempered with a tendency towards wayward hooves and sudden, bruising lurches of the head. Attempts to court his favour with sugar sticks or apples did nothing to assuage the beast's basic aggression. The only comfort in the pairing was the fact that Spit was even more badly behaved towards the others. Whatever his character faults, the beast proved fast at the gallop and fearless in practice, often snapping at the other mounts as they charged each other and never shying away from a melee.

Their lessons in mounted combat proved a gruelling affair as they attempted to unseat each other with lance or sword. Nortah's horsemanship and new-found love of the fight meant many tumbles from the saddle and more than a few minor injuries. They also began to learn the difficult art of mounted archery, a necessary element of the Test of the Horse, which they would have to pass in less than a year. Vaelin found the bow a hard discipline at the best of times but attempting to sink a shaft into a hay bale from twenty yards whilst twisting in a saddle was almost impossible. Nortah on the other hand hit the mark on his first try and hadn't missed since.

'Can you teach me?' Vaelin asked him, chagrined by another disastrous practice. 'Master Rensial's instruction is often hard to follow.'

Nortah stared at him with the empty passivity they had come to expect. 'That's because he's a gibbering loon,' he replied.

'He's clearly a troubled man,' Vaelin agreed with a smile. Nortah said nothing. 'So, any help you could provide . . .'

Nortah shrugged. 'If you wish.'

It turned out there was no real trick to it, just practice. Every day they would spend an hour or more after the evening meal with Vaelin consistently failing to hit the target and Nortah coaching him. 'Don't rise so high in the saddle before you loose . . . Make sure you get the string back to your chin . . . Only loose when you feel your mount's hooves leave the ground . . . Don't aim so low . . .' It took five days before Vaelin could put a shaft

in the hay bale and another three before his aim was true enough
to find the mark at almost every pass.

'My thanks, brother,' he said one night as they walked their
mounts back to the stables. 'I doubt I would have picked it up
without your help.'

Nortah gave him an unreadable glance. 'I owed you a debt,
did I not?'

'We are brothers. Debts mean nothing between us.'

'Tell me, do you really believe all this tripe you spout?' There
was no venom in Nortah's tone, just vague curiosity. 'We call each
other brother but we share no blood. We're just boys forced
together by this Order. Don't you ever wonder what it would have
been like if we had met on the outside? Would we have been
friends then, or enemies? Our fathers were enemies, did you know
that?'

Hoping silence would end the conversation, Vaelin shook his
head.

'Oh yes. When I was young I found a secret place in my father's
house where I could listen to the meetings in his study. He spoke
of your father often, and not with kindness. He said he was a
jumped-up peasant with no more brains than an axe blade. He
said Sorna should have been kept in a locked room until war
required his service and couldn't fathom why the King ever listened
to the counsel of such an oaf.'

They were halted now, facing each other. Nortah's eyes were
bright with the familiar hunger for combat. Sensing the tension,
Spit tossed his head and nickered in anticipation.

'You seek to provoke me, brother,' Vaelin said, patting his horse's
neck to calm him. 'But you forget, I have no father, so your words
mean nothing. Why is it the only joy you show these days is in
battle? Why do you hunger for it so? Does it make you forget?
Does it ease your pain?'

Nortah tugged his horse's reins and resumed the walk to the stables. 'It eases nothing. But it does make me forget, for a while at least.'

Vaelin kicked Spit into a canter, overtaking Nortah. 'Then mayhap a race will help you forget too.' He spurred into a gallop and headed for the main gate. Naturally, Nortah beat him by a clear length, but he was smiling when he did so.

It was late in the month of Jenislasur, a week after Vaelin's uncelebrated fifteenth birthday, when he was called to the Aspect's chambers.

'What now?' Dentos wondered. They were at the morning meal and he spat bread crumbs across the table as he spoke. Table manners were a lesson too far for Dentos. 'He must like you, you're never away from his rooms.'

'Vaelin is the Aspect's favourite,' Barkus said in a mock-serious tone. 'Everyone knows that. He'll be Aspect himself one day, you mark my words.'

'Piss off, the pair of you,' Vaelin responded, stuffing an apple in his mouth as he rose from the table. He had no idea why he had been called to the Aspect, likely it was another sensitive question regarding his father or a new threat to his life. He was often surprised at how the passage of time had made him immune to such fears. His nightmares had abated in recent months and he could look back on the dark events during the Test of the Run with cold reflection, although his dispassionate scrutiny did nothing to dispel the mystery.

He had munched his way through most of the fruit by the time he got to the Aspect's door, and concealed the core in his cloak before knocking. He would feed it to Spit later, doubtless earning a shower of slobber as a reward.

'Come in, brother.' The Aspect's voice came through the door.

Inside, the Aspect was standing next to the narrow window affording a view of the river, smiling his slight smile. Vaelin's nod of respect was cut short by the sight of the room's other occupant: a skeletally thin boy dressed in rags with bare, mud-stained feet dangling over the edge of the chair in which he was uncomfortably perched.

'That's 'im!' Frentis said, jumping to his feet as Vaelin entered. 'That's the brother that in-inspirated me! Battle Lord's son 'e is.'

'He is no-one's son, boy,' the Aspect told him.

Vaelin swore inwardly, closing the door. *Giving knives to a street urchin, a shameful episode. Not what is expected of a brother . . .*

'Do you know this boy, brother?' the Aspect enquired.

Vaelin glanced at Frentis, seeing eagerness under a mask of dirt. 'Yes, Aspect. He was of assistance to me during a recent . . . difficulty.'

'Y'see?' Frentis said urgently to the Aspect. 'Told ya! Told ya he knew me.'

'This boy has requested entry to the Order,' the Aspect went on. 'Will you vouch for him?'

Vaelin stared at Frentis in appalled surprise. 'You want to join the Order?'

'Yeh!' Frentis said, nearly jumping with excitement. 'Wanna join. Wanna be a brother.'

'Are you—?' Vaelin choked off at the word 'mad' and took a deep breath before addressing the Aspect. 'Vouch for him, Aspect?'

'This boy has no family, no-one to speak for him or formally place him in the hands of the Order. Our rules demand that all boys who join must be vouched for, either by a parent or, in the case of an orphan, a subject of recognised good character. The boy has nominated you.'

Vouched for? No-one had told him this. 'Was I vouched for, Aspect?'

'Of course.'

My father spoke to them before he brought me here. How many days or weeks before had he arranged it? How long had he known and not told me?

'Tell 'im I can be a brother,' Frentis was saying. 'Tell 'im I helped you.'

Vaelin drew a heavy breath and looked down at the frantic desperation in Frentis's eyes. 'May I have a moment alone with this boy, Aspect?'

'Very well. I shall be in the main keep.'

After he had gone, Frentis started again. 'Ya gotta tell 'im. Tell 'im I can be a brother . . .'

'Do you think this is a game?' Vaelin cut in, stepping close to grasp the rags covering Frentis's narrow chest, pulling him close. 'What do you want here? Safety, food, shelter? Don't you know what this place is?'

Frentis's eyes were wide with fear as he shrank back, his voice small now. ''S where they train the brothers.'

'Yes they train us. They beat us, they make us fight each other every day, they put us through tests that might kill us. I have fifteen years and more scars on my body than any seasoned soldier in the Realm Guard. There were ten boys in my group when I started here, now there are five. What are you asking me for? To agree to your death?' He released Frentis and turned back to the door. 'I won't do it. Go back to the city. You'll live longer.'

'I go back there, I'll be dead by nightfall!' Frentis cried, voice heavy with fear. He sank back into his chair and sobbed miserably. 'I got nowhere else to go. You send me away, and I'm dead. Hunsil's boys'll do for me for sure.'

Vaelin's hand lingered on the door handle. 'Hunsil?'

'Runs the gangs in the quarter, all the dippers, whores and

knifers pay 'im homage, five coppers a month. I couldn't pay last month so his boys gave me a beatin'.'

'And if you can't pay this month, he'll kill you?'

'It's too late for that. Not about the money anymore. 'S about 'is eye.'

'His eye?'

'Yeh, the right one. It ain't there no more.'

Vaelin turned back from the door with a heavy sigh. 'The knives I gave you.'

'Yeh, couldn't wait for you to teach me. Practised on me own. Got right good at it too. Thought I'd try it out on Hunsil, waited in the alley outside his tavern till he came out.'

'Taking him in the eye was an impressive throw.'

Frentis smiled weakly. 'Was aimin' for 'is throat.'

'And he knows it was you?'

'Oh 'e knows all right. Bastard knows everything.'

'I have some money, not much but my brothers will pitch in some more. We could buy you a berth on a merchant ship, a cabin boy. You would be safer on a ship than you could ever be here.'

'Thought about that, din't wanna. Don't like ships, get queasy just crossing the river in a flatboat. Besides, I've 'eard sailors'll do things to cabin boys.'

'I'm sure they'll leave you alone if we guarantee it.'

'But I wanna be a brother. I saw what you did to those Hawks. You and the other one. Never seen nothin' like it. I wanna be able to do that. I wanna be like you.'

'Why?'

''Cos it makes you someone, makes you matter. They're still yakkin' about it in the taverns y'know, how the Battle Lord's boy humbled the Blackhawks. You're almost as famous as your old man.'

'And that's what you want? To be famous?'

Frentis fidgeted. It was clear he was rarely asked for an opinion on anything and found this level of scrutiny disconcerting. 'Dunno. Wanna be someone, not just some dipper. Can't do that all me life.'

'All you are likely to earn here is an early death.'

Frentis no longer looked like a boy then, rather he seemed so aged and burdened by experience that Vaelin almost felt himself to be a child in the presence of an old man. 'That's all I've ever bin likely to earn.'

Can I do this? Vaelin asked himself. *Can I condemn him to this?* The answer came to him within a heartbeat. *At least he had a choice. He chose to come here. And what will I condemn him to if I send him away?*

'What do you know of the Faith?' Vaelin asked him.

''S what people believe 'appens when you die.'

'And what does happen when you die?'

'You join the other Departed and they, y'know, help us.'

Hardly the Catechism of Faith but succinctly put. 'Do you believe it?'

Frentis shrugged. 'S'pose.'

Vaelin leaned down and looked him in the eye, fixing him. 'When the Aspect asks you, don't suppose, be certain. The Order fights for the Faith before it fights for the Realm.' He straightened. 'Let's go and find him.'

'You're gonna tell 'im to let me in?'

May my mother's soul forgive me. 'Yes.'

'Great!' Frentis surged to his feet and ran to the door. 'Thanks . . .'

'Don't ever thank me for this,' Vaelin told him. 'Not ever.'

Frentis gave him a quizzical look. 'All right. So when do I get a sword?'

◆ ◆ ◆

It would be another three months before the next intake of recruits so Frentis was put to work. He ran errands, laboured in the kitchens or the orchard and swept the stables. They gave him a bunk in their north-tower room, the Aspect felt leaving him alone in one of the other rooms would be a poor welcome to the Order.

'This is Frentis,' Vaelin introduced him to the others. 'A novice brother. He'll bunk with us until the turn of the year.'

'Is he old enough?' Barkus asked, looking Frentis up and down. 'He's just rag and bone.'

'Up yours, fatso!' Frentis snarled in response, drawing back.

'How charming,' Nortah observed. 'An urchin of our very own.'

'Why's he bunking with us?' Dentos wanted to know.

'Because the Aspect commands it, and because I owe him a debt. And so do you, brother,' he said to Nortah. 'If he hadn't helped me, you'd be swinging in a wall cage.'

Nortah inclined his head but said no more.

'He's the one you knocked out,' Frentis said. 'The one that knifed that Blackhawk in the leg. Proper sharp that was. Are we allowed to knife Realm Guard then?'

'No!' Vaelin tugged him to his bunk, Mikehl's old bed, which had lain unused in the years since his death. 'This is yours. You'll get bedding from Master Grealin in the vaults, I'll take you there soon.'

'Do I get a sword from him?'

The others laughed. 'Oh you'll get a sword, right enough,' Dentos said. 'Finest blade ash can make.'

'Wanna proper sword,' Frentis insisted sullenly.

'You'll have to earn it,' Vaelin told him. 'Like the rest of us. Now, I want to talk to you about thieving.'

'I ain't gonna thieve nothin'. I'm done with that, I swear.'

More laughter from the others. 'Fine brother he'll make,' Barkus said.

'Thieving is . . .' Vaelin fumbled for the right words, 'accepted here, but there are rules. You never steal from any of us and you never steal from the masters.'

Frentis gave him a suspicious look. 'Is this one of them tests?'

Vaelin gritted his teeth. He was starting to understand why Master Sollis was so fond of his cane. 'No. You can steal from others in the Order provided they aren't a master and they're not in your group.'

'What? And no-one cares?'

'Oh no, they'll tan the hide off you if you get caught but that's for getting caught, not for stealing.'

A very small smile appeared on Frentis's lips. 'I only ever got caught once. Won't happen again.'

If Vaelin had expected Frentis to be quickly disillusioned by the rigours of Order life, he was to be disappointed. The boy happily scampered to every task given him, moving like a blur around the House, watching attentively during practice sessions and pestering them to teach him their skills. Mostly they were happy to oblige, training him in sword play and unarmed combat. He needed little instruction in knife throwing and soon began to rival Dentos and Nortah at the game. Seeing an opportunity, they quickly arranged a knives tournament and reaped a tidy sum in blades, which were shared out equally.

'How come I can't keep 'em?' Frentis whined as they counted the winnings.

''Cos you're not a real brother yet,' Dentos told him. 'When you are you'll get to keep all you win. Till then we all get a share, payment for our kind tutoring.'

The most surprising thing was Frentis's complete lack of fear when dealing with Scratch. Where the other boys were wary he was playful, wrestling the animal with happy abandon, giggling when the dog threw him around with ease. Vaelin had been concerned at first but saw that Scratch was exercising his own brand of caution, Frentis was never nipped or scratched.

'To him the boy's a cub,' Master Jeklin explained. 'Probably thinks he's one of yours. Sees himself as an older brother.'

Frentis also earned the distinction of being the only boy to never receive a beating from Master Rensial. For some reason the stable master never raised his hand to him, simply pointing him towards his allotted tasks and watching silently until they were complete, his expression even odder than usual; a curious mix of puzzlement and regret that made Vaelin resolve to keep Frentis out of the stables as much as possible.

'What's wrong with Master Rensial?' Frentis asked one evening as Vaelin taught him the basics of the parry. 'Is 'e funny in the head?'

'I know little about him,' Vaelin replied. 'He knows his horses, that's for sure. As for what goes on in his head, it's clear that the hardships of a life in the Order can do strange things to a man's mind.'

'Think it'll happen to you one day?'

Vaelin didn't answer, instead he sent an overhand swipe at Frentis's head that the boy only just managed to block with his wooden blade. 'Pay attention,' Vaelin snapped. 'You won't find the masters as forgiving as me.'

The months with Frentis passed quickly, his energy and blind enthusiasm making them forget their woes, even Nortah seemed enlivened by his time with the boy, taking on the task of showing him the bow. As with his tutelage of Dentos before the Test of Knowledge, Vaelin noted once again Nortah's facility for teaching, where the other boys would occasionally make their frustration with Frentis obvious, particularly Barkus, Nortah seemed to possess an abundance of patience.

'Good,' he said as Frentis managed to get his shaft within a yard of the target. 'Try pushing the stave at the same time as you pull the string, the bow will bend easier.'

It was thanks to Nortah that Frentis was able to begin his training as the only boy to hit the target during his first formal practice.

'Can't I stay with you lot?' Frentis had asked the night before he was due to move to the room he would share with his group.

'You must be in a group,' Vaelin said. They were in the kennels, watching Scratch as he stood guard over his heavily pregnant bitch. No-one else was allowed near his pen now, his mate's condition making him violently protective, even Master Jeklin was likely to provoke an attack if he came too close.

'Why?' Frentis said, the whine in his voice having abated somewhat but still noticeable.

'Because we cannot be with you throughout your training,' Vaelin told him. 'You will find brothers amongst the boys you meet tomorrow. Together you will help each other face the tests. It is how things are done in the Order.'

'What if they don't like me?'

'Like and dislike mean little here. The bond that binds us is beyond friendship.' He gave Frentis a nudge. 'Don't worry. You already know more than them, they will look to you for guidance, just don't be too cocky about it.'

'Are you and the others still gonna teach me?'

Vaelin shook his head. 'You will be under Master Haunlin's care. He will teach you now. We cannot interfere. He is a fair man, sparing with the cane as long as you don't push him. Mind him well.'

'Will I be allowed to steal for you, still?'

This was something Vaelin hadn't considered. Frentis's effortless ability to procure items of considerable value would be sorely missed. They were now rich in extra clothing, money, talismans, knives and myriad other sundries that made Order life a little more comfortable. True to his word, he had never been caught although the other boys had been quick to connect Frentis's arrival with the upsurge in missing valuables, leading to a particularly bloody fight in the dining hall one night. Luckily they now possessed both the skill and the strength to defend themselves, even from the older boys, and the incident hadn't been repeated although Master Sollis had told Vaelin to make Frentis lay off for a while.

'You'll have to steal for your own group now,' Vaelin told him, not without regret. 'But you can trade with us.'

'Thought I wouldn't be allowed to talk to you now.'

'We can still talk. Let's say we meet here every Eltrian eve.'

'Will Master Jeklin let me have one of the puppies?'

Vaelin looked at Scratch, noting the wary hostility of his gaze and the tension in his stance, knowing even he would earn a bite or two if he attempted to enter the pen. 'I don't think it's up to Master Jeklin.'

CHAPTER TWO

The Test of the Melee came after the Winterfall feast midway through the month of Weslin. Their swords were exchanged for wooden blades and they were divided, along with the fifty or so other boys of their age, into two equal contingents. On the practice field a lance adorned with a red pennant had been thrust into the frost-hard earth. Vaelin was surprised to see the other masters standing on the fringes of the field, even Master Jestin, who was rarely seen outside his forge.

'War is our sacred charge,' the Aspect told them when they had been arrayed before him. 'It is the reason for the Order's existence. We fight in defence of the Faith and the Realm. Today you will fight a battle. One contingent will seek to capture that pennant, another will defend it. Masters will observe the battle. Any brother failing to show sufficient courage and skill in battle will be required to leave on the morrow. Fight well, remember your lessons. Killing blows are not permitted.'

As the Aspect walked from the field the two contingents eyed each other with mingled trepidation and excitement. They all knew what this meant; no killing blows and wooden swords or not, this would be a bloody day.

Master Sollis came forward and handed Vaelin's contingent a number of red ribbons and told them to tie them to their left arm. Nearby Master Haunlin was handing out white ribbons to their nominal enemies. 'You will attack, the whites will defend,' Sollis told them. 'The battle is over when one of you gets his hands on the lance.'

As their white-ribboned enemies trooped off to arrange themselves in a loose line in front of the lance Vaelin saw the Aspect greeting three unfamiliar onlookers. There were two men, one large and broad the other lean and wiry, with long black hair trailing in the wind. The third figure was small, muffled in furs, and clung to the side of the large man.

'Who is that, Master?' he asked when Sollis handed him a ribbon, but it was clearly not a day for questions.

'Worry about the test, boy!' Sollis cuffed him angrily on the side of the head. 'Distraction will kill you this day.'

When they had all tied the ribbons to their arms they stood eyeing the defenders about a hundred yards away. Somehow they seemed to have grown in number.

'What do we do, Vaelin?' Dentos asked, looking at him expectantly.

Vaelin was about to shrug when he noticed they were all looking at him expectantly, not just the boys from his group, all of them. Nortah was the only exception, blithely tossing his wooden sword into the air and catching it again. He seemed bored. Vaelin struggled to formulate a plan; they were taught combat but not tactics. He had heard of flanking manoeuvres and frontal attacks but had no real idea how they worked. Most of the battle stories he knew concerned heroic brothers winning victory through individual effort and even then they were usually trying to storm a city wall or defend a bridge not capture a lance. *The lance . . . What value is there in a lance?*

'Vaelin?' Caenis prompted.

'This isn't really a battle,' Vaelin said, thinking aloud.

'What?'

Battles are not over when a man gets his hands on a lance, they're over when one army destroys the other. That's why it's called the Test of the Melee. They want to see us fight, that's all. The lance means nothing.

'We'll go straight into them,' he said, raising his voice, trying to sound both confident and decisive. 'We'll charge into the centre of their line, hard and fast. Break it open, and the lance is ours.'

'Hardly a subtle stratagem, brother,' Nortah observed.

'Do you want to lead this?'

Nortah inclined his head, smiling. 'I wouldn't dream of it. I'm sure your plan is sound.'

'Form up,' Vaelin told them. 'Keep it tight. Barkus, you're in front with me, and you, Nortah. You two as well.' He picked out two of the beefier boys he knew to be more aggressive than most. 'Caenis, Dentos, stay close, keep them off when we go for the lance. The rest of you heard what the Aspect said. If you don't want your coins in the morning, get in there, pick an enemy and beat him to the ground, when you've done that find another.'

The cheer surprised him, a ragged yell punctuated with a small forest of upraised wooden swords. He joined in, waving his sword and yelling and feeling silly. Incredibly, they yelled even louder, some of them even began shouting his name.

He kept it going as they began to advance, walking at first. The hundred yards to the enemy seemed to shrink in a few heartbeats.

'Vaelin! Vaelin!'

He took the pace up to a jog, hoping to save as much energy as possible for the fight.

'Vaelin! Vaelin!'

Some of the boys were almost screaming now, Caenis amongst them. The pace began to quicken as they covered more than half the distance to the enemy. Seemingly his small army was eager to get at their foes, some of them breaking into a run.

'Steady!' Vaelin shouted. 'Keep together!'

'Vaelin! Vaelin!' He glanced around, seeing faces distorted with rage. *Fear,* he understood. *They hide fear in rage.* He didn't feel enraged. In fact, his overriding concern was that he not get another scar. He had only just had the stitches removed from his last one, a deep cut on his thigh earned from a nasty fall when riding.

'Vaelin! Vaelin!'

They were all running now, their formation starting to break up. Dentos, despite instructions, was out in front, yelling with manic fervour.

Oh for Faith's sake! Vaelin broke into a sprint, pointing his sword at the centre of the enemy line. 'Charge! CHARGE . . .'

The two groups met with bone-crunching force, Vaelin's shoulder feeling like he had rammed it into a tree although he did manage to knock over two defenders. At first it seemed the shock of their charge would force a path straight through to the lance as five or six defenders went down under the combined weight, with Barkus trampling over their prone forms to charge for the pennant. However, their foes quickly gathered their wits and soon both sides were thrashing at each other with a savagery none had known before. Vaelin found himself assailed by two boys at once, both swinging their ash swords with a ferocity that made them forget their many lessons. He parried a blow, dodged another then hit back with a swipe at one boy's legs, sending him to the ground. The other thrust at Vaelin but overextended, allowing Vaelin to trap his sword arm beneath his own and send him reeling with a head-butt.

As the battle raged and the air filled with the mingled

cacophony of cracking wood and grunted pain it became harder to follow the chain of events, time seemed to fragment, the struggle becoming a series of confused, bruising fights in which he caught only the vaguest glimpses of his comrades. Barkus was laying about with his sword, two-handed blows landing with sickening thwacks on those who made the mistake of venturing too close. Dentos, forehead bloodied, had lost his sword and was exchanging punches with a boy a foot or more taller, he seemed to be winning. Caenis leapt on an opponent's back and proceeded to choke him with his sword, forcing him to the ground before one of the defender's boots caught him on the head, sending him sprawling. Vaelin fought his way through to him, hacking through the press of struggling boys, finding Caenis on his back desperately parrying blows from the boy he had tried to choke. Vaelin kicked the boy in the stomach and brought his sword up to connect with his temple, dropping him to the earth, where he stayed for the rest of the battle.

'Enjoying the glory of it, brother?' he asked Caenis, leaning down and offering a hand to help him up.

'Duck!' Caenis yelled.

Vaelin went down on one knee and felt the wind rush of a sword narrowly missing his head. He twisted, bringing his leg round to sweep the attacker off his feet, smacking his sword against his nose as he fell. They fought together after that, back-to-back, stumbling over unconscious or wounded comrades and enemies until they were within a few yards of the lance. One of the defenders, seeing a final chance to display his courage, charged at them wildly, screaming and hacking. Caenis parried his first slash and Vaelin sent him to the ground with a blow to the shoulder that made him wince at the audible crack of breaking bone.

Then it was done, no more enemies, no-one to fight. Just

groaning boys stumbling around and rolling on the ground amidst their immobile brothers and Nortah standing with the lance in his hands, blood streaming from wounds on his head and face. He smiled as Vaelin approached, a thick crimson bead swelling on the cut in his lip. 'It was a good plan, brother.'

Vaelin steadied him as he swayed, feeling more tired than he could remember, his arms felt like lead and the aftermath of violence left a ball of sickness in the pit of his stomach. He found he had no real idea how long it had lasted. It could have been an hour or a few minutes. It was like waking from a particularly draining nightmare. He was relieved to see that Barkus and Dentos were among the ten boys still left standing, although Dentos could only remain upright by virtue of Barkus's meaty hand on his neck. 'What's that, brother?' he said loudly for the benefit of the masters, leaning close as if to listen to Dentos's words although speech seemed to be beyond him at present. 'Yes! A fine fight indeed!'

'The test is concluded!' Master Sollis was striding across the field. 'Help the wounded to the infirmary. Leave the senseless ones lying, the masters will see to them.'

'Come on,' Vaelin told Nortah. 'Let's get you patched up.'

'I'd like that,' Nortah said. 'But I'm not too sure I can walk.' He swayed again and Vaelin had to catch him. Together he and Caenis helped him from the field, still clinging to the lance. Barkus followed, with Dentos dangling in his arms, feet dragging on the earth.

'Brother Vaelin.' It was the Aspect, standing alongside the three strangers.

Vaelin halted, struggling to keep Nortah from falling. 'Aspect.'

'Our guests have requested to meet you.' The Aspect gestured at the three strangers. Vaelin could see the smallest figure clearly now, a girl, wrapped in black furs like the large man to whose arm she clung. She was about his own age but small, pale skin and black hair . . . and very pretty. She hardly seemed to notice him, her eyes staying fixed on Nortah's barely conscious form. He wasn't sure if her expression was one of admiration or fear.

'Brother Vaelin, this is Vanos Al Myrna,' the Aspect said. The large man came forward and offered his hand. Vaelin shook it awkwardly, narrowly avoiding letting Nortah fall over. Caenis stiffened at the mention of the large man's name but it meant little to Vaelin. He had a dim memory of his father's mentioning it to his mother, it was not long before he had been made Battle Lord but Vaelin couldn't recall what the discussion was about.

'I knew your father,' Vanos Al Myrna told Vaelin.

'I have no father,' Vaelin replied automatically.

'Show Lord Vanos some respect, Vaelin,' the Aspect said, a thin smile on his lips. 'He is a Sword of the Realm and Tower Lord of the Northern Reaches. He honours us with his presence.'

Vaelin saw the ghost of a smile play on Vanos Al Myrna's lips. 'You fought well,' he said.

Vaelin nodded at Nortah. 'My brother fought better, he got the lance.'

Al Myrna studied Nortah for a second and Vaelin realised he had known his father too. 'This boy fights without fear. Not always a desirable trait in a soldier.'

'We are all fearless in service of the Faith, my lord.' *That was a good answer,* he decided. *I wish it wasn't a lie.*

The Tower Lord turned and gestured at the wiry, long-haired man. He had similar colouring to the girl, pale skin and dark hair, but his face was different, high cheekbones and a hawk nose. 'This is my friend Hera Drakil of the Seordah Sil.'

Seordah. Vaelin had never thought to see a Seordah with his own eyes. They were a truly mysterious people who, it was said, never ventured from the shelter of the Great Northern Forest and shunned outsiders. It was the Seordah Sil who made the forest a place of dark mystery for Realm folk, who rarely attempted to walk beneath its trees. Stories abounded of hapless travellers who had gone into the forest and never returned.

Hera Drakil nodded at Vaelin, his expression unreadable.

'And this' – Lord Vanos pulled the girl at his side forward a little, provoking a rueful smile – 'is my daughter Dahrena.'

She turned her smile on Vaelin, who wondered why his palms were suddenly sweating. 'Brother. You appear to be the only one uninjured.'

Vaelin realised she was right, he ached all over, and would no doubt ache worse in the morning, but he didn't have a cut. 'Luck smiles on me, my lady.'

She looked at Nortah again, her expression concerned. 'Will he be all right?'

'He's fine,' Caenis said, his tone sounding a little curt to Vaelin.

Nortah's head came up and he gazed blearily at the girl, frowning in confusion. 'You're Lonak,' he said, his head swivelling towards Vaelin. 'Are we in the north?'

'Easy, brother.' Vaelin patted him on the shoulder and was relieved when Nortah's head slumped forward again. 'My brother is not himself,' he told the girl. 'My apologies.'

'For what? I am Lonak.' She turned to the Aspect. 'I have some small healing skill. If I can be of any assistance . . .'

'We have a very capable physician, my lady,' the Aspect replied. 'But I thank you for your concern. Now, we must repair to my chambers and allow these brothers to see to their comrades.'

He turned and made for the keep, followed by the Tower Lord but the others lingered a moment. Hera Drakil gave them all a long look, his eyes moving from Dentos slumped in Barkus's arms to Caenis's blood-smeared nose and Nortah's sagging form, his unreadable expression turning into recognisable disgust. 'Il Lonakhim hearin mar durolin,' he said sadly and walked away.

The girl, Dahrena, seemed embarrassed by the words and gave them a brief glance of farewell before turning to follow.

'What did he say?' Vaelin asked, making her pause.

She hesitated and he wondered if she would plead ignorance of the Seordah language but he knew she had understood the words. 'He said, "The Lonak treat their dogs better."'

'And do they?'

Her mouth tightened a little and he saw a frown of anger before she turned away. 'I expect so.'

Nortah's head lolled back and he grinned at Vaelin. 'She's pretty,' he said before finally passing out.

'So how does the Tower Lord of the Northern Reaches come to have a Lonak for a daughter?' Vaelin asked Caenis.

They were walking the wall, the post-midnight shift, one of the drawbacks of achieving four years in the Order was a regular stint at guard duty. The wall was sparsely manned tonight with so many boys in the infirmary or too badly injured to take their turn, Barkus among them. He had waited until they were back in their room before revealing a deep cut across his back.

'I think someone put a nail through their sword,' he groaned.

They put Nortah in bed and cleaned him up as best they could. Luckily his cuts didn't seem serious enough to warrant stitches and they decided the best course of action was to bandage his head and leave him to sleep it off. Dentos was worse off, his nose seemingly broken again and he kept slipping in and out of consciousness. Vaelin decided he should go to the infirmary along with Barkus, whose wound was beyond their skill to stitch. Dentos was put to bed by a harassed Master Henthal and Barkus allowed to go after his cut had been stitched and smeared with corr-tree oil, a foul-smelling but effective guard against infection. They had left him watching over Nortah to take their turn on the wall.

'Vanos Al Myrna,' Caenis said, 'is not a man to be easily understood. But disloyalty is ever a difficult thing to fathom.'

'Disloyalty?'

'He was banished to the Northern Reaches twelve years ago. No-one knows why for sure but it is said he questioned the King's Word. He was Battle Lord then and King Janus may be kindly and just but he could not tolerate disloyalty from one so high in his court.'

'And yet here he is.'

Caenis shrugged. 'The King's forgiveness is famed. And there have been rumours of a great battle in the north, beyond the forest and the plains. Al Myrna supposedly defeated an army of barbarians who came across the ice. I must confess I gave it little credence but perhaps he is here to report to the King on the victory.'

He was Battle Lord before my father, Vaelin realised. He remembered now although he had been very young. His father came home and told his mother he would be Battle Lord. She had gone to her room and cried.

'And his daughter?' he asked, trying to dispel the memory.

'A Lonak foundling so they say. He came upon her lost in the forest. Apparently the Seordah allow him to travel there.'

'They must hold him in high esteem.'

Caenis sniffed. 'The regard of savages means little, brother.'

'The Seordah with Al Myrna seemed to have little regard for our ways. Perhaps to him we're the savages.'

'You give his words too much credence. The Order is of the Faith and the Faith cannot be judged by one such as him. Although I confess I am curious as to why the Tower Lord should bring him here to gawk at us.'

'I don't think that's why he came. I suspect he had business with the Aspect.'

Caenis looked at him sharply. 'Business? What could they possibly have to discuss?'

'You cannot be entirely deaf to word of the world outside these walls, Caenis. The Battle Lord has quit his post, the King's Minister has been executed. Now the Tower Lord comes south. It must all mean something.'

'This was ever an eventful realm. It's why our history is so rich in stories.'

Stories of war, Vaelin thought.

'Perhaps,' Caenis went on, 'Al Myrna had another reason for coming here, a personal reason.'

'Such as?'

'He said he and the Battle Lord had been comrades. Perhaps he wished to check on your progress.'

My father sent him here to see me? Vaelin wondered. *Why? To check I'm still alive? See how tall I've grown? To count my scars?* He had to force down the familiar well of bitterness building in his chest. *Why hate a stranger? I have no father to hate.*

CHAPTER THREE

O nly two boys were given their coins in the morning, both having been judged as displaying either cowardice or a chronic lack of skill during the battle. It seemed to Vaelin all the blood spilled and bones broken in the test had hardly been worth the outcome, but the Order never questioned its rituals, they were of the Faith after all. Nortah recovered quickly, as did Dentos, although Barkus would have a deep scar on his back for the rest of his life.

As winter's chill deepened, their training became more specialised. Master Sollis's sword scales acquired a daunting complexity and lessons with the pole-axe began to emphasise the discipline of close-order drill. They were taught to march and manoeuvre in companies, learning the many commands that formed a group of individuals into a disciplined battle line. It was a difficult skill to learn and many boys earned the cane for failing to know right from left or continually falling out of step. It took several months of hard training before they truly felt they knew what they were doing and a couple more before the masters appeared satisfied with their efforts. All through this they had to keep up their riding practice, most of which had to be done in the evening during the shortening hours of dusk. They had found their own racing course, a four-mile trail along the riverbank and back around the outer wall, which took in enough rough ground and obstacles to meet Master Rensial's exacting standards. It was during one of their evening races that Vaelin met the little girl.

He had misjudged a jump over a fallen birch trunk and Spit, with characteristic bad grace, had reared, dumping him from the saddle to connect painfully with the frosted earth. He heard the others laughing as they spurred on ahead.

'You bloody nag!' Vaelin raged, climbing to his feet and rubbing at a bruised backside. 'You're fit for nothing but the tallow mill.'

Spit bared his teeth in spite and dragged a hoof along the ground before trotting off to chew ineffectually at some bushes. In one of his more coherent moments Master Rensial had cautioned them against ascribing human feelings to an animal that had a brain no larger than a crab apple. 'Horses feel only for other horses,' he told them. 'Their cares and wants are not ours to know, no more than they can know a man's thoughts.' Watching Spit carefully show him his backside, Vaelin thought if that was true, then his horse had an uncanny ability to project the human quality of indifference.

'Your horse doesn't like you much.'

His eyes found her quickly, hands involuntarily moving to his weapons. She was about ten years old, wrapped in furs against the cold, her pale face poking out to peer at him with unabashed curiosity. She had emerged from behind a broad oak, mitten-clad hands clasping a small bunch of pale yellow flowers he recognised as winterblooms. They grew well in the surrounding woods and sometimes people from the city came to pick them. He didn't understand why since Master Hutril said they were no use as either medicine or food.

'I think he'd rather be back on the plains,' Vaelin replied, moving to the fallen birch trunk and sitting down to adjust his sword belt.

To his surprise the little girl came and sat next to him. 'My name's Alornis,' she said. 'Your name is Vaelin Al Sorna.'

'That it is.' He was growing accustomed to recognition since the Summertide Fair, drawing stares and pointed fingers whenever he ventured close to the city.

'Mumma said I shouldn't talk to you,' Alornis went on.

'Really? Why's that?'

'I don't know. I think Dadda wouldn't like it.'

'Then maybe you shouldn't.'

'Oh I don't always do what I'm told. I'm a bad girl. I don't do things girls should.'

Vaelin found himself smiling. 'What things are these?'

'I don't sew and I don't like dolls and I make things I'm not supposed to make and I draw pictures I'm not supposed to draw and I do cleverer things than boys and make them feel stupid.'

Vaelin was about to laugh but saw how serious her face was. She seemed to be studying him, her eyes roaming his face. It should have been uncomfortable but he found it oddly endearing. 'Winterblooms,' he said, nodding at her flowers. 'Are you supposed to pick those?'

'Oh, yes. I'm going to draw them and write down what they are. I have a big book of flowers I've drawn. Dadda taught me their names. He knows lots about flowers and plants. Do you know about flowers and plants?'

'A little. I know which ones are poison, which are useful for healing or eating.'

She frowned at the flowers in her mittens. 'Can you eat these?'

He shook his head. 'No, nor heal with them. They're not much good for anything really.'

'They're part of nature's beauty,' she told him, a small line appearing in her smooth brow. 'That makes them good for something.'

He laughed this time, he couldn't help it. 'True enough.' He glanced around for signs of the girl's parents. 'You aren't here alone?'

'Mumma's in the woods. I hid behind that oak so I could see you ride past. It was very funny when you fell off.'

Vaelin looked over at Spit, who artfully swung his head in the other direction. 'My horse thought so too.'

'What's his name?'

'Spit.'

'That's ugly.'

'So is he, but I have a dog that's uglier.'

'I've heard about your dog. It's as big as a horse and you tamed it after fighting it for a day and a night during the Test of the Wild. I've heard other stories too. I write them down but I have to hide the book from Mumma and Dadda. I heard you defeated ten men on your own and have already been chosen as the next Aspect of the Sixth Order.'

Ten men? he wondered. *Last I heard it was seven. By my thirtieth year it'll be a hundred.* 'It was four,' he told her, 'and I wasn't on my own. And the next Aspect cannot be chosen until the death or resignation of the current Aspect. And my dog isn't as big as a horse, nor did I fight him for a day and a night. If I fought him for five minutes, I'd lose.'

'Oh.' She seemed a little crestfallen. 'I'll have to change my book.'

'Sorry.'

She gave a small shrug. 'When I was little, Mumma said you were going to come live with us and be my brother but you never did. Dadda was very sad.'

The wave of confusion that swept through him was sickening. For a moment the world seemed to move around him, the ground swaying, threatening to tip him over. 'What?'

'ALORNIS!' A woman was hurrying towards them from the

woods, a handsome woman with curly black hair and a plain woollen cloak. 'Alornis, come here!'

The girl gave a small pout of annoyance. 'She'll take me away now.'

'I'm sorry, brother,' the woman said breathlessly as she approached, catching hold of the girl's hand and pulling her close. Despite the woman's evident agitation, Vaelin noted her gentleness with the girl, both arms closing over her protectively. 'My daughter is ever curious. I hope she didn't bother you overly.'

'Her name is Alornis?' Vaelin asked her, his confusion giving way to an icy numbness.

The woman's arms tightened around the girl. 'Yes.'

'And your name, lady?'

'Hilla.' She forced a smile. 'Hilla Justil.'

It meant nothing to him. *I do not know this woman.* He saw something in her expression, something besides the concern for her daughter. *Recognition. She knows my face.* He switched his gaze to the little girl, searching her face carefully. *Pretty, like her mother, same jaw, same nose . . . different eyes. Dark eyes.* Realisation dawned with the force of an icy gale, dispelling the numbness, replacing it with something cold and hard. 'How many years do you have, Alornis?'

'Ten and eight months,' she replied promptly.

'Nearly eleven then. I was eleven when my father brought me here.' He noticed her hands were empty and saw she had dropped her flowers. 'I always wondered why he did that.' He reached down to gather the winterblooms, being careful not to break the stems, and went over to crouch in front of Alornis. 'Don't forget these.' He smiled at her and she smiled back. He tried to fix the image of her face in his head.

'Brother . . .' Hilla began.

'You shouldn't linger here.' He straightened and went over to Spit, grasping his reins tight. The horse plainly read his mood because he allowed himself to be mounted without demur. 'These woods can be treacherous in winter. You should seek flowers elsewhere in future.'

He watched Hilla clutching her daughter and fighting to master her fear. Finally she said, 'Thank you, brother. We shall.'

He allowed himself a final glance at Alornis before spurring Spit into a gallop. This time he vaulted the log without the slightest hesitation and they thundered into the woods, leaving the girl and her mother behind.

I always wondered why he did that . . . Now I know.

The months passed, winter's frost became spring's thaw and Vaelin spoke no more than he had to. He practised, he watched the birth of Scratch's pups, he listened to Frentis's joyous tales of life in the Order, he rode his bad-tempered horse and he said almost nothing. Always it was there, the coldness, the numb emptiness left by his meeting with Alornis. Her face lingered in his mind, the shape of it, the darkness of her eyes. *Ten and eight months . . .* His mother had died a little under five years ago. *Ten and eight months.*

Caenis tried to talk to him, seeking to draw him out with one of his stories, the tale of the Battle of the Urlish Forest, where the armies of Renfael and Asrael met in bloody conflict for a day and a night. It was before the Realm was made, when Janus was a lord and not a king, when the four Fiefs of the Realm were split and fought each other like cats in a sack. But Janus united them, with the wisdom of his word and the keenness of his blade, and the power of his Faith. It was this that brought the Sixth Order into the battle, the vision of a Realm ruled by a king that put the Faith before all things. It was the charge of the Sixth Order that broke the Renfaelin line and won the day. Vaelin listened to it all without comment. He had heard it before.

'. . . and when they brought the Renfaelin Lord Theros before the King, wounded and chained, he spat defiance and demanded death rather than kneel before an upstart whelp. King Janus surprised all by laughing. "I do not require you to kneel, brother," he said. "Nor do I require you to die. Scant use you would be to this Realm dead." At this Lord Theros replied . . .'

'"Your Realm is a madman's dream,"' Vaelin cut in. 'And the King laughed again and they spent a day and a night arguing until argument became discussion and finally Lord Theros saw the wisdom of the King's course. Ever since he has been the King's most loyal vassal.'

Caenis's face fell. 'I've told you this before.'

'Once or twice.' They were near the river, watching Frentis and his group of youngsters play with Scratch's puppies. The hound bitch had produced six in all, four males and two females, seemingly harmless bundles of wet fur when she had licked at them on the kennel floor. They had grown quickly and were already half the size of a normal dog, though they gambolled around and tripped over their own paws like all pups. Frentis had been allowed to name them all but his choices proved somewhat unimaginative.

'Slasher!' he called to his favourite pup, the largest of the lot, waving a stick. 'Here boy!'

'What is it, brother?' Caenis asked him. 'Where does this silence come from?'

Vaelin watched Frentis being bowled over by Slasher, giggling as the pup slobbered over his face. 'He loves it here,' he observed.

'The Order has certainly been good for him,' Caenis agreed. 'Seems he's grown a foot or more since he came here, and he learns quickly. The masters think well of him since he never needs to be told anything twice. I don't think he's even had a caning yet.'

'What was his life like, I wonder, that this place is somewhere he could love?' He turned back to Caenis. 'He chose to be here.

Unlike the rest of us. He chose this. He wasn't forced through the gate by an unloving parent.'

Caenis moved closer and lowered his voice. 'Your father wanted you back, Vaelin. You should always remember that. Like Frentis, you chose to be here.'

Ten years, eight months . . . Mumma said you were going to come live with us and be my brother . . . but you never did . . . 'Why? Why did he want me back?'

'Regret? Guilt? Why does a man do anything?'

'The Aspect told me once that my presence here was a symbol of my father's devotion to the Faith and the Realm. If he had come into conflict with the King, perhaps withdrawing me would symbolise the opposite.'

Caenis's expression grew sombre. 'You think so little of him, brother. Although we are taught to leave our families behind, it bodes ill for a son to hate his father.'

Ten years, eight months . . . 'You have to know a man to hate him.'

CHAPTER FOUR

The coming of summer brought the traditional week-long exchange with brothers and sisters from different Orders. They were allowed to choose the Order in which they would be placed. It was usual for boys of the Sixth Order to trade places with brothers from the Fourth, the Order with which they would work most closely following confirmation. Instead Vaelin opted for the Fifth.

'The Fifth?' Master Sollis frowned at him. 'The Order of the Body. The Order of Healing. You want to go there?'

'Yes, Master.'

'What on earth do you think you can learn there? More importantly what do you think you can offer?' His cane tapped the back of Vaelin's hand, marked with the scars of practice and the splash of molten metal from Master Jestin's forge. 'These aren't made for healing.'

'My reasons are my own, Master.' He knew he was risking the cane but it had lost its sting long ago.

Master Sollis grunted and moved down the line. 'What about you, Nysa? Want to join your brother in mopping the brow of the sick and feeble?'

'I would prefer the Third Order, Master.'

Sollis gave him a long look. 'Scribblers and book hoarders.' He shook his head sadly.

Barkus and Dentos chose the safe option of the Fourth Order whilst Nortah took evident delight in electing for the Second. 'The Order of Contemplation and Enlightenment,' Sollis said tonelessly. 'You want to spend a week in the Order of Contemplation and Enlightenment?'

'I feel my soul would benefit from a period of meditation on the great mysteries, Master,' Nortah replied, showing his perfect teeth in an earnest smile. For the first time in months Vaelin felt like laughing.

'You mean you want a week of sitting on your arse,' Sollis said.

'Meditation is normally conducted in a sitting position, Master.'

Vaelin laughed, he couldn't help it. Three hours later, as he completed his fortieth lap of the practice ground, he was still chuckling.

'Brother Vaelin?' The grey-cloaked man at the gate was old, thin and bald, but Vaelin found himself disconcerted by the man's teeth, pearly white and perfect, like Nortah's, only the smile was genuine. The old brother was alone, wiping a mop across a dark brown stain on the cobbled courtyard.

'I am to report to the Aspect,' Vaelin replied.

'Yes, we were told you were coming.' The old brother lifted the catch on the gate and pulled it open. 'Rare for a brother from the Sixth to come to learn from us.'

'Are you alone, brother?' Vaelin said, stepping through the gate. 'I assume in a place such as this there is sore need for a guard.'

Unlike the Sixth, the House of the Fifth Order was situated within the walls of the capital, a large, cruciform building rising from the slums of the southern quarter, its whitewashed walls a bright beacon amidst the drab mass of closely packed, poorly built houses hugging the fringes of the docks. Vaelin had never been to the southern quarter before but quickly came to understand why it was rarely frequented by people with something worth stealing. The intricate network of shadowed alleyways and refuse-clogged streets provided ample opportunities for ambush. He had picked his way through the mess, not wishing to report to the Fifth Order with dirty boots, stepping over huddled forms sleeping off the previous night's grog and ignoring the unintelligible calls of those who had either had too much or not enough. Here and there a few listless whores gave him a disinterested glance but made no effort to entice his custom, Order boys had no money after all.

'Oh we never get bothered,' the old man told him. As he closed the gate Vaelin noted there was no lock. 'Been guarding this house for ten years or more, never a problem here.'

'Then why do you have to guard the gate?'

The old brother gave him a puzzled look. 'This is the Order of Healing, brother. People come here for help. Someone has to meet them.'

'Oh,' Vaelin said. 'Of course.'

'Still I do have my old Bess.' The old brother went into the small brick building that served as a guardhouse and returned with a large oak-wood club. 'Just in case.' He handed it to Vaelin, seemingly expecting an expert opinion.

'It's . . .' Vaelin hefted the club, swinging it briefly before handing it back, 'a fine weapon, brother.'

The old man seemed delighted. 'Made it meself when the Aspect gave me the gate to guard. My hands had gotten too stiff to mend bones or sew cuts, y'see?' He turned and walked quickly towards the House. 'Come, come, I'll take you to the Aspect.'

'You've been here a long time?' Vaelin asked, following.

'Only five years or so, apart from training o' course. Spent most of my brotherhood in the southern ports. I tell you there's no pox or disease on this earth that a sailor can't catch.'

Instead of leading him to the large door at the front of the house the old brother took him around the building and into a side entrance. Inside was a long corridor, bare of decoration and possessing a strong redolence of something both acidic and sweet.

'Vinegar and lavender,' the old man said, seeing him wrinkle his nose. 'Keeps the place free of foul humours.'

He took Vaelin past numerous rooms, where it seemed there was little but empty beds, and into a circular chamber tiled from floor to ceiling with white porcelain tiles. In the centre of the chamber a young man lay atop a table, naked and writhing. Two burly, grey-cloaked brothers held him down whilst Aspect Elera Al Mendah examined the crudely bandaged wound in his stomach. The man's screams were stopped by the strap of leather clamped into his mouth. The circumference of the chamber was lined with ascending rows of benches, where an audience of grey-robed brothers and sisters of varying ages looked down on the spectacle. There was a rustle of movement as they turned their gaze on Vaelin.

'Aspect,' the old man said, raising his voice, the echo of it incredibly loud in the chamber. 'Brother Vaelin Al Sorna of the Sixth Order.'

Aspect Elera looked up from the young man's wound, her smiling face adorned with a line of fresh blood-spatter across her forehead. 'Vaelin, how tall you've grown.'

'Aspect,' Vaelin replied with a formal nod. 'I submit myself to your service.'

On the table the young man arched his back, a plaintive whimper escaping the gag.

'You find me engaged in a most pressing case,' Aspect Elera

said, taking a pair of scissors from a nearby table to cut away the dirty bandage covering the young man's wound. 'This man took a knife in the gut in the early hours of the morning. An argument over the favours of a young lady apparently. Given the amount of ale and redflower already in his blood, we cannot give him any more for fear of killing him. So we must work while he suffers.' She put the scissors aside and held out her hand. A young, grey-robed sister placed a long-bladed instrument in her palm. 'Adding to his woes,' Aspect Elera went on, 'is the fact that the tip of the blade broke off inside his stomach and must be removed.' She raised her gaze to the audience on the benches. 'Can anyone tell me why?'

Most of the audience raised a hand and the Aspect nodded at a grey-haired man in the front row. 'Brother Innis?'

'Infection, Aspect,' the man said. 'The broken blade may poison the wound and cause it to fester. It may also be lodged close to a blood vessel or organ.'

'Very good, brother. And so we must probe the wound.' She bent over the young man and spread the lips of the cut with her left hand, applying the probe with the right. The young man's scream spat the gag from his mouth and filled the chamber. Aspect Elera drew back a little, glancing at the two burly brothers holding the young man to the table. 'He must be securely held, brothers.'

The young man began to thrash wildly, succeeding in wresting one of his arms free, his head banging on the table, madly kicking legs narrowly missing the Aspect, who was forced to retreat a few steps.

Vaelin moved to the table and placed his hand over the young man's mouth, forcing his head back onto the table, leaning close, meeting his eyes. 'Pain,' he said, fixing the man's gaze. 'It's a flame.' The young man's eyes filled with fear as Vaelin bore down on him. 'Focus. The pain is a flame inside your mind, see it. See it!' The man's breath was hot on Vaelin's palm but his thrashing had subsided. 'The flame grows smaller. It shrinks, it burns bright, but it's small. You see it?' Vaelin leaned closer. 'You see it?'

The young man's nod was barely perceptible.

'Focus on it,' Vaelin told him. 'Keep it small.'

He held him there, talking to him, fixing his eyes whilst Aspect Elera worked on his wound. The young man whimpered and his eyes flickered away, but Vaelin always brought them back until there was the dull clatter of metal falling into a pan and Aspect Elera said, 'Needle and catgut please, Sister Sherin.'

'Master Sollis teaches you well.'

They were in Aspect Elera's chamber, a room even more crammed with books and paper than Aspect Arlyn's. But where the room of the Aspect of the Sixth Order had a certain chaotic quality, this one was tightly ordered and meticulously tidy. The walls were adorned with overlapping diagrams and pictures; graphic, almost obscene depictions of bodies shorn of skin or muscle. He found his eye continually drawn to the image on the wall behind her desk, a man shown spread-eagled and split from crotch to neck, the flaps of the wound drawn back to reveal his organs, each expertly rendered with absolute clarity.

'Aspect?' he said, tearing his gaze away.

'The pain-control technique you used,' the Aspect explained. 'Sollis was always my most adept pupil.'

'Pupil, Aspect?'

'Yes. We served together on the northeastern border, years ago. On quiet days I would teach the brothers of the Sixth relaxation and pain-control techniques. It was a way to pass the time. Brother Sollis was always the most attentive.'

They knew each other, they served together. The idea of them even conversing felt incredible but an Aspect would never lie. 'I am grateful for Master Sollis's wisdom, Aspect.' It seemed the safest reply.

His eyes flicked to the drawing again, and she glanced at it over her shoulder. 'A remarkable work don't you think? A gift from Master Benril Lenial of the Third Order. He spent a week here drawing the sick and the recently expired, he said he wished to paint a picture that would capture the suffering of the soul. Preparatory work for his fresco commemorating the Red Hand. Of course we were happy to allow access and when he was done he gifted his sketches to our Order. I use them to teach the novice brothers and sisters the secrets of the body. The illustrations in our older books lack the same clarity.'

She turned back. 'You did well this morning. I feel the other brothers and sisters learned much from your example. The sight of blood didn't concern you? Make you feel ill or faint?'

Was she joking? 'I am accustomed to the sight of blood, Aspect.'

Her gaze clouded for a second before her customary smile returned. 'I cannot tell you how much it gladdens my heart to see how strong you've grown and that compassion is not absent from your soul. But I must know, why have you come here?'

He couldn't lie, not to her. 'I thought you might provide answers to my questions.'

'And what questions are these?'

There seemed little point in vagary. 'When did my father sire a bastard? Why was I sent to the Sixth Order? Why did assassins seek my death during the Test of the Run?'

She closed her eyes, her face impassive, breathing regular and even. She stayed that way for several minutes and Vaelin wondered if she was going to speak again. Then he saw it, a single tear snaking down her cheek. *Pain-control techniques,* he thought.

She opened her eyes, meeting his gaze. 'I regret I cannot answer your questions, Vaelin. Be assured that your service here is welcome. I believe you will learn much. Please report to Sister Sherin in the west wing.'

Sister Sherin was the young woman who had assisted the Aspect in the tiled room. He found her wrapping bandages around the waist of the wounded man in a room off the west-wing corridor. The man's skin had an unhealthy grey pallor and a sheen of sweat covered his flesh but his breathing seemed regular and he didn't appear to be in any pain.

'Will he live?' Vaelin asked her.

'I expect so.' Sister Sherin secured the bandage in place with a clasp and washed her hands in a water basin. 'Although service in this Order teaches us that death can often deny our expectations. Take those.' She nodded at a pile of bloodstained clothes lying in the corner. 'They need to be cleaned. He'll need something to wear when he leaves here. The laundry is in the south wing.'

'Laundry?'

'Yes.' She faced him with the smallest of smiles. Although he fought it, Vaelin found himself taking note of her form. She was slender, the dark curls of her hair tied back, her face displaying a youthful prettiness, but her eyes somehow bespoke a wealth of experience well beyond her years. Her lips formed the words with precision. 'The laundry.'

He was discomfited by her, preoccupied with the curve of her cheekbones and the shape of her lips, the brightness of her eyes, relishing confrontation. He quickly gathered the clothes and went to find the laundry. He was relieved to find he wasn't required to wash the clothes himself and, after Sister Sherin's cool reception, somewhat taken aback by the welcome he received from the brothers and sisters in the steam-filled laundry room.

'Brother Vaelin!' boomed a large, bearlike man, his hair-covered chest beaded with sweat. His hand felt like a hammer on Vaelin's back. 'I've waited ten years for a brother from the Sixth to come through our doors and when we finally get one it's their most famous son.'

'I am pleased to be here, brother,' Vaelin assured him. 'I have to clean these clothes . . .'

'Oh tosh.' The clothes were torn from his grasp and tossed into one of the large stone baths, where the laundry workers laboured. 'We'll do that. Come and meet everyone.'

The big man turned out to be a master, not a brother. His name was Harin and when he wasn't taking his turn in the laundry he taught the novices the finer points of bones. 'Bones, Master?'

'Yes, m'boy. Bones. How they work, how they fit together. How to mend them. I've snapped more arms back into sockets than I can remember. It's all in the wrist. I'll teach you before you leave, if I don't break your arm first.' He laughed, the sound easily filling the cavernous chamber.

The rest of the brothers and sisters gathered round to greet Vaelin and he found himself assailed with numerous names and faces, all of whom displayed a disconcerting enthusiasm for his presence, as well as a plethora of questions.

'Tell us, brother,' one brother said, a thin man named Curlis, 'is it true your swords are made from star silver?'

'A myth, brother,' Vaelin told him, remembering to keep Master Jestin's secret. 'Our swords are finely made, but of plain steel only.'

'Do they really make you live in the wilds?' a young sister asked, a plump girl called Henna.

'Only for ten days. It's one of our tests.'

'They make you leave if you fail, don't they?'

'If you live that long.' It was Sister Sherin, standing in the doorway, arms crossed. 'That's right isn't it, brother? Many of your brothers die in the tests? Boys as young as eleven years old.'

'A hard life requires hard training,' Vaelin replied. 'Our tests prepare us for our role in defending the Faith and the Realm.'

She raised an eyebrow. 'If Master Harin doesn't need to prolong your presence here, the teaching room needs mopping.'

And so he mopped the teaching room. He also mopped all the rooms in the west wing. When he was done she had him boil a mixture of pure spirit and water and soak the metal implements the Aspect had used to treat the young man's wound. She told him it eradicated infection. The rest of the day was spent in similar endeavours, cleaning, mopping, scrubbing. His hands were tough but he soon found them chafing with the work, the flesh red from soap and scrubbing by the time Sister Sherin told him he could go and eat.

'When do I learn how to heal?' he asked. She was in the teaching room, laying out a variety of instruments on a white cloth. He had spent two hours cleaning them and they shone brightly in the light from the overhead window.

'You don't,' she replied, not looking up. 'You get to work. If I think you won't get in the way, I'll let you watch when I tend to someone.'

A variety of responses flickered through his mind, some caustic, some clever, but all certain to make him sound like a petulant child. 'As you wish, sister. What hour do you require me?'

'We start at the fifth hour here.' She gave a conspicuous sniff. 'Before reporting for work, you are expected to wash thoroughly, which should help diminish your rather pungent aroma. Don't they wash in the Sixth Order?'

'Every three days we swim in the river. It's very cold, even in summer.'

She said nothing, placing a strange-looking implement on the cloth: two parallel blades fastened by a screw device.

'What is that?' he asked.

'Rib spreader. It allows access to the heart.'

'The heart?'

'Sometimes the beat of a heart will stop and can be recommenced by gentle massage.'

He looked at her hands, slim fingers moving with measured precision. 'You can do this?'

She shook her head. 'I've yet to learn such skills. The Aspect can though, she can do most things.'

'She'll teach you one day.'

She glanced up at him, her expression wary. 'You should eat, brother.'

'You're not eating?'

'I take my meals later than the others. I have more work to do here.'

'Then I'll stay. We can eat together.'

She barely paused in scrubbing at a steel basin. 'I prefer to eat alone, thank you.'

He stopped a sigh of exasperation before it escaped his mouth. 'As you wish.'

There were more questions at mealtime, more intense curiosity almost making him wish for Sister Sherin's disinterest. The masters of the Fifth Order ate with their students so he sat with Master Harin amongst a group of novice brothers and sisters. He was surprised by the variety in the ages of the novices at the table, the youngest little more than fourteen whilst the oldest clearly in his fifties.

'People often come to our Order later in life,' Master Harin explained. 'I didn't join until my thirty-second year. Was in the Realm Guard before then, Thirtieth Regiment of Foot, the Bloody Boars. You've heard of them no doubt.'

'Their renown does them credit, Master,' Vaelin lied, never

having heard of such a regiment. 'How long has Sister Sherin been here?'

'Been here since an infant that one, worked in the kitchens. Didn't start training till she turned fourteen though. That's the youngest we'll allow novices to join. Not like your Order, eh?'

'It's but one of many differences, Master.'

Harin laughed heartily and took a large bite from a chicken leg. Food in the Fifth Order was much the same as the Sixth, but there was less of it. Vaelin experienced a moment's embarrassment when he began wolfing down large helpings with habitual haste, drawing bemused glances from the others at the table. 'Have to eat quickly in the Sixth,' he explained. 'Wait too long and it'll all be gone.'

'I heard they starve you as punishment,' said Sister Henna, the plump girl he had met in the laundry. She asked even more questions than the others and whenever he looked up she seemed to be watching him.

'Our masters have more practical ways of punishing us than starvation, sister,' he told her.

'When do they make you fight to the death?' the thin man, Innis, asked. The question was voiced with such earnest curiosity Vaelin found he couldn't take offence.

'The Test of the Sword comes in our seventh year in the Order. It is our final test.'

'You have to fight each other to the death?' Sister Henna seemed shocked.

Vaelin shook his head. 'We will be matched against three condemned criminals. Murderers, outlaws and so forth. If they defeat us, they are considered to have been judged innocent of their crimes as the Departed will not accept them into the Beyond. If we defeat them, we are judged fit to carry a sword in service to the Order.'

'Brutal but simple,' Master Harin commented before belching loudly and patting his stomach. 'The ways of the Sixth Order may seem harsh to us, my children, but do not forget they stand between our Faith and those who would destroy it. In times past they fought to keep us safe. If not for them, we wouldn't be here to offer care and healing to the Faithful. Think well on that.'

There was a murmur of agreement around the table and, for once, conversation turned to other matters. The concerns of the Fifth Order seemed to revolve mainly around bandages, medicinal herbs, various forms of disease and the endlessly popular subject of infection. He wondered if he should be more upset at having to discuss the Test of the Sword but found it left him with little more than a vague sense of unease. He had known it was coming since his first days in the Order, they all had, it was an annual event, watched by a great many of the city's populace and, although novice brothers of the Order were forbidden to attend, he had heard many stories of prolonged combats and unfortunate brothers whose skills had failed to match the final test. However, set against what he had already experienced it seemed little more than one of many dangers ahead. Perhaps that was the point of the tests, to render them immune to danger, accepting fear as a normal part of their lives.

'Do you have tests?' he asked Master Harin.

'No, m'boy. No tests here. Novice brothers and sisters stay in the Order House for five years, where they are trained in our ways. Many will leave or be asked to leave but those who stay will have earned the skills to heal and will be appointed tasks that match their abilities. Myself, I spent twenty years in the Cumbraelin capital, seeing to the needs of the small Faithful community there. It's a hard thing, brother, to live amongst those who would deny the Faith.'

'The King's Edict tells us Cumbraelins are our brothers in the Realm, as long as they keep their beliefs within their own Fief.'

'Pah!' Master Harin spat. 'Cumbrael may have been forced into the Realm by the King's sword but always she seeks to promote her blasphemy. I was approached many times by god-worshipping clerics seeking my conversion. Even now she sends them across her borders to spread their heresy amongst the Faithful. I fear your Order and mine will have much work in Cumbrael in the years to come.' He shook his head sadly. 'A pity, war was ever a terrible thing.'

They gave him a cell in the south wing, bare apart from a bed and a single chair. He undressed quickly and slipped into the bed, enjoying the unfamiliar but luxuriant feel of clean, fresh linen. Despite the comfort, sleep was slow in coming; Master Harin's talk of Cumbrael had disturbed him. *War was ever a terrible thing.* But there was something in the master's eyes that seemed almost eager for war to be visited on the heretical Fief.

Sister Sherin's coldness was another concern. She clearly wanted little to do with him, which he found bothered him greatly, and had no regard for the Sixth Order, which he found bothered him not at all. He resolved to try harder to win her confidence in the morning. He would do everything she asked of him without question or complaint, he had a suspicion she would respect little else.

However, what kept him awake longest was Aspect Elera's refusal to answer his questions. He had been so sure she would provide the answers he craved that the prospect of a refusal hadn't even occurred to him. *She knows,* he thought with certainty. *So why won't she tell me?*

He fell asleep with the questions tumbling through his mind, finding no answers in his dreams.

He forced himself out of bed at first light, washed thoroughly in the trough in the courtyard and reported for work a good measure before the fifth hour. Sherin was there before him. 'Fetch bandages from the storeroom,' she said. 'People will soon be at the gate seeking treatment.' She frowned as he moved past her. 'You smell . . . better, at least.'

He borrowed a trick from Nortah and forced a smile. 'Thank you, sister.'

The first was an old man with stiff joints and endless tales of his time as a sailor. Sister Sherin listened politely to his stories as she massaged balm into his joints, giving him a jar of the substance to take home. The next was a thin young man with trembling hands and bloodshot eyes who complained of severe pains in the belly. Sister Sherin felt his stomach and the vein in his wrist, asked a few questions and told him that the Fifth Order did not give redflower to addicts.

'Up yours, Order bitch!' the young man spat at her.

'Watch your mouth,' Vaelin said, stepping forward to throw him out but Sherin stopped him with a glare. She stood impassively as the young man swore at her viciously for a full minute whilst casting wary glances at Vaelin before storming out, his profanity echoing through the hallway.

'I don't need a protector,' Sherin told Vaelin. 'Your *skills* are not required here.'

'I'm sorry,' he said, teeth gritted, failing to summon another Nortah smile.

They came in all ages and sizes, men and women, mothers with children, sisters with brothers, all cut, bruised, pained or sick. Sherin seemed to know the nature of their ailments instinctively, working without pause or rest, tending to them all with equal care. Vaelin watched, fetched bandages or medicine when he was told, trying to learn but instead finding himself pre-occupied with Sherin, fascinated by the way her face changed when she worked, the severity and wariness disappearing into compassion and humour as she joked and laughed with her charges, many of whom she clearly knew well. *That's why they come,* he realised. *She cares.*

And so he tried as hard as he could to help, fetching, carrying, restraining the fearful and the panicked, offering awkward words of comfort to the wives or sisters or children who brought the wounded to be healed. Most were in need of little more than medicine or a few stitches, some, the ones Sherin knew so well, had prolonged sicknesses and took the longest time to treat as she asked numerous questions and offered advice or sympathy. Twice, grievously wounded people came in. The first was a man with a crushed stomach who had walked into the path of a runaway cart. Sister Sherin felt the vein in his neck and began pumping at his chest with both fists clamped over his sternum.

'His heart stopped beating,' she explained. She kept at it until blood began to flow from the man's mouth. 'He's gone.' She moved back from the bed. 'Fetch a trolley from the storeroom and take him to the morgue. It's in the south wing. And clean the blood from his face. The family don't like to see that.'

Vaelin had seen death before but her coldness took him by surprise. 'That's all? There's nothing else you can do?'

'A cart weighing half a ton ran over his stomach, turning his guts to mush and his spine to powder. There is nothing else I can do.'

The second badly wounded man was brought in by the Realm Guard in the evening, a stocky fellow with a crossbow bolt through his shoulder.

'Sorry, sister,' the sergeant apologised to Sherin as he and two fellow guards hauled the man onto the table. 'Hate to waste your time with one such as this but we'll get hell from the captain if we turn up with another corpse.' He gave Vaelin a curious glance, taking in his dark blue robe. 'You appear to be in the wrong House, brother.'

'Brother Vaelin is here to learn how to heal,' Sherin informed him, leaning over the stocky man to examine his wound. 'Twenty feet?' she enquired.

'Closer to thirty.' One of the guards sniffed proudly, hefting his crossbow. 'And he was running.'

'Vaelin,' the sergeant murmured, his glance turning into a stare of scrutiny as he looked Vaelin up and down. 'Al Sorna, right?'

'That's my name.'

The three guards laughed, it wasn't a pleasant sound and Vaelin instantly regretted leaving his sword in the cell that morning.

'The boy brother who beat ten Hawks single-handed,' the younger guard said. 'You're taller than they said.'

'It wasn't ten . . .' Vaelin began.

'Wish I'd been there to see that,' the sergeant interrupted. 'Can't stand those bloody Hawks, strutting about the place. Hear they're making a plan of revenge though. You should watch your back.'

'I always do.'

'Brother,' Sherin cut in. 'I need catgut, needle, probe, a serrated knife, redflower and corr-tree oil, the gel not the juice. Oh, and another bowl of water.'

He did as he was told, grateful for the chance to escape the guardsmen's scrutiny. He went to the storeroom and filled a tray with the required items, returning to the treatment room to find it in uproar. The stocky man was on his feet, backed into a corner, his meaty fist clamped around Sister Sherin's throat. One of the guardsmen was down, a knife buried in his thigh. The other two had their swords drawn, shouting threats and fury.

'I'm walking out of here!' the stocky man shouted back.

'You're going nowhere!' the sergeant barked in response. 'Let her go and you'll live.'

'I go inside, One Eye'll have me done. Stand aside or I'll wring this bitch's n—'

The serrated knife Vaelin had fetched from the storeroom was heavier than he was used to but it wasn't a difficult throw. The man's throat was clearly open, but his death spasm might have caused him to snap Sister Sherin's neck. The blade sank into his forearm, causing his hand to open by reflex, allowing Sherin to collapse to the floor. Vaelin vaulted the bed, scattering the tray's contents across the room, and felled the stocky man with a few well-placed punches to the nerve centres in his face and chest.

'Don't,' Sherin gasped from the floor. 'Don't kill him.'

Vaelin watched the man slumping to the floor, his eyes vacant. 'Why would I?' He helped her to her feet. 'Are you hurt?'

She shook her head, pulling away. 'Get him back on the bed,' she told him, her voice hoarse. 'Sergeant, if you could help me get your comrade to another room.'

'Be doing the bastard a favour if you had killed him, brother,' the sergeant grunted as he and the other guardsman helped their fallen comrade to his feet. 'Hanging day tomorrow.'

Vaelin had to struggle to get the man off the floor, he seemed to be composed mainly of muscle and weighed accordingly. He groaned in pain as Vaelin let him fall back onto the bed, his eyes flickering open.

'Unless you've got another knife hidden,' Vaelin told him. 'I'd lie still.'

The man's gaze was baleful but he said nothing.

'So who's One Eye?' Vaelin asked him. 'Why does he want you dead?'

'I owe him money,' the man said, his face slicked with sweat and lined with pain from his wounds.

He recalled Frentis's tales of his time on the streets and the wayward throwing knife that had caused him to seek refuge in the Order. 'Your tax?'

'Three golds. I'm in arrears. We've all gotta pay. And One Eye hates those that don't pay with a passion.' The man coughed, staining his chin with blood. Vaelin poured a cup of water and held it to his lips.

'I have a friend who told me once about a man who lost his eye to a boy with a throwing knife,' Vaelin said.

The stocky man swallowed the water, his cough subsiding. 'Frentis. If only the little sod had killed the bastard. One Eye says he's gonna take a year to skin him alive when he finds him.'

Vaelin decided he would have to meet with One Eye sooner or later. He looked closely at the crossbow bolt still buried in the man's shoulder. 'Why did the Realm Guard do this?'

'Caught me coming out of a warehouse with a sackful of spice. Good stuff too, I'd've made meself six golds at least.'

He's going to die for a sackful of spice, Vaelin realised. *That and stabbing a guardsman and trying to choke Sister Sherin*. 'What's your name?'

'Gallis. Gallis the Climber they call me. Not a wall I can't scale.' Wincing, he lifted his forearm, the serrated knife still embedded there. 'Looks like I won't be doing that again.' He laughed then convulsed with pain. 'Any redflower going, brother?'

'Prepare a tincture.' Sister Sherin had returned with the sergeant in tow. 'One part redflower to three parts water.'

Vaelin paused to look at her neck, red and bruised from Gallis's grip. 'You should have that seen to.'

Momentary anger flashed in her eyes and he could tell she was biting back a sharp retort. He couldn't tell if she was angry that she had been proved wrong or that he had saved her life. 'Please prepare the tincture, brother,' she told him in a hard rasp.

She worked on Gallis for over an hour, administering the redflower then extracting the crossbow bolt from his shoulder, cutting the shaft in half then widening the wound and gently pulling the barbed point free, Gallis biting on a leather strap to

BLOOD SONG · 245

stifle his cries. She worked on the knife in his arm next, it was more difficult, being closer to major blood vessels, but came free after ten minutes' work. Finally she sewed the wounds shut after painting them with the corr-tree gel. Gallis had lost consciousness by then and his colour had noticeably paled.

'He's lost a lot of blood,' Sherin told the sergeant. 'He can't be moved yet.'

'Can't wait too long, sister,' the sergeant said. 'Got to have him in front of the magistrate for the morning.'

'No chance of clemency?' Vaelin asked.

'I've got a man with a knifed leg next door,' the sergeant replied. 'And the bugger tried to kill the sister.'

'I don't recall that,' Sherin said, washing her hands. 'Do you, brother?'

Is a sackful of spice worth a man's life? 'Not at all.'

The sergeant's face took on a deeply angry tinge. 'This man is a known thief, drunkard and redflower fiend. He would've killed us all to get out of here.'

'Brother Vaelin,' Sherin said. 'When is it right to kill?'

'In defence of life,' Vaelin replied promptly. 'To kill when not defending life is a denial of the Faith.'

The sergeant's lip curled in disgust. 'Softhearted Order sods,' he muttered before stalking from the room.

'You know they'll hang him anyway?' Vaelin asked her.

Sherin lifted her hands from the bloodied water and he passed her a towel. She met his eye for the first time that day, speaking with a certainty that was almost chilling: 'No-one is going to die on my account.'

He avoided the evening meal, knowing his actions would only have added to his celebrity and finding himself unable to face the torrent of questions and admiration. So he hid himself in the gatehouse with Brother Sellin, the aged gatekeeper who had greeted him the previous morning. The old brother seemed glad of the company and refrained from asking questions or mentioning the day's events, for which Vaelin was grateful. Instead, at Vaelin's insistence, he told stories of his time in the Fifth Order, proving that a man did not have to be a warrior to see much of war.

'Got this one on the deck of the *Seaspite*.' Sellin displayed an odd horseshoe-shaped scar on the underside of his forearm. 'I was stitching a wound in a Meldenean pirate's stomach when he rears up and bites me, nearly down to the bone. It was just after the Battle Lord had burned their city so I s'pose he had good reason to be angry. Our sailors threw him in the sea.' He grimaced at the memory. 'Begged them not to but men'll do terrible things when their blood's up.'

'How did you come to be on a warship?' Vaelin asked.

'Oh, I was Fleet Lord Merlish's personal physic for a number of years. He always had a soft spot for me since I cured his pox a few years before. A right fine old captain he was, loved the sea like a mother, loved all sailors, even had respect for the Meldeneans, best sailors in the world he said. Broke his heart when the Battle Lord burned their city. They had a mighty row about it, I can tell you.'

'They argued?' Vaelin was curious. Brother Sellin was one of the few people he had met who didn't initially refer to the Battle Lord as his father, in fact he appeared blithely unaware of the fact, although Vaelin suspected that the old man had been in service to the Faith for so long that disassociating its servants from their family connections was simply second nature.

'Oh yes,' Sellin continued. 'Fleet Lord Merlish called him a butcher, a killer of innocents, said he'd shamed the Realm forever. Everyone who heard it thought the Battle Lord would draw his sword but all he said was "Loyalty is my strength, my lord."' Sellin sighed, sipping from a leather flask Vaelin suspected contained a mixture not dissimilar to what Brother Makril had called Brother's Friend. 'Poor old Merlish. Stayed in his cabin all the way home, refused to report to the King when we docked. He died not long after, his heart gave out on a voyage to the Far West.'

'Did you see it?' Vaelin asked. 'Did you see the city burn?'

'I saw it.' Brother Sellin took a deep pull from his flask. 'I saw it all right. Lit up the sky for miles around. But it wasn't the sight of it that chilled you, it was the sound. We were anchored a good half mile offshore and still you could hear the screams. Thousands, men, women, children, all screaming in the fire.' He shuddered and drank again.

'I'm sorry, brother. I shouldn't have asked.'

Sellin shrugged. 'Times past, brother. Can't live in 'em. Just learn from 'em.' He peered out at the gathering dark. 'You'd best be getting back elst you'll not get a meal tonight.'

He found Sister Sherin in the meal hall, eating alone as was her habit. He expected a rebuke or outright rejection when he sat opposite her but she made no comment. The kitchen staff had placed a good selection on the table but she seemed content with a small plate of bread and fruit.

'May I?' he asked, gesturing at the array of food.

She shrugged so he helped himself to some ham and chicken, gulping it down ravenously, drawing a plainly disgusted glance.

He grinned, taking guilty enjoyment in her discomfort. 'I'm hungry.'

There was the faintest ghost of a smile as she looked away.

'No-one eats alone in the Sixth Order,' he told her. 'We all have our groups. We live together, eat together, fight together. We call each other brother with good reason. Here things seem to be different.'

'My brothers and sisters respect my privacy,' she said.

'Because you're special? You can do what they can't.'

She took a bite of apple and gave no reply.

'How's the thief?' he asked.

'Well enough. They moved him to the upper floor. The sergeant put two men on his door.'

'You intend to speak for him at the hearing?'

'Of course. Although it would help his case if you spoke as well. I feel your word would carry more weight than mine.'

He washed down a mouthful of ham with some water. 'What is it, sister, that makes you care so much for one such as him?'

Her face hardened. 'What is it that makes you care so little?'

Silence reigned at the table for a few moments. Finally, he said, 'Did you know my mother trained here? She was a sister, like you. She left the Fifth Order to marry my father. She never told me she had served here, she never told me about this part of her life. I came here seeking answers, I wanted to know who she was, who I was, who my father was. But the Aspect would tell me nothing. Instead she paired me with you, which I think was an answer in itself.'

'An answer to what?'

'Who my mother was, at least. Perhaps partly who I am. I'm not like you, I'm no healer. I would have killed that man today if I could, I've killed before. You couldn't kill anyone, and neither could she. That's who she was.'

'And your father?'

Thousands, men, women, children, all screaming in the fire . . . Loyalty is my strength. 'He was a man who burned a city because his king told him to.' He pushed his plate away and got up from the table. 'I'll speak for Gallis before the magistrate. See you at the fifth hour.'

In the morning it transpired that their presence at the magistrate's court would not be necessary; Gallis had escaped during the night.

The guards had entered his room on the top floor to find it empty and the window open. The wall outside was nearly thirty feet high with hardly any visible handholds.

Vaelin leaned out of the window to peer at the courtyard below. 'Gallis the Climber,' he murmured.

'With the wounds he had he shouldn't have been able to walk.' Sister Sherin moved close to inspect the wall outside. Vaelin found her proximity both intoxicating and uncomfortable but she seemed unconcerned. 'I'll never know how he managed it.'

'Master Sollis says a man doesn't know his true strength until he fears for his life.'

'The sergeant said he'd track the man down if it takes him all his days.' She moved away, leaving Vaelin in a confusion of regret and relief. 'He probably will. That or I'll see him again, dragged through the doors with another wound for me to heal.'

'If he's smart, he'll get himself on a ship and be far away by nightfall.'

Sherin shook her head. 'People don't leave this place, brother. No matter the threats against them, they stay and live out their lives.'

He turned back to the window. The southern quarter was waking up to the day, the pale morning sky just taking on the stain of chimney smoke that would hang over the rooftops until nightfall, the shortening shadows revealing streets soiled with mingled refuse and excreta, dotted here and there the huddled forms of the drunk, drugged or homeless. Already he could hear vague shouts of conflict or hatred and wondered how many more would come through the doors today.

'Why?' he wondered. 'Why stay in a place such as this?'

'I did,' she said. 'Why shouldn't they?'

'You were born here?'

She nodded. 'I was lucky enough to complete my training in

only two years. The Aspect offered me any posting in the Realm. I chose this one.'

The hesitancy in her voice told him he was probably the first person to hear her reveal so much of her past. 'Because this is . . . home?'

'Because I felt this is where I needed to be.' She moved to the door. 'We have work, brother.'

The next few days were hard but rewarding, not least because he was constantly in Sister Sherin's presence. The parade of injured and ill coming through the door provided plenty of opportunity to increase his meagre healing skills as Sherin began to impart some of her knowledge, teaching him the best pattern to use when stitching a cut and the most effective mix of herbs for aches in the stomach or head. However, it quickly became obvious the skills she possessed would never be his, she had an eye and an ear for sickness so unerring it reminded him of his own affinity for the sword. Luckily there was no further need for him to display his skills as the level of aggression amongst patients had declined considerably since his first day. Word had spread through the southern quarter that there was a brother from the Sixth here and most of the more shady characters turning up to request treatment wisely kept their tongues still and violent urges in check.

The only negative aspect to his time in the Fifth was the constant attention of the other brothers and sisters. He had continued to take his meals with Sister Sherin late in the evening and they soon found themselves joined by a cluster of novices eager for Vaelin's tales of life in the Sixth Order or a retelling of what they termed his 'rescue of Sister Sherin,' a tale that seemed to have become a minor legend in only a few days. As ever, Sister Henna was his most attentive audience.

'Weren't you scared, brother?' she asked, wide brown eyes

gazing up at him. 'When the big brute was going to kill Sister Sherin? Didn't it frighten you?'

Beside him, Sherin, who until now had borne the intrusion on her mealtime with stoic calm, pointedly let her cutlery fall onto her plate with a loud clatter.

'I . . . have been trained to control my fear,' he replied, instantly realising how conceited it sounded. 'Not as well as Sister Sherin, though,' he went on quickly. 'She remained calm throughout.'

'Oh she never gets bothered by anything.' Henna waved a hand dismissively. 'So, why didn't you kill him?'

'Sister!' Brother Curlis exclaimed.

She lowered her gaze, a flush creeping up her cheeks. 'I'm sorry,' she mumbled.

'It matters not, sister.' He patted her hand awkwardly, which seemed to make her blush even more.

'Brother Vaelin and I have had a long day,' Sister Sherin said. 'We would like to eat in peace.'

Although she wasn't a mistress, her word evidently commanded obedience because their small audience quickly dispersed back to their rooms.

'They respect you,' Vaelin observed.

She shrugged. 'Perhaps. But I am not liked here. I am envied and resented by most of my brothers and sisters. The Aspect warned me it might be this way.' Her tone indicated little concern, she was simply stating a fact.

'You could be judging them too harshly. Perhaps if you mixed with them more . . .'

'I am not here for them. The Fifth Order is the means by which I can help the people I need to help.'

'No room for friendship? A soul in whom to confide, share a burden?'

She gave him a guarded glance. 'You said it yourself, brother. Things are different here.'

'Well, although you may not welcome it, I hope you know you have my friendship.'

She said nothing, sitting still, eyes fixed on her half-empty plate.

Was this how it was for my mother? he wondered. *Was she so isolated by her abilities? Did they resent her too?* He found it hard to imagine. He remembered a woman of kindness, warmth and openness. She could never have been as closed to emotion as Sherin. *Sherin is formed by whatever happened to her beyond the gates,* he realised. *Out there in the southern quarter. My mother would have had a different life.* A thought occurred to him then, something he had never considered before. *Who was she before she came here? What was her family name? Who were my grandparents?*

Suddenly preoccupied, he rose from the table. 'Sleep well, sister. I'll see you in the morning.'

'It's your last day tomorrow, is it not?' she asked, looking up at him. Oddly her eyes seemed brighter than usual, it almost seemed she was tearful but the idea was absurd.

'It is. Although I still hope to learn more before I leave.'

'Yes.' She looked away. 'Yes of course. Sleep well.'

'And you, sister.'

Sleep was beyond him as he sat, legs crossed beneath him, and pondered the realisation that he knew almost nothing of his mother's past. She was a sister of the Fifth Order, she married his father, she bore him a son, she died. That was all he knew. For that matter he knew just as little about his father. A soldier elevated by the King for bravery, later Battle Lord, city burner, father of a son and a daughter by different mothers. But who had he been before? Vaelin had no knowledge of where his father had been born, whether his grandfather had been a soldier or a farmer or neither.

So many questions, raging in his mind like a storm. He closed his eyes and sought to control his breathing as Master Sollis had taught him, a skill no doubt learned from the Aspect of the Fifth Order, which in turn raised even more questions. *Focus,* he told himself. *Breathe, slow and even . . .*

An hour later, the beat of his heart slowed and the storm in his mind cooling, he was roused by a soft but insistent knock at his door. Pausing to pull his shirt over his head he went to the door, finding Sister Henna there, smiling shyly.

'Brother,' she said, her voice little above a whisper. 'Have I disturbed you?'

'I wasn't sleeping.' *Surely she can't want another story.* 'The hour is late, sister. If you require something of me, perhaps it could wait until morning.'

'Require something?' Her smile broadened a little and, before he could stop her, she stepped past him into his cell. 'I require your forgiveness, brother, for my thoughtless words this evening.'

Vaelin's calmed heart was beginning to thump again. 'There is nothing to forgive . . .'

'Oh, but there is!' she whispered fiercely, moving close to him, making him step back, the door forced closed behind him. 'I am such a stupid girl. I say such silly things. Thoughtless things.' She moved closer still, pressing against him, the feel of her ample breasts against his chest provoking an instant sheen of sweat and an unwelcome stirring in his groin. 'Say you forgive me,' she implored, a faint sob in her voice as she laid her head on his chest. 'Say you don't hate me!'

'Erm.' He searched urgently through his mind for an appropriate response but life in the Order had failed to equip him for such things. 'Of course I don't hate you.' Gently he put his hands on her shoulders and eased her away from him, forcing a smile. 'You shouldn't worry over such a trifle.'

'Oh, but I do,' she assured him breathlessly. 'The thought of offending you, of all people.' She looked away, ashamed. 'It's more than I could bear.'

'You care too much for my opinion, sister.' He reached behind him for the door handle. 'You should go now . . .'

Her hand reached out, touching his chest, feeling the muscle beneath his shirt. 'So hard,' she murmured. 'So strong.'

'Sister.' He put his hand over hers. 'This is not . . .'

She kissed him then, pressing close, her lips on his before he knew what had happened. The sensation was overwhelming, a torrent of unaccustomed feelings washing through his body. *This is wrong*, he thought as her tongue probed between his lips. *I should stop her. Right now . . . I must end this . . . Any second now . . .*

The sound that saved him was faint at first, a plaintive note on the wind seeping through his window, almost missed by his preoccupation with Sister Henna's lips, but something in it, something familiar, made him pause, pull away.

'Brother?' Sister Henna asked, the whisper of her breath caressing his lips.

'Can you hear that?'

A slight frown creased her brow. 'I hear nothing.' She giggled and pressed close again. 'But my heart beating, and yours . . .'

The sound grew, an unmistakable siren call.

'Wolf's howl,' he said.

'A wolf in the city?' Sister Henna giggled again. 'It's just the wind, or a dog . . .'

'Dog's don't howl like that. And it's not the wind. It's a wolf. I saw a wolf once, in the forest.' *Just before an assassin tried to kill me.*

It would have been easily missed had he not spent years studying his opponents' faces on the practice ground, searching for the tics and subtle changes in expression that warned of an attack. And he saw it in hers, a brief flicker of decision in her eyes.

'You shouldn't worry over such things,' she said, her left hand coming up to caress his face. 'Forget your worries, brother. Let me help you for—'

The knife in her right hand came free of her robes in a blur, the steel shining bright as it arced towards his neck. It was a practised move, executed with the speed and precision of an expert.

Vaelin twisted, the knife leaving a scratch on his shoulder, his right arm thrusting openhanded into her chest, propelling her back to collide with the far wall. She rebounded quickly, a look of feline hatred on her face, leaping, spinning a kick at his head and bringing the knife round to slash at his belly. He dodged the kick and caught her wrist, twisting, hearing the crack, forcing down a spasm of revulsion. *She's not a girl, she's not a sister, she's an enemy.*

Her free hand came round in a punch, palm flat and foreknuckles extended, aimed at the base of his nose, a blow he recognised from Master Intris's lessons, a killing blow. He moved his head, taking the punch on his brow, shaking off the sting of it and gripping her hard on the neck, forcing her against the wall. She thrashed, hissing, nails scraping at his face. He forced her head back, the bones of her neck straining, lifting her off her feet, tightening his grip to subdue her struggles.

'You are very skilled, sister,' he observed.

A grunt of pained fury escaped her throat. Her skin felt hot against his hand.

'Perhaps you could tell me where you learned such skills, and why you felt the need to practise them on me.'

Her eyes, shining bright amidst the flushed, red mask of her face, flicked to the rip in his shirt and the shallow scar beneath. A smile, ugly and full of malice, twisted her lips. 'Feeling . . . well, brother?' she grated through spittle. 'You don't . . . have time . . . to save her now.'

He felt it then, the heat rising in his chest, the fresh slick of sweat washing over him, a faint greyness creeping into the corners of his eyes. *Poison! Poison on the blade.*

He leaned close, his face inches from hers, meeting the hatred in her eyes. 'Save who?'

Her horrible smile widened into a grotesque laugh. 'Once . . . there were . . . seven!' she told him, the hatred in her eyes shining like a lantern in the dark.

Suddenly she jerked her head back, forcing her mouth open, then clamping it shut with a loud clack of colliding teeth. She began to writhe in his grasp, shuddering uncontrollably, froth spouting from her mouth. He released his grip, letting her fall to the floor where she thrashed, feet slapping the tiles, before lying still, eyes wide and unblinking, lifeless.

Vaelin stared at her, sweat beading his forehead, the heat in his chest building to a fire.

Poison on the blade . . . You don't have time to save her now . . . Once there were seven . . . You don't have time to save her . . . Save her . . . SAVE HER!

The Aspect!

He went to where his sword was propped against the wall, tearing it free of the scabbard, dragging the door open, sprinting along the corridor to the stairwell.

Poison on the blade . . . How long did he have? He chased the thought from his mind. *Long enough!* he decided fiercely, leaping up the steps three at a time. *I have long enough.*

The Aspect's rooms were on the top floor. He got there in seconds, running along the corridor, seeing her door ahead, finding no sign of a threat . . .

The blade was a sliver of light in the shadows, a half crescent of steel, wielded with speed and skill, it should have taken his head off at the shoulders. He ducked it, going into a roll, feeling the wind rush as the sword bit the air above him, coming to his feet, forming the parry stance in the same movement, the sword blade clashing with his own. He whirled, going down on one knee, sword arm fully extended, his arm jarring as his blade met flesh, drawing a stifled shout of pain and brief rainfall spatter of blood on floor tiles. His attacker wore cotton garments of black, a mask over his face, soot smeared on the brows and eyelids. His eyes glared up at Vaelin from the floor as he clutched at the deep gash in his thigh, not in anger but in shocked surprise.

Vaelin killed him with a slash to the neck, left him writhing in a welter of arterial blood as he ran on, the fire in his chest now an inferno of pain, his vision blurring, losing focus, fixing on the Aspect's door, no more than a few feet away now. He stumbled, colliding with the wall, pushing himself onwards with an angry grunt of self reproach.

SAVE HER!

Two more blades shimmered out of the darkness, another black-clad figure, a short sword in each hand, attacking in a frenzy of slashing blades. Vaelin parried the first two slashes, moved back to let the others whistle within an inch of his face, stepped inside the reach of the man's kick and killed him with a thrust to the sternum, guiding his sword blade up under the ribs, finding the heart. The black-clad man went into a brief spasm, blood gouting from his mouth, then sagged, doll-like, devoid of life, hanging on Vaelin's blade like a rag. The weight of it dragged him down, sword buried in the body up to the hilt, blood covering his arm in a thick red slick, bathing the floor. The smell would have made him gag but for the toxin raging in his blood.

Tired . . . He slumped against the corpse, a weight of

exhaustion greater than any he had known pressing down on him. The pain in his chest receding, displaced by this overwhelming need for sleep. *So tired . . .*

'You don't look well, brother.'

The voice was anonymous, without source or owner, lost amidst the shadows. *A dream?* he wondered. *A dream before death.*

'She found you, I see,' the voice went on. There was the faintest scrape of a blade tip on stone.

No dream. Vaelin gritted his teeth, grip tightening on his sword hilt. 'She's dead!' he shouted into the dark.

'I'm sure.' The voice was mild, devoid of accent or recognition. Neither cultured nor coarse. 'Pity. I always liked her in that guise. She was so wonderfully cruel. Did you bed her first? I think she would have liked that.'

It was only a slight note of tension in the tone, but Vaelin sensed the owner of the unseen voice was about to make his move.

Shaking with the effort, he got off his knees, standing, pulling his sword free of the corpse. *Waited too long,* he realised. *Should've killed me when I was vulnerable. Is he waiting for the poison to complete the task for him?*

'You're afraid,' Vaelin grunted into the darkness. 'You know you can't beat me.'

Silence. Silence and shadows, broken only by the drip of blood from his sword ticking on the floor. *No time,* he thought, his vision swimming, a dreadful, icy numbness creeping into this limbs. *No time to wait.*

'Once,' he said, his voice a dry rasp, making him cry it out. 'Once there were seven!'

There was a clatter of locks and latches followed by the creak of hinges as the Aspect's door opened behind him and her comely, faintly annoyed face appeared shrouded by candlelight.

'What *is* all this noise . . .'

The knife came spinning out of the dark, end over end, a precise throw, its tip certain to take the Aspect in the eye.

Vaelin's sword arm felt like lead as he brought his blade round in an arc, the blade meeting the knife, sending it spinning into the shadows. He never saw the assassin follow up his attack, he felt it, *knew* it, but he never saw it. His counter was automatic, unconscious, immediate. He spun, both hands on his sword hilt, the last vestiges of his strength in the blow, he never felt it meet the man's neck, heard rather than saw the geyser of blood painting the ceiling and walls as the headless corpse continued for a few steps before collapsing. All he knew was the inescapable, dominating need to sleep.

The floor tiles were cool against his cheek, his chest moving in a sedate rhythm. He wondered if he would dream of wolves . . .

'Vaelin!' Strong hands gripped him, shook him, many feet thundered on the floor, a babble of voices like a raging river. He groaned in annoyance.

'Vaelin! Wake up!' Something hard smacked across his face making him wince. 'Wake up! Don't sleep! Do you hear me?!'

More voices, tumbling together in a barely decipherable clamour. 'Fetch Sister Sherin, now! . . . Get him to the teaching room . . . Forget them, they're dead . . . What was he infected with? . . . Looks like a knife wound, where's the blade?'

'She wanted to apologise,' Vaelin said, deciding he should be helpful. 'Came to my room . . . Would've got me but for the wolf . . .'

'Check his room!' Sherin's voice, more shrill and panicked than he knew it could be. 'Look for a knife, make sure you don't touch the blade.'

There were more voices, a vague sensation of being carried, the coolness of the floor replaced by the hard smoothness of a treatment table. Vaelin groaned, his befuddled mind perceiving the pain to come.

'Dead?' the Aspect's voice. 'What do you mean dead?'

'Looks like poison,' Master Harin's deep rumble responded. 'A pellet hidden in one of her teeth. Haven't seen the like for a long time . . .'

Vaelin decided to open his eyes, seeing only a murky collage of shadows. He blinked, his vision clearing long enough to make out Sister Sherin, nostrils flared as she sniffed Sister Henna's knife. 'Hunter's Arrow,' she said. 'We need Joffril root.'

'That could kill him.' Vaelin knew he should have been shocked by the alarm in the Aspect's voice but found his mind filled with a question he had to ask.

'He'll die if we don't!' Sherin snapped, her face stricken, fearful, but determined. 'He's young and strong. He can stand it.'

A pause, a sigh of deep frustration. 'Fetch the root, and plenty of redflower . . .'

'No!' Sherin cut in. 'No, it diminishes the effect. No redflower.'

'Faith, sister.' Master Harin's hulking form moved into Vaelin's view for the first time. 'Do you know what that stuff does to a man?'

'She's right,' the Aspect said, her voice tight.

'Aspect?' Vaelin said.

She moved to him, her hand clasping his, fingers smoothing his brow. 'Vaelin, please lie still, we have to give you a physic to make you well. This will hurt . . . You must be strong.'

'Aspect,' he fought to keep his vision stable, locked on her eyes. 'Please, what was my mother's name?'

Vardrian.

It sang in his mind through a tumult of pain. *Vardrian.* Her name. Her family name. Sweat bathed him, his chest was a furnace, darkness clouded his eyes, but her name held him, an anchor in the world.

Sister Sherin had tied a leather strap around his arm and injected the tincture of Joffril root directly into his vein with a long needle. The agony was almost instantaneous. The room fractured and disappeared, the Aspect's soothing words fading away, Sherin's stricken face a pale smudge in the descending shadow.

Vardrian.

It was a curious effect of pain that time became infinite, every instant of agony prolonged to the ultimate. He knew that his back was arched, his spine tensed like a bow, strong hands holding him to the table as he raved and raged incoherently. He knew it, but he didn't feel it. It was far away, somewhere beyond the pain.

Ildera Vardrian. His mother. A plain name, a name without nobility or notoriety, a name that came from the fields or the streets. She was like his father, elevated by her talent. She was special. Suddenly he could see her face so clearly, the darkness fleeing before the brightness of her smile, the compassion in her eyes. She was a beacon in the pain, a focus for his will, his will to live.

He never knew how long it lasted, how long it took him to exhaust himself. They told him later he injured several of the Fifth Order's stronger brothers, that he even tried to bite the Aspect, that he screamed the most foul and terrible things, but he had no knowledge of it. All he knew was the name. *Ildera Vardrian.*

It saved him.

CHAPTER FIVE

I n his dream there was no pain. In his dream soft golden light streamed through the window and Sister Sherin's smile was radiant as she gazed down at him.

'You lived,' she said. 'I knew you would.'

A dream . . . a dream allows you to speak your heart. 'You're beautiful,' he told her.

Her smile became a laugh. 'You're delirious, brother. Try to sleep, you need to rest. There are a number of dangerous-looking young men outside who will be very angry with me if you don't recover.'

'We should go away together,' he went on blithely, rejoicing in the freedom of the dream. 'We should escape. Find a quiet part of the world where you can heal and I can learn to be something other than a killer . . .'

'Shhh!' Her fingers were on his lips, her smile gone now. 'Please, Vaelin . . .'

'I felt nothing when I killed those men. Nothing. That isn't right . . .'

'You saved the Aspect. You had no choice.'

The man in black clutched at the wound in his leg; when Vaelin's sword cut into his neck a faint, childlike whimper escaped his throat . . . 'I have shamed my mother. Compared to her, I'm nothing . . .'

'No.' Her hand caressed his brow, her face came close to his and a soft kiss played on his lips. 'You're a guardian, a warrior who fights in defence of the helpless. You are strong and you are just. Always remember that. And always remember that I will be here whenever you need me, whenever you call for me, my skills are yours.'

The dream began to fade, exhaustion dragging him to oblivion. 'I'd rather we just went away together . . .'

He woke to pain, not the agony of the Joffril root but the mingled ache of strained muscles and dehydration. Oddly shaped red-brown stains discoloured his bedsheets and the cut on his arm retained the sting of poison. His eyelids had begun to droop, the welcoming arms of his dream beckoning . . . when he noticed he was not alone.

Master Sollis sat in the corner of the room, arms folded, his sword resting on his knees. The redness of his eyes told of a sleepless night. 'Took you long enough to wake up,' he said.

'Sorry, Master,' Vaelin croaked.

Master Sollis rose and went to the table beside the bed to pour a cup of water from a large clay jug. 'Here.' He held the cup to Vaelin's lips. 'Small sips, don't gulp it.'

The water tasted better than water had ever tasted, flooding his mouth, banishing the dryness of his throat. 'Thank you, Master.'

'Sister Sherin said you should drink at least a cup every hour. She gave very strict instructions for your care.'

Sherin . . . We should go away together . . . A new pain tugged at his chest and he found himself wishing he had never had the dream, waking to find it hadn't been real was almost more than he could bear.

He looked down at the stains on his sheets. 'Did they have to cut me open?' He had a vividly unpleasant image of the rib spreader being plunged into his chest.

'Apparently Joffril root causes a man to sweat blood. Part of its useful purgative effect, so I'm told.' Sollis pulled his chair from the corner of the room and sat down next to the bed. 'I need to know what happened here.'

So Vaelin told him, omitting nothing. Sollis listened in silence, barely raising an eyebrow at Sister Henna's visit to his room and remaining impassive when Vaelin mentioned the wolf's howl that had saved him. His only reaction came at the mention of her words: *Once there were seven*. It was only a slight shift in the eyes, but it said much. *He knows,* Vaelin decided. *He knows what it means and I'd bet a sack of gold he isn't going to tell me.* Sollis showed no reaction to the rest of it, asking only a few questions. 'And how would you assess their skills, these assassins?'

'They could swing a blade but seemed to know nothing of tactics. I was poisoned, weak, they should've killed me, taken me in a rush. Instead they came at me in turn, each time from ambush.'

Master Sollis sat in silence, pondering the information. Vaelin felt a desperate need to sleep but forced himself to remain alert. Novice brothers did not sleep in a master's presence.

'Is Sister Sherin coming back?' Vaelin asked, hoping a break in the silence would keep him awake. 'I . . . I'd like to know how long I'll be laid up in this bed.'

'She's tending the wounded. She's likely to be busy for a while. The last two days have seen much trouble in the city.'

Two days. He had been dreaming and sweating blood for two days. 'Trouble, Master?'

'There have been riots. When word spread of the attacks rumours started about a Denier plot. Soon it was common knowledge a hidden army of Cumbraelins was waiting in the sewers to murder us all in our beds.' He shook his head in disgust. 'Ignorant people will believe anything if they're scared enough.'

Vaelin was puzzled. 'Attacks?'

'Elera Al Mendah was not the only Aspect to be attacked. The Aspects of the Fourth and Second Orders are dead. The others were lucky to survive. Aspect Hendrahl was sorely wounded, seems the knife wasn't long enough to reach his heart through the blubber.'

Vaelin's mind reeled. Two Aspects slain, it seemed so utterly incredible. He remembered Aspect Corlin Al Sentis well from his Test of Knowledge, the solemn, grave-faced man who had pressed him on the events in the forest. It was strange to think of him torn by daggers and poison. His chain of thought led him to an inevitable concern. 'Aspect Arlyn?'

'He's alive and well. They sent three men for him. They tunnelled into the vaults, where they were met by Master Grealin. It's always a mistake to underestimate a fat man in a fight.' It was the closest thing to a compliment Sollis had ever voiced about Master Grealin.

'Is he injured?'

'A few bruises only. Although he was sorely grieved he couldn't keep one of them alive to provide some answers.'

'My brothers?'

'They're all well. Brother Nortah managed to get himself expelled from the Second Order after only two days. As for the others, Brother Caenis distinguished himself by killing the assassin who had knifed Aspect Hendrahl and the others appear to have been sleeping off a vatful of ale when Aspect Corlin met his end. Half the novice brothers of the Sixth Order lolling about the House of the Fourth Order, and assassins slit the Aspect's throat and get away before anyone had noticed. Severe punishment was warranted.'

Vaelin sank back into his mattress, suddenly overwhelmed

by tiredness. 'Forgive me, Master,' he said. 'For not taking one of them alive. The poison dulled my wits somewhat . . .' He drifted away, seeing Master Sollis's lean, inexpressive face fade into shadow.

Barkus raged, Dentos joked, Nortah laughed and Caenis said little. Vaelin realised he had missed them all terribly.

'It's just so bloody daft,' Barkus said, bafflement creasing his brows. 'I mean what is going on?'

'Clearly there are enemies among us, brother,' Caenis said. 'We must be wary.'

'But why though? Why kill the Aspects?'

Vaelin was tired, the cut on his arm had darkened into a bluish scar and the agony instilled by the Joffril root had faded into a dull ache that lingered in his limbs. Throughout the morning he had had several visitors, Master Harin awkwardly complimenting him and forcing a booming laugh or two. Vaelin could tell the big man was gratified by his survival and saddened by Henna's betrayal. She had been something of a favourite in his group. Brother Sellin stayed for over an hour, gnarled hands clutching his wooden club and talking of how he would have used it on the assassins if he'd but had the chance. Vaelin had a brief vision of an elderly brother lying in a gatehouse with his throat cut but said, 'They were wise indeed to give you a wide berth, brother.' The old man seemed happy enough with this and said he would come back the next day with a healing broth of his own recipe. There had been other visitors but Sister Sherin had been conspicuous by her absence and he worried about any embarrassing ramblings he may have uttered in his sleep.

'How's Frentis?' he asked.

'Angry,' Nortah said. 'Doesn't know what to do with it, we've had to drag him out of three fights already. He begged the Aspect to let him come with us but got a day in the stables for his pains.'

'Keep an eye on him when you get back. I don't like his being around Master Rensial on his own. Tell him I'm well, I'll be back soon. And tell him to make sure he visits Scratch every day.'

Nortah nodded. It was unspoken but acknowledged that he would lead whilst Vaelin recovered. 'They said you killed four of them,' he said. 'Impressive.'

'Three. There was a girl, she had pretended to be a sister here for years. She killed herself when she failed to kill me.'

'A girl?' A faintly wicked smile played on Nortah's lips as he glanced at the scar on Vaelin's arm. 'How close did you let her get, brother?'

'Too close.' *A lesson I won't forget.*

'Brother Nillin had been at the Fourth Order for over twelve years,' Caenis said. 'He was one of their most respected scholars, author of three books on linguistics, teacher of languages to the novice brothers, and all the time he was waiting to kill Aspect Dendrahl.'

'The fat bastard's got you to thank he's still with us,' Nortah said. 'How did you reckon it out anyway?'

'I didn't. I was returning a book the Aspect had lent me. I kicked the door in when I heard him screaming.' He paused, his sombre mood deepening visibly. 'Brother Nillin put up a fair fight for a man in his forty-seventh year.'

'What'd you do him with?' Dentos asked.

'I didn't have a weapon, couldn't see the point of carrying one around the Fourth Order. I had to use my hands.'

'Couldn't have been easy,' Barkus commented. 'Facing off unarmed against a man with a knife.'

'The man was skilled but . . .' Caenis shrugged.

'He wasn't one of us,' Vaelin finished.

Caenis nodded. 'Which begs the question why wait until the Orders are full of boys from the Sixth Order before making their move.'

'Nothing about this makes sense,' Nortah said, yawning. 'Although I can understand someone wanting the Aspect of the Second Order dead. One more minute of the boring old fool's twaddle and I'd've strangled him myself.'

'Is that why you were expelled?' Vaelin asked.

Dentos snickered and Nortah's smile for once seemed to have some genuine humour in it. 'There was a misunderstanding with one of the sisters. Apparently relaxation massage has certain limitations. At least I think that's what she said before she slapped me and ran off.'

Vaelin let them laugh for a few seconds before cutting in, raising his gaze to meet each of their eyes in turn. 'I don't know what happened here, brothers. I don't understand it any better than you do. I do know that we live in perilous times, that the only trust we can have is in each other. Heed Master Sollis, obey the Aspect and, above all, guard each other well.'

The door opened and Sister Sherin entered with a bowl of steaming water, the first time he had seen her all day. 'Out!' she commanded. 'Time for Brother Vaelin's wash and you lot have been here long enough.'

'A wash, eh?' Nortah raised an eyebrow, leaning close to Sherin as she placed the bowl on the table, Vaelin noting how his gaze scanned her from head to toe. 'I trust you'll be *very* thorough, sister.'

Sherin gave Nortah the same wearied, uninterested glance he recognised from her encounters with amorous drunks in the treatment room. 'Don't you have to go and play with your sword somewhere, brother?'

Laughing wryly, Nortah followed the others from the room.

'Your friend could do with a lesson in manners,' Sherin observed, placing the bowl on the small table beside the bed. 'His demeanour is unseemly for a brother.'

'My Order has many different brothers within its ranks, some of them more seemly than others.'

She raised an eyebrow but said nothing, dipping her cloth into the bowl and making to pull back the covers. 'I'm strong enough now to wash myself, sister,' he told her, gently but firmly holding on to the blankets.

She gave him a bemused look. 'Trust me when I say, brother, you have nothing I haven't seen before. Who do you think washed you when you were unconscious?'

Vaelin drove the uncomfortable thought to the back of his mind and kept hold of the bedclothes. 'Even so. I'm stronger now.'

'As you wish.' She dropped the cloth into the bowl and moved back. 'Since you're so much stronger, you can meet with the Aspect today. She's been asking for you. In the gardens at noon. I'll help you, if you can stand to accept my help that is.'

She left the room without a backward glance. It took Vaelin a moment to realise he had actually hurt her feelings.

The gardens of the Fifth Order were extensive, covering several acres of rich soil where brothers and sisters tended the myriad variety of herbs and medicinal plants that played such an important role in their work. For the most part the gardens consisted of a series of rectangles, a monotonous chequer-board of green and brown, but here and there were islands of colour, clusters of flowers and cherry blossoms.

'We have gardens in our Order,' Vaelin told Sherin as she helped him along one of the gravel pathways between the allotments. His legs and chest still ached a good deal and he leaned on her shoulder more heavily than he would have wished, knowing the proximity made her uncomfortable. She had said nothing when she arrived at noon to take him to the Aspect and did her best to avoid his gaze. 'They aren't like this,' he went on when she didn't respond. 'Master Smentil tends them, mostly on his own. He only speaks in signs, lost his tongue to the Lonak . . .' His voice faded. Sister Sherin was clearly in no mood for conversation.

She halted at a small series of flowerbeds. He could see the slender figure of Aspect Elera moving between the blossoms.

'The Aspect will help you on the way back,' Sherin said, moving away to let his arm fall from her shoulder.

'Thank you, sister.'

She nodded and turned away.

'Sister,' he said, reaching out to touch her wrist. 'A moment please.'

She pulled her wrist away, avoiding his touch, but lingered, eyes guarded.

'I didn't thank you,' he said. 'For saving my life.'

'It is my role, brother.'

'When I was . . . undergoing my cure I had many strange dreams. I think I may have said things, things I would never say. If I said anything . . . offensive . . .'

'You said nothing, brother.' She raised her gaze, meeting his, forcing a small smile. 'Nothing offensive at least.' She folded her arms tightly across her chest, her smile fading. 'You'll be leaving soon, going back to that awful place, going to fight some dreadful war. We . . . we won't talk again, perhaps not ever.'

Involuntarily he moved closer, reaching out to grasp her hands. 'We'll talk again. I promise.'

'Vaelin!' It was Aspect Elera, standing at the edge of the flower garden, a small pruning knife in her hand. Her smile was bright. 'You're so much stronger.'

'Thanks to Sister Sherin's care, Aspect.'

'Indeed. Her care is valuable, as is her time.'

'Forgive me, Aspect.' Sherin bowed her head. 'I shouldn't loiter . . .'

'There is no rebuke, sister. But the city is still troubled. I fear your skills will be sorely needed again today.'

Sherin nodded, gave Vaelin a parting glance, a sad smile on her lips, before releasing his hands and making her way back to the Order House. Vaelin watched her until she was out of sight.

'What do you know of flowers, Vaelin?' Elera Al Mendah asked him, offering her arm for support and leading him into the flower garden.

'Master Hutril taught me to spot the poisonous ones. He said they're good for grinding up and smearing on arrowheads.' *And I have a sister who likes winterblooms.*

'Very useful I'm sure. Do you know what these are?' She stopped beside a short row of purple flowers with odd, curved heads framed by four long petals.

'I haven't seen them before, Aspect.'

'Marlian Orchids, from the far south of the Alpiran Empire. Actually, they're crossbreeds, I mixed in some of our native orchids to add a little hardiness, our climate is colder than they're used to. It's often the way with plants, take them out of the soil in which they've grown, and they wither and die.'

He felt a lesson was being taught, a lesson he didn't want to hear. 'I understand, Aspect.' He assumed it was the response she expected.

'Sherin is special,' the Aspect went on. 'She cares, you see. Cares more than most, even the brothers and sisters of this Order. Perhaps that's where her skill comes from. And she is very skilled, already she surpasses me in most things, but don't tell her that. Skill like that is bound to make her isolated. There aren't many who take the time or trouble to know her well enough to see how special she is. But you did, as I knew you would. It's why I placed you together. But I didn't expect your bond to be so strong.'

'I believe friendship is not forbidden those who serve the Faith.'

Aspect Elera raised an eyebrow at the impertinence but voiced no rebuke. 'Friendship is always to be valued. But it cannot inhibit the role you and Sherin are to play. Sherin is to this Order what you are to yours.'

'And what is that?'

'The future. It is necessary you both understand this. Your mother did not, or she refused to. Love can do that, blind you to the path the Faith has made for you. When she left this place to marry your father, the Fifth Order lost a future Aspect.'

'I am sure my mother knew her own heart.'

She winced a little, hearing his bitterness. 'Yes, she did. I meant no criticism, merely regret. She was my closest friend, when I first came here she taught me. Without her I would know nothing.'

She paused at a small plain wooden bench and bade him sit. He was grateful for the rest, his legs felt as if they would fold under him at any moment.

'May I ask, Aspect, have you learned anything of the men who attacked you?'

She shook her head. 'Very little. The bodies were examined, nothing of interest was found save that they all had poisoned pellets concealed in their teeth, like Sister Henna. Their faces were not known to anyone. The Realm Guard and the Fourth Order are investigating. I daresay they will provide answers in due course.'

For a woman who had recently escaped death, she seemed remarkably unconcerned about the identity of her attackers. 'You are not afraid others might try again?'

She frowned as if the thought had not occurred to her before. 'If they come, they come. There seems little I can do about it. The Faith tells us to accept those things we cannot change.'

'Sister Henna had been here a long time. Her betrayal must hurt.'

'Betrayal? I doubt she ever had any loyalty to this place so how could she betray it? She did what she was sent here to do. I must say I'm impressed with her dedication, all this time living a lie and she never faltered, never let her mask slip.'

'She said something, before she died. "Once there were seven." Do you know what it means?'

There was something there, some reaction but not the same recognition he had seen in Master Sollis, more like fear, but gone in an instant. 'You have many questions today, Vaelin. It seems to be a recurring feature of our conversations.'

Another one who'll tell me nothing. 'Forgive me, Aspect.'

She dismissed his concern with a laugh. 'After what you did for me I feel I owe you one answer at least. So, ask me, but one question only, mind.'

One question only. It almost seemed cruel, as if she was playing with him. He wanted answers to every one of the myriad questions that plagued him, but after a moment's frantic thought he settled on the one that had been at the forefront of his mind for months. 'What do you know of my sister?'

'Ah.' She paused for a moment, sadness lining her face. 'I know that she's a very bright little girl. I know her parents love her very much. I know that she was born a little over ten years ago.'

'When my mother was still alive.'

The Aspect sighed heavily. 'Vaelin, I don't wish to hurt you but you must understand that not every marriage is a happy story. Your mother and father loved each other greatly but they were also very different. Your mother hated war, she had seen enough of it in her service, but she accepted your father's role as Battle Lord because she loved him and because he was a man of justice who strove to keep the worst excesses of the Realm Guard in check. But when the third Meldenean war came she found she could stomach it no longer. She knew what he had been ordered to do and she begged him not to. But he had to obey his king.'

'The city.' *Men, women, children . . . screaming in the flames.*

'Yes. It haunted them both and it ended their union. She turned away from him. He began spending more time away from home, how he met the woman who would give him a daughter I don't know. But when your mother died and you were placed in the Sixth Order they were brought to live in his home. He asked for permission to marry and legitimise the girl but the King refused. The Battle Lord must be an example, a model for the people to follow. It was not long after this that your father left the King's service.'

'Did my mother know? About the girl.'

'I don't think so. Her health began to fail about the same time. She concerned herself with your future.' She reached up to smooth the hair from his forehead. 'She had many hopes for you. All the good she did, all the people she healed, but you were the proudest achievement of her life.'

'Then I am glad she did not live to see what I have become.'

The slap was slow by his standards but so unexpected he failed to block it.

'Don't ever say that!' Her voice was heavy with anger as he rubbed his stinging cheek. 'What have you become? A brave young man who saved my life. Not to mention Sister Sherin's. I know your mother's spirit sings with pride at who you are.'

'I am a killer. It's all I know how to do.'

'You are a warrior in the service of the Faith. Do not forget that. It may mean nothing to you now but it will in time.'

'It's not what she wanted. Putting me in that place so my father could move his whore into her house . . .'

'It wasn't his decision.'

'Another King's order, then. A symbol of his devotion . . .'

'It was your mother's dying wish.'

He felt he had been slapped again, only worse. His head spun, mind reeling. *LIES! She's lying! My mother would never have wanted this.*

'Vaelin?'

He rose from the bench, staggering away from her, nausea and confusion boiling inside him, but his weakened legs could only carry him a few steps before he collapsed, crushing precious orchids and finding himself blinded by tears.

'Vaelin.' She was holding him, cradling him as he sobbed. 'I'm sorry. You had to know.'

'Why?' he whispered into her breast. 'Why would she do that?'

'Because she was brave enough to look into your heart and see the man you were meant to be. She prayed to the Departed you would inherit her gift, that you would spend your life as a healer, but as you grew she knew it was your father's skill that ran in your blood. As your father's son you would have had a very different life, a life of service, true, but service to the King, not the Faith. The King had plans for you, did you know that? In time you would have been very useful to him. Your mother had lost her husband to his plans, she wouldn't lose a son. As her health worsened she realised she would not be there to protect you and your father would always obey his king. She knew Aspect Arlyn well from her time in the Cumbraelin wars and asked him to take you. Of course he agreed although he knew it meant conflict with the Crown. Your father raged when she told him, his anger was terrible, but your mother was dying and as his final service to her she made him promise he would give you to the Order when she was gone. It was his last act of loyalty to her.'

Loyalty is our strength . . . Loyalty to a king . . . Loyalty to a betrayed wife . . .

His voice came in a whisper, secrets rising from deep inside. 'I heard her once, my first night in the Order as I lay shivering in fear. I heard her say my name.'

Her arms tightened around him. 'She loved you so much. When I placed you in her arms she seemed to shine with it.'

He drew back a little, puzzled.

She smiled and placed a kiss on his forehead. 'I delivered you, Vaelin Al Sorna, and a big, squalling mass of flesh you were.'

Questions. Still so many questions. But somehow he felt content to leave them unasked. For now the answers she gave were enough. She held him for a while longer as his tears subsided then helped him back to the Order House. He left two days later amidst fond farewells from the brothers and sisters of the Fifth Order. Sister Sherin wasn't present, her Aspect having sent her to the southern coast the previous day, where fresh rioting left many people in need of healing. It would be nearly five more years before Vaelin saw her again.

CHAPTER SIX

He recovered in a few days with no lingering ailments save a tendency to cough on cold mornings and a lifelong suspicion of overly amorous women, something that did not concern a brother of the Sixth Order with any regularity. His return to the Order was greeted with studied indifference from the masters, a marked contrast to the joyous farewells he received from the brothers and sisters of the Fifth Order. His brothers, of course, acted differently, fussing over him with an embarrassing level of concern, confining him to bed for a full week and forcing food down his throat at every opportunity. Even Nortah joined in, although Vaelin detected a certain sadism in the way he tucked the blankets in and held the soup spoon to his mouth. Frentis was the worst, spending every spare minute in their tower room, anxiously watching over him and becoming agitated at the slightest cough or sign of ill health. He earned his first caning from Master Sollis for failing to appear at sword practice because he had been fretting over a slight fever Vaelin developed in the night. Finally, the Aspect decreed their room off-limits to him on pain of expulsion.

When Vaelin was strong enough to leave his bed without

assistance his first call was to the kennels, where Scratch's greeting was aggressively ecstatic, knocking him off his feet and painting his face with his stone-rough tongue as his rapidly growing brood of pups milled around them, yelping with excitement.

'Get off, you brute!' Vaelin grunted, managing to heave the dog's weight from his chest. Scratch whined a little at the reproach but laid his head affectionately on Vaelin's chest. 'I know.' Vaelin scratched his ears. 'I missed you too.'

When he visited the stables he found Spit also had a welcome waiting. It lasted a full two minutes and Master Rensial stated confidently it was the longest fart he had ever heard a horse produce.

'Bloody nag,' Vaelin muttered, holding a carrot up to the stallion's mouth. 'Test of the Horse soon. Don't let me down, eh?'

He found Caenis at archery practice, loosing as many arrows as possible in the shortest time, a skill crucial to the Test of the Bow. To Vaelin's eyes Caenis hardly needed the practice, his hands seeming to blur as he sent shaft after shaft into the butt thirty paces away. Vaelin had steadily improved with the bow but he knew he could never match the level of skill Caenis displayed with the weapon and even he was outshone by Dentos and Nortah.

'You're a few points off,' he observed, although in truth the inaccuracy was barely noticeable. 'The last few drifted to the left.'

'Yes,' Caenis agreed. 'My aim wanders after forty arrows or so.' He drew the bowstring back, the finely honed muscles of his arm straining before he sent the shaft into the centre of the target. 'A little better.'

'I wanted to ask you about the assassin you killed.'

Caenis's expression clouded. 'I've told the tale many times over, to you, the others and the masters. As I'm sure you've told your story many times.'

'Did he say anything?' Vaelin pressed. 'Before you killed him.'

'Yes, he said, "Get away from me, boy, or I'll gut you." Hardly worthy of a song, is it? I was wondering if I should change it when I write the tale.'

'You intend to write of this?'

'Of course. One day I will write the story of our service in the Faith. I feel our Order has been sadly remiss in recording its history. Do you know we are the only Order not to have its own library? I hope to start a new tradition.' He loosed another arrow, then two more in quick succession. Vaelin noted his aim had worsened.

Killing a man is not an easy thing to bear, or talk about, he realised. 'You liked him, this Brother Nillin?'

'He was an interesting man with many stories, although when I thought about it later I realised he had a fondness for the more ancient tales. The Old Songs they're called, from the time before the Faith was strong, sagas of blood and war and the practice of the Dark.'

The Dark . . . A wolf in the forest, a wolf howling outside my window. 'Once there were seven. Do you know what it means?'

Caenis had drawn his bow once again but slowly relaxed the tension. 'Where did you hear that?'

'Sister Henna said it before she took poison. What does it mean, brother? I know you know.'

Caenis took the arrow from the bow and returned it to the quiver at his hip, laying the bow down gently on his pack. 'It's a story. A tale like the Old Songs, but it concerns the Faith. Truth be told, I'd never given it credence. It's rarely told and the archives of the Orders make no mention of it.'

'No mention of what?'

'In our time there are six Orders serving the Faith. But once, so some say, there were seven. In the early years of the Faith, when the Orders were first formed and the first Aspects chosen, it's said there was a Seventh Order. The Orders were formed to serve each of the principal aspects of the Faith, and so the brother or sister chosen to lead an Order is called the Aspect. The Seventh Order, so it's claimed, was the Order of the Dark, its brothers and sisters would delve into the mysteries, seeking knowledge and power to better serve the Faith. Traditionally, practice of the Dark has been ascribed to the Denier creeds but, if this tale is to be believed, it was once part of our Faith. The tale has it that after one hundred years a crisis arose. The Seventh Order began to grow in power, using its knowledge of the Dark to seek dominion over the Orders, claiming their knowledge brought them closer to the Departed, claiming they could hear their voices, interpret their guidance more clearly than the lesser Orders. They said it was a privilege that gave them the right to lead, to have ascendancy in the Faith. Such a thing could not be tolerated of course, the Faith must have balance between the Orders, one cannot be set above the others. So there was war between the Faithful and in time the Seventh was destroyed but not before much blood had been spilled. It is said that so great was the chaos caused by this war that it brought the fracturing of the Realm into the four Fiefs not united again until the reign of our great King Janus. Whether any of this is true cannot be told. If true, it would have happened over six hundred years ago and the few books to survive the centuries say nothing of these events.'

'And yet you seem to know the tale well.'

'You know me, brother.' Caenis smiled faintly. 'I was always fond of stories. The more fanciful the better.'

'You believe it, don't you?' A sudden insight came to Vaelin then, a realisation spawned by the faintness of Caenis's smile and the immediacy with which he had told his tale. 'You already knew. You knew that this Seventh Order were behind this.'

'I suspected. There are tales, little more than fables, that claim the Seventh Order was never truly destroyed, that it survived, thrived in secret, awaiting its time to return and claim the ascendancy it sought so long ago.'

'We will go to Master Sollis and the Aspect, they must hear of this.'

'They already have, brother. I told them all I suspected as soon as I returned to the Order. I formed the impression I was telling them nothing they didn't already know.'

Vaelin remembered Master Sollis's reaction to Sister Henna's words and Aspect Elera's refusal to discuss it. *They know,* he realised. *They all know. A secret kept by the Aspects for centuries. Once there were seven. And the Seventh waits, it plots. They know.*

His limbs began to ache with a sudden chill although it was a bright, sunlit day. 'Thank you for sharing your knowledge with me, brother,' he said, crossing his arms and hugging himself for warmth.

'I always will, Vaelin,' Caenis replied. 'You know there are no secrets between us.'

The Test of the Horse came two months later, a mile-long course through woods and rough country followed by three arrows loosed from the saddle into the centre of three targets. Surprising no-one, Nortah excelled in the test, setting a new record in the process. The others all fared well, even Barkus, whose riding was scarcely better than Vaelin's. He struggled from the start, Spit was his usual fractious self and would only stir to a gallop after a tirade of heartfelt threats. They laboured over the course in the slowest time of the day and Vaelin's archery from the saddle was barely adequate, but at least he had passed. For once no other brothers failed the test and the evening meal became a raucous celebration complete with smuggled beer and much throwing of food. They were punished the next morning with a freezing swim in the river and five laps of the practice field at full pelt stark naked. No-one thought it hadn't been worth it.

Over the next few weeks there were more tales of riots and discord beyond the walls. Deniers, real or suspected, were being set upon by angry mobs, hundreds had died and the Realm Guard were hard-pressed to keep order. Eventually, as summer slipped into autumn, the Realm calmed. Contrary to the expectations of many there were no more assassinations, no hidden army of Cumbraelins beneath the streets, in fact the heretical Fief was calmer than it had been for over a decade. The Summer of Fire, as it became known, faded into memory, leaving only corpses, grief and ash in its wake.

The two prospective Aspects were led into the chamber, a woman in her early thirties and a sharp-faced man Vaelin had seen before. The woman was introduced as Mistress Liesa Ilnien of the Second Order, a plain and serene figure in a dun-coloured robe who met the combined gaze of the chamber's occupants with calm acceptance. The black-robed Tendris Al Forne of the Fourth Order was a contrast, staring back at his audience with a fierceness that could almost be defiance, the odd cheerfulness Vaelin had seen in him three years ago had disappeared but the fanaticism remained. He scanned the assembly with a narrow gaze, pausing when he saw Vaelin to offer a small nod.

Together with Caenis, he had been chosen to accompany Aspect Arlyn to the proceedings, ostensibly as guards, the Order House being short on confirmed brothers as continuing discord in the Realm had called most of them away. But Vaelin suspected the Aspect also wanted them to learn something of how the different Orders governed the Faith.

The Conclave convened in the debating hall of the House of the Third Order, a cavernous chamber of vaulted ceilings and long benches. In addition to the Aspects, many of the senior masters of each Order were also present and allowed a voice in the discussion. Caenis and Vaelin, however, had been left with no illusions as to the value of their own opinions.

'I never dreamt I would be allowed to come here, brother,' Caenis enthused in a whisper, almost shaking with excitement as they took their seats behind Aspect Arlyn. 'Present at the choosing of two new Aspects. A privilege indeed.'

Vaelin noted he had brought along a good supply of parchment and a stub of charcoal. 'Started the *Tale of Brother Caenis*, already?'

'Actually, I was going to call it *The Book of Five Brothers*.'

'It's six, counting Frentis.'

'Oh, he'll get a page or two, don't worry.'

Aspect Silla Colvis of the First Order was present, along with twenty or so of his white-robed masters. They were all men in their sixties or older, their deeply lined faces apparently lost in contemplation, either that or they were asleep. Aspect Elera was accompanied by only three brothers and two sisters, Vaelin's heart sinking when he saw that Sherin was not amongst them.

Aspect Dendrish Hendrahl's brush with death had clearly left its mark, his skin now a pallid grey contrasting with its previous porcine pinkness, his eyes sunken into the fleshy mass of his face like two stones pushed into soft dough. He had brought more masters than the other Aspects, over thirty, mostly men sharing a singular characteristic in that they seemed to be smelling the same foul odour. There was only the barest flicker of recognition when he caught sight of Caenis and no offer of a greeting to the young man who had saved his life. If anything, Vaelin sensed a resentment in the Aspect's demeanour. *It must have hurt almost as much as the poison*, he surmised, *to be saved by one of us*.

'These two come before us for recognition,' Aspect Silla told the assembled representatives of the Orders. 'The Faith requires we meet to consider the merits of their appointment. We will hear questions now.'

Aspect Dendrish was first to raise his hand, addressing his question to Liesa Ilnien. 'The lamented Aspect you wish to replace,' he began before pausing to cough loudly into a lace handkerchief, '. . . served as Aspect of the Second Order for over twenty years. Do you think you can offer the same level of experience?'

The woman responded without pause, the words flowing easily from her lips in precise, even tones. 'An Aspect does not require experience. An Aspect is a brother or sister who best embodies the values of his or her Order.'

'And you presume to judge yourself the embodiment of your Order's values?' the Aspect demanded, reddening a little, although Vaelin sensed his anger was somewhat forced.

'I presume to judge myself in all things,' Mistress Liesa Ilnien replied. 'The Faith teaches us to be our own judge, for who knows one's heart better than oneself?'

'Mistress Liesa,' Aspect Elera said before Hendrahl could respond. 'Have you journeyed far in this Realm?'

'I have visited all four Fiefs and I spent a year on a mission to the Northern Reaches, trying to bring the Faith to the horse tribes of the great plains.'

'A noble endeavour. Did you have any success?'

'Sadly, the horse folk tend to shun outsiders and cling to their delusions. If I am blessed by ascension to Aspect, it is my hope to send more missions north. The Faith is a blessing that must be shared beyond our borders.'

'Such concern for the outside world,' Aspect Silla said, 'would seem to contradict the values of your Order. Ever has it been the bastion of contemplation and meditation, sheltered from the many storms of our land. Would such work not suffer if you were to concern yourselves more with the harshness of the physical world?'

'In order to contemplate, one must *have* something to contemplate. A life without experience provides no chance of contemplation. Those who have not lived cannot meditate on the mysteries of life.'

Vaelin was impressed by the woman's logic but could sense the agitation of the assembled masters, a subdued rumble of conversation filling the benches. Next to him Caenis was busy scribbling.

Aspect Arlyn raised a hand and the murmuring of the crowd stopped immediately. 'Mistress Liesa, why do you think your Aspect was murdered?'

The mistress bowed her head for a moment, a momentary sadness passing over her face. 'There are those who wish to harm our Faith,' she said, raising her head to meet Aspect Arlyn's eye, her measured tone faltering slightly. 'Who they are or why they would do this is something I cannot imagine.'

Next to her, Brother Tendris Al Forne spoke for the first time. 'If our sister cannot imagine who would strike against us, perhaps I can.'

'You have not yet been questioned,' Aspect Silla pointed out.

'Show some respect for this occasion, young man,' Aspect Dendrish said, wheezing a little. Vaelin noted there were spots of blood on his handkerchief.

'I offer no disrespect,' Al Forne replied. 'Only truth, a truth some of us seem afraid to speak.'

'And what truth is this?' Aspect Elera asked.

Al Forne paused to take a deep breath as if gathering strength. Next to Vaelin, Caenis's charcoal stub was poised over his parchment in anticipation. 'We have been complacent,' Al Forne said eventually. 'We have allowed ourselves to become weak. The Sixth Order once fought only against the enemies of the Faith, now they police the frontiers of this Realm at the beck and call of the Crown and Denier sects gather in force without challenge.

'The Fifth Order once offered healing only to those who were true adherents of the Faith but now they open their arms to all, even the Unfaithful, and so they grow strong and confident in the knowledge that they may plot against us and we will still heal them.

'My own Order once kept records of Denier sects and practices going back centuries, but not more than three months ago they were destroyed to make yet more room for the royal accounts we are now required to keep. I know what I say may anger or shock many in this chamber, but believe me, brothers and sisters, we have tied the Faith too closely to the Realm and the Crown. And that is why we were attacked, because our enemies see our weakness if we do not.'

The silence was palpable, broken only by the choked rage of Aspect Dendrish, who managed to gasp, 'You come before us spouting this . . . this heresy and still expect to be made Aspect?'

'I come before you to speak the truth in the hope our Faith will return to its true path. As for your approval, I do not require it. I am the choice of my Order. My election was unopposed and no other will come before you. The articles of the Faith state you must be consulted before my ascension, that is all. Am I not correct, Aspect Silla?'

The aged Aspect nodded his grey head stiffly, either too shocked or too outraged to speak.

'Then we have consulted and I thank you all for your attention. I pray you will all heed my words. Now I must return to my Order, for I have much to do.' He bowed and turned to walk briskly from the chamber.

The Conclave exploded with rage, the assembly rising to their feet, shouting their anger at Al Forne's retreating back, the words 'heretic' and 'traitor' loudest amongst the cries. Al Forne didn't turn, leaving the chamber without breaking stride or sparing a backward glance. The tumult continued unabated, calls for action rising above the clamour, some masters imploring Aspect Arlyn to seize Al Forne and take him to the Blackhold. Aspect Arlyn, however, sat in silence throughout it all.

Vaelin noticed that Caenis had used up his supply of parchment and was feverishly searching his pockets for more. 'Has this ever happened before?' he asked him, finding he had to shout to be heard.

'Never,' Caenis replied. Locating a scrap of parchment, he began to write again, quickly covering it in script. 'Not ever in the history of the Faith.'

CHAPTER SEVEN

Autumn brought the Test of the Bow. Once again all the novice brothers passed. Predictably, Caenis, Nortah and Dentos excelled themselves whilst Barkus and Vaelin proved only adequate, at least by the standards of the Order. They were rewarded with permission to attend the Summertide Fair, delayed for two months due to the riots.

Both Vaelin and Nortah opted to remain behind. There were rumours that the Hawks continued to nurse their grievance and it seemed pointless to invite retribution at the scene of their humiliation. Besides, Nortah had no wish to revisit an event synonymous with his father's execution. They spent the day hunting in the woods with Scratch, the slave-hound's nose quickly leading them to a deer. Nortah put an arrow through the animal's neck from fifty paces. Instead of carrying the carcass back to the kitchens, they decided to butcher it on the spot and camp out for the night. It was a pleasant evening in the woods, the leaves of early autumn laying a greenish bronze blanket on the forest floor and shafts of sunlight streaming through the thinning branches.

'There are worse places to be,' Vaelin observed, cutting a slice from the haunch of venison spitted over their campfire.

'Reminds me of home,' Nortah said, tossing a slice of meat to Scratch.

Vaelin hid his surprise. Since his father's execution Nortah rarely spoke of his life before the Order. 'Where is it? Your home.'

'In the south, three hundred acres of land bordered by the Hebril River. My father's house was set on the shores of Lake Rihl. It had been a castle when he was a boy but he'd made many changes. We had over sixty rooms and a stable for forty horses. We'd often go riding in the woods, when he wasn't at Varinshold on the King's business.'

'Did he tell you what he did for the King?'

'Many times, he wanted me to learn. He said one day I would serve Prince Malcius the same way he served King Janus. It was the duty of our family to be the King's closest advisors.' He gave a short, bitter laugh.

'Did he ever tell you about the war with the Meldeneans?'

Nortah gave him a sidelong glance. 'When your father burned their city you mean? He only mentioned it once. He said the Meldeneans couldn't hate us any more than they already did. Besides they'd had ample warning of what would happen if they didn't leave our ships and our coast in peace. My father was a very pragmatic man, burning their city didn't seem to concern him greatly.'

'He didn't tell you why he sent you here, did he?'

Nortah shook his head. The hour was growing late and the glow of the fire shone brightly in his eyes, his handsome face sombre in shadow. 'He said I was his son and it was his wish that I join the Sixth Order. I remember he had argued with my mother the night before, which was strange because they never argued, in fact they rarely spoke at all. In the morning she wasn't at breakfast and I wasn't allowed to say good-bye when the cart came for me. I haven't seen her since.'

They lapsed into silence, Vaelin's line of thought leading him to questions he felt were best unasked.

'I know what you're thinking,' Nortah said.

'I wasn't thinking . . .'

'Yes you were. And you're right. My father sent me to the Order because you were sent here by *your* father. I told you they were rivals but I didn't tell you all of it. My father hated the Battle Lord, loathed him. For a while it seemed all he could talk about was how his position was constantly undermined by a gutter-born butcher. It irked him greatly that your father was so popular with the people, a thing my father could never achieve. He wasn't one of them, he was highborn, but your father was a commoner, risen to greatness on his own merits. When he sent you here it was a great symbol of devotion to the Faith and the Realm, a public sacrifice that could only be matched one way.'

'I'm sorry . . .'

'Don't apologise. You are as much a victim of your father as I am of mine. It took me years to reckon it, why he had done it, one day it just popped into my head. He gave me up to better his position at court.' He gave a wry, humourless smile. 'Our dear King, it seems, cared little for his gesture.'

I am not my father's victim, Vaelin thought. *My mother sent me here, to protect me*. He left the thought unsaid, suspecting Nortah would find it difficult to accept.

'It's ironic don't you think?' Nortah asked after a moment. 'If we'd never been given to the Order, most likely we'd have become enemies, like our fathers. And our sons would have been enemies, maybe even their sons, and on and on it would have gone. At least this way it ends before it could begin.'

'You sound almost content to be in the Order.'

'Content? No, just accepting. This is my life now. Who can say what the future will bring?'

Scratch yawned, his teeth gleaming in the firelight, then moved to Vaelin's side, snuggling close before settling down to sleep. Vaelin patted his flank and lay back on his bedroll, looking for shapes in the vast array of stars above and waiting for sleep to claim him.

'I . . . feel I owe you a debt, brother,' Nortah said.

'A debt?'

'For my life.'

Vaelin realised Nortah was trying to thank him, in the only way Nortah could thank anyone. Not for the first time he wondered what kind of man Nortah would have been had his father not sent him here. A future First Minister? A Sword of the Realm? Battle Lord even? But he doubted he would have been the kind of man who gave his son away just to better his rival.

'I don't know what the future will bring,' he told his brother eventually. 'But I suspect you'll have many chances to repay the debt.'

It was a curious fact of life in the Order that the older they got the harder their training became. It seemed their skills had to be raised ever higher, honed like a sword blade. And so as autumn became winter their sword practice doubled, then tripled until it seemed it was all they did. Master Sollis became their only master, the others now distant figures preoccupied with younger charges. The sword became their life. Why was no mystery. Next year would bring the Test of the Sword, when they would face three condemned men, sword in hand, and triumph or die.

Sword practice began after the seventh hour and continued for the rest of the day with a brief interlude for food and the relief of a short reacquaintance with the bow or their horses. In the morning Master Sollis would show them a sword scale, flashing through the dance of thrusts, parries and strokes in the space of a few heartbeats before commanding them to copy it. Failure to repeat the scale exactly earned a full-pelt run around the practice ground. Afternoons saw them swap their swords for wooden replicas and assail each other in contests that left them all with an increasingly spectacular collection of bruises.

Vaelin knew himself to be the best swordsman among them. Dentos was master of the bow, Barkus unarmed combat, Nortah the finest rider and Caenis knew the wild like a wolf, but the sword was his. He could never explain the feeling it gave him, the sense that the blade was part of him, an extension of his arm, his closeness to it accentuating his perception in combat, reading an opponent's moves before they were made, parrying blows that would have felled another, finding a way past defences that should have baffled him. It wasn't long before Master Sollis stopped matching him against the others.

'You'll fight me from now on,' he told Vaelin as they faced each other, wooden swords ready.

'An honour, Master,' Vaelin said.

Sollis's sword cracked against his wrist, the wooden blade flying from his grasp. Vaelin tried to step backwards but Sollis was too fast, the shaft of ash thudding into his midriff, forcing the air from his lungs as he collapsed to the ground.

'You should always respect an opponent,' Sollis was telling the others as Vaelin fought to contain his rising gorge. 'But not too much.'

With winter came Frentis's Test of the Wild and they gathered in the courtyard to see him off with a few choice words of advice.

'Stay out of caves,' said Nortah.

'Kill and eat everything you can find,' Caenis told him.

'Don't lose your flint,' Dentos advised.

'If there's a storm,' Vaelin said, 'stay in your shelter and don't listen to the wind.'

Only Barkus had nothing to say. Finding Jennis's body during his own test was still a raw memory and he confined his farewell to a soft pat on Frentis's shoulder.

'Lookin' forward to it, I am,' Frentis told them brightly, hefting his pack. 'Five days outside the walls. No practice, no canings. Can't wait.'

'Five days of cold and hunger,' Nortah reminded him.

Frentis shrugged. 'Been hungry before. Cold too. Reckon I'll get used to it again quick enough.'

Vaelin was struck by how strong Frentis had become in the two years since his joining. He was now almost as tall as Caenis and his shoulders seemed to grow broader by the day. Added to the change in his body was the change in his character, the whine that coloured his speech as a boy had mostly disappeared and he approached every challenge with a blind confidence in his own abilities. It was no surprise that he had emerged as leader of his group, although his reaction to criticism was often instant anger and occasional violence.

They watched him climb into the cart with the other boys. Master Hutril snapped the reins and steered the cart through the gate, Frentis waving, with a broad grin on his face.

'He'll make it,' Caenis assured Vaelin.

'Too right he will,' Dentos said. 'He's the type that comes back fatter than when he went out.'

The days passed slowly as they practised and nursed their bruises, Vaelin's concern for Frentis growing with every dawn. Four days after the boy's departure it had begun to dominate his thoughts, dulling his sword skills and leaving him with livid bruises he barely noticed. He couldn't shake the nagging knowledge that something was *wrong*. It was a familiar feeling by now, a shadow on his thoughts he had grown to trust, but stronger now, nagging, persistent, like a tune he couldn't quite remember.

When the fifth day passed he found himself hovering near the gates, clutching his cloak about him as he searched the gathering dark for sign of the cart bringing Frentis back to the safety of the Order House.

'What are we doing here?' Nortah asked, his face for once made ugly by the pinching chill of a winter's night. The others were back in their tower room. Today's practice had been hard, harder even than they were used to, and they had cuts to tend before the evening meal.

'I'm waiting for Frentis,' Vaelin replied. 'Go inside if you're cold.'

'Didn't say I was cold,' Nortah muttered but stayed put.

Finally, as the clear winter sky darkened to reveal its stars, the cart came into view, Master Hutril guiding it towards the gate, bearing four charges, three less than had left with him five days before. Vaelin knew even before the drays' shoes clattered on the courtyard cobbles that Frentis was not among them.

'Where is he?' he demanded of Master Hutril as he reined in.

Master Hutril ignored the discourtesy and gave Vaelin a rigidly neutral glance. 'Wasn't there,' he said, climbing down from the cart. 'Need to see the Aspect. Stay here.' With that he stomped off towards the Aspect's chambers. Vaelin managed to wait a full ten seconds before hastening after him.

Master Hutril was in the Aspect's rooms for several long minutes before he emerged, walking past Vaelin without a glance, ignoring his questions. The Aspect's door remained firmly closed and Vaelin found himself stepping forward to knock.

'No!' Nortah's hand was on his wrist. 'Are you mad?'

'I need to know.'

'You have to wait.'

'Wait for what? Silence? No sign that he had ever been here? Like Mikehl or Jennis? Light a fire, say some words and it's another one of us gone, forgotten.'

'The Test of the Wild is hard, brother . . .'

'Not for him! For him it was nothing . . .'

'You don't know that. You don't know what could have happened beyond the walls.'

'I know hunger and cold would never have laid him low. He was too strong.'

'For all his strength he was but a boy. As we were when they sent us out into the cold and the dark to fend for ourselves.'

Vaelin tore his wrist away, smoothing his hands through his hair in frustration. 'I don't think he was ever a boy.'

The sound of boots on stone snapped their attention to the corridor, seeing Master Sollis striding towards them. 'What are you two doing here?' he demanded, halting before the Aspect's door.

'Waiting for news of our brother, Master,' Vaelin replied evenly.

Sollis showed a brief spasm of anger before he reached for the door handle. 'Then wait.' With that he went inside.

It was only five minutes or so but seemed like an hour. Abruptly the door opened and Master Sollis jerked his head indicating leave to enter. They found the Aspect behind his desk, his long face as inexpressive as ever but there was a calculation in the gaze he levelled at Vaelin, as if what was about to transpire had more import than he could know.

'Brother Vaelin,' he said. 'Do you know if Brother Frentis has any enemies outside these walls?'

Enemies . . . Vaelin felt his heart plummet. *He found him. I couldn't protect him.* 'There is a man, Aspect,' he replied, his tone heavy with sorrow. 'The leader of Varinshold's criminal fraternity. Before Brother Frentis joined us he put a knife in his eye. I have heard that he still bears a grudge.'

Master Sollis gave a snort of exasperation and Nortah, for once, appeared lost for words.

'And it didn't occur to you,' the Aspect said, 'to share this information with myself or Master Sollis?'

Vaelin could only shake his head in numb silence.

'You arrogant idiot,' Master Sollis said, very precisely.

'Yes, Master.'

'What's done is done,' the Aspect said. 'Do you have any notion of where this man with one eye might take our brother?'

Vaelin's head snapped up. 'He's alive?'

'Master Hutril found a body, but it wasn't Brother Frentis, although the unfortunate fellow had one of our Order's hunting knives buried in his chest. There were signs of a fierce struggle, several blood trails, but no Brother Frentis.'

Somehow they knew he was here. So stupid to think One Eye's servants wouldn't find him. They must have followed the cart, taken him alive. The words of Gallis the Climber came back to him: *One Eye says he's gonna take a year to skin him alive when he finds him . . .*

'I will recover him,' he told the Aspect, his voice cold with certainty. 'I will kill those who took him and bring him back to the Order. Living or dead.'

The Aspect's eyes flicked to Master Sollis.

'What do you need?' Sollis asked.

'Half a day outside the walls, my brothers, and my dog.'

Scratch seemed to know what was expected of him, sniffing the sock they had found under Frentis's bunk and immediately sprinting off with a brief yelp. Vaelin had led him to the road leading to Varinshold's north gate before producing the sock, the slave-hound's evident joy at finding himself beyond the confines of the Order House muted by their grim mood. They ran after him, labouring to keep him in sight, the slave-hound setting a killing pace as he traced a winding route away from the road and towards the banks of the Brinewash. Vaelin found him pawing uncertainly at a patch of mud near some shallows, a plaintive whine coming from his throat as he pointed his nose at something lying in the river. Vaelin's heart plummeted at the sight of the body, facedown and covered with a blue cloak.

He jumped into the shallows and waded towards it, his brothers soon joining him to pull the body onto its back.

'Who's this bugger?' Dentos asked.

The dead man was short, only a little taller than Frentis, with a pock-marked face and a recent cut on his cheek.

'He's drained,' Nortah observed, noting the man's pallor and ripping open his shirt to reveal a stab wound to the lower belly. 'Our little brother's work perhaps.'

Vaelin pulled the cloak from the corpse and they searched it for any clue as to Frentis's whereabouts, finding nothing save some sodden pipe leaf.

'I make it five horses,' Caenis said, crouching to examine the tracks in the mud at the water's edge. 'He fell from his mount when they forded so they took anything of value and left him to bleed.'

'And I thought outlaws were such admirable folk,' Nortah commented.

'Brother,' Barkus said, nudging Vaelin and pointing to where Scratch was busily sniffing the grass on the bank. After a moment the slave-hound raised his head and bounded off, following the line of the river as they ran in pursuit. He paused again a few hundred paces short of the city walls, circling around some deep, parallel tracks ploughed into the earth.

'Cart wheels,' Caenis said. 'They hid him in a cart to get him through the gate.'

Scratch was already off again, making for the north gate. The city guards waved them through with puzzled expressions but no words. The Order was never to be questioned. It was no surprise to Vaelin when Scratch soon led them to the southern quarter.

The streets were mostly deserted save for the usual assortment of drunks and whores, most of whom found somewhere else to be when they saw five brothers from the Sixth Order running behind a very large dog. Eventually, Scratch stopped, standing tensed and still as he did when he was pointing out a trail when they hunted together. His nose pointed directly at a tavern nestled in a shadowed alleyway. The sign hanging over the door marked it as the Black Boar. Lamplight glowed dimly through the windows and they could hear the raucous babble of liquor-induced merriment.

Scratch began to growl, a soft but chilling rumble.

Vaelin knelt, patting him gently on the head. 'Stay,' he commanded.

The hound gave a plaintive whine as they moved towards the inn but did as he was told.

'What's the plan?' Dentos asked as they paused at the doorway.

'I thought I'd ask them where Frentis is,' Vaelin replied. 'After that I expect we'll find out if we're as well taught as we think we are.'

The vocal good humour of the inn's patrons died instantly at the sight of them. A room of mostly unwashed and prematurely aged faces stared at them with a mixture of fear and palpable hatred. The man behind the bar was large, bald and clearly less than happy to see them.

'Good evening, sir!' Nortah greeted him, striding towards the bar. 'A fine establishment you have here.'

'Order ain't welcome 'ere,' the barman said. Vaelin noted the thin sheen of sweat on his top lip. 'Ain't right you comin' in 'ere. 'Snot your place.'

'Oh don't fret, my fine fellow.' Nortah clapped the man on the shoulder. 'We want no trouble. All we want is our brother. The one who stuck a knife in your master's eye a few years ago. Be a good fellow and tell us where he is, and we won't kill you or any of your customers.'

A rumble of anger ran through the crowd and the barman licked his lips, his bald head now shining with sweat. For the briefest second his eyes flicked to his right before snapping back to Nortah. 'No brothers here,' he said.

Nortah gave one of his best smiles. 'Oh I beg to differ. Tell me, did you know a man can live for several hours, in agonising pain of course, after his stomach has been slit open?'

Vaelin followed the line of the barman's brief glance, seeing little but the shuffling feet of nervous patrons and a dusty floor, except for a clean patch near the fireplace, a patch about a yard square. As he moved forward to take a closer look a man rose from a table, a muscular man with the broad knuckles and indented nose common to prizefighters.

'Where're d'you think you're go—'

Vaelin punched him in the throat without breaking stride, leaving him choking on the dusty floorboards. There was a cacophony of scraping chairs as other patrons rose, a murmur of anger building in the crowd. Vaelin crouched to inspect the patch of dust-free floorboards, which quickly revealed itself as a trapdoor. *Well made,* he judged, his fingers tracing the joins.

'Got no right here!' the barman was shouting as he straightened. 'Comin' in here hittin' customers, makin' threats. Ain't right.'

There was a loud growl of assent from the inn's patrons, most now on their feet, many holding a variety of knives and cudgels.

'Order bastards,' one of them spat, brandishing a broad-bladed knife. 'Ventured where you shouldn't. Need cutting down to size.'

Nortah's sword came free of its scabbard in a blur, the man with the knife staring at his severed fingers as the blade clattered to the floor.

'No need for that kind of language, sir,' Nortah cautioned him sternly.

The rest of the crowd drew back a little and silence stretched, broken only by the knife-man's keening over his mutilated hand and the rasping chokes of the prizefighter Vaelin had punched. *They're afraid,* Vaelin decided, scanning the faces in the crowd. *But not scared enough to run. Numbers give them strength.*

He put his fingers to his mouth and whistled, once, sharp and loud. He had expected Scratch to use the door but the slave-hound apparently saw little obstacle in the window. Shattered glass exploded across the inn, the dark bulk of snarling muscle landing in the centre of the room, snapping viciously at any patrons unfortunate enough to be close by.

The inn emptied in a few seconds save for the two injured patrons and the barman, clutching a hefty cudgel, his chest heaving with fear.

'Why're you still here?' Dentos asked him.

'If I run without fightin', he'll kill me,' the bald man replied.

'One Eye'll be dead by morning,' Vaelin assured him. 'Get out of here.'

The barman gave them a last nervous glance before dropping his cudgel and running for the back door.

'Barkus,' Vaelin said. 'Help me with this.'

They jammed their hunting knives into the join between the floor and the trapdoor and levered it open. The hole it revealed went straight down into a dimly lit cellar. Vaelin could see firelight flickering on the stone floor about ten feet below. He stepped back, drawing his sword and preparing to jump. Scratch, however, had picked up a fresh trail and saw little reason to linger. He flashed past Vaelin and disappeared into the hole. After a second or two the mingled sound of shock, pain and Scratch's roaring growls left them in no doubt he had found some enemies.

'Think he'll save any for us?' Barkus asked, wincing.

Vaelin jumped into the hole, landing and rolling on the stone floor, coming to his feet with his sword levelled. His brothers followed him in quick succession. The cellar was large, at least twenty feet across, with torches set into the walls and a tunnel leading off to the right. There were two bodies in the cellar, both large men with their throats torn out. Scratch was sitting atop one of them, licking a bloodied snout. Seeing Vaelin, he yelped briefly and disappeared into the tunnel.

'He's still got the scent.' Vaelin lifted a torch from the wall and chased after the slave-hound.

The tunnel seemed to go on forever, though in truth it could only have taken a few minutes of racing after Scratch before they emerged into a large, vaulted chamber. It was clearly an old structure, finely pointed brickwork arching up on all sides to meet in an elegant ceiling high above. A terrace of tiled steps led down to a flat, circular area in which was placed a large oak-wood dining table decorated with a mismatched variety of gold and silver ware. There were six men seated at the table, playing cards in their hands and a scattering of coins between them. They stared at Vaelin and Scratch in stark amazement.

'Who in the name of the Faith are you?' one of them demanded, a tall man with a cadaverous face. Vaelin noted the loaded crossbow resting on the chair next to him. The other five men all had swords or axes within easy reach.

'Where is my brother?' Vaelin demanded.

The man who had spoken flicked his eyes from Vaelin to Scratch, taking note of the blood on his jaws, then blanching visibly as Barkus and the others emerged from the tunnel behind Vaelin.

'You're in the wrong place, brother,' the tall man said, Vaelin admiring the effort he put into keeping the tremble from his voice. 'One Eye doesn't take kindly to—' His hand flashed towards the crossbow. Scratch was a blur of muscle and teeth, leaping the table and fastening his jaws on the tall man's throat, the crossbow sending its bolt towards the ceiling. The other five men were on their feet, clutching their weapons, showing fear but no sign of fleeing. Vaelin saw little point in any further talk.

The burly man he charged attempted to feint to the left and bring his axe up under Vaelin's guard but was far too slow, the sword point taking him in the neck before he could begin his swing. Impaled on the blade he goggled, eyes bulging, blood seeping from his mouth. Vaelin withdrew his blade, letting him collapse to the floor, twitching.

He turned, finding that his brothers had already dispatched the other four. Barkus, grim-faced, was wiping his sword blade on the jerkin of the man he had killed, a pool of thick blood spreading over the tiles. Dentos knelt to pluck a throwing knife from the sternum of his enemy, Vaelin thought he may have been blinking away tears. Nortah was staring down at the man he had killed, blood dripping from his lowered sword, his face a frozen mask. Only Caenis appeared unaffected, flicking the blood from his sword and kicking the corpse at his feet to make sure he was dead. Vaelin knew that Caenis had killed before but still found his brother's coolness disconcerting. *Am I not the only true killer among us after all?* he wondered.

Scratch gave the tall man's neck a final twist, snapping the spine with a loud crack. Releasing the corpse, he trotted around the chamber, his nose twitching as he searched for Frentis's scent.

'This is an interesting structure,' Caenis observed, moving to one of the columns that stretched up to the vaulted ceiling and smoothing his palm over the brickwork. 'Fine, very fine. You don't see craftsmanship like that in the city these days. This is a very old place.'

'Thought it was part of the sewers,' Dentos said. His back was turned to the man he had killed and he stood with his arms tightly crossed, shivering as if chilled.

'Oh no,' Caenis responded. 'This is something else, I'm sure. See the motif here.' He pointed out a strange stone carving set into the brickwork. 'A book and a quill. An ancient emblem of the Faith signifying the Third Order, a sigil long out of use. This place dates from the earliest years of the city, when the Faith was still newborn.'

Vaelin's attention was mostly fixed on Scratch but he found himself drawn by Caenis's words. Looking around the chamber, he noted there were seven columns rising to the ceiling, each with a carved emblem set into the base. 'Once there were seven,' he murmured.

'Of course!' Caenis enthused, moving around the chamber to inspect each of the columns. 'Seven columns. This is proof, brother. Once there were seven.'

'What are you wittering about?' Nortah demanded, some colour returning to his cheeks. In contrast to Dentos he appeared unable to look away from the body of his slain enemy, his sword still bloody.

'Seven columns,' Caenis replied. 'Seven Orders. This is an ancient temple of the Faith.' He stopped beside a column to peer at the emblem it bore. 'A snake and a goblet. I'd wager this is the emblem of the Seventh Order.'

'Seventh Order?' Nortah finally looked up from the corpse. 'There is no Seventh Order.'

'Not now, no,' Caenis explained. 'But once . . .'

'A tale for another day, brother,' Vaelin told him. He turned to Nortah. 'Your blade'll rust if you don't clean it.'

Barkus was examining the riches piled on the table, running his hands over the gold and silver. 'Good stuff here,' he said in admiration. 'Would've brought a sack if I'd known.'

'Wonder where they got it all,' Dentos said, hefting an ornately engraved silver plate.

'They stole it,' Vaelin said. 'Take what you want but don't let it weigh you down.'

Scratch gave a short yelp, his nose pointed at a solid section of wall to Vaelin's left. Barkus moved to examine the wall, thumping his fist against the bricks a few times. 'Just a wall.'

Scratch scampered over and sniffed at the base of the wall, his paws chipping away at the mortar.

'A hidden doorway perhaps.' Caenis came over to run his hands over the wall's edges. 'Could be a catch or a lever somewhere.'

Vaelin pulled the axe from the limp hand of the man he had killed and walked over to smash it into the wall. He kept hacking until a hole appeared in the brickwork. Scratch yelped again but Vaelin didn't need the hound's senses to tell him what lay on the other side, he could smell it plain enough himself: sweet, sickening, corrupt.

He exchanged glances with Caenis, finding sympathy in his friend's eyes.

Frentis . . . Wanna be a brother . . . Wanna be like you . . .

He redoubled his efforts with the axe, bricks and mortar exploding in a cloud of red and grey dust. His brothers joined in with what tools they could find, Barkus using a hatchet taken from an enemy, Dentos a broken chair leg. Soon, enough of the wall was gone to allow them to enter.

The chamber beyond was long and narrow, torches set into the walls provided light enough to illuminate a scene from a nightmare.

'Faith!' Barkus exclaimed in shock.

The corpse hung from the roof, its ankles chained and arms secured with a leather strap across the chest. It had clearly been hanging for several days, greying flesh loosened and sagging from the bones. The gaping wound in the neck showed how the man had died. Placed beneath him was a bowl, black with dried blood. There were five more bodies hanging in the chamber, each with their throats cut and a bowl placed beneath. They swayed slightly in the draught from the demolished wall. The stench was overpowering. Scratch wrinkled his nose at the corruption staining the air and kept close to the wall, as far from the bodies as possible. Dentos found a corner to throw up in. Vaelin fought the desire to follow suit and moved from body to body, forcing himself to check each face, finding only strangers.

'What is this?' Barkus said in sick wonderment. 'You said this man was just an outlaw.'

'He appears to be an outlaw of considerable ambition,' Nortah observed.

'This isn't about thievery,' Caenis said softly, taking a closer look at one of the hanging corpses. 'This is . . . something else.' He looked down at the blood black bowl on the floor. 'Something else entirely.'

'What would . . . ?' Nortah began but Vaelin held up a hand to silence him.

'Listen!' he hissed.

It was faint, an odd sound, a man's voice, chanting. The words were indistinct, alien. Vaelin followed the sound to an alcove, where he found a door, slightly ajar. Sword held low, he eased the door open with the toe of his boot. Beyond was another chamber, this one roughly hewn from rock, bathed in the red glare of firelight, deep shadows flickering over a sight that made him stifle a shout of shock.

Frentis had been tied to a wooden frame in front of a roaring open fire. A gag was firmly secured in his mouth. He was naked, his torso marked by many cuts forming a strange pattern on the skin, blood flowing freely down his body. His eyes were wide open, alive with agony. At the sight of Vaelin, they widened further.

Next to Frentis was a man with a knife, bare-chested, his

strength evident in the knotted muscle of his arms and the hard, angular lines of his face, a face with only one eye. The empty socket had been filled with a smooth black stone, reflecting a single red point of firelight as he turned to Vaelin. 'Ah,' he said. 'And you must be the mentor.'

Vaelin had never truly wanted to kill before, never felt a real bloodlust. But now it raged in him, a song of fury blinding his reason. His fist tightened on his sword hilt as he stepped forward into a charge . . .

He never knew what happened, never truly understood the paralysis that seized his limbs, only that he found himself sprawled on the floor, his lungs suddenly empty of air, his sword clattering from his grasp. His hands and feet felt like ice. He tried to stand but could find no purchase on the floor, flailing like a senseless drunk as the one-eyed man moved away from Frentis, his knife a bloodstained yellow tooth in the fire's glow.

'Ho there!' Barkus shouted, charging along with the others. 'Time to die, One Eye!'

The one-eyed man raised his hand, an almost careless gesture, and a curtain of fire rose in front of Vaelin's brothers, sending them reeling back. The fire-wall spanned the chamber, rising from floor to ceiling, an unbroken barrier of swirling flame.

'I like fire,' the one-eyed man said, turning his angular face back to Vaelin. 'The way it dances, quite beautiful don't you think?'

Vaelin tried to reach inside his cloak for his hunting knife but found all his hand would do was shake uncontrollably.

'You're strong,' the one-eyed man observed. 'Usually they can't move at all.' He glanced over at Frentis, wide-eyed, blood streaming from his cuts, his naked form straining against his bonds with all his strength.

'You came here for him,' the one-eyed man continued. 'You're the one he said would come to kill me. Al Sorna, Blackhawk fighter, assassin killer, Battle Lord spawn. I've heard of you. Have you heard of me?' He gave a mirthless smile.

Vaelin found to his surprise he could still spit. It landed on the one-eyed man's boots.

The smile disappeared. 'I see you have. What did you hear I wonder? That I was an outlaw? An overlord of outlaws? True of course, but only in part. No doubt you had to kill several of my employees to get this far. Didn't you wonder why they wouldn't run? Why they were more afraid of me than you?'

The one-eyed man crouched, his face close to Vaelin's, hissing, 'You come here with your sword and your brothers and your dog, and you have no idea of your utter insignificance.'

He turned his face, displaying the black stone in his eye socket. 'You would be forgiven for thinking this a curse. But it was a gift, a wondrous gift for which I should thank your young brother. Oh, the power he gave me, power enough to set myself up over all the scum of this city. I have made myself a king of thieves and cut-throats, I've eaten off silver plates and slaked my lust on the finest whores. I have everything a man could want, but yet I find there is one thing I can't forget, one thing that troubles my sleep . . .' He rose and moved towards Frentis. 'The pain of a gutter-born whelp putting a knife through my eye.'

Frentis writhed in his bonds, his gagged face distorted with rage and hate. Vaelin could hear the muffled obscenities he attempted to spit through the gag.

'He wouldn't talk, you know,' the one-eyed man told Vaelin over his shoulder. 'You should be proud of him. Refused to share your Order's secrets, although now you're here in person I daresay my questions will be answered in full.' He placed the knife against Frentis's chest, pushing the point half an inch into the flesh and tracing a cut from the breast to the rib cage. Frentis's teeth were white on his gag as he screamed.

Vaelin tried to gather his arms under him, manoeuvring the ice-numb limbs beneath his chest, then trying to heave himself upright.

'Oh don't bother,' the one-eyed man said, turning back from Frentis, bloodied knife in hand. 'You're tightly bound I assure you.'

Teeth gritted, Vaelin managed to push himself off the stone floor, his entire body shaking with the effort.

'Strong indeed!' the one-eyed man said. 'But I can't have that.'

The same icy numbness seized him again, flooding his arms and legs, spreading into his chest and groin, forcing him back to the floor, exhausted.

'You feel my power?' The one-eyed man stood over him. 'At first it frightened me, even one such as I can feel the chill of looking into an abyss, but fear fades.' He held up the knife stained with Frentis's blood. 'I have the secret now. The knowledge to make myself immune to all enemies.' He placed a finger on the knife blade, drawing a bead of blood from the metal and placing it in his mouth. 'Who could have thought it would be so simple? To be a king amongst outlaws requires the spilling of much blood. These past years I have bathed in it as I sought victims to sate my anger against your young brother here. And as I bathed I found my power growing so that now, even one as strong as you cannot stand against my will. I was told your destiny lay elsewh—'

Caenis leapt through the wall of fire, his sword held high in a two-fisted grip. He brought it down as his feet touched the floor, the blade cleaving the one-eyed man from shoulder to sternum. The look on his face as he stood impaled on the sword was one of complete astonishment.

'Fire without heat,' Caenis said. 'Isn't fire at all.'

Vaelin's paralysis faded as the one-eyed man's corpse slipped to the floor, the fire-wall he had raised vanishing in an instant.

Vaelin felt hands lifting him, his limbs still shaking with lingering numbness. Barkus and Nortah cut Frentis's bonds and took the gag from his mouth. Free of his ties, the boy went wild, screaming hate-filled curses at the one-eyed man's inert form, taking up his knife and plunging it again and again into the body.

'You stinking bastard!' he screamed. 'Think you can cut me, you fucking filth!'

Vaelin waved the others back and let Frentis abuse the corpse until he collapsed from the effort, slumped over the body, bloody and exhausted.

'Brother,' he said, placing his cloak over Frentis's shoulders. 'Your wounds need attention.'

CHAPTER EIGHT

'Sister Sherin is still in the south,' Brother Sellin told Vaelin at the gate of the Fifth Order, his eyes flicking to Frentis, hanging bloody and unconscious between Barkus and Nortah. 'Master Harin has undertaken her duties. Come, brothers.' He opened the gate wide, beckoning them to enter. 'I will take you to him.'

Master Harin spent over an hour stitching and dressing the cuts on Frentis's body, ordering them from the treatment room when their unasked-for advice and constant questions became too irksome. Vaelin found Aspect Elera waiting in the corridor.

'I can see your day has been hard, brothers,' she said. 'There is food waiting for you in our dining hall.'

They ate in silence, their conversation stilled by the presence of so many members of the Fifth Order. The healers stared at the blue-robed, grim-faced interlopers, a few familiar faces offering greetings to Vaelin, receiving only a curt nod in response. Their table was piled high with food but Vaelin found he had no appetite. His hands retained a slight tremble from whatever the one-eyed man had done to him and the vision of Frentis tied and bleeding was still at the forefront of his thoughts.

Aspect Elera joined them an hour or so later. 'Master Harin tells me your brother will recover. He will have to stay with us for several days whilst he heals.'

'Is he awake, Aspect?' Vaelin asked her.

'Master Harin gave him a sleeping draught. He should wake in the morning. You can see him then.'

'My thanks, Aspect. May I request that word be sent to our Order? Aspect Arlyn will be expecting my report.'

She sent Brother Sellin to the House of the Sixth Order and gave them a room in the east wing. Vaelin insisted on sitting with Frentis, and Caenis waited with him whilst the others slept, cleaning his weapons to pass the time, laying his sword and knives out on the floor, metal gleaming in the candlelight as he ran cloth over each blade with meticulous care. Scratch had been confined to an empty pen in the stables. He ignored the food he had been given and howled continually, his plaintive cries reaching them through the walls.

Vaelin studied the long-bladed dagger he had taken from Frentis, the blade the one-eyed man had used to cut the web of scars into his body. It was Caenis's by right but he had refused to take it with a grimace of distaste. Vaelin decided to keep it on impulse, it was a finely made weapon of unfamiliar design, the blade well tempered and the handle elegantly fashioned with a silver pommel. The guard bore writing with unfamiliar letters. Clearly it was a weapon from across the sea. One Eye had a long reach it seemed.

'The fire was an illusion,' Vaelin said. His voice sounded listless and dull to his ears, reminding him of Brother Makril and his jaded tales of fire and slaughter.

Caenis glanced up from his weapons and nodded, his hands continuing to guide the cloth over the blades.

'The Dark,' Vaelin said. 'The blood, it gave him power. That's what the bodies were for.'

Caenis didn't look up but nodded once more, still cleaning his blades.

Vaelin felt the tremor return to his hands, his anger flaring at the memory of his helplessness before the one-eyed man. A helplessness not shared by Caenis. Caenis could leap through Dark-born fire and hack down the man who called it forth. *You know so much more than you tell me, brother,* Vaelin realised. *It's always been this way.* 'There are no secrets between us,' he said.

Caenis's hand paused in midstroke as he worked a cloth over his sword blade. His eyes met Vaelin's and for the briefest second there was something there, something different from the affection or respect he normally saw in his friend's eyes, something almost resentful.

The door opened and Master Sollis entered with Aspect Elera. 'You two should be resting,' he said shortly, moving to the bed to check on Frentis, his eyes tracing over the bloodstained bandages covering his chest and arms. 'Will he scar, Aspect?'

'The cuts were deep. Master Harin is skilled but . . .' She spread her hands. 'There is only so much we can do. Luckily his muscles are intact. He will be strong again soon.'

'The man who did this is dead?' Sollis asked Vaelin.

'Yes, Master.' Vaelin gestured at Caenis. 'My brother's stroke.'

Sollis glanced at Caenis. 'The man was skilled?'

'His skills were not with weapons, Master.' Caenis glanced uncertainly at Aspect Elera.

'Talk freely,' Sollis instructed him.

He told Master Sollis all that had transpired since their departure from the Order House, from the Black Boar Inn to their confrontation with the one-eyed man beneath the city. 'The man had knowledge of the Dark, Master. He could call up an illusion of fire and he bound Brother Vaelin by his will alone.'

'But not you?' Sollis asked with a raised eyebrow.

'No. I expect I surprised him by seeing through his illusion.'

'You made sure of the kill?'

'He's dead, Master,' Vaelin assured him.

Master Sollis and Aspect Elera shared a brief glance.

'I hear that the Aspect had been gracious enough to provide you with a room,' Sollis said, turning back to Frentis. 'She would feel insulted if you failed to use it.'

Recognising their dismissal, they rose and moved to the door. 'Tell no-one else of this,' Master Sollis ordered before they left. 'And do something to shut that bloody dog up!'

In the morning Master Sollis questioned them closely about the route to One Eye's chambers and the ancient temple to the Faith they had found. Vaelin offered to guide him but received only a stern refusal. When he was satisfied with their directions Sollis told them to return to the Order House.

'Brother Frentis . . .' Vaelin began.

'Will heal just as well with you at your training where you belong. The Test of the Sword is but eight weeks away and none of you are ready yet.'

They trudged back to the Order House without Master Sollis, who had given them another warning to keep silent before he went off to investigate their findings. Scratch had whined in protest when they led him away from the House of the Fifth Order, needing much reassurance from Vaelin before following their steps.

To Vaelin their tower room seemed to have shrunk in their absence. A night of fear and mystery made it feel so small, a child's room, even though it had been a long time since he felt like a child. He stowed his gear and lay back on his narrow bed, closing his eyes to see again the one-eyed man's wall of flame and Frentis's

314 · ANTHONY RYAN

tortured form. *I believed I had learned so much,* he thought. *But I know nothing.*

The boys from Frentis's group came asking questions but Vaelin followed Master Sollis's instructions and told them he had been attacked by a mountain lion during his Test of the Wild. He was recovering in the House of the Fifth Order and would return within a few days. Sollis himself said nothing about his investigations on return to the Order and the Aspect did not request their presence. Frentis's abduction was another non-event in the Order's history. *The Order fights, but often it fights in shadow.* As he grew older Vaelin found ever more truth in Master Sollis's words.

Frentis himself said nothing of the incident on his return, resuming his training with a disturbing vigour, as if rejecting the damage One Eye had done to him by ignoring the pain his exertions cost him. His demeanour had changed also; he was less apt to smile, and where he had been talkative before, now he was largely silent. His temper too had grown shorter and the masters had to drag him out of several fights. Even the other boys in his group seemed wary of him. Only with Scratch and Vaelin did he regain some vestige of his old self, taking an energetic part in training the now-grown pups. However, even then he continued to say nothing of his ordeal, although Vaelin sometimes caught him running his fingers over the pattern of scars carved into his skin, his face oddly thoughtful, as if trying to decipher their meaning.

'Do they hurt?' Vaelin asked him one Eltrian evening. The pups were tired from a day spent tracking with Master Hutril and could only snap lazily at the treats they tossed into their pens.

Frentis quickly pulled his hand away from his shirt. 'A little. Less and less as the weeks pass. Aspect Elera gave me a balm for 'em, helps a bit.'

'It was my fault . . .'

'Forget it.'

'If I had told the Aspect . . .'

'I said forget it!' Frentis's face was tense as he stared into the pens. Slasher, his favourite pup, sensed his mood and came over to lick at his hand, whining in concern. 'He's dead,' Frentis said, calmer now. 'And I'm not. So forget it. Can't kill him twice.'

They walked back to the keep together, cloaks wrapped against the chill although winter was fading fast and the surrounding trees were quickly taking on the verdant hues of spring.

'Test of the Sword next month,' Frentis said. 'Worried?'

'Why? Do you think I should be?'

'I've already bet my whole knife collection that you finish all three in less than two minutes. I meant what happens after. They'll send you away, right?'

'I expect so.'

'Think they'll let us serve together when I'm confirmed? I'd like that.'

'So would I. But I don't think we get a choice. It'll be a good while before we see one another again, that's for sure.'

They lingered at the courtyard, Vaelin sensing Frenfis had more to say. 'I . . .' he began then stopped, fidgeting uncomfortably. 'I'm glad you spoke for me, when I came here,' he said after a moment. 'I'm glad I'm in the Order. I feel like I was meant to be here. So you shouldn't feel bad about anything that happens to me, right? Whatever happens from now on, you don't have to feel bad and you don't have to come running when I'm in trouble.'

'Wouldn't you come running if I was in trouble?'

'That's different.'

'No, it's exactly the same.' He clapped Frentis on the shoulder. 'Get some rest, brother.'

He had taken a few steps when Frentis said something to make him stop, his voice barely above a whisper. 'The One Who Waits will destroy us.'

He turned to find Frentis hunched in his cloak, arms folded tightly against his chest, face wary. He wouldn't meet Vaelin's eye.

'What?' Vaelin asked.

'He told me.' Frentis winced, as if pained, and Vaelin knew he was reliving his torture at One Eye's hands. 'He got angry when I wouldn't tell him what he wanted to know. Kept asking about the tests, the skills we're taught here. Seemed to think we get taught how to practise the Dark. Stupid bastard. Wasn't going to tell him anything though. So he cut me some more, then he said, "The One Who Waits will destroy your precious Order, boy."'

The One Who Waits . . . 'Did he tell you want it meant?'

'I passed out when he started cutting me again. He'd only just managed to bring me round when you turned up.'

'Did you tell the Aspect of this?'

Frentis shook his head. 'Dunno why. Just felt that I shouldn't tell no-one except you.'

Vaelin felt a chill that had nothing to do with the deepening cold. For a moment he was back in the forest during the Test of the Run, listening to the men who had killed Mikehl as they debated the identity of their victim. *The other one . . . You heard what the other one said. Gave me the shivers he did.*

'Don't tell anyone else,' Vaelin said. 'One Eye told you nothing.' He watched Frentis shiver in his cloak and forced a smile. 'The man was a loon. His words mean nothing. But it's best we keep this between us. Telling our brothers would only cause foolish talk.'

He watched Frentis nod and walk away, still clutching himself beneath his cloak, his fingers no doubt playing over his scars. *Will he dream tonight?* Vaelin thought and felt a pang of mingled guilt and regret. *Why couldn't it have been me who killed One Eye?*

CHAPTER NINE

T he morning of the Test of the Sword brought a hard rain
that turned the earth to mud and did little to lighten
their spirits. The test was held in an arena in Varinshold's
northern quarter, an ancient structure of finely shaped granite,
worn with age and weathered by the elements. It was known only
as the Circle and Vaelin had never met anyone who could tell
him when or why it had been built. Looking at it now, he realised
there were similarities with the temple to the seven Orders they
had found beneath the city, the way the supporting columns curved
up to the tiers above echoed the elegance of the underground
structure. Here and there he glimpsed adornments in the stonework, carvings of faded intricacy that recalled the better-preserved
motifs of the temple. He drew Caenis's attention to them as Master
Sollis led them into the shade beneath the columns but he received
only a grunt in response. Today even Caenis was too preoccupied
to indulge in curiosity.

Vaelin could see the fear and uncertainty on his brothers' faces
but found he was unable mirror it. The emotions that made Dentos
vomit his breakfast and Nortah white-faced and closed-lipped
were something he simply didn't feel. He was unafraid and he

didn't understand why. Today he would face three men in armed combat. He would kill them or they would kill him. The prospect of death should have chilled him to the core. Perhaps it was the very simplicity of the situation that robbed him of his fear. There were no questions here, no mysteries, no secrets. He would live or he would die. But despite his inability to fear the ordeal something still nagged at him, a small, insistent voice at the very edge of his thoughts, whispering words he didn't want to hear: *Perhaps you don't fear the test because you relish it.*

Unwillingly, he recalled the Test of Knowledge, the awful truth the Aspects had forced from him. *I can kill. I can kill without hesitating. I was meant to be a warrior.* Images of the men he had killed came back to him in a rush: the archer in the forest, the faceless assassins in the House of the Fifth Order, the one-eyed man's hireling. It was true he had felt no hesitation in killing any of them, but had he truly relished it?

'You'll wait in here.' Master Sollis led them into a chamber set back from the main entrance. The walls were thick but they could hear the baying of the crowd in the Circle. The Test of the Sword was an ever-popular event in the city but only those with sufficient coin could purchase a ticket and typically it was the Realm's wealthier citizens who came to watch the three-day spectacle, often wagering huge sums on the outcome of each contest. The profits from the day would be donated to the Fifth Order to care for the sick. Vaelin couldn't help but smile at the irony of it.

'What's so funny?' Nortah demanded.

Vaelin shook his head and sat down on a stone bench to wait. There were twenty brothers in Vaelin's group today. The fifty other survivors of the three hundred who had started their training together as boys of ten or eleven had undergone their tests over the preceding two days. So far ten had been killed and another eight so badly maimed they could no longer serve the Order. Many others had serious cuts requiring weeks of healing. The parade of wounded and shocked brothers trooping through the gates over the past two days had added considerable weight to the burden of fear most of them now carried. Of all of them, only Vaelin and Barkus seemed unaffected.

'Sugar cane?' he offered Vaelin, taking the place next to his.

'Thank you, brother.' The cane was fresh and its sweetness tinged with a slight acidity, but still the sensation was a welcome distraction from the grim mood of the others.

'Wonder who'll be first,' Barkus said after a moment. 'Wonder how they choose.'

'We draw lots,' Master Sollis told them from the doorway. 'Nysa. You're first. Let's go.'

Caenis nodded slowly, face immobile, and got to his feet. When he spoke his voice was barely audible. 'Brothers . . .' he began, then stopped, choked. 'I . . .' He stammered for a moment before Vaelin reached out to grasp his forearm.

'We know, Caenis. I'll see you shortly. We all will.'

They stood, the five of them, grasping hands. Dentos, Barkus, Nortah, Vaelin and Caenis. Vaelin remembered how they had been as boys. Barkus beefy and clumsy. Caenis thin and fearful. Dentos loud and full of stories. Nortah sullen and resentful. Now he saw only shadows of those boys in the lean, stern-faced young men before him. They were strong. They were killers. They were what the Order had made them. *This is the end of something,* he realised. *Live or die, this is where things change, forever.*

'It's been a long road,' Barkus said. 'Never thought I'd get this far. Wouldn't have but for you lot.'

'Wouldn't change any of it,' Dentos said. 'Every day I thank the Faith for my place in the Order.'

Nortah's face was tense, his brows furrowed as he fought to

master his fear. Vaelin thought he wasn't going to speak but after a moment he said, 'I . . . hope you all make it through.'

'We will.' Vaelin clasped hands with all of them. 'We always do. Fight well, brothers.'

'Nysa,' Master Sollis said from the door. He sounded impatient and Vaelin was surprised he had allowed them this interlude. 'Let's go.'

Waiting to find out if your friends were dead, Vaelin discovered, was a singular form of agony that made the effects of Joffril root feel like a taste of lemon tea. One by one his brothers were called out by Master Sollis, there would be a short wait before the crowd erupted in cheers, the volume of which rose and fell with the fortunes of the fight. After a while he found he could gauge the course of a fight, if not the victor, by the crowd's reaction. Some were over quickly, a matter of seconds, Caenis's fight in particular had been very short. Vaelin found he couldn't decide if this was good or bad. Other fights were longer, Barkus and Nortah both enduring prolonged contests of several minutes.

Dentos was the last to be called before Vaelin. He forced a smile, took a firm grip on his sword hilt and followed Master Sollis from the chamber without a backward glance. Judging from the noise of the crowd, his fight was eventful, raucous cheers followed by hushed silence then an explosion of applause, repeated several times over. When the final wave of noise washed through the chamber Vaelin found he was unable to judge if Dentos had survived.

Luck to you, brother, he thought, alone in the chamber now. *Mayhap I'll join you soon.* His hand ached from gripping his sword hilt, the knuckles white on the leather. *Is this fear now?* he wondered. *Or just stage fright?*

'Sorna.' Master Sollis was in the doorway, his level gaze meeting Vaelin's eye with an intensity he hadn't seen before. 'It's time.'

The tunnel leading to the arena seemed long, much longer than he could have imagined. Time played tricks as he walked the length of the tunnel, the journey perhaps taking a minute or an hour. All the time the crowd's clamour rose in volume until he felt himself bathed in sound as he emerged onto the sandy floor of the arena.

The crowd bayed down at him from ascending tiers of seats on all sides, at least ten thousand in all. He was unable to distinguish a face amongst the multitude, they were simply a seething, gesticulating mass. None of them seemed to mind the rain, which was still falling in hard, wind-driven sheets. There was blood on the sand, raked to stop it pooling and dulled by the rain but still a stark red against the greenish yellow of the arena floor. Three men waited for him there, each holding a sword of the Asraelin pattern.

'Two murderers and a rapist,' Master Sollis said. Vaelin assumed it was the noise of the crowd that seemed to add a tremor to his voice. 'They deserve their end. Show them no mercy. Mark the tall one, he seems to know how to hold a blade.'

Vaelin's eyes found the tallest of the three, a well-built man in his mid-thirties with close-cropped hair and a natural balance in his stance; feet in line with his shoulders, sword held low. *Trained,* he realised. 'A soldier.'

'Soldier or healer, he's still a murderer.' The briefest pause. 'Luck to you, brother.'

'Thank you, Master.'

He drew his sword, handed the scabbard to Master Sollis and strode forward into the arena. The crowd's shouts redoubled as he entered, here and there he caught a word or two: 'Sorna! . . . Hawk-killer! . . . Kill them, boy! . . .'

He stopped ten feet or so from the three men, looking at each of them in turn as the crowd's noise dwindled to a hush of anticipation. *Two murderers and a rapist.* They did not look like criminals. The one on the left was simply a scared, unshaven man holding his sword in a shaking hand as rain pelted him and ten thousand souls awaited his death. *Rapist,* Vaelin decided. The man on the right was stockier and less afraid, shifting his weight constantly from one foot to the other, his eyes locked onto Vaelin's beneath deeply glowering brows as he twirled his sword in his right hand, rainwater spraying from the blade. He said something, water spouting from his lips, a curse or a challenge, the words lost amidst the rain and the wind. *Murderer.* The third man, the soldier, showed no fear and felt no need to twirl his sword or voice his aggression. He simply waited, his gaze unwavering, his stance the same sword fighter's stance Vaelin knew so well. *A killer certainly. But a murderer?*

The man on the right attacked first as Vaelin expected he would, charging into an easily turned thrust. Vaelin used the momentum of the parry to bring the blade round in a slash at the man's neck. The stocky man was fast though, dodging away with only his cheek laid open. The man on the left sought to take advantage of the distraction, screaming as he ran in, pulling his sword back over his head and hacking down at Vaelin's shoulder. Vaelin turned, the blade missing by less than an inch to thud into the sand. Vaelin's sword point took the unshaven man under the chin, forcing its way up through tongue and bone to find the brain. He withdrew the blade quickly and stepped away, knowing the soldier would attack now.

His thrust was fast and well placed, a killing stab at the chest. Vaelin's blade caught the tip and forced the sword point up, leaving an opening to the soldier's chest. Vaelin's counter was fast, fast enough to have caught any of his brothers, but the tall man parried it without apparent difficulty. He moved back in a slight crouch, sword close to the ground, his eyes never leaving Vaelin.

The stocky man was attempting to hold his slashed cheek together with one hand, his sword waving wildly as he staggered, spitting inaudible curses at Vaelin with bloodied lips.

Vaelin feinted towards the tall man, slashing at his legs to force him back, then attacking the stocky man in a move so fast there could be no defence, rolling under a wild defensive slash to deliver a killing thrust through the back. His sword point pierced the stocky man's heart and emerged from his chest. Vaelin put his foot to the dying man's back and heaved him off the blade in time to duck under another slash from the tall man. He fancied he saw a raindrop sliced in half by the blade's passage.

They drew back from each other, circling, swords levelled, eyes locked together. The stocky man took a few moments to die, struggling on the rain-sodden sand between them, spitting curses until his breath gave out and he sagged, lifeless in the rain.

Vaelin was suddenly struck by the same sense of wrongness that had assailed him before; in the forest, in the Fifth Order House when Sister Henna came to kill him, when he waited for Frentis to return from the Test of the Wild. There was something about his remaining opponent, something in the strength of his gaze and the set of his body, something in his *being* telling of a terrible, certain truth: *This man is no criminal. This man is no murderer!* How he knew he could not tell. But it was the strongest such feeling he had yet experienced and he had no doubt of its certainty.

He stopped, his sword point lowering as he straightened, the tensed, hard lines of his face softening. He could feel the rain for the first time, beating a chill into his skin. The tall man's brows knitted in puzzlement as Vaelin lost his fighting stance to stand, his sword held at his side, rain washing the blood from the blade. He raised his left hand, fingers open in a sign of peace.

'Who are—'

The tall man attacked in a blur, his sword as straight as an arrow, aimed directly at Vaelin's heart. It was a faster move than anything he had seen from Master Sollis and it should have killed him. But somehow he managed to turn in time for the sword point to pierce only his shirt, the edge of the blade marking his chest.

The tall man's head was resting on Vaelin's shoulder, the hard determination gone from his eyes, his lips parted in a small gasp, his skin rapidly draining of colour.

'Who are you?' Vaelin asked him in a whisper.

The tall man staggered back, Vaelin's sword making a sickening, ripping sound as it was dragged from his chest. He sank to his knees slowly, propping himself up with his own sword, resting his chin on the pommel. Vaelin saw that his lips were moving and knelt beside him to hear the words.

'My . . . wife . . .' the tall man said. It sounded like an explanation. His eyes met Vaelin's again and for moment there was something there, an apology? A regret?

Vaelin caught him as he fell, feeling the life go out of him in a shudder. He held the dead soldier as the rain beat down and the roar of the crowd crushed him with blood-crazed adulation.

Vaelin had never been drunk before. He found it an unpleasant sensation, not unlike the dizzy feeling he got when taking a hefty blow on the head during practice, just more prolonged. The ale was bitter in his mouth, his first taste making him screw up his face in disgust.

'You'll get used to it,' Barkus had assured him.

The tavern was near the western section of the city wall and frequented mainly by off-duty guardsmen and local traders. For the most part they seemed content to leave the five brothers alone, although there had been a few calls of congratulation to Vaelin.

'Best bet I ever made,' a cheery-faced old man called, lifting his tankard in salute. 'Made a packet on you today, brother. Got odds of ten to one when it looked like you'd get the chop . . .'

'Shut up!' Nortah told the old man flatly. His left arm was cradled in a sling, the forearm heavily bandaged, but his visage held sufficient menace to make the old man blanch and sit down without further comment.

They found a vacant table and Barkus bought the drinks. He was limping from a cut to the calf and spilled a fair amount of the ale on the way back from the bar.

'Clumsy sod,' Dentos grunted. 'Let me get them next time.' He was the only one to have gotten through the test unscathed, although his gaze had a bright, frightened look and he blinked rarely, as if scared of what he would see when he closed his eyes.

Caenis sipped his ale, frowning in puzzlement. 'From the way men lust after this so I'd expected it to taste better.' The line of his jaw was marked by a row of eight stitches. The brother from the Fifth Order who tended the cut had assured him he would carry the scar for the rest of his life.

'Well,' Nortah said, lifting his tankard. 'We're all here.'

'Yeh.' Dentos lifted his own mug, clacking it against Nortah's. 'Here's to . . . being here I s'pose.'

They drank, Vaelin forcing the ale down, draining his tankard.

'Easy, brother,' Barkus warned him.

He felt them exchanging uneasy glances across the table as he stared at the dregs at the bottom of the tankard. There had been an ugly scene with Master Sollis back at the Circle when Vaelin had demanded to know the identity of the tall man and received only a curt response: 'A murderer.'

'He was no murderer,' Vaelin insisted, a mounting anger dispelling his normal deference. The tall man's face as he slipped into death was fresh in his mind. 'Master, who was that man? Why was it necessary for me to kill him?'

'Every year the City Guard provide us with a selection of condemned men,' Sollis replied, his patience nearing its end. 'We choose the strongest and most skilled. Who they are is not our concern. Neither is it yours, Sorna.'

'It is today!' Vaelin took a step closer to Sollis, his fury mounting.

'Vaelin,' Caenis cautioned him, his hand on his arm.

'I killed an innocent man today,' Vaelin spat at Sollis, shaking off Caenis's hand, advancing further. 'For what? To show you I could kill? You knew that already. You chose him, didn't you? Knowing he was the most skilled. Knowing I'd be the one to face him.'

'A test is not a test if it's easy, brother.'

'EASY?' A red mist was staining his vision, he found his hand had gone to his sword.

'Vaelin!' Dentos and Nortah stepped between them, Barkus pulling him back and Caenis keeping a firm grip on his sword hand.

'Get him out of here!' Sollis commanded as they hustled him towards the exit, near-incoherent with rage. 'Take the rest of the evening. Help your brother cool off.'

Vaelin wasn't sure if ale was the best way to cool off. His anger hadn't dimmed at all; if anything, the way the room seemed to move around of its own volition was extremely aggravating.

'My Uncle Derv could drink more ale in a sitting than any man alive,' Dentos said after his fourth tankard, his head lolling. 'They'd 'ave a contest every shummertide fair. Folk from miles around'd come t'challenge 'im. Not one of 'em could ever beat 'im. Grand ale-drinking champion five years running. Woulda been six iffen he 'adn't drunk hisself t'death in the winter.' He paused to issue an extravagant burp. 'Silly old sod.'

'Aren't we supposed to be enjoying this?' Caenis asked, both hands gripping the table as if scared he was about to tip over.

'I'm happy enough,' Barkus said, grinning merrily. His shirt was damp with ale and he seemed oblivious to the rivulets that coursed down his chin every time he took a drink.

'Two brothers . . .' Nortah was saying. He had been rambling about his test for over an hour. From what Vaelin could gather, two of the men he had killed were brothers, both apparently condemned outlaws. 'Twins . . . I think. Looked just the same, even made the same sound when they died . . .'

Vaelin's stomach gave an uncomfortable lurch and he realised he was about to vomit. 'Going outside,' he mumbled, rising and making for the door on legs that seemed to have lost the ability to walk in a straight line.

The air outside chilled his lungs and made his nausea recede a little, but he was still obliged to spend a few minutes heaving into the gutter. Afterwards he rested his back against the tavern wall and sank slowly onto the cobbles, his breath steaming in the frigid air. *My wife*, the tall man had said. Maybe he had been calling to her. Or summoning a final memory as he struggled to take the image of her face with him into the Beyond.

'A man with so many enemies shouldn't make himself so vulnerable.'

The man standing over him was of average height but well built, with a lean, deeply lined face and a piercing stare.

'Erlin,' Vaelin said, releasing the hilt of his knife. 'You don't look any different.' He gazed blearily around the empty street. 'Did I pass out? Are you here?'

'I'm here.' Erlin reached down to offer him a hand. 'And I think you've had enough for one night.'

Vaelin took the hand and levered himself to his feet with difficulty. To his surprise he found he was at least half a foot taller than Erlin. When last they met he had barely come up to his shoulder.

'Thought you'd be a tall one,' Erlin said.

'Sella?' Vaelin asked.

'Sella's fine, last I saw her. I know she would want me to thank you for what you did for us.'

I'll fight but I won't murder. His boyhood resolve coming back to him, the promise he had made to himself after saving them in the wild. *I'll kill men who face me in battle but I won't take the sword to innocents.* It felt so hollow now, so naïve. He remembered his disgust at Brother Makril's tales of murdered Deniers and wondered if there was truly any difference between them now.

'I've still got her scarf,' he said, trying to force his thoughts in a more comfortable direction. 'Could you take it to her?' He fished clumsily inside his shirt for the scarf.

'I'm not sure I could find her if I chose to. Besides, I think she would want you to keep it.' He took Vaelin's elbow and guided him away from the tavern. 'Walk with me for a while. It should clear your head. And there is much I would like to tell you.'

They walked through the empty streets of the western quarter, tracing a route through the rows of workshops that characterised this as the craftsman's district. By the time they reached the river Vaelin knew from the ache building at the back of his skull and the increased steadiness of his legs that he was starting to sober up. They paused on the towpath overlooking the river, gazing down at the moonlight playing on the currents churning the ink black water.

'When I first came here,' Erlin said, 'the river stank so bad you couldn't go near it. All the waste of this city would flow into it before they built the sewers. Now it's so clean you can drink from it.'

'I saw you,' Vaelin said. 'At the Summertide Fair, four years ago. You were watching a puppet show.'

'Yes. I had business there.' It was clear from his tone he wasn't about to elaborate on what type of business.

'You risk much coming here. It's likely Brother Makril is still out hunting you somewhere. He's not a man to give up a hunt.'

'True enough, he caught me last winter.'

'Then how . . .?'

'It's a very long tale. In short he cornered me on a mountainside in Renfael. We fought, I lost, he let me go.'

'He let you go?'

'Yes. I was fairly surprised myself.'

'Did he say why?'

'He didn't say much of anything at all. Left me tied up through the night whilst he sat by the fire and drank himself unconscious. After a while I passed out from the beating he'd given me. When I woke in the morning my bonds were untied and he was gone.'

Vaelin remembered the tears shining in Makril's eyes. *Maybe he was a better man than I judged him to be.*

'I saw you fight today,' Erlin told him.

Vaelin felt the ache at the base of his skull deepen. 'You must be rich to have afforded a ticket.'

'Hardly. There's a way into the Circle few know of, a passage under the walls that affords a good view of the arena.'

Silence stretched between them. Vaelin had no wish to discuss his test and was increasingly preoccupied with the suspicion that he was about to throw up again. 'You said you had something to tell me,' he said, mainly in hope that further conversation would distract him from the burgeoning nausea in his gut.

'One of the men you killed, he had a wife.'

'I know. He told me.' He glanced at Erlin, noting the intense scrutiny in his eyes. 'You knew him?'

'Not well. My acquaintance was with his wife. She has assisted me in the past. I count her as a friend.'

'She's a Denier?'

'You would call her that. She calls herself Quester.'

'And her husband was also part of this . . . belief?'

'Oh no. His name was Urlian Jurahl. Once he had been called Brother Urlian. He was like you, a brother of the Sixth Order, but he gave it up to be with Illiah, his wife.'

Little wonder he fought so well. 'I took him for a soldier.'

'He took the trade of a boat builder after leaving the Order, became highly regarded, ran his own yard building barges, the finest on the river some say.'

Vaelin shook his head in sorrow. *I have served the Faith by killing an innocent builder of boats.* 'What was he doing in the arena? I know he wasn't a murderer.'

'It happened during the riots. Some locals got wind of Illiah's beliefs, quite how I don't know, mayhap her son spoke of it when at play, children can be so trusting. They came for her, ten men with a rope. Urlian killed two and wounded three more, the rest ran off, but they came back with the City Guard. Urlian was overpowered and taken to the Blackhold, his wife too.'

'Their son?'

'He hid at his father's bidding as the fight raged. He's safe now. With friends of mine.'

'If Urlian was defending his wife, then it wasn't murder. The magistrate would have seen that surely.'

'Surely. But the magistrate had some wealthy friends with an eye for an opportunity. Did you know the odds that you would survive your test were hardly worth a bet? The odds against were long indeed. With Urlian in the arena, it would be worth risking some gold on the long chance. They offered him a proposition, confess his crime and be chosen for the test, an easy thing to arrange as your masters would be quick to spot his skill. Once he had killed you he and his wife would be free.'

Vaelin realised he had sobered completely, the nausea fled in the face of the cold, implacable compulsion. 'His wife is still in the Blackhold?'

'She is. By now she will have heard of her husband's fate. I fear what her grief will make her do.'

'This magistrate and his wealthy friends, you have their names?'

'What would you do if I gave them to you?'

Vaelin fixed him with a cold stare. 'Kill them all. That is your intention, isn't it? To set me on this course for vengeance. Well, you'll get it. Just give me the names.'

'You misunderstand me, Vaelin. I have no wish for vengeance. In any case you couldn't kill them all. Wealthy men from noble families have many protectors, many guards. You might kill one, but not all. And Illiah would still be waiting her fate in the Blackhold once you have been cut down.'

'Then why tell me this when I can do nothing to set it right?'

'You can speak for her. Your word will carry much weight. If you went to your Aspect and explained . . .'

'She's a Denier. They won't help her unless she renounces her heresy.'

'She won't do that. Her soul is bound to her beliefs more closely than you could imagine. I doubt she could renounce them even if she wished to. I know your Aspect to be a compassionate man, Vaelin, he will speak for her.'

'Even if he does, the Blackhold is no longer guarded by the Sixth Order since the last Conclave. It falls under the control of the Fourth. I have met Aspect Tendris and he will not help an unrepentant Denier.' Vaelin turned back to the river, frustration raging in his chest, Urlian's pale face asking for his wife over and over again in his head.

'So there's nothing you can do?' Erlin asked. He sounded

resigned and Vaelin knew his visit had been a desperate act, undertaken at considerable risk.

'You put great trust in me coming here,' Vaelin said. 'Thank you.'

'I've lived long enough to judge a man's heart.' He stepped back from the river, offering Vaelin his hand. 'I'm sorry to have burdened you with this. I'll leave you in peace now.'

'As I grow older I'm learning that the truth is never a burden. It's a gift.' Vaelin shook his hand. 'Tell me the names.'

'I won't set you on a path to your own death.'

'You won't. Trust me. I've thought of something I can do.'

CHAPTER TEN

H e chose the gate on the eastern wall, assuming it would be the least busy. Even given the lateness of the hour the main palace gate would be too well guarded, too many mouths to speak of how Vaelin Al Sorna had appeared demanding an audience with the King.

'Piss off, boy,' the sergeant at the gate told him, not bothering to emerge from the shelter of the guardhouse. 'Go sleep it off.'

Vaelin realised he must smell like an alehouse. 'My name is Brother Vaelin Al Sorna of the Sixth Order,' he said, forcing authority into his voice as if he had every right to be here. 'I request an audience with King Janus.'

'Faith!' The sergeant sighed in exasperation. He came out to fix Vaelin with a fierce glare. 'You know a man could find himself flogged for giving a false name to an officer of the Royal Guard?'

A younger guardsman appeared behind the sergeant, staring at Vaelin with a disconcertingly awed expression. 'Uh, Sarge . . .'

'But it's late, and I'm in a good mood.' The sergeant was advancing on Vaelin with balled fists, his grizzled face tensed with impending violence. 'So it'll just be a beating before I send you on your way.'

'Sarge!' the younger man said urgently, catching hold of his arm. 'It's him.'

The sergeant's gaze swung to the younger man then back to Vaelin, looking him up and down. 'You sure?'

'Was on duty at the Circle this morning wasn't I? It's really him.'

The sergeant's fists uncurled but he didn't appear any happier. 'What's your business with the King?'

'For him alone. He'll see me if he's told I'm here. And I'm sure he'll be displeased if he hears I have been turned away.' *An accomplished lie,* he congratulated himself. In truth he had no certainty the King would see him at all.

The sergeant thought it over. His scars told of a lifetime of hard service and Vaelin realised he must resent any intrusion into what was no doubt a comfortable billet in which to await his pension. 'My compliments and apologies to the captain,' the sergeant told the younger guardsman. 'Wake him and tell him about our visitor.'

They stood regarding each other in wary silence after the guardsman had scampered off, hastily unlocking a small door set into the huge oak-wood gate and disappearing inside.

'Heard you killed five Denier assassins the night of the Aspect massacre,' the sergeant grunted eventually.

'It was fifty.'

It seemed an age before the door reopened and the young guardsman emerged followed by a trim young man, impeccably dressed in the uniform of a captain in the King's Horse Guard. He gave Vaelin a brief look of appraisal before offering his hand. 'Brother Vaelin,' he said in a slight Renfaelin accent. 'Captain Nirka Smolen, at your service.'

'Apologies for waking you, Captain,' Vaelin said, slightly distracted by the neatness of the young man's attire. Everything from the shine of his boots to the precise trim of his moustache spoke of a remarkable attention to detail. He certainly didn't appear to be a man just woken from his bed.

'Not at all.' Captain Smolen gestured at the open door. 'Shall we?'

Vaelin's boyhood memories of gleaming opulence were not matched by the interior of the eastern wing of the palace. After crossing a small courtyard, he was led into a warren of corridors crammed with a variety of dust-covered chests and cloth-wrapped paintings.

'This wing is used mostly for storage,' Captain Smolen explained, seeing his bemused expression. 'The King receives many gifts.'

He followed the captain through a series of corridors and chambers until they came to a large room with a chequered floor and several grand paintings on the wall. He found his attention immediately drawn to the paintings, each was at least seven feet across and depicted a battle. The setting changed with each painting but the same figure was at the centre of every one: a handsome, flame-haired man astride a white charger, sword held high above his head. *King Janus.* Though Vaelin's memory of the King was dim, he didn't remember his jaw being quite so square or his shoulders quite so broad.

'The six battles that united the Realm,' Captain Smolen said. 'Painted by Master Benril Lenial. It took him over three years.'

Vaelin remembered Master Benril's drawings in Aspect Elera's rooms, the fine detail with which each was rendered, the way the exposed viscera seemed to come out of the parchment. He saw none of the same clarity now. The colours were bright but not vibrant, the battling warriors clearly depicted but stilted somehow, not as if they were fighting at all, simply standing in a pose.

'Not his best, is it?' Captain Smolen commented. 'He was commanded to it, you see. I suspect he had little love for his subject. Have you ever seen his fresco in the Great Library commemorating the victims of the Red Hand? It's quite breath-taking.'

'I've never seen the Great Library,' Vaelin replied, thinking Captain Smolen would probably find much in common with Caenis.

'You should, it's a credit to the Realm. I'll need your weapons.'

Vaelin unclipped his cloak with the four throwing knives secured within its folds, unbuckled his sword, unhooked his hunting knife from his belt and removed the narrow-bladed dagger from his left boot.

'Nice.' Captain Smolen admired the dagger. 'Alpiran?'

'I don't know, I took it from a dead man.'

'These will be waiting for you here.' Smolen laid his weapons out on a nearby table. 'No-one will touch them.' With that he moved to a bare patch of wall and pushed, a section of the wall swinging inwards revealing a dark stairwell. 'Follow the stairs to the top.'

'He's in there?' Vaelin asked. He had expected to be led to a throne room or audience chamber.

'He is indeed. Best not keep him waiting.'

Vaelin nodded his thanks and entered the stairwell. Oil lamps set into the wall cast a dim light on the steps, the gloom deepening when Smolen closed the door behind him. As instructed he climbed the stairs, the fall of his boots on the stone steps loud in the confined space. The door at the top was slightly ajar, outlined in bright lamplight from the room beyond. It creaked loudly when Vaelin pushed it open but the man seated at the desk before him didn't look up. He sat crouched over a roll of parchment, his quill scratching over it, leaving a spidery script in its wake. The man was old, in his sixties, but still broad in the shoulder. His long hair hung over his face; once red, it was now grey but still had a faint tinge of copper. He wore a plain shirt of white linen, the sleeves stained with ink, his only adornment a gold signet ring on the third finger of his right hand, a signet ring bearing the symbol of a rearing horse.

'Highness—' Vaelin began, sinking to one knee.

The King raised his left hand, motioning for him to rise then pointing at a nearby chair. His quill didn't stop on the parchment. Vaelin moved to the chair, finding it piled high with books and scrolls. He hesitated then carefully gathered them together and placed them on the floor before sitting down.

He waited.

The only sound in the room came from the scratch of the King's quill. Vaelin wondered if he should speak again but something told him it was best to keep silent. Instead he surveyed the room. He had thought Aspect Elera's room to have been the most book-filled space he had ever seen but the King's room put it to shame. They lined the walls in great stacks rising nearly to the ceiling. In between the stacks were boxes of scrolls, some flaked and withered with age. The only decoration in the room was a large map of the Realm above the fireplace, its surface partly covered with short notations in a spidery script. Oddly some of the notations were written in red ink and others black. Down one edge of the map was a list of some kind, each item had been written in black but crossed through in red. It was a long list.

'You have your father's face but your mother's way of looking at things.'

Vaelin's gaze snapped back to the King. He had laid his quill aside and reclined in his chair. His green eyes were bright and shrewd in his craggy, weathered face. Vaelin found he couldn't stop his eyes straying to the livid red scars on the King's neck, the legacy of his childhood brush with the Red Hand.

'Highness?' he stammered.

'Your father was clever in the ways of war but in most other things I have to say he was as dumb as a rock. Your mother on the other hand was clever in almost everything. You had her look just now, when you were looking at my map.'

'I'm sure she would have been gratified to know you held such a high opinion of her, Highness.'

The King raised an eyebrow. 'Don't flatter me, boy. I have servants aplenty for that. Besides, you're no good at it. In that, at least, you are like your father.'

Vaelin felt himself flush and bit back an apology. *He's right, I'm no courtier.* 'Forgive my intrusion, Highness. I have come to ask for your help.'

'Most people who come before me do. Although, usually with obscenely expensive gifts and several hours' worth of grovelling. Will you grovel for me, young brother?' The King's mouth had curved in a small, humourless smile.

'No.' Vaelin found his trepidation was quickly disappearing in the face of a cold anger. 'No, Highness. I will not.'

'And yet you come here at this forsaken hour and demand favours.'

'I demand nothing.'

'But you do want something. What is it, I wonder? Money? I doubt it. It meant little to your parents, I daresay it means little to you. Help with a marriage proposal perhaps? Got your eye on some wench but her father doesn't want a penniless Order boy for a son-in-law?' The King angled his head, studying Vaelin closely. 'Oh no, hardly that. So what can it be?'

'Justice,' Vaelin said. 'Justice for a murdered man, justice for his family.'

'Murdered, eh? By whom?'

'By me, Highness. Today I killed a man in the Test of the

Sword. He was innocent, a victim of a false conviction brought simply to make him face me in the test.'

The humour faded from the King's face, replaced with something much more serious but otherwise unreadable. 'Tell me.'

Vaelin told him all of it, Urlian's arrest, his wife's imprisonment in the Blackhold, the names of those responsible: Jentil Al Hilsa, the magistrate who had condemned Urlian, and Mandril Al Unsa and Haris Estian, the two wealthy men who had sought to profit from his death.

'And how do you come by this intelligence?' the King asked when he had finished.

'A man came to me tonight, a man I trust.' Vaelin paused, gathering his will for the risk he knew he had to take. 'A man who knows much of the troubles besetting Deniers in the Realm.'

'Ah. For a member of an Order, you choose unusual friends.'

'The Faith teaches us that a man's mind should be open to truth, wherever he finds it.'

'It seems you have your mother's way with words as well.' The King pulled a fresh piece of parchment from a stack on his desk, dipped his quill in a bottle of black ink and wrote a short passage. He then wiped the quill on his shirtsleeve, dipped it in a pot of red ink and wrote a list below the black text. He completed the document with an elaborate signature, then took a candle and a block of sealing wax, touching the flame to the wax to melt a droplet onto the bottom of the parchment. He blew softly on the wax for a moment then pressed his signet ring into it.

'Every time I sign my name to one of these,' he said putting his quill aside, 'I have to amend my map.' Vaelin turned back to the chart on the wall, looking again at the list, black words crossed through with red. *Names,* he realised. *Names of men he's killed. Nortah's father must be there somewhere.*

'I'll execute these men,' the King said. 'On the strength of what you've told me. There will be no trial, the King's Word is above all law. Their families will hate me for what I've done, but since I intend to confiscate their property and render them penniless, it matters not.'

Vaelin met the King's gaze, trying to decide if this was some kind of bluff, but saw no deception. 'A family should not be punished for the crimes of but one of its members.'

'It is how it must be with nobles, leave the family its wealth and they'll use it against me sooner or later. Besides, I know these men and their families. They're a vile, greedy lot by and large. Life in the gutter will suit them well.'

'You put much stock in my word, Highness. I could be lying . . .'

'You're not. Thirty years a king teaches a man how to hear lies.'

A king's justice is hard indeed, Vaelin decided. Could he stomach it? Seeing the certainty in the King's expression, he realised he had no choice. The course had already been set as soon as he opened his mouth. 'And the man's wife?'

'Well there we have a problem. She's an unrepentant Denier. Aspect Tendris will no doubt seek to hang her from the walls in a cage. If she doesn't die under questioning first, of course.'

'Highness, you are the King of this Realm and the Champion of the Faith. There must be some influence . . .'

'*Must* there?' The King's expression was a mix of anger and amusement. 'I have done what I *must* this night.' He gestured to the death warrant he had written. 'It is a king's duty to dispense justice where he can. I will kill these men because they have broken the laws of this Realm and deserve their end. As for their victim's wife, her crimes fall outside my jurisdiction. Therefore, it is not a question of what I must do but what I may do, if it serves my purpose. So, Vaelin Al Sorna, tell me how saving this woman's life will serve my purpose. You used your name to get in here, do you have nothing else to say?'

Mother, forgive me. 'I know that Your Highness had plans for me, before my father sent me to the Order. If it pleases you, I will submit to your plans if you will secure the release of Urlian's wife.'

The King reached for a crystal decanter on his desk and poured a measure of red wine into a glass. 'Cumbraelin, ten years old. One of the benefits of Kingship is a well-stocked cellar.' He offered the decanter to Vaelin. 'Would you care for some?'

Vaelin's head still ached from his binge in the alehouse. 'No thank you, Highness.'

'You father wouldn't drink with me either.' The King sipped his wine slowly. 'But then he never sought to bargain with me. I commanded and he followed.'

'Loyalty is our strength.'

'Yes. A fine motto, one of my best. I chose it for him, even chose the hawk as your family crest. It was something of a joke actually. Your father hated hawking, it's a sport for nobles after all.' He took another sip from his wine, wiping the red stain from his lips with an ink-spattered sleeve. 'Do you know why he left my service?'

'I had heard there was discord between you over his wish to marry and legitimise my sister.'

'Know about her, eh? That must've been a shock. It's true enough that I refused your father's request to marry and he was angry over it. But in truth I believe he had resolved to leave my side when I had to kill my First Minister. They were at each other's throats for years but when Al Sendahl's thievery came to light it was your father who spoke for him when no other would. He had to die, of course, although it was a grievous loss. Few other men knew finance so well as Artis Al Sendahl.'

'I have served with his son since we were boys, Highness. He could never accept that his father stole from your purse.'

'Oh he wasn't a thief of coin, he was a thief of power. It's a terribly seductive thing, Vaelin. But to wield it well you have to hate it as much as you love it. Lord Artis never understood that, his actions became driven wholly by ambition, endangering the peace of the Realm, and so I killed him.'

'And took his family's wealth?'

'Of course. Made sure the wife and daughters were taken care of though, felt I owed him that much. Tower Lord Al Myrna was kind enough to take them in, gave the woman some land in the Northern Reaches, under a false name of course. Can't have my nobles thinking I'm softhearted.'

'It would ease my brother's mind greatly if I could tell him this.'

'I'm sure. But you won't.'

The King put down his wineglass and rose, rubbing and groaning at the stiffness of his legs, going to the map above the fireplace. 'The Unified Realm,' he said. 'Four Fiefs once divided by war and hatred now united in loyalty to me. Except, of course, they aren't. Nilsael sold itself to me because it was tired of armies raping its land for fodder every few years. Renfael lost half her knights in battle and Lord Theros saw that if he fought me any longer, he would soon lose the other half. Cumbrael hates and fears me in equal measure, but they fear the Faith more and will stay loyal as long as I keep it from their door. This is the Realm I spilled a sea of blood to build and through you I would have stopped it tearing itself apart when I die.

'You are right, I had many plans for you. The son of a Battle Lord and a former Mistress in the Fifth Order, both commoners at that. You would be the means by which I would bind the common folk to my line, not just in Asrael but in all the Fiefs. And when I had the hearts of the commons, their nobles could call for war but none would answer. I had plans for you indeed,

Young Hawk.' He scanned the map, his sigh heavy with regret. 'But your mother had plans of her own. When she persuaded Aspect Arlyn to take you into the Sixth Order she made you a brother, bound to the Faith, not to me.'

'Highness, if it is your wish that I leave the Order . . .'

'It's too late for that. It would be clear to all that you had left the Faith at my command. Robbing the Order of its most famous son would do little to make the people love me. No, the plans I had for you are long dead.'

Vaelin fumbled for something to say, some argument to secure the King's assistance. The prospect of leaving Urlian's wife to torture and slow execution was unbearable. Wild schemes flickered through his mind as panic gripped him. He would sneak into the Blackhold and rescue her, his brothers would help him, he was sure of it, although it probably meant death for all of them . . .

'I was not the first, you know?' the King said softly. Vaelin saw he was looking at a short list scribbled at the top of the map. 'There have been five before me.' The King tapped a finger to the five names on the list. 'Five Kings since Varin led our people to this land and drove the Seordah into the forests and the Lonak into the mountains. And in five hundred years no ruling family has held the Realm for more than a generation.'

'Prince Malcius is a good man, Highness.'

'My butcher is a good man, boy!' the King snapped, suddenly angry. 'So are my stable master and the man who sweeps dung from my courtyard. My son is a good man it is true, but it takes more than goodness to make a king. When he took the throne you were to be at his side to do what he could not. Now all I can do is make this Realm so great that those who would tear it down will fear being crushed by its fall.'

He returned to his chair, sitting down stiffly. 'And so I will make a new plan. And you, Brother Vaelin Al Sorna, will serve my purpose again.' He searched through a pile of papers on his desk, extracting a sheaf of documents sealed with black wax. 'Aspect Tendris keeps me busy with his loyal guidance and humble requests for new measures to combat the scourge of the Unfaithful. Here' – the King selected the topmost document – 'he suggests the Realm Guard flog any subject who cannot recite the Catechism of Faith on command.'

'Aspect Tendris is zealous in his beliefs, Highness.'

'Aspect Tendris is a deluded fanatic. But even a fanatic can be bargained with.' The King held up another document and began to read: '"I would most humbly remind Your Highness of the regular reports that the Unfaithful are gathering in unprecedented numbers in the Martishe forest. I have heard from the most reliable sources that these are adherents of the Cumbraelin form of god worship and are most vehement in their heresy. They are well armed and, my sources assure me, resolved to meet any attempt to dislodge them with the utmost violence. I implore Your Highness, with the greatest respect, to heed my calls to act decisively in this matter."'

The King tossed the parchment aside. 'What do you make of this?'

'The Aspect wishes you to send the Realm Guard to the Martishe to root out Deniers.'

'Indeed, as if my soldiers have little better to do than run around the woods for months with Cumbraelin longbowmen waiting behind every tree. Oh no, the Realm Guard will not go within ten miles of the Martishe. But you will.'

'Me, Highness?'

'Yes. I will prevail upon Aspect Arlyn to send a small contingent of brothers to the Martishe, you will be among them. As will a young man named Linden Al Hestian. You know this name?'

'Al Hestian.' Vaelin recalled the furious man lashing his way through the crowd at the Summertide Fair where Nortah's father had met his end. 'I once met a Lord Marshal of that name.'

'Lakrhil Al Hestian, Lord Marshal of my Twenty-seventh Regiment of Horse. A capable officer and one of my wealthier nobles. Like my late First Minister, a man of great ambition, particularly where his son is concerned. His elder son, Linden.'

Vaelin felt a hard ball of dread form in the pit of his stomach. 'His son, Highness?'

'A fine young man with many admirable qualities, sadly humility and intelligence are not among them. The fellow has a wide circle of friends, in truth a gang of admirers and sycophants. Nothing attracts friends like wealth and arrogance. He is currently the darling of my esteemed court, winning tournaments, bedding ladies, fighting duels. It's a rather tediously familiar story, I'm afraid. A young man achieves great fame and success at an early age and begins to believe his own legend, not helped by the indulgence of an ambitious father. He is by far the most popular young man in court, far more popular than my own son, who has never been gifted in the ways of artifice. Every day I'm beset with entreaties to give the younger Al Hestian a commission, something to help him prove his worth, set him on the path to glory. And so I will. He will be made a Sword of the Realm and commanded to raise his own regiment, which he will take into the Martishe to root out the Deniers currently infesting it. Sadly, I predict this will be a long and arduous campaign and after' – the King paused to think – 'six months or so he will, tragically, meet his end in a Denier ambush.'

Their eyes met, Vaelin's stomach churning with mingled anger and despair. *I am a fool,* he decided. *A mouse seeking bargains with an owl.* 'Urlian's wife, Highness?' he grated.

'Oh, I daresay Aspect Tendris will be in a more amenable frame of mind when I tell of him of my plans for a crusade in the

Martishe, especially since you will be part of it. He's fond of you, you know. I'll vouch for the woman, tell him I'm convinced of her redemption, provided she says nothing to the contrary, she will be free by tomorrow evening.'

'I need assurance she and her son will be provided for.' Vaelin forced himself to keep his eyes locked on the King's. 'If I'm to be part of your crusade.'

'I'm sure Tower Lord Al Myrna can find room for another exile or two. The distinction between Faithful and Denier means little in the Northern Reaches.' The King turned back to his desk, lifting his quill and smoothing a blank parchment out before him. 'You will receive your orders in the next few days.' He began to write again, his quill scratching its path across the page.

It took a moment for Vaelin to realise he had been dismissed. He got to his feet, finding himself slightly dizzy, whether with anger or sorrow he couldn't tell. 'My thanks for your time, Highness.' He forced the words out and moved to the door.

'Remember, Young Hawk,' the King said, not looking up from his parchment. 'This is not the whole of my plan for you. Merely the beginning. I command, you follow. That is the bargain you made this night.' He glanced up, meeting Vaelin's eyes again. 'You understand?'

'I understand perfectly, Highness.'

The King held his gaze a moment longer, then returned to his writing, saying nothing as Vaelin left.

Captain Smolen was waiting for him when he emerged from the wall. 'Your visit is concluded, brother?'

Vaelin nodded and collected his weapons from the table, reequipping himself quickly, possessed by a strong desire to be away from this place. He needed time alone to think. The enormity of his bargain with the King had stirred his thoughts into a confused jumble. He followed Smolen back along the myriad corridors lined with forgotten gifts, his mind continually repeating the King's final words. *This is not the whole of my plan for you. Merely the beginning.*

'You'll forgive me if I leave you here,' Smolen said at the corner to what Vaelin recognised as the corridor leading to the east gate. 'I have pressing duties elsewhere.'

Vaelin peered at the shadowy end of the corridor then turned back to Smolen, seeing a faint discomfort in the set of the man's face. 'Pressing duties, Captain?'

'Yes.' Smolen coughed. 'Very pressing.' He took a step backwards, nodded formally then turned and strode back the way they had come.

Vaelin took another look at the corridor ahead of him, a faint sensation of wrongness making his heart beat faster. *Ambush,* he decided. *The King has untrustworthy servants.* He considered going after the captain and forcing him to walk ahead into whatever was waiting but found he couldn't summon the will. It had been a very long night. Besides he could always find him later. He palmed a throwing knife from the folds of his cloak and started along the corridor.

He expected the attack to come at the darkest point, near the corridor's end, but nothing happened. No black-clad men with curved swords leaping out to challenge him. But there was a faint scent in the air, subtle, sweet, like flowers on a hot day . . .

'I'd heard you were handsome.'

He pivoted towards the sound of the voice, the knife half-out of his hand before he saw her. A girl, standing half in shadow. He managed to move his hand at the last instant, sending the throw wide, the knife thudding into the wall an inch from her head. She glanced at it briefly before stepping forward into the light. Vaelin had seen beautiful women before, he had always thought Aspect

Elera the most beautiful woman he was likely to meet, but this girl was different. Everything about her, from the flawless porcelain of her skin, to the soft curve of her face and the lustrous red-gold of her hair, spoke of effortless perfection.

'You're not,' she said, coming closer, head angled as she studied him with bright green eyes. 'But your face is interesting.' She reached up, fingers extended into a caress.

Vaelin took a step back before her hand could touch his face. He dropped to one knee and bowed low. 'Highness.'

'Please get up,' said Princess Lyrna Al Nieren. 'We can't talk properly if your face is constantly pointed at the floor.'

Vaelin rose. Waiting and trying not to stare.

'I'm sorry if I surprised you,' the princess apologised. 'Captain Smolen was kind enough to inform me of your visit. I thought we should talk.'

Vaelin said nothing, his sense of wrongness hadn't faded. Something about this encounter was dangerous. He knew he should make an excuse and leave but found himself unable to find the words. He wanted her to talk to him, he wanted to be near her. It was a compulsion that provoked a sudden and deep resentment.

'I had intended to watch you fight today,' the princess went on. 'My father wouldn't let me, of course. I was told it was a very stirring contest.'

Her smile was dazzling, performed with a precise affectation of sincerity that put Nortah to shame. *She expects me to be flattered,* he realised. 'Is there something you wish of me, Highness? Like Captain Smolen, I have pressing business elsewhere.'

'Oh don't be angry with the captain. He's normally so correct in his duties. I'm afraid I may be corrupting him terribly.' She turned and went to the wall, where his throwing knife was embedded, and worked it loose with difficulty. 'I like trinkets,' she said, examining the blade, running her delicate fingers over the metal. 'Young men give them to me all the time. None of them have yet given me a weapon though.'

'Keep it,' Vaelin told her. 'If you'll excuse me, Highness.' He bowed and turned to go.

'I won't,' she said flatly. 'We haven't finished our talk. Come,' she beckoned to him with the knife, moving away from the wall. 'We will talk together beneath the stars, you and I. It will be as if we are in a song.'

I could just leave, he realised. *She couldn't stop me . . . could she?* After briefly considering the prospect of fighting off hordes of guardsmen summoned to prevent his leaving, he followed her back along the corridor. She led him to a door in an unobtrusive alcove, pushing it open and gesturing for him to enter. The garden beyond was small but even in moonlight the beauty on display in its flowerbeds was remarkable. There seemed to be an endless variety of blooms, far more than in Aspect Elera's garden.

'It should really be seen in daylight,' Princess Lyrna said, closing the door and stepping past him, pausing to examine a rosebush. 'And it's a little late in the year, many of my darlings are already shrinking in the cold.'

She walked to a low stone bench in the centre of the garden, her gown swaying gracefully. Vaelin distracted himself by searching the flowerbeds for something vaguely familiar, to his surprise he found it in the shape of yellow buds nestling beneath a small maple tree. 'Winterblooms.'

'You know flowers?' The princess sounded surprised. 'I was told brothers of the Sixth Order knew nothing beyond the arts of war.'

'We are taught many things.'

She sat on the bench and raised her hands, gesturing at the flowerbeds. 'Well, do you like my garden?'

'It's very beautiful, Highness.'

'When I was little my father asked me what I wanted as a Winterfall gift. Growing up in the palace meant I was never alone, there were always guards or maids or tutors, so I said I wanted somewhere to be alone. He brought me here. It was just an old empty courtyard then, I made it a garden. No-one else is allowed here and I have never shown this place to anyone, before now.' She was studying him intently, gauging his reaction.

'I am . . . honoured, Highness.'

'I'm glad. So, as I have honoured you with a confidence, perhaps you will honour me with one in return. What business did you have with my father?'

He was tempted to say nothing but knew he couldn't simply ignore her. Various lies flicked through his mind but he had a sense that the princess had her father's ear for untruth. 'I don't think King Janus would wish me to discuss it,' he said after a moment.

'Really? Then I am forced to guess. Please tell me if I guess well. You found out that one of the men you killed today had been forced into the fight. You came here asking my father for justice. Am I correct?'

'You know much, Highness.'

'Yes. But sadly, I find that I never know enough. Did my father grant your request?'

'He was gracious enough to dispense justice.'

'Oh.' There was a faint note of pity in her voice. 'Poor Lord Al Unsa. He always used to make me laugh at the Warding's Night ball, the way he would stumble about the dance floor.'

'I'm sure your fond memories will be a great comfort to him on the gallows, Highness.'

Her smile faded. 'You think me cold? Perhaps I am. I've known many lords over the years. Smiling, friendly men who gave me sweets and presents and told me how pretty I am, all seeking to win my father's favour. Some he sent away, some he allowed to remain in his service and some he killed.'

He realised his own father must have been among the many lords she had met and wondered if she had aroused as much uncertainty in him. 'Did my father give you presents?'

'All your father ever gave me was a hard stare. Though not as hard as the stare your mother gave me. My father's plan for us made them wary of me I suppose.'

'Us, Highness?'

She raised an eyebrow. 'We were to be married. Didn't you know?'

Married? It was absurd, ridiculous. Married to a princess. Married to *her*. He recalled the rude little girl from his boyhood visit to the palace. *I'm not marrying you, you're dirty.* Was this really how the King intended to bind him to his line?

'No, I never liked the idea much either,' Princess Lyrna said, reading his face. 'But now I can appreciate the elegance of it. My father's designs often take years before their intent is revealed. In this case he intended to place you at my brother's side and enhance my standing. Together we would guide my brother in his rule.'

'Perhaps your brother will need no guidance.'

She raised her perfect face to the sky, studying the spectacular array of stars. 'Time will tell. I should come here at night more often. The view is really quite lovely.' She turned to him, her face serious now. 'What does it feel like when you take a life?'

Her tone was one of simple curiosity. Either she didn't know her question might cause offence or didn't care. Oddly, he found he wasn't offended. It was something no-one had ever asked him. Although he knew the answer all too well.

'It feels like your soul has been soiled,' he said.

'And yet you continue to do it.'

'Until today it has always been . . . necessary.'

'And so you come to my father seeking to assuage your guilt. What price did he extract I wonder? I expect he took you into his service. A spy within the Sixth Order would be an asset indeed.'

A spy? If only that were all. 'Did you lead me here simply to ask questions to which you already know the answer, Highness?'

To his surprise she laughed, it sounded rich, genuine. 'How refreshing you are. You offer me no flattery, you sing me no songs and quote me no sonnets. You are singularly without charm or calculation.' She looked down at the throwing knife in her hand. 'And you are the only man I've met that has succeeded in making me afraid. As ever I am amazed at my father's foresight.' Her gaze was uncomfortably direct and he had to force himself to meet it, keeping silent.

'What I have to say to you is simple,' she told him. 'Leave the Order, serve my father at court and in war, in time you will become a Sword of the Realm, and we may fulfil the plan he laid for us.'

He searched her face for some sign of mockery or deceit but found only serious intent. 'You wish us to marry, Highness?'

'I wish to honour my father.'

'Your father believes his plan for me dead. Leaving the Order would be of no value to him now. If I followed your command, I would be acting against his wishes.'

'I will speak to him. He listens to my counsel in most things, he will hear the wisdom of my course.' He saw it then, the faint glimmer in her eyes. The wrongness deepened as he realised he had seen it before, in Sister Henna's eyes when she tried to kill him. It wasn't malice exactly, more calculation mixed with desire. But where Sister Henna had desired his death the princess wanted more, and he doubted it was the delightful prospect of being his wife.

'You honour me greatly, Highness,' he said, his tone as formal as he could make it. 'But I'm sure you will understand that I have given my life in service to the Faith. I am a brother of the Sixth Order and this meeting is unseemly. I would be very grateful if you would permit me to withdraw.'

She looked down, a small wry smile on her lips. 'Of course, brother. Please forgive my discourtesy in delaying you.'

He bowed and turned to leave, reaching the door before she stopped him.

'I have much to do, Vaelin.' Her tone was devoid of humour or affectation, entirely serious and sincere. *Her true voice,* he thought.

He paused at the door and didn't turn. Waiting.

'What I have to do would have been easier with you at my side but I will do it nevertheless. And I will tolerate no obstacle. Believe me when I say I should hate us to be enemies.'

He glanced back at her. 'Thank you for showing me your garden, Highness.'

She inclined her head and turned her gaze back to the sky. He was dismissed. The most beautiful woman he had ever seen, bathed in moonlight. It was a truly captivating sight, one he found himself fervently wishing he never saw again.

PART III

It pleases me to report the excellent progress made by Lord Al Hestian's command in recent months. Many Deniers have paid the appropriate price for their heresy or fled the forest in fear of their lives. The spirits of the men are high, rarely have I encountered soldiers so enthused by their cause.

—BROTHER YALLIN HELTIS, FOURTH ORDER,
LETTER TO ASPECT TENDRIS AL FORNE
DURING THE MARTISHE FOREST CAMPAIGN,
FOURTH ORDER ARCHIVES

VERNIERS' ACCOUNT

He had fallen silent as my quill continued its fevered track across the parchment. About me lay the ten scrolls I had filled with his story. Outside, night had descended and our only illumination came from a single lantern swaying from a deck beam above our heads. My wrist ached from hours of writing and my back was strained with hunching over the barrel on which I had chosen to rest my papers. I scarcely noticed.

'Well?' I prompted.

His face was sombre in the dim glow of the lantern, his expression distant. I had to speak again before he roused himself.

'I'm thirsty,' he said, reaching for the flask the captain had allowed him to fill from the water barrel. 'Haven't said more than a few words a day for five years. My throat hurts.'

I put my quill down and rested my aching spine on the hull. 'Did you see her again?' I asked. 'The princess.'

'No. I expect she had no use for me since I refused her plan.' He lifted the flask to his mouth, drinking deep. 'But her fame grew over the years, the legend of her beauty and her kindness spread far and wide. Often she was seen in the poorer quarters of the city and the wider Realm, giving alms to the needy, providing funds for new schools and Fifth Order sick-houses. Many nobles courted her but she refused them all. There was talk that the King was angry with her for failing to wed a conveniently powerful husband but she defied his will, though it pained her greatly.'

'You think she still waits for you?' The tragedy of it stirred my writer's soul. 'That she mends her broken heart with good deeds, knowing that only this will win your approval. Although, for all she knows, you have been dead these past five years.'

The look he gave me was one of amused incredulity. After a moment he began to laugh. He had a deep, rich laugh. A laugh that was both loud and, on this occasion, very lengthy.

'One day, my lord,' he said when his mirth had subsided. 'If your gods curse you, you may get to meet Princess Lyrna. If you do, take my advice and run very fast in the opposite direction. Your heart, I think, she would find far too easy to crush.'

He tossed the water flask to me. I drank quickly, hoping it disguised my anger. Everything he had told me about the princess bespoke a woman of intelligence and duty, a woman who wished to honour her father and serve her people. I suspected I could find much to discuss with such a woman.

'She hasn't wed because a husband would be a shackle for her,' Vaelin Al Sorna told me. 'She does good deeds to curry favour with the common folk. Win their hearts, and she wins power. If she has a heart, then it's power that stirs it, not passion.'

Silently I resolved to make my own researches into the life of Princess Lyrna. The more this Northman told me the greater my compulsion to travel to his homeland. Although I suspected he had little appreciation for the artistry and learning evident in the culture he described, I lusted for it. I wanted to read the books in the Great Library and view Master Benril Lenial's frescoes of the Red Hand. I wanted to see the ancient stones of the Circle, where he had spilled the blood of three men. We had thought the people of the Unified

BLOOD SONG · 359

Realm little more than illiterate savages, and in truth, many of their warriors had been just that. But now I could see there was more to their story than simple barbarism and war lust. In a few short hours I had learned more of his realm than in all the years of study for my history of the war. He had kindled something in me, the desire to write another history, greater and richer than all my previous work. A history of his realm.

'Did the King keep his promise?' I asked. 'Did he impose his justice and save the woman in the Blackhold?'

'The men I named were executed the next day. The woman and her son were packed off to the Northern Reaches within the week.' He paused, his face heavy with sorrow. 'I went to see her before she left, Erlin arranged the meeting. I begged her for forgiveness. She spat at me and called me a murderer.'

I took up my quill and wrote down his words, taking the liberty of exchanging 'spat at me' with 'cursed me with all the power of her Denier gods.' I like to add a little colour where I can.

'And your part of the bargain?' I continued. 'Did you do what the King had commanded? Did you kill Linden Al Hestian?'

He looked down at his hands – resting on his knees – flexing the fingers, the veins and sinews standing out clearly amidst the scars. Killer's hands, I thought, knowing they could choke the life from me in a few seconds.

'Yes,' he said. 'I killed him.'

CHAPTER ONE

A Cumbraelin longbow was over five feet long when
unstrung and fashioned from the heart-wood of a yew
tree. It could propel an arrow over two hundred paces,
almost three hundred in skilled hands, and was quite capable
of piercing plate armour at close range. The one Vaelin held
was slightly thicker than most, the smoothness of the stave
evidence of the extensive use it had seen. Its owner had a keen
eye, sending his steel-tipped arrow clean through the armoured
chest of one Martil Al Jelnek, an affable young noble with a
fondness for poetry and a somewhat tiresome inclination to
talk constantly about his betrothed, who he claimed to be the
fairest and kindest maid in all of Asrael, if not the world. Sadly,
he would never see her again. His eyes were open but had lost
all vestige of life. His mouth was stained with blood and
vomit, the signs of a painful death; Cumbraelin archers tended
to coat their arrowheads in a mixture of joffril root and adder
venom. The bow's owner lay a few yards away with Vaelin's shaft
in his arm, his neck broken by the fall from the birch in which
he had hidden.

'Nothing,' Barkus said, trudging through the snow, flanked by

Caenis and Dentos. 'Looks like he was the only one.' He kicked the dead archer's head, making it swivel on a twisted spine, before kneeling to divest the corpse of any valuables.

'Where'd all the soldiers go?' Dentos asked.

'Scattered,' Vaelin said. 'Probably find most of them in the camp when we get back.'

'Bloody cowards.' Dentos peered down at Martil Al Jelnek. 'Didn't they like him? Thought he was a nice enough fellow, meself. For a highborn.'

'These supposed soldiers are the sweepings of the Varinshold dungeons, brother,' Caenis told him. 'They have no loyalty to any man save themselves.'

'Did you find his horse?' Vaelin asked. He didn't relish the prospect of carrying the dead noble back to the camp.

'Nortah's bringing it,' Barkus said, straightening from the archer, jingling the few coppers he had found. He tossed the Cumbraelin's quiver to Vaelin. The arrows it held were stained ash black and fletched with raven's feathers. Their enemies liked to sign their work. 'You keeping that?' He nodded at the bow. 'I could get ten silvers for it when we get back to the city.'

Vaelin kept hold of the weapon. 'Thought I'd see if I could master it.'

'Good luck. These buggers train for a lifetime from what I hear. Their Fief Lord makes them practice every day.' He looked down at the meagre collection of coppers in his hand. 'Doesn't seem keen on paying them much though.'

'This lot fight for their god not their lord,' Caenis said. 'Money holds little interest for them.'

They stripped the armour from Al Jelnek and heaved him onto the back of his horse, Nortah slapping Barkus's hand away when it strayed to the dead man's purse.

'He won't need it, will he?'

'We left the House seven months ago, for Faith's sake!' Nortah snapped. 'You don't need to steal any more.'

Barkus shrugged. 'It's a habit.'

Seven months, Vaelin thought as they made their way back to camp. Seven months of hunting Cumbraelin Deniers in the Martishe forest aided, in the loosest sense, by Linden Al Hestian and his newly raised regiment of infantry. Linden Al Hestian, who was conspicuously alive a full month longer than the King had ordained. With every passing day Vaelin felt the burden of his bargain weigh a little more heavily.

His mood was not lightened by his surroundings. The Martishe was not the Urlish, being both darker and denser, the trees so close to each other in some places that it was practically impassable. Added to this was the broken nature of the ground, dotted with hollows and gullies that made perfect ambush sites and forced them to abandon their horses. They walked everywhere with bows ready and arrows notched. Only the nobles amongst their contingent continued to ride, making themselves easy targets for the Cumbraelin archers who haunted the trees. Of the fifteen young nobles who had accompanied Linden Al Hestian to the Martishe, four were dead and another three wounded so badly they had had to be carried out. Their men had suffered worse, six hundred had been enlisted or pressed into the regiment but over a third were gone; killed or lost amidst the trees, some undoubtedly deserting when the chance arose. Often they would find men who had been missing for weeks, frozen in the snow or tied to a tree and tormented to death. Their enemies had no use for captives.

Despite the losses, their small Order contingent had won a few victories. A month ago Caenis led them in tracking a group of over twenty Cumbraelins as they moved along a creek, a clever move but of little value if Caenis was on their trail. They followed for hours until their enemies paused to rest, hard-faced men in buckskin and sable pelts, their longbows on their backs, not expecting trouble. The first volley cut down half, the rest turning and fleeing back along the creek bed. The brothers drew their swords and hunted them down, none had escaped and none had asked for quarter. Caenis was right, their enemies fought for their god and displayed little reluctance in dying for him.

The camp came into view a few miles later, in truth it was a stockade rather than an encampment. When they first arrived they had tried mounting a sentry picket, which had simply provided their enemies with an opportunity for some nighttime archery practice. Linden Al Hestian had been forced to order trees felled to provide timber for a stockade, a grim circle of spiked trunks sitting in one of the few clearings to be found in the Martishe. Vaelin and most of the Order contingent hated the damp oppression of the place and spent most of their time in the forest, patrolling in small groups, making their own camps, which they moved every day, playing their deadly game of chase with the Cumbraelins whilst Al Hestian's soldiers sheltered in their stockade. The sortie by the unfortunate Martil Al Jelnek had been the first for weeks, even then the men he led had to be threatened with a flogging before they would march. In the event, it had taken a single arrow to set them to flight.

A stocky brother with bushy, frost-adorned eyebrows and a fierce glower was waiting at the gate to the stockade. At his side was a very large mongrel with a grey-flecked coat and a gaze that could match its master's for fierceness.

'Brother Makril.' Vaelin greeted him with a short bow. Makril wasn't much for formalities but as commander of their contingent he deserved a show of respect, especially in front of Al Hestian's soldiery, some of whom were loitering near the gate, fearful eyes tracking from Al Jelnek's corpse to the dark wall of the forest as if a Cumbraelin arrow might come hissing at them from the shadows at any moment.

Vaelin had managed to hide his surprise when the Aspect had called him to his room and he found Makril waiting, staring at the red, diamond-shaped cloth in his hand, a bemused expression on his blunt features.

'You two are acquainted, I believe,' the Aspect said.

'We met during my Test of the Wild, Aspect.'

'Brother Makril has been appointed commander of our expedition to the Martishe forest,' the Aspect told him. 'You will follow his orders without question.'

Apparently few men knew the Martishe as well as Makril, save for Master Hutril, who couldn't be spared from his duties at the Order House. Their contingent numbered only thirty brothers, mostly experienced men from the northern border who seemed to share Vaelin's wariness of Makril, but he quickly proved himself an adept tactician, albeit with a somewhat abrupt style of leadership.

'One fucking hour,' he growled. 'You were supposed to sweep to the south for two days.'

'Lord Al Jelnek's men ran away,' Nortah said. 'Didn't seem much point staying out there.'

'Was I asking you, snot-boy?' Makril demanded. He had taken an instant dislike to all of them but reserved most of his bile for Nortah. Beside him his mongrel, Snout, gave a growl of agreement. Where he found the animal Vaelin had no idea, apparently Makril had given up on slave-hounds after his experience with Scratch and opted for the largest and most-ill-tempered hunting dog he could find, regardless of breeding. Several soldiers bore scars as evidence of Snout's dislike of petting or eye contact.

Nortah stared back at Makril with fully reciprocated dislike. Vaelin worried continually what would happen if the two were left alone together.

'We thought it best to return with the body, brother,' Vaelin said. 'We will patrol ourselves this evening.'

Makril turned his glower on Vaelin. 'Some of the men made it back. Said there had been at least fifty scum out there.' Makril always referred to the Cumbraelins as scum. 'How many did you get?'

Vaelin hefted the longbow in his hand. 'One.'

Makril's bushy eyebrows knitted together. 'One out of fifty?'

'One out of one, brother.'

Makril sighed heavily. 'We better report to his lordship. He's got another letter to write.'

Lord Linden Al Hestian was tall and handsome with an easy smile and a lively sense of humour. He was courageous in battle and skilled with sword and lance. Contrary to the King's description, he also turned out to possess a quick mind and his apparent arrogance was merely the swagger of a young man who had achieved much in his short life and saw little reason to hide his self-satisfaction. Vaelin, much to his regret, found himself liking the young noble, although he had to admit the man made a terrible leader, his nature simply lacked the necessary ruthlessness. He had threatened the men with flogging many times but had yet to inflict any punishment at all despite obvious cowardice, drunkenness and a camp that was a disgrace to soldierly conduct.

'Brothers!' He greeted them with a broad smile as they approached his tent, the smile fading as he saw the body slung over the horse. Clearly none of the fleeing men had bothered to tell him the news.

'My condolences, my lord,' Vaelin said. He knew the two men had been friends since childhood.

Linden Al Hestian moved to the corpse, his face stricken with grief, and gently touched his dead friend's hair. 'Did he go down fighting?' he asked after a moment, voice thick with emotion.

Vaelin saw Nortah open his mouth to reply and cut in quickly. Nortah had a tendency to indulge his cruel streak where Lord Al Hestian was concerned, voicing barely concealed insults and criticism without hesitation. 'He was very brave, my lord.'

Martil Al Jelnek had wept like a child with the arrow buried in his gut, his hands clutched at Vaelin in brief, desperate spasms as the light of life faded from his eyes and effluent spouted from his mouth. He had tried to say something at the end, Vaelin was sure of it, his mouth stumbling over a torrent of bile-choked gibberish. Perhaps some message for his beloved. They would never know.

'Brave,' Al Hestian repeated with a faint smile. 'Yes, he was always that.'

'His men ran,' Nortah said. 'One arrow and they ran. This regiment of yours is no more than a rabble of criminal scum.'

'Enough!' Brother Makril barked.

Sergeant Krelnik approached, snapping a smart salute at Al Hestian. He was a stocky man nearing his fiftieth year, with a heavily scarred face and a fearsome disposition towards the men. As he was one of the few experienced soldiers to enlist in the regiment, having served in the Realm Guard since the age of sixteen, Al Hestian had wisely made him Master Sergeant, responsible for discipline. But despite his best efforts Nortah's description was accurate, the regiment remained a rabble.

'I'll order the pyre built, my lord,' Sergeant Krelnik said. 'We should give him to the flames tonight.'

Al Hestian nodded, stepping back from the corpse. 'Yes. Thank you, Sergeant. And you, brothers, for bringing him back.' He returned to his tent. 'Brother Makril, Brother Vaelin, may I have a moment?'

Al Hestian's tent was free of the luxuries found in the quarters of the other nobles, the available space taken up with his weapons and armour, which he cleaned and maintained himself. Most of the other nobles had brought along a servant or two but apparently Lord Al Hestian was capable of seeing to his own needs.

'Please, brothers.' He gestured for them to take a seat and moved to the small portable desk where he dealt with the numerous administrative tasks that beset regimental commanders. 'A royal missive,' he said, lifting an opened envelope from the desk. Vaelin's heart began to beat a little faster at the sight of the King's seal.

"'To Lord Linden Al Hestian, commander of the Thirty-fifth Regiment of Foot, from His Highness Janus Al Neiren,'" Al Hestian read. "'My lord, please accept my congratulations for keeping a regiment in the field for such a protracted period. Lesser commanders would no doubt have opted for the more obvious course of concluding the Realm's business in the Martishe forest with the utmost dispatch. You, however, clearly have a more subtle stratagem in mind, so subtle in fact that I am unable to discern its substance from this distance. You will recall Aspect Arlyn's gracious provision of a contingent from the Sixth Order, brothers for whom the Aspect is keen to find other employment. I hear my former Battle Lord's son is among them and I feel sure he has inherited his father's appreciation for urgency in carrying out his king's commands. Perhaps you should discuss your plans with these brothers, who may be of sufficiently generous disposition to offer some advice.'"

Vaelin was appalled to find his hands trembling and hid them in his cloak, hoping the others assumed he was feeling the chill.

'So, brothers,' Al Hestian said, regarding them with an expression of honest despair. 'I must seek your counsel, it seems.'

'I've given you my counsel several times, my lord,' Makril said. 'Flog some men, force the laziest and most cowardly through the gates without weapons, and allow Sergeant Krelnik a free hand in discipline.'

Al Hestian massaged his temples, fatigue evident in his brows. 'Such measures would hardly win the men's hearts, brother.'

'Bugger their hearts. It's a rare commander that can win the love of his men. Most rule by fear. Make them fear you and they'll respect you. Then perhaps they'll start killing some Cumbraelins.'

'I suspect from the tone of His Highness's letter we may have little more than a few weeks to conclude matters here. And, despite the King's assumption, I confess I have no stratagem for bringing down Black Arrow and his cohorts. Even if I adopt the measures you recommend, it will take more time than we have to win victory in this blighted forest.'

Black Arrow. They got the name from the only prisoner they had taken in seven months, an archer brought down by Nortah. He lived long enough to spit hate and defiance at them, calling on his god to accept his soul and begging forgiveness for his failure. He laughed at their questions; there were few threats that could be made to a dying man. In the end Vaelin had sent the others away, sitting down to offer the man his water bottle.

'Drink?'

The man's eyes were bright with defiance but the maddening thirst as his life-blood seeped away made him bite back a refusal. 'I'll tell you nothing.'

'I know.' Vaelin held the bottle to the man's lips as he drank. 'Do you think he will forgive you? Your god.'

'The World Father is great in His compassion.' The dying man spoke fiercely, spitting the words. 'He will know my weaknesses and my strengths and love me for both.'

Vaelin watched the man clutch at the arrow in his side, a small whimper escaping his lips.

'Why do you hate us?' Vaelin asked. 'Why do you kill us?'

The man's whimper of pain turned into a rasping laugh of bitterness. 'Why do you kill *us*, brother?'

'You came here in defiance of treaty. Your lord agreed you would not bring word of your god to the other Fiefs . . .'

'*His* words cannot be bound by borders, nor by the servants of a false faith. Black Arrow brought us here to defend those you would slaughter in service to your heresy. He knew the peace between us was a betrayal, a vile blasphemy . . .' He choked off, coughing uncontrollably. Vaelin had tried to coax more information from him but the man would only ramble on about his god, his words becoming less coherent as his life ebbed away. He soon slipped into unconsciousness, his breathing faltering to stillness within a few minutes. For some reason Vaelin found himself wishing he had asked his name.

'And you, Brother Vaelin?' Al Hestian's question brought him back to the present with a start. 'Our King seems to have faith in your judgement. Can you advise a method for bringing this campaign to a close?'

Call an end to the whole bloody farce and go home. He left the thought unsaid. Al Hestian couldn't leave the forest without victory, or at least a claim to victory. *And the King does not wish him to leave the forest at all,* he reminded himself. *You have a bargain to keep. Who's to say His Highness cannot undo what he has done?*

'Your men are hunted by Black Arrow's archers whenever they leave the camp,' he said. 'But my brothers and I are not, we are the hunters in this forest and the Cumbraelins fear us. Your men must become hunters also, at least those who can be taught.'

Makril snorted. 'This lot couldn't be taught to piss straight, never mind hunt.'

'There must be some men here who can be trained, the Faith teaches us there is worth even in the most wretched. I suggest we select a few, thirty or so. We will train them, they will answer to us. We will organise a raid, find one of Black Arrow's encampments and destroy it. When they have their first success against the

Cumbraelins the rest of the men will be inspired.' He paused, gathering the will for what he had to do. 'It would further inspire the men if you were to lead the raid personally, my lord. Soldiers will respect a leader who shares their dangers.' *And much can happen in the confusion of a raid, an arrow can easily go astray . . .*

Al Hestian stroked the sparse stubble on his chin. 'Brother Makril, you agree with this course of action?'

Makril gave Vaelin a sidelong glance, his heavy brows creased with suspicion. *He knows something isn't right,* Vaelin realised. *He can smell it, like a hound catching an unfamiliar scent.*

'It's worth a try,' Makril said after a moment. 'Finding their encampment though. That'll be a pretty trick. The scum cover their tracks well.'

'Brothers of the Sixth are considered the finest woodsmen in the Realm,' Al Hestian said. 'If the camp can be found, you will find it, I'm sure.' He slapped his knee, enlivened by the prospect of some resolution to his dilemma. 'Thank you, brothers. This plan will do very well.' He rose, sweeping a wolf fur from the back of his chair and fastening it over his shoulders. 'Let's be about it. We have much to do!'

None of the soldiers seemed to have a family name. They were known mostly by the criminal appellations of their past: Dipper, Red Knife, Fast Hands and so on. They had chosen the thirty trainees by the simple expedient of making the whole regiment run around the stockade and picking those who dropped last. They stood in three ranks of ten, staring balefully at Makril as he set out the rules that would govern their lives from here on.

'Any man found drunk without permission will be flogged. Those found drunk more than once will be dismissed from the regiment. Any of you shitheads thinking that means a free passage home should know that dismissed men will have to walk out of the

Martishe on their own two feet with no weapons.' Makril paused a moment to let the import of his words sink in. A lone man walking through the Martishe with no means of defence was likely to find himself lashed to a tree and disembowelled in short order.

'Understand this, you miserable bunch of thieving scum,' Makril growled. 'Lord Al Hestian has given the Sixth Order leave to train you as we see fit. You belong to us now.'

'Didn't sign up for this,' a sallow-faced man in the front row muttered sullenly. 'S'posed to be in the King's serv—'

Makril's fist smashed into the man's jaw, felling him instantly. 'Brother Barkus!' he barked, stepping over the prostate soldier. 'Ten lashes for this man. No rum for a week.' He glared at the remaining trainees. 'Anyone else want to discuss their terms of service?'

Caenis and Dentos slipped into the forest the next day with instructions to find the Cumbraelins' camp whilst the men were trained. The combined threat of flogging and death proved an excellent stimulus to both discipline and exertion. Their trainees scrambled to obey every order, running for miles through the snow, enduring bruising lessons in swordsmanship or unarmed combat, listening in respectful silence as Makril attempted to teach them the basics of woodcraft. If anything, they seemed too respectful, too cowed by fear, and Vaelin knew fearful soldiers made bad soldiers.

'Don't fret it,' Makril told him. 'As long as they're more scared of us than they are of the scum they'll do fine.'

Vaelin took charge of the sword lessons whilst Barkus made himself a figure of dread with his rough-and-tumble approach to unarmed combat. Nortah quickly abandoned attempts to teach the men the bow, none of them had the muscle or the skill for it, and concentrated instead on the crossbow, a weapon even the clumsiest oaf could master in a few days. By the end of the first week their small company could run five miles without complaint, had lost their fear of sleeping outside the stockade, and most could hit a mark at twenty paces with a crossbow. Their sword skills and basic fighting ability were still lacking but Vaelin felt they had at least learned enough to survive an initial encounter with Black Arrow's men.

As usual, Vaelin's legend had preceded him and the men regarded him with a mixture of awe and fear. They would occasionally exchange a word or two with Nortah and Barkus but maintained a rigid silence in Vaelin's presence, as if one wrong word could earn a swift death. Their fear was deepened by Vaelin's black mood, making him short-tempered and prone to dishing out painful slaps with the wooden stave he used for sword practice. At times he found himself sounding like Master Sollis. It did nothing to lighten his mood.

Al Hestian had chosen to train with the men, running with them and sharing their bruises in practice. He proved a skilled swordsman and was sufficiently tall and strong to at least compete with Barkus in unarmed combat. All the while he strove to encourage the men, dragging slackers to their feet and pulling them along during the runs, applauding their meagre progress with the sword. Vaelin noticed their growing regard for the young noble, where before he had been 'that snot-nosed lackwit' behind his back, now he was simply 'his lordship.' The mood of the men was still sullen, they had no affection for Vaelin and his brothers, but Al Hestian had become a figure worthy of their solidarity. Watching him as he sparred with some of the men, Vaelin felt his depression deepen yet further. *Murderer.*

The voice had begun to plague him the day they began the training, a soft, knowing murmur at the back of his thoughts, whispering awful truths. *Assassin. You're no better than the scum who killed Mikehl. The King has made you his creature . . .*

'What do you think, brother?' Al Hestian was striding towards him through the snow, face flushed with exertion but also bright with optimism. 'Will they do?'

'At least another ten days, my lord,' Vaelin replied. 'They still have much to learn.'

'But they have improved greatly, wouldn't you say? At least now we can call them soldiers.'

Fodder more like. A mask for your deceit, bait for your trap. 'Indeed, my lord.'

'Pity Brother Yallin didn't live to see this, eh?' Brother Yallin had been the Fourth Order's addition to their expedition. Nominally responsible for reporting their progress to Aspect Tendris, he had spent the first weeks in the forest claiming he couldn't venture outside the stockade because his attempts to teach the men the Catechism of Devotion were of primary importance. Sadly he soon succumbed to a virulent bout of dysentery and died shortly after. It was fair to say he hadn't been greatly missed.

'It seems odd that Aspect Tendris didn't send a replacement for Brother Yallin,' Vaelin commented.

Al Hestian shrugged. 'Perhaps he thought the journey too perilous.'

'Perhaps. Or he could be in complete ignorance of Brother Yallin's death. One might almost think someone has been sending Aspect Tendris regular reports in Brother Yallin's name.'

'Such a thing would be unthinkable, brother.' Al Hestian laughed and went off to shout encouragement at a group of men grappling nearby. *Why couldn't you have been hateful?* Vaelin wondered. *Why couldn't you have made my task easy?* The voice's response was immediate, implacable: *Should murder ever be easy?*

CHAPTER TWO

'About seventy men all told,' Dentos said around a mouthful of salt beef. 'Ten miles west of here. It's a well-chosen site, a gully to the east, rocks to the south and a steep slope to the north and west. Hard to take unawares.'

They had returned on the fourteenth day of the training, Caenis bearing a sketched map showing the layout of the Cumbraelins' camp. They huddled around the campfire with Al Hestian and Makril to plan the attack.

'Seventy's a lot for these lads to face, brother,' Barkus advised Makril. 'Even with our brothers they'll still have numbers in their favour.'

'Each brother's worth at least three of theirs,' Makril replied. 'Besides, a surprised man is usually defeated before he even draws his sword.' He paused to ponder Caenis's map, tracing a stubby finger over the gully leading to the camp's eastern edge. 'How well do they guard this?'

'Three men during the day,' Caenis replied. 'Five at night. Black Arrow is a cautious man it seems, knows we're most likely to come for him in darkness. There is a route in.' He pointed to the cluster of rocks covering the camp's southern border. 'I got close enough to smell their pipe smoke. But it's a path for one man only. Any more would be seen.'

'Five men guarding the best way in and only one man to open the door,' Makril mused. 'That's if he can get across the camp unseen.'

'We've kept some of their clothing and weapons,' Vaelin said. 'In the dark they might take me for one of their own.'

'You mean me, brother,' Caenis said.

'Five men at once . . .'

'As brother Makril says, surprised men are easier to kill. Besides, I'm the only one who knows the way.'

'He's right,' Makril said. 'I'll take our brothers through the gully. My lord' – he glanced at Al Hestian – 'I suggest you take your company to the southern approach, wait until you hear the clamour of our attack then charge straight in. We'll have drawn most of their strength to us so you should catch them on their blind side.'

Al Hestian nodded. 'A good plan, brother.'

'I should go with Lord Al Hestian,' Vaelin said. 'The men may be less inclined to tarry in the charge if one of us is with them.'

He could tell from Makril's narrowed eyes that his suspicion still lingered. *He knows,* the voice hissed in his mind. *The others would never suspect but he knows, he smells it on you like blood.*

'It'd be better if Sendahl and Jeshua went with his lordship,' Makril said, his narrow gaze still fixed on Vaelin. 'Your sword will be much needed when we breach the camp.'

'They're more afraid of Vaelin than they are any of us,' Barkus commented. 'Lot less likely to run if he's with them.'

'And I would be honoured to fight at Brother Vaelin's side!' Al Hestian enthused. 'I believe it's a fine idea.'

Makril slowly returned his gaze to the map. 'As you wish, my lord.' He pointed at the slope north of the camp. 'If this goes right, they'll flee down the hill towards the river. The perfect place to trap them. If the Departed favour us, we should get them all.' He looked up, his expression suddenly fierce. 'Even so this'll be a hard and bloody fight. The scum don't ask for quarter and won't give any. Tell the men to get close, use their swords, don't give them a chance to get their bows into play. Make sure they know defeat will mean death for all of us. There's no retreat from this place, we kill them all or they'll be sure to kill us.'

He rolled the map into a scroll and got to his feet. 'Five hours' sleep then we move out. We'll march in the dark so their scouts won't see us. Ten miles is a lot of ground to cover in the snow so we'll have to press hard. Any man who talks without permission or falls out on the march will have his throat slit. No rum ration until this is done.' He tossed the map to Caenis. 'Brother, you'll lead the way.'

The march was hard, taxing the men to the extreme, but the promise of death for any too exhausted to continue was sufficient to keep them moving. The Order was at the head of the column, arrows notched to their bowstrings, eyes peering into the dark for any sign of Cumbraelin scouts. Although Black Arrow's men sometimes came to harass the camp at night with a fire arrow launched over the stockade, their visits had trailed off when Caenis and Makril had taken to hunting after sundown, collecting four bows in as many nights. Now the Cumbraelins rarely ventured close at night and their march was not interrupted.

It took eight hours of hard going before they came to the edge of a clearing where a small slope led up to the mound of rocks behind which the Cumbraelins had made their camp. Off to the right they could glimpse the dark shadow of the gully where Makril would lead the Order contingent. There was little preamble, Makril made the sign of good luck and led the eighteen brothers off across the clearing in a loose skirmish formation.

Need anything? Vaelin signed to Caenis.

His brother shook his head, pulling a cord tight on his sable-pelted jerkin. In his captured garments he fitted his role well, the disguise completed by exchanging his strongbow for a longbow and hitching a hatchet into his belt. He opted to keep his sword strapped to his back, their enemies had captured many Asraelin blades from Al Hestian's soldiers so it was unlikely to look out of place.

Luck to you, brother, Vaelin signed, touching his shoulder. Caenis grinned briefly and was gone, covering the distance to the rocks in a dead run. *He'll be fine,* Vaelin reassured himself. Their time in the Martishe had given him a new appreciation of Caenis's skills, the slight boy who had shivered in fear at Master Grealin's tall tales of monstrous rats was now a lithe, deadly warrior who seemed to fear nothing and killed without hesitation.

There was a crunch of snow as Al Hestian crouched beside him. 'How long do you think, brother?' he whispered.

Vaelin fought down a surge of guilt at the sight of the young noble's earnest face. *You hope he won't realise it was you,* his ever-present watcher told him. *You hope he'll go into the Beyond believing the lie that you were friends . . .*

'An hour or so, my lord,' he whispered back. 'Perhaps less.'

'It'll give the men a chance to rest at least.' He moved away to check on his soldiers, murmuring reassurance and encouragement. Vaelin tried not to listen and concentrated on the dim silhouette of the rocks. The sky was still dark but had taken on the blue tinge heralding the onset of daylight. Makril had favoured a dawn attack, when the guards at the mouth of the gully would be tiring at the end of their shift.

Vaelin steadied his breathing, counting the passing seconds, gauging the right moment to set his scheme into motion, forcing away any thought that might deflect him from his course. His hand ached as his grip tightened on his bow. When he was sure at least a half hour had passed he moved to Al Hestian, crouching to whisper in his ear.

'There are sure to be guards in the rocks,' he said. 'My brother will have let them be to avoid raising the alarm. Although there won't be enough of them to stop our attack, their bows are likely to thin our ranks.' He hefted his bow. 'I'll go ahead now, when the attack starts I'll make sure they don't trouble us.'

Al Hestian rose. 'I'll come with you.'

Vaelin restrained him with a firm grasp on his forearm. 'You must lead the men, my lord.'

Al Hestian cast a glance round at the tense, drawn faces of his men and nodded reluctantly. 'Of course.'

Vaelin forced a smile. 'We'll share breakfast in Black Arrow's tent.' *Liar!*

'Luck go with you, brother.'

He found he couldn't meet Al Hestian's eye, nodding and setting off for the rocks at a run, covering the ground in what seemed like a few heartbeats, sheltering amidst the huge boulders that rose out of the snow like slumbering monsters. He cast a quick eye around for any sentries but saw nothing. From the camp came the faint scent of woodsmoke but no sound of any alarm. Caenis had yet to move against the guards at the gully. Vaelin reached for his quiver and extracted a cloth-wrapped arrow, discarding the covering to reveal an ash-black shaft and raven fletching, a Cumbraelin arrow taken from the archer who had slain poor Lord Al Jelnek, his instrument of murder. A single arrow would claim Lord Al Hestian's life as he heroically led his men in a charge against an enemy encampment. *A fine end indeed,* the voice said. *His father will be proud, I'm sure. Remember your words? Remember your vow? I'll kill, but I won't murder . . .*

Leave me be! Vaelin spat back. *I do what I must. There is no choice in this. I cannot break a contract with the King.*

His hands shook as he notched the arrow to the string, his heart a booming drum in his chest. *Enough!* He flexed his hands, forcing the tremor away. *I do what I must. I've killed before. What is one more death?*

From behind him came a faint clash of metal on metal followed by the snap of bowstrings and a sudden clamour of alarmed voices. The sounds of battle were soon echoing across the clearing and Vaelin saw Al Hestian's command emerge from the trees and begin their charge. The young noble was easy to pick out, leading his men by a good few strides, long sword held high, his cloak trailing. Vaelin could hear his calls to the men, urging them forward. He was strangely gratified to see that the whole company had followed Al Hestian, having expected many to flee.

He dragged in a deep draught of air, the chill burning his lungs, and raised his bow, drawing the string back, the raven's feathers in the shaft caressing his cheek, the bead centred on Al Hestian's rapidly approaching form. *Murder is easy,* he realised, the string slipping over his fingers. *Like snuffing out a candle.*

Something growled in the darkness. Something shifted its weight and scraped at the snow. Something made the hairs on the back of his head prickle.

The familiar sense of wrongness built within him like a fire, the tremor returning to his hands as he lowered the bow and turned.

The wolf's teeth were bared in a snarl, its eyes bright in the gloom, raised hackles like spikes of silver. As their eyes met, its growl subsided and it raised itself from the aggressive crouch it had assumed, regarding him with the same silent intensity he remembered from the Test of the Run all those years ago.

The moment seemed to stretch, Vaelin captured by the animal's gaze, unable to move, a thought singing in his mind: *What am I doing? I am no murderer!*

The wolf blinked and turned, sprinting away across the snow, a blur of silver and frost, gone in a heartbeat.

The approaching shouts of Al Hestian's charging men brought him back to his senses, turning to see they were almost at the rocks. Less than twenty feet away a figure rose, garbed in sable, a drawn longbow aiming a shaft straight at Al Hestian's chest. Vaelin's arrow took the archer in the belly. He was on him in seconds, his long-bladed dagger stabbing down to make sure of the kill.

'My thanks, brother!' Al Hestian called, leaping past to charge on to the camp. Vaelin surged after him, tossing his bow aside and drawing his sword.

The camp was a chaos of death and flame. The Cumbraelins could equal the Order's bow skills but at close quarters they were hopelessly outmatched, bodies littered the snow amidst burning tents. A wounded Cumbraelin stumbled out of the smoke, a bloodied arm hanging useless at his side, his good limb swinging a hatchet wildly at Al Hestian. The noble easily side-stepped the blow and hacked the man down with his long sword. Another came at Vaelin, eyes wide with panic and fear, jabbing a long-bladed boar spear at his chest. Vaelin ducked under the weapon, grasping the haft below the blade and pulling its owner onto his sword. One of Al Hestian's soldiers charged forward and rammed his sword into the Cumbraelin's chest, his scream of exultant fury merging with the shouts of the other men as they followed Al Hestian onwards, killing all they could find.

Vaelin saw Al Hestian charge off into the smoke and followed, seeing him cut down two men in quick succession. A third leapt onto his back, wrapping his legs around the noble's chest, dagger raised high. Vaelin's throwing knife took the Cumbraelin in the back, Al Hestian shrugging him off as he convulsed in pain, the long sword slashing down to cleave his chest. Al Hestian raised his sword in a silent gesture of thanks and ran on.

The bloodshed became frenzied as the company killed their way through the camp, hacking down the few Cumbraelins still able to offer resistance or knifing those found lying wounded. Vaelin ran past a series of nightmarish tableaux: a soldier raising the severed head of a Cumbraelin to let the blood bathe his face, three men taking turns to slash at a man writhing on the ground, men laughing at a Cumbraelin as he tried to stuff his guts back into the hole in his belly. He had seen men drunk before but never on blood. After months of fear and misery Al Hestian's soldiers were taking full measure of retribution from their tormentors.

He caught up with Al Hestian, finding the noble standing uncertainly over the kneeling figure of a young Cumbraelin, a boy of no more than fifteen years. The boy's eyes were closed, his lips moving in a murmured prayer. His weapons lay at his side and his hands were clasped in front of his chest.

Vaelin paused, catching his breath and wiping blood from his sword. From the direction of the river he could hear the clamour of weapons and shouts of combat as his brothers finished the last of Black Arrow's men. Dawn was rising fast now, revealing the horrid spectacle of the camp. Bodies lay all around, some still twitching or writhing in pain, streaks of blood discolouring the snow between the blazing tents. Al Hestian's men wandered through the destruction, looting the dead and finishing off the wounded.

'What should we do with him?' Al Hestian said. He face was streaked with sweat and ash, his expression grim. The bloodlust evident in his men has not reached him, he did not relish the killing. Vaelin was very glad he had abandoned his bargain with the King.

He will be angry, his watcher told him.

I'll answer to the King, he replied. *He can have my life if he wants it. At least I won't die a murderer.*

Vaelin glanced at the boy. He seemed oblivious to their words or the sounds of death around him, intent on his prayer. He spoke a language Vaelin didn't know, the prayer flowing from his lips in a soft, almost melodious tone. Was he asking his god to accept his soul or deliver him from impending death?

'It seems we have our first prisoner, my lord.' He nudged the boy with his boot. 'Stand up! And stop yammering.'

The boy ignored him, his expression unchanged as he continued to pray.

'I said get up!' Vaelin reached down to grab the boy's pelt. There was a rush of air on his neck as something flicked past his ear followed by the hard smack of an arrow finding flesh. He looked up to see Al Hestian staring at the black shaft buried in his shoulder, his eyebrows raised in a faint expression of surprise. 'Faith,' he breathed and collapsed heavily to the snow, his limbs already twitching as the poison mingled with his blood.

Vaelin whirled, catching a blur of powdered snow in a nearby cluster of trees. Rage filled him then, sprinting in pursuit of the archer, with red mist clouding his vision. 'You there!' he called to a group of soldiers. 'See to his lordship, he needs a healer!'

He ran full pelt into the trees, all senses alive to the song of the forest, searching, hunting. There was a faint crunch of snow off to the left and he sprinted after it, his nostrils finding the scent of fear-born sweat. He had never been so alive to the song of the forest before, never so possessed by the desire to kill. His mouth was flooded with drool and his mind devoid of all thought but the need for blood. How long he hunted would always be lost to him, it was a dream of blurred trees and half-remembered scents as his quarry led him deeper into the forest. He ran tirelessly, immune to any strain. He knew only the hunt and the prey.

The song of the forest changed as he entered a small clearing. The birdsong greeting the dawn was muted here, stilled by an unwelcome presence. He stopped, fighting to control his heaving chest, searching with all his senses, straining for the faintest sign. The clearing was well lit by the rising sun, the sunlight playing over an oddly shaped stone in its centre. Something about the stone drew his attention, lessening his concentration on the forest's song. It stood about four feet in height with a narrow base rising to a wide flat top in a roughly mushroomed shape, part overgrown with creepers. Looking closer, he realised it was not a natural feature at all but fashioned, chiselled from one of the many granite boulders that littered the Martishe.

If his senses hadn't been so alive, he would have missed the faint creak of the bowstring. He ducked, the arrow passing over his head in a black streak. The archer leapt from the bushes, hatchet raised high, his war cry shrill and savage. Vaelin's sword slashed into the man's wrist, his hatchet spinning away along with the hand that held it, the backswing laying his throat open as he staggered back in shock. He took only seconds to bleed to death.

Vaelin sagged as his body woke to the end of the hunt, the ache of the battle and the chase seeping into his limbs, his pulse raging in his ears as he fought for breath. He stumbled away, slumping against the stone, sinking to the ground, wanting nothing more than sleep. His eyes were drawn to the archer's corpse. The lines and weathering in his slack features betrayed him as a man with more years than most of their enemies. *Black Arrow?* Vaelin wondered but found he was too tired to search the body for any evidence of the man's identity.

The song of the forest returned as he lay there, head sagging to his chest, the birdsong louder now. A sudden warmth in his limbs roused him and he looked up to find the clearing bathed in bright sunlight. Oddly the sun was now high overhead, and he realised he must have surrendered to sleep. *Fool!* He climbed to his feet, making to brush the snow from his cloak . . . Except there was none. No snow on his cloak or his boots. No snow on the ground or the trees. Instead the ground was covered in lush green grass and the trees were liberally adorned with leaves. The air had lost the sharp chill of winter and through the forest canopy the sky was a deep shade of blue. *Summer . . . It's summer!*

He looked around wildly. Black Arrow's body, if it was indeed his, was gone. The stone structure that had drawn his gaze when he first entered the clearing was now bare of foliage, revealing a finely carved plinth of grey granite, its top perfectly flat save for a circular indentation in the centre. He moved closer, reaching out to trace a finger along the surface.

'You shouldn't touch that.'

He whirled, levelling his sword at the source of the voice. The woman was of medium height and dressed in a simple robe of loosely woven fabric, the design of which was completely unfamiliar. Her hair was black and long, tumbling over her shoulders and framing an angular, pale-skinned face. But it was her eyes that fixed him, or rather the fact that she had no eyes. They were a milky pink in colour, devoid of pupils. As she neared he saw they were shot through with a fine web of veins, like two orbs of red marble regarding him above a faint smile. *Blind?* But how could she be? He could tell she was *seeing* him, she had seen him reach out to the stone. Something about the set of her features triggered a memory from a few years ago, a grave, hawk-faced man shaking his head sadly and speaking in a language Vaelin didn't know.

'Seordah,' he said. 'You're of the Seordah Sil.'

Her smile widened a little. 'Yes. And you are Beral Shak Ur of the Marelim Sil.' She raised her arms, encompassing the clearing. 'And this is the place and time of our meeting.'

'My . . . name is Vaelin Al Sorna,' he said, mystification making him stumble over the words. 'I am a brother of the Sixth Order.'

'Really? What's that?'

He stared at her. The Seordah were renowned for their insularity but then how could she know his language but not know of the Order?

'I am a warrior in service to the Faith,' he explained.

'Oh, you're still doing that.' She came closer, her brows furrowed, head angled, red marble eyes regarding him for a moment of unblinking scrutiny. 'Ah, still so young. I always assumed you would be older when we met. There is still so much for you to do, Beral Shak Ur. I wish I could tell you it will be an easy road.'

'You speak riddles, lady.' He glanced around at the impossible summer day. 'This is a dream, a phantom in my mind.'

'There are no dreams in this place.' She moved past him, reaching out to the stone plinth, her hand hovering over the circular indentation in the centre. 'Here there is only time and memory, trapped in this stone until the ages turn it to dust.'

'Who are you?' he demanded. 'What do you want of me? Did you bring me here?'

'You brought yourself.' She withdrew her hand and turned back to him. 'As for who I am, my name is Nersus Sil Nin and I want many things, none of which you can give me.'

He realised he was still holding his sword and sheathed it, feeling faintly foolish. 'The man I killed, where is he?'

'You killed a man here?' She closed her eyes and a note of sadness coloured her voice. 'How weak have we become? I had hoped I was wrong, that my sight had failed me. But if blood can be spilled here, then it has all happened.' She opened her eyes again. 'My people are scattered, are they not? They hide in the forests whilst you hunt them to extinction?'

'You do not know of your own people?'

'Please. Tell me.'

'The Seordah Sil dwell in the Great Northern Forest. My people do not go there. We do not hunt the Seordah. It is said they are greatly feared. Even more than the Lonak.'

'Lonak? So they survived the coming of your kind. I should have known the High Priestess would find a way.' She turned her blank gaze on him once more, the impression of scrutiny was overpowering, his sense of wrongness flaring with it. But the sensation was different this time, not so much a warning of danger, more a feeling of disorientation, as if he had climbed a cliff and found himself awed by the sight of the ground far below.

'So,' said Nersus Sil Nin, her head tilted. 'You can hear the song of your blood.'

'My blood?'

'The feeling you just experienced. You have felt it before, yes?'

'Several times. Mostly in times of danger. It has . . . saved me in the past.'

'Then you are fortunate to be so Gifted.'

'Gifted?' He didn't like the tone she used when speaking the word, there was a gravity to it that made him uncomfortable. 'It is simply an instinct for survival. All men have it I'm sure.'

'All men do, but not all can hear it as clearly as you can. And the blood-song has more to its music than simply a warning of danger. In time you'll learn its tune well enough.'

Blood-song? 'You're saying I'm afflicted with the Dark, somehow?'

Her mouth twitched in faint amusement. 'The Dark? Ah yes, the name your people will give to what they fear and refuse to understand. The blood-song can be dark, Beral Shak Ur, but it can also shine very brightly indeed.'

Beral Shak Ur . . . 'Why do you call me that? I have a name of my own.'

'Men such as yourself tend to collect names like trophies. Not all the names you'll earn will be so kind.'

'What does it mean?'

'My people believe the raven to be a harbinger of change. When the raven's shadow sweeps across your heart your life will change, for good or ill, there is no way to know. Our word for raven is Beral and our word for shadow is Shak. And you, Vaelin Al Sorna, warrior in service to the Faith, are the Shadow of the Raven.'

The sensation, the blood-song she called it, was still singing in him. It was stronger now, the feeling was not unpleasant but it did make him wary. 'And your name?'

'I am the Song of the Wind.'

'My people believe that the wind can carry the voices of the Departed from the Beyond.'

'Then your people know more than I gave them credit for.'

'This' – Vaelin gestured around him at the clearing – 'this is the past, isn't it?'

'In a way. It is my memory of this place trapped in the stone. I trapped it there because I knew one day you would come and touch the stone, and we would meet.'

'How long ago is this?'

'Many, many summers before your time. This land belongs to the Seordah Sil and the Lonak. Soon your people, the Marelim Sil, the children of the sea, will come to our shores and take it all from us, and back to the forest we will go. I have seen it, the blood-song is your gift but mine is the sight that can pierce time. Only when I use my gift can my eyes see, it is the price I pay.'

'You're using your gift now? I am . . .' He fumbled for the right word. '. . . a vision?'

'In a way. It was necessary that we meet. And now we have.' She turned and began to walk back to the trees.

'Wait!' He reached out to her but his hand grasped nothing, passing through her robe like mist. He stared at it in bewilderment.

'This is my memory, not yours,' Nersus Sil Nin told him without pausing. 'You have no power here.'

'Why was it necessary for us to meet?' The blood-song had raised its pitch now, forcing the questions from his lips. 'What was your purpose in calling me here?'

She walked to the edge of the clearing and turned, her expression sombre but not unkind. 'You needed to know your name.'

'VAELIN!'

He blinked and it was all gone, the sun, the lush grass beneath his boots, Nersus Sil Nin and her maddening riddles. Gone. The air felt shockingly cold after the warmth of that summer's day uncountable years ago, the whiteness of the snow making him shield his eyes.

'Vaelin?' It was Nortah, standing over him, his face a mixture of bemusement and worry. 'Are you hurt?'

He was still slumped against the plinth, now once again covered in weeds. 'I . . . needed to rest.' He accepted Nortah's hand and hauled himself upright. Nearby Barkus was rifling the corpse of the old archer Vaelin had killed.

'You tracked me here?' he asked Nortah.

'It wasn't easy without Caenis. You don't leave much of a trail.'

'Caenis is hurt?'

'He earned a cut on the arm when he took care of the sentries. It's not too bad but he's laid up for a while.'

'The battle?'

'It's over. We counted sixty-five Cumbraelin bodies. Brother Sonril lost an eye and five of Al Hestian's men have gone to join the Departed.' Nortah's eyes showed the same haunted look that had clouded them when he first killed a man during their hunt for Frentis. Unlike Caenis and the others, Nortah did not appear to be growing accustomed to killing. He gave a mirthless laugh. 'A victory, brother.'

Vaelin recalled the sound of the arrow as it flew past his ear and embedded itself in Linden Al Hestian. *A victory . . . It feels like the worst of defeats.*

'Did he linger for long?'

Nortah frowned. 'Who?

'Lord Al Hestian. Did he suffer?'

'He suffers still, poor bastard. The arrow didn't kill him. Brother Makril doesn't know if he'll live. He's been asking for you.'

Vaelin fought down a shudder of guilt-ridden despair. Seeking a distraction, he moved to where Barkus was busily stripping the archer's corpse of any valuables. 'Anything to say who he was?'

'Not much.' Barkus quickly pocketed a few silver coins and extracted a sheaf of papers from the small leather satchel slung over the man's shoulder. 'Found some letters. Might tell you something.'

Nortah took the papers, his eyebrows rising as he read the first few lines.

'What is it?' Vaelin asked.

Nortah carefully folded the papers away. 'Something for the Aspect's eyes. But I think this little war of ours may be about to grow beyond this forest.'

Lord Linden Al Hestian lay on a bed of wolf fur, dragging air into his lungs with long, rasping breaths, his skin grey and moist with sweat. Brother Makril had extracted the arrow from his shoulder and dressed the wound with a herb poultice to draw out the poison, but this was only to ease the noble's mind, there was no saving him. They had forced redflower on him despite his objections, taking the edge from his pain but still he suffered as the poison worked its way through his veins. The men had erected a tent for him, the stench inside stirring Vaelin's memory of his agonised recovery from the Joffril root.

'My lord?' Vaelin said, sitting down next to him.

'Brother.' There was a ghost of a smile on the young noble's pale lips. 'They told me you went after Black Arrow. Did you get him?'

'He's . . . with his god now,' Vaelin replied, though in truth he still didn't know for certain who the man had been.

'Then we can go home, eh? I think the King will be satisfied, don't you?'

Vaelin looked into Al Hestian's eyes, seeing the pain and the fear there, the knowledge that there would be no homecoming for him, he would soon be gone from this world. 'He will be satisfied.'

Al Hestian slumped back into the furs. 'They killed the boy, you know. I told them to leave him be, but they cut him to pieces. He didn't even cry out.'

'The men were angry. They respect you greatly. As do I.'

'To think my father warned me against you.'

'My lord?'

'My father and I have many differences, many arguments. Truth to tell, I confess I like him not, father or no. Sometimes I think he hates me for not matching his ambition with my own. And men of ambition see enemies everywhere, especially at court, where intrigue abounds. Before I left he warned me of rumours, tales of a hidden hand moving against me, although he refrained from telling me whose hand. But he said I should mind you well.'

Rumours of a hidden hand . . . The princess has been busy it seems.

'Why you would seek to hurt me I cannot imagine,' Al Hestian went on in his pained rasp. 'You'll tell him for me, won't you? You'll tell him we were friends.'

'You'll tell him yourself.'

Al Hestian's laugh was faint. 'Humour me not, brother. There is a letter in my tent, back at the camp. I wrote it before we left. I would be grateful if you would see to its delivery. It's . . . for a lady of my acquaintance.'

'A lady, my lord?'

'Yes, Princess Lyrna.' He paused, sighing in sorrow. 'Coming here was to be the means by which I would finally win the King's favour. Our union would have had his blessing.'

Vaelin gritted his teeth to forestall a curse at his own stupidity. He had known since meeting Al Hestian that the King's description of him had been fanciful at best but hadn't realised the true reason for his mission here. He was to rid the princess of an unsuitable match.

'The princess must have regretted seeing you ride into danger,' he said.

'She is a lady of great fortitude. She said love must risk all or perish.'

I have much to do and I will tolerate no obstacle . . . Vaelin felt a wave of self-loathing course through him. *Princess, between us we have killed a very good man.*

'I have a younger brother, Alucius,' Al Hestian was saying. 'I would like him to have my sword. Tell him . . . tell him it would be best if he leaves it sheathed. I find war is not much to my liking . . .' He paused, face tensing as a tremor of pain swept through him. 'Lyrna . . . Don't tell her it was like thi—' He choked off, convulsed in pain, blood staining his chin. Vaelin reached for him but could only watch helplessly as Al Hestian writhed in his furs. Unable to bear it, he fled the tent, finding Brother Makril by the fire, his flask in his hand, gulping Brother's Friend.

'Is there no hope?' Vaelin pleaded. 'Nothing you can do?'

Makril barely glanced at him. 'He's had all the redflower we can give him. If we move him, he dies. A healer from the Fifth Order could ease his passing but even they couldn't halt it.'

Vaelin winced as a shout of pain came from the tent behind him.

'Here.' Makril held out his flask. 'It'll dull your hearing.'

'We can't leave him to suffer like this.'

Makril looked up, meeting his eyes. The suspicion was still there, his instinctive knowledge of Vaelin's guilt. After a moment he looked away and started to rise. 'I'll take care of it.'

'No.' Vaelin turned back to the tent. 'No . . . it's my duty.'

'The jugular. It's the quickest way. I doubt he'll even feel the cut.'

He nodded, walking back to the tent on numb legs. *So the King has made me a murderer after all . . .*

Al Hestian's eyes were glazed and unfocused as Vaelin knelt beside him, only coming back to life when they caught the glimmer of the dagger's blade. There was a moment of fear, then a sigh, whether of sorrow or relief Vaelin would never know. He met Vaelin's eye, smiled and nodded. Vaelin held him, cradling his head in his arm, laying the blade against his neck.

Al Hestian spoke, forcing the words out through a fresh grimace of pain. 'I'm . . . glad it was you . . . brother.'

CHAPTER THREE

'And these letters were found on the body of this Black Arrow?'

The Aspect's hands were splayed on the letters before him like two pale spiders, his long face intent as he stared up at Vaelin and Makril. Vaelin supposed they must look dreadful, grimy and worn from the twelve-day trek back from the Martishe, but the Aspect seemed indifferent to their appearance. After listening to their report he demanded the letters, his eyes scanning them quickly.

'We believe the man may have been Black Arrow, Aspect,' Vaelin replied. 'There is no way to know for sure.'

'Yes. Perhaps you shouldn't be so quick with the killing blow next time, brother.'

'I was remiss. My apologies, Aspect.'

The Aspect dismissed the admission with a barely perceptible shake of his head. 'You understand the import of these letters?'

'Sendahl read them to us,' Makril said.

'Did anyone outside the Order hear him?'

'We gave Al Hestian's men a double rum ration that night. I doubt they could hear anything.'

BLOOD SONG · 395

'Good. Pass the word to your brothers: they are not to discuss this with anyone, including each other.' He gathered the letters together and placed them in a solid wooden chest on his desk, shutting it firmly and securing a heavy lock on the latch. 'You must be tired, brothers. On behalf of the Order I thank you for your service in the Martishe. Brother Makril, you are confirmed as a Brother Commander. You will reside with us here for the time being. Master Sollis is currently commanding a company on the southern shore, the local smugglers are becoming excessively violent in resisting the King's excise men. You will take over his lessons. You still remember enough of the sword to teach it, I'm sure.'

'Of course, Aspect.'

'Brother Vaelin, report to the stables at the eighth hour on the morrow. You will accompany me to the palace.'

'Congratulations, brother,' Vaelin offered as they made their way towards the practice ground, where Al Hestian's regiment was encamped. There were no barracks available for them so the Aspect had granted permission to remain at the Order House. Vaelin suspected no provision had been made for them in the city because the King hadn't expected any to return.

Makril paused, regarding him with silent scrutiny.

'A commander and a master,' Vaelin went on, discomfited by the tracker's silence. 'An impressive achievement.'

Makril stepped close to him, his nostrils flared, drawing the air in. Vaelin resisted the impulse to reach for his hunting knife.

'Never did like your scent, brother,' Markil said. 'Something not quite natural about it. And now you stink of guilt. Why is that?' Without waiting for a reply, he turned and walked off, a stocky figure in the gloom. He gave a brief, shrill whistle and his hound emerged from the shadows to pad alongside as he made his way to the keep.

The tower room Vaelin had shared with the others for so many years was now occupied by a fresh group of students so they had been obliged to camp with the regiment. He found his brothers clustered around the fire, regaling Frentis with tales of their time in the Martishe.

'. . . went straight through two men,' Dentos was saying. 'A single arrow, I swear. Never seen nothing like it.'

Vaelin took a seat next to Frentis. Scratch, who had been curled up at Frentis's feet, rose and came to him, nuzzling his hand in search of petting. Vaelin scratched his ears, realising he had missed the slave-hound greatly but had no regrets about leaving him behind. The Martishe would have been a fine playground for him but Vaelin felt he had tasted enough human blood already.

'The Aspect thanks us for our service,' he told them, stretching his hands out to the fire. 'The letters we found are not to be discussed.'

'What letters?' Frentis asked. Barkus threw a half-eaten chicken leg at him.

'Did he say where we're going next?' Dentos asked, passing him a cup of wine.

Vaelin shook his head. 'I'm to accompany him to the palace tomorrow.'

Nortah snorted and gulped a mouthful of wine. 'You don't need the Dark to see the future for us.' His words were loud and slurred, chin stained red with spilled drink. 'On to Cumbrael!' He got to his feet, raising his cup to the air. 'First the forest then the Fief. We'll bring the Faith to them all, the Denier bastards. Whether they like it or not!'

'Nortah—' Caenis reached up to pull him down but Nortah shrugged him off.

'It's not as if we've slaughtered enough Cumbraelins already, is it? Only killed ten of them myself in that bloody forest. How about you, brother?' He swayed towards Caenis. 'Bet you can beat that, eh? At least twice as many, I'd say.' He swung towards Frentis. 'Should've been there, m'boy. We bathed in more blood than your friend One Eye ever did.'

Frentis's face darkened and Vaelin gripped his shoulder as he tensed. 'Have another drink, brother,' he told Nortah. 'It'll help you sleep.'

'Sleep?' Nortah slumped back to the ground. 'Haven't done much of that recently.' He held up his cup for Caenis to pour more wine, staring morosely into the fire.

They sat in uncomfortable silence for a while, Vaelin grateful for the distraction provided by one of the soldiers at a neighbouring fire. The man had found a mandolin somewhere, probably looted from a Cumbraelin corpse in the forest, and played it with considerable skill, the tune melodious but sombre, the whole camp falling quiet to listen. Soon the player had an audience clustered around him and began to sing a tune Vaelin recognised as 'The Warrior's Lament':

> *A warrior's song is a lonely tune*
> *Full of fire and gone too soon*
> *Warriors sing of fallen friends*
> *Lost battles and bloody ends . . .*

The men applauded loudly when he finished, calling for more. Vaelin made his way through the small crowd. The player was a thin-faced man of about twenty years. Vaelin recognised him as one of the thirty chosen men who had taken part in their final battle in the forest, the stitched cut on his forehead testified that he had done some fighting. Vaelin struggled to remember his name but realised with shame that he hadn't bothered to learn the names of any of the men they had trained. Perhaps, like the King, he hadn't expected any to live.

398 · ANTHONY RYAN

'You play very well,' he said.

The man gave a nervous smile. The soldiers had never lost their fear of Vaelin and few made any effort to speak to him, most taking care to avoid catching his eye.

'I was apprenticed to a minstrel, brother,' the man said. His accent differed from that of his comrades, the words precisely spoken, the tone almost cultured.

'Then why are you a soldier?'

The man shrugged. 'My master had a daughter.'

The gathered men laughed knowingly.

'I think he taught you well, in any case,' Vaelin said. 'What's your name?'

'Janril, brother. Janril Norin.'

Vaelin spied Sergeant Krelnik in the crowd. 'Wine for these men, Sergeant. Brother Frentis will take you to Master Grealin in the vaults. Tell him I'll meet the expense, and make sure he gives you the good stuff.'

There was an appreciative murmur from the men. Vaelin fished in his purse and dropped a few silvers into Janril's hand. 'Keep playing, Janril Norin. Something lively. Something fit for a celebration.'

Janril frowned. 'What are we celebrating, brother?'

Vaelin clapped him on the shoulder. 'Being alive, man!' He raised his cup, turning to the assembled men. 'Let's drink to being alive!'

The King convened his Council of Ministers in a large chamber with a polished marble floor and ornate ceiling decorated in gold leaf and intricately moulded plaster, the walls adorned with fine paintings and tapestries. Immaculately turned-out soldiers of the Royal Guard stood to attention in a wide circle around the long, rectangular table where the Council sat. King Janus himself was markedly different from the ink-spattered old man with whom Vaelin had made his bargain, seated at the centre of the table, an ermine-lined cloak about his shoulders and a band of gold on his brow. His ministers were seated on either side, ten men dressed in varying degrees of finery, all staring intently at Vaelin as he finished his report, with Aspect Arlyn at his side. At a smaller table nearby two scribes sat writing down every word spoken. The King insisted on a precise recording of every meeting and each Council member had been required to state his name and appointed role before sitting down.

'And the man who carried these letters,' the King said. 'His identity remains unknown?'

'There were no captives to name him, Highness,' Vaelin replied. 'Black Arrow's men were not given to surrender.'

'Lord Al Molnar.' The King handed the letters to a portly man on his left who had stated his name and office as Lartek Al Molnar, Minister of Finance. 'You know Fief Lord Mustor's hand as well as I. Do you see a similarity?'

Lord Al Molnar examined the letters closely for a few moments. 'Regretfully, Highness, the hand that penned these missives seems so similar to the Fief Lord's that I can discern no difference between the two. More than that, the way the letter is phrased. Even without a signature I would know it as the work of Lord Mustor.'

'But why?' asked Fleet Lord Al Junril, a large, bearded man on the King's right. 'Faith knows I've scant love for the Fief Lord of Cumbrael, but the man's no fool. Why sign his name to letters of free passage for a fanatic intent on fracturing our Realm?'

'Brother Vaelin,' Lord Al Molnar said. 'You fought these heretics for several months, would you say they were well fed?'

'They did not seem weakened by hunger, my lord.'

'And their weapons, of good quality would you say?'

'They had finely crafted bows and well-tempered steel, although some of their weapons were taken from our fallen soldiers.'

'So, well equipped and well fed, and this in the dead of winter when game would be scarce in the Martishe. I submit, Highness, that this Black Arrow must have had considerable support.'

'And now we know from where,' said a third minister, Kelden Al Telnar, Minister of Royal Works and, next to the King, the most finely dressed man at the table. 'Fief Lord Mustor has condemned himself. Long have I warned that his observance of the peace was but a mask for future treachery. Let us not forget that the Cumbraelins were forced into this Realm only after the bloodiest of defeats. They have never stopped hating us, or our beloved Faith. Now the Departed have guided brave Brother Vaelin to the truth. Highness, I implore you to act . . .'

The King raised a hand, silencing the man. 'Lord Al Genril.' He turned to a grey-bearded man seated at his right hand. 'You are my Lord of Justice and Chief Judge of my courts, and perhaps the wisest head at this Council. Are these papers evidence enough for trial or merely investigation?'

The Lord of Justice stroked his silver-grey beard thoughtfully. 'If we consider this as only a matter of law, Highness, I would say the letters require question and any charges would depend on the answers. If a man came before me charged with treason based solely on this evidence, I could not send him to the gallows.'

Lord Al Telnar started to speak again but the King waved him to silence. 'What questions, my lord?'

Lord Al Genril took up the letters and scanned them briefly. 'I note that these letters grant the bearer free passage across the borders of Cumbrael and require any soldier or official of the Fief to render whatever assistance the bearer may require. And indeed, if the signature and seal are genuine, they have been signed by the Fief Lord himself. But they are not addressed to any individual.

Indeed we do not even know the name of the man who carried them to his death. If they were penned by the Fief Lord, did he intend them for use by Black Arrow or were they perhaps stolen and used for a different purpose?'

'So then,' Lord Al Molnar said. 'You would have us put the Fief Lord to the question?'

The Chief Judge took several seconds to reply and Vaelin could see from the tension in his face that he recognised the grave import of his words. 'I believe question is warranted, yes.'

The door to the chamber opened abruptly and Captain Smolen entered, coming to attention before the King and saluting smartly.

'Found him, have you?' the King asked.

'I have, Highness.'

'Whorehouse or redflower palace?'

Captain Smolen's only sign of discomfort was to blink twice. 'The former, Highness.'

'Is he in a fit state to talk?'

'He has made efforts to sober himself, Highness.'

The King sighed and rubbed his forehead wearily. 'Very well. Bring him in.'

Captain Smolen saluted and strode from the room, returning a few seconds later with a man dressed in expensive but soiled clothes. He walked with the precise gait of one who worries he might tip over at any moment, the redness of his eyes and sallowness of his stubbled complexion bespoke several hours of excess. He looked to be in his forties but Vaelin guessed him to be younger, a man aged by indulgence. He halted next to Aspect Arlyn, greeted him with a cursory nod, then bowed extravagantly, but unsteadily, to the King. 'Highness. As ever I am honoured by your summons.' Vaelin noted the man's accent: Cumbraelin.

The King turned to his scribes. 'Let the record show that His

Honour, Lord Sentes Mustor, heir to the Fiefdom of Cumbrael and appointed representative of Cumbraelin interests to the court of King Janus, is now in attendance.' He turned a level gaze on the Cumbraelin. 'Lord Mustor. And how are you this morning?'

Lord Al Telnar gave a muted snort of amusement.

'Very well, Highness,' Lord Mustor replied. 'Your city has always been very kind to me.'

'I am glad. Aspect Arlyn you know of course. This young man is Brother Vaelin Al Sorna, recently returned from the Martishe forest.'

Lord Mustor's gaze was guarded as he turned to Vaelin, nodding a formal greeting, but his tone remained cheerful, if forced. 'Ah, the blade that won me ten golds at the Test of the Sword. Well met, young sir.'

Vaelin nodded back but said nothing. Mention of the Test of the Sword tended to darken his mood.

'Brother Vaelin has brought us some documents.' The King took the letters from Lord Al Genril. 'Documents that raise questions. I believe your opinion of their content would be valuable in discerning their intent.' Vaelin took note of Lord Mustor's momentary hesitation before stepping forward to take the papers from the King's hand.

'These are letters of free passage,' he said after scanning the pages.

'And they are signed by your father, are they not?' the King asked.

'That . . . would appear to be the case, Highness.'

'Then perhaps you can explain how Brother Vaelin came to find them on the body of a Cumbraelin heretic in the Martishe forest.'

Lord Mustor's gaze swung to Vaelin, his reddened eyes suddenly fearful, then back to the King. 'Highness, my father would never place documents of such import in the hands of a rebel. I can only imagine they were stolen somehow. Or perhaps forged . . .'

'Perhaps your father could provide a more absolute explanation.'

'I – I have no doubt he could, Highness. If you would care to write to him . . .'

'I would not. He will come here.'

Lord Mustor took an involuntary step backwards, fear now obvious in his face. Vaelin could tell the situation dwarfed him, he was being tested and found wanting. 'Highness . . .' he stammered. 'My father . . . It is not right . . .'

The King let out a long sigh of exasperation. 'Lord Mustor, I fought two wars against your grandfather and found him an enemy of considerable courage and cunning. I never liked him but I did respect him greatly and I feel he would be grateful he is no longer here to see his grandson gabble like the whoring drunkard he is when his Fief stands on the brink of war.'

The King raised a hand to beckon Captain Smolen over. 'Lord Mustor will be our guest in the palace until further notice,' the King told him. 'Please escort him to suitable quarters and ensure he is untroubled by unwanted visitors.'

'You know that my father will not come here,' Lord Mustor stated flatly. 'He will not be put to the question. Imprison me here if you must but it will make no difference. A man doesn't place his favoured son in the hands of his enemy.'

The King paused, regarding the Cumbraelin lord with a narrow gaze. *Surprised you,* Vaelin realised. *Didn't think he had the stomach to speak up.*

'We'll see what your father does,' the King said. He nodded to Captain Smolen and Lord Mustor was led from the room, two guards following close behind.

The King turned to one of his scribes. 'Draft a letter to the

Fief Lord of Cumbrael commanding his presence here within three weeks.' He pushed his chair back and got to his feet. 'This meeting is over. Aspect Arlyn, Brother Vaelin, please join me in my rooms.'

Everything in the King's quarters gave an overwhelming impression of order, from the angle of the finely woven carpets on the tiled marble floor to the papers on the large oaken desk. Vaelin found nothing to compare to the cramped, hidden room of books and scrolls he had been led to eight months before. *That was where he worked*, he realised. *This is where he wants people to think he works.*

'Sit, please, brothers.' The King gestured at two chairs as he settled behind his desk. 'I can send for refreshment if you wish.'

'We are content, Highness,' Aspect Arlyn replied in a neutral tone. He remained standing, obliging Vaelin to follow suit.

The King's gaze lingered on the Aspect for a moment before he turned to Vaelin, his lips forming a smile beneath his beard. 'Note the tone, my boy. No respect but no defiance either. You'd do well to learn it. I suspect your Aspect is angry with me. Why can that be I wonder?'

Vaelin looked at the Aspect, who stood expressionless, offering no reply.

'Well?' the King pressed. 'Tell me, brother. What could have aroused the anger of your Aspect?'

'I cannot speak for my Aspect, Highness. The Aspect speaks for me.'

The King snorted a laugh and smacked his palm on the desk. 'You hear it, Arlyn? His mother's voice. Clear as a bell. Don't you find it chilling at times?'

Aspect Arlyn's tone was unchanged. 'No, Highness.'

'No.' The King shook his head, chuckling slightly and reaching for a wine decanter on his desk. 'No, I don't suppose you do.' He poured himself a glass of wine and settled back into his chair. 'Your Aspect,' he told Vaelin, 'is angry because he believes I have set the Realm on the road to war. He believes, with some justification I might add, that the Fief Lord of Cumbrael will happily let me hack his drunken son's head from his shoulders before setting foot outside his own borders. This in turn will force me to send the Realm Guard into his Fief to root him out. Battles and bloodshed will result, towns and cities will burn, many will die. Despite his vocation as a warrior, and therefore a practitioner of death in all its many forms, the Aspect believes this to be a regrettable action. And yet he will not tell me so. It has always been his way.'

Silence reigned as the two men matched stares and Vaelin experienced a sudden revelation: *They hate each other. The King and the Aspect of the Sixth Order detest the sight of one another.*

'Tell me, brother,' the King went on, addressing Vaelin but keeping his eyes on the Aspect. 'What do you think the Fief Lord will do when he hears I have taken his son and commanded his presence?'

'I do not know the man, Highness . . .'

'He's not a complicated fellow, Vaelin. Reckon it out. I daresay you've enough of your mother's wit for that.'

Vaelin found himself disliking the way the King's tongue twisted around the mention of his mother but forced out a reply. 'He will be . . . angry. He will see your action as a threat. He will be put on guard, gathering his forces and watching his borders.'

'Good. What else will he do?'

'It seems he has but two choices, to follow your command or ignore it and face war.'

'Wrong, he has a third choice. He can attack. With all his might. Do you think he will do that?'

'I doubt Cumbrael would have the strength to face the Realm Guard, Highness.'

'And you would be correct. Cumbrael has no actual army beyond a few hundred guardsmen loyal to the Fief Lord. What it does have is thousands of peasant bowmen it can call upon in time of need. A formidable force, having ridden through an arrow storm or two in my time, I would know. But no cavalry, no heavy infantry. No chance, in fact, of attacking Asrael or matching the Realm Guard in open field. The Fief Lord of Cumbrael is far from being an admirable character but he does have enough of his father's brains to heed a reminder of his weakness.'

The King smiled again, turning away from the Aspect and waving a hand in placation. 'Oh don't worry, Arlyn. In a fortnight or so, the Fief Lord will send his messenger with a suitably grovelling apology for not attending in person and a plausible, if not very convincing, explanation for the letters, probably attached to a chest full of gold. I will be persuaded by my wise and peace-loving son to withdraw my command and release the drunkard. Thereafter, I doubt the Fief Lord will be giving any more letters of free passage to Denier fanatics. More importantly, he'll have remembered his place in this Realm.'

'Am I to take it, Highness,' the Aspect said, 'that you are convinced the Fief Lord is the author of the letters?'

'Convinced? No. But it seems likely. The man may not be a fanatic like the fools Brother Vaelin dispatched in the Martishe but he does have a weakness for his god. Probably fretting over his place in the Eternal Fields now he's passed his fiftieth year. In any case, whether he wrote the letters or not makes little difference, the problem lies in the mere fact of their existence. Once they came to light I had little choice but to act. At least this way the Fief Lord will feel a debt to my son when he ascends the throne.'

The King quickly downed the rest of his wine and rose from

his desk. 'Enough statecraft, I have other business with you brothers. Come.' He beckoned them into a smaller adjoining room no less ornately decorated, but in place of paintings or tapestries the walls were adorned with swords, a hundred or more gleaming blades. A few were of the Asraelin pattern but there were many others the style of which Vaelin had never seen. Great two-handed broadswords nearly six feet in length. Sicklelike sabres with blades that curved almost in a semicircle. Long needlelike rapiers with no edge and bowl-shaped guards. Swords with blades fashioned of gold or silver despite the fact that such metals were too soft to ever make useful weapons.

'Pretty, aren't they?' the King commented. 'Been collecting them for years. Some are gifts, some are the spoils of war, some I bought simply because I liked the look of them. Every so often I give one away' – he turned to Vaelin, smiling again – 'to a young man like you, brother.'

Vaelin experienced a sudden resurgence of the unease that had gripped him during his first meeting with the King. The unsettling knowledge that he was a small part of a larger, unseen design. The wrongness, what Nersus Sil Nin had called the blood-song, was singing faintly at the back of his mind. *If he gives me a sword . . .*

'I am a brother of the Sixth Order, Highness,' he said, trying to match the Aspect's neutral tone. 'Royal honours are not for one such as me.'

'Royal honours are precisely for one such as you, Young Hawk,' the King replied. 'Sadly, I'm usually obliged to hand them out to the undeserving. Today will be a welcome change.' He gestured expansively at the collection of swords around them. 'Choose.'

Vaelin turned to the Aspect, seeking guidance.

Aspect Arlyn's eyes had narrowed slightly but his expression was otherwise unchanged. He remained silent for a moment and when he spoke his tone was the same as before, void of both deference and defiance. 'The King honours you, brother. In so doing he honours the Order. You will accept.'

'But can it be right, Aspect? Can a man be both a brother and a Sword of the Realm?'

'It has happened before. Many years ago.' The Aspect's gaze shifted from the King to Vaelin and softened somewhat but his voice held no room for further discussion. 'You will accept the King's honour, Brother Vaelin.'

I don't want it! he thought fiercely. *It's payment, payment for a murder. This scheming old man wishes to bind me to him even more.*

But he could see no escape. The Aspect had commanded him. The King had honoured him. He had to take the sword.

Swallowing a sigh of frustration, he scanned the walls, eyes flicking from one blade to another. He toyed with the idea of choosing one of the golden blades, he could always sell it later, but decided a weapon of some practical use would be the wisest choice. He saw little point in taking an Asraelin sword, it could hardly be better than his own star-silver blade, and the more exotic weapons seemed too unwieldy to his eye. His gaze finally fell on a broad-bladed short sword with a simple plain bronze guard and wooden hilt. He took it down from the wall and tried a few experimental swings, finding it well balanced with a comfortable weight. The edge was keen, the steel bright and unscarred.

'Volarian,' the King said. 'Not very pretty but a solid weapon, useful in the press of battle when a man can't raise his arm. A good choice.' He held out his hand and Vaelin passed him the sword. 'Normally there would be a ceremony, lots of oaths and kneeling but I think we can dispense with that. Vaelin Al Sorna, I name you Sword of the Realm. Do you pledge your sword in service to the Unified Realm?'

'I do, Highness.'

'Then use it well.' The King handed him the sword. 'Now, as Sword of the Realm I must find you a commission. I name you commander of the Thirty-fifth Regiment of Foot. Since the Aspect has been gracious enough to allow the use of the Order House to accommodate my regiment, I think it only proper that the Order retain command of it. You will train the soldiers and command them in war, when the time comes.'

Vaelin looked to the Aspect for some reaction but saw nothing but the same rigid lack of expression.

'Forgive me, Highness, but if the regiment is to come under Order control, then Brother Makril would seem a better choice . . .'

'The famous Denier hunter? Oh, I don't think so. Could hardly give him a sword could I? Only one ennobled by the Crown can command a regiment of the Realm Guard. How long before they're ready do you think?'

'Our losses in the Martishe were heavy, Highness. The men are weary and haven't been paid for weeks.'

'Really?' The King looked at the Aspect with raised eyebrows.

'The Order will meet the cost,' the Aspect said. 'It would only be right if the regiment is to be ours to command.'

'Very generous, Arlyn. As for the losses, you can have your choice from the dungeons plus any men you can recruit from the streets. I daresay more than a few boys will come seeking service in a regiment commanded by the famous Brother Vaelin.' He chuckled ruefully. 'War is always an adventure to those who've never seen it.'

CHAPTER FOUR

'No rapists, no murderers, no redflower fiends.' Sergeant Krelnik handed the Chief Gaoler the King's order with the smallest of bows. 'No weaklings either. Got to make soldiers out of this lot.'

'Life in a dungeon doesn't do much for a man's fitness,' the Chief Gaoler replied, checking the seal on the King's order and briefly reading the contents. 'But we always endeavour to do the best for His Highness, especially since he's sent the Realm's most famous warrior.' He gave Vaelin a smile that was intended as either ingratiating or ironic, it was difficult to tell under the grime. Vaelin had initially taken the Chief Gaoler as a prisoner from the meanness of his garb and the dirt that covered his flesh, but the width of his girth and the extensive set of keys jangling at his belt bespoke his rank.

The Royal Dungeons were a set of old, interconnected forts near the harbour that would have fallen into disuse with the construction of the city walls two centuries ago. However, succeeding rulers had found their cavernous vaults an ideal storage space for the city's criminal element. The exact number of prisoners was apparently unknowable. 'They die so often, you can't keep count,' the Chief Gaoler explained. 'Biggest and meanest last the longest, can fight for the food, y'see.'

Vaelin peered into the darkness beyond the solid iron grate secured over the entrance to the vaults, resisting the urge to hide his face in his cloak against the almost overpowering stench. 'Do you give many to the Realm Guard?' he asked.

'Depends on how troubled the times are. When the Meldenean war was on the place was almost empty.' The Chief Gaoler's keys jangled as he moved forward to unlock the grate, gesturing at the four burly guards nearby to follow. 'Well, let's see how rich the pickings are today.'

The pickings consisted of a little under a hundred men, all in varying stages of emaciation, dressed in rags and soiled with a thick layer of dirt, blood and filth. They blinked in the sunlight, casting wary glances at the guards on the walls above the main courtyard, each aiming a loaded crossbow at the knot of prisoners.

'This really the best you could do?' Sergeant Krelnik asked the Chief Gaoler sceptically.

'Hanging day yesterday,' the man replied with a shrug. 'Can't keep 'em forever.'

Sergeant Krelnik shook his head in stoic disgust and started whipping the men into line. 'Let's have some order here, scum! No use to the Realm Guard if you can't stand up straight.' He continued to abuse them until they were arrayed in two uneven lines, then turned to Vaelin, snapping off a salute. 'Recruits for your inspection, my lord.'

My lord. The title still sounded strange to his ears. He didn't feel like a lord, he felt and looked like a brother of the Sixth Order. He had no lands, no servants, no wealth and yet the King had proclaimed him a lord. It felt like a lie, one of many.

He nodded to Sergeant Krelnik and walked along the line, finding it hard to meet the many frightened eyes that tracked his progress. Some men stood straighter than others, some were cleaner, some so thin and wasted it was remarkable they could still stand upright. And they all stank, a thick, cloying stench he knew so well. These men stank of their own death.

He continued down the line until something made him pause, one set of eyes that didn't follow him but remained fixed on the ground. He stopped and moved closer to the man. He was taller than most of the prisoners, broader too, the sagging flesh on his chest indicating a once-muscular torso weakened by a long period of malnutrition. Just visible under the filth covering his forearm was the deep indentation of a badly healed scar.

'Still climbing?' Vaelin asked him.

Gallis looked up, reluctantly meeting his eyes. 'On occasion, brother.'

'What was it this time? Another sackful of spice?'

There was a faint tick of amusement in Gallis's haggard face. 'Silver. From one of the big houses. Would've made it too if my lookout had kept his head.'

'How long have you been here?'

'Month or two. Can't really keep track of time in the vaults. Was s'posed to get hung yesterday but the cart was full.'

Vaelin nodded at his scarred arm. 'Does that give you any trouble?'

'Aches a little in the winter months. But I can still scale a wall better than any man. Don't you worry.'

'Good. I can find a use for a climber.' Vaelin took a step closer, holding the man's gaze. 'But you should know I'm still unhappy at what you tried to do to Sister Sherin, so if you run . . .'

'Wouldn't think of it, brother. I may be a thief but my word is iron.' Gallis made an effort to look soldierly, puffing out his chest and pulling his shoulders back. 'Why, it'd be an honour to march with . . .'

'All right.' Vaelin waved him to silence and moved back, lifting his voice so they could all hear. 'My name is Vaelin Al Sorna, brother of the Sixth Order and commander by the King's Word of the Thirty-fifth Regiment of Foot. King Janus has graciously consented to commute your sentence to the privilege of serving in the Realm Guard. In return you will march and fight at his word for the next ten years. You will be fed, you will be paid and you will follow my orders without question. Any man guilty of indiscipline or drunkenness will be flogged. Any man who deserts will be executed.'

He scanned their faces for some reaction to his words but saw mostly dumb relief. Even the hardships of a soldier's life were preferable to another hour in the dungeons. 'Sergeant Krelnik.'

'My lord!'

'Get them back to the Order House. I have business in the city.'

The seat of the noble house of Al Hestian was in the northern quarter, the city's richest district. It was an impressive red sandstone manse of many windows and extensive grounds surrounded by a solid wall topped with wicked iron spikes. The impeccably attired servant at the gate listened to Vaelin's enquiry with practised disinterest before asking him to wait and going inside for instructions. He returned after a few minutes.

'Young master Al Hestian is in the garden at the rear of the house, my lord. He bids you welcome and asks that you join him presently.'

'And the Lord Marshal?'

'Lord Al Hestian was called to the palace this morning. He is not expected until this evening.'

Vaelin gave an inward sigh of relief. The ordeal ahead would have been even more onerous if he had had to face the father as well as the brother.

Once through the gate he found a squad of Royal Guardsmen loitering on the lawn, one holding the reins of a handsome white mare. His relief evaporated as he surmised the meaning of their presence. The guardsmen gave him a formal bow as he passed. It seemed word of his new rank had spread quickly. He returned the bow and hurried on, anxious to be done with this and return to the Order House, where he could busy himself with training his regiment. *My regiment.* He wondered at the fact of it. Barely in his nineteenth year and the King had given him a regiment and, although Caenis had been quick to reel off a list of famous warriors who had risen to command at an early age, to Vaelin it still seemed absurd. He had sought an explanation from the Aspect as they travelled back to the Order House after the meeting at the palace but his questions were met with a simple instruction to follow his orders. But the preoccupied frown on the Aspect's brow told him the King's actions had left him much to consider.

The gardens were a protracted maze of hedgerows and flowerbeds blossoming in the onset of spring. He found them sheltering from the sun under a maple tree. The princess was as lovely as ever, smiling radiantly and tossing her red-gold hair as she listened to the earnest youth on the bench beside her reading aloud from a small book. Vaelin saw only the faintest resemblance to his brother in Alucius Al Hestian, a thin boy of fifteen years or so, his youthful features delicate, almost feminine, topped by a mane of black curls that cascaded over his shoulders. He wore black in mourning. Vaelin took a firm grip on the scabbard of the longsword he carried, drew in a deep draught of air and strode forward with all the confidence he could muster. As he drew nearer he could hear the lilting refrain of the boy's words: *'I pray you weep no more my love, let no tears fall for my demise, lift your face to the sky above, and let the sun dry your eyes . . .'*

He fell silent as Vaelin's shadow fell upon them.

'My Lord Al Sorna!' Alucius rose to greet him, offering his hand without regard to the lordly formalities Vaelin was finding so irksome. 'This is indeed an honour. My brother's letters spoke so highly of you.'

Vaelin's confidence withered and drifted away with the wind. 'Your brother was an overly generous man at times, sir.' He shook the boy's hand, and offered a short bow to Princess Lyrna. 'Highness.'

She inclined her head. 'A pleasure to see you again, brother. Or do you prefer "my lord" these days?'

He met her gaze, a mounting rage threatening to spill unwise words from his lips. 'Whatever pleases you, Highness.'

She made a show of contemplation, stroking her chin, her nails were painted pale blue and adorned with inlaid jewels that glittered in the sun. 'I think I'll keep calling you "brother." It seems more . . . seemly.'

There was a barely perceptible edge to her voice. He couldn't tell if she was angry, still smarting over his rejection, or simply mocking a man she thought a fool for passing up the chance to share in the power she craved.

'A fine verse, sir.' He turned to Alucius, seeking escape. 'One of the classics?'

'Hardly.' The boy seemed a little embarrassed and quickly put aside the small book he was holding. 'Merely a trifle.'

'Oh don't be so modest, Alucius,' the princess chided him. 'Brother Vaelin, you are honoured to witness a reading by one of the Realm's most promising poets. I'm sure it will be a proud boast in years to come.'

Alucius gave a sheepish shrug. 'Lyrna flatters me.' His gaze fell on the longsword in Vaelin's hand, sorrow clouding his face in recognition. 'Is that for me?'

'Your brother wanted you to have it.' Vaelin held the sword out to him. 'He asked that you leave it sheathed.'

The boy took the sword after a moment's hesitation, gripping the hilt tightly, his expression suddenly fierce. 'He was always more forgiving than I. Those who killed him will pay. I vow it.'

Boy's words, Vaelin thought, feeling very old. *Words from a story, or a poem*. 'The man who killed your brother is dead, sir. There is no vengeance to seek.'

'The Cumbraelins sent their warriors into the Martishe, did they not? Even now they plot against us. My father has heard word of it. The Cumbraelin Fief Lord sent the heretics who slew Linden.'

Word flies fast from the palace indeed. 'The matter is in the King's hands. I'm sure he will steer the Realm on the correct course.'

'The course to war is the only course I will follow.' The boy's sincerity was intense, tears gleaming in his eyes.

'Alucius.' Princess Lyrna laid a gentle hand on his shoulder, her tone soothing. 'I know Linden would never have wanted your heart to be burdened with hatred. Listen to Brother Vaelin's words; there is no vengeance to be had. Cherish Linden's memory and leave his sword in its sheath, as he wished.'

Her concern sounded so genuine Vaelin almost forgot his anger, but the vivid image of Linden's marble-white face as he pressed the knife against his neck dispelled any regard. However, her words seemed to have a calming effect on the boy, the anger draining from his face, although his tears continued.

'I beg your forgiveness, my lord,' he stammered. 'I must be alone now. I should . . . I should like to speak to you again, about my brother and your time with him.'

'You can find me at the House of the Sixth Order, sir. I would be glad to answer any questions you have.'

Alucius nodded, turned to press a brief kiss against the princess's cheek and walked back to the house, still weeping.

'Poor Alucius,' the princess sighed. 'He does feel things so, ever since we were children. You realise he intends to ask for a commission in your regiment?'

Vaelin turned to her, finding her smile gone, her flawless face serious and intent. 'I had not.'

'There are rumours of war. He has visions of following you to the Cumbraelin capital, where together you will visit justice upon the Fief Lord. It would please me greatly if you were to refuse him. He is just a boy, and even as a man I doubt he would ever be much of a soldier, just a pretty corpse.'

'There are no pretty corpses. If he asks, I will refuse him.'

Her face softened, rosebud lips curving in a soft smile. 'Thank you.'

'I couldn't accept if I wanted to. My Aspect has decided all the officers in the regiment will be brothers of the Order.'

'I see.' Her smile became rueful, acknowledging his refusal to engage with her game of favours. 'Will there be war do you think? With the Cumbraelins?'

'The King thinks not.'

'What do you think, brother?'

'I think we should trust the King's judgement.' He bowed stiffly and turned to go.

'Recently I had the good fortune to meet a friend of yours,' she went on, making him pause. 'Sister Sherin, is it not? She runs a healing house for the Fifth Order in Warnsclave. I went to make a gift of alms on behalf of my father. Sweet girl, though terribly dedicated. I mentioned that we had become friends and she asked to be remembered to you. Although she seemed to think you may have forgotten her.'

Say nothing, he told himself. *Tell her nothing. Knowledge is her weapon.*

'Do you have no reply for her?' she pressed. 'I could have the

King's Messenger carry it. I do so hate to see friendships end needlessly.'

Her smile was bright now, the same smile he remembered from their talk in her private garden, the smile that told of an unassailable confidence and knowledge far beyond her years. The smile that told him she thought she knew his mind.

'I'm glad fate has brought us together once more,' she continued when he didn't answer. 'I've been thinking recently, pondering a problem that may interest you.'

He said nothing, meeting her gaze and refusing to play whatever game she had in mind.

'Puzzles are a hobby of mine,' she went on, 'I once solved a mathematical riddle which had confounded the Third Order for over a century. I never told anyone of course, it doesn't do for a princess to outshine brilliant men.' Her voice had changed again, taking on a bitter edge.

'Your keenness of mind does you credit, Highness,' he said.

She inclined her head, apparently deaf to the emptiness of the compliment. 'But what has puzzled me lately is an event in which you were closely involved; the Aspect massacre, although why it's called that when only two of them died I can't imagine.'

'Why should such an unpleasant event concern you, Highness?'

'It's the mystery of course. The enigma. Why would the assassins attack the Aspects on that particular night, a night when novice brothers from the Sixth Order are present in three of the Order Houses? It seems a singularly poor strategy.'

Despite himself, his interest was piqued. *She has something to share. Why? What advantage does she gain by this?* 'And what conclusions have you drawn, Highness?'

'There's an Alpiran game called *Keschet*, which means "cunning" in our language. It's highly complex, twenty-five different pieces played on a board of one hundred squares. The Alpirans have a great love of strategy, in business and in war. Something I hope my father remembers in times to come.'

'Highness?'

She waved a hand. 'No matter. Games of *Keschet* can last for days and wise men have been known to devote their whole lives to mastering its intricacies.'

'A task I'm sure you've already accomplished, Highness.'

She shrugged. 'It wasn't so hard, it's all in the opening. There are only about two hundred variations, the most successful being the Liar's Attack, a series of moves designed to appear essentially defensive but which in fact conceal an offensive sequence bringing victory in only ten moves, if done right. The success of the attack is dependent on fixing the opponent's attention on a separate overt move in another region of the board. The key is in the narrow focus of the hidden offensive, it has but one objective, to remove the Scholar, not the most powerful piece on the board but crucial to a successful defence. The opponent, however, has been convinced that he's facing a varied attack on a broad front.'

'Attacking all the Aspects was a diversion,' he said. 'They only intended to kill one of them.'

'Perhaps, or perhaps two. In fact if you apply the theory more widely, it could be that you were the intended victim and the Aspects merely incidental.'

'Is that your conclusion?'

She shook her head. 'All theories require an assumption, in this case I assume that whoever orchestrated this attack was seeking to damage the Orders and the Faith. Simply killing the Aspects would of course meet this end, but new Aspects can be appointed to replace them, like Aspect Tendris Al Forne, and it is not unreasonable to conclude that his ascension has driven a wedge between the Orders. Damage has been done.'

'You're saying the whole attack was aimed at elevating Al Forne to Aspect of the Fourth Order?'

She raised her face to the sky, closing her eyes as the sun warmed her skin. 'I am.'

'You speak dangerous words, Highness.'

She smiled, her eyes still closed. 'Only to you, and I do wish you'd call me Lyrna.'

The promise of power wasn't enough, he thought. *So now she tempts me with knowledge.* 'What did Linden call you?'

There was only the smallest pause before she turned away from the sun to meet his gaze. 'He called me Lyrna, when we were alone. We had been friends since childhood. He sent me many letters from the forest so I know how much he admired you. My heart ached to hear . . .'

'Love must risk all or perish.' He was aware that his voice was hard with anger and his face set in a fierce glower. He was also aware that she had stopped smiling. 'Isn't that what you told him?'

It was only for a moment, but he was sure something like regret passed across her face, and for the first time there was uncertainty in her voice. 'Did he suffer?'

'The poison in his veins made him scream in agony and sweat blood. He said he loved you. He said he had gone to the Martishe to win your father's approval so you could wed. Before I slit his throat he asked me to give you a letter. When we gave him to the fire I burned it.'

She closed her eyes for a second, a picture of beauty and grief, but when she opened them again it was gone and there was no emotion in her answer: 'I follow my father's wishes in all things, brother. As do you.'

The truth of it lashed at him. They were complicit. Murder entangled them both. He may have resisted loosing the bowstring but he had placed Linden in the path of the fatal arrow, just as she had set him on the road to the Martishe. It occurred to him this may have been the King's plan all along, sordid murder binding them together in guilt.

He knew now his enmity for her was a deceit, an attempt to avoid his own share of blame, but even so found himself holding to it. *She is cold, she is scheming, she is untrustworthy.* But more than that, he hated the lingering hold she had over him, her effortless ability to engage his interest.

There was the faintest glimmer of something behind her eyes then as he realised the intensity of the gaze he had turned on her. *Fear,* he decided. *The only man who can make her afraid.*

He bowed again, guilt mingling with satisfaction in his breast. 'By your leave, Highness.'

Sister Gilma was plump and friendly, with a quick smile and bright blue eyes that seemed to sparkle continually with mirth. 'In the name of the Faith, cheer up, brother!' she had said when they first met, tweaking Vaelin's chin with a mock punch. 'You'd think the cares of the Realm were on your shoulders. Brother sour-face they call you.'

'Are you really sure you want a healer attached to the regiment?' Nortah had asked.

Sister Gilma laughed. 'Oh I see I'm going to like you!' she said in her thick Nilsaelin brogue, giving Nortah a punch on the arm that was less playful.

Vaelin had concealed his disappointment that Aspect Elera hadn't seen fit to appoint Sister Sherin in answer to his request, although he was hardly surprised. 'Whatever you require will be provided, sister.'

'It better be.' She laughed. In the month since her arrival he had noticed she tended to laugh when she was being serious, employing a humourless tone when indulging her weakness for gentle but effective mockery.

'Another two broken arms today,' she told him with a chuckle and wry shake of her head as he entered the large tent that served as her treatment room. Four men were lying abed, bandaged and sleeping. Another two were being tended by the assistants she had insisted on recruiting from the ranks. To Vaelin's surprise she had chosen two of the pressed men from the dungeons, slight fellows with quick minds and careful hands who would probably have made poor soldiers in any case.

'Keep driving these men so hard, and there'll be few left to face a battle a month from now.' She was smiling her bright smile, blue eyes twinkling.

'Battle is a hard business, sister. Soft training will make for soft soldiers, who will in turn become soft corpses.'

Her smile faded a little. 'Battle is coming then? There will be a war?'

War. The question was on everyone's lips. It had been four weeks since the King had summoned the Fief Lord of Cumbrael and no answer had come. The Realm Guard had been confined to barracks and leave cancelled. Rumours flew with alarming speed. Cumbraelins were massing on the border. Cumbraelin archers had been seen in the Urlish. Hidden Denier sects were plotting all manner of hideous Dark-fuelled villainy. Everywhere the air was thick with expectation and uncertainty, making Vaelin drive the men as hard as he dared. If the storm broke, they had to be ready.

'I know no more than you, sister,' he assured her. 'Any more pox cases?'

'Not since my visit to the ladies' encampment.'

An outbreak of pox amongst the men had been traced to a camp of enterprising whores recently established in the woods a scant two miles away. Fearing the Aspect's reaction to the news of a nest of whores so close to the Order House, Vaelin had ordered

Sergeant Krelnik to put together a squad of the more trustworthy men to evict the women and send them back to the city. However, the old soldier had surprised him by hesitating. 'Are you sure about this, my lord?'

'I've got twenty men too poxed to train, Sergeant. This regiment is under the command of the Order, can't have the men sneaking off to . . . indulge their lust in this way.'

The sergeant blinked, his grizzled, scarred face impassive but Vaelin felt sure he was suppressing a grin. There were times when talking to the sergeant he felt himself a child giving orders to his grandfather. 'Erm, with respect, my lord. The regiment may belong to the Order but the men don't. They ain't brothers, they're soldiers, and soldiers expect to be shown a woman now and again. Take away their . . . indulgence and there could be trouble. Not saying the men don't respect you, my lord, they surely do, never seen a bunch as terrified of their commander as this lot, but these fellows ain't exactly the cream of the Realm and we've been working them pretty hard. They get too hacked off, they could start taking to their heels, hanging or no.'

'What about the pox?'

'Oh the Fifth Order's got remedies aplenty for that. Sister Gilma'll sort it, get her to pay a visit to these women, sort them in no time she will.'

So they had gone to Sister Gilma and Vaelin had stammered out a request whilst she regarded him with an icy visage.

'You want me to go into a camp full of whores to cure them of the pox?' she said coldly.

'Under guard of course, sister.'

She looked away, closing her eyes whilst Vaelin fought the desire to flee.

'Five years training at the Order House,' she said softly. 'Four more on the northern border assailed by savages and ice storms.

And what is my reward? To live amongst the dregs of the Realm and tend to their doxies.' She shook her head. 'Truly the Departed have cursed me.'

'Sister, I meant no offence!'

'Oh good!' she said, beaming suddenly. 'I'll get my bag. The guard won't be necessary, though I'll need someone to show me the way.' She arched an eyebrow at Vaelin. 'You don't know it do you, brother?'

He grimaced at the memory of his stuttering denial. Sergeant Krelnik had been right, the incidents of pox fell away quickly and the men stayed content, or as content as they could be after weeks of training under his brothers' bruising tutelage. He opted to forget to apprise the Aspect of the incident and there was a tacit agreement it was not to be discussed amongst the brothers.

'Is there anything you need?' he asked Gilma. 'I can send a cart to your Order House for supplies.'

'My stocks are sufficient for now. Master Smentil's herb garden has been a great help. He's such a dear. Been teaching me to sign, look.' She made a series of signs with her plump but nimble hands that roughly translated as: *I am a bothersome sow.* 'It means "My name is Gilma."'

Vaelin nodded, his face expressionless. 'Master Smentil is a gifted teacher.'

He left her with the wounded and went outside. Everywhere, men were training, clustered in companies around brothers struggling to impart skills learned over a lifetime in the space of a few months. It was an often frustrating task, their recruits seemed so slow and clumsy, ignorant of the most basic tenets of combat. So much so that his brothers had complained bitterly when Vaelin forbade use of the cane. 'Can't train a dog if you can't whip it,' Dentos had pointed out.

'They're not dogs,' Vaelin replied. 'Not boys either, most of them anyway. Punish them with extra training or menial duties, cut their rum ration if you think it appropriate. But no beatings.'

The regiment was now at full strength, numbers swelled by the pressed men from the dungeons and a steady flow of new recruits who, true to the King's prediction, had been drawn to a soldier's life by Vaelin's legend, some having travelled great distances to enlist.

'More times than not it's the rumble in a man's belly makes him enlist,' Sergeant Krelnik observed. 'This lot seem hungry only for the glory of serving under the Young Hawk.'

As the weeks passed, the training began to take hold, the men growing visibly stronger, aided by a healthy diet, which many had never known before. They stood straighter and moved faster, handling their weapons with greater skill, although they still had much to learn. Gallis the Climber soon recovered much of his physique, his spirits brightened by repeated visits to the whores' camp. He became one of the regiment's characters, ever ready with a cynical quip to draw laughter from his comrades, although he was wise enough to curb his tongue during the training sessions. The brothers may have been forbidden the cane but they knew a thousand ways to hurt a man in the tumble of a sparring match. Most gratifying for Vaelin was their discipline, they rarely fought amongst themselves, never questioned an order and there had been no attempts at desertion. He was yet to order a flogging or a hanging and lived in dread of the day when he had no option. *War will be the test,* he decided, recalling the miserable months in the Martishe and the many men who had chosen to risk escape through the Cumbraelin-infested forest rather than face another day in the stockade.

He found Nortah teaching the bow to a group of their more burly recruits. All newly enlisted soldiers had been tested at the butts and most found wanting, the more keen-eyed collected into a company of crossbowmen, but a few had shown sufficient skill and strength to warrant further tuition. They numbered only thirty or so, but even a small number of skilled bowmen would be a valuable asset to the regiment. Nortah again proved an able teacher; all his charges could now sink a shaft into the centre of the butt from forty paces and one or two could repeat the feat with the rapidity usually displayed only by brothers of the Order.

'Don't kiss the string,' Nortah told a student, a brawny fellow Vaelin recalled from his trip to the dungeons. His name was Drak or Drax, a renowned poacher before the King's Foresters had caught him quartering a freshly felled deer in the Urlish. 'Get the arrow back behind your ear for every loosing.'

Drak or Drax forced the extra effort into his muscles and let fly, the shaft striking home a few inches higher than the bull's-eye. 'Not bad,' Nortah told him. 'But you're still letting the stave swing out after you loose. Remember, this is a war bow, you're not hunting game with it. Get that string back as quick as you can.' He noticed Vaelin's approach and clapped his hands to get the attention of his company. 'All right. Move the butts back another ten paces. First man to hit the bull gets an extra inch of rum tonight.'

He turned to give Vaelin an extravagant bow as his men went to move the butts. 'Greetings, my lord.'

'Don't do that.' Vaelin glanced at the men, joking and laughing as they worked their shafts from the butts. 'They're in good humour.'

'With good reason. Plenty of food, rum every day and cheap harlots a short walk through the forest. More than most of them could ever hope for.'

Vaelin took a close look at his brother, seeing the familiar haunted look that had continued to cloud his eyes ever since their time in the Martishe. He seemed tired and distant when off duty, taking an excessive interest in the various rum-based concoctions the men would brew of an evening. Not for the first time Vaelin found himself on the verge of telling him the fate of his family but as ever the King's order stilled his tongue. *He seems so aged,* Vaelin thought. *Not yet twenty and he has the eyes of an old man.*

'Where's Barkus?' Vaelin asked him. 'He's supposed to be teaching the pole-axe.'

'In the smithy, again. Hardly away from the place these days.'

Since their return from the Martishe, Barkus had lost his reluctance to work metal, presenting himself to Master Jestin and spending many an hour in the smithy helping to fashion the new weapons needed by the regiment. Master Grealin's armoury was extensive but even the racks of weapons in the vaults were insufficient to arm every man and still provide for the Order's needs. Vaelin did not object to Barkus taking up the hammer once again, especially since it seemed to make him so happy, but found it irksome that it took him away from his duties with the regiment. He would have to speak to him, as he had to speak to Nortah.

'How much did you have last night?'

Nortah shrugged. 'Stopped counting after my sixth cup. Slept well though.'

'I'll bet.' He sighed, hating the necessity of saying what he had to say. 'I don't begrudge a man a drink, brother, but you are an officer in this regiment. If you must get drunk, please do so out of sight of the men.'

'But the men like me,' Nortah protested with mock sincerity. '"Come sup with us, brother," they say. "You're not like the Young Hawk. We're not scared shitless of you, oh no." They even invited me to come roger some whores with them. I was touched.' He laughed at Vaelin's appalled expression. 'Don't worry, I've not quite sunk that far. Besides, from what I hear a visit to the camp will most likely leave a man with a fire raging in his britches.'

Vaelin decided it best not to enlighten Nortah with the news that the pox outbreak was now under control. He nodded at the bowmen. 'How long till they're ready?'

'In about seven years they'll be as good as we are. Think the Cumbraelins will give us that long?'

'I can only hope so. I meant will they stand? Will they fight?'

Nortah looked at his men, his haunted eyes distant, no doubt picturing them in battle, hacked and bloodied. 'They'll fight,' he said eventually. 'Poor bastards. They'll fight all right.'

CHAPTER FIVE

He was dreaming of the Martishe, back in the clearing listening to the maddening enigma woven by Nersus Sil Nin, when Frentis came to wake him. But now the red marble pattern of her eyes was jet-black, like the stone that sat in the empty socket of the one-eyed man. The warm summer sun that had bathed the clearing in his vision was gone now, the ground thick with snow, the air cutting with its chill. And her words, whilst still mysterious, were cruel.

'You will kill and kill again, Beral Shak Ur,' she told him with a sickening smile, small points of light gleaming in the black orbs of her eyes. 'You will witness the harvest of death under a blood-red sun. You'll kill for your faith, for your King and for the Queen of Fire when she arises. Your legend will cover the world and it will be a song of blood.'

He was kneeling in the snow, his hands entwined on the hilt of his dagger, the blade slick with blood that shone black in the moonlight. Behind him there was a corpse; he could feel its heat seeping away into the snow. He knew the face of the corpse, he knew it was someone he loved. And he knew he had killed them. 'I didn't ask for this,' he said. 'I never wanted it.'

'Want is nothing. Destiny is everything. You are a plaything of fate, Beral Shak Ur.'

'I'll choose my own fate,' he said, but the words were faint, empty, a child's defiance to an indifferent parent.

Her laugh was a mocking cackle. 'Choice is a lie. The greatest of lies.'

Her spite-filled features faded as a hand shook his shoulder. 'Brother!' He came awake with a start, Frentis's pale, worried face swimming into clarity through clouded eyes. 'There's a messenger here,' his brother said. 'From the palace. The Aspect wants you.'

He dressed quickly and forced the lingering nightmare from his mind as he made his way to the keep. He found the Aspect in his rooms, reading from a scroll bearing the King's seal. 'The Fief Lord of Cumbrael is dead,' the Aspect told him without preamble. 'It appears his son, his second son, has murdered him and claimed Lordship of the Fief. He calls for all loyal Cumbraelins and true servants of their god to rally to him and throw off the hated oppressor and heretic King Janus. He orders all adherents of the Faith to leave the Fief or face righteous execution. Reportedly some are already burning in their bonfires.' He paused, watching Vaelin's face closely. 'You know what this means, Vaelin?'

The conclusion was obvious if chilling. 'There will be war.'

'Indeed. Battles and bloodshed, towns and cities will burn.' The Aspect's voice was bitter as he tossed the King's message onto his desk. 'His Highness has ordered the Realm Guard to muster. Our regiment is to be at the north gate by noon tomorrow.'

'I'll see to it, Aspect.'

'Are they ready?'

Vaelin recalled Nortah's words and his own assessment of their discipline. 'They will fight, Aspect. If we had more time, they would fight better, but they will fight.'

'Very well. Brother Makril will command a scout troop of

thirty brothers to accompany the regiment and provide reconnaissance. I would have liked a more sizeable contingent but our
commands are scattered about the Realm and there is no time
to recall sufficient numbers.'

The Aspect came closer, his face as serious as Vaelin had ever
seen it. 'Remember this above all. The regiment is under the King's
Word but is a part of this Order and this Order is the sword of
the Faith. The sword of the Faith cannot be stained with innocent
blood. In Cumbrael you will see many things, many terrible things.
They are a people who deny the Faith and indulge in the falsehood
of god-worship but they are still subjects of this Realm. There will
be great temptation to indulge your rage, to allow your men to
abuse the people you find there. You must resist it. Rapists and
thieves and any who abuse the people are to be flogged and hanged.
You will show every kindness to the common folk of Cumbrael. You
will show them that the Faith is not vengeful.'

'I will, Aspect.'

The Aspect moved back to his desk, sitting down heavily, his
long fingers clasped together in his lap, his thin face drawn and
tired, eyes mournful. 'I had hoped I would not see this Realm
once again rent by war in my lifetime,' the Aspect said eventually.
'It was why we joined him, you see? Why we wedded the Faith to
the Crown. For peace and' – a faint smile curled his narrow lips –
'for unity.'

'I . . . doubt the King wished this crisis to end in war, Aspect,'
Vaelin offered.

The Aspect turned to him sharply and the sorrow was gone
in an instant, replaced by the immobile certainty Vaelin had known
since his boyhood. 'The King's wishes are not for us to know. Do
not forget my instructions, Vaelin. Keep to the Faith and may the
Departed guide your hand.'

◆ ◆ ◆

The regiment marched under a slate-grey sky, the late-summer sun hidden by a bank of angry cloud that matched the grim mood of the men. It had taken longer to get them assembled and marching than Vaelin had liked and he found his temper flaring continually during the march to the city.

'Pick it up, lackwit!' he snarled at one unfortunate soldier who dropped his pole-axe. 'It's worth more than you are. Sergeant, no rum for this man tonight.'

'Aye, my lord!' Sergeant Krelnik was always at his side, eyeing him with wary respect. Vaelin suspected the sergeant might not always be punctilious in enforcing his punishments, something he chose to ignore, although today he felt markedly less inclined to do so.

They arrived at the north gate an hour before noon, the men falling out on the side of the road, some grumbling at the lack of rest on the march, but not too loudly.

'Where are they all?' Barkus asked, looking at the empty plain. 'Isn't the whole Realm Guard supposed to be here?'

'Maybe they're late,' Dentos suggested. 'We beat them here 'cos we march faster.'

'Brother Commander Makril may have some answers.' Caenis nodded at the gate, where Makril had appeared, leading his small company of mounted scouts at the gallop.

'The Realm Guard are mustering on the Western Road,' the Brother Commander told them as he reined in, scattering dust before him. 'The Battle Lord orders us to wait here.'

'Battle Lord?' Vaelin asked. There hadn't been a Battle Lord in the Realm since his father left the King's service.

'Lord Marshal Al Hestian has been honoured by the King. He leads the Realm Guard to Cumbrael with orders to take the capital with all dispatch.'

Al Hestian . . . The King has put the Realm Guard in the hands of Linden's father. Vaelin wished now he had met with the Lord Marshal when he delivered his sword to Linden's brother. He would have given much to gauge the man's temper, to know if he lusted for vengeance. If so, the Aspect's fears for the innocent people of Cumbrael would be well-founded.

He turned to Sergeant Krelnik. 'Make sure the men go easy on the water. No fires. We don't know how long we'll be here.'

'Aye, my lord.'

They waited under the threatening sky, the men clustering together to play dice or toss board, the Order game having been enthusiastically adopted by the regiment. As in the Order, throwing knives had become a form of currency and a sign of status amongst the soldiers, although Vaelin had been keen to ensure other Order traditions, such as thievery and frequent mealtime brawling, did not cross over into the ranks.

'Faith, Barkus! What is that?'

Dentos was staring at the object Barkus had unfurled from his saddlebag. It was about a yard long with a spiralled iron haft and a double-headed blade that seemed to shine unnaturally in the meagre daylight. 'Battle-axe,' Barkus replied. 'Master Jestin helped me forge it.'

Looking at the weapon, Vaelin experienced a murmur of disquiet from the blood-song, his unease deepened by what he knew of Barkus's Dark affinity for metal.

'Star silver in the blade?' Nortah asked as they gathered round to inspect the weapon.

'Of course, only on the edges though. The haft is hollow to keep it light.' He tossed the axe into the air, where it turned end over end before landing in his palm. 'See? Could bring down a sparrow in flight with this. Try it.'

He handed the weapon to Nortah, who gave it a few practice swings, his eyebrows rising at the fluid passage of the blade through the air. 'Sounds like it's singing. Listen.' He swung the axe again and there was a faint, almost musical note in the air. Vaelin felt the pitch of the blood-song deepen at the sound and found himself edging away involuntarily, a dull nausea building in his gut.

'Want to try, brother?' Nortah offered him the axe.

Vaelin's gaze was drawn to the axe blade, its gleaming star-silver edge and the broad centre of the blade indented with an inscription. 'You gave it a name?' he asked Barkus, not taking the axe.

'Bendra. For my . . . A woman I used to know.'

Nortah peered closely at the blade. 'Can't read it. What language is this?'

'Master Jestin said it was old Volarian. It's a smith's tradition to use it when inscribing blades. Dunno why.'

'Volarian smiths are counted the best in the world,' Caenis said. 'It's said they were the first race to smelt iron. Most of the secrets of the smithy originate with them.'

'Enough play, brothers,' Vaelin said, seized by a desire to be away from the weapon. 'See to your companies. Make sure they haven't contrived to lose any heavy gear on the march.'

It was an hour before another party came through the gate, twenty men of the mounted Royal Guard led by a tall red-haired young man on an impressive black stallion. Vaelin recognised the impeccably neat figure of Captain Smolen riding at his side.

'Get them into ranks!' Vaelin barked at Sergeant Krelnik. 'Make it tidy. We have a royal visitor.'

He strode forward to greet the prince as the regiment quickly formed companies and stood to attention, raising a thick cloud of dust in the process. The prince's party reined in as Vaelin sank to one knee, head bowed. 'Highness.'

'Get up, brother,' Prince Malcius told him. 'We have scant time for ceremony. Here.' He tossed Vaelin a scroll bearing the King's seal. 'Your orders. This regiment is at my disposal until further notice.' He glanced over his shoulder and Vaelin's gaze was drawn to the hunched figure mounted in the front rank of the guards, a sallow-faced man with red-rimmed eyes and heavy brows denoting an extended period of overindulgence. 'You've met Lord Mustor before, I believe,' Prince Malcius said.

'I have. My condolences on your father's passing, my lord.' If the heir to Cumbrael noticed his offer of commiseration, he gave no sign, squirming uncomfortably in his saddle and yawning.

'Lord Mustor will be accompanying us,' the prince informed him. He glanced around at the neatly arranged ranks. 'Are they ready to march?'

'At your command, Highness.'

'Then let's not dally. We will take the Northern Road and be at the bridge over the Brinewash by nightfall.'

Vaelin did a rough calculation of the distance. *Nearly twenty miles, and on the Northern Road, away from the Realm Guard's route.* He pushed the torrent of questions to the back of his mind and gave a formal nod. 'Very well, Highness.'

'I will proceed ahead and make camp.' The prince favoured him with a brief smile. 'We'll talk tonight. No doubt you'll wish an explanation for all this.'

He spurred his horse and rode off at the gallop, followed closely by the company of guardsmen. As they rode past, Vaelin picked out another familiar face amongst the riders, a thin youthful face framed by a mane of black curls. His eyes met Vaelin's briefly, an earnest expression seeking recognition, approval. *Alucius Al Hestian. So he will ride to war after all.* Vaelin turned away and began shouting orders.

Night was already drawing in when the regiment reached the timber bridge over the broad torrent of the Brinewash River. Vaelin ordered the camp raised and pickets posted. 'No rum ration until this is over,' he told Sergeant Krelnik, dismounting from Spit and rubbing the ache in his back. 'I expect several more days of hard marching. Don't want the men's feet slowed by liquor. Any man who complains can take it up with me personally.'

'There'll be no complaints, my lord,' Krelnik assured him before striding off, his harsh, gravelled voice casting forth a torrent of orders.

Leaving Spit in the care of a brother in Makril's command, he found the prince's party encamped near a willow tree close to the bridge. 'Lord Vaelin.' Captain Smolen greeted him formally, snapping off a precise salute. 'Good to see you again.'

'Captain.' Vaelin was still cautious of the captain after his part in placing him in Princess Lyrna's company. Still, it seemed churlish to hold it against him, he could understand how a man would find it all too easy to accede to her persuasion.

'Must say I'm glad of the chance to be a soldier again.' Captain Smolen inclined his head at the campfire, where a huddled, cloaked figure stared into the flames, taking occasional sips from a wine bottle. 'I feel I have been nurse-maiding the new Fief Lord long enough.'

'He is a demanding charge then?'

'Hardly. My duties consist mainly of keeping him supplied with wine and refusing to procure him a whore. If he's not asking for either, he rarely says anything.' The captain gestured at the tent pitched nearby. 'His Highness said to bid you enter as soon as you arrive.'

He found the prince hunched over a table, his gaze fixed on the map spread out before him. Seated in the corner of the tent, Alucius Al Hestian looked up from the scroll on which he had been writing.

'Brother,' the prince greeted him warmly, coming forward to take his hand. 'Your men made good time. I didn't expect you for another hour or two.'

'The regiment marches well, Highness.'

'I'm very glad to hear it. They'll have many more miles to cover before we're done.' He moved back to the table, glancing at Alucius. 'Some wine for Brother Vaelin, Alucius.'

'Thank you, Highness, but I would prefer water.'

'As you wish.'

The young poet poured a goblet of water from a flask and handed it to Vaelin, his expression was guarded but still eager for acknowledgment. 'I am glad to see you again, my lord.'

'And I you, sir.' His tone was neutral but, from the way Alucius drew back, he knew his face must have betrayed his thoughts.

'Check on the horses will you, Alucius?' the prince asked. 'Ranger gets feisty when he's not groomed properly.'

'I will, Highness.' Alucius bowed and departed, casting another guarded look in Vaelin's direction before the tent flap closed behind him.

'He begged me,' Prince Malcius said. 'Said he would follow us even if I commanded him not to. I made him my squire, what else could I do?'

'Squire, Highness?'

'A Renfaelin custom. Younger nobles are apprenticed to seasoned knights to learn their trade.' He paused, noting Vaelin's expression. 'I see you share my sister's disapproval.'

'His brother didn't want this for him. It was his dying wish.'

'Then I am sorry. But a man must make his own path in life.'

'A man yes. But he is still a boy. All he knows of war comes from a book.'

'I had barely fourteen years when I accompanied our fleet to the Meldenean Islands. I thought of war as a grand escapade. I soon learned I was wrong. And so will Alucius. It is the lessons we learn that change us from boys to men.'

'Has he been trained at least?'

'His father attempted to have him tutored in the sword, but apparently he made a poor student. I've asked Captain Smolen to give him some instruction.'

'Captain Smolen appears a fine officer, Highness, but I would consider it a favour if I could be permitted to train the boy.'

Prince Malcius considered a moment. 'So, friendship with one brother extends to the other?'

'More like obligation.'

'Obligation. I know a little about that. Very well, train the boy if you wish. Though where you'll find the time I can't imagine. Look here.' He turned back to the map. 'Our mission is like to prove arduous.'

The map was a detailed depiction of the border between Cumbrael and Asrael, from the southern coast to the mountains forming the northern boundary with Nilsael. 'We are currently encamped here.' The prince pointed to the crossing at the western branch of the Brinewash. 'Whilst Battle Lord Al Hestian leads the Realm Guard along the Western Road to the ford north of the Martishe. From there he will make for the Cumbraelin capital, no doubt spreading fire and terror in his wake. Most likely he will reach the capital in twenty days, perhaps twenty-five if the Cumbraelins muster sufficient force to meet him in the field. Have no doubt, when he gets to Alltor it will burn, and many innocent souls will burn with it.' Prince Malcius met Vaelin's eyes, his gaze unblinking and intent. 'Would the Orders of our Faith rejoice or weep at such an outcome, brother? So many Deniers given to the fire to trouble us no more.'

'The truly Faithful could never rejoice at the spilling of innocent blood, Highness. Denier or not.'

'Then you would agree that we should seize any chance we have to halt such slaughter before it begins?'

'Of course.'

'Good!' The prince's fist thumped the table and he moved to the tent flap. 'Fief Lord Mustor! Your attention please.'

It took the Fief Lord of Cumbrael several moments to answer the summons, his unshaven visage even more drawn and wasted than Vaelin remembered. The man was clearly still drunk and Vaelin was surprised at the steadiness of his voice.

'Brother Vaelin. I understand congratulations are in order.'

'Congratulations, my lord?'

'You are made a Sword of the Realm, are you not? It seems your elevation coincides with my own.' His laugh was loaded with irony.

'I was acquainting Brother Vaelin with our design, Lord Mustor,' Prince Malcius informed him. 'He agrees with the intent of our mission.'

'I'm so glad. Really would rather not inherit a Fief composed mostly of ash and corpses.'

'Quite,' the prince muttered, moving back to the map. 'Fief Lord Mustor has been gracious enough to provide us with what he believes to be sound intelligence regarding the dispositions of his usurping brother. Although the Battle Lord will no doubt expect to find him at the Cumbraelin capital, Lord Mustor is certain we will in fact find him here.' His finger tapped at a point to the north, a narrow pass in the Greypeaks, the mountain range forming the natural border between Cumbreal and Asrael.

Vaelin peered closely at the map. 'There's nothing there, Highness.'

Fief Lord Mustor snorted a short laugh. 'Won't find it on any map, brother. My father and all his father's fathers made sure of that. It's called the High Keep, with good reason I assure you. The most impregnable fortification in the Fief, if not the Realm. Granite walls a hundred feet high and commanding views over all approaches. It's never been taken. My poor deluded little brother will be there, no doubt surrounded by a few hundred loyal fanatics. Probably spending their time quoting the Ten Books at the top of their lungs and whipping each other for impious thoughts.' He paused to look hopefully around the tent. 'Do you perchance have anything to drink, Prince Malcius? I find myself quite parched.'

Vaelin saw the prince bite back an irritated retort as he pointed at the wine bottle on a small table. 'Ah, most kind.'

'Forgive me, my lord,' Vaelin said. 'But if this keep is impregnable, how are we to gain access to the usurper?'

'By means of my family's most cherished secret, brother.' Fief Lord Mustor smacked his lips as he tasted a generous sip of wine. 'Ah, a fine red from the Werlishe Valley. My compliments on your cellar, Highness.' He took another, more generous sip.

'Secret, my lord?' Vaelin prompted.

The Fief Lord's brows knitted in momentary puzzlement. 'Oh, the keep. Yes, the family secret, only entrusted to the firstborn son. The keep's only weakness. Many years ago, when the keep was the main seat of our house, one of my forebears became somewhat fearful of his own subjects and convinced himself the House Guards were in league with plotters to bring about his downfall. In need of an escape route in a time of crisis, he had a tunnel hewn through the mountain and, having had all the miners who did the hewing quietly poisoned, entrusted the secret of its location to his firstborn son. Ironically, it appears his constant fear of plotters was merely a symptom of the black pox, which can affect a man's mind as much as his member, and from which he expired a few months later.' He drained his wineglass. 'This really is a rather excellent vintage.'

'So you see,' Prince Malcius said. 'The Fief Lord will lead us to the tunnel, your men will storm the keep and the usurper will be taken into custody to face the King's justice.'

'Hardly likely, Highness,' Lord Mustor said, reaching for the bottle again. 'I'm sure my brother will make every effort to martyr himself in service to the World Father. Still, I daresay Brother Vaelin and his band of cut-throats are more than up to the task.'

'I am puzzled, Lord Mustor,' Vaelin said. 'Your brother has murdered your father in order to claim the Fief as his own, yet he secludes himself in a remote castle whilst the Realm Guard march on his capital.'

'My brother Hentes is a fanatic,' Lord Mustor replied with a shrug. 'When it became clear my father was going to bend the knee to King Janus he called him to a secret meeting and stuck his sword in his heart as a service to the World Father. No doubt the more vehement priests and followers would have approved but Cumbrael is not a land that could tolerate a Fief Lord who ascends by the murder of his own father. Whatever the thoughts of the commoners, the vassals who followed my father would not follow Hentes. They'll fight your army, they have little choice after all, but only in defence of the Fief. My brother will be at the keep, he can go nowhere else.'

'And once the usurper is . . . dislodged?' Vaelin asked Prince Malcius.

'The reason for this war will have disappeared. But it all depends on time.' He turned his attention back to the map, his finger tracing the route from the Brinewash bridge to the pass where the High Keep waited. 'Best guess, the pass is two hundred miles distant. If we are to accomplish our goal, we must get there in sufficient time to allow word to be taken to the Battle Lord.' He reached for a sealed parchment on the table. 'The King has already set down a command for the Realm Guard to return to Asrael in the event we are successful.'

Vaelin quickly calculated the distance between the pass and the Cumbraelin capital. *Nearly a hundred miles, two days' ride for a fast horse. Nortah could do it, maybe Dentos too. Getting to the keep in time, that's the hard part. The regiment will have to cover at least twenty miles a day.*

'Can it be done, brother?' the prince asked.

Vaelin's gaze turned to the Cumbraelin villages laid out on the map in precise, neat lines. He wondered how many people in those hamlets along the Western Road had any notion of the storm that would soon descend. When this war was done perhaps another map would have to be drawn. *In Cumbrael you will see many things. Many terrible things.* 'It will be done, Highness,' he said with flat certainty. *I'll whip them all the way there if I have to.*

And so they marched, four hours at a stretch, twelve hours a day. They marched. On through the grass lands north of the Brinewash, into the hills and valleys beyond and the foothills that signalled entry into border country. Men who fell out on the march were kicked to their feet and hounded into movement, those who collapsed given half a day on the wagon then put back on the road. Vaelin had decreed the only men left behind would be ready to join the Departed and counted on their fear of him to keep them moving. So far it had worked. They were sullen, weighed down by weapons and provisions, their mood soured by his order cancelling the rum ration until further notice, but they were still afraid, and they still marched.

Every night Vaelin would seek out Alucius Al Hestian for two hours of training. The boy was initially delighted by the attention. 'You honour me, my lord,' he said gravely, standing with his long sword held out in front of him as if he were holding a mop. Vaelin slashed it from his grip with a flick of his wrist.

'Don't be honoured, be attentive. Pick that up.'

An hour later it had become obvious that as a swordsman Alucius made a fine poet. 'Get up,' Vaelin told him, having sent him sprawling with a flat-bladed blow to the legs. He had repeated the same move four times and the boy had failed to notice the pattern.

'I, um, need some more practice . . .' Alucius began, his face flushed, tears of humiliation shining in his eyes.

'Sir, you have no gift for this,' Vaelin said. 'You are slow, clumsy and have no appetite for the fight. I beg you, ask Prince Malcius to release you and go home.'

'*She* put you up to this.' For the first time, there was some hostility in Alucius's tone. 'Lyrna. Trying to protect me. Well I won't be protected, my lord. My brother's death demands a reckoning, and I will have it. If I have to walk all the way to the usurper's keep myself.'

More boy's words. But there was a strength to them nonetheless, a conviction. 'Your courage does you credit, sir. But proceeding with this will only result in your death . . .'

'Then teach me.'

'I've tried . . .'

'You have not! You've tried to make me leave, that's all. Teach me properly, then there will be no blame.'

It was true of course. He had thought an hour or two of humiliation would be enough to convince the boy to go home. Could he really train him in the time left? He looked at the way Alucius held his sword, how he held it close to his body to balance the weight of it. 'Your brother's sword,' he said, recognising the bluestone pommel.

'Yes. I thought it would honour him if I carried it to war.'

'He was taller than you, stronger too.' He thought for a moment then went to his tent, returning with the Volarian short sword King Janus had given him. 'Here.' He tossed the weapon to Alucius. 'A royal gift. Let's see if you fare any better with it.'

He was still clumsy, still too easily fooled, but at least had gained some quickness, parrying a couple of thrusts and even managing a counterstroke or two.

'That's enough for now,' Vaelin said, noting the sweat on Al

Hestian's brow and his heaving chest. 'Best if you strap your brother's sword to your saddle from now on. In the morning, rise early and practice the moves I showed you for an hour. We'll train again tomorrow evening.'

For nine more nights they trained, after an arduous day's march, Vaelin would try to turn a poet into a swordsman.

'You don't block the blade, you turn it,' he told Alucius, annoyed he sounded so much like Master Sollis. 'Deflect the force of the blow, don't absorb it.'

He feinted a thrust at the boy's belly then swept the blade up and around, slashing at the legs. Alucius stepped back, the blade missing by inches, and countered with a lunge of his own, it was clumsy, unbalanced and easily parried, but it was quick. Despite his continual misgivings, he was impressed.

'All right. That'll do for now. Sharpen your edge and get some rest.'

'That was better, wasn't it?' Alucius asked. 'I am getting better?'

Vaelin sheathed his sword and gave the boy a pat on the shoulder. 'It seems there's a warrior in you after all.'

On the tenth day one of Brother Makril's scouts reported the pass less than half a day's march distant. Vaelin ordered the regiment to camp and rode ahead with Prince Malcius and Lord Mustor to locate the tunnel entrance, Makril's command riding as escort. The green hills soon gave way to boulder-strewn slopes on which the horses could find scant purchase. Spit grew fractious, tossing his head and snorting loudly.

'Foul-tempered animal you have there, brother,' Prince Malcius observed.

'He doesn't like the ground.' Vaelin dismounted, taking his bow and quiver from the saddle. 'We'll leave the horses here with one of Brother Makril's men, proceed on foot.'

'Must we?' Lord Mustor asked. 'It's miles yet.' His sagging features showed the signs of yet another night's indulgence and Vaelin was surprised he had managed to remain in the saddle for the duration of the march.

'Then we had best not linger, my lord.'

They struggled upwards for another hour or so, the dark majesty of the Greypeaks an oppressive, dominating presence above. The summits seemed ever shrouded in mist, hiding the sun, the muted light making the landscape uniformly grey. Although it was late summer, the air was chilled, possessed of a cloying dampness that seeped into their clothes.

'By the Father, I hate this place,' Lord Mustor gasped when they had paused for a rest. He slumped against a rocky outcrop and slid to the ground, unstoppering a flask. 'Water,' he said, noting the prince's disapproving glare. 'Truth be told, I had hoped I'd never see Cumbrael again at all.'

'You are the heir to the lordship of this land,' Vaelin pointed out. 'It seems an unlikely ambition never to return to it.'

'Oh, I was never meant to sit on the Chair. That honour would have been afforded Hentes, my murderous sibling, whom my father loved dearly. Must've broken the old bastard's heart when he lost him to the priests. He was always the favoured son, you see. Best with the bow, best with the sword, quick of wit, tall and handsome. Sired three bastards of his own by his twenty-fifth year.'

'He doesn't sound like the most devout of men,' Prince Malcius observed.

'He wasn't.' Lord Mustor took a long gulp from his flask, causing Vaelin to suspect it contained more than water. 'But that was before he took an arrow in the face during a skirmish with some outlaws. My father's surgeon removed the arrowhead but my brother took a fever and lay near death for several days, at one point it's said his heart stopped beating. But the Father saw fit to spare him, and once recovered he was a changed man. The handsome carousing, wench-chasing warrior became a scarred, pious devotee of the Ten Books. Hentes Trueblade they called him. He cut himself off from his old friends, shunned his many lovers, sought out the company of the most ardent and radical priests. He began to preach, passionate sermons describing the visions he had seen as he lay dying. He claimed the World Father had spoken to him, shown him the glorious path to redemption. Much of which apparently involves converting you foreign heathens to the teachings of the Ten Books, at sword point if necessary. My father had little choice but to send him away, along with his ever-growing band of followers.'

'And you say he believes your god told him to assassinate your father?' the prince asked.

'My brother's beliefs are not always easily understood, even by his disciples. But the very notion of the Fief Lord of Cumbrael abasing himself to King Janus would have been anathema, especially since it resulted from what he sees as Brother Vaelin's persecution of the holy warriors in the Martishe. So he invited my father to a meeting, under the pretence of seeking a return from exile, and there, with no guards to protect him, he killed him.'

He paused to drink again, his gaze lingering on Vaelin. 'My sources write that your name is known in Cumbrael now, brother. Hentes may be the Trueblade, but you are the Darkblade. It's from the Fifth Book, the Book of Prophecy. Centuries ago a seer spoke of a near-invincible heretic swordsman: "He will smite the holy and strike down those who labour in the service of the World Father. Know him by his blade for it was forged in an unnatural fire and guided by the voice of the Dark."'

Darkblade? Vaelin thought of the blood-song and what Nersus

Sil Nin had told him of its origins. *Perhaps they have it right.* He got to his feet. 'We'd best press on.'

'Well that's a lot of fucking use!' Brother Commander Makril spat on the ground near Lord Mustor's feet.

The Fief Lord drew back, a glimmer of fear in his eyes. 'It was open ten years ago,' he said, a faint whine colouring his voice.

Vaelin peered into the tunnel entrance, a narrow crack in a windswept cliff-face they would have barely noticed if Lord Mustor hadn't pointed it out. In the gloom of the tunnel entrance he could just make out the source of Makril's anger; a pile of huge boulders sealed the passage from floor to ceiling. The mass of rock was far too heavy to move with their small force. Makril was right, the tunnel was useless.

'I don't understand it,' Lord Mustor was saying. 'It was as well built as it could be. No-one save my father and I knew of its existence.'

Vaelin moved into the tunnel, running a hand over the surface of one of the boulders, feeling how it was smooth in one place and rough in another, his fingers finding the hard edges left by a chisel. 'This stone has been worked loose. Recently, if I'm any judge.'

'It appears your greatest secret has been betrayed, my lord,' Prince Malcius observed. 'If, as you say, your father favoured your brother over you, he may have felt it appropriate to share the secret with him.'

'What are we to do?' Lord Mustor asked plaintively. 'There is no other way into the High Keep.'

'Except by siege,' the prince said. 'And we have not the time, men or engines for that.'

Vaelin emerged from the tunnel. 'Is there a vantage point nearby where we can view the keep without being seen?'

It was a perilous climb up a narrow, rock-strewn path but they made good time, despite Lord Mustor's constant grumbling about his blistered feet. Eventually they came to a ledge shielded from the wind by a large outcrop of rock.

'Best stay low,' Lord Mustor advised. 'I doubt any sentry will have eyes keen enough to see us, but we shouldn't trust to chance.' He crept to the shoulder of the outcrop and pointed. 'There, hardly the most elegant of architecture, is it?'

The High Keep was hard to miss, its walls rose from the mountain like a blunted spear-point thrust up through the rock. Lord Mustor was right in noting the building's lack of elegance. It was devoid of any decoration, unadorned by statuary or minarets, the smooth plane of the walls broken only by a scattering of arrow slits. A single banner bearing the holy white flame of the Cumbraelin god snapped atop a tall lance on the bastion above the gate. The only approach to the keep was a single narrow road rising steeply from the floor of the pass. They were level with the top of the wall and Vaelin could see the black specks of sentries atop the battlements.

'You see, Lord Vaelin?' Mustor said. 'It's unassailable.'

Vaelin edged closer, peering down at the base of the keep; irregular rock giving way to smooth walls. *The rocks aren't a problem, but the wall?* 'How tall did you say the walls are, my lord?'

'Are you sure you can do this?'

Gallis the Climber lifted the coil of rope over his head, settling the weight on his shoulders, and glanced up at the towering keep above. 'I do like a challenge, milord.'

Vaelin pushed his doubts to the recess of his mind and handed the man a dagger. 'Do this for me and I might forget I'm angry with you.'

'I'll settle for that flagon of wine you promised me.' Gallis grinned, pushing the dagger into his boot and turning to the rock face, his hands exploring the granite for holds, dextrous fingers tracing over the irregular surface with intuitive precision. After a few seconds he took hold and began to climb, his body moving fluidly over the cliff, his hands and feet finding purchase seemingly of their own volition. Ten feet or so off the ground he paused to look down at Vaelin, smiling broadly. 'Easier than a merchant's house by far.'

Vaelin watched him ascend from the cliff to the wall, growing smaller the higher he climbed until he seemed like an ant struggling on the trunk of a great tree. He never faltered, never slipped. Satisfied he wasn't actually going to fall, Vaelin turned to the brothers and soldiers crouched in the darkness about him. They were a mixture of Nortah's best archers and brothers from Makril's command, twenty men in all. It was scant force against the numbers guarding the usurper but any more would increase the risk of detection. The rest of the regiment was waiting at the foot of the long uphill road to the keep's gate, Brother Makril had the command and would lead a mounted charge with Prince Malcius when the gate was opened. Caenis would follow with the main body on foot. Vaelin had endured strenuous objections against leading the assault on the gate, Caenis stating flatly that his place was with the men.

'I was sent for the usurper,' Vaelin replied. 'I intend to get him, alive if possible. Besides, I'd like the chance to talk to him. I'm sure he has many interesting things to say.'

'You mean you want to test his sword,' Makril said. 'His lordship's tales made you wonder, did they? Want to know if he's as good as you.'

Is that it? Vaelin wondered. In truth he felt no hunger for matching steel with the Trueblade. In fact he harboured no doubts that he could defeat the man when he found him. But he did want to confront him, hear his voice. Lord Mustor's story had indeed made him curious. The usurper believed he was doing the work of his god, like the Cumbraelin he had watched die in the Martishe. *What drives them to this? What makes a man murder for his god?* But there was something more, ever since he had first glimpsed the High Keep: the blood-song. It was faint at first, but grew in power as night fell. It was not a note of warning exactly, more an urgency, a need to discover what waited inside.

He beckoned Nortah and Dentos closer, his whispered words misting the air in the dark mountain chill. 'Nortah, take your men along the battlements. Kill the sentries and cover the courtyard. Dentos, take the brothers to the gatehouse, get the gate raised and hold it until the regiment arrives.'

'And you, brother?' Nortah asked with a raised eyebrow.

'I have business in the keep.' He glanced up at Gallis's shrinking form. 'Nortah, tell your men not to scream if they fall. The Departed won't accept a coward into the Beyond. Luck to you, brothers.'

He was first to follow Gallis up the rope, the wind a howling, unseen monster threatening to tear him from the wall at any moment. His arms were burning with the effort and his hands gripped the rope with ice-numb fingers by the time he came upon Gallis. The onetime thief was perched just below the lip of the battlement, his fingertips clamped on the edge of the stone, legs braced against the wall. Vaelin could only marvel at the strength it must have taken to remain in such a position for so long. As Vaelin dragged himself level with the iron grapple lodged on the battlement, Gallis nodded, his 'Milord' of greeting lost to the wind. Vaelin took a one-handed grip on the grapple and flexed the fingers of his right hand to regain some feeling. He turned to Gallis with a questioning glance.

'One,' Gallis mouthed, inclining his head at the battlement. 'Looks bored.'

Vaelin inched himself up for a quick glance over the wall. The guard was a few yards away, huddled in his cloak in the shelter of a small alcove in the battlements, a flaming torch guttered in the wind above his head, scattering sparks into the black void. The sentry's spear and bow were propped against the wall as he rubbed his hands vigorously, breath steaming in the air. Vaelin reached over his shoulder to draw his sword, breathed deeply then hauled himself over the wall in a single fluid motion. He had counted on surprise to prevent the guard calling out the alarm but was surprised himself when the man failed even to reach for his weapons, simply standing in shocked immobility as the star-silver blade took him in the throat.

Vaelin lowered the body to the rampart floor and beckoned Gallis over the wall. 'Here,' he whispered, stripping the blood-sodden cloak from the corpse and tossing it to the climber. 'Put this on and walk around a bit. Try to look Cumbraelin. If any of the other guards talk to you, kill them.'

Gallis grimaced at the blood dripping from the cloak but pulled it about his shoulders without complaint, tugging the hood over his head so his face was concealed in shadow. He strolled slowly out of the shelter of the small alcove and moved along the battlements, rubbing his hands beneath his cloak, giving every impression of being nothing more than a bored sentry walking a wall on a cold night.

Vaelin moved to the grapple and tugged hard on the rope, once then twice. It took an age before Nortah's head appeared above the wall and even longer before the men followed him. Dentos was the last, struggling over the battlement and sinking slowly to the floor, the tremble in his hands not only a symptom of the cold, he had never liked heights.

Vaelin did a head count, grunting in satisfaction that there had been no fallers. 'No time for rest, brother,' he whispered to Dentos, tugging him to his feet. 'You know what to do. Keep it as quiet as you can.'

The two parties separated to pursue their missions, Nortah leading his bowmen along the battlements to the left, arrows notched, Dentos taking the brothers in the opposite direction towards the gatehouse. Soon there came the hard snap of bowstrings as Nortah's men dealt with the sentries. There were a few stifled shouts of alarm but no screams and no answering clamour from the keep. Vaelin found the steps to the courtyard and hurried downwards. Lord Mustor's description of the keep had been vague, the man's memory for detail was somewhat dulled, but he had been clear on one thing: his brother would be in the Lord's Chamber, the hub of the High Keep, which could be reached by the door directly opposite the main gate.

Vaelin moved quickly, the blood-song louder now, an edge of warning colouring the tune: *find him*. He encountered two men upon opening the door, burly fellows leaning close to one another as they shared a candle flame, pipe smoke billowing. They were seated at a small table, a half-empty bottle of brandy and an opened book between them. The first died as he surged to his feet, the sword sweeping across his chest, slicing through flesh and bone in a silver blur. The second managed to get a hand to the dagger in his belt before Vaelin cut him down with a slash to the neck. It was an untidy blow and the man lingered for a moment, a scream rising from his ruined throat. Vaelin clamped his hand over the man's mouth to smother the sound, blood gouting through his fingers, punching the sword blade hard into the man's guts. He held him down as he twitched, watching the life fade from his eyes.

He wiped his bloodied hand on the man's jerkin and took stock of his surroundings. A small room with a passage leading deeper into the keep and a stairway off to the left. Lord Mustor had told him the Lord's Chamber was at ground level so he took the passage, moving slower now, each shadowed corner a potential threat. Soon he found himself before a large oaken door, slightly ajar, outlined by the torchlit chamber beyond.

How many guards with him? he wondered, his hand already reaching out to push the door open. *This is foolish. I should wait for the others . . .* But the blood-song was so loud now, forcing him forward. *FIND HIM!*

There were no guards, just a large stone chamber, the walls shrouded in shadow beyond the six stone pillars that supported the ceiling. The man seated on a dais at the far end of the chamber was tall and broad-shouldered, his handsome face marred by a deep scar on his left cheek. A naked sword lay across his knees, a plain, narrow-bladed weapon Vaelin recognised as Renfaelin from the absence of a guard; Cumbraelins were renowned bowsmiths but reputedly knew little of forging steel. The man said nothing as Vaelin entered, remaining seated and regarding him with silent intent, his eyes empty of fear.

Now he stood confronted by his quarry the blood-song lost its shrillness, diminishing to a soft but steady murmur at the back of his mind. *Am I where it wants me to be?* he thought. *Or where I need to be?* In either case, he saw little reason for preamble.

'Hentes Mustor!' he said, striding forward. 'You are called by the King's Word to answer charges of treason and murder. Give up your sword and stand ready to be shackled.'

Hentes Mustor remained seated as Vaelin approached, neither speaking nor reaching for his weapon. It was only when Vaelin came within the last few yards that he noticed a chain coiled around his left wrist and traced the dark links of iron from his hand to the shadows between the pillars. Mustor's hand jerked in a quick, skilful motion, the chain snapping like a whip, striking sparks from the flagstones as a figure was dragged from the darkness, a slender figure, gagged with wrists shackled. She stumbled to her knees before Mustor, and Vaelin had time to note the grey robe she wore and the dark tumble of her hair before the usurper was on his feet with his sword at her throat.

'Brother,' he said in a soft, almost sorrowful voice. 'I believe this young woman is known to you.'

Her eyes were bright, fearful, pleading. Her shouts stopped by the gag but the meaning was clear in the emphatic, frantic shake of her head. Her eyes locked onto his and he read them clearly. *Do not sacrifice yourself for me!* The gag and the passage of years meant nothing. He would have known her anywhere. *Sherin!*

CHAPTER SIX

'Your sword, brother,' Hentes Mustor said in his soft voice. There should have been rage, desperate, bloody rage sending a throwing knife into Mustor's arm and a sword cleaving deep into his neck. But something choked it off as it rose in his breast. It wasn't just caution, although the man was quick, far quicker than Gallis the climber had been all those years ago, it was something more. For a second he was lost in confusion then it came to him: the blood-song's tune hadn't changed. The same soft, steady murmur still sang in his head, devoid of the warning or wrongness he knew so well.

His sword landed with a clatter at Mustor's feet, the sound mingling with Sherin's muffled sob of despair.

'And so.' Mustor kicked the sword away into the shadows, his tone heavy with reverence. 'The truth of His word is shown again.' His eyes fixed on Vaelin. 'Your other weapons, throw them away. Slowly.'

Vaelin did as he was bid, his knives and the dagger in his boot tossed into the shadows. 'Now I am disarmed,' he said. 'Is there any reason to threaten my sister so?'

Mustor glanced at Sherin's reddened face, as if remembering

she was there. 'Your sister. He told me that's not how you think of her. She is your love, is she not? The key by which your faith can be unlocked.'

'My faith cannot be unlocked, my lord. I've given you my sword, that's all.'

'Yes.' Mustor nodded, his voice flat with certainty. 'As He said you would.'

Is he mad? Vaelin wondered. The man was a patent fanatic but did that make him insane? He recalled Sentes Mustor's story of his brother's conversion. *He claimed the World Father had spoken to him . . .* 'Your god? He told you I would come here?'

'He is not *my* god! He is the World Father, who created all and knows all in His love, even heretics like you. And I am blessed by His voice. He warned me of your coming and that your Dark skill with the blade would undo me, though in my sinful pride I longed to face you without this trickery. He guided me to the mission where this woman could be found. And it was all as He foretold.'

'Did he foretell that you would kill your father?'

'My father . . .' The certainty faded from Mustor's eyes and he blinked, his expression guarded. 'My father lost his way. He turned away from the World Father's love.'

'He didn't turn away from you. He gave you this keep, did he not? Gave you letters of safe passage to ensure you could travel here unmolested. He even told you the most cherished secret of your family: the passage through the mountain. He did all this to ensure you would be safe. You are to be envied to have been so loved. And you repaid him with a blade in his heart.'

'He strayed from the law of the Ten Books. His toleration of your heretic dominion could not be borne forever. I had no choice but to act . . .'

'A strange god that loves you so much he makes you murder your own father.'

'SHUT UP!' Mustor screamed in a voice that almost sobbed with sorrow, flinging Sherin away as he advanced on Vaelin, sword levelled. 'Shut your mouth! I know what you are. Don't think He did not tell me. You are a practitioner of the Dark. You shun the Father's love. You know *nothing*.'

Still the blood-song's tune failed to change, even as the usurper's blade came within a hand's-breadth of his chest. 'Are you ready?' Mustor asked. 'Are you ready to die, Darkblade?'

Vaelin noted the way Mustor's sword tip trembled, the moist redness of his eyes and the hard clench of his jaw. 'Are you ready to kill me?'

'I will do what I must.' His voice was grating now, forced out through clenched teeth. His whole body appeared to tremble, his chest heaving, seeming to Vaelin like a man at war with himself. The sword tip wavered but did not move, neither forward nor back.

'Forgive me, my lord,' Vaelin said. 'But I doubt you have any killing left in you.'

'Just one more,' Mustor whispered. 'Just one more, He told me. Then at last I could rest. The Eternal Fields would finally be opened to me where I was denied before.'

From beyond the door came the first sounds of battle, many voices raised in alarm soon drowned in the clatter of iron-shod hooves and the hard ring of clashing steel.

'What?' Mustor seemed bewildered, his gaze flicking continually between Vaelin and the door. 'What is this? Do you seek to distract me with some Dark illusion?'

Vaelin shook his head. 'My men are storming the keep.'

'Your men?' His face took on an expression of deep confusion. 'But you came alone. He said you would come alone.' His sword fell to his side as he stumbled back a few steps, his gaze distant, unfocused. 'He said you would come alone . . .'

458 · ANTHONY RYAN

Kill him now! A voice shouted in Vaelin's mind, a voice he had
thought lost in the Martishe, the voice that had endlessly mocked
his preparations for Al Hestian's murder. *He's within reach, take
his sword away and break his neck!*

The voice was right, it would be an easy kill. Whatever madness
or disturbance clouded Mustor's thoughts had left him defenceless.
But the blood-song's tune was unchanged . . . And his words raised
so many questions.

'You have been deceived, my lord,' Vaelin told Mustor softly.
'Whatever voice speaks in your mind has played you false. I came
here with a full regiment of foot and a company of mounted
brothers. And I doubt my death, or any death, would buy you a
place in the Beyond.'

Mustor staggered, almost falling to the floor. He froze, only
for a moment, but it was a moment of complete stillness, standing
as if carved from ice. When he moved again the depth of confusion marring his features had vanished, replaced by the face of
a man in full possession of his faculties, one eyebrow raised in
amused consternation, but the eyes cold with hatred. A voice
Vaelin had heard before issued from Mustor's lips in a tone of
calm certainty. 'You do continue to surprise me, brother. But this
ends nothing.'

Then it was gone, Mustor's face once again the mask of confusion from a second before. It was clear to Vaelin that Mustor had
no knowledge of what had just transpired. *Something lives in his
mind,* he realised. *Something that can speak with his voice. And he
doesn't know.*

'Hentes Mustor,' he said. 'You are called by the King's Word to
answer charges of treason and murder.' He held out his hand.
'Your sword, my lord.'

Mustor looked down at the sword in his hand, turning the
blade so it gleamed in the torchlight. 'I washed it and washed it.

Ground the blade on the stone for hours. But I can still see it, the blood . . .'

'Your sword, my lord,' Vaelin repeated, stepping closer, hand outstretched.

'Yes . . .' Mustor said faintly. 'Yes. Best if you take it . . .' He reversed his hold on the hilt and lifted the sword towards Vaelin's hand.

There was a sound like the beating of a hawk's wing, a soft rush of air on Vaelin's cheek, and a blur of spinning steel. The blood-song roared, full of wrong and warning, making him stagger with the force of it. He found himself instinctively reaching for the empty scabbard on his back and felt an instant of complete and utter helplessness as Hentes Mustor took the axe full in the chest. The impact lifted him off his feet, laying him arms outstretched on the chamber floor.

'Got the bastard!' Barkus exclaimed, advancing from the shadows. 'A fine throw, if I say so—'

Vaelin's blow caught him on the jaw, spinning him to the floor. 'He was giving up!' Anger boiled in him, stoked by the blood-song, making his hands itch for his weapons. 'He was surrendering, you stupid bloody oaf!'

'Thought—' Barkus coughed red spit on the floor. 'Thought he was going to kill you . . . Had a sword, you didn't . . . Saw the sister lying there. I didn't know.' He seemed more bewildered than angry.

The certain, awful truth that Vaelin had been entirely willing to kill Barkus in that moment shocked the anger from him. He reached down, offering his hand. 'Here.'

Barkus stared up at him for a moment, a red swelling already forming on his jawline. 'That really hurt, you know.'

'I'm sorry.'

Barkus took his hand, hauling himself upright. Vaelin looked

460 · ANTHONY RYAN

over at Mustor's body and the dark pool now spreading out from it. 'See to our sister,' he told Barkus, moving to the body, Barkus's hateful axe still buried in his chest. *Is this why I couldn't touch it? Did the song know this is what it would be used for?*

He had hoped there would be some vestige of life lingering in Mustor's breast, enough breath to impart a final answer to the mystery of his murderous and deceitful god. But there was no light in Mustor's eyes, no movement in his slack features. Barkus's axe had done its work all too well.

He knelt next to the body, recalling the man's fevered words: *The Eternal Fields would finally be opened to me where I was denied before.* He laid his hand on Mustor's chest, reciting softly, 'What is death? Death is but a gateway to the Beyond. It is both ending and beginning. Fear it and welcome it.'

'I hardly think that's appropriate.' Sentes Mustor, undisputed Fief Lord of Cumbrael, was looking down at his brother's body with a mixture of anger and distaste. A naked, untarnished sword dangled from his hand and his chest heaved with unaccustomed exertion. Vaelin was impressed he had made his way here so quickly, apparently by failing to trouble himself with any part of the battle. 'He would want the Prayer of Leaving from the Tenth Book,' Lord Mustor said. 'The words of the World Father . . .'

'A god is a lie,' Vaelin quoted harshly. He rose, offering the Fief Lord the most cursory of bows. 'I think your brother knew that.'

'How many?'

'Eighty-nine in all.' Caenis nodded at the bodies laid out in the courtyard below. 'No quarter asked and none given. Just like the Martishe.' He turned back to Vaelin, his expression sombre. 'We lost nine men. Another ten injured. Sister Gilma's seeing to them.'

'Impressive,' Prince Malcius commented. He had his fur-trimmed cloak tight about his shoulders, his red hair fluttered in the chill wind sweeping the battlements. 'To lose so few against so many.'

'Between our pole-axes and Brother Nortah's archers on the walls . . .' Caenis shrugged. 'They had little chance, Highness.'

'Does the Fief Lord have any instructions regarding the Cumbraelin dead?' Vaelin asked the prince. Lord Mustor had been notably absent since the conclusion of the battle, apparently busying himself with a close inspection of the keep's wine cellar.

'Burn them or throw them from the walls. I doubt he's sober enough to care much either way.' There was a hard edge to the prince's voice this morning. Vaelin knew he had been at the forefront of the charge through the gate, Alucius Al Hestian close behind him. There had been a brief but frenzied defence of the courtyard by twenty or so of the usurper's followers, Alucius tumbling from his horse and disappearing under the crush. After the battle he was pulled from beneath a pile of bodies, alive but unconscious, his short sword dark with dried blood and a large lump on his head. He was in Sister Gilma's care now and still hadn't woken.

Make him play with a sword for ten days and lie to him that he's a warrior, Vaelin thought heavily. *Better if I'd tied him to his saddle on the first day and set the horse on the road back to the city.* Vaelin pushed the guilt away and turned to Caenis.

'Do you know anything about how the Cumbraelins treat their dead?'

'Burial, usually. Sinners are dismembered and left in the open to rot.'

'Sounds fair,' Prince Malcius grunted.

'Form a party,' Vaelin told Caenis. 'Cart them to the base of the mountain and have them buried. The map shows a village five miles to the south of the pass. Send a rider for the local priest. He can say the appropriate words.'

Caenis cast an uncertain glance at the prince. 'The usurper too?'

'Him too.'

'The men won't like it . . .'

'I could give a dog's fart for what they like!' Vaelin flushed, fighting down the anger he knew came from his guilt over Alucius. 'Ask for volunteers,' he told Caenis with a sigh. 'Double rum ration and a silver for the first twenty to step forward.' He bowed to Prince Malcius. 'With your permission, Highness. I have other business . . .'

'You dispatched your best riders I take it?' the prince asked.

'Brother Nortah and Brother Dentos. With a fair wind the King's command will be in the Battle Lord's hands within two days.'

'Good. I should hate for all of this to have been for nothing.'

Vaelin thought of Alucius's earnest face, red from exertion after another clumsy hour attempting to master the blade. 'And I, Highness.'

His skin was pallid and clammy to the touch, black hair clinging to his sweat-damp scalp. The regular, untroubled rise and fall of his chest did nothing to assuage Vaelin's guilt.

'He will be well again soon enough.' Sister Sherin placed a hand on Alucius's forehead. 'The fever broke quickly, the lump on his head is already diminished and see.' She gestured at his closed eyes and Vaelin saw the impression of his pupils moving beneath the lids.

'What does it mean?'

'He's dreaming, so his brain is likely undamaged. He'll wake in a few hours, feeling awful. But he will wake.' She met his eyes, her smile bright and warm. 'It's very good to see you again, Vaelin.'

'And you, sister.'

'It seems ever your curse to be my rescuer.'

'If not for me, you would never have been in danger.' He glanced around the meal hall Sister Gilma had converted to a temporary hospital. She was by the fireplace laughing heartily at Janril Norin, the onetime apprentice minstrel, stitching a wound on his arm as he regaled her with one of his more ribald pieces of doggerel.

'Can we talk?' Vaelin asked Sherin. 'I would know more of your time as a captive.'

Her smile faded a little, but she nodded. 'Of course.'

He led her to the battlements, away from curious ears. In the courtyard below, men were busy loading the Cumbraelin bodies onto carts, exchanging forced but lively humour amidst the drying blood and stiffening limbs. From the uncertain gait of some, he surmised Caenis had been somewhat free with the extra rum ration already.

'You're burying them?' Sherin asked. He was surprised at the absence of shock or disgust in her voice but realised life as a healer made her no stranger to the sight of death.

'It seemed right.'

'I doubt even their own people would do that. They are sinners against their god, are they not?'

'They didn't think so.' He shrugged. 'Besides, it's not for them. News of what happened here will spread across the Fief. Many Cumbraelin fanatics will be quick to call it a massacre. If it becomes known that we showed respect for their customs in caring for the dead, it may dull the hatred they wish to stir.'

'You almost sound like an Aspect.' Her smile was so bright, so open, stirring an old, familiar ache in his chest. She was different; the guarded, severe girl he had met near five years ago was now a confident young woman. But the core of her remained, he had seen in it the way she laid her hand on Alucius's forehead and her frantic pleading behind the gag when she thought he was giving up his life for her. Compassion, it burned in her.

'We always seem to be at different ends of the Realm,' she went on. 'I had the fortune to meet Princess Lyrna last year. She said you were friends, I asked her to send my regards.'

Friends. The woman lies like others breathe. 'She did that.' It was clear that she didn't know, Aspect Elera had never told her why they were always so far apart. Abruptly he decided she would never know.

'Did he hurt you?' he asked. 'Mustor. Did he . . . ?'

'A bruise here and there when I was captured.' She showed him the marks of the shackles on her wrists. 'But otherwise I am unharmed.'

'When did he take you?'

'Seven, eight weeks ago. Maybe longer. I've lost track of time within the walls of this keep. I had finally been called back to the Order House from Warnsclave, looking forward to taking up my old post but Aspect Elera put me to work on researching new curatives. It's a deadly dull task, Vaelin. Endless grinding of herbs and mixing concoctions, most of which smell quite appalling. I even complained to the Aspect but she told me I needed to gain a broader grasp of the workings of the Order. In any case I was actually glad when a messenger arrived from my former mission with word of an outbreak of the Red Hand. I had been working on a compound that may offer some hope of a cure, or at least relief from the symptoms. So the local master sent for me.'

The Red Hand. The plague that had swept through the four Fiefs before the King forged the Realm, claiming the lives of thousands in the two hellish years of its reign. No family had escaped untouched and no other sickness was more feared. But the sickness had not been seen in the Realm for nearly fifty years.

'It was a trap,' he said.

She nodded. 'I went alone for fear the sickness had taken hold. But there was no sickness, only death. The mission was quiet, empty I thought. Inside there were only corpses, but not taken by the Red Hand. Hacked and slashed, even the sick in their beds. Mustor's followers were waiting, and they had spared no-one. I tried to run but they caught me of course. I was shackled and taken here.'

'I'm sorry.'

'There is no blame for you in this. It would hurt me to think that you thought so.'

Their eyes met again and the ache in his chest lurched once more. 'Did Mustor say anything to you? Anything that might explain his actions?'

'He would come to my cell most days. At first he seemed concerned for my welfare, making sure I had sufficient food and water, even bringing me books and parchment when I asked. But always he would talk, as if driven to it, but his words rarely made sense. He rambled on about his god, quoting whole passages from the Ten Books the Cumbraelins revere so much. I thought at first he was trying to convert me but I came to realise that he wasn't really talking to me, he cared nothing for my opinion. He merely needed to speak words he couldn't speak to his followers.'

'What words?'

'Words of doubt. Hentes Mustor doubted his god. Not its existence but its reasoning, its intention. I didn't know then that he had murdered his father, apparently at his god's behest. Perhaps the guilt had driven him mad. I told him as much. I told him if he thought he could use me to kill you, then he was truly mad. I told him you would kill him in an instant. It appears I was wrong.' She looked at him intently. '*Was* he mad, Vaelin? Is that what drove him? Or was it . . . something else? I sense you know more than you tell.'

He wanted to tell her, the compulsion burned in his breast, the need to share it all with someone. The wolf in the Urlish and the Martishe, his meeting with Nersus Sil Nin, the One Who Waits, and the voice, the same voice he had heard from the lips of two dead men. But something held it back. It wasn't the blood-song this time, it was something more easily understood. *Such knowledge is dangerous. And she has seen enough danger on my account.*

'I am but a brother with a sword, sister,' he told her. 'As the years pass I realise I know very little.'

'You knew enough to save my life. You knew Mustor had no more stomach for killing. I was so sure you would cut him down when you saw he had me . . . I was proud of you, proud you didn't. Mad or not, murderer or not, I could sense no evil in him. Only grief, and guilt.'

From below came the sound of a commotion. Vaelin glanced down to see Fief Lord Mustor upbraiding Caenis, the bottle in his hand sloshing wine onto the cobbled courtyard. The Fief Lord was dishevelled, unshaven and, judging from the slur of his words, considerably more drunk than usual. 'Let them rot! You hear me, brother! Sinnersh are not buried in Cumbrael, oh no! Hack off their heads and leave them for the crowsh—' He staggered onto a patch of still-wet blood and slipped heavily to the cobbles, dousing himself in wine. He swore extravagantly, slapping Caenis's helping hands away. 'Let those sinners rot, I say! This is my keep. Prince Malsiush? Lord Vaelin? This is my keep!'

'Who is that man?' Sherin asked. 'He seems . . . troubled.'

'The Cumbraelins' rightful Fief Lord, Faith help them.' He gave her a smile of apology. 'I should go. My regiment will remain here awaiting orders from the King. I'll have Brother Commander Makril provide an escort to take you back to your Order.'

'I would prefer to wait here for a while. I think Sister Gilma would be glad of the help. Besides, we've barely had time to exchange news. I have much to share.'

The same open smile, the same ache in his chest. *Send her away,* his inner voice commanded. *Only pain can result if you keep her here.*

'Lord Vaelin!' Fief Lord Mustor's cry dragged his attention back to the courtyard. 'Where are you? Shtop these men!'

'I have much to share also,' he said before turning away.

At first, Fief Lord Mustor raged at Vaelin's refusal to stop the burial of the bodies, loudly restating his ownership of the keep and the primacy of his authority in his own lands. When Vaelin replied simply that he was a servant of the Faith and therefore not bound by the word of a Fief Lord, Mustor's mood degenerated into a baleful sulk. After his appeals to Prince Malcius earned only a stern look of disapproval he took himself off to his dead brother's quarters, where he had amassed a large proportion of the keep's wine cellar.

They remained at the High Keep for another eight days, anxiously awaiting word of the war's end. Vaelin occupied the men with constant training and patrols into the mountains. There was little grumbling, morale was high, boosted by triumph and the shared spoils of the keep and the dead which, though meagre, fulfilled a basic soldierly desire for loot. 'Give 'em victory, gold in their pockets and a woman every now and again,' Sergeant Krelnik told Vaelin one evening, 'and they'll follow you forever.'

As Sister Sherin had promised, Alucius Al Hestian recovered quickly, waking on the third day and passing the basic tests that showed his brain was not permanently damaged, although he could remember nothing of the battle or how he came by his wound.

'So he's dead?' he asked Vaelin. They were in the courtyard, watching the men at evening drill. 'The Usurper.'

'Yes.'

'Do you think he gave Black Arrow the letters of free passage?'

'I can't see how else they could have fallen into his hands. It seems the old Fief Lord went to great lengths to protect his son.'

Alucius wrapped his cloak tightly around his shoulders, his hollowed eyes making him seem an old man peering out from behind a young man's face. 'All of this blood spilled over a couple of letters.' He shook his head. 'Linden would have wept to see it.' He reached inside his cloak and unhitched Vaelin's short sword from his belt. 'Here,' he said, offering the hilt. 'I won't need this anymore.'

'Keep it. A gift from me. You should have a souvenir of your time as a soldier.'

'I can't. The King gave you this . . .'

'And now I'm giving it to you.'

'I don't . . . It shouldn't be given to one such as I.'

Seeing the way the boy gripped the sword hilt, the tremble of his fingers, Vaelin recalled the red slick that covered the blade when he had been pulled from beneath the pile of corpses near the gate. *The face of battle is always most ugly when seen for the first time.* 'Who better to give it to?' he said, putting his hand over the hilt, gently pushing it away. 'Put it on your wall when you get home. Leave it there. I will not take it back.'

The boy seemed about to say more but restrained himself, returning the sword to his belt. 'As you wish, my lord.'

'Will you write about this? Is it worth a poem, do you think?'

'It's worth a hundred, I'm sure, but I doubt I'll write any of them. Since my awakening, words don't seem to come to me as they once did. I've tried, I sit with pen and parchment but nothing comes.'

'It takes a while for a man to return to himself after a wound. Rest and eat well. I'm sure your talent will return.'

'I hope so.' The boy gave a faint smile. 'Perhaps I'll write to Lyrna. I'm sure I can find some words for her.'

Vaelin, who had plenty of words of his own for the princess, nodded and turned back to the drill, venting his sudden anger at a man who held his pole-axe too high in the defensive formation. 'Lower it, lackwit! How are you supposed to gut a horse with your weapon stuck up in the air? Sergeant, an extra hour's drill for this man.'

Each evening was spent in Sherin's company. They would sit in the Lord's Chamber exchanging stories about their experiences over the last few years. He discovered she had travelled far more widely than he, visiting Fifth Order missions in all four Fiefs of the Realm, even taking a ship to the enclave in the Northern Reaches, where Tower Lord Vanos Al Myrna ruled in the King's name.

'A lively place, despite the cold,' she told him. 'And home to so many different people. Most of the farming folk are in fact exiles from the southern Alpiran Empire. Tall, handsome people with black skin. Apparently they angered the Emperor and had to take ship or face extermination, fetching up in the Northern Reaches more than fifty years hence. Most of the Tower Lord's Guard is made up of exiles, they have a fearsome reputation.'

'I met the Tower Lord once, and his daughter. I don't think she liked me much.'

'The famous Lonak foundling? She was absent when I visited, away in the forest with the Seordah. They seem to revere her and her father greatly. Something to do with the great battle against the Ice Horde.'

He told her of his months in the Martishe, sharing the painful memory of Al Hestian's passing, feeling like a coward and a liar for leaving out his murderous scheming.

'It was a mercy, Vaelin,' she said, taking his hand, reading the guilt in his face. 'Leaving him to suffer would have been wrong, against the Faith.'

'I have done much in the name of the Faith.' He looked at the scarred flesh of his hand next to the pale smoothness of her own. *Killer's hands, healer's hands. Faith, why does she feel so warm?*

'All any of us can ask of ourselves is have we done wrong in the name of the Faith,' Sherin said. 'Have you, Vaelin?'

'I've killed men, men I didn't know. Some were criminals, some assassins, scum really. But some, like the deluded fanatics who dwelt here, were men who simply followed another belief. Men who may have been my friends if we'd met in a different time or place.'

'The men who dwelt here were murderers. They slaughtered an entire mission of my Order merely to take me captive. Could you ever do the same?'

She doesn't see it, he realised. *Doesn't see the killer in me.* 'No,' he said, for some reason again feeling like a liar. 'No. I couldn't.'

As the days passed he began to indulge in the dream that the King and the Order might allow them to remain here, a permanent garrison in Cumbraelin lands. He would be master of the keep, a reminder to any Cumbraelin fanatics of the price of rebellion. Sherin could establish a mission to administer to the sick in this remote and bitter land and they could serve the Faith and the Realm in happy isolation for years. Although he recognised its impossibility, the dream lingered in his mind, a bright and enticing hope that grew with every deluded imagining. Caenis would take over the keep's library, establish a school for local children, teaching them letters and the truth of the Faith. Barkus would occupy the smithy, Nortah the stables, Dentos would become Huntmaster. He would bring Scratch and Frentis from the Order House to join them. He knew it was a delusion, a lie he told himself after every evening spent in Sherin's company. Because he didn't want it to end, because he wanted the peace he felt in her presence to last for as long as he could make it. He even began to compose a formal proposal to Aspect Arlyn in his head, rephrasing it over and over but putting off the moment when he would ask Caenis to pen it for him. Speaking it aloud would reveal the absurdity of it, and he preferred the dream.

The scale of his delusion became apparent on the morning of the ninth day. He had woken early, briefly inspected the guard on the gate and was taking a tour of the sentries on the battlements before going to find some breakfast. The sentries were chilled but cheerful enough, making him suspect they had been indulging in a tot or two of Brother's Friend whilst on duty. He paused for a moment before descending to the courtyard, taking in the brooding majesty of the view. *A forbidding place to serve out the rest of your days. But quiet, blessedly quiet.*

For years to come he would remember it clearly, the brightness of the morning sun shimmering blue-silver on the fresh snowfall that covered the surrounding mountain tops, the clear blue of the sky, the sharp wind on his face. He never forgot it, the moment before everything changed.

He was about to turn away when his gaze was drawn to the long, narrow road ascending from the valley floor: a rider, making haste. Even from this distance he could see the bright plume of the horse's breath as it laboured up the road at the gallop. *Dentos,* he realised as the rider drew nearer. *Dentos without Nortah.*

Dentos's face was grey with fatigue as he dismounted in the courtyard, a livid bruise discolouring his cheek. 'Brother.' He greeted Vaelin in a voice heavy with sorrow and exhaustion. 'I must talk to you.' He staggered a little and Vaelin reached out to steady him.

'What it is?' Vaelin demanded. 'Where's Nortah?'

Dentos gave an entirely humourless grin. 'Many miles away I reckon.' His face clouded and he looked down, as if fearing to meet Vaelin's eye. 'Our brother tried to kill the Battle Lord. He's a fugitive with half the Realm Guard on his tail.'

'There was a battle,' Dentos said, a cup of brandy-laced warm milk clutched in his hands as he sat by the fire in the meal hall. Vaelin had called Barkus and Caenis to hear his story along with Prince Malcius and Sister Sherin, who had applied a balm to his bruise. 'The Cumbraelins had gotten together about five thousand men to oppose the Realm Guard at Greenwater Ford. Not much of a force to stand against so many but I guess they were trying to buy time for their city to muster its defences. Could've cut down many guardsmen as they forded the river but the Battle Lord was too wily for 'em. Drew up all his cavalry on the south bank to fix their sight and sent half his infantry downstream to ford in deep water in the early hours of the morning, lost fifty men to the current doing it but they got across. Fell on the Cumbraelin right flank whilst they were still unwrapping their arrows. It was all but over by the time me and Nortah got there, place looked like a charnel house, the river was red with it.'

Dentos paused to sip some milk, his face more sombre than Vaelin had ever seen it. 'They'd captured a few hundred in the final rout,' he went on. 'We found the Battle Lord reading sentence of death over them. Don't think he was pleased to hear our news.'

'You gave him the King's signed order?' Prince Malcius asked.

'That we did, Highness. He looked at the seal then called us into his tent. When he read it he wanted to know if we'd seen the Usurper's body ourselves, was his death certain and such. Nortah assured him it was but the Battle Lord cut him off. "The words of a traitor's son mean no more than pig shit to me," he said.'

'Nortah tried to kill him for that?' Barkus asked.

Dentos shook his head. 'Nortah was angry right enough, looked ready to kill the bastard right there, but he didn't. Just gritted his teeth and said, "I'm no-one's son, my lord. The King's Word is given to you that this war is over. Will you abide by it?"' Dentos fell silent, his eyes distant.

'Brother?' Caenis prompted. 'What is it?'

'The Battle Lord said he needed no advice in how to serve the King. Before he marched the Realm Guard home across this Faithless land he had justice to administer to those who had risen in arms against the Crown.'

'He meant to continue with the execution of the prisoners,' Vaelin said. He recalled Nortah after their return from the Martishe, the weary despair in his eyes as he drank to dull the pain in his heart. *We'll bring the Faith to them all, the Denier bastards.*

'Yeh.' Dentos sighed. 'Nortah told him he couldn't. Told him it was against the King's Word. The Battle Lord laughed and said the King's message said nothing about how best to deal with captured Denier scum. Told Nortah to take himself off or he'd send him to the Beyond along with his traitor father, brother or not.'

Vaelin closed his eyes, forcing himself to ask. 'How badly was the Battle Lord injured?'

'Well,' said Dentos. 'He'll have to wipe his arse with his left hand from now on.'

'Faith!' breathed Caenis.

'Shit!' said Barkus.

'Why didn't he finish him?' Vaelin asked.

'Stopped him, didn't I?' Dentos replied. 'Managed to block his next swing. I was pleading with him, begging him to give up his sword. I don't think he even heard me. Nortah was out of his mind,

I could see it in his eyes, like a dog gone rabid, desperate to get at the Battle Lord. That bugger was on his knees, just staring at the stump where his hand used to be, watching the blood spurt. Nortah and me fought.' He rubbed at the bruise on his cheek. 'I lost. Lucky for the Battle Lord, his guards came in to see about the ruckus. Nortah killed two and wounded the others. More came running. He killed a couple more and ran for his horse. Managed to ride through the whole of the Realm Guard encampment, after all, who'd think a brother had just hacked off the Battle Lord's hand? I snuck off in the confusion. Didn't think I'd be too popular when the dust settled. Spent a day or so hiding in woodland then struck out for the keep. I heard rumours on the road about the mad brother, how half the Realm Guard were hunting him. Last seen heading west, so they said.'

'Which means he'll really be heading anywhere else,' Barkus said. 'They'll never catch him.'

'This is a bad business, brother,' Prince Malcius said to Vaelin, his face grave. 'The Order affords great protection to its brothers but this . . .' He shook his head. 'The King will have no choice but to issue a death warrant.'

'Then let's hope our brother finds his way quickly to safer lands,' Caenis said. 'He's possibly the finest rider in the Order, and has great skill in the wild. He won't be easily caught by the Realm Guard . . .'

'He won't be caught by the Realm Guard at all,' Vaelin said. He went to the table where his sword rested and buckled it on quickly, tugging the straps tight before pulling his cloak over his shoulders. He could feel Sherin's eyes following him but found himself unable to look at her. 'Brother Caenis, the regiment is yours. You will send a messenger to Aspect Arlyn informing him I am in pursuit of Brother Nortah and will bring him to justice. The regiment will wait here for orders from the King.'

'You're going after him?' Barkus seemed astonished. 'You heard the prince. If you bring him back, they'll hang him. He's our brother . . .'

'He's a fugitive from the King's justice and a disgrace to the Order. And I doubt he'll give me the chance to bring him back.' He forced himself to look at Sherin, searching for some words of farewell but nothing came. Her eyes were bright and he could tell she was close to tears. *I'm sorry,* he wanted to say, but couldn't, the weight of what he had to do pressed down too heavily.

'What makes you think you could hunt him down anyway?' Barkus demanded. 'He's a better rider than you by far, better in the wild too.'

He doesn't have a blood-song to guide him. It had begun as soon as Dentos began his story, a flat tone flaring whenever Vaelin's thoughts turned to the north. 'I'll find him.'

He turned and bowed to Prince Malcius. 'By your leave, Highness.'

'You're not going alone?' the prince asked.

'I'm afraid I must insist on it.' He looked in turn at his brothers, Barkus angry, Caenis confused, Dentos sorrowful, and wondered if they would ever forgive him. 'Take care of the men,' he said and walked from the chamber.

CHAPTER SEVEN

The Renfaelin city of Cardurin had been built on one of the foothills to the northern mountains. Approaching the walls with Spit at a sedate walk, Vaelin was struck by the complexity of its construction, every cobbled street sloping upwards in what seemed tighter and ever-steeper curves. Tall, rectangular, sandstone buildings topped by clay-tiled roofs rose on each side. The town was an interconnected whole, each block joined to another by a walkway, high arches curving elegantly between the walls. It felt as if he were staring up at a forest of stone.

He was waved through the gate by a spearman who favoured him with a respectful nod. The Order had always been held in high esteem in Renfael, a regard that had remained undiminished despite the Wars of Unification, when the Aspects had taken the King's part. People in the streets beyond the gate gave him a few curious glances but there was none of the open staring or recognition he dreaded when traversing the streets of Varinshold.

He left Spit with a stableman near the gate, who gave him directions to the Sixth Order mission. 'It's a bit of a climb, brother,' the man said, taking hold of Spit's reins and making to give him a scratch on the nose.

'Don't!' Vaelin pulled the man's hand away, Spit's teeth chomping on empty air. 'He's got a temper and we've ridden a long way these past two weeks.'

'Oh.' The stableman moved back a little, grinning at Vaelin. 'Bet you're the only one can handle him, eh?'

'No, he bites me too.'

The Sixth Order mission house was near the summit of the city and the stableman hadn't exaggerated the climb, Vaelin's legs were aching with the effort by the time he jangled the bell suspended next to the door. The brother who opened it was broad and heavily bearded, staring at Vaelin with shrewd blue eyes beneath his bushy brows.

'Brother Vaelin?' he asked.

Vaelin frowned in surprise. 'I am expected, brother?'

'A galloper arrived from the capital two days ago. The Aspect gave notice of your mission and ordered me to give any assistance you require should you call here. I expect similar missives were sent to missions throughout the Realm. Unfortunate business.' He stepped aside. 'Please, you must be hungry.'

Vaelin was led along a dimly lit corridor and up a flight of stairs, then another flight, and another after that. 'Brother Commander Artin,' the bearded man introduced himself as they climbed. 'Sorry about the stairs. Renfaelins call Cardurin the city of many bridges. Really should call it the city of countless stairs.'

'May I ask why you have no guard on the door, brother?' Vaelin enquired.

'Don't need one. Safest city I've ever been to. No outlaws in the wilds either, Lonak won't tolerate them.'

'But don't the Lonak themselves pose a danger?'

'Oh they never come here. Don't like the stink of the town; apparently, bad smell means bad luck. When they raid, they go for the smaller settlements near the border. Every couple of years one of the War Chiefs will get a few thousand of them worked up enough for a large-scale raid, but even then they rarely come close to the city walls. Not much for siege-craft, the Lonak.'

He was led to a large room that served as the mission's meal hall and ate a plate of stew Brother Artin had brought up from the kitchens. After the meal the Brother Commander unfurled a large map on the table. 'The most recent effort from our brother map-makers in the Third Order,' he explained. 'A detailed rendering of the borderlands. Here.' He pointed to a pictogram of a walled city. 'Cardurin. Directly north will take you to the Skellan Pass, fortified and permanently manned by three companies of brothers. A truly unassailable barrier for any fugitive. The Lonak gave up on it decades ago.'

'How do they make their way south?' Vaelin asked.

'The foothills to the west and east. It's a long journey and makes them vulnerable to pursuit but they've little choice if they want to keep raiding. How can you be sure your brother will venture into Lonak lands?'

He's my brother no longer, Vaelin wanted to say but held his tongue. He felt a profound anger whenever he thought of Nortah and it would do no good to voice it. 'Is there a safe way in?' he asked the Brother Commander, avoiding his question. 'A way a man travelling alone wouldn't be seen?'

Brother Artin shook his head. 'The Lonak know whenever we venture into their lands, alone in the dead of winter or in a full company of brothers in high summer, it makes no difference. They always know. Something Dark about it, I reckon. Make no mistake, brother, if you follow him in there, you'll meet them, sooner or later.'

Vaelin scanned the map, from the solid mass of jagged peaks that formed the northern mountains and the heart of Lonak lands to the Skellan Pass, fortified a century ago when the Renfaelin

Lord decided the Lonak were a real threat rather than a continual nuisance. It was when he turned his attention to the western foothills that the blood-song flared. His finger picked out a small, unfamiliar pictogram on the map. 'What's this?'

'The fallen city? He won't go there. Even the Lonak don't go there.'

'Why?'

'It's a bad place, brother. All ruins and bare rock. Only ever seen it from a distance and it gave me the frights. Something in the air . . .' He shook his head. 'Just feels bad. The Lonak call it *Maars Nir-Uhlin Sol*, the Place of Stolen Souls. They have plenty of stories about people going there and never coming back. There was a party of brothers from the Fourth Order about a year ago, come in search of Deniers fleeing north. It was after the appointment of their new Aspect and our Order's refusal to assist any longer in the Fourth's Denier hunting. They insisted on going to the fallen city, claimed they had intelligence leading them there, although from where they wouldn't say. They were deaf to my warnings. "Servants of the Faith need fear no savage superstition," they said. We only ever found one of them, or rather part of him, frozen solid in the snow three months later. Something had been at him. Something hungry.'

'Perhaps they simply got lost and froze to death. A wolf or a bear could have come upon the body.'

'The man's face was frozen, brother, in a scream. Never seen such a look on any man, alive or dead. He was eaten alive, by something bigger and far meaner than any wolf. And bears don't leave marks like those.'

Vaelin turned back to the map. 'How many days' ride to the fallen city?'

Brother Artin's shrewd eyes regarded Vaelin closely. 'You really think he's there?'

I know he's there. 'How many days' ride?'

'Three, if you push hard. I'll send a bird to the wall for a party to accompany you. May take a few days. You can rest here . . .'

'I'll be travelling alone, brother. In the morning.'

'Alone into Lonak lands? Brother, to say that is unwise is a gross understatement.'

'Did the Aspect's missive contain any injunction against my travelling alone?'

'No. It merely ordered that you be given every assistance.'

'Well' – Vaelin moved back from the table and clapped Brother Artin on the shoulder – 'a good night's sleep, provisions for the journey and you will have assisted me very well.'

'If you go in there alone, you will die,' Brother Artin stated flatly.

'Then let's hope I complete my mission before I do.'

The western foothills were rocky and barren, broken by a seemingly unending series of gullies through which Vaelin was obliged to navigate his way north. Winter was coming on quickly and a hard, chill rain swept the hills with dreary regularity. Spit was more fractious than ever, tossing his head and snorting every time Vaelin mounted him, his mood unleavened by a regular supply of sugar lumps from the mission-house stores. Vaelin covered barely fifteen miles the first day and made camp beneath an overhang of rock, huddling in his cloak and resisting the urge to ignore Brother Artin's stern warning against lighting a fire. Sleep, when it came, was fitful and troubled by dreams he could barely recall on waking to the dull glimmer of dawn. The blood-song was more muted now but still clear, still leading him on to the fallen city, where he knew that Nortah would be waiting.

Nortah . . . The anger returned, fierce and implacable. *How could he do this? HOW COULD HE?* It had been building ever since Dentos related the tale, ever since the sickening realisation that he would have to hunt down and kill his brother. He found himself unable to muster much regret over Battle Lord Al Hestian's severed hand, it was hard to pity a man intent on venting his grief on helpless captives. But Nortah . . . *He'll fight*, he knew with a dread certainty. *He'll fight, and I'll kill him.*

He ate a breakfast of dried beef and set off through a light morning drizzle, leading Spit on foot as the ground was too rocky for riding. He had gone only a few miles when the Lonak attacked.

The boy leapt from the rocks above in an impressive display of acrobatics, turning over in midair and landing nimbly on his feet in front of Vaelin, war club in one hand and a long, curved knife in the other. He was bare-chested and lean as a greyhound, Vaelin guessing his age at somewhere between fourteen and sixteen. His head was shaven, with an ornate tattoo above his left ear. His smooth, angular face tensed in anticipation of combat as he voiced a harsh challenge in a tongue Vaelin had never heard.

'I'm sorry,' Vaelin said. 'I don't know your language.'

The Lonak boy evidently took this as either an insult or an acceptance of his challenge since he attacked without further delay, leaping in the air, war club above his head, his knife hand drawn back for a slash. It was a practised move performed with elegant precision. Vaelin side-stepped the club as it came down, caught the knife hand in midslash and knocked the boy unconscious with an open-handed blow to the temple.

His hand went to his sword as he looked around for further enemies, eyes scanning the rocks above. *Where there's one, there's more*, Brother Artin had warned him. *There are always more.* There was nothing, no sound or scent on the wind, nothing to disturb the faint patter of rain on rock. Spit clearly sensed nothing either as he began to nibble at the unconscious boy's leather-clad feet.

Vaelin pulled him away, earning a near-miss kick from a

forehoof, and crouched to check on the boy. His breathing was regular and there was no blood coming from his ears or nose. Vaelin positioned him so he wouldn't choke on his tongue and tugged Spit onwards.

After another hour the gullies gave way to what Brother Artin had called the Anvil of Stone. It was the strangest and most un-familiar landscape he had seen, a broad expanse of mostly bare rock, pocked by small pools of rainwater and rocky tors rising from the undulating surface like great deformed mushrooms. He could only marvel at whatever design of nature had produced such a scene. The Cumbraelins claimed their god had made the earth and all it held in a blinking of his eye, but seeing the weather-fashioned channels in the tors rising above, he knew this place had taken many centuries to reach such a state of profound strangeness.

He remounted Spit and headed north at a walk, covering another ten miles before nightfall. He camped in the shelter of the largest tor he could find, his cloak once again tight around him as he sought sleep. His eyelids were drooping when the Lonak boy attacked again.

The boy raged in his unfathomable language as Vaelin tied the rope around his chest, his hands already bound behind his back. A livid bruise marred his temple and another was forming beneath his nose, where Vaelin's fore-knuckles had found the nerve cluster which sent him senseless.

'Nisha ulniss ne Serantim!' the boy screamed at Vaelin, his bruised face rigid with hate. 'Herin! Garnin!'

'Oh shut up,' Vaelin said tiredly, pushing a rag into the boy's mouth.

He left him writhing in his bonds and led Spit onwards, careful of his footing in the dark, although the half-moon was bright enough for him to make his way without misstep. He kept going until the boy's muffled cries were no longer audible and found shelter next to a large boulder, lying down to let sleep claim him.

The next day brought his first glimpse of sunlight, intermittent rays breaking through the clouds to play across the frozen rock of the Anvil, drawing huge shadows from the tors, their weathered surfaces seeming to shimmer. *Beautiful,* he thought, wishing he had come here on a different mission. His heavy heart seemed to forbid enjoyment of simple things.

The Anvil stretched on for another five miles, eventually giving way to a series of low hills dotted with the stunted pine, which seemed to proliferate in the north. Spit spurred into an unbidden gallop as soon as his hooves touched the grass, snorting his relief at leaving the unyielding rock of the Anvil. Vaelin gave him his head and let him run. Spit was ever a mean-spirited animal and it was a novelty to feel the joy in him as he raced up and down the hills, churning sod in their wake. By nightfall they were in sight of the broad plateau where the fallen city waited. Vaelin found a campsite atop the last of the hills, affording a good view of the approaches and cover from a cluster of pine near the summit.

He tethered Spit to a low-hanging branch and gathered wood, arranging it within a circle of rocks, adding pine shavings for kindling. He struck his flint and blew softly on the flames until the fire built. Sitting cross-legged, his sword still on his back and his bow within reach, an arrow already notched, he waited. He had become aware of being followed in the early evening so there seemed little point in observing Artin's stricture against lighting a fire.

Night came on quickly, the clouded sky making the darkness deep and impenetrable beyond the firelight. It was another hour before the soft scrape of hooves on sod told of a visitor. The man who walked into the camp stood at least six and a half feet tall, with broad shoulders and thickly muscled arms, his chest confined within a bearskin vest that reached to his waist, where a war club and a steel-bladed hatchet hung on his belt. He wore deerskin trews and leather boots. Like the boy who had attacked Vaelin earlier his head was shaven and tattooed, an intricate mazelike design that circled his head from temple to temple. More tattoos covered his arms, strange whirls and barblike shapes stretching from shoulder to wrist. His face was lean and angular, making it difficult to judge his age, but his eyes, dark and hostile beneath a heavy frown, spoke of many years and, if Vaelin was any judge, many battles. He was leading a sturdy pony that bore something slung across its back, something writhing and moaning in tight-bound rope.

The Lonak pulled the hatchet and war club from his belt in a quick and skilful movement Vaelin almost didn't catch. He watched the man whirl the weapons expertly for a second or two, feeling the rush of displaced air and resisting the impulse to reach for his sword. The man's eyes never left his, studying, calculating. After a moment he grunted in apparent satisfaction and laid both weapons on the ground near the fire. Taking a step backwards, hands raised, his expression no less hostile.

Vaelin unbuckled his sword from his back and placed it before him, also raising his hands. The Lonak grunted again and went to the pony, pulling the bound boy from its back and dumping him unceremoniously next to the fire.

'This is yours,' he told Vaelin, his words thickly accented but clearly spoken.

Vaelin glanced at the boy, his mouth securely gagged with a leather strap, eyes dim with exhaustion. 'I don't want it,' he told the Lonak.

The big man regarded him in silence for a moment then moved to the opposite side of the fire, spreading his hands to the warmth.

'Among my people, when a man comes to your fire in peace it is custom to offer him meat and something to slake his thirst.'

Vaelin reached for his saddlebags and extracted some dried beef and a waterskin, tossing them to the Lonak across the fire. He took a small knife from his boot and cut a strip from the beef, chewing and swallowing quickly. Drinking from the waterskin, however, made him grimace and spit on the ground. 'Where is the wine you *Merim Her* love so much?' he demanded.

'I rarely drink wine.' Vaelin glanced again at the boy. 'Aren't you going to let him eat too?'

'Whether he eats is your choice. He belongs to you.'

'Because I defeated him?'

'If you defeat a man and don't deign to kill him, he is yours.'

'And if I don't take him?'

'He will lie here until he starves or the beasts come to claim him.'

'I could just cut his bonds, set him free.'

The Lonak barked a harsh laugh. 'There is no freedom for him. He is *varnish*, defeated, destroyed, worth no more than dog shit to my people.' The man's gaze was fixed on the boy now, a fierce, implacable glower. 'A fitting punishment for one who disobeys *Her* word, who allows his misplaced pride to blind him to his obeisance. Cut his bonds and he will wander here, weaponless, friendless, my people will shun him and he will find no shelter.'

His gaze swung back to Vaelin, the tension of his jaw and the set of his lips telling of something more than anger, something too keenly felt to be hidden. *Concern. He fears for the boy.*

'If he's mine,' Vaelin said, 'then I may do with him as I wish?'

The Lonak's eyes flicked back to the boy for an instant. He nodded.

'Then I give him to you. A gift of thanks for allowing me to cross your lands.'

486 · ANTHONY RYAN

The Lonak's face remained impassive but Vaelin could read the relief in his eyes. 'You *Merim Her* are soft,' he sneered. 'Weak and craven. Only your numbers give you strength, and that will not last forever. One day we will sweep you back to the sea and the waves will turn red with your blood.' He rose and went to the boy, using the boot knife to sever his bonds. 'I'll take your worthless gift, since it's all you have to offer.'

'You're welcome.'

Free of the ropes, the boy was listless, sagging as the Lonak dragged him to his feet, whimpering as the big man slapped him awake with a chorus of curses in his own language. Once roused, the boy's gaze swung to Vaelin, the same hatred and bloodlust colouring his features again. He bridled, tensing himself for another attack. The big Lonak struck him, a hard, backhanded cuff across the face, drawing blood from his lip, then pushed him roughly to the waiting pony, hoisting him onto its back and pointing sternly back down the hill. The boy favoured Vaelin with a last glare of naked animosity before spurring away into the darkness.

The Lonak returned to the fire and reached for the dried beef once more, his face sombre as he ate.

'A good father suffers much for his son,' Vaelin observed.

The Lonak's eyes flashed at him, the hostility shining once again. 'Do not think there is a debt between us. Do not think you have bought passage through our lands with my son's life. You live because *She* wishes it.'

'She?'

The Lonak shook his head in disgust. 'You have fought us for centuries and you know so little of us. *She* is our guide and our protection. *She* is our wisdom and our soul. *She* rules us and serves us.'

Vaelin recalled his dream-meeting with Nersus Sil Nin in the

Martishe. What had she said about the Lonak? *I should have known the High Priestess would find a way.* 'The High Priestess. She leads you?'

'High Priestess.' The Lonak spoke the words as if tasting unfamiliar fare. 'As good a name as any. Your bastard tongue does not fit easily with our ways.'

'You speak my bastard tongue very well. Where did you learn it?'

The Lonak shrugged. 'When we raid we take captives, although they have little uses. The men are too weak to work the seams for more than a season without perishing and the women bear sickly children. But once we took a man in a grey robe. Called himself Brother Kellin. He could heal and he could learn. Came to speak our tongue like his own in time, so I made him teach me his.'

'Where is he now?'

'Sickened last winter. He was old, we left him out in the snow.'

Vaelin was starting to understand why the Lonak were so widely despised. 'So your High Priestess told you to let me pass?'

'Word came from the Mountain. One of the *Merim Her* would come alone into our lands, their greatest warrior seeking the blood of his brother. No harm will come to him.'

The blood of his brother . . . The High Priestess sees much it seems. 'Why?'

'*She* does not explain. Words from the Mountain are not to be questioned.'

'And yet your son tried to kill me.'

'Boys seek renown in forbidden deeds. He had visions of defeating you and winning glory, the keenest sword of the *Merim Her* taken by his knife. How could I have angered the gods so that they visit me with a fool for a son?' He hawked and spat into the fire, glancing up at Vaelin. 'Why did you spare him?'

'There was no need to kill him. Killing without need is against the Faith.'

'Brother Kellin spoke often of your Faith, endless lies. How can a man have a creed but no god to punish him if he breaks it?'

'A god is a lie, and a man cannot be punished by a lie.'

The Lonak chewed some more beef and shook his head, he seemed almost sorrowful. 'I have heard the voice of the fire god, Nishak, deep in the dark places under the smoking mountain. There was no lie in it.'

Fire god? Obviously the man had confused an echoing cavern for the voice of one of his gods. 'What did he tell you?'

'Many things. None of them for your ears, *Merim Her.*' He tossed the beef and waterskin back to Vaelin. 'It's ill luck for a man to seek the death of his brother. Why do you do it?'

Vaelin was tempted to ignore the question and sit in silence until the Lonak left, there seemed little left to talk about and he certainly didn't cherish the man's company, but something made him voice the feelings that pained him so much. *Easier to unburden yourself to a stranger.* 'He's not my brother in blood, but in the Faith. We are of the same Order and he has committed a great offence.'

'And so you will kill him?'

'I will have to. He will not let me take him back to face judgement. Did the High Priestess tell you to let him pass also?'

The Lonak nodded. 'The yellow hair rode through seven days ago, making for the *Maars Nir-Uhlin Sol.* You intend to follow him there?'

'I have to.'

'Then you'll most likely find a yellow-haired corpse waiting for you. There is only death in those ruins.'

'I've heard. Do you know what it is that deals death in the fallen city?'

The Lonak's face twitched in annoyance. Fear was clearly a touchy subject. 'Our people do not go there, haven't for more than five winters, even before then we didn't like the place, there's a weight to the air that bears down on a man's soul. Then the bodies started appearing. Seasoned hunters and warriors torn and rent by something unseen, their faces frozen in fear. A shameful end to be taken by a beast, even a beast of magic.' He glanced up at Vaelin. 'You go there, you'll soon be as dead as your brother.'

'My brother isn't dead.' He knew it, felt it in the constant note of the blood-song. Nortah was still alive. Waiting.

Abruptly, the Lonak reached for his weapons and rose to his feet, fixing Vaelin with a hostile glare. 'We've talked long enough, *Merim Her*. I'll soil myself no longer with your company.'

'Vaelin Al Sorna,' Vaelin said.

The Lonak squinted at him suspiciously. 'What?'

'My name. Do you have one?'

The Lonak regarded him in silence for a long time, the hostility fading from his gaze. Eventually he shook his head. 'That is not your name.'

Then he was gone, into the blackness beyond the fire without a sound.

The tower must have stood over two hundred feet high and Vaelin could only imagine how impressive it had once looked: an arrow of red marble and grey granite pointing straight to the heavens. Now it was a broken and cracked road of weed-dotted rock leading him to the heart of the fallen city. Looking closer, he noticed that the rubble was adorned with fine relief carvings showing a myriad collection of beasts and frolicking, naked humans. The stone friezes that decorated the older buildings of the capital were all martial in character, warriors fighting forgotten battles with archaic weaponry. But there were no battles here, the carvings seemed joyous, often carnal, but never violent.

The morning sun had dawned behind a thick layer of cloud,

bringing flurries of snow driven by a stiff wind he knew would only gain in strength as the day wore on. He closed his cloak against the chill and urged Spit onwards. Although he was less fractious than usual, there was a tension in the animal Vaelin hadn't sensed before, his eyes were wide and he nickered nervously at the slightest sound. It was the city, he knew. The Lonak and Brother Artin hadn't exaggerated the oppression in the air. It thickened as he drew closer to the jagged outline of the ruins ahead, a dull ache building at the base of his skull. The blood-song was different too, less constant in its tone, more urgent in its warning.

He began to guide Spit towards a central archway near to where the fallen tower appeared to have had its base. They had only gone a few paces when Spit began to tremble, his eyes widening further, rearing and casting his head about in alarm.

'Easy!' Vaelin tried to calm him with a soft stroke to the neck but the horse was uncontrollable with fear, giving a shrill whinny and tipping Vaelin from his back with a sudden lurch then thundering away before Vaelin could grab at the reins.

'Come back, you bloody nag!' he raged. The only answer was the distant drum of hooves. 'Should've cut his throat years ago,' Vaelin muttered.

'Don't move, brother.'

Nortah stood beneath the part-collapsed archway. His blond hair was longer, reaching nearly to his shoulders, and the beginnings of a youthful beard showed on his chin. Instead of his brother's garb he wore a set of buckskin trews and a leather jerkin. Apart from the hunting knife in his belt he was unarmed. Vaelin had expected defiance, plus a modicum of the usual scorn and mockery, so was surprised that Nortah's expression was one of grave concern.

'Brother,' he addressed Nortah formally, 'Aspect Arlyn commands your immediate return . . .'

Nortah barely seemed to hear him, edging closer with his hands raised, and Vaelin noticed how his eyes kept flicking to the side, focusing on something to the rear . . .

Vaelin whirled, his sword coming free from the scabbard in a blur.

'DON'T!' Nortah's shout came too late as something large and immensely strong slammed into Vaelin's side, the force of the charge jarring his sword from his grip and sending him into the air to land a good ten feet away, his breath forced from his lungs by the impact.

He scrabbled for the dagger in his boot, dragging air into his lungs and trying to ignore the sharp pain in his chest, which told of at least one broken rib. He pushed himself upright, shouting with pain, and promptly fell again as a wave of nausea blurred his vision and tipped the ground beneath his feet. *More than just a broken rib.* He struggled, waving his dagger wildly, trying to rise and finding Nortah standing over him. Vaelin drew back expecting an attack, reversing his hold on the dagger to parry a thrust . . .

Nortah had his back to him, standing with his hands raised above his head, waving frantically. 'NO! No! Leave him!'

There was a sound, like a snarl mixed with a growl. But it was not a sound any dog would ever make.

Vaelin had seen wildcats in the Urlish and the Martishe but the beast that confronted him now was so different in size and shape he almost concluded it was from another species altogether. It stood over four feet tall at the shoulder, its lean, powerful frame covered in snow-white fur shot through with dark black stripes. Massive paws scraped at the ground with claws more than two inches long, and its eyes, bright green and shining out from the complex striped mask of its face, seemed to glow with malevolent intent. Meeting his gaze, it hissed, bearing fangs like ivory daggers.

'NO!' Nortah yelled, placing himself between the cat and Vaelin. 'No!'

The cat snarled again, raising a paw to slash the air in annoyance then shifted to the left, seeking to edge past Nortah. Vaelin was amazed. *Does it fear him?*

A handclap sounded, loud and sharp in the chilled mountain air. Vaelin tore his gaze from the snarling cat and saw a young woman standing a short distance away, a slender young woman with auburn hair and a familiar and very pretty oval face.

'Sella?' he said, wincing as a fresh wave of pain swept through him, his vision swimming. When it cleared he found her standing over him, smiling warmly, the cat was at her side now, nuzzling her leg as she played a hand through its fur. Behind her he could see other figures emerging from the ruins, dozens of people, young and old, men and women.

'Brother?' Nortah was kneeling next to him, his face pale with concern. 'Are you hurt?'

'I . . .' Meeting Nortah's gaze and seeing the worry in his eyes, he felt a great swell of shame in his breast. *I came here to kill you, my friend. What kind of man am I?* 'I'm fine,' he said, pushing himself upright and promptly passing out from the savage flare of agony in his chest.

CHAPTER EIGHT

H e was woken by voices, softly spoken but tense with
conflict.

'. . . a danger to us all,' a man was whispering
heatedly.

'No more than I,' answered a familiar voice.

'You are as much a fugitive as we are, brother. *He* is a member
of an Order that kills our kind.'

'This man is under my protection. No harm will come to him.'

'I'm not talking about harming him. There are other ways, we
can keep him sleeping . . .'

'A bit late for that,' Vaelin said, opening his eyes.

He lay on a bed of furs in a large, bare room, the walls and
the ceiling richly decorated with faded paintings of animals and
strange sea creatures he couldn't name. The floor was covered in
an elaborate mosaic showing a pear tree laden with fruit surrounded
by unfamiliar symbols and intricate swirling patterns. Nortah
stood near the door, accompanied by a slightly built man with
greying hair and wary eyes.

'Brother,' Nortah said with a smile. 'You are well?'

Vaelin felt at his side, expecting to find it tender to the touch but there was no pain. Pulling down the furs, he saw the livid bruise he expected was absent, his flesh smooth and unmarked. 'It appears so. Thought that beast had broken a rib at least.'

'She did more than that,' the slightly built man said. 'Weaver had to spend half the night on you. Snowdance is not an easy animal to control, even for Sella.'

'Snowdance?'

'The cat,' Nortah explained. 'A war-cat left behind by the Ice Horde. It seems some of them made the mistake of wandering into Lonak lands after the Tower Lord sent them packing. Sella found her when she was a kitten. Apparently she's not yet fully grown.'

'Grown large and ferocious enough to keep us safe,' the other man said, giving Vaelin a cold look. 'Until now.'

'This is Harlick,' Nortah said. 'He's scared of you. Most of them are.'

'Them?'

'The people who live here, and a very strange bunch they are too.' He went to a corner where Vaelin's clothes and weapons were neatly arranged and tossed him a shirt. 'Get dressed and I'll give you a tour of the fallen city.'

Outside, the sun was bright and high, warming the air and banishing shadows from the ruins. They emerged from what appeared to have been an official building of some kind, its size and the cluster of symbols carved into the lintel above the entrance marked it out as a place of importance.

'Harlick thinks it was a library,' Nortah said. 'He should know, used to be a man of importance in the Great Library in Varinshold. What became of all the books, however . . .' He shrugged.

'Gone to dust ages past, most like,' Vaelin said. Looking around, he was struck by an impression of beauty despoiled. The elegance of the buildings, evident in every line and carving, had been displaced and disfigured by the city's fall. His eyes picked out marks in the stonework and the broken statues, not cracks of age but scars hewn into the stone. Elsewhere he noted the way all the taller buildings had fallen in different directions, as if pulled down at random. There was a violence to the destruction that spoke of more than the deprivations of passing years and harshness of the elements.

'This place was attacked,' he murmured. 'Torn down centuries ago.'

'Sella said the same thing.' Nortah's face clouded a little. 'She has dreams sometimes. Bad dreams, about what happened here.'

Vaelin turned to face him, searching his face for signs of wrongness. Nortah was certainly different, the weariness that had dulled his eyes since their time in the Martishe was gone, replaced by something Vaelin took a moment to recognise. *He's happy.*

'Brother,' he said. 'I must know. Has she touched you?'

Nortah's expression was both amused and guarded. 'My father once told me there are some things a true nobleman does not discuss.'

Vaelin was momentarily undecided whether to be jealous or angry that Nortah could throw off his vows so easily. He surprised himself by finding he was neither. 'I meant . . .'

There was a rapid scrape of claws on stone and Vaelin fought to contain his alarm as the war-cat Snowdance bounded toward them, leaping a fallen column and nearly knocking Nortah from his feet as she pressed her great head against him, purring loudly.

'Hello, you vicious beast,' Nortah greeted her, tickling her behind the ears, for all the world as if he were petting a kitten. Vaelin couldn't stop himself edging away. The obvious power of the animal made even Scratch look weak in comparison.

'She won't hurt you,' Nortah assured him, scratching the cat's jaw as she angled her head. 'Sella won't let her.'

496 · ANTHONY RYAN

Nortah led him through the ruins to a cluster of buildings that seemed more intact than the others. There were people there, about thirty in all of varying ages, with a few children running about. Most of the adults regarded Vaelin with a mixture of fear and suspicion, a few were openly hostile. Oddly, they showed no fear of Snowdance, a couple of children even running over to pet her.

'Why didn't you take his sword?' a tall man with a black beard demanded of Nortah. He was clutching a heavy quarterstaff, and a little girl was peering out from behind his legs, eyes wide with fear and curiosity.

'It's not mine to take,' Nortah replied in a placid tone. 'And I'd advise you not to try, Rannil.'

Vaelin was struck by the way the people avoided his gaze as they moved through the camp, a couple even covered their faces although he knew none of them. There was also a murmur from the blood-song, a tone he hadn't heard before, it felt almost like recognition.

Nortah paused next to a heavily built young man who, unlike the others, paid them no attention at all. He sat surrounded by piles of rushes, his hands moving deftly as he worked them together, interlacing the long stems with unconscious skill. A number of completed conical baskets lay nearby, each one seemingly identical.

'This is Weaver,' Nortah told Vaelin. 'You have him to thank for your unbroken ribs.'

'You are a healer, sir?' Vaelin asked the young man.

Weaver stared up at Vaelin with blank eyes and a vague smile on his broad face. After a moment he blinked, as if recognising Vaelin for the first time. 'All broken up inside,' he said in a rapid tumble of words Vaelin almost didn't catch. 'Bones and veins and muscles and organs. Needed fixing. Long time fixing.'

'You fixed me?' Vaelin asked.

'Fixed,' Weaver repeated. He blinked again and returned to his task, his fingers resuming their expert work without further pause. He didn't look up as Nortah drew Vaelin away.

'He's slow of mind?' Vaelin asked.

'No-one's quite sure. He sits weaving his baskets all day, rarely speaks. The only time he's not weaving is when he's healing.'

'How can he have learned the healing arts?'

Nortah paused and rolled up the shirtsleeve on his left arm. There was a thin scar running along the forearm, faded and barely noticeable. 'When I cut my way out of the Battle Lord's tent one of his Hawks caught me with a lance. I stitched it best I could but I'm no healer. By the time I made it into the mountains the gangrene had set in, the flesh around the cut was black and stinking. When I found myself among these people Weaver put down his rushes, came over and put his hands on my arm. It felt . . . warm, almost like burning. When he took his hands away the wound looked like this.'

Vaelin looked back at Weaver, sitting surrounded by his rushes and baskets, and felt the blood-song murmur again. 'The Dark,' he said. As he glanced around at the wary faces of the others, the meaning of the song's new tone became clear. 'They all have it.'

Nortah leaned close, speaking softly. 'So do you, brother. How else could you find me?' He grinned at the shock on Vaelin's face. 'You hid it so well, all these years. None of us had any idea. But you couldn't hide it from her. She told me what you did for her, for which I thank you most humbly. After all, we'd never have met if you hadn't. Come on, she's waiting.'

They found Sella encamped in a large plaza in the centre of the city, smoke rising from a campfire, above which a steaming pot of stew was suspended. She wasn't alone, Spit snorting happily as she ran a hand over his flanks. His snorts turned to a familiar whinny of irritation as Vaelin approached, as if he resented the intrusion.

Sella's embrace was warm and her smile wide, although he noted she wore gloves and avoided contact with his skin. Her hands moved with the clean fluency he remembered. *You're taller,* she said.

'And you.' He nodded at Spit, now nuzzling a gorse bush with studied indifference to his master. 'He likes you. Usually he hates everyone on sight.'

Not hate, her hands said. *Anger. His memory is long for a horse. He remembers the plains where he grew up. Endless grass, boundless skies. Hungers to return.*

She paused to press a kiss to Nortah's lips as he pulled her close with easy familiarity, provoking a moment of unease. *So, she has touched him.*

Spit gave an abrupt whinny of alarm when Snowdance came bounding into view and would have fled if Sella hadn't calmed him with a handstroke to his neck. She turned her gaze to the war-cat, halting her in midstride. Vaelin felt a whisper of the blood-song as Sella's gaze remained locked on the cat. After the briefest pause Snowdance blinked, shaking her head in confusion, then bounded off in another direction, quickly disappearing into the ruins.

Wants to play with your horse, Sella said. *She'll stay away from him now.* She moved to the campfire, lifting the stewpot from its tripod.

'Will you eat with us, brother?' Nortah asked.

Vaelin realised he was fiercely hungry. 'Gladly.'

The stew was goat meat seasoned with thyme and sage, which apparently grew in abundance amidst the ruins. Vaelin wolfed down a bowl with his customary lack of manners, noting Nortah's wince of apology in Sella's direction. She just smiled and shook her head.

'How's Dentos?' Nortah asked.

BLOOD SONG · 499

'Bruised. You nearly broke his cheekbone.'

'He damn near broke mine. The Hawks didn't get him then?'

'He made it safely back to the High Keep.'

'I'm glad. He and the others, were they angry?'

'No they were worried. *I* was angry.'

Nortah's smile was tight, almost wary. 'Did you come here to kill me, brother?'

Vaelin met his gaze squarely. 'I knew you wouldn't let me take you back.'

'You were right. And now?'

Vaelin pointed to the medallion chain around Nortah's neck and gestured for him to hand it over. Nortah hesitated briefly then took out the small metal icon of the blind warrior, hooking the chain over his head and tossing it into Vaelin's palm.

'Now there is no need,' Vaelin said, putting the chain around his own neck. 'Since you unwisely fled into Lonak territory weakened by your wound. Having fought off several Lonak attacks, you sadly fell victim to an unnamed but famously savage beast known to dwell near the fallen city.' He touched a hand to the medallion. 'I could scarcely recognise your remains but for this.'

Will they believe you? Sella asked.

Vaelin shrugged. 'They believed what I told them about you. Besides, it's the King's belief that matters, and I suspect he will choose to take my word without further investigation.'

'So you do have the King's ear,' Nortah mused. 'We always suspected. Did the Battle Lord live?'

'So it seems. The Realm Guard have returned to Asrael and Lord Mustor is now installed as Fief Lord in the Cumbraelin capital.'

'And the Cumbraelin prisoners?'

Vaelin hesitated. He had heard the story from Brother Artin and wasn't sure how Nortah would react to the news but decided he deserved to hear the truth. 'The Battle Lord is popular with the Hawks, as you know. After what you did to him they rioted, the prisoners were slaughtered to a man.'

Nortah's face sagged with sorrow. 'All for nothing then.'

Sella reached over to clasp his hand briefly. *Not for nothing,* her hands told him. *You found me.*

Nortah forced a smile and got to his feet. 'I should hunt.' He planted a kiss on her cheek and shouldered his bow and quiver. 'We're running short of meat, and I suspect you both have much to discuss.'

Vaelin watched him walk off towards the northern edge of the city. After a moment Snowdance emerged to pad alongside him.

I know what you're thinking, Sella said when he turned back.

'You touched him,' Vaelin replied.

Not how you think, her hands insisted. *You have something of mine.*

Vaelin nodded, fishing inside his collar for the silk scarf she had given him. He untied it from his neck and handed it to her, feeling oddly reluctant. It had been his talisman for so long its absence felt strange, unnerving.

Sella smiled sadly as she laid the scarf out on her knees, her fingers tracing over the delicate gold-thread pattern. *Mother wore this all her life,* she signed. *When she passed it came to me. Its message is precious to those who believe as we do. See.* She pointed at the sigil woven into the silk, a crescent encircled by a ring of stars. *The moon, the sign of calm reflection, from where reason and balance are derived. Here.* She pointed to a golden circle ringed with flame. *The sun, source of passion, love, anger.* Her finger traced to the tree in the centre of the scarf. *We exist here, between the two. Grown from the earth, warmed by the sun, cooled by the moonlit night. Your brother's heart had been pulled too far into the realm of the sun, fired with anger and regret. Now he has cooled and he looks to the moon for guidance.*

'By his own choice or by your touch?'

Her smile became shy. *I feared him when Snowdance called to me with news of his coming. We found him fallen from his horse, raving with fever from his wound. The others wanted to kill him but I wouldn't let them. I knew what he was, a man with his skills may have been useful to us, and so I touched him.* She paused, looking down at her gloved hands. *Nothing happened. For the first time, no rush of power, no sense of control.* A slow flush crept up her cheeks. *I can touch him.*

Something for which I'm sure he's very grateful, Vaelin thought, fighting a pang of envy. 'He does not do your bidding? He is not' – he fumbled for the right words – 'enslaved?'

Mother told me it would be this way. One day I would meet someone who would be immune to my touch, and we would be bound together. It is always this way for those with our gift. Your brother is as free as he ever was. Her smile faded, sympathy colouring her eyes. *More free than you, I think.*

Vaelin looked away. 'He told me what Weaver did for him,' he said, desiring a change of subject. 'All the people here are touched by the Dark, are they not?'

Her hands twitched in annoyance and a frown creased her brow. *The Dark is a word for the ignorant. The people here are Gifted. Different powers, different abilities. But Gifted. Like you.*

He nodded. 'That's what you saw in me, all those years ago. You knew it before I did.'

Your gift is rare and precious. My mother called it the Hunter's Call. In the days of the Four Fiefs it was known as the Battle Sight. The Seordah . . .

'Blood-song,' he said.

She nodded. *It's grown since our last meeting. I can feel it. You have honed it, learned its music well. But there is still so much to learn.*

'You can teach me?' He was surprised at the hope evident in his voice.

She shook her head. *No, but there are others, older and wiser, with the same gift. They can guide you.*

'How do I find them?'

Your song links you to them. It will find them. All you must do is follow. Remember, it is a rare gift you hold. It may be years before you find one who can guide you.

Vaelin hesitated before asking his next question, he had kept the secret so long it was a habit he found hard to break. 'There is something I need to know. How can it be that I have faced two men, now dead, who both spoke with the same voice?'

Her face was suddenly guarded and it was a moment before her hands spoke again. *They wished you ill, these men?*

He thought of the assassin in the House of the Fourth Order and the murderous desperation of Hentes Mustor. 'Yes, they wished me ill.'

Sella's hands now moved with a strange hesitancy he hadn't seen before. *There are stories among the Gifted . . . Old stories . . . Myths . . . Of Gifted who could return . . .*

He frowned. 'Return from where?'

From the place where all journeys end . . . From the Beyond . . . From death. They take the bodies of the living, wear them like a cloak. Whether such a thing can truly be done I don't know. Your words are . . . troubling.

'Once there were seven. You know what this means?'

There were once seven Orders of your Faith. An old story.

'A true story?'

She shrugged. *Your Faith is not mine, I know little of its history.*

He glanced back at the camp and its fearful inhabitants. 'These people all follow your beliefs?'

She gave a small laugh and shook her head. *Only I follow the path of the Sun and the Moon here. Amongst us are Questers, Ascendants, followers of the Cumbraelin god and even some adherents of your Faith. Belief does not bind us, our gifts do that.*

'Erlin guided all these people here?'

Some. There were only Harlick and a few others when he first brought me here. Others came later, fleeing the fears and hatreds our kind attracts, called by their gifts. This place. She gestured at the surrounding ruins. *Once there was great power here. The Gifted were protected in this city, vaunted even. The echo of that time is still strong enough to call us. You can feel it, can't you?*

He nodded, the atmosphere seemed less oppressive now he knew its meaning. 'Nortah said you have bad dreams of this city. Of what happened here.'

Not all bad. Sometimes I see it how it was before the fall. There were many wonders here; a city of artists, poets, singers, sculptors. They had mastered so much, learned so much, they felt themselves invulnerable, thinking the Gifted among them all the protection they needed. They had lived in peace for generations and had no warriors, so when the storm came they were naked before it.

'Storm?'

Many centuries ago, before our kind came to these shores, before even the Lonak and the Seordah, there were many cities like this, this land was rich in people and beauty. Then the storm came and tore it all down. A storm of steel and twisted power. They swept aside the Gifted who fought them and vented all their hate on this city, the city they hated most of all. She paused, a shudder making her pull her shawl around her shoulders. *Rape and massacre, the burning of children, men ate the flesh of other men. Every horror imaginable was visited here.*

'Who were they? The men who did this?'

She shook her head vaguely. *The dreams tell me nothing of who they were or from where they came. I think it's because the people who lived here didn't know either. The dreams are the echo of their lives, they only show me what they knew.*

She closed her eyes for a moment, clearing her head of the memory, then deftly folded the scarf on her knees and held it out to him.

'I can't,' he said. 'It was your mother's.'

Her gloved hands took his and pressed the scarf into them. *A gift. I have much to thank you for and only this to show it.*

In the evening they shared a brace of rabbits Nortah had brought back from his hunt, regaling Sella with the more humorous tales of their days in the Order. Strangely, the stories felt dated, as if they were two old men spinning yarns of long ago. It occurred to him that for Nortah the Order was now part of his past, he had progressed, Vaelin and his brothers were no longer his family. He had Sella now, Sella and the other Gifted, huddling in their ruin.

'You know it's not safe to stay here,' he told Sella. 'The Lonak will not tolerate your war-cat forever. And sooner or later Aspect Tendris is bound to send a stronger expedition to solve the mystery of this place.'

She nodded, hands moving in the firelight. *We will have to leave soon. There are other refuges we can seek.*

'Come with us,' Nortah suggested. 'You do have more right to join this odd company than I, after all.'

Vaelin shook his head. 'I belong with the Order, brother. You know that.'

'I know there's nothing but war and killing in your future if you stay with them. And what do you think they'll do when they find out your secret?'

Vaelin shrugged to mask his discomfort. Nortah was right of course, but his conviction was unshaken. Despite the burden of many secrets and the blood he had spilled, despite his ache for

Sherin and the sister he would never know, he knew he belonged with the Order.

He hesitated before saying what he knew he had to say next, the secret had been kept too long and the guilt weighed heavily. 'Your mother and your sisters are in the Northern Reaches,' he told Nortah. 'The King found a place for them there after your father's execution.'

Nortah's face was unreadable. 'How long have you known this?'

'Since the Test of the Sword. I should have told you before. I'm sorry. I hear Tower Lord Al Myrna is tolerant of other faiths within his lands. You may find refuge there.'

Nortah stared into the fire, his face tense. Sella put her arm around his shoulders and laid her head on his chest. His face softened as he stroked her hair. 'Yes, you should have told me,' he said to Vaelin. 'But thank you for telling me now.'

Some children came running out of the darkness, laughing and clustering around Nortah. 'Story!' they chanted. 'Story! Story!'

Nortah tried to placate them, saying he was too tired but they pestered him even more until he relented. 'What kind of story?'

'Battles!' a little boy cried as they sat around the fire.

'No battles,' insisted a little girl Vaelin recognised as the fearful, wide-eyed child from the camp. 'Battles are boring. Scary story!' She climbed into Sella's lap and settled into her arms.

The other children took up the cry and Nortah waved them to silence, his face taking on a mock-serious countenance. 'Scary story it is. But' – he held up a finger – 'this is not a story for the faint at heart or the weak of bladder. This is the most terrible and frightful of tales and when I am done you may curse my name for ever having voiced it.' His voice dropped to a whisper and the children leaned closer to catch his words. 'This is the tale of the Witch's Bastard.'

It was an old tale Vaelin knew well: a Dark-afflicted witch from a Renfaelin village snared the local blacksmith into lying with her and of their union a vile creature in the shape of a human boy was born, destined to bring about the ruin of the village and the death of his father. He thought it an odd choice of story for these children, given as it was often used to warn of the dangers of dabbling in the Dark, but they listened avidly, eyes wide as Nortah set the scene. 'In the darkest part of the darkest woods in old Renfael, before the time of the Realm, there stood a village. And in this village there dwelt a witch, comely to the eye but with a heart blacker than the blackest night . . .'

Vaelin rose quietly and made his way through the darkened ruins to the main camp, where suspicious eyes stared at him from makeshift shelters. There were a few guarded nods of greeting but none of the Gifted spoke to him. *They must know I'm one of them,* he thought. *But still they fear me.* He continued on to the building where he had awoken that morning, the place Nortah called a library. There was a faint glow of firelight in the doorway and he lingered outside a moment to ensure there were no voices. He wanted a private conversation with Harlick, the one-time librarian.

He found the man reading by his fire, the smoke escaping through a hole in the ceiling. Looking closer at the fire, Vaelin noted it had an unusual fuel. Instead of wood, the flames licked at curled, blackened pages and blistered leather bindings. His suspicions were confirmed when Harlick turned the last page of his book, closed it and tossed it into the flames.

'I was once told to burn a book is a heinous crime,' Vaelin observed, recalling one of his mother's many lectures on the importance of learning.

Harlick jerked to his feet in fright, taking a few wary backward steps. 'What do you want?' he demanded, the quaver in his voice draining any threat from the words.

'To talk.' Vaelin entered and crouched next to the fire, warming his hands and watching the books burn. Harlick said nothing, crossing his arms and refusing to meet his gaze.

'You are Gifted,' Vaelin continued. 'You must be or you wouldn't be here.'

Harlick's eyes flashed at him. 'Don't you mean *afflicted*, brother?'

'You have no need to fear me. I have questions, questions a man of learning might be able to answer. Especially a man with a gift.'

'And if I can't answer?'

Vaelin shrugged. 'I shall seek answers elsewhere.' He nodded at the fire. 'For a librarian you seem to have little respect for books.'

Harlick bridled, anger overcoming his fear. 'I have given my life to the service of knowledge. I will not justify myself to one who does little but litter the Realm with corpses.'

Vaelin inclined his head. 'As you wish, sir. But I should still like to ask you my questions. You may answer or no, the choice is your own.'

Harlick pondered in silence for a moment then moved back to the fur-covered stool beside the fire, resuming his seat and cautiously meeting Vaelin's eye. 'Ask then.'

'Is the Seventh Order of the Faith truly extinct?'

The man's gaze dropped immediately, fear once more clouding his face. He didn't speak for a long time and when he did his words were a whisper. 'Have you come here to kill me?'

'I am not here for you. You know that.'

'But you are in search of the Seventh Order.'

'My search is in service to the Faith and the Realm.' He frowned, realising the import of what Harlick had said. '*You* are of the Seventh Order?'

Harlick seemed shocked. 'You mean to say you do not know? Why else would you be here?'

Vaelin was undecided whether to laugh or cuff the man in frustration. 'I came in search of my fugitive brother,' he told Harlick patiently. 'Not knowing what I would find. I know a little of the Seventh Order and wish to know more. That is all.'

Harlick's face became rigid, as if he feared any display of emotion could betray him. 'Would you reveal the secrets of your Order, brother?'

'Of course not.'

'Then do not expect me to divulge the secrets of mine. You can torture me, I know. But I'll tell you nothing.'

Vaelin saw how the man's hands trembled in his lap and couldn't help admiring his courage. He had thought the Seventh Order, if it still existed, a malign group of Dark-afflicted conspirators, but this frightened man and his simple courage spoke of something different.

'Did the Seventh Order orchestrate the killing of Aspects Sentis and Morvin?' he demanded, more harshly than intended. 'Did they try to assassinate me during the Test of the Run? Did they deceive Hentes Mustor into murdering his father?'

Harlick flinched, gasping out a noise that was half a sob and half a laugh. 'The Seventh Order guards the Mysteries,' he said, the words sounding like a quotation. 'It practises its arts in service of the Faith. It has always been thus.'

'There was a war, centuries ago. Between the Orders, a war begun by the Seventh Order.'

Harlick shook his head. 'The Seventh went to war with itself. It was sundered from within, the other Orders were drawn into the conflict. The war was long and terrible, thousands died. When it was over those of the Seventh who remained were feared beyond reason by the people and the nobility. Conclave decided the Seventh would disappear from the Fiefs and be seen no more by the people. Its House was destroyed, its books burned, its brothers and sisters scattered and hidden. But the Faith requires there to be a Seventh Order, visible or no.'

'You mean the Seventh was never truly destroyed? It works in secret?'

'I've told you too much. Ask me no more.'

'Do the Aspects know?'

Harlick shut his eyes tight and said nothing.

Suddenly furious, Vaelin grabbed the man, lifting him clear of the stool, forcing him against the wall. 'DO THE ASPECTS KNOW?'

Harlick shrank from him, quailing in his grasp, words bubbling from his lips amidst panicked spittle. 'Of course they know. They know everything.'

Memories came in a flood as Harlick's words struck home. The shift in Master Sollis's eyes when he first said, 'Once there were seven,' Aspect Elera's instant of fear at the same words, the way Sollis had exchanged glances with her after they told the tale of One Eye's Dark abilities. And the knowledge behind Aspect Arlyn's eyes. *Am I a fool?* he wondered. *For not seeing this? The Aspects have been lying to the Faithful for centuries.*

He released Harlick and went back to the fire. The books were little more than ash now, the leather bindings curled and charred black amidst the embers. 'The other Gifted, they don't know, do they?' he asked, glancing back at Harlick. 'They don't know what you are.'

Harlick shook his head.

'You have a mission here?'

'I cannot tell you anything further, brother.' Harlick's voice was strained but determined. 'Please do not ask me.'

'As you wish, brother.' He went to the doorway, gazing out at the moonlit ruins. 'I would be grateful if you would omit mention of Brother Nortah's survival in any report you make to your Aspect.'

Harlick shrugged. 'Brother Nortah is not my concern.'

'Thank you.'

He wandered the ruins for hours, memories playing though his mind in a torrent. *They knew, all this time. They knew.* He couldn't decide if his confusion was born of betrayal or something deeper. *The Aspects embody the virtues of the Faith. They* are *the Faith. If they have lied . . .*

'I really wish you'd come with us.' He looked up finding Nortah perched atop a massive piece of fallen statuary. It took Vaelin a moment to recognise it as the marble head of a bearded man, his carved expression one of deep contemplation. Surely one of the city's luminaries commemorated in stone. Was he a philosopher or a king? A god perhaps. Vaelin leaned against the statue's forehead, running a hand over the deep lines in his brows. Whoever or whatever he had been was forgotten now. No more than a great stone head waiting for the ages to turn him to dust in a city where no-one was left to remember his name.

'I . . . can't,' he told Nortah eventually.

'You don't sound so certain now.'

'Perhaps I'm not. Even so, there is much I need to know. I'll only find answers in the Order.'

'Answers to what?'

There's something growing. A threat, a danger, something that threatens us all. I've felt it for a long time, although it's only now I realise it. Vaelin left it unsaid. Nortah had a new path now, a new family. Sharing would only burden him. 'We're all looking for answers, brother,' he said. 'Though you appear to have found yours.'

'That I have.' Nortah leapt down from the statue and held out his sword. 'You should take this as well as the talisman. It'll add to your proof.'

'You may need it, the road to the Northern Reaches will be long and hazardous. These people will need your protection.'

'There are other forms of protection. I've spilled enough blood with this. I intend to live the rest of my days without taking another life.'

Vaelin took the sword. 'When will you leave?'

'There's no point waiting for winter. Convincing the others may be difficult though. Some of them have been here for years.' He paused, his expression oddly sheepish. 'I didn't kill the bear.'

'What?'

'During the Test of the Wild. I didn't kill it. The shelter I built collapsed in the wind. I was desperate, freezing, wandering in the snow. I found a cave and thought the Departed had guided me to shelter. Unfortunately, the bear who lived there didn't appreciate visitors. It chased me for miles, all the way to the edge of a cliff. I managed to grab on to a branch, the bear wasn't so lucky. Kept me fed for a while though.'

Vaelin laughed, the sound was strange amidst the ruins, out of place. 'You bloody liar.'

Nortah grinned. 'Next to the bow it was my major talent.' His smile faded. 'I'll miss you, and the others. Can't say I'm sorry about the Battle Lord though.'

They walked back to the camp, fed the waning fire and talked of the Order and their brothers for hours. When Nortah finally went to the shelter he shared with Sella, Vaelin settled down in his cloak, knowing that in the morning he would wake early and leave without a farewell. The reason came to him before he tumbled into sleep: *I want to stay.*

PART IV

In addition to his many lies regarding the supposed perfidy of Alpiran interlopers, King Janus had need of a legal device to supplement his premise for war. Accordingly, extensive digging into the royal archive unearthed an obscure treaty dating back some four hundred years. What was in fact a lapsed and fairly standard trade agreement on tariffs between the Lord of Asrael and the then-independent city states of Untesh and Marbellis enabled the King's Lord of Justice to seize on a minor clause formalising arrangements to co-operate in suppressing Meldenean pirates. Through a mixture of inventive translation from the original Alpiran text and basic sophistry, this clause was twisted into an invitation to assume sovereignty. Thus was the lie fabricated that the invasion was simply a seizure of property that already belonged to the King.

The invasion fleet arrived off the Alpiran coast on the ninety-sixth day of Emperor Aluran's reign (all praise his wisdom and benevolence). Although the recent deterioration in relations between our Empire (may it live forever) and the Unified Realm had caused some Imperial advisors to

warn of a possible invasion, the comparative smallness of King Janus's fleet led many to discount their fears. The Imperial mathematician Rerien Alturs calculated that to deposit the Realm Guard on our coast would require a fleet of at least fifteen hundred ships and the Realm possessed barely five hundred, of which only half were warships. Sadly, no word had reached our ears of the treacherous actions of the Meldenean pirate nation (may the ocean rise to swallow their islands) in agreeing to ferry the Realm forces across the Erinean Sea. Sources disagree on the price paid by Janus for this service, opinion ranging from no less than three million gold pieces to the offer of his daughter in marriage to a Meldenean of suitable rank, but the cost must have been high indeed for the pirates to set aside their hatred of the Northmen born of the destruction of their city twenty years earlier.

It was the greatest misfortune that the Hope was at that very moment engaged in a ceremonial visit to the Temple of the Goddess Muisil in Untesh, accompanied by one hundred men of the Imperial Horse Guard. He was therefore only ten miles from the landing site when a terrified fisherman arrived with news of a Meldenean raiding party of previously unseen size. The Hope immediately mobilised the local garrison, some three thousand horse and five thousand spears, setting out in the dead of night to confront the invaders and sweep them back into the sea. It took several hours to assemble the

force and march to the coast. If his force had moved only fractionally quicker, the Hope would have had a chance to deal a serious, possibly fatal blow to the forces still assembling on the beach. However, the first Realm Guard regiment to land had already formed ranks to defend the narrow track through the dunes leading to the beach. At their head was the most fanatical and ferocious warrior priest of the Unified Realm's heretic faith: Valin il Sorna (curse his name for all the ages).

—VERNIERS ALISHE SOMEREN,
THE GREAT WAR OF SALVATION,
VOL. 1 (UNREVISED TEXT),
ALPIRAN IMPERIAL ARCHIVES

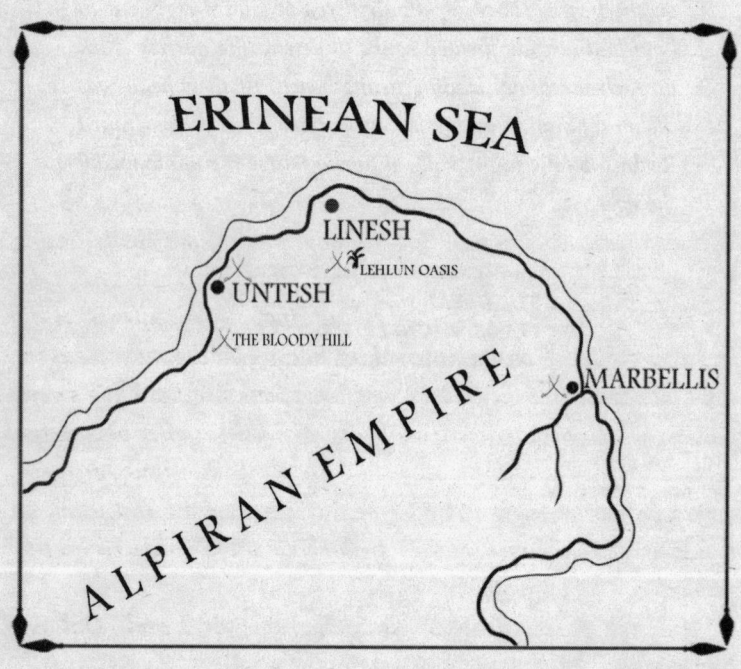

ERINEAN SEA

LINESH

LEHLUN OASIS

UNTESH

THE BLOODY HILL

MARBELLIS

ALPIRAN EMPIRE

VERNIERS' ACCOUNT

'It must have pained you,' I said, 'finding your brother's body. Seeing him so . . . mutilated.'

The Northman got to his feet, rubbing at the stiffness in his legs and groaning as he stretched his back. 'Not the most pleasant sight,' he agreed. 'I gave what was left to the fire, took his sword and his medallion back to the Order. The King and Aspect Arlyn accepted my word without question. The Battle Lord, understandably, was less trusting, naming me a traitor and a liar. I think he would have challenged me too if the King hadn't ordered him to silence.'

'And the mysterious beast that killed Nortah,' I said. 'Did you ever discover what manner of creature it was?'

'They say wolves grow large in the north. In the eastern crags there are ferocious apes twice the size of a man, with faces like dogs.' He shrugged. 'There are many dangers in nature.'

He moved to the stairs leading to the deck and began to ascend. 'I feel the need of some fresh air.'

I followed him out into the night. The sky was cloudless and the moon bright, painting the ship's rigging a pale blue as it swayed in the stiff sea breeze. The only crewmen I could see were the helmsman and the dim shape of a boy perched high on the mainmast. 'Captain told you to stay in the hold,' the helmsman growled.

'Then go and wake him,' I suggested before joining Al Sorna. He stood resting his forearms on the rail, staring out at the moonlit sea, his expression distant.

'The Teeth of Moesis,' he said, pointing to a cluster of white specks in the distance, where waves were breaking on a series of jagged rocks. 'Moesis is the Meldenean god of the hunt, a great serpent who fought Margentis, the giant orca god, for a day and a night. So great was their struggle they made the sea boil and forced the continents apart. When it was over and Moesis floated dead in the surf his body rotted away but his teeth were left to mark his passing. His spirit joined with the sea and when the Meldeneans rose to hunt the waves it was to him they looked for guidance, for his teeth mark the way to their homeland. We're in Meldenean waters now. Where I believe your ships never venture.'

'Meldeneans are pirate scum,' I said simply. 'Any of our ships would make a valuable prize.'

'And yet the Lady Emeren's vessel was taken here.'

I said nothing. I had unsettling questions of my own on this matter but was reluctant to discuss them with him.

'I understand the ship and crew were allowed to sail on their way,' he went on. 'Only the lady was taken.'

I coughed. 'The pirates no doubt recognised her value for ransom.'

'Except they asked for no ransom. Only for me to come and fight their champion.' His mouth twitched and I realised I was being baited.

I recalled Emeren's bitter audience with the Emperor after the Northman's trial, where she had begged for his sentence to be changed. 'A death demands a death,' she had railed, her fine features contorted with rage. 'The gods demand it. The people demand it. My fatherless son demands it. And I demand it, Sire, as widow to the murdered Hope of this Empire.'

In the chill silence that followed her tirade the Emperor sat silent and unmoving on his throne, the attending guards and courtiers shocked and stiff with trepidation, their eyes fixed firmly on the floor. When the Emperor finally spoke his voice was toneless and devoid of anger as he decreed the Lady Emeren had offended his person and was banished from court until further notice. As far as I knew they hadn't exchanged a single word since.

'Suspect what you wish,' I told Al Sorna. 'But know the Emperor does not scheme, he would never indulge in revenge. His every action is in service to the Empire.'

He laughed. 'Your Emperor has sent me to the Islands to die, my lord. So the Meldeneans can have their revenge on my father and the lady can witness the death of the man who killed her husband. I wonder if it was her idea or theirs.'

I couldn't fault his reasoning. He was, of course, expected to die. The Hope Killer's end would be the final act in the trauma of our war with his people, the epilogue to the epic of conflict. Whether this had been in the Emperor's mind when he agreed to the Meldeneans' offer I truly don't know. In any case, Al Sorna seemed free of fear and resigned to his fate. I wondered if he actually expected to survive his duel with the Shield, reputedly the finest swordsman ever to wield a blade. The Hope Killer's story had left me in little doubt as to his own deadly abilities but they were sure to have been dulled by his years of captivity. Even if he did prevail, the Meldeneans were unlikely simply to allow the son of the City Burner to sail away unmolested. He was a man going to his doom. I knew it, and so, apparently, did he.

'When did King Janus tell you of his plans to attack the Empire?' I asked, keen to extract as much of his story as possible before we made landfall.

'About a year before the Realm Guard embarked for Alpiran shores. For three years the regiment had roamed the Realm putting down rebels and outlaws. Smugglers on the southern shore, bands of cut-throats in Nilsael, ever more fanatics in Cumbrael. We spent a winter in the north fighting the Lonak when they decided it was time for another round of raiding. The regiment grew larger, adding two companies to the roster. After our Cumbraelin adventure the King had given us a banner of our own, a wolf running above the High Keep. And so the men began calling themselves the Wolfrunners. I always thought it sounded silly but they seemed to like it. For some reason young men flocked to our banner, not all of them poor either, and we had no further reason to recruit from the dungeons. So many turned up at the Order House the Aspect was forced to insti-gate a series of tests, mainly tests of strength and speed, but tests in the Faith as well. Only those with the soundest Faith and the strongest bodies were taken. By the time we came to board the fleet for the invasion I had command of twelve hundred men, probably the best trained and most experienced soldiers in the Realm.' He looked down at the blue-white froth of the ocean as it collided with the hull, his expression sombre. 'When the war ended less than two-thirds were left. For the Realm Guard it was even worse, maybe one man in ten made it back to the Realm.'

Deservedly so, I thought but didn't say. 'What did he tell you?' I asked instead. 'What reason did Janus give for the invasion?'

He lifted his head, staring at the Teeth of Moesis as they faded towards the dim horizon. 'Bluestone, spices and silk,' he said, his tone faintly bitter. 'Bluestone, spices and silk.'

CHAPTER ONE

T he bluestone sat in Vaelin's palm, a king's gift, the dim light from the crescent moon gleaming on its smooth surface, a thin vein of silver-grey marking the otherwise flawless blue. It was the largest bluestone ever found, most were little bigger than a grape, and Barkus had informed him, with barely concealed greed, that it would fetch enough gold to buy most of Renfael.

'Can you hear that?' Dentos's voice was steady but Vaelin saw the twitch below his eye. It had begun a year ago, when they cornered a large Lonak raiding party in a box canyon in the north. As ever the Lonak had refused to surrender and charged straight for their line, screaming death songs. It had been a brief but ugly fight, Dentos in the thick of it, emerging unscathed but for the twitch. It tended to flare up just before a battle. 'Sounds like thunder.' He grinned, still twitching.

Vaelin pocketed the bluestone and looked out over the broad plain stretching away from the beach, sparse grass and scrub barely visible in the gloom. It seemed the northern coast of the Alpiran Empire was not overly blessed with vegetation. Behind him the din of thousands of Realm Guard assembling on the beach mingled with the roar of the surf and the creak of countless oars as their fleet of Meldenean hirelings ferried ever more to the shoreline. Despite the noise, he could hear it clearly: distant thunder, out in the darkness.

'Didn't take them long,' Barkus observed. 'Maybe they knew we were coming.'

'Meldenean bastards.' Dentos hawked and spat on the sand. 'Never trust 'em.'

'Perhaps they simply saw the fleet coming,' Caenis suggested. 'Eight hundred ships would be hard to miss. It's barely a couple of hours' ride from here to the garrison at Untesh.'

'It scarcely matters how they know,' Vaelin said. 'What matters is that they do and we have a busy night ahead of us. Brothers, to your companies. Dentos, I want the archers on that rise.' He turned to Janril Norin, one-time failed minstrel and now regimental bugler and standard-bearer. 'Form ranks by company.'

Janril nodded, bringing the bugle to his lips and sounding the urgent call to arms. The men responded instantly, rising from their resting places amidst the dunes and hurrying into their ranks, twelve hundred men forming into neat ranks in barely five minutes, the rapid, unconscious actions of professional soldiers. There was little talk and no panic. Most had done this many times before and the new recruits took their lead from the veterans.

Vaelin waited until the men had assembled then walked the length of the regiment, checking for gaps, nodding encouragement or berating those he found with loose mail or poorly strapped helmets. The Wolfrunners were the least armoured soldiers in the Realm Guard, eschewing the usual steel breastplate and wide-brimmed helm for mail shirts and caps of leather lined with iron plates. The light armour befitted a force usually employed to pursue small bands of Lonak raiders or outlaws across rough country or thick forest.

Vaelin's inspection was really Sergeant Krelnik's job but had become something of a pre-battle ritual, giving the men a chance to see their commander before the chaos started, a distraction from the impending bloodshed, and it spared him the chore of making a rousing speech as other commanders were apt to do. He knew the men's loyalty to him was mostly born of fear and a wary respect for his ever-growing reputation. They didn't love him, but he never doubted they would follow him, speech or not.

He paused before a man once known as Gallis the Climber, now Sergeant Gallis of the Third Company. Gallis greeted him with a smart salute. 'Milord!'

'You need a shave, Sergeant.'

Gallis grinned. It was an old joke, he always needed a shave. 'Prepare for cavalry, milord?'

Vaelin glanced over his shoulder, darkness still shrouded the landscape but the thunder grew ever louder. 'Indeed, Sergeant.'

'Hope they're easier to kill than the Lonak.'

'We'll find out soon enough.'

He moved to the rear, where Janril Norin was waiting with Spit, holding his reins with nervous hands and keeping as far away as possible from his infamously vicious teeth. Spit snorted as Vaelin approached, allowing him to mount without the usual shudder of annoyance. He was always like this before a fight, for some reason the impending violence seemed to calm him. Whatever his faults as an obedient mount, the last four years had shown Spit to be a formidable warhorse. 'Bloody nag,' Vaelin said, patting his neck. Spit gave a loud whinny and dragged a hoof along the sandy soil. The confinement and discomfort of the voyage across the Erinean had been hard for him and he appeared to rejoice in the space and the promise of battle.

Reined in nearby were fifty mounted men of the scout troop, at their head a muscular young brother with lean, handsome features and bright blue eyes. Seeing Vaelin, Frentis gave a tight smile and raised a hand in greeting. Vaelin nodded back, pushing away a rush of guilt. *I should have contrived to spare him this.* But there had been no way to keep Frentis in the Realm, a newly confirmed brother with already renowned skills made too fine an addition to the regiment.

Janril Noren quickly mounted his own horse and reined in alongside. 'Signal prepare for cavalry,' Vaelin told him. The call quickly rang out, three short blasts of the bugle followed by one long peel. There was a ripple in the ranks as the men fumbled for the caltrops they wore at their belts. It had been Caenis's idea, back when the Lonak had taken to charging the regiment's patrols on their sturdy ponies. The caltrops had worked remarkably well, so well the Lonak abandoned their tactic, but would it work now against these Alpirans?

Out in the gloom the thunder stopped. Vaelin could see them now, barely visible in the predawn light, a long line of mounted men, horses' breaths steaming in the cool air amidst the flicker of bared sabres and lance points. A quick calculation of their numbers did little to lighten his mood.

'Must be well over a thousand, my lord,' Janril said, his strong, melodious voice showing the strain of the wait. He had proved himself a brave soldier many times in the past four years, but the wait before the killing could unnerve the strongest heart.

'Closer to two,' Vaelin grunted. 'And that's just what we can see.' Two thousand or more trained cavalry against twelve hundred infantry. The odds were not good. Vaelin glanced over his shoulder at the dunes, hoping the spear-points of the Realm Guard would suddenly rise above the sand. The riders he had sent to the Battle Lord must have reached him by now, although he had doubts about Al Hestian's keenness to send aid. The man's enmity remained undimmed, his eyes gleamed with it every time Vaelin had the misfortune to be in his presence, as did the barbed-steel spike the Battle Lord now wore in place of his hand. *Will he lose a war just to see me dead?*

The line of Alpiran horsemen paused, shimmering in the gloom as they dressed their ranks in preparation for the charge. A lone voice could be heard shouting orders or encouragement, answered by the horsemen as they roared out a single word in unison: 'SHALMASH!'

'It means victory, my lord,' Janril said, sweat shining on his upper lip. 'Shalmash. Met a few Alpirans in my time.'

'Good to know, Sergeant.'

The Alpirans were moving now, at a trot at first then increasing the pace to a canter, three lines coming on in good order, each man garbed in chain-mail, a spiked helm and a white cloak. Their discipline was impressive, not a rider was out of place and their lines moved forward at a precisely observed pace. Vaelin had rarely seen it done better, even the King's Mounted Guard would have been pressed to match the feat away from the parade ground. When they had closed to within two hundred paces a fresh tumult of shouts and bugle calls sounded and they surged into the charge, lances levelled, each rider hunched forward, spurring their mounts onwards, the precision of their lines fragmenting, becoming a mass of horseflesh and steel, thundering towards the regiment like a giant mailed fist.

There was no need for further orders, the Wolfrunners had done this before, although never on such a scale. The first rank stepped forward and threw their caltrops as far as they could, kneeling as the second rank repeated the manoeuvre, then the third, the ground directly in front of them now seeded with spiked metal the oncoming horsemen could not avoid. The first horse went down within fifty yards of their lines, bringing down another as it fell shrieking, blood on its hooves, the riders behind having to rein in or fall themselves. All along the Alpiran line the charge faltered as horses fell or reared in pain, the forward movement slowing, although the momentum of so many horses at the gallop kept them coming.

On the dunes behind, Dentos judged the time right and unleashed his archers. Over the years the company of bowmen had grown to two hundred men, slow-loading crossbows long since abandoned for the Order's strongbow. Skilled and practised veterans, they took down at least fifty riders with the first volley before commencing their arrow storm, drawing and loosing as fast as they could. The Alpiran's charge stalled and then stopped under the relentless rain of arrows, the three proud lines now a confused jumble of wavering lances and rearing riders.

Vaelin nodded to Janril once more and the bugler sounded the three long blasts that signalled the charge of the whole regiment. A shout rose from the ranks and all four companies surged forward at the run, pole-axes raised to stab at the riders, many dropping their lances to draw sabres in the press of the fight, clashing steel adding to the din of the battle. Vaelin could see Barkus in the thick of the struggle, his hateful two-bladed axe rising and falling amidst the chaos, cutting down men and horses alike. Over on the left Caenis had led his company in an oblique charge against the edge of the Alpiran line, hedging them in and preventing a manoeuvre around the regiment's flank.

As the two sides thrashed at each other, Vaelin watched with a practised eye, waiting for the inevitable moment of crisis, when the tide of battle would turn in favour of friend or foe. He had seen it happen many times now, men would assail each other with seemingly boundless ferocity then abruptly turn and flee, as if some primal instinct warned them of impending defeat. Seeing the way the white-cloaked Alpiran cavalry continued to hack at the Wolfrunners despite their mounting losses and the continual rain of arrows, he knew instinctively there would be no sudden rout here. These men were determined, disciplined and, if he was any judge, resolved to fight to the death if necessary. The regiment had killed many but they remained outnumbered, and the Alpirans were beginning to build up on the right flank, where Brother Inish's company had started to bow under the pressure, riders forcing their mounts through the crush to slash down at the hard-pressed infantry. The barrage from Dentos's archers continued unabated but soon their arrows would be exhausted whilst the Alpirans still had plenty of men.

Vaelin glanced behind him once more, seeing no sign of rein-forcements cresting the dunes. *I might kill Lord Al Hestian if I live through this.* Drawing his sword, he scanned the field once more, seeing a tall pennant waving in the centre of the Alpiran throng, blue silk emblazoned with a silver wheel. He waved to get Frentis's attention and pointed his sword at the pennant. Frentis nodded and drew his own sword, barking a command at his men to follow suit.

'Stay close,' Vaelin told Janril then spurred Spit into a gallop, Frentis and his scout troop following. He led them around Brother Inish's wavering company, keeping a good distance from the fight so as not to be drawn in too soon, then turned sharply towards the naked Alpiran flank. *Fifty horse against two thousand. Still, an adder can kill an ox if it finds the right vein.*

The first Alpiran he killed was a well-built man with ebony-dark skin and a neatly groomed beard showing beneath the chin guard of his helm. He was an excellent rider and a fine swordsman, nimbly bringing his mount around and raising his sabre in an impeccable parry as Vaelin closed. The star-silver blade took his arm off above the elbow. Spit reared and bit at the Alpiran's mount, trampling the rider as he slipped from the saddle, dark blood jetting from the stump of his arm. Vaelin spurred on, cutting down a second rider, slashing through his leg then hacking at his face until he fell, his jaw hanging loose from his skull, his scream a silent gush of blood. A third rider came for him at the gallop, lance levelled, face livid with rage and bloodlust. Vaelin reined Spit to a halt, twisted in the saddle to let the lance-point miss him by inches, bringing his sword up and down to cleave into the neck of the charging horse. The animal went down in a welter of blood, the rider tumbling free of the saddle to surge to his feet, sabre drawn. Spit reared again, his hooves sending the Alpiran reeling, his helm flying.

Vaelin paused to gauge the impact of the charge. Nearby, Frentis was running his sword through a dismounted Alpiran whilst the rest of the scout troop were cutting their way through the throng, although he could see three blue-cloaked bodies lying amidst the carnage. Looking over at Brother Inish's company, he saw that the ranks had stiffened, the line straightening as the Alpiran advance lost momentum.

A warning shout from Frentis dragged his attention back to the battle. Another Alpiran was charging, sabre outstretched, then abruptly pitching from the saddle as a well-aimed arrow from the regiment's archers on the dunes punched through his chest. However, the man's horse kept coming, eyes wide with panic and fear, ploughing into Spit's flank, the force of the impact sending them both sprawling to the ground.

Spit was up quickly, snorting in rage, kicking and biting at the offending horse then chasing after the terrified animal as it fled. Vaelin found himself dodging determined sabre thrusts from an Alpiran mounted on a grey stallion, parrying desperately until Frentis spurred between them to cut the man down. 'Wait there, brother!' he called above the din, reining in to dismount. 'Take my horse.'

'Stay in your saddle!' Vaelin shouted back, pointing again at the tall pennant in the centre of the Alpiran host. 'Keep cutting!'

'But, brother—'

'GO!' Hearing the implacable note of his command, the young brother hesitated before reluctantly riding away, quickly swallowed by the swirl of battle.

Glancing round, he saw that Janril was also dismounted, his horse lying dead nearby. The minstrel's leg was gashed and he supported himself with the regimental standard, slashing clumsily at any Alpiran who came close. Vaelin sprinted to his side, dodging lances, casting a throwing knife at the face of a rider who raised his sabre to hack down the minstrel, the man wheeling away with the steel dart embedded in his cheek.

'Janril!' He caught the man before he fell, noting the bleach white of his skin, the pained sag of his features.

'Apologies, my lord,' Janril said. 'Not so fast a rider as you . . .'

Vaelin jerked him to one side as an Alpiran bore down, his lance-point gouging the earth. Vaelin hacked the lance in two then half severed the rider's leg with the backswing, grabbing his mount's reins to bring the animal to a halt as its owner collapsed, screaming. He calmed the panicked horse as best he could then hauled Janril onto its back. 'Back to the beach,' he commanded. 'Find Sister Gilma.' He slapped the flat of his sword against the horse's flank to send them on their way, the minstrel swaying alarmingly as they sped through the confusion of flesh and metal.

Vaelin grasped the standard and thrust it into the earth, leaving it upright, the sigil snapping in the stiff morning breeze. *Defend the flag*, he thought, smiling in wry amusement. *Test of the Melee indeed.*

About twenty yards away he saw a sudden convulsion in the Alpiran ranks, men reining in to wheel to one side as a rider on a magnificent white charger forced his way through, waving his sabre for them to clear a path, his voice raised in command. The rider was clad in a white enamel breastplate adorned in gold with an intricate circular design that echoed the wheel sigil on the pennant still standing tall in the Alpiran centre. He wore no helm and his bearded, olive-skin features were tense with rage. Oddly the men around him seemed intent on restraining him, one even reaching out to grab his reins, then shrinking back in servile deference as the white-clad man barked a harsh rebuke. He cantered forward, halting briefly to point his sabre at Vaelin in challenge, then spurred into a charge.

Vaelin waited, sword held low, legs balanced, breathing slow and even. The white-clad man came on, teeth bared in a snarl, rage burning in his eyes. *Anger.* Vaelin recalled Master Sollis's words, a lesson from years ago. *Anger will kill you. A man who attacks a prepared enemy in anger is dead before he makes the first thrust.*

As ever, Sollis was right. This man with his fine white armour and excellent horse, this brave, rage-filled man, was already dead. His courage, his weapons, his armour meant nothing. He had killed himself the moment he began his charge.

It was one of the more hazardous lessons they learned at the hands of mad old Master Rensial; how to defeat a headlong charge by a mounted opponent. 'When you are afoot a mounted enemy has but one advantage,' the wild-eyed horse-master had told them on the practice field years ago. 'The horse. Take the horse away and he is just a man like any other.' That said, he had spent the next hour chasing them around the practice field on a fleet hunter, attempting to ride them down. 'Dive and roll!' he kept calling out in his shrill, madman's voice. 'Dive and roll!'

Vaelin waited until the white-clad man's sabre was an arm's reach away then shifted to the right, diving past the thunderous drum of hooves, rolling to his knees and bringing the sword round to cleave through the charger's rear leg. Blood bathed him as the horse screamed, crashing to the earth, the white-clad man struggling free of the tangle as Vaelin leapt the thrashing animal, his sword sweeping the sabre aside then slashing down, the enamel breastplate parting with the force of the blow. The white-clad man fell, coughed blood and died.

And the Alpirans stopped.

They stopped. Upraised sabres hovered then fell limply to their owners' sides. Charging riders reined in to stare in shock. Every Alpiran within sight of the scene simply stopped fighting and stared at Vaelin and the corpse of the white-clad man. Some were still staring as arrows took them or the Wolfrunners hacked them down.

Vaelin glanced down at the corpse, the sundered golden wheel on the bloodied breastplate gleamed dully in the gathering dawn light. *A man of some importance, perhaps?*

'Eruhin Makhtar!' Words spoken by a dismounted Alpiran, stumbling nearby, clutching at a wound in his arm, tears streaking his bloodied face. There was something in his tone, something beyond anger or accusation, a depth of despair Vaelin had rarely heard. *'Eruhin Makhtar!'* Words he would hear a thousand times in years to come.

The wounded man staggered forward, Vaelin making ready to knock him unconscious with his hilt guard, he was unarmed after all. But he made no move to attack, stumbling past Vaelin to collapse beside the body of the white-clad man, sobbing like a child. *'Eruhin ast forgallah!'* he howled. Vaelin watched in horror as the man pulled a dagger from his belt and drove it without hesitation into his own throat, slumping across the white-clad corpse, unstaunched blood gouting from his wound.

The suicide seemed to break the spell gripping the Alpirans, a sudden fierce shout rising from the ranks, every eye fixed on Vaelin, sabres and lances levelling as they stirred themselves and began to close, murderous hate writ on every face.

There was a sound like a thousand hammers striking a thousand anvils and the Alpiran ranks convulsed again, Vaelin could see men thrown into the air by the impact of whatever had struck their rear. The Alpirans struggled to turn their mounts and meet the new threat, but too late as a wedge of burnished steel skewered their host.

A hulking figure clad head to toe in armour and seated on a tall black charger smashed his way through the lighter mounts of the Alpirans, his mace a blur as it clubbed the life from men and horses alike. Behind him hundreds more steel-clad men wreaked similar havoc, long swords and maces rising and falling with deadly ferocity. The enraged Alpirans fought back savagely, more than a few knights disappeared under the mass of stamping hooves, but they had neither the numbers nor the steel to stand against such an onslaught. Soon it was over, every Alpiran dead or wounded. None had fled.

The hulking figure on the black charger hitched his mace to his saddle and trotted over to Vaelin, pushing his visor back to reveal a broad weathered face distinguished by a twice-broken nose and eyes deeply lined with age.

Vaelin bowed formally. 'Fief Lord Theros.'

'Lord Vaelin.' The Fief Lord of Renfael glanced round at the carnage and barked a laugh. 'Bet you've never been so glad to see a Renfaelin, eh boy?'

'Indeed, my lord.'

A tall young knight reined in beside the Fief Lord, his handsome face smeared with sweat and blood, dark blue eyes regarding Vaelin with clear but unspoken malevolence.

'Lord Darnel,' Vaelin greeted him. 'My thanks, and the thanks of my men, to you and your father.'

'Still alive then, Sorna?' the young knight replied. 'At least the King will be pleased.'

'Still your tongue, boy!' snapped Lord Theros. 'My apologies, Lord Vaelin. The boy was ever spoiled. I blame his mother, meself. Three sons she bore me and this is the only one not still-born, Faith help me.'

Vaelin saw how the young knight's hands twitched on the hilt of his long sword and the red flush of fury that coloured his cheeks. *Another son who hates his father,* he observed. *A common ailment.*

'If you'll excuse me, my lord.' He bowed again. 'I must see to my men.'

Striding back towards the beach, stepping over the dead and the dying as the morning sun rose on the field of blood, he reached again for the bluestone, lifting it to let the rising sunlight play on the surface, thinking about the day the King had pressed it upon him, the day Lord Darnel came to hate him, the day Princess Lyrna had cried.

The day the blood-song fell silent.

'Bluestone, spices and silk,' he said softly.

CHAPTER TWO

The inclusion of Renfaelin knightly contests in the Summertide Fair was a relatively recent innovation but had quickly become hugely popular with the people. The crowd was roaring their appreciation for a particularly spectacular joust as Vaelin made his way towards the royal pavilion, his hood pulled over his face to spare himself the burden of recognition. On the field a knight sailed from his saddle amidst a cloud of splinters, his opponent tossing his shattered lance to the crowd.

'That's one snotty bastard won't be getting up again!' a florid-faced man commented, making Vaelin wonder if it was the spectacle of combat they appreciated or the chance to witness the maiming of rich folk.

The guards at the pavilion entrance favoured him with a deeper bow than his rank required and glanced only briefly at the King's warrant he proffered, pulling the flap aside and bidding him entry with barely a pause. He was only two days back from the north but the legend of his supposedly great victory over the Lonak was already widespread.

After being relieved of his weapons he was led to the royal box, where he was unsurprised to find Princess Lyrna, alone.

'Brother.' She greeted him with a smile, holding her hand out for him to kiss. He was momentarily disconcerted, this was something she hadn't done before, a sign of favour rarely bestowed, and made in front of the assembled population of the capital. Nevertheless he went to one knee and pressed his lips against her knuckles. Her flesh was warmer than he'd expected and he angered himself by enjoying the sensation.

'Highness,' he said straightening, attempting a neutral tone and not quite managing it. 'I was summoned to your father's presence . . .'

She waved a hand. 'He'll be along. It seems he mislaid his favourite cloak. Never ventures outdoors without it these days.' She gestured to the seat next to her own. 'Will you sit?'

He sat, distracting himself with the knights' contest. Two groups were assembling at opposite ends of the field, about thirty in each, one under a red-and-white-check banner with an eagle motif, the other under a flag displaying a red fox on a green background.

'The melee is the climax of the Renfaelin tourney,' the princess explained. 'The red fox is the banner of Baron Hughlin Banders, that's him in the rusty armour, once chief retainer to Fief Lord Theros. The eagle belongs to Lord Darnel, the Fief Lord's heir. Apparently the melee will settle a long-standing grievance between the two.' She picked up a white silk scarf from a nearby table. 'I have been begged to give this to whichever oaf I think more violent than the others. Apparently the sight of large men in metal suits beating each other senseless is supposed to make my womanly heart swell.'

'A singular misjudgement, Highness.'

She turned to him and grinned. 'Not one you are likely to make, brother.'

'I would hope not.' He watched the two sides line out, exchange salutes then charge towards each other at full gallop, swords and maces whirling. They met in such a crash of metal and horseflesh that both Vaelin and the princess winced. The subsequent fight was a confused morass of tumbling knights and clashing weapons. Vaelin knew the knights were only supposed to strike with the flat of the blade but most appeared to be ignoring this rule and he saw at least three steel-clad figures lying immobile amidst the chaos.

'So this is battle,' Lyrna commented.

'Of a sort.'

'So what do you make of him? The Fief Lord's heir.'

Vaelin watched Lord Darnel smash his sword hilt into an opponent's helmet, the man slipping to the churned earth, blood spouting from his visor. 'He fights well, Highness.'

'Though not as well as you, I'm sure. And he has none of your insight, or integrity. Women will bed him for the influence and wealth he holds, not for love. Men will follow him for pay or duty, not devotion.' She paused, her expression one of faint irritation. 'And my father thinks he will make me a fine husband.'

'I'm sure your father wants the best . . .'

'My father wants me to breed. He wants the palace filled with the squalling of Al Neiren brats, all of them sharing blood with the Renfaelin Fief Lord. The final seal on his alliance. All I have done in service to this Realm and my father still sees me as no more than a brood-sow.'

'The Catechism of Joining is clear, Highness. No-one, man or woman, can be forced to marry against their will.'

'My will.' She laughed bitterly. 'With every year that passes without a marriage my will erodes further. You have your sword and your knives and your bow. My only weapons are my wits, my face and the promise of power that lies in my womb.'

The openness of their conversation was disconcerting. Where was the tension, the knowledge of shared guilt? *Don't forget,* he warned himself. *Do not forget what she is. What we did.* He noted the way her eyes tracked Lord Darnel in the melee, gauging, assessing, saw how she barely concealed the sneer of distaste that curled her lips. 'Highness,' he said. 'I doubt you engineered this encounter to ask my opinion of a man you have no intention of ever marrying. Do you have another theory for me, perhaps?'

'If you mean the Aspect massacre, I'm afraid my opinion is unchanged. Although I have uncovered another factor. Tell me, have you heard of the Seventh Order?'

She was watching his face closely and he knew she would see a lie. 'It's a story.' He shrugged. 'A legend really. Once there was an order of the Faith devoted to study of the Dark.'

'You give it no credence then?'

'I leave history to Brother Caenis.'

'The Dark.' The princess tasted the word softly. 'A fascinating subject. All superstition of course, but terribly persistent in the historical record. I went to the Great Library and requested all the books they have on the subject. It transpired I caused a bit of a stir since most of the older volumes were found to have been stolen.'

Vaelin thought of Brother Harlick tossing books into his fire in the fallen city. 'And how does this legend connect to the Aspect massacre?'

'Stories are plentiful about the unfortunate event. I've made it my business to collect all I can, discreetly of course. The tales are mostly nonsense, exaggerations that grow with every telling, especially where you're concerned, brother. Did you know you killed ten assassins single-handed, each of them armed with magic blades that drank the blood of the fallen?'

'I can't say I recall that, Highness.'

'I doubted you would. Nonsense these tales may be, but they all share a theme, an element of the Dark colours each one, and the more fanciful include references to the Seventh Order.'

For all his wariness he couldn't deny the sharpness of her mind. What he had previously taken for low cunning was but a facet of a considerable intellect. Many times over the past three years he had pondered the meaning of Harlick's confession in the fallen city, trying to draw together the different strands of knowledge. But nothing gelled; the Aspects' apparent betrayal of the Faithful, One Eye's power, the familiar voice of whatever had lived behind the eyes of Hentes Mustor. Try as he might he could see no link. There was a continual sense of something hovering out of reach, a profound conclusion even the blood-song couldn't divine. *But can she? And if she can, could she be trusted with the knowledge?* The idea of trusting her was absurd, of course. But even the untrustworthy could be useful.

'Tell me, Highness,' he said. 'Why would a man devoted to learning read a book then immediately throw it on the fire?'

She frowned quizzically. 'Is this relevant?'

'Would I ask you if it wasn't?'

'No. I doubt you would ask me anything if you didn't need to.'

On the field the number of knights still fighting had dwindled to a dozen or so, Lord Darnel now exchanging blows with Baron Banders, the stiffness of his rust-stained armour apparently doing little to stem his ferocity.

'If such a man were truly devoted to learning,' the princess continued as if her previous comment had remained unspoken, 'then the burning of a book would seem to him a terrible crime. Books have been burned before, King Lakril the Mad once famously made a bonfire of every book in Varinshold, pronouncing any subject who could read as disloyal and worthy of execution. Luckily the Sixth Order deposed him shortly after. However, there was wisdom in Lakril's madness. A book's value rests in the knowledge it contains, and knowledge is ever a dangerous thing.'

'So, burning the book removes the danger posed by the knowledge.'

'Perhaps. This man was learned you say. How learned?'

Vaelin hesitated, unwilling to part with the name. 'He was once a scholar in the Great Library.'

'Learned indeed.' She pursed her lips. 'Do you know I never read a book twice? I don't need to. I remember every word perfectly.'

Her tone was so matter-of-fact he knew this was no boast. 'So a man with the same skill would have no need to keep a book, a dangerous book. Once read he has possession of the knowledge.'

She nodded. 'Perhaps this man was attempting to preserve such knowledge, not destroy it.'

So that was Harlick's mission. He stole the Dark books from the Great Library. Destroying them to hide their knowledge, first reading them to keep it, protect it. But why?

'You're not going to tell me, are you?' the princess asked. 'Who he was. Where you found him.'

'Just a curious incident I witnessed . . .'

'I know my regard for you is not returned, brother. I know your opinion of me is not high. But my opinion of you has always been based on the fact that you do not lie to me. Your truth may be harsh, but it is always truth. Tell me the truth now, please.'

He met her eyes and was shocked to see tears shining there. *Are they real? Can they be?* 'I don't know if I can trust you,' he told her simply. 'We once did a terrible thing together . . .'

'I didn't know!' she whispered fiercely. She leaned close, her tone urgent. 'Linden came to me with his mad idea for an expedition to the Martishe. My father ordered me to bless his endeavour. I made no promises to Linden, I did love him but as a sister loves a brother. But he loved me more than any sister and he heard what he wanted to hear. I swear I didn't know my father's true design. After all *you* were going too, and I knew you were not capable of murder.' The tears spilled from her eyes and traced along the perfect oval of her face. 'I made my own researches, Vaelin. I know you didn't murder him, I know you spared him a horrible end. I tell you these truths because you must believe me now. You must heed my words. You *must* refuse to do what my father asks of you this day.'

'What does he ask of me?'

'Princess Lyrna Al Nieren!' A strong voice. A voice of command. A king's voice. Vaelin hadn't seen Janus for over a year and found him yet more aged, the lines in his face deeper, more grey streaking the copper mane of his hair, the stoop of his shoulders more pronounced. But still, he retained a king's voice. They both rose and bowed, suddenly aware of the vast silence of the crowd.

'Daughter of the royal line of Al Nieren,' the King continued. 'Princess of the Unified Realm and second in line to the throne.' A thin, liver-spotted hand appeared from beneath the King's ermine robes, jabbing at the field behind them. 'You forget your duty.'

Vaelin turned to see Lord Darnel, crouched on one knee before the royal pavilion. Beyond him the fallen knights of the melee were stumbling away or being carried from the field, Baron Banders in his rust-stained armour among them. Despite the servility of his bow, Lord Darnel's head was not lowered and his helm was clasped at his side. His eyes were locked onto Vaelin's, shining with an intense and disconcerting fury.

Lyrna quickly wiped the tears from her face and bowed again. 'Forgive me, Father,' she said in a tone of forced frivolity. 'I haven't spoken with Lord Vaelin in such a long time . . .'

'Lord Vaelin does not command your attention here, my lady.' A flash of anger flickered across her face but she mastered it quickly before forcing a smile. 'Of course.' Turning, she held out the silk scarf, beckoning Lord Darnel forward. 'Well fought, my lord.'

Lord Darnel gave a rigidly formal bow, reaching up to take the scarf in his gauntleted hand, flinching visibly as the princess withdrew her hand before he could kiss it. Stepping back, he fixed his furious gaze on Vaelin once again. 'I understand, Lord Vaelin,' he said, anger making his voice quiver, 'that brothers of the Sixth Order are forbidden to accept challenges.'

'That is correct, my lord.'

'A great pity.' The knight bowed once again to Lyrna and the King and strode from the field without a backward glance.

'You seem to have aroused the shiny boy's dislike,' the King observed.

Vaelin met the King's gaze, seeing that same owlish calculation he remembered from their first hateful bargain. 'I am used to being disliked, Highness.'

'Well we like you, don't we, daughter?' the King asked Lyrna.

Her face was expressionless as she nodded, saying nothing.

'Possibly too much, it seems. When she was little I worried that her heart would prove too icy to allow attachment to any man. Now, I find myself wishing it would freeze again.'

Vaelin was unused to embarrassment and found it hard to bear. 'You sent for me, Highness.'

'Yes.' The King held Lyrna in his gaze for a second longer. 'Yes I did.' He turned and gestured to the pavilion door. 'There is someone I should like you to meet. Daughter, please stay and try to remind the assembled commons that, despite appearances, we are in fact their betters.'

The princess's voice was devoid of emotion as she said, 'Of course, Father.'

Vaelin went to one knee, accepting her hand when she offered it, pressing another kiss to the warmth of her skin. *Even the untrustworthy can be useful.* 'Highness,' he addressed her rising, all too aware of the King's presence, 'I'm not sure you are correct.'

'Correct?'

It was wrong in many ways, an appalling breach of etiquette, but he stepped closer and planted a kiss on her cheek, whispering in her ear. 'The Dark is not superstition. Look in the western quarter for the tale of the one-eyed man.'

'Do you seek to test me, Young Hawk?'

They were walking from the rear of the pavilion, alone but for two guards. The King trudged through the mud, the hem of his ermine robes heavily stained. He seemed shorter somehow, stunted by age, his head barely reaching Vaelin's shoulder.

'Test you, Highness?' Vaelin asked.

The King rounded on him. 'Do not play with me, boy!' His eyes bored into him. 'Do not!'

Vaelin met his gaze squarely. The King might still be an owl but he was no longer a mouse. 'My friendship with Princess Lyrna offends you, Highness?'

'You have no friendship with her. You cannot stand the sight of her, with good reason.' The King angled his head, eyes narrowed in contemplation. 'She wanted to show you the shiny boy, arouse your jealousy. Yes?'

Keschet. Vaelin recalled her words in Al Hestian's garden. *The Liar's Attack. Hide one stratagem within another.* Lord Darnel was a distraction, something her father expected. *You must refuse to do what my father asks of you this day.*

He shrugged. 'I expect so.'

'What did you say to her? I know you weren't stealing a kiss.'

He gave a tight, sheepish smile. 'I told her that beauty fades, along with opportunity.'

The King grunted, resuming his stooped trudge through the mud. 'You shouldn't bait her so. It's necessary that you don't become enemies. For the Realm, you understand?'

'I understand, Highness.'

'She's not going to marry him, is she?'

'I very much doubt it.'

'Knew she wouldn't.' The King sighed in weary frustration. 'If only the fellow weren't such a dolt. What a burden it is to have an intelligent daughter. It goes against nature for wit to be bound up in so much beauty. It's my experience that truly beautiful women are either bestowed with great charm or mountainous spite. Her mother, my dear departed queen, was a renowned beauty and had all the spite you could ever need but mercifully little brain.'

This isn't candour, Vaelin surmised. *Just another mask. He makes a lie of honesty to trap me in another design.*

They came to an ornately decorated carriage, intricately carved wood shining with gold leaf, its windows curtained in black velvet. A team of four dappled greys waited at the tethers. The King gestured for him to open the door and climbed inside, groaning with the effort, beckoning him to follow. The King settled himself into a soft leather couch and rapped his bony fist against the wall behind. 'Palace! Not too fast.'

From outside came the snap of a whip, the carriage jerking into motion as the four greys took the strain. 'It was a gift,' the King explained. 'The carriage, the horses. From Lord Al Telnar, you remember him?'

Vaelin recalled the finely dressed man from the Council Chamber. 'The Minister of Works.'

'Yes, snide little bastard wasn't he? Wanted me to seize a quarter of the Cumbraelin Fief Lord's lands, punishment for his brother's rebellion. Of course, he would generously take on the burden of stewardship, together with all the attendant rents. I thanked him for his carriage and seized a quarter of his own lands, gave the rents to Fief Lord Mustor. Should keep him in wine and whores for a while. A reminder to Lord Al Telnar that a true king cannot be bought.'

The King fished inside his cloak, coming out with a leather pouch about the size of an apple. 'Here.' He tossed the pouch to Vaelin. 'Know what this is?'

Vaelin tugged the pouch open to find a large stone of blue, veined with grey. 'Bluestone. A big one.'

'Yes, the largest ever found, dug out of the mines in the Northern Reaches seventy-odd years ago when my grandfather, the twentieth Lord of Asrael, built the tower and established the first colony. Know what it's worth?'

Vaelin glanced at the stone again, the lamplight gleamed on its smooth surface. 'A large amount of money, Highness.' He closed the bag and held it out to the King.

The old man kept his hands within his cloak. 'Keep it. A king's gift to his most valued sword.'

'I have no need of riches, Highness.' *I can't be bought either.*

'Even a brother of the Sixth Order may one day find himself in need of riches. Please, think of it as a talisman.'

Vaelin returned the stone to the bag and hooked it to his belt.

'Bluestone,' the King went on, 'is the most precious mineral in the world, highly prized by peoples of all nations, Alpirans, Volarians, the merchant kings of the Far West. It commands a better price than silver, gold or diamonds, and most of it is to be found in the Northern Reaches. The Realm has other riches of course, Cumbraelin wine, Asraelin steel and so on, but it was with bluestone that I built my fleet and with bluestone that I forged the Realm Guard, the two pins that hold this Realm in unity. And Tower Lord Al Myrna tells me the bluestone seams are beginning to thin. Within twenty years there won't be enough left to pay the miners to dig it out. And then what will we do, Young Hawk?'

Vaelin shrugged, commerce not being a familiar subject. 'As you say, Highness, the Realm has other riches.'

'But not enough, not without taxing nobles and commons to such an extent that they'd both happily see me and my children hung from the palace walls. You've seen how troubled this land can be, even with the Realm Guard to hold it together, imagine the blood that will flow when it's gone. No, we need more, we need spices and silk.'

'Spices and silk, Highness?'

'The main trade route for spices and silk runs through the Erinean Sea, spices from the southern provinces of the Alpiran Empire, silk from the Far West, they come together at the Alpiran ports on the northern coast of the Empire. Every ship that docks must pay the Emperor for the privilege and a share in the value of their cargo. Alpiran merchants have grown wealthy off this trade, some more wealthy than even the Merchant Kings of the West, and they all pay tribute to the Emperor.'

Vaelin's unease deepened. *He can't be thinking it.* 'You wish to lure this trade to our ports?' he ventured.

The old man shook his head. 'Our ports are too few, our harbours too small. Too many storms lash our coast and we are too far north to capture so much trade. If we want it, we'll have to take it.'

'Highness, I know little of history but I cannot recall any occasion when this Realm or any of the Fiefs was threatened by Alpiran invasion or even raid. There is no blood between our peoples. The catechisms tell us that war is only justified in defence of land, life or Faith.'

'Alpirans are god worshippers, are they not? A whole empire in denial of the Faith.'

'The Faith can only be accepted, not forced, especially not on an empire.'

'But they scheme to bring their gods here, to undermine our Faith. Their spies are everywhere, disguised as merchants, whispering denial, defiling our youth in Dark rites. And all the time their army grows and the Emperor builds more ships.'

'Is any of this true?'

The King gave a small smile, owl eyes glittering. 'It will be.'

'You expect the whole Realm to believe this nonsense?'

'People always believe what they want to, true or not. Remember the Aspect massacre, all those Deniers and suspected Deniers slaughtered in the riots on the basis of mere rumour. Give them the right lie and they'll believe it.'

Vaelin regarded the King in silence as the carriage rattled over the cobbled streets of the northern quarter, the certainty of his realisation was chilling. *There's no lie here, he actually means to do it.* 'What do you want of me, Highness? Why share this with me?'

The King spread his bony hands. 'I need your sword, of course. Could hardly go to war without the Realm's most famous warrior now can I? What would the commons think if you were to refuse to bring the sword of the Faith to the Empire of Deniers?'

'You expect me to make war on a people with whom this Realm has no quarrel on the basis of lies?'

'I most certainly do.'

'And why would I?'

'Loyalty is your strength.'

Linden Al Hestian's face, turning marble white as the blood drained from the gash in his neck . . . 'Loyalty is another lie you use to trap the unwary in your designs.'

The King frowned, at first he seemed angry then barked a laugh. 'Of course it is. What do you think Kingship is for?' His mirth faded quickly. 'You forget the bargain we made. I command and you follow. You remember?'

'I've already broken our bargain, Highness. I didn't do what you commanded of me in the Martishe.'

'And yet Linden Al Hestian still resides in the Beyond, taken by your knife.'

'He was suffering. I had to end his pain.'

'Yes, very convenient.' The King waved a hand in irritation, apparently bored with this subject. 'It matters not. You made a bargain. You're mine, Young Hawk. This attachment to the Order is a fiction, you know it as well as I do. I command, you follow.'

'Not to the Alpiran Empire. Not without a better reason than a shortage of bluestone.'

'You refuse me?'

'I do. Execute me if you must. I will make no declamation in my defence. But I'm tired of your schemes.'

'Execute you?' Janus barked another laugh, even louder than the first. 'How noble, especially since you are fully aware I can do no such thing without arousing rebellion amongst the commons and war with the Faith. And I think my daughter hates me enough as it is.'

Abruptly, the King pulled aside the velvet curtain covering the window, his face suddenly lighting up. 'Ah, the widow Nornah's bakery.' He rapped on the carriage roof again, raising his king's voice. 'STOP!'

Climbing out of the carriage, he waved away the assistance of the two soldiers of the Mounted Guard who had ridden in escort, grinning at Vaelin, almost like an overgrown child. 'Come join me, Young Hawk. Finest pastries in the city, possibly the Fief. Indulge an old man's weakness.'

Widow Nornah's bakery was warm and thick with the smell of oven-fresh bread. On seeing the King, she hurried from behind her counter, a tall, thickset woman with heat-reddened cheeks and flour-speckled hair. 'Highness! Sire! You bless my humble enterprise again!' she gushed, bowing awkwardly and shouldering shocked customers aside. 'Move! Move for the King!'

'My lady.' The King took her hand and kissed it, the redness of her cheeks deepening. 'A chance to enjoy your pastries can never be ignored. Besides Lord Vaelin here is curious. He has scant opportunity for cakes, do you, brother?'

Vaelin saw the way her eyes roamed his face, drinking in the sight of him, the way her customers, now bowed to one knee, stole furtive glances, almost hating them for their adulation. 'My knowledge of cakes is scant indeed, Highness,' he replied, hoping his annoyance didn't colour his tone.

'Do you perhaps have a back room where we can enjoy your wares?' the King enquired of the widow. 'I should hate to disturb your business further.'

'Of course, Highness. Of course.'

She led them to the rear of the bakery, ushering them into what appeared to be a storage room, shelves laden with jars and sacks of flour lining the walls, furnished with a table and chairs. Seated at the table was a buxom young woman wearing a gaudy dress of cheap material, her hair dyed red, lips painted scarlet and her blouse open at the neck to reveal ample cleavage. She rose as the King entered, executing a perfect bow. 'Highness.' Her voice was coarse, the vowels clipped. A voice from the streets.

'Derla,' the King greeted her before turning to the baker. 'The apple snaps I think, Mistress Nornah. And some tea if you could.'

The widow bowed and retreated from the room, the door closing firmly behind her. The King lowered himself into a chair and gestured for the buxom woman to rise. 'Derla, this is Lord Vaelin Al Sorna, renowned brother of the Sixth Order and Sword of the Realm. Vaelin, this is Derla, unrenowned whore and highly distinguished spy in my service.'

The woman gave Vaelin a long look of appraisal, a half smile playing on her lips. 'An honour, my lord.'

Vaelin nodded back. 'Lady.'

Her smiled widened. 'Hardly.'

'Don't waste your wiles on him, Derla,' the King advised. 'Brother Vaelin is a true servant of the Faith.'

She arched a painted eyebrow and pouted. 'Pity. Do some of my best trade with Order folk. Specially the Third, randy lot those bookish types.'

'Delightful, isn't she?' the King asked. 'A woman of keen mind but no moral scruple whatever. And an occasionally violent temper. Just how many times did you stab that merchant, Derla? I forget.'

Vaelin studied Derla's face closely, seeing no artifice in her lack of expression. 'Fifty or so, Highness.' She gave Vaelin a wink. 'Wanted to beat me to death and fuck my corpse.'

'Yes, a perverted wretch indeed,' the King conceded. 'But a rich one, and a popular figure at court. Once I'd recognised how useful you might be it took considerable expense to arrange your supposed suicide and actual release.'

'For which I shall always be grateful, Highness.'

'As you should be. You see, Vaelin, it is a king's duty to seek out the talented among his subjects so that he might put them to useful service. I have a few like Derla secreted around the four Fiefs, all reporting directly to me. They get a good deal of gold and the satisfaction of knowing their efforts preserve the security of this Realm.' The King seemed suddenly weary, resting his chin on his palm, rubbing at his hooded eyes. 'Your report from last week,' he said to Derla. 'Repeat it to Lord Vaelin.'

She nodded and began speaking in formal, practised tones. 'On the seventh day of Prensur I was in the alley behind the

Rampant Lion tavern, observing a house I know to be frequented by Deniers of the Ascendant sect. Close on midnight a number of people entered the house, including a tall man, a woman and a girl of about fifteen years who arrived together. After they had entered the house I gained access to the premises via the coal chute into the cellar. Whilst in the cellar I was able to hear the heretical rites being conducted in the room above. After roughly two hours I deduced the meeting was about to end and left the cellar, returning to the alley, where I observed the same three people leaving together. Something about the tall man seemed familiar so I resolved to follow them. They proceeded to the northern quarter, where they entered a large house overlooking the mill at Watcher's Bend. As the man entered the house the light from the lamps inside illuminated his face and I was able to confirm his identity as Lord Kralyk Al Sorna, former Battle Lord and First Sword of the Realm.'

She regarded Vaelin with an incurious gaze, void of fear or concern. The King scratched idly at the grey stubble on his chin. 'It wasn't always this way, you know?' he said. 'With the Deniers. When I was a boy they lived among us, wary but tolerated. My first tutor in swordplay was a Quester, and a fine man he was. The Orders warned against them but never advocated forbidding their practices, we are a land of exiles after all, driven to these shores centuries ago by those who would kill us for our Faith and our gods. The Faith was always dominant, of course, first in the rank of beliefs, but others lived alongside it, and whilst there were many amongst the Faithful who didn't like it, most folk didn't seem to care that much. Then came the Red Hand.'

The King's hand shifted to the pattern of livid red marks on his neck, his eyes distant with the memory. 'They called it the Red Hand for the mark it leaves, like a claw scarring the flesh on your neck. Once the marks appeared you knew you were as good as dead. Imagine it, Vaelin, a land laid waste in a few months. Think of everyone you know, man, woman, child, rich or poor, it doesn't matter. Think of them all then imagine half of them gone. Imagine them dead from a wasting illness that makes them rave and thrash and scream as they vomit out their own insides. The bodies were piled like chaff, no-one was safe, fear became the only faith. It couldn't just be another plague, not this. This had to be Dark work. And so our eyes shifted to the Deniers. They suffered as we did but because they were fewer in number, it seemed they suffered less. Mobs roamed the cities and the fields, hunting, murdering. Some sects were wiped out and their beliefs lost for all time, the rest driven into the shadows. By the time the Red Hand faded all that was left was the Faith and the Cumbraelin god. The others were hidden, worshipping in the dark, ever fearful of discovery.'

The focus returned to the King's eyes, fixing Vaelin with cold calculation. 'Your father appears to have developed unhealthy interests, Young Hawk.'

The blood-song returned, loud and harsh, as strong as he had ever known it, its meaning more clear than he could remember. There was great danger in this room. Danger from the knowledge this spying whore possessed. Danger from the King's design. But most of all the danger of the blood-song, telling him to kill them both.

'I have no father,' he grated.

'Perhaps. But you do have a sister. Bit young to be hung from the walls with her tongue ripped out, after receiving the Fourth Order's ministrations in the Blackhold. Her mother too I shouldn't wonder, caged side by side, gabbling nonsense at each other until starvation weakens them and the crows come to peck at their flesh whilst they still live. You wanted a better reason. Now you have one.'

Dark eyes, like his own, small hands clutching winterblooms. *Mumma said you were going to come live with us and be my brother* . . .

The blood-song howled. His hands twitched. *Never killed a woman before,* he thought. *Or a king.* Watching the old man yawn and rub at his pained knees he saw how easy it would be to take his fragile neck and snap it like a twig. How *satisfying* it would be . . .

He clenched his fists, stilling the twitch, sitting down heavily at the table.

And the blood-song died.

'Actually,' the King said, levering himself upright. 'I don't think I'll stay for the cakes after all. Please enjoy them with my compliments.' He placed a bony hand on Vaelin's shoulder. *An owl's talon.* 'I assume I don't have to coach you in what to say when Aspect Arlyn seeks your counsel.'

Vaelin refused to look at him, worried the blood-song would return, nodding stiffly.

'Excellent. Derla, please linger awhile. I'm sure Lord Vaelin has more questions.'

'Of course, Highness.' She gave another perfect bow as he left. Vaelin remained seated.

'May I sit, my lord?' Derla asked him.

He said nothing so she took the seat opposite. 'Quite a treat for me to meet so distinguished a Lordship as yourself,' she went on. 'Done business with lords aplenty of course. His Highness is always interested in their habits, the more beastly the better.'

Vaelin said nothing.

'Are all the stories about you true, I wonder?' she continued. 'Seeing you now I think they might be.' She waited for him to speak and fidgeted in discomfort when he gave no reply. 'The baking widow is taking her time with those cakes.'

'The cakes aren't coming,' Vaelin told her. 'And I don't have any questions. He left you here so I would kill you.'

He met her eyes, seeing genuine emotion there for the first time: fear.

'The widow Nornah is no doubt skilled in the quiet disposal of corpses,' he elaborated. 'I expect he's led quite a few unsuspecting fools here over the years. Fools like the two of us.'

Her eyes flicked to the door then back to his. Her mouth twisted, biting back challenges and provocation. She knew she couldn't brawl with him. 'I am not defenceless.'

'You keep a knife in your bodice and another at the small of your back. I assume the pin in your hair is fairly sharp too.'

'I have served King Janus loyally and well for five years—'

'He doesn't care. The knowledge you possess is too dangerous.'

'I have money . . .'

'I have no need of riches.' The bag holding the bluestone was heavy on his belt. 'No need at all.'

'Well.' She leaned back from the table, letting her hands fall to her side, lifting her skirts to show her parted knees, another half smile playing on her lips, no more genuine than the first. 'At least show me the courtesy of fucking me before rather than after.'

A laugh died on his lips. He looked away, clasping his hands together on the tabletop. 'You're safe from me but not from him. You should leave the city, the Realm if you can. Don't ever come back.'

She rose slowly, moving cautiously to the door, reaching for the handle, her other hand behind her back, no doubt clutching her knife. Turning the handle, she paused. 'Your father is fortunate in his son, my lord.' And she was gone, the door swinging closed on poorly oiled hinges.

'I have no father,' he said softly to the empty room.

CHAPTER THREE

A way from the Alpiran coast, scrubland gave way to broad, trackless desert, swept by a stiff southerly wind that stirred the sands into funnels of dust, drifting over the dunes like wraiths. The army kept to the fringes of the desert, advancing towards Untesh in a column more than two miles long. Watching the army, Vaelin was reminded of a great snake he had once seen slip from a cage on a ship from the Far West, it had stretched across the width of the deck, scales glittering in the sun like the spears of the Realm Guard now.

He was perched on a rock-studded rise a few miles ahead of the main column, drinking from his canteen whilst Spit chewed at the meagre leaves of a desert shrub nearby. Frentis and his scout troop, what was left of them after the battle near the beach, were encamped about the rise, keeping watch on the eastern horizon.

He thought of the battle two days ago, of the white-clad man and the party that came to ask for his body, four stern-faced men of the Imperial Guard who appeared out of the desert and demanded to see the Battle Lord. Al Hestian rode out to greet them with the luminaries of the army in tow, making a show of formal etiquette, which the Alpirans ignored by staying in their saddles. He was reading out the King's proclamation of annexation of the three cities of Untesh, Linesh and Marbellis when one of the guardsmen cut him off in midsentence, a well-built man with ash-grey hair, speaking near-perfect Realm tongue: 'Save your prattle, Northman. We come for the *Eruhin's* body. Give it to us or kill us, we won't leave without it.'

Al Hestian's composure faltered, his face flushing with anger. 'What is this *Eruhin*?'

'The man in white,' Vaelin said. He hadn't been asked to join the parley but had reined in on the fringes anyway, knowing that the Battle Lord wouldn't wish to make a scene by sending him away, not at such an auspicious moment as his first meeting with the enemy. 'The *Eruhin*, yes?' he asked the guardsman.

The guardsman's eyes locked onto him, scanning him from head to toe, searching his face. 'It was you? You slew him?'

Vaelin nodded. Snarling, one of the other guardsmen half drew his sabre before the grey-haired man restrained him with a harsh order.

'Who was he?' Vaelin asked.

'His name was Seliesen Maxtor Aluran,' the guardsman replied. 'The *Eruhin*, the Hope in your language. Chosen heir of the Emperor.'

'Our commiserations to your Emperor,' the Battle Lord broke in smoothly. 'Such a grievous loss is to be regretted, but we come only for what is rightfully . . .'

'You come for conquest and plunder, Northman,' the grey-haired man told him. 'You will find only death in these lands. There will be no further parleys, no more talk, we will kill you all as you have killed our Hope. Expect no quarter. Now give us his body.'

Lord Darnel drank from a flask and swilled wine around his mouth before spitting it on the hooves of the guardsman's horse. 'He breaks the rules of parley with his discourtesies, my lord,' he observed to Al Hestian. 'His life is clearly forfeit.'

'No it isn't.' Vaelin spurred between the two parties, addressing the guardsman. 'I'll escort you to the body.'

He could feel the Battle Lord's fury as they rode over to the corpse, sensing Lord Darnel's hate, remembering something Aspect Arlyn had told him, *Men who love themselves hate those who would dim their glory.*

The guardsmen dismounted and lifted the body of their Hope onto a packhorse. The grey-haired guardsman tightened the straps securing the body to the horse and turned to Vaelin, his eyes shining with tears. 'What is your name?' he demanded hoarsely.

He could think of no reason not to tell him. 'Vaelin Al Sorna.'

'Your consideration does not dim my hate, Vaelin Al Sorna, *Eruhin Makhtar*, Hope Killer. My honour tells me I should take my own life, but my hate will keep me alive. From now on my every breath will be drawn with but one purpose, to see your end. My name is Neliesen Nester Hevren, Captain of the Tenth Cohort of the Imperial Guard. Do not forget it.'

With that he and his comrades had mounted and ridden away.

Sometimes the Faith requires all we have. The Aspect's words again, spoken that day last winter when he walked with Vaelin on the snow-covered practice field listening to what he had to say about the King's plans. It had been cold that day, colder than usual even for Weslin, the novice brothers stumbling in the snow as they ran and fought and bore the sting of their masters' canes.

'This will be a war unlike any we have known,' the Aspect had said, his breath steaming the air. 'A great sacrifice will be made. Many of our brothers will not return. You understand this?'

Vaelin nodded, he had listened to the Aspect for a long time and found he had no more words.

'But you must return, Vaelin. Fight as hard as you have to, kill as much as you have to. No matter how many of your men and your brothers fall, you will return to this Realm.'

Vaelin nodded again and the Aspect smiled, the only time Vaelin had seen him do so since that first day at the Order House gate all those years ago. Somehow it made him seem old, the way it creased the lines around his eyes and his thin lips. He had never seemed old before.

'Sometimes, you remind me so much of your mother,' the Aspect said sadly, then turned and walked away, his tall form moving through the snow without the slightest misstep.

Scratch came loping up the rise, a cloud of dust ascending in his wake, a hare dangling from his mouth. Large, wide-footed hares seemed to proliferate in the scrublands and, like Scratch, the Realm Guard had been quick to take advantage of easy game. The slave-hound dropped the hare at Vaelin's feet and gave one of his short, rasping barks.

'Thanks, daft dog.' Vaelin scratched at his neck. 'But you can have it.' He lifted the hare and threw it down the hill, Scratch scampering after with a joyful yelp.

'You usually leave him behind when we go on campaign,' Frentis said, sitting down and unstoppering his flask.

'Thought he would appreciate a new hunting ground.'

'So he was their Emperor's son, was he?' Frentis asked. 'The man in the white armour.'

'His chosen heir. It seems the Emperor chooses his successor from amongst his subjects.'

Frentis frowned. 'How's he do that then?'

'Something to do with their gods, I believe.'

'Think he would've chosen someone who could fight better. The silly sod couldn't even sit on his horse right.' Despite his young brother's levity, Vaelin could sense his concern. 'Had no business being there really.'

'Do not worry over me, brother.' He gave Frentis a grin. 'My heart does not weigh so heavily.'

Frentis nodded and turned his gaze on the vast expanse of desert to the south. 'Not really sure why the King wants this place so bad. It's all dust and scrub. Haven't seen a tree since we landed.'

'We come in search of what is rightfully ours by ancient treaty and to avenge the wrongs done us by the Denier Empire.'

'Yeh, been wondering about that. Y'know, the only Alpirans I ever saw were sailors and merchants around the docks. They dressed funny but they didn't seem no different from all the other sailors and merchants, chasing whores and money the way such folk do, bit more polite about it than most though. Can't remember any of my fellow no-good urchins getting abducted and tortured in Dark rites, 'cept me o' course, and One Eye wasn't no Alpiran.'

'You question the King's Word, brother?'

Frentis's hands moved inside his cloak, no doubt once again exploring the pattern of scars. 'His and everyone else's, if I think I have to.'

Vaelin laughed. 'Good, keep doing that.'

'My lord!' one of the scouts called to him, standing and pointing to the eastern horizon.

Vaelin moved to the other side of the rise and peered into the distance, seeing a faint shimmer in the heat haze rising from the sun-warmed sands. 'What am I looking for?'

'I see it.' Frentis had his spyglass at his eye. It was an expensive item, brass tubes and a sharkskin cover. Vaelin thought it best not to enquire where he got it although he remembered that the captain of the Meldenean galley that brought them to these shores had possessed a similar item. Like Barkus, Frentis's thieving instincts had never completely faded.

'How many?'

'Not good with figurin', brother, as you know. But I'll be buggered if there ain't at least our number and a third more besides.'

◆　◆　◆

'I know you know where he is.' The Battle Lord's gaze was dark with boundless enmity.

'My lord?' Vaelin was distracted by the spectacle on the plain before them, thousands of Alpiran soldiers drawn up in offensive formation, advancing at a steady march towards the rise where they stood. The Battle Lord had ordered Vaelin to bring his full regiment to the rise and put his standard on as tall a pole as could be found. On the western slope, out of sight of the Alpirans, were five thousand Cumbraelin archers. Officially the archers were Fief Lord Mustor's contribution to the campaign, a show of allegiance after what had become known as the Usurper's Revolt, but in fact they were mercenaries selling their bow skills to the King and no Cumbraelin noble was counted among their number. On either side of the rise the Realm Guard infantry were arrayed in regiments, four ranks deep. To the rear the Nilsaelin contingent of five thousand light infantry waited, flanked by the ten thousand horse of the Realm Guard cavalry on the right and the Renfaelin knights on the left. Behind them stood four mounted companies from the Sixth Order alongside Prince Malcius, commanding three companies of the King's Mounted Guard. It was the largest army ever fielded by the Unified Realm and was about to fight its first major engagement, something that seemed to concern the Battle Lord hardly at all.

'The bastard who left me with this,' Al Hestian raised his right arm, the barbed spike protruding from the leather cap covering the stump glinted in the bright midday sun. His gaze was fixed on Vaelin, seemingly oblivious to the advancing Alpiran host. 'Al Sendahl, I know you didn't find him taken by some imaginary beast.'

Vaelin had been surprised the Battle Lord had chosen to place himself on the rise, although he supposed it gave him a good view of the field. But he was more surprised at the man's choice of time to pursue a grievance. 'My lord, perhaps this discussion can wait . . .'

'I know my son's death was no mercy killing,' the Battle Lord continued. 'I know who wished him ill and I know you were their instrument. I will find Al Sendahl, be assured of that. I will settle accounts with him. I'll win this war for the King, then I'll settle with you.'

'My lord, if you hadn't been so intent on slaughtering helpless captives, you would still have your hand and I would still have my brother. Your son was my friend and I took his life to spare him pain. The King is satisfied with my account in both cases and as a servant of the Crown and the Faith I have nothing else to say on either subject.'

They regarded each other in cold silence, the Battle Lord's rage making his features tremble. 'Hide behind the Order and the King if you wish,' he said through clenched teeth. 'It will not save you when this war is won. You or any of your brothers. The Orders are a blight on the Realm, setting up gutter-born scum to lord it over their betters . . .'

'Father!' A tall, fine-featured young man stood nearby, his expression strained with embarrassment. He wore the uniform of a captain in the Twenty-seventh Cavalry, a black tail feather fluttering from the top of his breastplate, a long sword with a bluestone pommel strapped across his back. At his belt he wore a Volarian short sword. 'The enemy,' Alucius Al Hestian said, inclining his head at the host advancing across the plain, 'doesn't seem inclined to dally.'

Vaelin expected the Battle Lord to explode at his son but instead he almost seemed chagrined, biting back his anger, nostrils flaring in frustration. With a final, baleful glance at Vaelin he strode off to stand beneath his own standard, an elegant scarlet rose at odds with the character of its owner, his personal guard of Blackhawks closing protectively on either side, casting suspicious glances at the Wolfrunners surrounding them. The two regiments shared a mutual detestation and were like to turn taverns and streets into battlefields when encountering one another in the capital. Vaelin was keen to ensure they were kept well apart in the line of march.

'Hot day's work ahead, my lord,' Alucius said, Vaelin noting the forced humour in his voice. He had been disappointed to find that Alucius had taken a commission in his father's regiment, hoping the young poet had seen enough slaughter at the High Keep. They had met infrequently in the years since, exchanging pleasantries at the palace when the King called him there for some meaningless ceremony or other. He knew Alucius had recovered his gift, that his work was now widely read and young women were eager for his company. But the sadness still lingered in his eyes, the stain of what he had seen in the High Keep.

'Your breastplate should be tighter,' Vaelin told him. 'And can you even draw that thing on your back?'

Alucius forced a smile. 'Ever the teacher, eh?'

'Why are you here, Alucius? Has your father forced you to this?'

The poet's false smile faded. 'Actually my father said I should stay with my scribblings and my highborn strumpets. Sometimes I think I owe my way with words to him. However, he was persuaded that a chronicle of his glorious campaign, penned by the Realm's most celebrated young poet no less, would add greatly to our family's fortunes. Don't concern yourself with me, brother, I'm forbidden from venturing more than an arm's length from his side.'

Vaelin looked at the oncoming Alpiran army, the myriad flags of their cohorts rising from the throng like a forest of silk, their trumpets and battle chants a rising cacophony. 'There will be no safe place on this field,' he said, nodding at the short sword on Alucius's belt. 'Still know how to use that?'

'I practice every day.'

'Good, stay close to your father.'

'I will.' Alucius offered his hand. 'An honour to serve with you once again, brother.'

Vaelin took the hand, more firmly than he intended, meeting the poet's eyes. 'Stay close to your father.'

Alucius nodded, gave a final sheepish smile and walked back to the Battle Lord's party.

Design within design, Vaelin concluded, pondering the Battle Lord's words. *Janus promises him my death in return for victory. I get to save my sister, the Battle Lord gets vengeance for his son.* He calculated the many bargains and deceits the King must have spun to bring them to these shores. The entreaties made to Fief Lord Theros to bring so many of his finest knights. The unnamed price agreed with the Meldeneans to carry the army across the sea. He wondered if Janus ever lost track of the web he wove, if the spider ever mislaid one of his threads, but the notion was absurd. Janus couldn't forget his designs any more than Princess Lyrna could forget the words she read. He thought about the Aspect again, about the orders he had been given and how, for all its complexity, the old man's web amounted to nothing.

'ERUHIN MAKHTAR!'

The shout went up from every man in the regiment, loud enough to carry to the oncoming Alpirans, loud enough to be heard above their own chants and exhortations.

'ERUHIN MAKHTAR!' The men brandished their pole-axes, steel catching the sun, shouting as one the words they had been taught. 'ERUHIN MAKHTAR!' On the summit of the rise, Janril was waving the standard on a pole twenty feet high, the running wolf rippling in the wind for the whole plain to see. 'ERUHIN MAKHTAR!'

Already the Alpiran cohorts nearest the hill were beginning to react, the ranks wavering as soldiers increased their pace, their drummers' steady beat unheeded as the Wolfrunners' taunt drew them on. 'ERUHIN MAKHTAR!'

The Battle Lord was right, Vaelin decided, seeing the discipline of the leading Alpiran cohort give way completely, ranks dissolving as the men broke into a run, charging the hill, their own shouts a burgeoning growl of rage. *The guardsman gave us a weapon. The words and the banner. Eruhin Makhtar. The Hope Killer is here, come and get him.*

And they came. The cohorts on either side of the charging men broke ranks and followed suit, the madness spreading rearwards as more and more formations forgot their discipline and charged head-long for the hill.

'Little point waiting,' Vaelin told Dentos. He had stationed himself with the archers, his own bow ready, arrow notched. 'Loose as soon as they're in range. Might make them run faster.'

Dentos lifted his bow, sighted carefully, his men following his lead, then drew and let fly, the shaft arching down on the charging Alpirans, a cloud of two hundred arrows close behind. Men fell, some rose and charged on, others lay still. Vaelin fancied he saw a few still trying to crawl forward despite shafts buried deep in chest or neck. He loosed off four arrows in quick succession as the archers' arrow storm began in earnest, all the time the regiment maintaining its taunt. *'ERUHIN MAKHTAR!'*

At least a hundred Alpirans must have fallen by the time they were halfway up the hill but they showed no sign of faltering; if anything, their charge had gathered pace, the base of the hill now thick with men struggling to climb the rise and slay the Hope Killer. Vaelin saw how the whole Alpiran line had been disrupted by the charge, how the flanking cohorts were wavering, undecided as to whether to assault the Realm Guard before them or turn and try for the hill. *This battle is already won,* he realised. The Alpiran army was like an ox tempted into the killing pen with a bale of fresh hay. *All that remains is the slaughter.* Whatever his faults, it was plain the Battle Lord had a gift for tactics.

When the tide of onrushing Alpirans had come to within two

hundred paces the Battle Lord had his own flag-men give the signal for the Cumbraelin archers to move to the summit. They came at a run, longbows ready, reaching into the thicket of arrows already thrust into the sandy soil on the summit, notching and loosing without preamble as they had been ordered.

Vaelin had fought Cumbraelins on many occasions, acquiring an intimate knowledge of their deadly skills with the longbow, but he had never seen their massed arrow storm before. Air hissed like the breath of a great serpent as five thousand shafts arched into the charging mass, producing a huge groan of shock and pain as they struck home. It seemed as if all the Alpirans in the lead companies fell at once, five hundred men or more, driven to the sand by the mass of arrows. The air above Vaelin's head became thick with arrows as the Cumbraelins continued to loose. Glancing back, he marvelled at the speed with which they plucked shafts from the soil, notched and loosed, seeing one man put five arrows in the air before the first fell to earth.

In the face of the storm the Alpiran rush slowed as men fought to climb over the bodies of dead and wounded comrades, arms and shields raised to ward off the deadly rain, although these seemed to offer scant protection. But still they came on, fuelled by rage, some still stumbling forward over the thickening carpet of dead with multiple arrows protruding from their mail. When they had struggled to within fifty paces of the summit the Battle Lord signalled the command for the Realm Guard regiments flanking the hill to advance. They moved forward at the double, spears levelled, pushing the disrupted Alpiran line back. The Alpiran cohorts wavered but soon rallied, their line holding as horse-borne archers to their rear responded, galloping along the line of battle to loose their shafts at the Realm Guard over the heads of their embattled comrades.

On the right a cloud of dust rose as Alpiran horse massed for a countercharge at the Realm Guard's flank. The Battle Lord saw the danger, his flag-men signalling frantically to set their own cavalry in motion. The neatly arranged ranks of the Realm Guard horsemen stirred, more dust rising as they manoeuvred to face the mass of Alpiran cavalry. The discordant peal of a hundred trumpets signalled the charge, ten thousand horse hurtling towards the oncoming Alpiran lancers, meeting head-on in a thunderous collision. Through the dust it was just possible to glimpse the whirling spectacle of the melee, men and horses falling and rearing amidst the din of clashing weapons, before the cloud became so thick it was impossible to gauge the course of the struggle, although it was clear the Alpiran charge had been checked. The Realm Guard infantry continued their assault without interference, the Alpiran line on the right beginning to buckle under the pressure.

Whoever commanded the Alpiran host belatedly started to exert control over his forces, sending what infantry reserves remained to bolster the disintegrating line, five cohorts running forward to halt the momentum of the Realm Guard advance. But it was too late, the Alpiran line bowed, wavered and broke, the Realm Guard streaming through the gap to assault the neighbouring Alpirans from the rear, the whole line breaking apart under the strain in the space of a few minutes. Not a man to miss an opportunity, the Battle Lord unleashed Fief Lord Theros's knights, the mass of armour and horse-flesh thundering through the remnants of the Alpiran right then wheeling around, wreaking slaughter on the Alpirans still thronging at the base of the hill despite the Cumbraelin arrow storm.

On the left, the Alpiran line started to collapse as the soldiers saw the havoc being wrought on their comrades at the hill. Panic took hold of one cohort, the whole complement fleeing despite the exhortations of their leaders. The Realm Guard surged into the gap, more cohorts taking to flight as the whole line crumbled. Soon thousands of Alpirans were streaming away across the plain, raising a cloud of dust tall enough to obscure the sun and cast the battle in shadow.

On the slope before Vaelin the surviving Alpirans were at last attempting to escape the combined fury of the arrow storm and the onslaught of the Renfaelin knights. Seemingly too exhausted to run, many simply stumbled away, clutching wounds or embedded shafts, too spent even to defend themselves when knights spurred amongst them to hack down with mace or long sword. Here and there knots of men fought on, islands of dogged resistance amidst the tide of steel and horse, but they were soon overwhelmed. Not one man had made it to within sword reach of the summit and the Wolfrunners hadn't lost a single soldier.

Over on the right the ever-burgeoning dust-cloud spoke of an undiminished fury from the Alpiran cavalry and the Battle Lord ordered the Order companies into the fray. The blue-cloaked brothers were soon swallowed by the dust and it was only a matter of minutes before Alpiran riders began to emerge, galloping westwards, foam streaming from the flanks and mouths of their horses. There were only a few hundred survivors from the thousands of horsemen that had sought to turn the flank of the Realm Guard.

Vaelin glanced up at the pale disc of the sun, tinged red by the dust. *You will witness the harvest of death under a blood-red sun . . .* Words from a dream, spoken by the spectre of Nersus Sil Nin. The thought that the dream's portent might have a claim on his future left an unwelcome chill in his breast. The body cooling in the snow, the body of someone he had loved, someone he had killed . . .

'Faith!' Dentos exclaimed at Vaelin's side, gazing at the spectacle before them with a mixture of awe and repulsion. 'Never seen the like.'

'Don't expect to see it again,' he replied, shaking his head to clear away the vestiges of the dream. 'What we faced today was but a gathering of the garrisons of the northern coast. When the Emperor's real army comes north I doubt they'll offer us so easy a triumph.'

CHAPTER FOUR

The Governor's mansion at Untesh stood on a picturesque hill-top overlooking the harbour, where the masts of the city's scuttled merchant fleet jutted from the water like a submerged forest. The mansion's gardens were rich in olive groves, statuary and avenues of acacia trees, tended by a small army of gardeners who had continued their daily labours without interruption following the Battle Lord's assumption of residence. The rest of the mansion staff had acted similarly, going about their duties with mute servility, which had done little to alleviate the Battle Lord's insecurity. His guards watched the servants with a glowering vigilance and his meals were tasted twice before proceeding to his table. The dumb obedience of the mansion staff was, for the most part, mirrored in the city's wider population. There had been some trouble with a few dozen wounded soldiers, survivors of what had become known as the Bloody Hill, mounting a shambolic attack on the main gate when the first Realm Guard regiments had trooped through, and meeting a predictable end. But for the most part the Alpirans were quiescent, apparently at the order of their governor who, before drinking poison along with his family, had issued a proclamation ordering no resistance.

568 · ANTHONY RYAN

Apparently the man had been in command of Alpiran forces the day of the Bloody Hill and, feeling he had enough slaughter on his conscience, had no wish to face the gods with yet more weighing the scales against him.

Despite the lack of resistance, Vaelin could see the resentment of the people in every snatched glance they cast in his direction, marking the shame that made them shuffle wordlessly about their business and avoid the gaze of their neighbours. Many had no doubt lost sons and husbands to the Bloody Hill and would nurse their grudges in silence, waiting for the Emperor's inevitable response. The atmosphere in the city was oppressive, made worse by the mood of the Realm Guard, which had soured by the time they marched through the gate, the jubilation of victory fading in the face of the Battle Lord's decision to leave the most badly wounded behind and the lack of plunder to be had in the Realm's newest city. The day after their arrival a gallows had appeared in the central forum, three corpses dangling from the scaffold, all Realm Guard, with signs hung about their neck proclaiming one a thief, one a deserter and the other a rapist. The King's orders had been clear, they were to take the cities, not ruin them, and the Battle Lord felt no compunction in ensuring his orders were followed without demur. The men had taken to calling him Blood Rose in grim mockery of his family emblem. It seemed Al Hestian's facility for victory was matched by his talent for making his men hate him.

Vaelin guided Spit along the acacia-lined avenue leading from the mansion gate to the courtyard, dismounting and offering the reins to a nearby groom. The man stood still, head bowed, eyes downcast, sweat shining on his skin in the hot afternoon sun. Vaelin noted the way his hands trembled. Glancing around, he saw that the other grooms had adopted the same stance, all standing immobile, refusing to look at him or see to his horse, accepting the consequences. *Eruhin Makhtar,* he thought with a sigh, tying Spit to a post with enough slack to reach the trough.

The council was already underway in the mansion's main hall, a large marble chamber impressively decorated with mosaics on the walls and floor illustrating scenes from the legends of the principal Alpiran gods. As usual, the council discussion had quickly degenerated into a heated argument. Baron Banders, whom Vaelin had once seen beaten unconscious by Lord Darnel at the Summertide Fair and who had since regained his position of chief retainer to Fief Lord Theros, was exchanging insults with Count Marven, captain of the Nilsaelin contingent. The words 'jumped-up peasant' and 'horse-shagging dullard' could be heard amidst the tumult as the two men jabbed fingers at each other and shrugged off the restraining hands of their companions. There had been some bad blood between the Nilsaelins and the rest of the army since the Bloody Hill, their contingent hadn't been ordered forward until the enemy were already in flight and most had seemed more interested in looting Alpiran corpses than pursuing their broken army.

'You are late, Lord Vaelin.' The Battle Lord's voice cut through the commotion, silencing the argument.

'I had far to ride, my lord,' Vaelin replied. Al Hestian had ordered his regiment to camp at an oasis a good five miles outside the city walls, ostensibly to guard a supply of fresh water for their next march but also a sensible precaution against the potentially violent reaction of the city folk to Vaelin's continued presence within the walls. It also afforded the Battle Lord an opportunity to rebuke him for lateness every time he convened a council.

'Well ride faster,' the Battle Lord told him curtly. 'Enough of this,' he commanded the two fractious lords, now glowering at each other in furious silence. 'Save your energies for the enemy. And before you ask Baron Banders, no I will not lift the stricture on challenges. Return to your seats.'

Vaelin took the only remaining chair and surveyed the rest of the council. Prince Malcius and Fief Lord Theros were present along with most of the army's senior captains, joined by a comparatively junior figure from the Sixth Order, although he still outranked Vaelin in the Order's hierarchy. Master Sollis was as lean as ever, with only a few more lines creasing his forehead and some grey in his close-cropped hair to show the passing of the years. His cold grey eyes regarded Vaelin with neither warmth nor enmity. They had met only once in the years since the Test of the Sword, a brief, tense exchange of greetings at the Order House when the Aspect had summoned him for an account of the most recent Lonak raids. Vaelin knew he now commanded a company of brothers but had made no effort to seek him out, not trusting himself to control his anger at the inevitable rush of memories the sight of the sword-master provoked. *My wife,* Urlian Jurahl's last breath. *My wife . . .*

'I have called you here,' the Battle Lord began, 'to issue orders for the next phase of our campaign.' He spoke with a slightly theatrical air, imparting his words with a grave importance, although the impression was spoiled somewhat when he glanced over at his son, seated at a desk outside the circle, to ensure he was making notes. Alucius smiled at his father and jotted down a line or two in his leather-bound notebook. Vaelin noticed he stopped as soon as Al Hestian turned back to the council.

'We have won perhaps the greatest victory in the history of our Realm,' the Battle Lord went on. 'But only a fool could imagine this war is over. We must strike swiftly if we are to fulfil our king's commands. In six months the winter storms will sweep across the Erinean and our line of supply will be tenuous at best. Linesh and Marbellis must be in our hands before then. Word has come from the King that reinforcements will dock at Untesh within the month, some seven freshly raised regiments, five of foot and two of horse.

They will make good our losses and garrison the city against siege. When they get here, we march. It only remains to decide where. Luckily we have new intelligence with which to formulate a strategy.' He turned to Sollis. 'Brother?'

Sollis's voice was coarser than Vaelin remembered, years of shouted commands adding a dry rasp to his tone. 'At the Battle Lord's order I conducted a reconnaissance of the defences at Linesh and Marbellis,' Sollis began. 'From the scale of additional fortifications and numbers of troops visible it appears the remnants of the army defeated at the Bloody Hill have concentrated on Marbellis; as the largest city on the northern coast it offers the greatest chance for defence. To judge by the number of abandoned houses and villages in the environs, it appears the common folk have also sought refuge there, no doubt swelling the garrison but also denuding supplies. In comparison Linesh appears less well prepared, I counted only a few dozen sentries on the walls and her garrison stays in the city, making no patrols. The walls are in a poor state of repair, although there appears to have been some effort to remedy this. However, there are no new fortifications and the ditch around the wall has not been deepened.'

'Ripe for the plucking, eh?' Fief Lord Theros commented. 'Linesh first then on to Marbellis.'

'No,' the Battle Lord said. He assumed a thoughtful pose, a finger stroking his chin, although it was clear to Vaelin his strategy had been decided well in advance of this meeting. 'No. It appears Linesh can be taken easily but to do so would add precious weeks to our march. The road between Untesh and Marbellis is more direct, and Marbellis is the pin on which ultimate victory rests, without it our efforts will have been for nothing. Our way is clear, we must divide the army. Lord Vaelin.'

Vaelin met the Battle Lord's gaze, wishing for perhaps the

thousandth time that the blood-song had not deserted him. At times like this he sorely missed its counsel. 'My lord?'

'You will take command of three regiments of foot, Count Marven's forces and one-fifth of the Cumbraelin archers. You will proceed to Linesh immediately, take the city by storm and hold it against siege. Prince Malcius and his guard will remain in Untesh to govern the city according to Realm Law. The main force will proceed to Marbellis when the King's reinforcements arrive. We will therefore have all three cities in our hands well before the dawn of winter.'

There was a moment's uncomfortable silence, several attendees registering surprise or confusion, but Prince Malcius was the first to voice concern. 'I am to be left here whilst the Realm Guard march onwards into even greater peril?'

'The decision was not mine, Highness. King Janus gave me specific orders before we sailed. I have written copies if you want them.'

The prince's jaw clenched and Vaelin saw how he fought to control his fury and humiliation. After a moment he spoke again, a barely concealed choke in his voice. 'You expect Lord Vaelin to take a city with barely eight thousand men?'

'A poorly defended city by all accounts,' the Battle Lord countered. 'And I'm sure so vaunted a commander as Lord Vaelin is equal to the task.'

Count Marven coughed several times, face flushed. In accordance with Nilsaelin custom his head was shaven to grey stubble, which, along with the gold ring he wore in his mutilated left ear, gave him the look of an outlaw, a trait he shared with most of his men. 'My lord,' he addressed Al Hestian. 'I mean no disrespect to Lord Vaelin, but I would point out my rank . . .'

'Rank is unimportant when set against ability and experience,' the Battle Lord interrupted. 'Lord Vaelin has fought and won many battles whilst you, I believe, have merely engaged in skirmishes with the many outlaw bands haunting the highways of your Fief.'

Count Marven glowered but his mouth remained closed despite his obvious anger.

'I cannot believe,' Prince Malcius said, 'that my father would countenance this plan.'

'King Janus gave command of this army to *me*, Highness.' Al Hestian's tone was one of forced civility but his entirely reciprocated dislike of the prince was palpable.

The argument continued, rising in volume as Vaelin pondered the plan. From what Sollis had said, taking the city might not be a major problem but holding it was another matter. So far no mention had been made of the Alpiran forces, which were probably already marching northwards, no doubt in considerable numbers, and Linesh stood at the extreme end of the principal route through the hills fringing the eastern edge of the desert. It would almost certainly be the first target before the Alpirans turned to Marbellis, made all the more tempting by the presence of the Hope Killer. To call it a vulnerable position was a considerable understatement, as the Battle Lord well knew.

He rids himself of a rival for glory, Vaelin thought. *Knowing that the Alpirans will assail Linesh with all their might to revenge themselves on the Hope Killer, thinning their ranks in the process, whilst he wins eternal fame by taking Marbellis and holding it against siege. And by rendering me so vulnerable, he provides the Alpirans ample opportunity to give him the revenge he craves.* He frowned, remembering the Aspect's instructions. *Vulnerable . . . Away from the main body of the army, away from so many curious eyes. A tempting target . . .*

'I believe this is an excellent plan,' he said brightly, quelling the blossoming fracas.

Prince Malcius stared at him, appalled. 'My lord?'

'Battle Lord Al Hestian has difficult choices to make. Yet none can doubt his gifts for strategy after our recent victory. We should not lose faith in him now. I will happily accept this commission, and' – he gave Al Hestian a grave bow of respect – 'I thank the Battle Lord for the honour.'

'You do see the trap in this, I assume?'

Vaelin unhitched Spit's reins from the post and led him onto the gravel path, not looking at Sollis. 'I see many things these days, Master.'

'Brother,' Sollis corrected. 'Brother Commander if you must. The days when you called me master are long past us.'

'And yet' – Vaelin checked the saddle strap and palmed away the dust on Spit's flank – 'it seems to me like yesterday.'

'You are no longer a child, brother. Sulking ill becomes a Sword of the Realm.'

Vaelin turned on him then, anger rising in his breast. Sollis met his gaze and made no backward step. One of the few men who would never be afraid of him. He knew he should welcome the company of such a man, but the Test of the Sword hung between them like a curse.

'I have my orders from the Aspect,' he told Sollis. 'As, I'm sure, do you. I am merely attempting to follow them.'

'The Aspect ordered me to take my company into this carnival of fools. He did not say why.'

'Really? He told me more than I wanted to hear.' He fixed his eyes on Sollis's face, ready to read the reaction to his words. 'What do you know of the Seventh Order, brother? What can you tell me of the One Who Waits? What intelligence have you on the Aspect massacre?'

Sollis blinked. It was his only reaction. 'Nothing. Nothing you don't already know.'

'Then leave me to my trap.' He put a foot in the stirrup and hauled himself into the saddle. Glancing down at Sollis, he saw something in his face he had never expected to see: uncertainty. 'If you see the Realm again, and I do not,' Vaelin said, 'tell the Aspect I did what I could. The Aspects, all seven of them, should seek counsel with Princess Lyrna, she is the hope of the Realm.'

He spurred Spit into a gallop and tore away, a cloud of gravel in his wake, exultant in the finality of his course. *Linesh, I will have answers in Linesh.*

'It was a clever plan.'

Holus Nester Aruan, governor of Linesh, was a portly man of about fifty with a jewelled ring on each of his stubby fingers and a mingled expression of fear and anger on his fleshy face. They had found him in a small study off the mansion's main hallway and his wrist bore a bruise from when Frentis had twisted a dagger from his grasp. He offered no reply to Vaelin's words and spat on the intricate floor mosaic, closing his eyes and breathing a heavy sigh, obviously expecting death.

'Gutsy bugger, isn't he?' Dentos observed.

'Leaving a gap in the wall,' Vaelin went on. 'Only making a show of repairs whilst you prepare a spiked ditch behind for us to fall into. Clever.'

'Just kill me and have done,' the governor grated. 'I am dishonoured enough without suffering your empty platitudes.' He gave a conspicuous sniff, wrinkling his nose. 'Is shit the natural aroma for Northmen?'

Vaelin glanced at his heavily stained clothing. Frentis and Dentos were similarly besmirched and exuded an equally appalling stench. 'Your sewers need some attention,' he replied. 'There are several blockages.'

The governor gave a small moan and grimaced in realisation. 'The drain in the harbour.'

'Indeed, easily accessible at low tide, once the bars were removed. Brother Frentis here spent four nights creeping across the sands at low tide to scrape away the mortar.' Vaelin went to the window and gestured at the tower above the main gate. A flaming torch could be seen waving back and forth in the darkness. 'The signal confirming our success. The walls are in our hands and your garrison is captured. The city is ours, my lord.'

The governor looked at Vaelin closely, scrutinising his face and clothing. 'A tall warrior in a blue cloak,' he murmured, eyes narrowing. 'Eyes of black with a jackal's cunning. Hope Killer.' A profound expression of sorrow covered his features. 'You have doomed us all by coming here. When the Emperor learns you are within our walls his cohorts will burn the city to the ground just to burn you.'

'That won't happen,' Vaelin assured him. 'My king will be angry if I oversee the destruction of his newest dominion.'

'Your king is a madman and you are his rabid dog.'

Frentis bridled. 'Watch your mouth . . .'

Vaelin held up a hand to silence him. 'If insulting me relieves your guilt, then feel free to do so. But at least allow me to present our terms.'

The governor frowned in puzzlement. 'Terms? What terms can there be? You have conquered us.'

'You and your fellow citizens are now subjects of the Unified Realm, with all the rights and privileges that entails. We are not here as slavers or thieves. This is a thriving port and King Janus desires it remains so, with as little disturbance as possible to its current administration.'

'If your king expects me to serve him, he truly is mad. My life is already forfeit, the Emperor will expect me to take the honourable course, as well he should.'

'*Hasta!*' There was a shout from the doorway and a girl burst into the room. She was in her mid-teens and dressed in a white cotton shift. Her eyes were wide with fear and a small knife was clutched in her hand. Frentis moved to intercept her but Vaelin waved him back and she rushed to the governor's side, positioning herself between them, waving her knife at Vaelin and glaring defiance. Her words were heavily accented and it took him a moment to comprehend them. 'Leave my father alone!'

The governor put his hands on her shoulders, speaking softly into her ear. She trembled, eyes brimming with tears, the knife shuddering in her hand. Vaelin noted the gentleness with which the governor calmed her, taking the knife from her and pulling her close as she collapsed in tears.

'In Untesh,' Vaelin said, 'the governor's family were obliged to join him in death. This land has some strange customs.'

The governor shot him a guarded look of resentment and continued to cradle his daughter.

'How old is she?' Vaelin asked. 'Is she your only child?'

The governor gave no reply but his embrace tightened on the girl.

'She has nothing to fear from me or any of my men,' Vaelin told him. 'They have orders to avoid bloodshed wherever possible. They will be quartered within strictly ordered limits and will not patrol the streets. We will pay for any food or goods we require. If any of my men abuses one of your citizens, you will report it to me and I will see him executed. You will continue to administer the city and see to the needs of the population. Existing taxes will continue to be collected. One of my officers, Brother Caenis, will meet with you tomorrow to discuss the details. Do I have your agreement, my lord?'

The governor stroked his daughter's hair and gave a curt nod, shame bringing tears to his eyes. Vaelin gave a formal bow of respect. 'Please forgive the intrusion. We will speak again soon.'

They were moving to the door when it hit him, the blood-song, a hammerblow in his mind, louder and clearer than he had ever heard it. Vaelin tasted iron in his mouth and licked his upper lip, finding blood gushing from his nose in a thick stream. He felt himself growing colder and stumbled to his knees, Dentos reaching out to steady him as blood spattered onto the mosaic. A fresh wetness on his cheeks told him his ears were also bleeding.

'Brother?' Dentos's voice was pitched high in alarm. Frentis was on the verge of panic, sword drawn and glaring warningly at the governor, who looked down at Vaelin with a mixture of terror and bafflement.

His vision swam and the mansion faded, mist and shadow closing around him. There was a sound in the gloom, a rhythmic clunk of metal on stone and a vague image of a chisel chipping at a block of marble. The chisel moved unceasingly, faster and faster, faster than any human hand could wield it, and a face began to emerge from the stone . . .

ENOUGH!

The voice was a blood-song. He knew it instinctively. Another blood-song. The tone was different from his own, stronger and more controlled. Another voice speaking in his mind. The marble face dissolved and drifted away like sand on the wind, the sound of the chisel stopped and did not resume.

Your song is unschooled, the voice said. *It makes you vulnerable. You should be wary. Not every Singer is a friend.*

He tried to answer but the words choked him. *The song,* he real-ised. *He can only hear the song.* He struggled to summon the music, to sing his reply, but all he could produce was a thin trill of alarm.

Don't fear me, the voice said. *Find me when you recover from this. I have something for you.*

He summoned all his remaining strength, forcing the song into a single word. *Where?*

The image of the chisel and the stone returned, but this time the marble block was whole, the face it contained still hidden, the chisel lay atop it, waiting. *You know where.*

CHAPTER FIVE

He awoke to a smell more foul than even the sewers of Linesh. Something wet and rough scraped over his face and he became aware of a crushing weight on his chest.

'Get off him, you filthy brute!' Sister Gilma's stern command made his eyes flutter open, finding himself face-to-face with Scratch, the slave-hound giving a happy rasp of greeting.

'Hello, you daft dog,' Vaelin groaned in response.

'OFF!' Sister Gilma's shout sent Scratch skulking from the bed, slinking into a corner with a petulant whine. He had always treated the sister with a wary respect, perhaps because she had never shown the slightest fear of him.

Vaelin scanned the room, finding it mostly bare of furniture save for the bed and a table, where Sister Gilma had arranged the variety of vials and boxes that held her curatives. From the open window came the keening of gulls and a breeze tinged with the combined odours of salt and fish.

'Brother Caenis commandeered the old offices of the Linesh Merchants Guild,' Sister Gilma explained, pressing a hand to his forehead and feeling for the pulse in his wrist. 'All roads in the city led to the docks and the building was standing empty so it seemed a good choice for a headquarters. Your dog was frantic until we let it in the room. He's been here the whole time.'

Vaelin grunted and licked at his dry lips. 'How long?'

Her bright blue eyes regarded him with a moment's wariness before she went to the table, pouring a greenish liquid into a cup and mixing in a pale white powder. 'Five days,' she said without turning. 'You lost a lot of blood. More than I thought a man could lose and still live, in fact.' She gave a wry chuckle, the inevitable bright smile on her lips when she turned back, holding the cup to his lips. 'Drink this.'

The mixture had a bitter but not unpleasant taste and he felt his weariness receding almost immediately. *Five days.* He had no sense of it, no lingering memory of dreams or delusions. *Five days lost. To what?* The voice, the other blood-song, he could still hear it, a faint but persistent call. His own song answering, the vision of the marble block and chisel vivid in his mind. Sella's words in the fallen city becoming clearer. *There are others, older and wiser with the same gift. They can guide you.*

'I have to . . .' He raised himself up, trying to draw back the covers.

'No!' Gilma's tone brooked no argument, her plump hand pushing him back into the softness of the bed. He found he didn't have the strength to resist. 'Absolutely not. You will lie there and rest, brother.' She pulled the covers up and secured them firmly under his chin. 'The city is quiet. Brother Caenis has things well in hand. There is nothing requiring your attention.'

She drew back, for once her face was entirely serious. 'Brother, do you have any idea what happened to you?'

'Never seen the like, eh?'

She shook her head. 'No, I never have. When someone bleeds there has to be an injury, a cut, a lesion, something. You show no sign of any injury. A swelling in your brain that could cause you to bleed like that would have killed you, yet here you are. There was some wild talk amongst the men about Governor Aruan trying to kill you with a Dark curse or some such. Caenis had to put a guard on his mansion and hand out a few floggings before they calmed down.'

Floggings? he thought. I *never have to flog them.* 'I don't know, sister,' he told her honestly. 'I don't know why it happened.' *I just know what caused it.*

It was another two days before Sister Gilma released him, albeit with stern warnings about overexerting himself and making sure he drank at least two pints of water a day. He convened a council of captains atop the gatehouse, from where they could observe the progress of the defences. A thick pall of dust was rising from the workings as men toiled to deepen the ditch surrounding the city and make good the decades-long neglect of the walls.

'It'll be fifteen feet deep when completed,' Caenis said of the ditch. 'We're down to nine feet so far. Work on the walls is slower, not too many skilled masons in this little army.'

Vaelin spat dust from his parched throat and took a gulp of water from his canteen. 'How long?' he asked, hating the croak in his voice. He knew his appearance was not one to inspire great confidence, his eyes deeply shadowed with fatigue and his pallor pale and clammy. He could see the concern in the eyes of his brothers and the uncertainty of Count Marven and the other captains. *They wonder if I'm fit to command,* he decided. *Perhaps with good reason.*

'At least two more weeks,' Caenis replied. 'It would go quicker if we could conscript labour from the town.'

'No.' Vaelin's tone was emphatic. 'We have to win the confidence of these people if we are to rule this place. Pushing a shovel into their hands and forcing them to backbreaking toil will hardly do that.'

'My men came here to fight, my lord,' Count Marven said, his tone light but Vaelin could see the calculation in his gaze. 'Digging is hardly a soldier's work.'

'I'd say it's most certainly a soldier's work, my lord,' Vaelin replied. 'As for fighting, they'll get plenty of that before long. Tell any grumblers they have my leave to depart, it's only sixty miles of desert to Untesh. Perhaps they'll find a ship home from there.'

A wave of weariness swept through him and he rested against a battlement to disguise the unsteadiness of his legs. He was finding the burden of command, with all the petty concerns of both allies and subordinates, increasingly irksome. His irritation was made more acute by the insistence of the blood-song calling him to the voice and the marble block he knew lay somewhere in the city.

'Are you unwell, my lord?' Count Marven asked pointedly.

Vaelin resisted the urge to punch the Nilsaelin squarely in the face and turned to Bren Antesh, the stocky archer who commanded the Cumbraelin bowmen. He was the most taciturn of the captains, barely speaking in meetings and the first to leave when Vaelin called a halt. His expression was perpetually guarded and it was plain he neither wanted nor needed their approval or acceptance, although any resentment he may have felt over serving under a man the Cumbraelins still referred to as the Darkblade was kept well hidden. 'And your men, Captain?' he asked him. 'Any complaints about the workload?'

Antesh's expression remained unchanged as he replied with what Vaelin suspected was a quote from the Ten Books, 'Honest labour brings us closer to the love of the World Father.'

Vaelin grunted and turned to Frentis. 'Anything from the patrols?'

Frentis shook his head. 'Nothing, brother. All approaches remain clear. No scouts or spies in the hills.'

'Perhaps they're making for Marbellis after all,' offered Lord Al Cordlin, commander of the Thirteenth Regiment of Foot, known as the Blue Jays for the azure feathers painted on their breastplates. He was a sturdily built but somewhat nervous man, his arm still rested in a sling after being broken at the Bloody Hill, where he had lost a third of his men in the fierce fighting on the right flank. Vaelin suspected he had little appetite for the coming battle and was unable to blame him.

He turned to Caenis. 'How goes it with the governor?'

'He's cooperative but hardly pleased about it. He's kept the people quiet so far, made speeches to the merchants guild and the civic council, pleading with them to stay calm. He tells me the courts and the tax collectors are operating as well as can be expected in the circumstances. Trade is down, of course. Most of the Alpiran ships put to sea when news spread we had taken the city, the remainder refuse to sail and threaten to fire their ships if we try to seize them. The Volarians and Meldeneans seem keen to take advantage of the opportunity though. Prices for spice and silk have risen considerably, which means they've probably doubled back in the Realm.'

Lord Al Trendil, commander of the Sixteenth Regiment, gave a suppressed huff of annoyance. Vaelin had forbidden the army to have any part in the local trade for fear of accusations of corruption, severely disappointing the few nobles in his command with money to spend and an eye for profit.

'What about the food stores?' Vaelin asked, choosing to ignore Al Trendil.

'Full to the brim,' Caenis assured him. 'Enough for two months of siege at least, more if it's carefully rationed. The city's water supply comes primarily from wells and springs within the walls so we're unlikely to run short.'

'Provided the city folk don't poison them,' Bren Antesh said.

'A good point, Captain.' Vaelin nodded at Caenis. 'Put a guard on the main wells.' He straightened, finding his dizziness had subsided. 'We'll meet again in three days. Thank you for your attention.'

The captains departed leaving Caenis and Vaelin alone on the battlements. 'Are you all right, brother?' Caenis asked.

'A little tired is all.' He gazed out at the trackless desert, the horizon wavering in the midday haze. He knew he would one day look out at this scene and behold the spectacle of an Alpiran host. The only question was how long it would take them to arrive. Would they leave him enough time to accomplish his task?

'Do you think Al Cordlin could be right?' Caenis ventured. 'The Battle Lord will have Marbellis under siege by now, it is the largest city on the northern coast.'

'The Hope Killer isn't in Marbellis,' Vaelin said. 'The Battle Lord drew his plans well, he'll have a free hand at Marbellis whilst the Emperor's army deals with us. We should have no illusions.'

'We'll hold them,' Caenis said with flat certainty.

'Your optimism does you credit, brother.'

'The King requires this city to fulfil his plans. We are taking but the first step on a glorious journey towards a Greater Unified Realm. In time the lands we have secured will become the fifth Fief of the Realm, united under the protection and guidance of King Janus and his descendants, free from the ignorance of their superstitions and the oppression of lives lived at the whim of an Emperor. We have to hold.'

Vaelin tried to discern some irony in Caenis's words but could detect only the familiar blind loyalty to the King. Not for the first time he was tempted to give his brother a full account of his meetings with Janus, wondering whether Caenis's devotion to the old man would survive knowledge of his true nature, but he held back as always. Caenis was defined by his loyalty, he cloaked himself in it as protection against the many uncertainties and lies that abounded in their service to the Faith. Quite why Caenis was so devoted Vaelin had never been able to divine but he was loath to rob him of his cloak, delusion though it might be.

'Of course we'll hold,' he assured Caenis with a grim smile, thinking, *Whether it makes a thimble-worth of difference to anything is another matter.*

He moved to the stairway at the rear of the battlement. 'I think I'll take a tour of the town, barely seen it yet.'

'I'll fetch some guards, you shouldn't walk the streets alone.'

Vaelin shook his head. 'Worry not, brother. Not so weakened that I can't defend myself.'

Caenis was still unsure but gave a reluctant nod. 'As you wish. Oh,' he said as Vaelin began to descend the stairs. 'The governor requested we send a healer to his house. Apparently his daughter's taken ill and the local physicians lack the skills to help her. I sent Sister Gilma this morning. Perhaps she can foster some goodwill.'

'Well if anyone can, it's her. Assure the governor of my best wishes for his daughter will you?'

'Of course, brother.'

The woman who answered the door to the stonemason's shop regarded him with naked hostility, her smooth brow set in a frown and her dark eyes narrowed as she listened to his greeting. She seemed a year or so shy of thirty, with long dark hair tied back in a ponytail and a dust-stained leather apron covering her slender form. From behind her came the rhythmic thud of metal on stone.

'Good day, madam,' he said. 'Please forgive the intrusion.'

She folded her arms and gave a curt reply in Alpiran. From her tone he assumed she wasn't welcoming him inside with an offer of iced tea.

'I . . . was told to come here,' he went on, her stern gaze giving no insight as to her understanding, her mouth fixed in a hard line, offering nothing.

Vaelin glanced around at the mostly empty street, wondering if he could have misread the vision somehow. But the blood-song had been so implacable, its tone so certain, compelling his course through the streets, only subsiding when he happened upon this door beneath the sign of a chisel and hammer. He resisted an impulse to push his way inside and forced a smile. 'I have business to discuss.'

Her frown deepened and she spoke in heavily accented but unmistakable words, 'No business here for Northmen.'

Vaelin felt a faint murmur from the blood-song and the hammering from the interior of the shop fell silent. A male voice called out in Alpiran and the woman gave a grimace of annoyance before glaring at Vaelin and stepping aside. 'Sacred things here,' she said as he entered. 'Gods curse you if you steal.'

The interior of the shop was cavernous, the ceiling high and the marble-tile floor covering thirty paces square. Sunlight streamed through opened skylights, illuminating a space filled with statuary. Their size varied, some a foot or two in height, others life-sized, one was at least ten feet tall of an impossibly well-muscled man wrestling a lion. Vaelin was struck by the vitality of the form, the precision with which it had been carved, seemingly freezing the giant and the lion at the moment of greatest violence. There was another smaller statue nearby, a life-sized woman of arresting beauty, her arms outstretched in supplication and her fine features frozen in an expression of depthless sorrow.

'Herlia, goddess of justice, weeping as she passes her first judgement.' On hearing the voice, the blood-song rose in pitch, not in warning but in welcome. The man stood with his hands on his hips, a chisel and hammer hanging from the pockets of his apron. He was short but well built, his bare arms knotted with muscle. His face was angular, with high cheekbones, almond-shaped eyes, and the parts of his skin not covered in dust had a faint, golden sheen.

'You are not Alpiran,' Vaelin said.

'Neither are you,' the man replied with a laugh. 'Yet here we both are.' He turned to the woman and said something in Alpiran. She gave Vaelin a parting glare and disappeared into the rear of the shop.

Vaelin nodded at the statue. 'Why is she so sad?'

'She fell in love with a mortal man, but his passion for her drove him to commit a terrible crime and so she judged him, consigning him to the depths of the earth, chained to a rock, where his flesh is eternally eaten by vermin.'

'It must have been quite a crime.'

'Indeed, he stole a magic sword and with it slew a god, thinking him a rival for her affections. In fact he was her brother, Ixtus, god of dreams. Now, whenever we suffer nightmares it is the shade of the fallen god taking his revenge on mortal kind.'

'A god is a lie. But it's a good story.' He held out his hand. 'Vaelin Al Sorna . . .'

'Brother of the Sixth Order, Sword of the Unified Realm and now commander of the foreign army occupying our city. An interesting fellow indeed, but we Singers usually are. The song leads us down so many paths.' The man shook his hand. 'Ahm Lin, humble stonemason, at your service.'

'All your work?' Vaelin asked, gesturing at the array of statuary.

'In a manner of speaking.' Ahm Lin turned and moved deeper into the workshop, Vaelin following, his gaze drinking in the carnival of fantastic shapes, the seemingly endless variety of form and tableaux. 'Are they all gods?' he asked.

'Not all. Here—' Ahm Lin paused next to a bust of a grave-faced man with a hook-nose and heavy, deeply furrowed brows. 'Emperor Cammuran, the first man to sit on the throne of the Alpiran Empire.'

'He seems troubled.'

'He had good reason. His son tried to kill him when he realised he wasn't going to be the next emperor. The idea of choosing a successor from amongst the people, with the gods' help of course, was a dramatic break with tradition.'

588 · ANTHONY RYAN

'What happened to the son?'

'The Emperor stripped him of his wealth, had his tongue cut out and his eyes blinded, then sent him forth to live out his days as a beggar. Most Alpirans think he was being unduly lenient. They are a fine people, courteous and generous to a fault, but unforgiving when roused. You should remember that, brother.' He gave Vaelin a sidelong glance when he failed to reply. 'I must say I'm surprised your song led you here. You must know this invasion is doomed.'

'My song has been . . . inconsistent of late. It has told me little for a long time. Until I heard your voice, it had been silent for over a year.'

'Silent.' Ahm Lin seemed shocked, his gaze becoming curious. 'What was it like?' He sounded almost envious.

'Like losing a limb,' Vaelin replied honestly, realising for the first time the depth of loss he had felt when his song fell silent. It was only now it had returned that he accepted the truth, the song was not an affliction. Sella had been right; it was a gift, and he had grown to cherish it.

'Here we are.' Ahm Lin spread his arms wide as they arrived at the rear of the workshop, where a large bench was covered in a bewildering array of neatly arranged tools, hammers, chisels and oddly shaped implements Vaelin couldn't name. Nearby a ladder was propped against a large block of marble from which a partly completed statue emerged. Vaelin drew up in shock at the sight of it. The snout, the ears, the finely carved fur, and the eyes, those unmistakable eyes. His song was singing a clear and warm note of recognition. The wolf. The wolf that had saved him in the Urlish. The wolf that had howled its warning outside the House of the Fifth Order, when Sister Henna came to kill him. The wolf that had restrained him from murder in the Martishe.

'Ah . . .' Ahm Lin rubbed at his temples, his expression pained. 'Your song is strong indeed, brother.'

'Sorry.' Vaelin concentrated, trying to calm the song, but it was a few seconds before it subsided. 'Is it a god?' he asked Ahm Lin, gazing up at the wolf.

'Not quite. One of what the Alpirans call the Nameless, spirits of the mysteries. The wolf features in many of the named gods' stories, as guide, protector, warrior or spirit of vengeance. But it is never named. It is only ever just the wolf, feared and respected in equal measure.' He regarded Vaelin with an intent gaze. 'You've seen it before, haven't you? And not captive in stone.'

Vaelin was momentarily wary of disclosing too much to this man, a stranger with a song that had nearly killed him after all. But the warmth of his own song's welcome overcame his distrust. 'It saved me. Twice from death, once from something worse.'

Ahm Lin's expression showed a brief flicker of something close to fear but he quickly forced a smile. '"Interesting" seems an inadequate term for you, brother. This is for you.' He gestured to a nearby workbench where a block of marble rested, a chisel sitting atop it. The block was a perfect cube of white marble, the same block from his vision when Ahm Lin's song had laid him low, its surface smooth under Vaelin's fingers.

'You obtained this for me?' he asked.

'Many years ago. My song was most emphatic. Whatever rests inside has been waiting a long time for you to set it free.'

Waiting . . . Vaelin flattened his palm against the stone, feeling a surge from the blood-song, the tune a mix of warning and certainty. *The One Who Waits.*

He lifted the chisel, touching the blade tentatively to the stone. 'I've never done this,' he told Ahm Lin. 'Can't even carve a decent walking stick.'

'Your song will guide your hands, as mine guides me. These statues are as much the work of my song as my skill.'

He was right, the song was building, strong and clear, guiding the chisel over the stone. Vaelin hefted a mallet from the bench and tapped the butt of the chisel, chipping a small piece of marble from the edge of the cube. The song surged, and his hands moved, Ahm Lin and the workshop fading as the work consumed him. There were no thoughts in his head, no distractions, there was just the song and the stone. He had no sense of time, no perception of the world beyond the song and it was only a rough shake to the shoulder that brought him back.

'Vaelin!' Barkus shook him again when he didn't respond. 'What *are* you doing?'

Vaelin looked at the tools in his dust-caked hands, noting his cloak and weapons lying nearby and having no memory of removing them. The stone was radically altered, the top half now a roughly hewn dome with two shallow indentations in the centre and the ghost of a chin forming at the base.

'Standing here hammering away with no weapons and no guard.' Barkus sounded more shocked than angry. 'Any passing Alpiran could have stuck you without breaking sweat.'

'I . . .' Vaelin blinked at him in confusion. 'I was . . .' He trailed off, realising any explanation was pointless.

Ahm Lin and the woman who had answered the door were standing nearby, the woman glaring at the two soldiers Barkus had brought with him. Ahm Lin was more relaxed, idly guiding a whetstone over the tip of one of his chisels, favouring Vaelin with a slight smile of what might have been admiration.

Barkus's gaze shifted to the stone then back to Vaelin, a frown creasing his heavy brows. 'What's that supposed to be?'

'Doesn't matter.' Vaelin reached for a piece of linen and draped it over the stone. 'What do you want, brother?' He was unable to keep the irritation from his tone.

'Sister Gilma needs you. At the Governor's mansion.'

Vaelin shook his head impatiently, reaching again for his tools. 'Caenis deals with the governor. Send him.'

'He has been sent for. She needs you as well.'

'I'm sure it can wait . . .' Barkus's hand was tight on his wrist, putting his lips close to Vaelin's ear and whispering two words, which made him drop his tools and reach for his cloak and weapons without further demur, despite the immediate howl of protest from the blood-song.

'The Red Hand.' Sister Gilma stood on the other side of the mansion gate, having forbidden them from coming any closer. For once there was no trace of mirth in her tone or bearing. Her face was pale, her usually bright eyes dimmed with fear. 'Just the governor's daughter for now, but there'll be others.'

'You're certain?' Vaelin asked her.

'Every member of my Order is taught to look for the signs from the moment we join. There's no doubt, brother.'

'You examined the girl? You touched her?'

Gilma nodded wordlessly.

Vaelin fought down the sorrow clutching at his chest. *No time for weakness now.* 'What do you need?'

'The mansion must be sealed and guarded. No-one can be allowed in or out. You must be watchful for any more victims in the city at large. My orderlies know what to look for. Any found to have the sickness must be brought here, by force if necessary. Masks and gloves must be worn when dealing with them. You must also seal the city, no ships can sail, no caravans can leave.'

'There'll be panic,' Caenis warned. 'The Red Hand killed as many Alpirans as Realm folk in its time. When word spreads they'll be desperate to flee.'

'Then you'll have to stop them,' Sister Gilma said flatly. 'We cannot allow this plague loose again.' She fixed her gaze on Vaelin. 'You understand, brother? You must do whatever is required.'

'I understand, sister.' Through his sorrow a dim memory began to surface, Sherin at the High Keep. He tended to avoid thinking of that time, the sense of loss was too great, but now he fought to recall her words that morning after the death of Hentes Mustor. The Usurper's followers had trapped her with a false report of an outbreak of the Red Hand in Warnsclave. *I had been working on a cure . . .*

'Sister Sherin,' he said. 'She told me once she had a cure for the sickness.'

'A possible cure, brother,' Gilma replied. 'Based on theory only and beyond my skills to formulate in any case.'

'Where is Sister Sherin stationed these days?' Vaelin persisted.

'At the Order House, last I heard. She is mistress of curatives now.'

'Twenty days' sailing with a good wind,' Caenis said. 'And twenty days back.'

'For an Alpiran or Realm vessel,' Vaelin mused softly. He turned back to Gilma. 'Sister, ask the governor to write a proclamation confirming your measures and ordering the city folk to cooperate. Brother Caenis will have it copied and distributed about the city.' He turned to Caenis. 'Brother, see to the guarding of the gates and the mansion. Double the guard on the walls. Use our men only where possible.' He glanced back at Sister Gilma and forced an encouraging smile. 'What is hope, sister?'

'Hope is the heart of the Faith. Abandonment of hope is a denial of the Faith.' Her own smile was faint. 'I have certain instruments and curatives in my quarters. I should like them brought to me.'

'I'll see to it,' Caenis assured her.

Vaelin turned to go, hurrying along the stone-paved path. 'What about the docks?' Caenis called after him.

Vaelin didn't look back. 'I'll see to the docks.'

◆ ◆ ◆

The Meldenean captain was compact and wiry, sitting across the table from Vaelin with his lean features drawn in a suspicious glare. He wore gloves of soft leather, his hands clasped in a double fist on the table. They were in the map room of the old merchants guild building, alone save for Frentis, who guarded the door. Outside, night was drawing on quickly and the city would soon be sleeping, still blissfully unaware of the crisis that would greet them in the morning. If the captain had any complaints about how he and his crew had been hauled from their bunks, forced to strip and submit to an inspection by Sister Gilma's orderlies before being brought here, he clearly felt it best to keep them to himself.

'You are Carval Nurin?' Vaelin asked him. 'Captain of the *Red Falcon*?'

The man gave a slow nod. His eyes flickered continually between Vaelin and Frentis, occasionally lingering on their swords. Vaelin felt no desire to alleviate the man's unease, it suited his purpose to keep him scared.

'Your ship is reputed to be the fastest vessel to sail from this port,' Vaelin went on. 'Finest lines of any hull ever crafted in the Meldenean yards, so they say.'

Carval Nurin inclined his head but remained silent.

'You have no reputation for piracy or dishonesty, unusual for a captain from your islands.'

'What do you want?' The man's voice was harsh, rasping, and Vaelin noticed the pale edge of a scar protruding from the black silk scarf he wore around his throat. Pirate or not, he had seen his share of trouble on the seas.

'To engage your services,' Vaelin replied mildly. 'How fast can you get to Varinshold?'

The captain's unease lessened but suspicion still clouded his face. 'Done it in fifteen days before. Udonor was kind with the northerlies.'

Udonor, Vaelin knew, was one of the Meldenean gods said to have dominion over the winds. 'Can it be done quicker?'

Nurin shrugged. 'Maybe. With an empty hold and a few more hands to run the rigging. And two goats for Udonor, of course.'

It was common practice for Meldeneans to sacrifice animals to their favoured gods before a hazardous voyage. Vaelin had been witness to a mass slaughter of livestock before their invasion fleet left port, the blood had flowed so freely the harbour waters turned red.

'We'll provide the goats,' he said and gestured for Frentis to come forward. 'Brother Frentis and two of my men will be your passengers. You will carry him to Varinshold, where he will collect another passenger. You will then return here. The whole voyage cannot take more than twenty-five days. Is it possible?'

Nurin considered for a moment and nodded. 'Possible, yes. But not for my ship.'

'Why not?'

Nurin unclasped his hands and slowly removed his gloves, revealing mottled and discoloured skin from fingers to wrist. 'Tell me, land-bound,' he said, holding his hands up for Vaelin's inspection. The lamplight gleamed on the waxy, misshapen flesh. 'Have you ever beaten at flames with your bare hands whilst your sister and mother burn to death?' A grim smile twisted the Meldenean's lips. 'No, my ship will not sail in your service. The Alpirans call you the Hope Killer, to me you are the spawn of the City Burner. The Ship Lords may have whored themselves to your king but I will not. Whatever threats or torments you employ will make no—'

The bluestone made a soft thud as Vaelin placed it on the table, spinning it around, lamplight flickering on the silver-veined surface. Carval Nurin stared at it in astonished and unbridled greed.

'I'm sorry about your mother and your sister,' Vaelin said. 'And your hands. It must have been very painful.' He continued to spin the bluestone. Nurin's eyes never left it. 'But I sense you are, above all, a man of business, and sentiment is hardly profitable.'

Nurin swallowed, his scarred hands twitching. 'How much do I get?'

'If you return within twenty-five days, all of it.'

'You lie!'

'On occasion, but not right now.'

Nurin's eyes finally shifted from the bluestone, meeting Vaelin's. 'What surety do I have?'

'My word, as a brother of the Sixth Order.'

'Pox take your word and your Order. Your ghost-worshipping nonsense means nothing to me.' Nurin pulled his gloves on, frowning in calculation. 'I want a signed assurance, witnessed by the governor.'

'The governor is . . . indisposed. But I'm sure the Grand Master of the Merchants Guild will be happy to oblige. Good enough?'

The *Red Falcon* differed markedly from any other ship Vaelin had seen. She was smaller than most, with a narrow hull and three masts instead of the usual two. There were only two decks and she carried a crew of just twenty men.

'Built for the tea trade,' Carval Nurin explained gruffly when Vaelin remarked on the unusual design. 'Fresher it is, the more profit you make. Small cargo of fresh tea makes three times the price of the stuff shipped in bulk. Quicker you get from one port to another, the more money you make.'

'No oars?' Frentis asked. 'Thought all Meldenean ships had oars.'

'Got 'em right enough.' Nurin pointed at the sealed ports on the lower deck. 'Only use 'em when the wind dies, which it rarely does in northern waters. In any case, the *Falcon*'ll shift with even the smallest breeze.'

The captain paused to cast his gaze around the docks, taking in the rows of silent and empty ships and the cordon of Wolfrunners guarding the quayside. The crews had been ordered from their vessels during the night, not without some trouble, and were now nursing their bruises under heavy guard in the warehouses nearby. 'Can't remember the Linesh docks ever being so quiet,' Nurin observed.

'War is bad for trade, Captain,' Vaelin replied.

'Ships came and went at their leave over the past month and now they sit empty with their crews imprisoned. And yet the *Falcon* alone is permitted to sail . . .'

'We can't be too careful.' Vaelin clapped him on the back affably, provoking a shudder of fearful repugnance. 'Plenty of spies about. When do you sail, Captain?'

'Another hour, when the tide's right.'

'Then don't allow me to delay your preparations.'

Nurin suppressed a sneering response and nodded, walking up the gangplank to assail his crew with a barrage of curse-filled orders.

'Do you think he knows?' Frentis asked.

'He suspects something, but he doesn't know.' He gave Frentis an apologetic smile. 'I'd send more men with you, but it might arouse even more suspicion. Sister Gilma's orderlies told you what to look for?'

Frentis nodded. 'Swelling in the neck, sweats, dizziness and rashes on the arms. If any of them have it, they'll start showing within three days.'

'Good. You understand, brother, that if any of the crew, including yourself, shows signs of the Red Hand, this ship cannot land in Varinshold, or anywhere else?'

Frentis nodded. Vaelin could detect no fear or reluctance in him. The blood-song spoke of only a basic and unshakeable trust, an almost unreasoning loyalty. The thin, ragged boy who had pleaded for his support all those years ago in the Aspect's room was gone now, forged into a seasoned and fearfully skilled warrior who would never question his orders. There were times when having command of Frentis felt more of a burden than a blessing. He was a weapon to be used only with great care, for there was no sheathing him once unleashed.

'I . . . regret the necessity of this, brother,' he said. 'If there were any other course . . .'

'You never gave me that lesson,' Frentis said.

Vaelin frowned. 'Lesson?'

'The throwing knife, you said you'd teach me. Thought I'd learned enough myself. Was wrong about that.'

'You've been taught much since.' Vaelin felt a sudden surge of guilt. All the battles fought by this blindly trusting young man, the wounds suffered. All the lives he had taken. 'You wanted to be a brother,' he said, failing to keep the guilt from his voice. 'Did we do right by you?'

To his surprise Frentis laughed. 'Do right by me? When did you ever do wrong?'

'One Eye scarred you. The Tests hurt you. You followed me here to war and pain.'

'What else was there for me? Hunger and fear and a knife in an alley to leave me bleeding in a gutter.' Frentis gripped his shoulder. 'Now I have brothers who would die in my defence, as I would die for them. Now I have a Faith.' His smile was fierce, unwavering, complete in its conviction. 'What is Faith, brother?'

'The Faith is all. The Faith consumes us and frees us. The Faith shapes my life, in this world and in the Beyond.' As he spoke the words, Vaelin was struck by the conviction in his own voice, the depth of his own belief. He had seen so much of the world now, so many gods, yet the words came from his lips with absolute conviction. *I heard my mother's voice . . .*

CHAPTER SIX

The days following the departure of the *Red Falcon* quickly took on a tense monotony. Every morning Vaelin went to speak to Sister Gilma at the mansion gate. So far the only new case had been the daughter's maid, a woman of middle years who wasn't expected to last the week. The girl herself, aided by her youth, was suffering the symptoms with great fortitude but was unlikely to live out the month.

'And you, sister?' he asked every morning. 'Are you well?'

She would smile her bright smile and give a small nod. He dreaded the day he climbed the path to the gate and found she wasn't there to greet him.

Once word of the outbreak spread, the mood in the city became palpably fearful, although reactions varied. Some, mainly the richer citizens, collected their valuables and close relatives together before proceeding immediately to the nearest gate, demanding to be allowed to leave and resorting to threats or bribes when refused. When the bribes failed some conspired to rush the gates at nightfall in company with armed bodyguards and servants. The Wolfrunners had easily repulsed the assault, clubbing them back with the staves Caenis had had the foresight to issue when the crisis arose. Luckily, there had been no deaths but the mood of the city's elite remained resentful and often desperately fearful. Some had barricaded themselves in their houses, refusing all visitors and even loosing arrows or crossbow bolts at trespassers.

The less well-off were equally fearful but more stoic in facing their fear and so far there had been no riots. For the most part people went about their normal business, albeit spending as little time on the streets or in the company of neighbours as possible. All submitted to the regular inspections for signs of the sickness with a resigned trepidation. As yet there had been no cases in the city itself, though Sister Gilma seemed certain it was only a matter of time.

'The Red Hand always started in the port towns,' she said one morning. 'Carried by ships from across the sea. No doubt that's how it came here. Governor Aruan tells me the girl liked to go to the docks and watch the ships coming and going. If you find another case, it'll most likely be a sailor.'

Fearful as the townspeople were, he found himself more worried by his own soldiers. The Wolfrunners' discipline was holding well but the others were more restive. There had been several ugly brawls between Count Marven's Nilsaelins and the Cumbraelin archers, producing some serious injuries on both sides and forcing him to flog the worst offenders. The only desertions had been from the Realm Guard, five of Lord Al Cordlin's Blue Jays slipping over the wall with looted provisions in the hope of making it to Untesh. Vaelin had been tempted to let them perish in the desert but knew an example had to be made so sent Barkus after them with the scout troop. Two days later he returned with the bodies, Vaelin having instructed him to administer sentence on the spot to spare the spectacle of a public hanging. He had the corpses burned within sight of the main gate to ensure the guards on the wall got the message and spread it to their comrades: no-one was going anywhere.

In the afternoons he toured the walls and the gates, forcing conversation on the men despite their obvious discomfort. The Realm Guard were rigidly respectful but scared, the Nilsaelins sullen and the Cumbraelins clearly detested the very sight of the Darkblade, but he spent time with all of them, asking questions about their families and their lives before the war. The answers were the standard, clipped responses soldiers always gave to the ritual pleasantries of their commanders but he knew his distance from them was immaterial, they needed to see him and know he was unafraid.

One day he found Bren Antesh near the western gate, a hand shielding his eyes from the sun as he gazed up at a bird hovering overhead.

'Vulture?' Vaelin asked.

As was his custom the Cumbraelin leader gave no formal greeting, something Vaelin found irked him not at all. 'Hawk,' he replied. 'Of a type I haven't seen before. Looks a little like the swift-wing from home.'

Of all the captains, Antesh had reacted with the greatest calm to the crisis, placating his men and assuring them they were in no danger. His word clearly held considerable sway as there had been no attempts at desertion by any of the archers.

'I wanted to thank you,' Vaelin said. 'For the discipline of your men. They must trust you greatly.'

'They trust you too, brother. Almost as much as they hate you.'

Vaelin saw little reason to argue the point. He moved next to Antesh, resting against a battlement. 'I have to say I was surprised the King was able to recruit so many men from your Fief.'

'When Sentes Mustor took the Fief Lord's chair his first act was to abolish the law requiring daily practice with the longbow and the monthly stipend that came with it. Most of my men are farmers, the stipend helped supplement their income, without it many couldn't feed their families. They may hate King Janus with a passion, but hatred doesn't put food in the mouth of your children.'

'Do they really believe I'm this Darkblade from your Ten Books?'

'You slew Black Arrow, and the Trueblade.'

'Actually, Brother Barkus killed Hentes Mustor. And to this day I still don't know if the man I killed in the Martishe was really Black Arrow.'

The Cumbraelin captain shrugged. 'In any case, the Fourth Book relates how no godly man can kill the Darkblade. I have to say, brother, you do seem to fit the description quite well. As for the use of the Dark . . . Well, who can say?' Antesh's face was cautious, as if expecting some sort of rebuke or threat.

Vaelin decided a change of subject was appropriate. 'And you, sir. Did you enlist to feed your children?'

'I have no children. No wife either. Just my bow and the clothes I'm wearing.'

'What of the King's gold? Surely, you have that too.'

Antesh seemed agitated, looking away, his eyes searching the sky once again for the hawk. 'I . . . lost it.'

'As I understand it, every man was paid twenty golds up front. That's a lot to lose.'

Antesh didn't turn back. 'Do you require something of me, brother?'

The blood-song gave a short murmur of unease, not the shrill warning of impending attack but a suggestion of deception. *He hides something.* 'I'd like to hear more of Darkblade,' Vaelin said. 'If you would care to tell me.'

'That would mean learning more of the Ten Books. Aren't you afraid your soul will be sullied by such knowledge? Your Faith undone?'

The Cumbraelin's words summoned Hentes Mustor from his memory, seeing again the guilt and the madness in the Usurper's

602 · ANTHONY RYAN

eyes. The blood-song's murmur grew louder. *Did he know him? Had he been one of his followers?* 'I doubt any knowledge could sully a man's soul. And as I told your Trueblade, my Faith cannot be undone.'

'The First Book tells us to teach the truth of the World Father's love to any who wish to hear it. Find me again and I'll tell you more, if you wish.'

In the evenings he would make his way to Ahm Lin's shop, where his wife would scowl murderously as she poured tea and the stone-mason would coach him in the ways of the song.

'Amongst my people it's called the Music of Heaven,' Ahm Lin explained one night. They were in the workshop, sipping tea from small porcelain bowls next to the statue of the wolf, which appeared more unnervingly real every time Vaelin visited. The mason's wife wouldn't allow Vaelin into the house itself, where she invariably secluded herself after pouring the tea. He had once made the mistake of suggesting they pour it themselves, which had provoked such an outraged glare that he waited until Ahm Lin took a sip from his own cup for fear she had poisoned the beverage.

'Your people?' Vaelin asked. He had deduced that the mason hailed from the Far West but knew little of the place beyond the tales of sailors, fanciful stories of a vast land of endless fields and great cities, where the Merchant Kings held sway.

'I was born in the province of Chin-Sah under the benevolent rule of the great Merchant King Lol-Than, a man who knew well the value of those with unusual gifts. When mine became known to the village elders I was taken from my family at age ten and brought to the king's court, to be tutored in the Music of Heaven. I remember I was terribly homesick but never tried to run away. It was the law that the treason of the son extends to the father and I didn't wish him to suffer for my disobedience, though I longed to return to his shop and work the stone again. He was a mason too, you see.'

'There is no shame in the Dark in your homeland?'

'Hardly, it is seen as a blessing, a gift from Heaven. A family with a Gifted child gains great honour.' His expression clouded. 'Or so it was said.'

'So you were taught the song? You know how to use it, you know where it comes from.'

Ahm Lin smiled sadly. 'The song cannot be taught, brother, and it doesn't come from anywhere. It is simply what you are. Your song is not another being living inside you. It *is* you.'

'The song of my blood,' he murmured, recalling the words of Nersus Sil Nin in the Martishe.

'I have heard it called that, a name that suits well enough.'

'So, if it cannot be taught, what could they teach you?'

'Control, brother. It is like any other song, to sing it well, it must be practised, honed, perfected. My tutor was an old woman called Shin-La, so old she had to be carried around the palace on a litter and couldn't see more than a foot or two beyond her nose. But her song . . .' He shook his head in wonder at the memory. 'Her song was like fire, burning so bright and loud you felt blinded and deafened by it all at once. The first time she sang to me I nearly fainted. She cackled and called me Rat, little Singing Rat, *Ahm Lin* in the language of my people.'

'She sounds a harsh teacher,' Vaelin observed, reminded of Master Sollis.

'Harsh, yes she was that, but she had much to teach me and little time left in which to do it. Our gift is extremely rare, brother, and in all her long life of service to the Merchant King and his father before him, she had never met another Singer. I was her replacement. Her lessons were harsh, painful. She needed no stick to strike me, her song could hurt me well enough. It started with the truth-telling, two men would be brought in, one having committed a crime of some sort. Each would claim innocence and she would ask me which was guilty. Every time I got it wrong, and it happened often at first, her song would lash me with its fire. "Truth is the heart of the song, Rat," she would say. "If you cannot hear truth, you cannot hear anything."

'Once I had mastered the art of hearing truth, the lessons became more complex. A servant would be given a token, a precious jewel or ornament, and told to hide it somewhere within the palace. If I didn't find it by nightfall, the servant could keep it, and I would be punished for its loss. Later, a large group of people would mill around one of the courtyards, talking at the top of their voices, with one of them carrying a dagger beneath his robes. I had only five minutes to find it before her song would stab me as the dagger would have stabbed our master. For, as she never failed to remind me, I owed all to him and to fail him would be my eternal shame.'

'The Merchant King made use of your song?'

'Indeed he did. Commerce is the life-blood of the Far West, those who trade well become great men, even kings of men, and successful commerce requires knowledge, especially knowledge others wish to keep hidden.'

'You were a spy?'

Ahm Lin shook his head. 'Merely a witness to the affairs of greater and richer men. At first Lol-Than would have me sit in the corner of his throne room, playing with his children; if anyone asked, I was said to be his ward, orphan son of a distant cousin. Naturally, most assumed I was his bastard, an unimportant but nonetheless honoured position at court. As I played, men would come and go with varying degrees of ceremony and protracted effusions of respect or regret at besmirching the king's palace with their unworthy presence. I noted that the richer the man's clothes or the larger his entourage, the more he would proclaim his abject unworthiness, at which Lol-Than would assure them no insult had been suffered and offer his apologies for not providing a more ostentatious welcome. It could take an hour or more before the true reason for the visit became apparent, and it was almost always about money. Some wanted to borrow it, others were owed it, and all wanted more of it. And as they talked, I would listen. When they were gone, with an assurance the king would give them a swift answer and an apology for the appalling discourtesy of delaying response to their request, he would ask me what song the Music of Heaven had sung during the conversation.

'Being but a boy, I had little notion of the true import of these affairs, but my song didn't need to know why a man lied or deceived, or hid hatred behind smiles and great respect. Lol-Than knew why, of course, and in knowing saw the road to either profit or loss, or occasionally the axe-man's block.

'And so I lived my life at the Merchant King's palace, learning from Shin-La, telling the truth of my song to Lol-Than. I had few friends, only those permitted me by the courtiers appointed my guardians. They were a dull lot mostly, happy but unquestioning children from the minor merchant families who had bought a place at court for their offspring. In time I came to realise my playmates were chosen for their dullness, their lack of guile or cunning. Friends with sharper minds would have sharpened my own thoughts, made me consider that this pleasant life of luxury and plenty was in reality nothing more than an ornate cage, and I a slave within it.

'There were rewards of course, as I grew to manhood and the lusts of youth took me. Girls if I wanted, boys if I wanted. Fine wine and all manner of bliss-giving potions if I asked, though never enough to dull the sound of my song. When I grew too old to play with Lol-Than's children I became one of his scribes, there were always at least three at every meeting and no-one seemed to notice that my calligraphy was clumsy and often barely legible. Life in my cage was simple, untroubled by the trials of the world beyond the tall walls that surrounded me. Then Shin-La died.'

His gaze had become distant, lost in the memory, shrouded in sorrow. 'It is not an easy thing for a Singer to hear another's death song. It was so loud I wondered the whole world couldn't hear it. A scream of such anger and regret, it sent me reeling into oblivion. Sometimes I think she was trying to take me with her, not out of spite, but duty. In hearing her final song, I understood that her devotion to Lol-Than was a lie, the greatest of lies since she managed to keep it from her song throughout all the years she had taught me. Her final song was the scream of a slave who had never escaped her master and didn't wish to leave me there alone. And she showed me something, a vision, born of the song, a village, ruined, smoking, littered with corpses. My village.'

He shook his head, his voice laden with such sadness that Vaelin realised he was the first person to hear this story. 'I was so blind,' Ahm Lin continued after a moment. 'I failed to realise that the value in my gift lay in no-one's knowing of its existence. No-one save Lol-Than and the old woman I would replace. I remembered all the people Shin-La had used in her lessons, all the suspected criminals and servants, there must have been hundreds over the years. I knew they could never be allowed to live with the knowledge of my gift. I had killed them merely by being in their presence.

'When I woke from the oblivion Shin-La had dragged me to, I found I had a new sensation burning in my soul.' He turned to Vaelin, an odd glint in his eye, like a man recalling his own madness. 'Do you know hate, brother?'

Vaelin thought of his father's disappearing into the morning mist, Princess Lyrna's tears and his barely suppressed urge to break the King's neck. 'Our Catechism of Faith tells us hate is a burden on the soul. I have found much truth in that.'

'It weighs on a man's soul true enough, but it can also set you free. Armed with my hate, I began to take note of the meetings Lol-Than had me attend, to write down what was said with meticulous care. I began to conceive of just how vast his dominions were, to learn of the thousand ships he owned and the thousand more in which he had an interest. I learned of the mines where gold, jewels and ore were hewn from the earth, of the vast fields in which lay his true wealth, the countless acres of wheat and rice that underwrote every transaction he made. And, as I learned, I searched, poring over my papers for some flaw in the great web of trade. Four more years passed and I learned and searched, barely distracted by the comforts of the court, left to my efforts by the guardians I now knew to be my gaolers, who saw no threat in my new-found studiousness, and all the time the truth of my song never wavered and I faithfully related to Lol-Than all it told me, every deceit and every secret, and his trust grew with every plot or fraud uncovered so that I became more than his truth-teller. In time I was as trustworthy a secretary as a man such as he could have, given more knowledge, more strands to the web, all the time searching, waiting, but finding nothing. The Merchant King knew his business too well, his web was perfect. Any lie I told him would be swiftly uncovered, and my death would follow swiftly after.

'There were times when I considered simply taking a dagger and sinking it into his heart, I had ample opportunity after all, but I was still young and though my hatred consumed me, I still lusted for life. I was a coward, a prisoner whose captivity was made worse by his knowledge of the vastness of his prison. Despair began to rot my heart. I fell to indulgence again, seeking escape in wine and drugs and flesh, an indulgence that would have seen me dead before long, had not the foreigners arrived.

'In all my years in Lol-Than's palace, I had never seen a foreigner. I had heard stories, of course. Tales of strange, white- or black-skinned people who came from the east and were so uncivilised

608 · ANTHONY RYAN

their very presence in the Merchant King's domain was insulting and only tolerated because of the value of the cargoes they carried. The party that came to treat with Lol-Than were certainly strange to me with their odd clothes and impenetrable language, to say nothing of their clumsy attempts at etiquette. And to my amazement, one of them was a woman, a woman with a song.

'The only women allowed in the presence of the Merchant King were his wives, daughters or concubines. In my homeland they have no role in business and are forbidden from owning property. Through the interpreter I was given to understand that this woman was of high birth and to refuse her admittance would be a grave insult to her people. The likely profits from whatever proposal these foreigners intended must have been great indeed for Lol-Than to allow her entry to the audience chamber.

'The interpreter continued but I could barely follow his words, the woman's song filled my mind and I couldn't help staring at her. This was a beautiful woman, brother, but beautiful in the way a leopard is beautiful. Her eyes glittered, her black hair shone like polished ebony and her smile was one of cruel amusement as she heard my song.

'"So the slant-eyed pig has a Singer of his own," her song said, the hollow laughter that coloured it making me tremble. She was powerful, I could sense it, her song was stronger than mine. Shin-La may have been able to match her but not I, the rat had met a cat and was helpless before it. "What can you tell me, I wonder?" she sang in my mind, the song plunging deeper, reaching into memory and feeling with brutal ease, dragging up all my hate and my scheming. My intended betrayal seemed to make her exultant, fiercely triumphant. "And the Council told me this would be difficult," she sang. Her gaze lingered on mine for a moment longer. "If you want the Merchant King dead, tell him to reject our offer." Then it was gone, her intrusion into my mind withdrawn, leaving behind a chill of certainty. She was here to kill Lol-Than if he refused whatever they proposed, and she *wanted* to kill him, the outcome of the negotiations meant nothing to her. She had travelled across half the world for blood and would not be denied it.'

Ahm Lin's face was tense with remembered pain. 'Sometimes the song lets us touch the minds of others, in all the years since I must have touched thousands, but never have I felt anything to compare with the black stain of that woman's thoughts. For years afterwards I had nightmares, visions of slaughter, murder practised with sadistic precision, faces screaming or frozen in fear, men, women, children. And visions of places I had never seen, languages I couldn't understand. I thought I was going mad until I realised she had left some of her memories with me, either out of indifference or casual malice. They faded over time, mostly. But even now there are nights when I wake screaming and my wife holds me as I weep.'

'Who was she?' Vaelin asked. 'Where did she come from?'

'The name spoken by the interpreter was a lie, I sensed that even before I heard her song, and the memories she left gave no clue as to name or family. As for where she was from, it meant nothing to me at the time but the delegation presented greetings from the High Council of the Volarian Empire. What I've learned of the Volarians since leads me to conclude she would have been most at home there.'

'Did you do it? Did you tell the Merchant King to reject their proposal?'

Ahm Lin nodded. 'Without a moment's hesitation. Shocked as I was, my hatred was undimmed. I told him they were full of lies, that their scheme was an attempt to spend his treasure and save their own. In truth I had barely any understanding of what they had proposed or if their word was true. As always, however, he trusted my verdict implicitly.'

'And did she keep her word?'

'At first I thought she had betrayed me. Lol-Than gave them his answer the next morning, after which they boarded their ship and sailed away. He appeared to be in fine health and gave every impression of remaining so. Disappointment and fear crushed me. For the first time I had lied to the Merchant King. Surely, I would be discovered and an ugly death would follow. A month passed as I worried and fought to conceal my fear, and then Lol-Than slowly began to sicken. It was nothing at first, a small but persistent cough that of course no-one would dare to mention, then his colour became paler, his hands began to tremble, within weeks he was coughing blood and raving in fits. By the time he died he was a wasted bundle of bone and skin that couldn't remember its own name. I felt no pity at all.

'He had a successor, of course. His third son, Mah-Lol, the two older brothers having been quietly poisoned in early manhood when it became clear they lacked their father's acumen. Mah-Lol was truly his father's son, highly intelligent, exceptionally well educated and possessed of all the cunning and ruthlessness needed to sit on a Merchant King's throne. But, to my great delight, he knew nothing of my gift. Lol-Than's illness had left him in no state to enlighten his son as to the nature of my role at court. To Mah-Lol I was simply an unusually trusted secretary, and he had his own man for that. I was consigned to a bookkeeping position in the palace stores, moved from my fine quarters and paid a fraction of the salary I had received before. Apparently, I was expected to kill myself in shame at my fall from royal favour, as many of Lol-Than's now-redundant servants had already done. Instead, I simply left, telling the guard at the palace gate that I had an errand to run in the city. He barely glanced at me as I walked out. I was twenty-two years old and a free man for the first time. It was the sweetest moment of my life.

'Freedom brought a change in my song, made it soar, seeking out wonders and novelty. I followed its music across the breadth of Mah-Lol's kingdom and beyond. It guided me to a stonemason in a small village high in the mountains, who, lacking sons or apprentices, agreed to teach me his craft. I think he was disturbed by the speed with which I learned, not to say the unusual quality of my work, and he seemed relieved when it became clear he had no more to teach me and I moved on.

'The song guided me to a port, where I took ship to the east. For the next twenty years I travelled and worked, from city to city, town to town, leaving my mark on houses, palaces and temples. I even spent a year in your Realm, carving gargoyles for a Nilsaelin lord's castle. I never wanted for anything, in lean times the song guided me to food and work, when times were fraught it sought out peace and solitude. I never questioned it, never resisted it. Five years ago it guided me here, where Shoala, my most excellent wife, was struggling to keep her late father's shop going. She had the skills but richer Alpirans don't like to deal with women. I've been here ever since. My song has never signalled a need to move on, for which I am grateful.'

'Even now?' Vaelin wondered. 'With the Red Hand in the city?'

'Did your song raise its voice when you first heard the sickness was here?'

Vaelin remembered the despair he felt at Sister Gilma's likely fate but realised it hadn't been coloured by the blood-song. 'No. No it didn't. Does this mean there is no danger?'

'Hardly. It means that, for whatever reason, this is where we are both supposed to be.'

'This is . . .' Vaelin fumbled for the right words. 'Our destiny?'

Ahm Lin shrugged. 'Who can say, brother? Of destiny I know little but to say I've seen so much of the random and unexpected in my life as to doubt there is such a thing. We make our own path, but with the song's guidance. Your song is you, remember. You can sing it as well as hear it.'

'How?' Vaelin leaned forward, discomfited by the hunger for knowledge he knew coloured his voice. 'How do I sing?'

Ahm Lin gestured at the workbench, where Vaelin's partly carved block still sat, untouched since his first visit. 'You've already started. I suspect you've been singing a long time, brother. The song can make us reach for many different tools; the pen, the chisel . . . or the sword.'

Vaelin glanced down at his sword, resting within easy reach against the edge of the table. *Is that what I've been doing all these years? Cutting my path through life? All the blood spilled and lives taken, just verses in a song?*

'Why haven't you finished it?' Ahm Lin enquired. 'The sculpture?'

'If I pick up the hammer and chisel again, I won't put them down until it's done. And our current circumstance requires my full attention.' He knew this to be only partly true. The roughly hewn features emerging from the block had begun to take on a disturbing familiarity, not yet recognisable but enough to make him conclude the finished version would be a face he knew. Perversely, the arrival of the Red Hand had been a welcome excuse for delaying the moment of final clarity.

'It's not advisable to ignore one's song, brother,' Ahm Lin cautioned him. 'You recall the harm I did when I called to you the first time? Why do you think that was?'

'My song was silent.'

'That's right. And why was it silent?'

The King's fragile neck . . . The whore's dangerous secrets . . . 'It called on me to do something, something terrible. When I couldn't do it my song fell silent. I thought it had deserted me.'

'Your song is your protection as well as your guide. Without it you are vulnerable to others who can do as we do, like the Volarian woman. Trust me, brother, you wouldn't wish to be vulnerable to her.'

Vaelin looked at the marble block, tracing the rough profile of the unformed face. 'When the *Red Falcon* returns,' he said. 'I'll finish it then.'

Twenty days after the *Red Falcon*'s departure the sailors rioted, breaking out of their makeshift prisons in the warehouse district, killing their guards and making for the docks in a well-planned assault. Caenis was quick to respond, ordering two companies of Wolfrunners to hold the docks and drafting in Count Marven's men to seal off the surrounding streets. Cumbraelin archers were placed on the rooftops, cutting down dozens of sailors as their attack on the docks faltered in the face of disciplined resistance and they went reeling back into the city. Caenis ordered an immediate counter-attack, and the brief but bloody revolt was all but over by the time Vaelin got to the scene.

He found Caenis fighting a large Meldenean, the big man swinging a crudely fashioned club at the lithe brother as he danced around him, sword flicking out to leave cuts on his arms and face. 'Give up!' he ordered, his blade slicing into the man's forearm. 'It's over!'

The Meldenean gave a roar of pain-fuelled rage and redoubled his efforts, his useless club meeting only air as Caenis continued his vicious dance. Vaelin unlimbered his bow, notched an arrow and sent it cleanly through the Meldenean's neck from forty paces. One of his better feats of archery.

'Not a time for half measures, brother,' he told Caenis, stepping over the Meldenean's corpse and drawing his sword. Within the hour it was done, nearly two hundred sailors were dead and at least as many wounded. The Wolfrunners had lost fifteen men, among them the one-time pickpocket known as Dipper, one of the original thirty chosen men from their days in the Martishe. They herded the sailors back into their warehouses and Vaelin had the surviving captains brought to the docks. Forty men or so, all with the blunt and weathered features common to sea captains. They were lined up on the quayside, kneeling before him, arms bound, most staring up with sullen fear or open defiance.

'Your actions were stupid and selfish,' Vaelin told them. 'If you had reached your ships, you would have carried plague to a hundred other ports. I have lost good men in this pathetic farce. I could execute you all, but I won't.' He gestured at the harbour where the many ships of the city's merchant fleet were at anchor. 'They say a captain's soul rests with his ship. You killed fifteen of my men. I require fifteen souls in recompense.'

It took a long time, with boat-loads of Realm Guard hauling at the oars as they towed the vessels out of the harbour and anchored them offshore, spreading pitch on the decks and dousing the sails and rigging with lamp oil. Dentos's archers finished the job with volleys of fire arrows and by nightfall fifteen ships were burning, tall flames fountaining embers into the starlit sky and lighting up the sea for miles around.

Vaelin surveyed the captains, taking dull satisfaction from the grief in their weathered faces, some with tears gleaming in their eyes. 'Any repeat of this foolishness,' he said, 'and I'll have you and your crews lashed to the masts before I burn the rest of the fleet.'

In the morning Vaelin found Governor Aruan at the mansion gate. There was no sign of Sister Gilma and an icy claw of fear gripped his insides.

'Where is my sister?' he asked.

The governor's once-fleshy face was sagging from worry and a too-sudden weight loss, although he showed no sign of the

Red Hand. His gaze was guarded and his voice flat. 'She succumbed yesterday evening, much more quickly than my daughter or her maid. I recall my mother saying that was how it was with the sickness, years ago. Some last for days, weeks even, others fade in a matter of hours. Your sister wouldn't let me near my daughter, insisted on caring for her alone, my servants and I were forbidden from even venturing into that wing of the mansion. She said it was necessary, to stop the spread of the sickness. Last night I found her collapsed on the stairs, barely conscious. She forbade me from touching her, crawled back to my daughter's room on her own . . .' He trailed off as Vaelin's expression darkened.

'I spoke to her yesterday,' he said stupidly. He searched the governor's face for some sign he was mistaken, finding only wary regret. His voice was thick as he voiced the redundant question, 'She's dead?'

The governor nodded. 'The maid too. My daughter lingers though. We burned the bodies, as your sister instructed.'

Vaelin found himself gripping the wrought iron of the gate with white-knuckled fists. *Gilma . . . Bright-eyed, laughing Gilma. Dead and lost to the fire in a matter of hours whilst I tarried with those idiot sailors.*

'Were there any words?' he asked. 'Did she leave any testament?'

'She faded very fast, my lord. She said to tell you to keep to her instructions, and you will see her again in the Beyond.'

Vaelin looked closely at the governor's face. *He's lying. She said nothing. She just sickened and died.* Nevertheless, he found himself grateful for the deceit. 'Thank you, my lord. Do you require anything?'

'Some more salve for my daughter's rash. Perhaps a few bottles of wine. It keeps the servants happy, and our stocks are running low.'

'I'll see to it.' He unclasped his hands from the gate and turned to go.

'There was a great fire in the night,' the governor said. 'Out to sea.'

'The sailors rioted, tried to escape. I burned some ships as punishment.'

He was expecting some kind of admonishment but the governor simply nodded. 'A measured response. However, I advise you to compensate the merchants guild. With me confined here they are the only civil authority in the city, best not to antagonise them.'

Vaelin was more inclined to flog any merchant who made the mistake of raising his voice within earshot but, through the fog of his grief, saw the wisdom in the governor's words. 'I will.' For some reason he paused, feeling compelled to add something, some reward for the governor's kindly lies. 'We will not be here long, my lord. Maybe a few more months. There will be blood and fire when the Emperor's army arrives, but win or lose, we will soon be gone and this city will be yours again.'

The governor's expression was a mixture of bafflement and anger. 'Then why, in the name of all the gods, did you come here?'

Vaelin gazed out at the city. The light of the morning sun played over the houses and empty streets below. Out to sea the ocean shimmered with gold, white-topped waves swept towards the coast and the sky above was a cloudless blue . . . and Sister Gilma was dead, along with thousands of others and thousands more to come. 'There is something I have to do,' he said, walking away.

He found Dentos atop the lighthouse at the far end of the mole forming the left shoulder of the harbour entrance. He sat with his legs dangling over the lip of the lighthouse's flat top, staring out to sea and sipping from a flask of Brother's Friend. His bow lay nearby, the quiver empty. Vaelin sat down next to him and Dentos passed him the flask.

'You didn't come to hear the words for our sister,' he said, taking a small sip and handing the flask back, grimacing slightly as the mingled brandy and redflower burned its way down his throat.

'Said my own words,' Dentos muttered. 'She heard me.'

Vaelin glanced down at the base of the lighthouse, where numerous lifeless seagulls bobbed in the water, all neatly skewered with a single arrow. 'Looks like the gulls heard you too.'

'Practising,' Dentos said. 'Filthy scavengers anyhow, can't stand them, bloody noise they make. Shite-hawks my Uncle Groll called 'em. He was a sailor.' He grunted a laugh and took another drink. 'Could be I killed him last night. Can't rightly remember what the bastard looked like.'

'How many uncles do you have, brother? I've always wondered.'

Dentos's face clouded and he said nothing for a long time. When he finally spoke there was a sombre tone to his voice Vaelin hadn't heard before. 'None.'

Vaelin frowned in puzzlement. 'What about the one with the fighting dogs? And the one who taught you the bow . . .'

'I taught myself the bow. There was a master hunter in our village but he wasn't my uncle, neither was that vicious shit-bag with the dogs. None of them were.' He glanced at Vaelin and smiled sadly. 'My dear old mum was the village whore, brother. She called the many men who came to our door my uncles, made them be nice to me or they weren't getting in her bed, any one of them could have been my dad after all. Never did find out which one, not that I give a dog's fart. They were a pretty worthless bunch.

'Whore or not, my mum always did her best for me. I was never hungry and I always had clothes on my back and shoes on my feet, unlike most of the other children in the village. Bad enough being the whore's whelp, worse to be an envied whore's whelp. It was common knowledge my dad could've been one of thirty-odd men in the village, so the other kids called me "Whose bastard?" I was about four when I first heard it. "Whose bastard? Whose bastard? Where'd you get your shoes from, Whose bastard?" On and on it went, year after year. There was this one lad, Uncle Bab's boy, mean little shit he was, always the first to start shouting. One day him and his gang started throwing stuff at me, sharp stuff some of it, I got all cut up, it made me angry. So I took my bow, put an arrow through that boy's leg. Can't say I was sorry to watch him bleed and cry and flail around. After that' – he shrugged – 'couldn't really stay there any more. No-one was going to apprentice a whore's bastard, a dangerous bastard at that, so my mum packed me off to the Order. I can still remember her crying when the cart took me away. I've never been back.'

Watching him swig from his flask, Vaelin was struck by how old Dentos looked. Deep lines marked his brows and premature grey coloured in the close-cropped hair at his temples. Years of battle and hard living had aged him and his grief for Sister Gilma was palpable. Of all the brothers, she had been closest to him. *When we return to the Realm I'll ask the Aspect to give him a position at the Order House,* Vaelin decided, then realised that there was every chance neither of them would see the Realm again. All he had to offer Dentos were yet more opportunities for a bloody end. His thoughts turned again to the marble block waiting in Ahm Lin's shop and he knew he had delayed too long. It was time he did what he had been sent here to do. If he could achieve it before the Alpiran army arrived, then perhaps another slaughter could be avoided, if he was willing to pay the price.

He got to his feet, touching Dentos on the shoulder in farewell. 'I have business . . .'

Dentos's weary eyes were suddenly bright with excitement and his finger shot out to point at the horizon. 'A sail! You see it, brother?'

Vaelin shielded his eyes to scan the sea. It was the merest speck, a smudge of grey between water and sky, but unmistakably a sail. The *Red Falcon* was back.

Captain Nurin was first down the gangplank, his lean, weathered face drawn with exhaustion, but the light of triumph burned in his eyes along with the greed Vaelin remembered so well from their first meeting. 'Twenty-one days!' he exulted. 'Wouldn't have thought it possible so late in the year, but Udonor heard our calls and made a gift of the winds. Would have been eighteen if we hadn't had to tarry so long in Varinshold, nor carry so many passengers back.'

'So many passengers?' Vaelin asked. His gaze was fixed on the gangplank, expecting a slender, dark-haired form to appear at any second.

'Nine in all. Though why a girl whose head barely reaches my shoulder needs seven men to guard her is beyond me, I must say.'

Vaelin turned to him, frowning. 'Guards?'

Nurin shrugged, gesturing at the gangplank. 'See for yourself.'

The heavyset man descending the gangplank had a squat, brutish face, unleavened by the scowl with which he regarded Vaelin and the surrounding Wolfrunners. More disconcerting still was the fact that he wore the black robe of the Fourth Order and a sword at his belt.

'Brother Vaelin?' he enquired in a flat tone, devoid of civility.

Vaelin nodded, growing unease dispelling any urge to offer a greeting.

'Brother Commander Iltis,' the black-robed man introduced himself. 'Faith Protection Company of the Fourth Order.'

'Never heard of you,' Vaelin told him. 'Where are Sister Sherin and Brother Frentis?'

Brother Iltis blinked, clearly unused to disrespect. 'The prisoner and Brother Frentis are aboard ship. We have some issues to discuss, brother. Certain arrangements must be made . . .'

Vaelin had heard only one word. 'Prisoner?' His voice was soft but he was aware of the menace it possessed. Brother Iltis blinked again, his scowl fading to an uncertain frown. 'What . . . prisoner?'

The sound of creaking wood made him turn back to the ship. Another brother of the Fourth Order, also armed with a sword, was leading a dark-haired young woman by a chain attached to shackles on her wrists. Sherin was paler than he remembered, also somewhat thinner, but the bright, open smile that lit her face as their eyes met remained unchanged. Another five brothers followed her onto the quay, spreading out on either side and eyeing Vaelin and the Wolfrunners with cold distrust. Last to descend was Frentis, his face drawn in shame and his eyes averted.

'Sister.' Vaelin moved towards Sherin but found his path suddenly blocked by Iltis.

'The prisoner is forbidden discourse with the Faithful, brother.'

'Get out of my way!' Vaelin ordered him, precisely and deliberately enunciating each word.

Iltis paled visibly but held his ground. 'I have my orders, brother.'

'What is this?' Vaelin demanded, rage building in his chest. 'Why is our sister shackled so?'

Behind Iltis, Sherin lifted her shackled wrists, grimacing ruefully. 'I'm sorry you find me in chains once again . . .'

'The prisoner will not speak unless permitted!' Iltis barked, rounding on her, tugging sharply on her chain, the shackles chafing her flesh, producing a wince of pain. 'The prisoner will not sully the ears of the Faithful with her heresy or treachery!'

Sherin's eyes flicked to Vaelin, imploring. 'Please don't kill him!'

CHAPTER SEVEN

She was angry, he could tell. Her expression rigid, eyes avoiding his gaze as they walked the track to the Governor's mansion, her heavy chest of curatives weighing on his shoulder.

'I didn't kill him,' Vaelin offered when the silence became unbearable.

'Because Brother Frentis stopped you,' she replied, eyes flashing at him.

She was right, of course. If Frentis hadn't stopped him, he would have continued to beat Brother Iltis to death on the quayside. The other brothers from the Fourth Order had unwisely begun reaching for their weapons when Vaelin's first blow sent the man sprawling to the ground, quickly finding themselves disarmed by the surrounding Wolfrunners. They could only stand and watch helplessly as Vaelin continued to smash his fist into Iltis's increasingly bloody and distorted face, deaf to Sherin's pleading and leaving off only when Frentis hauled him away.

'What is this?' he snarled, wrenching himself free. 'How could you allow this?'

Frentis looked more shamed and miserable than Vaelin could remember. 'The Aspect's orders, brother,' he replied in a soft murmur.

'Excuse me!' Sherin jangled her chains, glaring at Vaelin. 'Do you think I might be freed to tend to our brother before he bleeds to death?'

And so she had tended to Brother Commander Iltis, ordering her chest be carried from the ship and applying balms and salves to his cuts before stitching the gash Vaelin had left in his brow when he pounded his forehead against the cobbles. She worked in silence, her deft hands doing their work with the clean efficiency he remembered, but there was a sharpness to her movements that bespoke a restrained anger.

She didn't like seeing it, Vaelin realised. *Didn't like seeing the killer in me.*

'Get this lot to the gaol,' he told Frentis, waving a hand at the Fourth Order brothers. 'If they give you any trouble, flog them.'

Frentis nodded, hesitating. 'Brother, about the sister . . .'

'We'll talk later, brother.'

Frentis nodded again and moved away to take command of the prisoners.

Nearby, Captain Nurin cleared his throat. 'What?' Vaelin demanded.

'Your word, my lord,' the wiry captain said. He was unnerved by the display of violence but refused to be daunted, forcing himself to meet Vaelin's glare. 'Our arrangement, as noted before witnesses.'

'Oh.' Vaelin tugged the bag containing the bluestone from his belt and tossed it to Nurin. 'Spend it wisely. Sergeant!'

The Wolfrunner sergeant quickly snapped to attention. 'My lord!'

'Captain Nurin and his crew are to be detained with the other sailors. Search the ship thoroughly to ensure none are hiding aboard.'

The sergeant saluted smartly and moved off, shouting orders.

'Detained, my lord?' Nurin raised his eyes reluctantly from

the bluestone now grasped tightly in his fist. 'But I have urgent business . . .'

'I'm sure you do, Captain. However, the presence of the Red Hand in the city requires you remain with us a little longer.'

The greed in the captain's eyes transformed abruptly into naked fear, and he took a few rapid backward steps. 'The Red Hand? Here?'

Vaelin turned back to Sister Sherin, watching her tie off the suture and snip away the stray threads with a small pair of scissors. 'Yes,' he murmured. 'But, I suspect, not for much longer.'

'I told you once,' Sherin said as they paused on the track to the Governor's mansion, 'no-one is going to die on my account. And I meant it, Vaelin.'

'I'm sorry,' he said, surprised at his sincerity. He had hurt her, made her feel every blow he landed on Iltis, made her see the killer.

She sighed, some of the anger leaching from her face. 'Tell me about the Red Hand. How many have died?'

'So far, only Sister Gilma and a maid at the Governor's mansion. His daughter still lingers, although she may have expired by now.'

'No other cases? No sign of it anywhere else in the city?'

He shook his head. 'We followed Sister Gilma's instructions to the letter.'

'Then she may have saved the city by acting so quickly.'

They came to the mansion gate, where one of the guards rang the bell to call the governor. Vaelin eyed the mansion's dim windows as they waited. Since Sister Gilma's passing the place had taken on a sinister aspect, made worse by the shabby appearance of the untended gardens. He was half expecting no-one to answer the bell, for the Red Hand to have finally run rampant through the house, leaving it an empty husk awaiting the torch. He was ashamed to find himself almost hoping it was over, with no

624 · ANTHONY RYAN

outbreaks elsewhere in the city it could end here and there would be no need to send Sherin into danger.

'Is that the governor?' she asked.

'That it is.' Vaelin's shameful hope faded as Governor Aruan's portly form emerged from the mansion. 'He hates us but he loves his daughter. It's how I got him to surrender the city.'

'You threatened her?' Sherin gaped at him. 'Faith, this war has made you a monster.'

'I wouldn't have hurt her . . .'

'Don't say any more, Vaelin.' She shook her head, eyes closed in disgust, turning away from him. 'Just stop talking, please.'

They stood in icy silence as the governor approached, the guards scrupulously looking elsewhere and Vaelin feeling Sherin's anger like a knife. When the governor arrived Vaelin made the introductions and worked the key in the heavy padlock securing the gate. 'She grows weaker,' Aruan said, hauling the gate open, his voice frantic with hope and desperation. 'She was still talking last night, but this morning . . .'

'Then we'd best not linger, my lord. If you could help me with this.'

Vaelin set the chest down and Sister Sherin and the governor hefted it together and started back towards the mansion. She offered no word of farewell.

'How long will this take, sister?' he asked.

She halted, glancing back, her face devoid of emotion. 'The curative requires several hours' preparation. Once administered the improvement should be immediate. Come back in the morning.' She turned away again.

'Why were you shackled?' he demanded before she could leave. 'Why were you under guard?'

She didn't turn back, her answer so soft he almost missed it. 'Because I tried to save you.'

◆   ◆   ◆

He sent the guards away and settled down to wait, lighting a fire and huddling in his cloak, the onset of winter added a chill to the wind sweeping in from the sea. The hours stretched as he pondered Sherin's words and brooded on her anger. *I tried to save you . . .*

As the sun faded towards the horizon, Frentis appeared, sitting opposite and adding some wood to the fire. Vaelin glanced up at him but said nothing.

'Brother Commander Iltis will live,' Frentis said, his tone deliberately light. 'More's the pity. Can't talk yet though, just grunts and moans on account of his jaw. No great loss, heard enough of his guff during the voyage.'

'You said the Aspect ordered you to allow her to be treated like that,' Vaelin said. 'Why?'

Frentis's expression was pained, reluctant to share what he knew would be unwelcome information. 'Sister Sherin is a convicted traitor to the Realm and a Denier of the Faith.'

Sherin in the Blackhold. The thought of it sent waves of guilt and worry coursing through him. *What had she suffered there?*

'I went straight to Aspect Elera when we docked,' Frentis continued. 'Like you told me. When she heard what I had to say we went to Aspect Arlyn. He was able to talk the King into releasing the sister from the palace.'

'The palace? She wasn't in the Blackhold?'

'Seems she was kept there when the Fourth Order first arrested her but Princess Lyrna got her out. Apparently she just marched in and demanded they release the sister to her custody. The warden thought she was acting on the King's orders so handed her over. Rumour is Aspect Al Tendris was hopping mad when he heard, but there wasn't much he could do about it. Sister Sherin was still a prisoner anyway, just had a nicer prison.'

'What could she have done that could ever be considered treason, let alone denial of the Faith?'

'She spoke against the war. Not just once either. Many times, to anyone who'd listen. Said the war was founded on lies and contrary to the Faith. Said you and all the rest of us had been sent to our doom for no good reason. Wouldn't have mattered so much if it'd been some nobody spouting off, but she's well-known in the poorer parts of the capital, well liked too, on account of all the people she's helped. When she spoke people listened. Seems neither the King nor the Fourth Order liked what she had to say.'

More of the old man's scheming? Vaelin wondered. Perhaps he knew about his attachment to Sherin and her arrest was another means of applying pressure. He felt it unlikely, Janus had already secured his obedience. Sherin's arrest seemed an act born of simple fear; his war could not be undone by a dissenting voice. Vaelin knew well the King's ruthlessness but to publicly arrest a well-liked sister of the Fifth Order was hardly the subtle, insidious move he favoured. *He must have tried something else,* Vaelin concluded. *Some other way to silence her or buy her loyalty. So, she had the strength to resist him where I did not.*

'The King only agreed to Sherin's release on condition she be shackled and kept under constant guard,' Frentis went on. 'She's also forbidden to talk to anyone without permission.' Frentis tugged an envelope from his cloak and held it out to Vaelin. 'The details are here. Aspect Arlyn said we should observe them . . .'

Vaelin took the envelope and tossed it on the fire, watching the wax of the King's seal bubble and run in the flames.

'It seems the King has reprieved Sister Sherin and ordered her immediate release,' he told Frentis in a tone that didn't invite argument. 'In recognition of her long years of service to the Realm and the Faith.'

Frentis's eyes flicked to the now-charred envelope but didn't linger. 'Of course, brother.' He shifted nervously, clearly debating whether to voice something more.

'What is it, brother?' Vaelin prompted tiredly.

'There was a girl, came to the dockside when we were getting ready to leave. Asked if I could give you this.' His hand emerged from his cloak again, clutching a small package wrapped in plain paper. 'Pretty thing, she was. Almost made me sorry I joined the Order.'

Vaelin took the package, opening it to find two thin wooden blocks tied together with a blue silk ribbon. Inside was a single winterbloom, pressed flat on a white card. 'Did she say anything?'

'Only that I should convey her thanks. Didn't say what for.'

Vaelin was surprised to find a smile on his lips. 'Thank you, brother.' He retied the ribbon and consigned the blocks to his pocket. 'Didn't happen to bring some food did you? I'm quite starved.'

Frentis made a journey back down the hill and returned a half hour later with Caenis, Barkus and Dentos, each laden with provisions and bedrolls.

'Haven't slept under the stars for weeks now,' Caenis commented. 'I find I miss it.'

'Oh, quite,' Barkus drawled, unfolding his bedroll. 'My backside has indeed missed the joys of hard earth and sudden rain.'

'Don't you lot have duties?' Vaelin enquired.

'We've decided to shirk them, *my lord*,' Dentos replied. 'Going to flog us?'

'Depends on what kind of meal you've brought me.'

They roasted a haunch of goat over the fire and shared bread and dates. Dentos opened a bottle of Cumbraelin red and passed it round. 'This is the last one,' he said, his voice laden with regret. 'Had Sergeant Gallis pack twenty bottles before we left.'

'Men do seem to drink more in time of war,' observed Caenis.

'Can't imagine why,' Barkus grunted.

For a while it was almost as it had been all those years ago, when Master Hutril would lead them into the woods and they would camp out, boys sharing stories and mockery around the fire. Except there were fewer of them now, and the humour had a bitter edge. Even Frentis, in his way the most guileless soul among them, was becoming prone to cynicism, regaling them with the news that the dungeons were once again empty as the King attempted to add ever more regiments to the Realm Guard. 'More cut-throats ready to get their throats cut.'

'Seems fitting,' Caenis said. 'Those who have besmirched the King's peace should be obliged to make recompense. What better way than through service in war? And I have to say, former outlaws do make excellent soldiers.'

'No illusions,' Barkus agreed. 'No expectations. When you live your whole life in hardship, a soldier's life doesn't seem so bad.'

'Ask those poor bastards we left behind at the Bloody Hill how much they liked a soldier's life,' Dentos said.

Barkus shrugged. 'Soldier's life often means a soldier's death. Least they get paid, what do we get?'

'We get to serve the Faith,' Frentis put in. 'It's enough for me.'

'Ah, but you're still young, in mind and body. Give it another year or two and you'll be reaching for Brother's Friend to silence those pesky questions, like the rest of us.' Barkus tipped the wine bottle into his mouth, grimacing in disappointment as the last drops dribbled out. 'Faith, I wish I were drunk,' he grumbled, hurling the bottle into the darkness.

'Don't you believe it then?' Frentis went on. 'What we're fighting for?'

'We're fighting so the King can double his tax income, oh innocent urchin.' Barkus pulled a flask of Brother's Friend from his cloak and took a long pull. 'That's better.'

'That can't be right,' Frentis protested. 'I mean, I know all that stuff about Alpirans stealing children was so much horse-dung, but we're bringing the Faith here, right? These people need us. That's why the Aspect sent us.' His gaze swivelled to Vaelin. 'Right?'

'Of course that's right,' Caenis told him with his accustomed certainty. 'Our brother sees the basest motives in the purest actions.'

'Pure?' Barkus gave a long and hearty laugh. 'What's pure about any of this? How many corpses are lying out there in the desert because of us? How many widows and orphans and cripples have we made? And what about this place? You think the Red Hand appearing here after we seize the city is just some huge coincidence?'

'If we brought it with us, then it would have laid us low as well,' Caenis snapped back. 'You speak such nonsense sometimes, brother.'

Vaelin glanced back at the mansion as they continued to bicker. A dim light was burning in one of the upstairs windows, vague shadows moving behind the blinds. Sherin at work, most probably. He felt a sudden lurch of concern, feeling her vulnerability. If her curative failed to work, she was naked before the Red Hand, like Sister Gilma. He would have sent her to her death . . . and she was so angry.

He rose and went to the gate, eyes locked on the yellow square of the window, helplessness and guilt surging in his breast. He found he was already turning the key in the lock. *If it works, then there is no danger, if it doesn't, then I can't linger here whilst she dies . . .*

'Brother?' Caenis, voice heavy with warning.

'I have to . . .' The blood-song surged, a scream in his mind, sending him to his knees. He clutched at the gate to keep from falling, feeling Barkus's strong hands bear him up.

'Vaelin? Is it the falling sickness again?'

Despite the pain throbbing in his head, Vaelin found he could stand unaided, and there was no tang of blood in his mouth. He wiped at his nose and eyes, finding them dry. *Not the same, but it was Ahm Lin's song.* A sudden, sick realisation struck him, and he tore away from Barkus's grasp, eyes scanning the dark mass of the city, finding it quickly, a bright beacon of flame shining in the artisan's quarter. Ahm Lin's shop was burning.

The flames were reaching high into the sky when they arrived, the roof of the shop was gone, the blackened beams wreathed in fire. The heat was so intense they couldn't go within ten yards of the door. A line of townsfolk relayed buckets from the nearest well, although the water they cast at the inferno had little effect. Vaelin moved among the crowd, searching frantically. 'Where's the mason?' he demanded. 'Is he inside?'

People shrank from him, fear and animosity on every face. He told Caenis to ask them for the mason and a few hands pointed to a cluster of people nearby. Ahm Lin lay on the street, his head cradled in his wife's lap as she wept. Livid burns glistened on his face and arms. Vaelin knelt next to him, gently touching a hand to his chest to check he still drew breath.

'Get away!' His wife lashed out, catching him on the jaw, pushing his hand away. 'Leave him alone!' Her face was blackened with soot and livid with grief and fury. 'Your fault! Your fault, Hope Killer!'

Ahm Lin coughed, lurching on the ground as he fought for breath, eyes blinking open. *'Nura-lah!'* his wife sobbed, pulling him close. *'Erha ne almash.'*

'Thank the Nameless, not the gods,' Ahm Lin rasped. His eyes found Vaelin and he beckoned him closer, whispering in his ear. 'My wolf, brother . . .' His eyelids flickered and he lost consciousness, Vaelin sighing in relief at the sight of his swelling chest.

'Get him to the guild house,' he ordered Dentos. 'Find a healer.'

Caenis came to him as they carried Ahm Lin away, his wife clutching his hand. 'They found the man who did this,' he said, gesturing at another knot of people. Vaelin rushed over, pushing through the cordon and finding a battered corpse lying on the cobbles. He kicked the body onto its back, seeing a bruised and completely unfamiliar face. An Alpiran face.

'Who is he?' Vaelin asked, his gaze tracking the crowd as Caenis translated. After a moment a swarthy man stepped forward and spoke a few words, glancing uneasily at Vaelin.

'The mason is well thought of,' Caenis related. 'The work he does is considered sacred. This man shouldn't have expected mercy.'

'I asked who he is,' Vaelin grated.

Caenis relayed the question to the man in his halting but precise Alpiran, receiving only a blank shake of the head. Questions to the rest of the crowd elicited only meagre information. 'No-one seems to know his name, but he was a servant in one of the big houses. He took a blow to the head when they tried to break out a few weeks ago, hasn't been the same since.'

'Do they know why he did this?'

This produced a babble of seemingly unanimous responses. 'He was found standing in the street with a flaming torch in his hand,' Caenis said. 'Shouting that the mason was a traitor. It seems the mason's friendship with you caused some bad talk, but no-one expected this.'

Vaelin's scrutiny of the crowd intensified under the blood-song's guidance. *The threat lingers. Someone here had a hand in this.*

The sound of falling masonry made him turn back to the shop. The walls were crumbling as the fire ate the timbers inside. With the walls gone the many statues inside were revealed, gods, heroes and emperors serene and unmoving amidst the flames. The murmur of the crowd fell to hushed reverence, a few voices uttering prayers and supplications.

It's not there, Vaelin realised, sweat beading on his brow as he moved closer to scan the blaze. *The wolf is gone.*

◆ ◆ ◆

632 · ANTHONY RYAN

In the morning he searched amidst the wreckage, sifting ash under the impassive gaze of the blackened but otherwise undamaged marble gods. It had taken hours for the fire to subside, despite the countless water buckets heaved at it by the townsfolk and gathered soldiery. Eventually, when it became clear the surrounding houses were in no danger, he called a halt and let it burn. As dawn lit the city he sought out the block with its vital secret, finding nothing but ash and a few shattered pieces of marble that might have been anything. The blood-song was a constant mournful throb at the base of his skull. *Nothing*, he thought. *This has all been for nothing.*

'You look tired.' Sherin stood nearby, grey-cloaked and pale in the lingering smoke rising from the charred ruin. Her face was still guarded but he saw no anger there, just fatigue.

'As do you, sister.'

'The curative worked. The girl will be fully recovered in a few days. I thought I should let you know.'

'Thank you.'

She gave a barely perceptible nod. 'It's not quite over yet. We need to keep watch for more cases, but I'm confident any outbreak can be contained. Another week and the city can be opened once more.'

Her eyes surveyed the ruins then seemed to notice the statues for the first time, her gaze lingering on the massive form of the man and the lion locked in combat.

'Martual, god of courage,' he told her. 'Battling the Nameless great lion that laid waste to the southern plains.'

She reached up to caress the god's unfeasibly muscled forearm. 'Beautiful.'

'Yes, it is. I know you're tired, sister, but I would be grateful if you could look at the man who carved it. He was badly burned in the fire.'

'Of course. Where do I find him?'

'At the guild house near the docks. I've had quarters prepared for you there. I'll show you.'

'I'm sure I can find it.' She turned to go then paused. 'Governor Aruan told me about the night you took the city, how you secured his cooperation. I feel my words may have been overly harsh.'

She held his gaze and he felt the familiar ache in his chest, but this time it warmed him, dispelling the blood-song's sorrowful dirge and bringing a smile to his lips, though the Departed knew he had little to smile about.

'You have been released on the King's orders,' he said. 'Brother Frentis brought a royal command.'

'Really?' She arched an eyebrow. 'May I see it?'

'Sadly, it has been lost.' He gestured at the smoking mess around them by way of explanation.

'Unusually clumsy of you, Vaelin.'

'No, I'm often clumsy, in my deeds and my words.'

A brief answering smile lit Sherin's face before she looked away. 'I should see to this artistic friend of yours.'

The gates were opened seven days later. Vaelin also ordered the sailors released, though only one crew at a time. It provoked little surprise when most chose to leave port with the earliest tide, the *Red Falcon* amongst the first to depart, Captain Nurin hounding his crew with desperate urgency as if afraid Vaelin would attempt a last-minute retrieval of the bluestone.

Some of the richer citizens also chose to leave, fear of the Red Hand did not fade quickly. Vaelin managed to intercept the one-time employer of the man who had set fire to Ahm Lin's shop, a richly attired if somewhat bedraggled spice merchant, chafing under guard at the eastern gate as Vaelin questioned him. His

634 · ANTHONY RYAN

family and remaining servants lingered nearby, packhorses laden with assorted valuables.

'His name was Carpenter, as far as I knew,' the merchant said. 'I can't be expected to remember every servant in my employ. I pay people to remember for me.' The man's knowledge of the Realm tongue was impeccable, but there was an arrogant disdain to his tone Vaelin didn't like. However, the fellow's evident fear made him suppress the urge to deliver an encouraging cuff across the face.

'He had a wife?' he asked. 'A family?'

The merchant shrugged. 'I think not, seemed to spend most his free time carving wooden effigies of the gods.'

'I heard he was injured, a blow to the head.'

'Most of us were that night.' The merchant lifted a silken sleeve to display a stitched cut on his forearm. 'Your men were very free with their clubs.'

'The carpenter's injury,' Vaelin pressed.

'He took a blow to the head, a bad one it seems. My men carried him back to the house unconscious. In truth we thought him dead, but he lingered for several days, barely breathing. Then he simply woke up, showing no ill effects. My servants thought it the work of the gods, a reward for all his carvings. The next morning he was gone, having said no words since his awakening.' The merchant glanced back at his waiting family, impatience and fear showing in the tremble of his hands.

'I know you were not complicit in this,' he told the merchant, stepping aside. 'Luck to you on your journey.'

The man was already moving away, shouting commands to put his household on the road.

He lingered for days, Vaelin mused and the blood-song stirred, sounding a clear note of recognition. He felt the familiar sense of fumbling for something, some answer to the many mysteries of his life, but once again it was beyond his reach. Frustration seized him and the blood-song wavered. *The song is you,* Ahm Lin had said. *You can sing it as well as hear it.* He sought to calm his feelings, trying to hear the song more clearly, trying to focus it. *The song is me, my blood, my need, my hunt.* It swelled within him, roaring in his ears, a cacophony of emotion, blurred visions flicking through his mind too fast to catch. Words spoken and unspoken rose in an incomprehensible babble, lies and truth mingling in a maelstrom of confusion.

I need Ahm Lin's counsel, he thought, trying to focus the song, forcing harmony into the discordant din. The song swelled once more, then calmed to a single, clear note and there was a brief glimpse of the marble block, the chisel resuming its impossibly rapid work, guided by an unseen hand, the face emerging, features forming . . . Then it was gone, the block blackened and shattered amidst the wasted ruin of the mason's home.

Vaelin moved to a nearby step and sat down heavily. It appeared there had been but one chance to know what message the block contained. This verse was over and he needed a new tune.

CHAPTER EIGHT

He was called to the gate at midnight, Janril Norin limping to his room in the guild house to wake him. 'Scores of horsemen on the plain, my lord,' the minstrel said. 'Brother Caenis requested your presence.'

He quickly strapped on his sword and mounted Spit, galloping to the gatehouse in a few minutes. Caenis was already there, ordering more archers onto the walls. They climbed the stairs to the upper battlements, where one of Count Marven's Nilsaelins pointed to the plain. 'Near five hundred of the buggers, my lord,' the man said, voice shrill with alarm.

Vaelin calmed him with a pat to the shoulder and moved to the battlement, looking down on a small host of armoured riders, steel gleaming a faint blue in the dim light from the crescent moon. At their head a burly figure in rust-stained armour glared up at them. 'You ever going to open this bloody gate?' Baron Banders demanded. 'My men are hungry and I've got blisters on my arse.'

Shorn of his armour, the baron was smaller in stature but no less bullish. 'Pah!' He spat a mouthful of wine onto the floor of the guild-house chamber which served as their meal hall. 'Alpiran piss. Don't you have any Cumbraelin to offer an honoured guest, my lord?'

'I regret my brothers and I are guilty of exhausting our reserves, Baron,' Vaelin replied. 'My apologies.'

Banders shrugged and reached for the roasted chicken on the table, tearing off a leg and chomping into the flesh. 'I see you managed to leave most of this place standing,' he commented around a mouthful. 'Locals couldn't have put up much of a fight.'

'We were able to effect a stealthy seizure of the city. The governor has proved a pragmatic man. There was little bloodshed.'

The baron's face became sombre, and he paused for a moment before washing down his food and reaching for more. 'Couldn't say the same about Marbellis. Thought the place was going to burn forever.'

Vaelin's disquiet deepened. The baron's unexpected appearance was unsettling, and it seemed he had dark news to impart. 'The siege was difficult?'

Banders snorted, pouring himself more wine. 'Four weeks of pounding with the engines before we had a practical breach. Every night they'd sally out, small parties of dagger men, sneaking through our lines to cut throats and hole the water barrels. Every bloody night a sleepless trial. The Departed know how many men we lost. Then the Battle Lord sent three full regiments into the breach. Maybe fifty men made it out again, all wounded. The Alpirans had set traps in the breach, spiked pits and so forth. When the Realm Guard got held up by the pits they sent bundles of kindling rolling in, all soaked in oil. Their archers set them blazing with fire arrows.' He paused, eyes closed, a small shudder ran through him. 'You could hear the screams a mile away.'

'The city is not taken?'

'Oh it's taken. Taken and taken again like a cheap whore.'

Banders belched. 'Blood Rose licked his wounds and drew his plan well. In truth I think his assault on the breach was a grand ruse, a sacrifice to convince the Alpirans they were facing a fool. Two nights later he drew up four regiments opposite the breach, making ready to assault. At the same time he sent the entire remaining Realm Guard infantry against the eastern wall with scaling ladders. He gambled the Alpirans were concentrating their strength at the breach and didn't leave enough men to defend the walls. Turns out he was right. Took all night and the cost was high but by morning the city was ours, what was left of it.'

Banders lapsed into silence, concentrating on his meal. Vaelin let him eat and found his gaze lingering on the baron's perennially rust-stained armour. On seeing it up close for the first time, he noticed that those parts of steel plate not besmirched with corrosion gleamed with a polished sheen and the rust itself had an odd, waxy texture.

'It's paint,' he said aloud.

'Mmmm?' Banders glanced over at his armour and grunted. 'Oh that. A man should try to live up to his legend, don't you think?'

'The legend of the rusty knight?' Vaelin asked. 'Can't say I've heard it, my lord.'

'Aha, but you're not Renfaelin.' Banders grinned. 'My father was a boisterous, kindhearted fellow, but overfond of dice and harlots and consequently unable to leave me much more than a crumbling hold-fast and a rusty suit of armour, which I was obliged to wear when answering the Lord's call to war. Luckily my father had managed to pass on something of his skill with the lance and so my standing grew with every battle and tourney. I was famed as the Rust Knight, loved by the commons for my poverty. The armour became my banner, made me easy to find in the melee, something for the peasants to cheer and my men to rally to, once I had fortune enough to hire some of course.'

'So this is not the original armour?'

Banders laughed heartily. 'Faith no, brother! That's all rusted to uselessness years ago. Even the best armour rarely lasts more than a few years in any case, battle and the elements take their toll. We have a saying in Renfael: if you want to be richer than a lord, become a blacksmith.' He chuckled and poured himself more wine.

'Why are you here, Baron?' Vaelin asked him. 'Do you bring word from the Battle Lord?'

The baron's expression sobered once again. 'I do. I also bring myself and my men. Three hundred knights and two hundred armed retainers and assorted squires, if you'll have us.'

'You and your men are most welcome, but will Fief Lord Theros not have need of your services?'

Banders set aside his wine and sighed heavily, meeting Vaelin's eyes with a level gaze. 'I have been dismissed from the Fief Lord's service, brother. Not for the first time, but I suspect the last. The Battle Lord bid me offer my command to you.'

'You quarrelled with the Fief Lord?'

'Not with him, no.' His mouth was set in a hard, unyielding line and Vaelin sensed it was best to let the matter drop.

'And the Battle Lord's word?'

Banders pulled a sealed letter from his shirt and tossed it on the table. 'I know the contents, to save you reading it. You are instructed to make the city safe against imminent siege. Order patrols from Marbellis spied a great host of Alpirans making its way north. They appear intent on bypassing Marbellis and seizing Linesh with all dispatch.' He took another, deep gulp of wine, wiping his mouth and belching again. 'My advice, brother, commandeer the merchant fleet and sail your men back to the Realm. There isn't a hope of holding this place against so many.'

◆ ◆ ◆

'At least ten cohorts of infantry, another five of horse and assorted savages from the southern provinces of the Empire. Near twenty thousand in all.' Banders's voice was light but all present could sense the weight behind his levity. Vaelin had called a council of captains in the guild house, having had Caenis search the city archive for the largest and most accurate map of the northern Alpiran coast.

'I thought there would be more,' Caenis said. 'The Emperor's army is supposed to be beyond counting.'

'Indeed there are more, brother,' Banders assured him. 'This is just the vanguard. The few prisoners we took in Marbellis were happy to confirm it. The force marching on this city is the elite of the Alpiran army. The finest infantry and cavalry he can muster, all veterans of the border wars with the Volarians. Don't underestimate the savages either, all warriors born. It's said they spend their lives worshipping the Emperor like a god and fighting each other over petty insults, which they're happy to put aside when he calls them to war. Seems they like the taste of defeated enemies.'

'Siege engines?' Vaelin asked.

Banders nodded. 'Ten of them, much taller and heftier than anything we have, can sling a boulder the size of a musk-ox over three hundred paces.'

Vaelin glanced around the table, gauging the reaction of the other captains to the baron's words. Count Marven was rigidly controlled, seemingly wary of betraying any emotion that might undermine his jealously guarded status. Lord Marshal Al Cordlin had paled visibly and kept clutching his recently healed arm, a faint sheen of sweat beginning to show on his upper lip. Lord Marshal Al Trendil seemed lost in thought, stroking his chin, eyes distant. Vaelin assumed he was calculating if he could escape with all the spoils he had looted at Untesh. Only Bren Antesh seemed unaffected, arms folded and regarding Banders with only a mild interest.

'How long do we have?' Caenis asked the baron.

'Brother Sollis put them here.' Banders tapped a finger to the map spread out on the table before them, picking out a point about twenty miles southwest of Marbellis. 'That was twelve days ago.'

'An army that size couldn't cover more than fifteen miles a day,' Count Marven mused in a deliberately measured tone. 'Less in the desert.'

'Gives us maybe another two weeks,' Lord Marshal Al Cordlin said, his voice was pitched slightly high and he coughed before continuing. 'Ample time, my lord.'

Vaelin frowned at him. 'Ample time for what?'

'Why, evacuation of course.' Al Cordlin's eyes cast around the table, seeking support. 'I know there aren't sufficient ships remaining to carry the whole of the army, but the senior officers could be got away easily. The men can march to Untesh . . .'

'We are ordered to hold this city,' Vaelin told him.

'Against twenty thousand?' Al Cordlin gave a short and some-what hysterical laugh. 'More than three times our number, and elite troops at that. It would be madness to . . .'

'Lord Marshal Al Cordlin I hereby relieve you of your command.' Vaelin nodded at the door. 'Leave this room. In the morning you will be escorted to the harbour, where you will take ship for the Realm. Until then keep to your quarters, I don't want the men infected with your cowardice.'

Al Cordlin rocked back on his heels as if struck, beginning to babble. 'This is . . . Such insults are unwarranted. My regiment was given to me by the King . . .'

'Just get out.'

The stricken lord cast one more final glance at the rest of the captains, finding either indifference or wary discomfort, before moving to the door and making his exit. 'Any more suggestions of evacuation will receive the same response,' Vaelin told the council. 'I trust that's understood.'

He turned his attention back to the map, ignoring the chorus of affirmation. Once again he was struck by the barrenness of the region, marvelling that three large cities such as Untesh, Linesh and Marbellis could exist on the fringes of such trackless desert. *All dust and scrub,* as Frentis had said. *Haven't seen a tree since we landed . . .* 'No trees.'

'My lord?' Baron Banders asked.

Vaelin gave no reply and kept his attention on the map as something stirred, the seed of a stratagem nurtured by a faint murmur from the blood-song, building to a chorus as his eyes picked out a pictogram about thirty miles south of the city; a copse of palm trees surrounding a small pool. 'What's this?' he asked Caenis.

'The Lehlun Oasis, brother. The only sizeable source of water on the southern caravan route.'

'Meaning,' Count Marven said, 'the Alpiran army will have to stop there on the way north.'

'You mean to poison the water, my lord?' Lord Marshal Al Trendil asked. 'An excellent notion. We could spoil it with animal carcasses . . .'

'I don't mean to do any such thing,' Vaelin replied, continuing to let the blood-song feed his design. *The risks are great, and the cost . . .*

'We should seal the city, my lord,' Count Marven said, breaking the silence, which Vaelin realised had lasted several minutes. 'The southbound caravans will surely pass word of our numbers to the enemy.'

'People have been leaving by the dozen since the threat of the Red Hand faded,' Vaelin said. 'I'd be greatly surprised if the Alpiran commander doesn't already possess a full picture of our numbers and our preparations. Besides, letting him think us weak could work to our advantage. An overconfident enemy is prone to carelessness.'

He gave the map a final glance and moved back from the table. 'Baron Banders, I apologise for asking you to take to the saddle again so soon after your arrival, but I require you and your knights on the morrow.' He turned to Caenis. 'Brother, have the scout troop assemble at dawn, I will take command personally. In my absence the city is yours. Make every effort to deepen the ditch around the walls and double its width.'

'You intend to ambush an army of twenty thousand with a few hundred men?' Count Marven was incredulous. 'What can you hope to achieve?'

Vaelin was already moving to the door. 'An axe without a blade is just a stick.'

Further inland the northern desert sands rose into tall dunes, stretching to the horizon like a storm-swept sea frozen in gold under a cloudless sky. The sun was too intense to permit marching during the day and they were obliged to travel by night, sheltering under tents in daylight whilst the knights grumbled and their warhorses nickered and stamped hooves in irritation at the unaccustomed heat.

'Noisy buggers, this lot,' Dentos observed on the second day out.

Vaelin glanced over at a clutch of knights, bickering and shoving each other over a game of dice. Nearby, another knight was loudly berating his squire for the lack of polish on his breastplate. He had to agree that the knights were hardly the most stealthy soldiers and he would have gladly exchanged them all for a single company from the Order, but there were no brothers to be had and he needed cavalry for this to work.

'It shouldn't matter,' he replied. 'They only have to make one charge.' *Though, I couldn't say how many will be left after that.*

'What about patrols?' Frentis asked. 'The Alpirans would be fools not to scout their flanks.'

'This far out from the city, I'm hoping they're foolish enough to do just that. If not, we'll only have to linger for one day in any case. Any patrol that finds us will have to be silenced and we'll hope they aren't missed by nightfall.'

It took another two nights before the oasis came into view, shimmering into solidity amidst the baking dunes. Vaelin was surprised by the size of it, expecting little more than a pond and a few palms, but in fact finding a small lake surrounded by lush vegetation, a near-irresistible jewel of green and blue.

'No sign of the Alpirans, brother,' Frentis said, reining in with the scout troop at the foot of the dune, where he had halted to survey the oasis. 'Seems we beat them to it, like you said.'

'Caravans?' Vaelin asked him.

'Nothing for miles around.'

'We saw scant sign of traders on our journey north, my lord,' Baron Banders commented. 'War is never good for commerce. 'Less you're trading in steel o' course.'

Vaelin surveyed the desert, spying a tall, almost mountainous dune two miles to the west. 'There,' he said, pointing. 'We'll camp on the westward slope. No fires, and it would be greatly appreciated, Baron, if your men refrained from excessive noise.'

'I'll do what I can, my lord. But they're not peasants, y'know. Can't just flog them like your lot.'

'Maybe you should, milord,' Dentos suggested. 'Remind 'em they bleed the same colour as us peasants.'

'They'll bleed well enough when the Alpirans come, brother,' Banders snapped back, his already flushed face colouring further.

'Enough,' Vaelin cut in. 'Brother Dentos, go with Brother Frentis.

Fetch as much water as you can carry, leave as little sign as possible. I don't want our foes to think anything bigger than a spice caravan has passed here in weeks.'

It was two more days before the Emperor's army appeared, heralded by a tall column of dust rising above the southern horizon. Vaelin, Frentis and Dentos lay atop a high dune to observe their advance to the oasis. The cavalry appeared first, small parties of outriders followed by long columns riding two abreast. Vaelin counted four regiments of lancers plus an equal number of horse-borne archers. Their discipline and efficiency was impressive, evident in the speed with which they established their camp, tents and cooking fires appearing amidst the palms of the oasis within an hour of their arrival. He borrowed the spyglass from Frentis and picked out officers and sergeants amongst the throng, marking their stern visage and easy authority as they posted pickets in a tight and well-placed perimeter. *Veterans indeed,* he decided, regretting he hadn't had time to say his good-byes to Sherin before they left. Although he had sensed a softening in her regard at their last meeting, he still had much to explain.

He tracked the spyglass away from the oasis and focused on a second dust cloud rising to the south, the wavering, stick figures of the Alpiran infantry materialising out of the desert heat with unwelcome clarity.

It took over an hour for the infantry to file into the oasis and make camp. Master Sollis's estimate had been conservative; there were in fact twelve cohorts of infantry, swelling the Alpiran force to at least thirty thousand and making Vaelin consider, for only the briefest second, if Lord Marshal Al Cordlin hadn't been right after all.

'See there?' Frentis pointed, lifting his eye from the spyglass. 'Battle Lord maybe?'

Vaelin took the glass and followed his finger to a large tent pitched to the north of the oasis. A group of soldiers were erecting a tall standard bearing a red banner adorned with an emblem of two crossed sabres in black. They were overseen by a tall man in a gold cloak with hard, ebony features and grey-peppered hair. *Neliesen Nester Hevren, Captain of the Tenth Cohort of the Imperial Guard. Come to keep a promise.*

He watched the captain turn and bow to a stocky man with a pronounced limp. He wore old but serviceable armour and a cavalry sabre at his belt. His skin had the olive hue of the northern provinces and his head was shaven bald. He listened to Hevren for a few moments as the captain appeared to make some kind of report, then cut him off with a dismissive wave of his hand, stomping off to the tent without sparing him another glance.

'No, the limping man is the Battle Lord,' Vaelin said. He noted the weary slump of Hevren's shoulders before he straightened and marched away. *Shamed,* he decided. *Shunned because you lost the Hope. What were you suggesting, I wonder? More patrols, more guards? More regard for the cunning of the Hope Killer? Wouldn't listen, would he?* For the first time since leaving the city, Vaelin felt his mood begin to lighten.

It was early evening by the time the siege engines came into view. He had been nurturing the faint hope that Banders had exaggerated Sollis's report with the telling but knew now the baron had spoken true. The Realm Guard had engines of its own, mangonels and catapults for slinging boulders and fireballs at or over castle walls, but even the largest and most carefully crafted could not compare to the obvious power of the devices the emperor had sent to bring down the walls of Linesh. Lumbering giants in the gathering gloom, their weighted arms swayed as great teams of oxen drew them onwards.

The engines were escorted by perhaps three thousand men,

from their loose formation and nonuniform appearance clearly the tribesmen Banders had described. Their costume varied in colour, from garish red silk and blue-feathered head-dresses to sober black or blue robes devoid of decoration. Their weaponry and armour was equally diverse. He picked out a few breastplates and mail shirts but most seemed unarmoured save for round wooden shields decorated with unfathomable sigils. Weapons seemed to consist mainly of long spears with serrated iron blades augmented with viciously spiked clubs and maces worn at the belt along with daggers and short swords.

Vaelin watched as the oxen hauled the engines to the southern edge of the oasis, the drovers unlimbering the teams to lead them to the water and the tribesmen making their camp around the tall frames.

'That's a lot of savages to cut through, brother,' Dentos commented.

'If it works, we won't have to.' Vaelin handed the spyglass back to Frentis. 'Let's pack the horses. We'll move out with the moon rise.'

Spit, to Vaelin's complete lack of surprise, proved unsuited to the role of packhorse, the stallion's ill temper taking a dangerous turn as he attempted to hoist the pack onto his back, his hooves stamping with perilous disregard for toes and feet. It took several precious minutes of cajoling, threatening and bribing with sugar lumps before he was sufficiently settled to allow the pack to be secured in place, by which time the bright crescent of the moon was high overhead.

'Why you hold on to that beast is a mystery, brother,' Dentos observed, his voice slightly muffled by the muslin scarf covering the lower half of his face.

'He's a fighter,' Vaelin replied. 'It makes up for the bruises.' He scanned the assembled scout troop, each man similarly garbed in the white muslin robes typical of the traders who tracked spice and other valuables across the desert to the northern ports. Every mount was laden with packs, each bulging with the round red clay pots used for carriage of spices, although tonight they were filled with a different cargo. He knew they were unlikely to fool an experienced eye, their mounts too tall and their garb showing too many unfamiliar details, not to mention the odd bulge of a concealed weapon. But, for a few vital moments, they should be convincing enough in the dark. He hoped it would be enough.

He glanced to the north, marking the winding trail of the caravan route through the dunes to the oasis. The desert was a strange sight under the moon, the sand painted silver by the light. Taken with the chill of the nighttime desert it was almost like looking upon a snowfield, once more calling forth the half-forgotten dream, Nersus sil Nin's cruel mockery, a body cooling in the snow . . .

'Brother?' Frentis asked, breaking the reverie.

Vaelin shook his head to clear the vision, turning to the scout troop and raising his voice. 'You all know the importance of our mission tonight. Once it's done, ride for Linesh and don't look back. They'll be on our heels like starved wolves so don't tarry, not for anything.'

He turned back to the north and tugged on Spit's reins. 'Come on, you bloody nag.'

They lit torches and approached at a steady pace, calling greetings in memorised Alpiran to the tribesmen guarding the southern perimeter. They were all tall, lean men with pointed beards and skin like polished mahogany, their garb a mixture of red-dyed cloth and loose armour fashioned from ivory. Each carried one of the long spears with serrated blades Vaelin had noted when they surveyed the camp earlier. They were clearly suspicious but not overly alarmed and Vaelin was relieved when no tumult erupted at the appearance of a small but unknown party. Five of them gathered to obstruct their path as they approached the camp, spears levelled but their manner not overly threatening.

'*Ni-rehl ahn!*' Dentos greeted the tribesmen. Next to Caenis he had the best ear for Alpiran, although he could hardly be said to be fluent. Despite having been extensively coached by Caenis in the few hours before their departure from Linesh, he was unlikely to fool a native of the northern empire. It was their fortune that the tribesmen hailed from the southern provinces and probably knew less of the local dialect than they did.

One of the tribesmen shook his head in confusion, saying something in his own language to his fellows, who replied with shrugs of bafflement.

'*Unterah.*' Dentos gave the word for trader, patting his chest, then gestured broadly at their makeshift caravan. '*Onterish.*' Spice.

The tribesman who had spoken stepped past Dentos, eyes scanning their company with careful scrutiny. He approached Vaelin, ignoring the affable nod he offered and giving Spit a long look of examination, his eyes narrowing at the sight of the many scars covering the warhorse's legs and flanks.

A shout came from one of the other tribesmen and the man confronting Vaelin stepped back quickly, hands tight on his spear, crouching into a fighting stance. Vaelin held up his hands in placation, pointing to the west. The tribesman risked a glance over his shoulder, straightening in confusion at the sight of a large number of torches appearing out of the desert, about three hundred teardrops of light flickering in the gloom, accompanied by the growing telltale rumble of a cavalry charge in full tilt and the peel of multiple trumpets.

The tribesman turned to his fellows, mouth opening to voice a command, and died as Vaelin's throwing knife sank into the base of his skull. The snap of bowstrings and the whistle of thrown blades filled the air as the scout troop freed their weapons to dispatch the remaining sentries.

'Douse the torches! Get to the engines!' Vaelin barked, tugging Spit into a run.

The cacophony of battle erupted as they entered the camp, the thunderclap crash of Baron Banders's knights striking the hastily formed line of defending tribesmen soon replaced by the familiar din of shrieking horses and clashing metal. Everywhere, tribesmen were gathering weapons and rushing to join the battle, war cries and the harsh, grating peel of their own horns calling them forth. By the time Vaelin's party were among the tents, most had gone to join the fray and the few who lingered to trouble them were quickly cut down.

They found the engines bare of defenders save for the artisans who tended them, mostly middle-aged men in leather smocks with few weapons save for carpentry tools. Vaelin was sorry they didn't have the good sense to run, killing one who swung at him with a mallet and leaving another clutching a partly severed hand.

'Get out of here!' he commanded the man, sheathing his sword and unhitching the pack of clay pots from Spit's back. The man just looked up at him in dumb shock before the loss of blood made him collapse limply into the sand. Vaelin cursed and left him there, opening the pack and heaving the pots at the nearest engine as fast as he could. They broke against the sturdy wooden frames and spilled their clear, viscous liquid over every surface. Vaelin quickly exhausted the contents of one pack and hauled another to a second engine, already partly doused by Frentis, who grinned wolfishly.

'Going to make quite a sight, brother.'

'That it will.' He emptied the second pack and surveyed the progress of the rest of the party, noting with satisfaction the shattered remains of numerous pots on all ten engines. 'Right, that's enough!' he shouted. 'Get them lit!'

They retreated twenty yards or so, Vaelin dragging the wounded artisan behind him, unwilling to let him burn. Dentos and Frentis unlimbered their bows, lit fire arrows and sent them arching towards the engines, the flames catching the lamp oil instantly, and soon ten great fires were raging in the midst of the camp, flames engulfing the tall engines in a few moments, ropes and bindings disintegrating in the heat, the great arms of the engines tumbling like pine caught in a forest fire.

The flames were bright enough to illuminate the battle raging on the western perimeter, where Baron Banders was now rallying his men for the withdrawal, although the battle-maddened tribesmen were in no mood to let them go. Vaelin saw several knights pulled from their horses and speared to death in quick succession as they vainly sought to extricate themselves from the struggle.

Vaelin mounted Spit and drew his sword. 'Ride for the city!' he called to the scout troop.

'And you, brother?' Frentis asked.

Vaelin nodded at the battle. 'The baron needs some help. I'll be along presently.'

'Let me—'

He fixed Frentis with a look that brooked no argument. 'Take your men home, brother.'

Frentis bit down on no doubt bitter words and nodded. 'If you're not back in two days . . .'

'Then I'm not coming back and you will look to Brother Caenis for command.' Vaelin spurred Spit into a gallop and hurtled towards the battle, feeling the warhorse tense beneath him in anticipation of combat. He skirted the edge of the throng, lashing out to strike down unwary tribesmen, wheeling away as they swarmed at him, galloping on then repeating the process, seeking to divert their fury enough to allow the knights some relief. '*Eruhin Makhtar!*' he shouted repeatedly, hoping they knew what it meant. 'I am the *Eruhin Makhtar*! Come and kill me!'

The words were clearly understood by at least some of the tribesmen, judging by the ferocity with which they pursued him, hurling spears and hatchets with sometimes unnerving accuracy. One showed a remarkable turn of speed, sprinting after Vaelin as he wheeled away from another pass, leaping onto Spit's back with his war club raised then tumbling to the sand with an arrow speared through his torso.

'I don't think we should linger much longer, brother!' Dentos called, notching and releasing another shaft as he galloped along-side, a tribesman spinning to the ground a short distance away.

'Thought I sent you back to the city,' Vaelin called.

'No, you sent Frentis.' Dentos loosed another arrow and ducked a spear. 'We really need to go!'

Vaelin glanced at the main throng, seeing a broad figure in red-stained armour riding away from the fight, the baron choosing to be the last to leave. He pointed to the west and they turned away, spurring their mounts to even greater speed, the still-burning engines casting long shadows over the sands, fading as they were swallowed by the desert.

They rode on through the night, keeping a westward course until sunrise then turning to the north, only dismounting to walk the horses when the heat began to make them stagger. They stripped the mounts of all excess weight, throwing their mail away but keeping their weapons and the remaining canteens of water.

'No sign of 'em,' Dentos said, shielding his eyes as he scanned the southern horizon. 'Not yet anyway.'

'They'll be along,' Vaelin assured him. He held a canteen to

Spit's mouth, the animal snatching it between his teeth and tipping the contents down his throat in a few gulps. Vaelin wasn't sure how much longer the stallion could last in the heat, the desert was a cruel environment for a north-born animal, evidenced by the foam that covered his flanks and the weary blink of his normally bright and suspicious eye.

'With any luck they're following the baron's trail,' Dentos went on. 'More of 'em to follow after all.'

'I think we used up our share of luck last night, don't you?' Vaelin waited until Spit had finished drinking then took hold of his reins. 'We keep walking. If we can't ride in this heat, neither can they.'

It was early evening when they saw it, small and faint in the distance, but undeniably real.

'Fifteen miles, maybe?' Dentos wondered, eyeing the dust cloud.

'Closer to ten.' Vaelin hauled himself into the saddle, wincing at Spit's weary snort of annoyance. 'Seems they can ride in the heat after all.'

They kept to a canter for most of the night, wary of pushing the horses to collapse, glancing continually to the south, seeing only the desert and the star-rich sky but knowing their pursuers were gaining with every mile.

The northern shore came into sight with the dawn, the desert sands giving way to scrub and, six miles to the east, the white walls of Linesh gleaming in the morning light.

'Brother,' Dentos said softly.

Vaelin turned his gaze southwards, the dust cloud was larger now, the riders raising it clearly visible. He leaned forward to pat Spit's neck, whispering in his ear. 'Sorry.' Leaning back he kicked his heels against the horse's flanks and they spurred into a gallop. He had expected Spit to have lost much of his speed, but if anything he seemed to find some kind of relief in the gallop, tossing his head and snorting either in pleasure or anger. His hooves churned the dusty ground and they quickly outdistanced Dentos and his struggling mount, so much so that Vaelin was forced to rein in after four miles. They had crested a small rise overlooking the plain before the city walls. The gates were open and a line of horsemen were making their way inside, sunlight gleaming on their armour.

'Seems the baron made it back,' Vaelin observed as Dentos reined in.

'Glad someone did.' Dentos upended a canteen and let the water bathe his face. Behind him Vaelin could see their pursuers were closing fast, barely a mile behind. He was right, they weren't going to make it.

'Here,' he said, making to dismount. 'I have the faster horse. It's me they want.'

'Don't be fucking stupid, brother,' Dentos said wearily. He unhitched his bow from the saddle and notched an arrow, wheeling his horse around to face the oncoming horsemen. Vaelin knew there was no dissuading him.

'I'm sorry, brother,' he said, voice laden with guilt. 'This fool's war, I . . .'

Dentos wasn't listening, looking off to the south, a puzzled frown on his brow. 'Didn't know they had them here. Big bugger too, isn't he?'

Vaelin followed his gaze and felt the blood-song surge in a fiery tumult of recognition as his eyes picked out the form of a large grey wolf sitting a short distance away. It regarded him with the impassive, green-eyed stare he remembered so well from that first meeting in the Urlish. 'You can see him?' he asked.

'Course, he's hard to miss.'

BLOOD SONG · 655

The blood-song was raging now, a piercing cacophony of warning. 'Dentos, ride for the city.'

'I'm not going anywhere . . .'

'Something's going to happen! Please, just go!'

Dentos was going to argue further but his gaze was drawn by something else, a great dark cloud rising above the southern horizon, ascending from the desert to at least a mile into the sky, swallowing sunlight in its billowing fury as it swept towards the city, dunes disappearing as it gathered them to its hungry breast.

An arrow thumped into the ground a few feet away. Vaelin turned to see their pursuers now barely fifty yards distant, at least a hundred men, preceded by a swarm of arrows launched at the gallop, a desperate attempt to end the chase before the sandstorm bore down.

'RIDE!' Vaelin shouted, taking hold of Dentos's reins and pulling him along as he kicked Spit into a gallop, arrows raining down as they descended the rise and rode for the city. The storm hit before they had covered a third of the distance, the sand blasting into face and eyes like a cloud of vicious needles. Dentos's mount reared in the fury of it and Vaelin lost his grip on the reins, horse and rider disappearing in the whirling red mist. He tried to call for him but instantly choked on the sand, which sought to fill his mouth. He could only do his best to shield his face and cling on as Spit ran blindly through the storm.

In desperation he turned to the blood-song, trying to calm it, master it enough to guide its music, to sing. At first there was only the discordant shriek of wrongness and alarm that had erupted at the sight of the wolf, but as he exerted his will the confusion began to calm, a few clear notes forming amongst the storm raging in his mind. *Dentos!* he called, seeking to cast the song into the storm like a grapple. *Find him!*

The song changed again, more notes forming, the music

656 · ANTHONY RYAN

becoming more melodious, almost serene but tinged with something more, a tone so strange as to be vastly unknowable. The realisation dawned like a blow. *This is not my song! This is not the song of any man!*

Who? he sang. *Who are you?*

The other song changed again, all music fading to be replaced by a single impatient growl.

Please! he begged. *My brother . . .*

The wolf's growl became a shout in his mind, strong enough to make him reel in the saddle. Spit whinnied and reared in alarm as he heaved himself upright, feeling blood begin to pour from his nose. *NO!* he screamed back with every fibre of strength he could force into the song. *I DO NOT WANT YOUR HELP!*

Instantly the wind dropped, the harsh blast of grit on his face dissipating to a faint breeze, the wind-tossed sands slowly descending with a sound like a thousand whispering voices. Through the fading mist he saw the dark shape of a rider, no more than ten yards away, Dentos clearly recognisable from the sword on his back. Relief flooded Vaelin as he trotted over, reaching out to clasp his brother's shoulder.

'Not a good time to linger, brother . . .'

Dentos pitched from the saddle and fell heavily to the ground. His eyes were open, face pale with a familiar pallor, the arrow that had killed him jutting from his chest, the steel barb wet with blood.

They told him later how he had sat there, still and frozen, like one of Ahm Lin's creations appearing out of the ebbing sandstorm, raising shouts from the sentries on the walls and compelling Caenis to frantic efforts to reopen the gate. The Alpiran pursuers, scattered by the storm, were quick to recover their wits and close in on the immobile Hope Killer. One galloped to within twenty yards, leaning low over his stallion's neck, bow drawn and shaft ready, teeth bared with hate and triumph. Bren Antesh leapt atop the gatehouse battlements, put an arrow clean through the rider's chest then barked an order at his archers. A thousand arrows rose from the walls and descended on the Alpirans in a black hail. Near a hundred riders cut down by a single volley.

Vaelin had no knowledge of any of it. There was only Dentos, his slack, empty face, and the arrowhead, gleaming metal shining amongst the red gore. Voices called to him from the walls but he heard nothing. Caenis and Barkus sprinted through the reopened gate, stumbling to a halt in shock. Vaelin couldn't hear their grief or their questions. *Dentos and the arrow . . .*

'Vaelin.'

It was the only voice he could have heard. Sherin was at his side, reaching up to clasp his wrist, his knuckles white as they gripped the reins. 'Vaelin, please.'

He looked down at her, drinking in the sight of her compassion, the familiar ache dispelling his numbness with a desperate need and hopeless shame. 'I am a murderer,' he said, forming each word with cold precision.

'No . . .'

'I am a murderer.' He gently pulled her hand away and kicked Spit into a walk, guiding him through the gate and into the city.

CHAPTER NINE

He stayed in his room for two days, slumped fully clothed on his bunk. Janril knocked and left food outside his door but he ignored it. Caenis, Barkus and Frentis each came in turn to call through the door but he barely heard them. He felt no need of sleep, no hunger, no thirst. There was only Dentos and the arrowhead, and the song, the great unknowable song of the wolf like a deafening echo in his mind. And the truth of course, the hateful truth. *I am a murderer.*

He remembered when he had gone to Dentos to ask for his presence on the mission. 'You're the best horse archer we have . . .' he had begun but Dentos was already packing his kit.

'Nortah was better,' he said, stringing his bow.

'Nortah's dead.'

Dentos had simply smiled and for the first time Vaelin realised he had never believed his lie about Nortah's fate. How much more had he known? What other secrets had he kept? All of his knowledge gone in an instant, stolen by an arrow loosed by a stranger who probably thought he had felled the Hope Killer himself. Vaelin wondered if the man had died happy under the hail of Cumbraelin arrows, perhaps expecting a hero's welcome from the gods. It must have been a terrible disappointment.

Towards evening of the second day his attention was finally drawn by a scratching at the door, accompanied by a plaintive whine. He blinked, gazing at the dim room with blurred eyes, fingers scraping the stubble on his chin, smelling his own stink. 'I need a bath,' he muttered, rising to open the door.

Scratch's weight bore him down effortlessly, his harsh tongue scraping over face and chin with desperate affection. 'All right daft dog!' he groaned, pushing the slave-hound away with some difficulty. 'I'm all right.'

'Really?' Sherin was standing in the doorway, arms folded, her expression an echo of the severity he remembered from their first meeting. 'Because you look terrible.'

She turned and descended the steps, returning a few minutes later with a cloth and a steaming bowl of water. She closed the door and sat on the bed as he stripped to the waist and washed, Scratch's head in her lap as she rubbed the fur behind his ears. He could feel her gaze on his torso, knowing her eyes lingered on his scars, sensing her sorrow. 'Nothing I didn't earn, sister,' he told her, reaching for his razor. 'All of it, and more besides.'

'So you hate yourself now?' There was an edge of anger to her tone. Clearly her bitterness at his beating of Brother Commander Iltis was taking a while to fade.

'The things I've done. This war . . .' He trailed off, closing his eyes briefly before lathering his face and lifting the razor to his skin.

'Here.' Sherin rose and moved to his side, taking the razor from him. 'You haven't slept, your hands are unsteady.' She pulled over a stool and made him sit. 'Relax, I've done this more times than I can remember.' He had to admit many barbers would envy the skill with which she wielded the razor, sliding the blade over his skin with deft precision, her healer's hands gentle and soothing. For a moment he was lost in the scent and the closeness of her, the grief and self-loathing vanished by this new intimacy. He knew he should tell her to stop, that this was inappropriate, but found himself too intoxicated to care.

'There.' She moved back, smiling down at him, a finger tracing over his chin. 'Much better.'

Possessed by a sudden and nearly irresistible impulse to pull her close again, he reached instead for the cloth to wipe away the remaining soap. 'Thank you, sister.'

'Brother Dentos was a good man,' she said. 'I'm sorry.'

'He was the son of a whore who grew up in a place where everyone hated him. For him there was no other role in this world than to fight and die in service to the Order. But you're right, he was a good man, and he deserved a longer life and a better death.'

'Why did you come here, Vaelin?' Her voice was soft, the anger gone now, her tone merely sorrowful. 'You detest this war, I can see it. Your skills, like mine, were not meant for this. We are supposed to serve a Faith that defends against greed and cruelty. What are we defending here? What did the King promise or threaten to force you to this?'

The impulse to lie, to continue to wallow in secrets as he had for years, was only the faintest whisper now, a nagging sense of stepping too far on an uncharted path, easily overridden by the need to tell her. If he couldn't hold her, at least he could find some comfort in confidence. 'He discovered my father has become a Denier. The Ascendant sect, I believe. Whatever that is.'

'We leave our ties of blood behind when we give ourselves in service to the Faith.'

'Do we? Did you? Your compassion was born somewhere, sister. In those streets you came from, amongst those beggared people you try so hard to save. Do we ever really leave anything behind?'

She closed her eyes, face downcast, unspeaking.

'I'm sorry,' he said. 'Your past is your own. I don't mean to . . .'

'My mother was a thief,' she said, eyes open now, meeting his gaze, a harsh, unfamiliar accent colouring her tone. 'Finest dipper the quarter ever saw. Hands like lightning, could have a ring off a merchant's finger quicker than a snake takes a rat. Never knew my father, she said he was a soldier, lost to the wars, but I knew she done some whorin' before she learned the trade. She taught me, y'see, said I had the hands for it.' She looked down at her hands, the deft, slender fingers clenching. 'I was her darlin' little thief, she said, and a thief never needs to be a whore.

'Turns out I wasn't quite the thief she thought I was. Fat old rich man with a fat old wife managed to corner me when I lifted her brooch. Was beating on me with his walking stick when my mum knifed him. "No-one hits my Sherry!" she said. She could've run but she stayed.' She crossed her arms, hugging herself. 'She stayed for me. She was still stabbin' away when the Guard came. They hanged her the next day. I was eleven years old.

'After the hanging I sat down and waited to die. Couldn't steal any more y'see, just couldn't. And it was all I knew how to do. No mum, no trade. I was done. Next morning a pretty lady in a grey robe asked if I needed help.'

He couldn't recall standing or pulling her close, but found her head was on his chest, breath catching as she fought down tears. 'I'm sorry, sister . . .'

She breathed deeply, her sobs fading, lifting her face, a small wry smile on her lips, whispering, 'I'm not your sister,' before she pressed them against his.

◆　◆　◆

'You taste' – Sherin's tongue played over his chest – 'of sand and sweat.' She wrinkled her nose. 'And you smell of smoke.'

'I'm sorry . . .'

She giggled a little, raising herself to kiss his cheek before pressing her nakedness against him, her head resting on his chest. 'I'm not complaining.'

His hands played over the slim smoothness of her shoulders, drawing a sigh of pleasure. 'I had heard that one had to be experienced at this to find it truly enjoyable,' he said.

'I heard that true devotion to the Faith would blind me to the lure of such pleasures.' She kissed him again, longer this time, tongue probing his lips. 'It appears you can't believe all you hear.'

They had lain together for hours, making love with urgent, whispered intimacy, Scratch posted outside the door to discourage visitors. The wonderful, electrifying feel of her against him, the caress of her breath on his neck as he moved in her, was overpowering, amazing. Despite the grief and the guilt and knowledge of what waited beyond this room, for now he was, perhaps for the first time he could remember, truly happy.

The dim light of dawn was filtering through the shutters on the window and he could see her face clearly, her smile of serene bliss as she drew back. 'I love you,' he told her, fingers tracing through her hair. 'I always have.'

She nuzzled against him, her hand playing over the hard muscle of his chest and belly. 'Really? After all these years apart?'

'I don't think love like that can ever really fade.' He clasped her hand, fingers entwining. 'The Blackhold. Were you . . . did they hurt you?'

'Only if terror is a kind of torture. I was only there for one night, but the things I heard.' She gave a small shudder and he pressed a kiss to her forehead.

'I'm sorry, I had to know. Your words must have carried great weight to have worried the King and Aspect Tendris so.'

'This war is more than just a mistake, Vaelin. It sullies our souls. It is against the Faith in every way. I had to speak out. No-one else would, not even Aspect Elera, though I begged her to. I started standing up in market squares and shouting it out to anyone who'd listen. To my surprise some did, especially in the poorer quarters. My words were written down, reproduced with that new ink-and-block device the Third Order uses. Pamphlets were being passed around in growing numbers, saying things like "End the War and Save the Faith."'

'Has a ring to it.'

'Thank you. It took two weeks for them to come for me, Brother Iltis and his men storming into the Order House with a King's warrant for my arrest. Brother Iltis is not the kindest of men, as you noticed, and took great delight in explaining to me in detail what was in store in the Blackhold. I lay awake all that night, listening to the screams. When the cell door opened I nearly fainted with fear, but it was Princess Lyrna with fresh clothes and a King's order for my release into her custody.'

Lyrna. What stratagem lay behind this I wonder? 'Then I am in her debt.'

'And I. Such a kindly and courageous soul is rare. She made sure I had everything I needed, a fine room of my own, books and parchment. We spent many hours talking in her secret garden. You know, I think she's a little lonely. When I left on receiving your summons she even cried. She said to give you her warmest regards by the way.'

'Kind of her.' He was keen to change the subject. 'What did he offer you? Janus, I know he must have tried to ensnare you in some kind of bargain.'

'Actually, I only met him once. The Guard Captain, Smolen, took me to his room. Rumours were flying around the city and the palace that he's not a well man these days, and I could see it clear as day in the greyness of his skin, the way his flesh hung on his bones. Probably the onset of age coupled with some wasting illness. I offered to examine him but he said he had physicians aplenty. After that he stared at me for a moment or two and asked me just one question. When I gave him an answer he laughed and told the captain to take me back to Princess Lyrna's quarters. It was a sad laugh, full of regret.'

'What did he ask you?'

She shifted, rising to her knees, the sheets falling away to reveal her slender form, her eyes glittered and he realised she was crying. 'He asked if I loved you. I said I did. And I do.' Her hands caressed his face with trembling fingers. 'I do. I should have gone away with you when you asked, all those years ago.'

The morning he awoke after the agony of her cure, after the Aspect massacre, after she had saved his life. 'I thought it was a dream.'

'Then it was one we shared.' Her hands stopped in midcaress, her tone suddenly hesitant. 'One we could still share. There is no longer a place for me in the Realm, and there is a whole world I've yet to see. We could see it together. Perhaps find a place where there are no kings, no wars, no people killing each other over faith and gods and money.'

He pulled her close, enfolding her in his arms, rejoicing in the warmth of her, inhaling the smell of her hair. 'There is something I have to do here. Something that has to happen.'

He felt her stiffen. 'If you mean to win this war, you must know that is a fool's hope. The Empire stretches for thousands of miles, from desert to frozen mountains, with more people than there are stars in the sky. Fight off one army and the Emperor is sure to send another, and another after that.'

'No, not the war. A task given to me by my Aspect. And I can't run from it, though I want to. When it's done, our dreams will be our own.'

She pressed closer, her lips touching his ear, whispering. 'You promise?'

'I promise.' He meant it, with all his soul, and couldn't understand why it felt like a lie.

The moment was broken by a loud growl from the hallway. Janril Noren, voice unnerved in the face of the angry slave-hound, called to him through the door.

Sherin put her hands to her lips to suppress a laugh and shrank into the covers as Vaelin reached for his trews. 'What is it?' he demanded, pulling the door open.

'There's an Alpiran at the gates demanding you come and fight him, my lord.' Janril's eyes slid from Vaelin's face to snatch a glance at the room beyond, before fixing on the still-growling Scratch. 'Captain Antesh offered to feather him but Brother Caenis thought you might want him alive.'

'What does he look like, this Alpiran?'

'Big fellow, greying hair. Dressed like one of those horsemen we fought at the beach. Seems in a bad way, having a hard time staying in the saddle. Too long in the desert I think.'

'How many with him?'

'None, my lord. He's all alone, if you can believe such a thing.'

'Tell Brother Frentis to muster the scout troop and inform Brother Caenis I'll be there directly.'

'My lord.'

He closed the door and began to dress.

'Are you going to fight him?' Sherin asked, emerging from the covers.

'You know I'm not.' He pulled his shirt on and leaned over to kiss her. 'I need you to do something for me.'

Captain Neliesen Nester Hevren sat slumped in his saddle, a desolate fatigue marring his unshaven face. However, as the gates swung open and he caught sight of Vaelin, his evident exhaustion was replaced by grim satisfaction.

'Found the courage to face me, Northman?' he called as Vaelin approached.

'I had no choice, my men were starting to lose all respect for me.' He looked beyond the captain at the empty desert. 'Where's your army?'

'Fools led by a coward!' Hevren spat. 'No stomach for what needed to be done here. Gods curse Everen, desert-born scum. The Emperor will take his head.' He fixed Vaelin with a stare of pure, unbridled hatred. 'But I'll have yours first, Hope Killer.'

Vaelin inclined his head. 'As you wish. Care to dismount or do you want it said you had an unfair advantage?'

'I need no advantage.' Hevren slid from his saddle with difficulty, desert sand shifting from his clothes, his horse giving a snort of relief. Vaelin surmised he had been in the saddle for days and noted how his legs sagged for a moment before he straightened.

'Here.' Vaelin unslung the canteen on his shoulder, removing the cap and taking a drink. 'Quench your thirst, lest people say *I* had the advantage.' He replaced the cap and tossed the canteen to Hevren.

'I need nothing from you,' Hevren said, but Vaelin saw how his hand shook as it held the canteen.

'Then stay here and rot,' he replied, turning to go.

'Wait!' Hevren uncapped the canteen and drank, gulping down the water until it was empty, then tossing it aside. 'No more talk,

Hope Killer.' He drew his sabre, planting his feet in a fighting stance, flicking a sudden rush of sweat from his brow.

'I'm sorry, Captain,' Vaelin told him. 'Sorry for the Hope, sorry we came here, sorry I can't give you the death you hunger for.'

'I said no more talk!' Hevren took a step forward, sabre drawing back for a thrust, then stopped, blinking in confusion, eyes suddenly unfocused.

'Two parts valerian, one part crown root and a pinch of camomile to mask the taste.' Vaelin held up the canteen cap he had switched for the one containing Sherin's sleeping draught. 'Sorry.'

'You . . .' Hevren stumbled forward a few steps before collapsing. 'No!' he grunted, desperately trying to heave himself upright. 'No . . .' He thrashed for a while longer then lay still.

Vaelin called to the Nilsaelin soldiers manning the gate. 'Find him somewhere comfortable but secure, and make sure you take all his weapons.'

Frentis arrived with the scout troop, reining in beneath the arch of the gatehouse. 'Couldn't have been much of a fight,' he observed as the Nilsaelins carried off Hevren's unconscious form.

'I've taken enough from him,' Vaelin replied. 'His army's nowhere in sight. Circle out to the west, see if you can pick up their trail.'

'You think they're making for Untesh?'

'Either there or back to Marbellis. Stay out for one day only, and take no chances. If you're spotted, ride back to the city.'

Frentis nodded and spurred his horse forward, the scout troop following close behind. Vaelin watched them ride towards the west and tried to ignore the faint trill of unease from the blood-song.

Night came with no sign of Frentis. He waited atop the gatehouse, gazing out at the desert, marvelling again at the clearness of the sky here, the vast array of stars shimmering above the night black sands.

'You worry about him.' Sherin appeared at his side, her fingers briefly touching the back of his hand before she folded her arms beneath her robe.

'He's my brother,' he replied. 'The captain still sleeps?'

'Like a child. He's as well as a man could be after days in the desert with little water.'

'Don't get too close to him when he wakes, he'll be angry.'

'He hates you very much.' Her voice was heavy with regret. 'They all do, these people, despite what you did for them . . .'

'I killed the heir to their Empire and brought a foreign army to their city. For all I know the Red Hand too. Let them have their hate, I earned it.'

She moved closer, casting a wary glance at the guard nearby, who seemed more preoccupied with the grit under his fingernails. 'The mason heals well but his sleep is troubled, his burns still cause him pain. I dull it as best I can but still he rants in his dreams, speaking languages I've never heard for the most part, but some in our tongue.' Her gaze was intent, questing. 'Some of the things he says . . .'

He raised an eyebrow. 'What does he say?'

'He talks of a song, of Singers, of a living wolf fashioned from stone, of a vile and deadly woman, and he talks of you, Vaelin. Maybe it's just nonsense, delusions and dreams born of drugs and pain, but they scare me. And you know I am not easily scared.'

He put his arm around her shoulders and pulled her close, ignoring her glance of alarm at the guard. 'What does it matter, now?' he asked.

'Your position, your role here.'

'Let them mutiny, depose me if they like.' He had raised his voice so the guard could hear, although the man was now intensely interested in looking anywhere but at him. If he was any judge of soldierly gossip, it would be all over the barracks by morning. He found he couldn't care a jot.

'Stop it.' She shrugged free of him, flustered but also suppressing a laugh.

The guard cleared his throat and Vaelin turned to find him pointing out at the desert. 'Troop returning, my lord.'

The gates swung open to allow the scout troop to enter at a weary trot, Vaelin instantly alarmed that Frentis was not among them. 'The Alpiran host was less than ten miles from Untesh when we found it, my lord,' explained Sergeant Halkin, Frentis's second in command. 'Brother Frentis elected to ride ahead and warn Prince Malcius of the danger. He ordered us to return here to bring word to you.'

Vaelin briefly clasped Sherin's hand and strode off towards the stables, calling over his shoulder. 'Fetch Brother Barkus and Brother Caenis!'

CHAPTER TEN

'Well, that's that,' Barkus said.

'Clever,' Caenis murmured. 'We didn't give this Alpiran enough credit, it seems.'

A thick column of smoke rose from the city of Untesh to stain the morning sky. Hundreds of corpses littered the ground before the walls, where scaling ladders reached up to the battlements like stacked kindling. Through the smoke Vaelin could see a standard snapping in the breeze, crossed sabres of black on a red background, the same standard he had seen at the oasis. The Alpiran Battle Lord had eschewed siege for an all-out assault, accepting dreadful losses to reclaim the city for the Emperor. Untesh had fallen. Prince Malcius and Frentis were dead or captured.

I am a murderer . . .

'We should keep this from the men,' Caenis said. 'The effect on morale . . .'

'No,' Vaelin said. 'We tell them the truth. They know I won't lie to them. Trust is more important than fear.'

'He could've made it out,' Barkus suggested, although his tone lacked conviction. 'Got to a ship, maybe.'

Vaelin closed his eyes, trying to calm his thoughts, attempting to cast the blood-song forth as he had when he lost Dentos in the sandstorm. The note was even, unwavering, and found no answer. 'He's not there,' he whispered, hope surging in his breast. He had entertained a half-mad notion of waiting until darkness then finding a way over the walls to search for Frentis amidst the aftermath of the battle, although he was fully aware the most likely outcome would be a swift death. *But if he's not here, then where? He wouldn't have deserted the prince.*

'Outriders,' Caenis said, pointing to the plain before the city, where a body of horsemen were raising a thick cloud of dust as they galloped towards their position.

'Can't be more than a dozen.' Barkus unhitched his axe from his saddle and unfastened the leather cover on the blades. 'A little recompense, for the prince and our brother.'

'Leave it.' Vaelin pulled on Spit's reins, turning him away from the city. 'Let's go.'

Another month passed as they waited for the storm. He trained the men hard, drilling them until they sagged with exhaustion, ensuring each man knew his place on the walls and was fit and skilful enough to at least survive the first assault when it came. He sensed their fear and growing resentment but had no answer to it but more training and sterner discipline. To his surprise, their mingled fear and respect held true and there were no desertions, even after Barkus returned from a reconnaissance to Marbellis with news that it too had fallen.

'Place is near a ruin,' the big brother related, swinging down from his horse. 'Walls breached in six places, half the houses wrecked by fire and I lost count of the Alpirans camped outside.'

'Prisoners?' Vaelin asked.

His brother's usually cheerful visage was entirely grim. 'There were spikes on the walls, lots of spikes, each one topped with a head. If they spared anyone, I didn't see them.'

The Battle Lord . . . Alucius . . . Master Sollis . . .

'What fools we were to let the old bastard send us here,' Barkus was saying.

'Get some rest, brother,' Vaelin told him.

At night Sherin would come to him and they would make love, finding blessed relief in intimacy, lying coiled together in the dark afterwards. Sometimes she would cry small, jerking sobs she tried to hide. 'Don't,' he would whisper. 'All be over soon.'

After a while her sobs would subside and she would cling to him, lips covering his face with a desperate urgency. She, like every other soul in the city, knew what was coming. The Alpirans would break over the walls like a wave and he and every other Realm subject in arms would die here.

'We can go,' she said one night, imploring. 'There are still ships in the harbour. We can just sail away.'

His hand traced over her smooth brow, the fine curve of her cheek and the elegant line of her chin. It was wonderful to touch her face, to feel her shiver at his touch before a warm flush crept over her skin. 'Remember my promise, my love,' he said, thumbing a tear from her eye.

He was touring the walls the next morning when Caenis came with word of Realm vessels approaching the harbour. 'How many?'

'Near forty.' His brother appeared unsurprised by the turn of events. The idea that the King would leave them to wither unsupported seemed not to have occurred to him at all. 'We're to be reinforced.'

'There has been talk,' Caenis said as they waited on the quayside watching the first ship steer its way past the mole and into the harbour. His tone was uncomfortable but determined. 'About Sister Sherin.'

Vaelin shrugged. 'Well there might. We've hardly been discreet.' He glanced at Caenis, regretting his levity in the face of his brother's discomfort. 'I love her, brother.'

Caenis avoided his gaze, his tone heavy. 'According to the tenets of the Faith, you aren't my brother now.'

'Excellent. Feel free to depose me. I'll happily hand this city over to you . . .'

'Your position as Lord Marshal of the regiment and commander of this garrison was given you by the King, not the Order. I have no power to depose you. All I can do is report your . . . transgression to the Aspect for judgement.'

'If I live to be judged.'

Caenis gestured at the approaching ship. 'We're being reinforced. The King has not failed us. I think we'll all live awhile yet.'

In the distance Vaelin could see the rest of the fleet bobbing sluggishly on the swell. *Why do they linger out there?* he wondered, a realisation dawning as the ship drew nearer and he saw how high it sat in the water. This vessel carried no reinforcements.

Sailors threw ropes to soldiers on the quay as the ship tied up to the dock, a gangplank quickly heaved over the railing. He had expected some senior Realm Guard marshal to descend and was surprised by the appearance of a figure clad in the expensive garb of Realm nobility making an uncertain passage from ship to shore. It took a moment before Vaelin pulled the man's name from his memory, Kelden Al Telnar, one-time Minister of Royal Works. The man following Al Telnar was more to Vaelin's expectation, tall and simply dressed in a robe of blue and white with a neatly trimmed beard and mahogany dark skin.

'Lord Vaelin.' Al Telnar bowed as Vaelin came forward to greet them.

'My lord.'

'May I present Lord Merulin Nester Velsus, Grand Prosecutor of the Alpiran Empire, currently acting as Ambassador to the Court of King Janus.'

Vaelin gave the tall man a bow. 'Prosecutor, eh?'

'A poor translation,' Merulin Nester Velsus replied in near-perfect Realm tongue, his tone cool and his eyes tracking over Vaelin with predatory scrutiny. 'More accurately, I am the Instrument of the Emperor's Justice.'

Vaelin wasn't sure why he started laughing, but it took a long time to subside. Eventually he sobered and turned to Al Telnar. 'I take it you have a royal order for me?'

'These orders are clear to you, my lord?' Al Telnar was nervous, a faint sheen of sweat on his upper lip, his hands clasped tightly together on the table before him. But his clear satisfaction at being involved in a moment of such importance appeared to override any trepidation he might have harboured about delivering these orders to such a famously dangerous man.

Vaelin nodded. 'Quite clear.' They were in the council room at the merchants guild, the tall Alpiran Grand Prosecutor the only other occupant. The lack of witnesses had peeved Al Telnar, making him enquire as to the whereabouts of a scribe to record the proceedings. Vaelin hadn't bothered to answer.

'I have the King's Word in writing.' Al Telnar produced a leather satchel and extracted a sheaf of papers bearing the King's seal. 'If you would care to . . .'

Vaelin shook his head. 'I hear the King is unwell. Did he give you these orders himself?'

'Well, no. Princess Lyrna has been appointed Chamberlain, until such time as the King recovers of course.'

'But his illness doesn't prevent him issuing orders?'

'Princess Lyrna struck me as a very conscientious and dutiful daughter,' Lord Velsus put in. 'If it is any consolation, I discerned a considerable reluctance in her bearing when she reported her father's word.'

Vaelin found himself unable to suppress a chuckle. 'Ever played *Keschet*, my lord?'

Velsus narrowed his eyes, his lips curling in anger, and he leaned across the table. 'I do not understand your meaning, you ignorant savage. Nor do I care to. Your king has given his word, will you abide by it or not?'

'Erm,' Al Telnar cleared his throat. 'Princess Lyrna did ask me to pass on word of your father, my lord.' He balked at the intensity of the gaze Vaelin turned on him but forged ahead valiantly. 'It seems he too is unwell, the various maladies of age, I'm told. Although she wished to assure you she does all she can to sustain him. And hopes to continue to do so.'

'Do you know why she chose you, my lord?' Vaelin asked him.

'I assumed she recognised the good service I have provided . . .'

'She chose you because it will be no loss to the Realm if I kill you.' He turned to the Alpiran. 'Wait outside. I have business with Lord Velsus.'

Alone with the Alpiran Grand Prosecutor he could feel the man's hatred like fire, his eyes were alive with it. Al Telnar may have relished the import of the moment, but he could see Lord Velsus cared nothing for history, only justice. Or was it vengeance?

'I'm told he was a good man,' he said. 'The Hope.'

Velsus's eyes flashed and his voice was a hard rasp. 'You could never understand the greatness of the man you killed, the enormity of what you took from us.'

He remembered the clumsy charge of the man in the white armour, the blind disregard for his own safety as he sped towards death. Had that been greatness? Courage certainly, unless the man had expected the fabled favour of the gods to protect him. In any case, the frenzy of battle left little room for admiration or reflection. The Hope had been just another enemy in need of killing. He regretted it but could still find no room for guilt in the memory, and the blood-song had ever been silent on the subject.

'I began this war with four brothers,' he told Velsus. 'Now one is dead and the other lost to the mists of battle. The two that remain . . .' His voice faded. *The two that remain . . .*

'I care nothing for your brothers,' Velsus replied. 'The Emperor's mercy is a great agony to me. If it were within my gift, I would see your entire army flayed and driven into the desert as a feast for the vultures.'

Vaelin met his gaze squarely. 'If there is the slightest attempt to interfere with the safe passage of my men . . .'

'The Emperor's Word has been given, written and witnessed. It cannot be broken.'

'To do so would be against the gods' will?'

'No, the law. We are an Empire of laws, savage. Laws that bind even the greatest of us. The Emperor's Word is given.'

'Then it seems I have no choice but to trust it. I request it be noted that Governor Aruan gave no assistance to my forces during our tenure here. He has remained a loyal servant of the Emperor throughout.'

'The governor will give his own testimony, I'm sure.'

Vaelin nodded. 'Very well.' He rose from the table. 'Tomorrow at dawn then, a mile south of the main gate. I assume there are some Alpiran forces nearby awaiting your word. It would be best if you spent the night with them.'

'If you think I will allow you out of my sight until . . .'

'Do you want me to flog you from this city?' His tone was mild but he knew the Alpiran could hear its sincerity.

Velsus's features quivered with a mixture of fury and fear. 'Do you know what awaits you, savage? When you are mine . . .'

'I have to trust your Emperor's Word. You'll have to trust mine.' Vaelin turned to the door. 'There is a captain of the Imperial Guard in our custody. I'll ask him to act as your escort. Please be out of the city within the hour. And feel free to take Lord Al Telnar with you.'

He had the men assembled in the main square, Renfaelin knights and squires, Cumbraelin archers, Nilsaelins and Realm Guard all drawn up in ranks awaiting his word. His dislike of speech-making was still undimmed and he saw little point in preamble.

'The war is over!' he told them, standing atop a cart and casting his voice towards the rear ranks so they all heard clearly. 'His Highness King Janus agreed to a treaty with the Alpiran Emperor three weeks ago. We are ordered to quit the city and return to the Realm. Ships are now berthing in the harbour to take us home. You will proceed to the docks in companies, taking only your packs and weapons. No Alpiran property is to be removed on pain of execution.' He scanned the ranks briefly. There were no cheers, no rejoicing, just surprised relief on nearly every face. 'On behalf of King Janus, I thank you for your service. Stand at ease and await orders.'

'It's really over?' Barkus asked as he stepped down from the cart.

'All over,' he assured him.

'What made the old fool give it up?'

'Prince Malcius lies dead in Untesh, the bulk of the army was destroyed at Marbellis and trouble brews in the Realm. I assume he wants to preserve as much of his army as he can.'

He noticed Caenis standing nearby, possibly the only man not joining his voice to the massed babble of relief. His brother's slender face showed a mix of mystification and what could only be described as grief. 'It seems there's to be no Greater Unified Realm, brother,' he said, keeping his tone gentle.

Caenis's gaze was distant, as if deep in shock. 'He does not make mistakes,' he said softly. 'He never makes mistakes . . .'

'We're going home!' Vaelin laid hands on his shoulders, giving him a shake. 'You'll be back at the Order House in a couple of weeks.'

'Bugger the Order House,' Barkus said. 'I'll be making for the nearest dockside tavern, where I intend to stay until this whole bloody farce has become a bad dream.'

Vaelin clasped hands with them both. 'Caenis, your company will take the first ship. Barkus, take the second. I'll keep order while the rest of the men embark.'

Lord Al Telnar opted to take the first ship home rather than wait for the climax of this moment in history, his face stiff with resentment when Vaelin delayed him at the gangplank. 'Tell my brother nothing of the treaty until you reach the Realm.' He glanced over at where Caenis stood on the prow of the ship, his bearing still so forlorn. They had all lost more than they should in this war, friends and brothers, but Caenis had lost his delusion, his dream of Janus's greatness. He wondered if his desolation would turn to hate when he heard the full details of the treaty.

'As you wish,' Al Telnar replied shortly. 'Anything further, my lord, or may I depart?'

He felt he should give him some message for Princess Lyrna but found he had nothing to say. As he could feel no guilt over killing the Hope, he was surprised to discover he also had no more anger towards her.

He stood aside to let Al Telnar board and waved to Caenis as the gangplank was hauled aboard and the ship began to pull away from the quay. Caenis answered with a brief and distracted wave of his own before turning away. 'Good-bye, brother,' Vaelin whispered.

Barkus was next to go, urging his men aboard with a hearty bluster that failed to mask the haunted look his eyes had taken on since his return from Marbellis. 'Come on, step faster, you lot. Whores and innkeepers won't wait forever.' His mask almost slipped completely when Vaelin approached, his face tense as he fought to suppress tears. 'You're not coming, are you?'

Vaelin smiled and shook his head. 'I can't, brother.'

'Sister Sherin?'

He nodded. 'There's a ship waiting to take us to the Far West. Ahm Lin knows of a quiet corner of the world where we can live in peace.'

'Peace. Wonder what that's like. Think you'll like it?'

Vaelin laughed. 'I have no idea.' He extended his hand, but Barkus ignored it to enfold him in a crushing embrace.

'Any message for the Aspect?' he asked, stepping back.

'Only that I've decided to leave the Order. He can keep the coins.'

Barkus nodded, hefted his hateful axe and strode up the gangplank without a backward glance. He stood unmoving on the foredeck as the ship pulled away, like one of Ahm Lin's statues, a great and noble warrior frozen in stone. Vaelin would always prefer to think of him like this in the years that followed.

He stayed on the quay to watch them all leave, Lord Al Trendil hounding his regiment onto the ships with a flurry of waspish insults, offering Vaelin the most cursory of bows before boarding. It seemed he had never quite forgiven him for taking away the chance of profiting from the war. Count Marven's Nilsaelins scrambled aboard the ships with unabashed eagerness, a few calling jocular farewells to Vaelin as they sailed away. The count himself seemed unusually cheerful, now all chance of glory had evaporated, it seemed he had no more cause for enmity. 'I lost more men to brawls than to battle,' he said, offering Vaelin his hand. 'For which I think my Fief owes you its thanks, my lord.'

Vaelin shook his hand. 'What will you do now?'

Marven shrugged. 'Go back to hunting outlaws and wait for the next war.'

'You'll forgive me if I hope you have a long wait.'

The count grunted a laugh and strolled onto his ship, accepting a bottle of wine from his men, who sang heartily as the ship drew away,

Desert winds blow hard at me
Till we reach the shining sea.
And borne away across the waves
My lover's life I'll sail to save.

Baron Banders and his knights laboured onto the ships under the weight of their disassembled armour. Of all the contingents their mood was the most varied, a few weeping openly over the loss of the great warhorses, which had had to be left behind, others clearly drunk and laughing uproariously.

'A sorry spectacle they make without armour and horses, eh?' Banders asked, his own faux-rusted plate balanced on the shoulders of an unfortunate squire who stumbled several times before successfully heaving it onto the ship.

'They're fine men,' Vaelin told him. 'Without them this city would have fallen and there would be no homecoming for any of us.'

'True enough. When you return to the Realm I hope you'll visit me. Always a full table in my manor.'

'I shall, and gladly.' He shook the baron's hand. 'You should know Al Telnar brought details of events at Marbellis. It seems the Battle Lord and a few others managed to fight their way to the docks when the walls fell. About fifty men managed to escape in all, Fief Lord Theros was not among them but his son was.'

The baron's laugh was harsh and his face grim. 'Vermin always find a way to survive, it seems.'

'Forgive me, Baron, but what happened at Marbellis to cause the Fief Lord to dismiss you? You've never told me.'

'When we finally fought our way in the slaughter was terrible, and not confined to Alpiran soldiery. Women and children . . .' He closed his eyes and sighed. 'I found Darnel and two of his knights raping a girl next to the bodies of her parents. She couldn't have been more than thirteen. I killed the two others and was trying to geld Darnel when the Fief Lord's mace laid me low. "He's scum, right enough," he told me the next day. "But he's also the only son I have." So he sent me to you.'

'Have a care when you return to your lands. Lord Darnel doesn't strike me as a forgiving soul.'

Banders replied with a grim smile, 'Neither am I, brother.'

Sergeants Krelnik, Gallis and Janril Noren were the last of the Wolfrunners to leave. He shook hands with each of them and thanked them for their service. 'It's been less than ten years,' he told Gallis. 'But if you wish to be released, it is within my discretion.'

'We'll see you in the Realm, my lord!' Gallis said, snapping off an impeccable salute and marching onto the ship, quickly followed by Krelnik and Noren.

The Cumbraelin archers were the last contingent onto the ships. He had offered to place them ahead of the Renfaelins for fear they might suspect some perfidious Darkblade plot to abandon them to the Alpirans, but Bren Antesh had surprised him by insisting they wait until all others had gone. He supposed there was a possibility of ambush, he was alone with a thousand men who saw him as an enemy of their god after all, but they all trooped onto the ships without trouble, most either ignoring him or offering nods of wary respect.

'They're grateful for their lives,' Antesh said, reading his expression. 'But they'll be dammed if they'll say it. So I will.' He bowed, Vaelin realising it was the first time he had done so.

'You're welcome, Captain.'

Antesh straightened, glanced at the waiting ship and then back at Vaelin. 'This is the last ship, my lord.'

'I know.'

Antesh raised his eyebrows as realisation dawned. 'You don't intend to return to the Realm.'

'I have business elsewhere.'

'You shouldn't linger here. All these people have to offer you is an ugly death.'

'Is that what happens to the Darkblade in the prophecy?'

'Hardly. He is seduced by a sorceress, who makes herself a queen with the power to conjure fire from the air. Together they wreak terrible ruin on the world until her fire consumes him in the throes of their sinful passion.'

'Well, at least I have that to look forward to.' He returned Antesh's bow. 'Luck to you, Captain.'

'I have something to tell you,' Antesh said, his normally placid features sombre. 'I did not always carry the name Antesh. Once I had another name, one you know.'

The blood-song surged, not in warning, but clear and strident triumph. 'Tell me,' he said.

Ahm Lin's burns had healed well but his scars would linger for the rest of his life. A large patch of puckered, discoloured tissue marred the right side of his face from cheek to neck and similarly ugly scars were visible on his arms and chest. Despite this, he appeared as affable as ever, although his sadness at what Vaelin asked of him was obvious.

'She has preserved me, cared for me,' he said. 'To do such a thing . . .'

'Would you do any less for your wife?' Vaelin asked.

'I would follow my song, brother. Are you?'

He recalled the pure, triumphant note of the blood-song as he had listened to what Antesh had to say. 'More closely than I ever have before.' He met the mason's gaze. 'Will you do this thing I ask?'

'It seems our songs are in agreement, so I have little choice.'

Sherin knocked at the door and entered, bearing a bowl of soup. 'He needs to eat,' she said, placing the bowl next to the mason's bed and turning to Vaelin. 'And you need to help me pack.'

Vaelin touched Ahm Lin briefly on the hand by way of thanks and followed her from the room. She had taken over Sister Gilma's old quarters in the basement of the guild house and was busily sorting out which of the myriad bottles and boxes of curatives to take with her. 'I've managed to procure a small chest for your things,' she told him, moving to a shelf where her hand traced along the line of bottles, picking out some, leaving others.

'I only have these,' he replied, taking a bundle from his cloak and handing it to her, the wooden blocks Frentis had brought him wrapped in Sella's scarf. 'Not much of a dowry, I know.'

She gently undid the scarf, fingers pausing to play over the intricate design. 'Very fine. Where did you come by this?'

'A gift of thanks from a beautiful maiden.'

'Should I be jealous?'

'Hardly. She's half a world away and, I suspect, married to a handsome blond fellow we used to know.'

Sherin pulled the blocks apart. 'Winterbloom.'

'From my sister.'

'You have a sister? A blood sister?'

'Yes. I only met her once. We spoke of flowers.'

She reached to clasp his hand, summoning an overpowering need for her, so fierce and powerful as to almost make him forget what he had asked of Ahm Lin, forget the Aspect, the war, the whole sorry blood-soaked tale. Almost.

'Governor Aruan is arranging the ship, but we have hours yet,' he said, moving to the table where she prepared her concoctions, sitting down to unstopper a bottle of wine. 'Quite possibly the last bottle of Cumbraelin red left in the city. Will you drink with a former Lord Marshal of the Thirty-fifth Regiment of Foot, Sword of the Realm and brother of the Sixth Order?'

She arched an eyebrow. 'Have I saddled myself with a drunkard, I wonder?'

He reached for two cups and poured a measure of red in each. 'Just have a drink, woman.'

'Yes, my lord,' she said in mock servility, sitting opposite and reaching for a cup. 'Did you tell them?'

'Just Barkus. The others think I'm following on the last ship.'

'We could still go back. With the war over . . .'

'There's no place for you there, now. You said so yourself.'

'But you're losing so much.'

He reached across the table and grasped her hand. 'I'm losing nothing and gaining everything.'

She smiled and sipped her wine. 'And the task the Aspect set you, is it complete?'

'Not quite. By the time we leave here it will be.'

'Can you tell me now? Am I finally allowed to know?'

He squeezed her hand. 'I don't see why not.'

It had been cold that day, colder than usual even for Weslin. Aspect Arlyn stood at the edge of the practice field, watching Master Haunlin teach the staff to a group of novice brothers. Vaelin judged them as third-year survivors from their age and the comparative smallness of the group. In the distance, mad Master Rensial was trying to ride down another group of boys, his shrill tones carrying well in the chill air.

'Brother Vaelin,' the Aspect greeted him.

'Aspect. I request lodging for the Thirty-fifth Regiment of Foot during the winter months.' At the Aspect's insistence it had become a ritual between them to formally request lodging every time the regiment returned to the Order House, recognition of the fact that, funding and equipment notwithstanding, it remained a part of the Realm Guard.

'Granted. How was Nilsael?'

'Cold, Aspect.' They had spent the better part of three months on the Nilsaelin border with Cumbreael, hunting a particularly savage and fanatical band of god worshippers calling themselves the Sons of the Trueblade. One of their less savoury habits was the abduction and forcible conversion of Nilsaelin children, many of whom had been subjected to various forms of abuse to force their adherence, some killed outright when they proved too intractable or troublesome. The pursuit through the hill country and valleys of southern Nilsael had been difficult but the regiment had harried the band with such ferocity they were down to barely thirty men by the time they were cornered in a deep gulley. They immediately killed their remaining captives, a brother and sister of eight and nine stolen from a Nilsaelin farmhouse a few days before, then loosed arrows at the Wolfrunners whilst singing prayers to their god. Vaelin left it to Dentos and his archers to wipe them out to a man, something he found troubled his conscience not at all.

'Casualties?' the Aspect enquired.

'Four dead, ten injured.'

'Regrettable. And what did you learn about these, what was it, Sons of the Trueblade?'

'They considered themselves followers of Hentes Mustor, believed by many Cumbraelins to embody the prophesied Trueblade from their Fifth Book.'

'Ah, yes. Apparently there is an eleventh book being touted around Cumbrael, The Book of the Trueblade, telling the tale of the Usurper's life and martyrdom. The Cumbraelin bishops have condemned it as heretical but many of their followers are clamouring to read it. It's always the way with such things, burn a book and the ashes spawn a thousand copies. It seems by killing one lunatic we have grown another branch to their church. Ironic, don't you think?'

'Very, Aspect.' He hesitated, gathering strength for what he had to say, but as ever the Aspect was ahead of him.

'King Janus wants my support for his war.'

Does anything ever surprise you? Vaelin wondered. 'Yes, Aspect.'

'Tell me, Vaelin, do you believe Alpiran spies lurk in every alleyway and bush preparing the way for their armies to invade our lands?'

'No, Aspect.'

'And do you believe Alpiran Deniers abduct our children to defile in unspeakable god-worshipping rites?'

'No, Aspect.'

'In that case do you think that the future wealth and prosperity of this Realm is dependent on securing the three principal Alpiran ports on the Erinean Sea?'

'I do not, Aspect.'

'And yet you come to ask for my support on behalf of the King?'

'I come to ask for guidance. The King has placed my father and his family under threat in order to ensure my obedience, but I find I cannot preserve them whilst thousands die in a pointless war. There must be some way to steer the King away from this course, some pressure that can be brought against him. If all the Orders were to speak as one . . .'

'The time when the Orders spoke as one is long past. Aspect Tendris hungers for war against the Unfaithful like an ale-starved drunkard whilst our brothers in the Third Order lose themselves in their books and watch the events of the world with cold detachment. The Fifth Order by custom takes no part in politics and as for the First and Second, they consider communion with their souls and the souls of the Departed to take precedence over all earthly concerns.'

'Aspect, I am given to believe there is another Order, with possibly more power than all the others combined.'

He was expecting some register of shock or alarm, but the Aspect's only expression was a slightly raised eyebrow. 'I see this is the day all secrets are to be revealed, brother.' He clasped his long-fingered hands together and concealed them within his robe, turning and gesturing with his head. 'Come, walk with me.'

Frost crunched underfoot as they walked together in silence. From the practice field came the shouts and grunts of pain and triumph he remembered so well. It made him ache with unexpected nostalgia, for all the pain and the loss of his years within these walls it had been a simpler time, before the schemes of kings and the secrets of the Faith brought darkness and confusion into his life.

'How did you come by this knowledge?' the Aspect asked eventually.

'I met a man in the north, a brother of an order long thought to be a myth by the Faithful.'

'He told you of the Seventh Order?'

'Not without persuasion and only up to a point. He did confirm that the continued existence of the Seventh Order is a secret known to all the Aspects. Although, given the recent rift with the Fourth Order, I suspect Aspect Tendris remains in ignorance of this information.'

'Indeed he does, and it is vital his ignorance continues. Wouldn't you agree?'

'Certainly, Aspect.'

'What do you know of the Seventh Order?'

'That it is to the Dark as we are to war and the Fifth Order is to healing.'

'Quite so, although our brothers and sisters in the Seventh Order do not refer to the Dark. They regard themselves as guardians and practitioners of dangerous and arcane knowledge, much of which defies such mundane concepts as names or categories.'

'And would they use such knowledge to aid us?'

'Of course, they always have and continue to do so to this day.'

'The man I met in the north spoke of a war within the Faith, of some within the Seventh Order becoming corrupted by their power.'

'Corrupted or deluded. Who can say? There is much that remains known only to the vanished years. What is clear is that members of the Seventh Order came to possess knowledge best left hidden, that somehow they reached into the Beyond and touched something, some spirit or being of such power and malice that it came close to destroying our Faith and the Realm with it.'

'But it was defeated?'

'"Contained" might be a better word. But it lurks there still, in the Beyond, waiting, and there are those called to do its bidding, plotting and killing at its instruction.'

'The Aspect massacre.'

'That and more.'

Vaelin thought back to his confrontation with One Eye beneath the city, of what he had told Frentis as he carved the complex pattern of scars into his chest. 'The One Who Waits.'

This time the Aspect's surprise was clear. 'You have been busy haven't you?'

'Who is he?'

The Aspect paused, turning to regard the boys on the practice field. 'Perhaps he's Master Rensial, his apparent madness all these years merely a cloak for his true design. Or he's Master Haunlin, who never did say how he came by those burns. Or is he you, I wonder?' There was an unnerving intensity to the Aspect's gaze as he turned to Vaelin. 'What better disguise could there be, after all? Son of the Battle Lord, courageous in all things, apparently without flaw, loved by the Faithful. What better disguise indeed.'

Vaelin nodded. 'Quite. It would only be surpassed by you, Aspect.'

The Aspect blinked slowly and turned away to resume his walk. 'My point is that he remains too well hidden and no device or effort by the Seventh Order has yet revealed him. He could be a brother of the Order or a soldier in your regiment. Or even someone with no connection to the Order at all. The prophecies are vague on the method but are clear that it is the purpose of the One Who Waits to destroy this Order.'

Vaelin frowned in puzzlement. The concept of prophecy was not a feature of the Faith. Prophets and their visions were the province of false beliefs, of god worshippers and Deniers who clung to superstition they mistook for wisdom. 'Prophecies, Aspect?'

'The One Who Waits was foretold to us many years ago by the Seventh Order. There are some within their ranks who have the gift of scrying the future, or at least the ever-changing clouds of shadow that make up the future, so they tell me. It is rare for the visions produced by such people to concur, for the shadows to coalesce into a recognisable whole, but they all agreed on two things: we will have only one chance to discover the One Who Waits and if we fail to do so, then this Order will fall, and without this Order so falls the Faith and the Realm.'

'But we have a chance to stop it?'

'One chance, yes. The last brother to make a prophecy on the subject lived over a century ago, it's said he would slip into a trance and write his visions in script more precise and artful than the most skilled scribe in the land, even though he was unable to read or write when the trance was not upon him. Shortly before he died he reached once more for his pen and left a short passage. "War will unmask the One Who Waits when a king sends his army to fight beneath a desert sun. He'll seek the death of his brother and mayhap find his own.'"

The death of his brother . . .

'You survived two attempts on your life whilst still in training,' the Aspect went on. 'We believe both were carried out by those in service to whatever malignance lurks in the Beyond. For some reason it greatly desires your death.'

'If the One Who Waits is concealed within the Order, why not simply have him kill me?'

'Either because no such opportunity has yet arisen or because to do so would have risked revealing his face, and he still has much to do. But amidst the chaos of war, surrounded by so much death, he may well take his chance.'

Vaelin felt a chill that owed nothing to the icy winds sweeping across the practice field. 'The King's war is our chance?'

'Our only chance.'

'Foretold by a man scribbling in a trance more than a hundred years ago. You are willing to commit the Order to war on the basis of this alone?'

'After all you have seen, all you have learned, can you really doubt it? This war will happen whether we support it or not. The King has set his course and will not be dissuaded.'

'If it happens, the Realm could fall in any case.'

'And if it doesn't, it will certainly fall. Not to warring Fiefs once more but to utter ruin, the earth scorched, the forests burned to cinder and all the people, Realm folk, Seordah and Lonak, dead. What else would you have us do?'

'I couldn't think of anything to say,' Vaelin told Sherin, his thumb tracing over the smooth skin of her hand. 'He was right. It was horrible, terrible, but he was right. He told me this would be a war unlike any we have known. A great sacrifice would be made. But I must return. No matter how many of my men and my brothers fell, I must return to the Realm once I had completed my task. As he walked away he told me I reminded him of my mother. I often wondered how they came to know each other, now I suppose I'll never find out.'

Her head lay on the table, eyes closed, lips parted, her hand still holding the wine cup he had given her. 'Two parts valerian, one part crown root and a pinch of camomile to mask the taste,' he said, stroking her hair. 'Try not to hate me.'

He dressed her in her cloak, tucking the scarf and blocks in the folds, and carried her to the harbour. She was light in his arms, fragile. Ahm Lin waited on the quay next to a large merchant vessel, his wife Shoala clutching his hand, her face tight with suppressed tears as she cast a forlorn gaze at the city she would likely never see again. Governor Aruan was negotiating with the vessel's captain, a stocky man from the Far West who grew alarmed at the sight of Vaelin. Perhaps he had been one of the captains forced to watch the burning ships after the sailors' escape attempt, Vaelin couldn't remember, but he quickly concluded his haggling with the governor and stomped off up the gangplank.

'The price is agreed,' the governor told Ahm Lin. 'They sail direct for the Far West, first port of call . . .'

'It's better if I don't know,' Vaelin cut in.

Ahm Lin came forward to take Sherin from him, lifting her easily in his muscular mason's arms.

'Tell her they killed me,' Vaelin said. 'As the ship pulled away from the dock, the Emperor's Guard arrived and killed me.'

The mason gave a reluctant nod. 'As the song wills it, brother.'

'She could stay here,' Governor Aruan offered. 'The city owes her a great debt after all. She would be in no danger.'

'Do you really think Lord Velsus will share your gratitude, Governor?' Vaelin asked him.

The governor sighed. 'Perhaps not.' He took a leather purse from his belt and handed it to Shoala. 'For her, when she wakes. With my thanks.'

The woman nodded, cast a final hateful glare at Vaelin then a tearful glance at the city, before turning and striding up the gangplank.

Vaelin reached out to trace his fingers through Sherin's hair, trying to burn the image of her sleeping face into his memory. 'Take care of her,' he told Ahm Lin.

Ahm Lin smiled. 'My song would have it no other way.' He turned to go then hesitated. 'My song holds no note of farewell, brother. I can't help but think that one day we'll sing together again.'

Vaelin nodded, stepping back as Ahm Lin carried Sherin onto the ship. He stood with the governor as the ship pulled away from the dock, riding the tide to the harbour mouth, sails unfurling to catch the northerly winds, taking her away. He waited and watched until the sail was a faint smudge on the horizon, until it had vanished completely and there was only the sea and the wind.

He unbuckled his sword and held it out to Aruan. 'Governor, the city is yours. I am commanded to wait for Lord Velsus beyond the walls.'

Aruan looked at the sword but made no move to take it. 'I will speak for you, I have some influence at the Emperor's court. He is famed for his mercy . . .' He faltered and stopped, perhaps hearing the emptiness of his words. After a moment he spoke again, 'Thank you for my daughter's life, my lord.'

'Take it,' Vaelin insisted, again holding out the sword. 'I'd rather you than Lord Velsus.'

'As you wish.' The governor took the sword in his plump hands. 'Is there nothing I can do for you?'

'Actually, about my dog . . .'

PART V

In longer games, where the Liar's Attack or one of the other openings outlined above has failed, the complexity of Keschet is fully revealed. The following chapters will examine the most effective stratagems to be employed in the long game, beginning with the Bowman's Switch, taking its name from a manoeuvre employed by Alpiran horse archers. Like the Liar's Attack, the Bowman's Switch employs misdirection but also retains the potential for exploiting unforeseen opportunity. A skilled player can move offensively against two objectives, leaving the opponent ignorant of the ultimate target until the most fruitful opportunity presents itself.

—AUTHOR UNKNOWN, KESCHET – *RULES AND STRATEGIES*,
GREAT LIBRARY OF THE UNIFIED REALM

VERNIERS' ACCOUNT

'And?'

Al Sorna had fallen to silence after relating his final words to the governor. 'And what?' he enquired.

I bit down my exasperation. It was becoming increasingly apparent that the Northman took no small pleasure from vexing me. 'And what followed?'

'You know what followed. I waited outside the walls, in the morning Lord Velsus came with a troop of Imperial Guards to take me into custody. Prince Malcius was duly delivered to the Realm unharmed. Janus died shortly after. Your history was fulsome in its description of my trial. What else can I tell you?'

I realised he was right; insofar as recorded history could relate, he had told me the entirety of his tale, providing a great deal of previously unknown information and clarification on the origins of the war and the nature of the Realm that had spawned it. But I found myself possessed of a conviction that there was more, an unshakeable sense that his tale was incomplete. I recalled moments when his voice had faltered, only slightly but enough to assure me he had been holding back, perhaps concealing truths he had no desire to reveal. As I looked at the wealth of words adorning the sheets that now covered the deck around my bedroll, my mood darkened as I considered the work involved in verifying this narrative, the extensive research that would be needed to corroborate such a story. Where is the truth amongst all this? I wondered.

'So,' I said, gathering my papers, taking care to keep them in order. 'This is the answer to the war? Simply the folly of a desperate old man?'

Al Sorna had settled onto his bedroll, hands clasped behind his head, eyes cast to the ceiling, his expression sombre and distant. He yawned. 'That's all I can tell you, my lord. Now, if you'll allow me some rest, I have to face certain death tomorrow and would prefer to meet it fully refreshed.'

I sifted through the pages, my quill picking out those passages where I suspected he had been less than forthcoming. To my dismay I found there were more than I would have liked, even a few contradictions. 'You said you never met her again,' I said. 'Yet you say Princess Lyrna was present at the Summertide Fair where Janus embroiled you in his warmongering scheme.'

He sighed, not turning. 'We exchanged a cursory greeting only. I didn't think it worth mentioning.'

A dim memory came to me, a fragment from my own researches undertaken whilst preparing my history of the war. 'What about the mason?'

It was only the briefest hesitation but it told me a great deal. 'Mason?'

'The mason at Linesh you befriended. His house was set alight because of it. It was a well-known story when I researched your occupation of the city. Yet you make no mention of him.'

He rolled onto his back and shrugged. 'Hardly a friendship. I wanted him to carve a statue of Janus for the town square. Something to confirm his ownership of the city. Needless to say the mason refused. Didn't stop someone burning his house down though. I believe he and his wife left the city when the war ended, with good reason it seems.'

'And the sister of your faith who stopped the red plague from ravaging the city,' I pressed, angrier now. 'What of her? The city folk I interviewed told many tales of her kindness and her closeness to you. Some even thought you were lovers.'

He shook his head wearily. 'That is absurd. As for what became of her, I assume she returned to the Realm with the army.'

He was lying, I was sure of it. 'Why relate this tale if you have no intention of telling me all of it?' I demanded. 'Do you seek to make me a fool, Hope Killer?'

Al Sorna grunted a laugh. 'A fool is any man who doesn't think he's a fool. Let me sleep, my lord.'

In the twenty years since its destruction the Meldeneans had made strenuous efforts to rebuild their capital on a grander and more ornate scale, perhaps seeking defiance in architectural achievement. The city clustered around the wide natural harbour on the southern shore of Ildera, the largest island in the archipelago, a vista of gleaming marble walls and red-tiled rooftops interspersed with tall columns honouring the islanders' myriad sea gods. I had read how Al Sorna's equally formidable father had overseen the toppling of the columns when his army stormed ashore bringing fire and destruction. Survivors spoke of Realm Guards urinating on the fallen statues that sat atop the columns, drunk on blood and victory, chanting, 'A god is a lie!' as the city burned around them.

If Al Sorna felt any remorse at the destruction his father had wrought, he failed to show it, gazing at the fast-approaching city with only the faintest interest, hateful sword in hand, ignored by the sailors as he rested against the rail. It was a bright, cloudless day and the ship ploughed easily through the still waters with sails furled, the sailors hauling on their oars under the bosun's harsh exhortations.

We exchanged no greeting when I joined him at the rail. My head still buzzed with questions but my heart was chilled by the certain knowledge that he would provide no answers. Whatever purpose he had pursued in telling me his tale was now fulfilled. He would tell me nothing more. I had lain awake most of the night, my mind poring over his story, seeking answers and finding only more questions. I wondered if his intention had been to take some cruel revenge for the harsh condemnation of him and his people that had coloured nearly every line of my history of the war, but, despite the fact that I could never feel any warmth for him, I knew he was not truly vindictive. A deadly enemy, certainly, but rarely a vengeful one.

'Can you still use that?' I asked eventually, tiring of the silence.

He glanced at the sword in his hand. 'We'll soon see.'

'Apparently, the Shield is insisting on a fair contest. I expect they'll give you a few days to practise. So many years of inactivity would hardly make you the most fearsome opponent.'

His black eyes played over my face, faintly amused. 'What makes you think I've been inactive?'

I shrugged. 'What is there to do in a cell for five years?'

He turned back to the city, his reply a vague whisper nearly lost to the wind. 'Sing.'

All business on the dockside gradually died away as we tied up to the quay. Every stevedore, fisherman, sailor, fishwife and whore ceased activity and turned to regard the son of the City Burner. The silence was instantly thick and oppressive, even the constant keening of the innumerable gulls seemed to fade in an atmosphere now heavy with an unspoken, universal hatred. Only one figure amongst the throng seemed immune to the mood, a tall man standing arms wide in welcome at the foot of the gangplank, perfect teeth gleaming in a broad smile. 'Welcome, friends, welcome!' he called in a rich, deep baritone.

I took in his full stature as I descended to the quay, noting the expensive blue silk shirt that clad his broad, lean torso and the gold-hilted sabre at his belt. His hair, long and honey blond, trailed in the wind like a lion's mane. He was, quite simply, the most handsome man I had ever seen. Unlike Al Sorna, his appearance was entirely in keeping with his legend and I knew his name before he told me, Atheran Ell-Nestra, Shield of the Isles, the man the Hope Killer had come to fight.

'Lord Verniers, is it not?' he greeted me, his hand engulfing my own. 'An honour, sir. Your histories have pride of place on my shelves.'

'Thank you.' I turned as Al Sorna made his way down the gang-plank. 'This . . .'

'Is Vaelin Al Sorna,' Ell-Nestra finished, bowing deeply to the Hope Killer. 'The tale of your deeds flies before you, of course . . .'

'When do we fight?' Al Sorna cut in.

Ell-Nestra's eyes narrowed a little but his smile never wavered. 'Three days hence, my lord. If it suits you.'

'It doesn't. I wish to conclude this farce as quickly as possible.'

'I was under the impression that you had been languishing at the Emperor's pleasure for the last five years. Do you not require time to refresh your skills? I should feel dishonoured if folk were to say I had too easy a victory.'

Watching them stare at each other, I was struck by the contrast they made. Although roughly equal in stature, Ell-Nestra's masculine beauty and blazing smile should have outshone Al Sorna's stern, angular visage. But there was something about the Hope Killer that defied the islander's commanding presence, an innate inability to be diminished. I knew why, of course, I could see it in the false humour Ell-Nestra painted on his face, the way his eyes scanned his opponent from head to toe. The Hope Killer was the most dangerous man he would ever face, and he knew it.

'I can assure you,' Al Sorna said. 'No-one will ever say you had an easy victory.'

Ell-Nestra inclined his head. 'Tomorrow then, midday.' He gestured at a group of armed men nearby, hard-eyed sailors festooned with a variety of weapons, all glaring at the Hope Killer with undisguised antipathy. 'My crew will escort you to your quarters. I advise you not to linger on the way.'

'Lady Emeren,' I said as he made to walk away. 'Where is she?'

'Comfortably situated at my home. You'll see her tomorrow. She sends you her warmest regards, of course.'

It was a bald lie and I wondered what she had told him about me and how close was their association. Could it perhaps amount to more than just a convenience between two vengeful souls?

Our quarters were a soot-blackened building near the centre of town, the finely pointed brickwork and ruined mosaics on the floor indicated it had probably once been a dwelling of considerable status. 'Ship Lord Otheran's house,' one of the sailors explained in gruff response to my query. 'The Shield's father.' He paused to glare at Al Sorna. 'He died in the fire. The Shield commanded it be left as it is, a reminder for both him and the people.'

Al Sorna didn't appear to be listening, his gaze roaming over the ruined, grey-black walls, a strange distance in his eyes.

'Food has been provided,' the sailor told me. 'In the kitchen, take the stairs over there to the lower floors. We'll be outside if you need anything.'

We ate at a large mahogany table in the dining room, an oddly perfect furnishing in so wasted a house. I had found cheese, bread and an assortment of cured meats in the kitchen, together with some very palatable wine Al Sorna recognised as originating from the southern vineyards of Cumbrael.

'Why do they call him the Shield?' he asked, pouring himself a cup of water. I noticed he hardly touched the wine.

'After your father's visit the Meldeneans decided they needed to look to their defences. Every Ship Lord must contribute five ships to a fleet that constantly patrols the Islands. The captain given the honour of commanding the fleet is known as the Shield of the Isles.' I paused, watching him carefully. 'Do you think you can beat him?'

His eyes wandered around the dining room, lingering on the peeled remains of a wall painting, whatever it had depicted now lost in a black-streaked smear of once-vibrant colours. 'His father was a rich man, bringing an artist from the Empire to paint a mural of the family. The Shield had three brothers, all his elders, and yet he knew his father loved him more than the others.'

There was an unnerving certainty to his words, provoking the suspicion that we sat eating amidst the ghosts of the Shield's murdered family. 'You see much in a patch of faded paint.'

He set his cup down and pushed his plate away. If this was his last meal, it seemed to me he had approached it with little enthusiasm. 'What will you do with the story I told you?'

The unfinished story you told me, I thought but said, 'It has given me much to think about. Although, if I were to publish it, I doubt many would be convinced by the picture of the war as simply the deluded agency of a foolish old man.'

'Janus was a schemer, a liar and, on occasion, a murderer. But was he truly a fool? For all the blood and treasure spilled into the sand in that hateful war, I'm still not sure it wasn't all part of some great design, some final scheme too complex for me to grasp.'

'When you talk of Janus you tell of a callous and devious old man, and yet I hear no anger in your voice. No hatred for the man who betrayed you.'

'Betrayed me? The only loyalty Janus ever felt was to his legacy, a Unified Realm ruled in perpetuity by the House of Al Nieren. It was his only true ambition. Hating him for his actions would be like hating the scorpion that stings you.'

I drained my wine cup and reached for the bottle. I found I had a liking for the fruit of Cumbrael and felt a sudden desire to be drunk.

The stress of the day and the prospect of witnessing bloody combat on the morrow left an unease in my gut I was keen to drown. I had seen men die before, criminals and traitors executed at the Emperor's command, but however bright my hatred burned for this man I found I could no longer relish the impending violence of his end.

'What will you do if you gain victory tomorrow?' I asked, aware I was slurring a little. 'Will you return to your Realm? Do you think King Malcius will welcome you?'

He pushed back from the table and got to his feet. 'I think we both know there will be no victory for me here, whatever transpires tomorrow. Good night, my lord.'

I refilled my cup, listening to him climb the stairs and make his way to one of the bedrooms. I marvelled that he could sleep, knowing that without the wine's assistance I was unlikely to find any rest this night. And yet I knew he would sleep soundly, untroubled by fearful nightmares, untroubled by guilt.

'Would you have hated him, Seliesen?' I asked aloud, hoping he was among the ghosts crowding this house. 'I doubt it. Grist for another poem, no doubt. You always did relish their company, these sword-swinging brutes, though you could never truly be one of them. Learn their tricks, learn to ride, learn to make pretty patterns with that sabre they gave you. But you never learned to fight, did you?' Tears were coming now. Here I was, a drunken scribbler weeping in a house of ghosts. 'You never learned to fight, you bastard.'

Among the few attractions the Meldenean Islands have to offer the more educated visitor are the many impressive ruins to be found on the coastline of the larger isles. Although varying in scale and purpose, they display a uniformity of design and articulation clearly indicative of construction by a single culture, an ancient race possessed of an aesthetic sophistication and elegance entirely absent from the archipelago's modern inhabitants.

By far the most impressive surviving example of this once-great architecture is the amphitheatre situated some two miles from the Meldenean capital. Carved from a depression in the red-veined yellow marble cliffs on the island's southern shore, the amphitheatre has proven immune to the depredations wrought by successive generations of islanders who display scant reluctance in cannibalising other sites for building materials. A great bowl of terraced seating looking down upon a wide oval stage where, no doubt, great oratory, poetry and drama had once been the delight of a more enlightened audience, the amphitheatre was now the perfect venue for modern islanders to publicly execute miscreants or watch men fight to the death.

We had been roused by the Shield's crew just as dawn broke over the city. They explained it would be best if we were conveyed to the venue before the populace woke to throng the streets and bay their hatred at the City Burner's spawn.

As I had come to expect, Al Sorna showed no outward concern as we waited for the sun to climb to its midway place in the sky. He sat in the lowermost tier, sword resting beside him as he gazed out to sea. A stiff breeze was blowing from the south although the absence of cloud foretold a day free of rain. I wondered if Al Sorna felt it was a good day to meet his death.

The Lady Emeren arrived an hour short of noon, accompanied by two more of the Shield's crewmen, dressed simply as always in a plain white-and-black robe, her fine features unadorned by paint or jewellery. But for the sapphire ring on her finger there was no outward sign of her rank. However, her innate dignity and poise were unchanged. I rose to greet her as she strode into the oval arena, bowing formally. 'My Lady Emeren.'

'Lord Verniers.' Her voice had lost none of the rich timbre I remembered, coloured by a faint trace of the peculiar lilting accent unique to those raised in the Emperor's court. I was struck once again by her beauty, the flawless skin, the full lips and bright green

eyes. She had long been regarded as the perfection of Alpiran woman-hood, as dutiful as she was comely, daughter of a noble bloodline and favoured by the Emperor since girlhood, educated at court alongside his own sons, a daughter to him in all but name. When Seliesen was called to his destiny it was inevitable that they would marry. Who else was worthy of her after all?

'You are well?' I asked. 'You have suffered no mistreatment, I trust.'

'My captors have been more than generous.' Her gaze shifted to the Hope Killer and I saw again the expression of cold, fathomless malice that marred her perfect features whenever she spoke of him. Al Sorna returned her gaze with a short incline of his head, his face showing only the mildest interest.

'There are no guards with you,' the Lady Emeren observed.

'The prisoner gave his word to the Emperor that he would meet the Shield's challenge. Guards were not deemed necessary.'

'I see. My son is well?'

'Very. Happily at play last I saw him. I know he hungers for your return. As do we all.'

Her eyes flashed at me, burning with almost the same flame of hatred she showed to the Hope Killer, and I found I could not meet them. She always knew, I recalled. Why would she not hate me too?

'When I return to the Empire my son and I will continue to live in quiet seclusion,' the Lady Emeren told me. 'I desire no return to court. Nor do I expect any thanks for finally securing justice for my husband.'

I sighed heavily. 'So it's true then? This circumstance is your doing.'

'The Meldeneans desire justice too. The Shield watched his parents and brothers burn to death before his eyes. His assistance required little persuasion. These Northmen have a rare gift for stoking hatred in others.'

'And do you really believe your hatred will die with him? What if it doesn't? What comfort will you find then?'

Her green eyes narrowed. 'Do not preach at me, scribe. You are a godless man, we both know it.'

'So it's to the gods you look for comfort now? Begging gifts from heedless stone. Seliesen would have wept . . .'

Her sapphire ring left a cut on my cheek as she slapped me. I staggered a little. She was a strong woman and felt no need of restraint. 'Do not speak my husband's name!'

Many words came to me then as I stood clutching my bleeding face, many bile-filled, loathsome words sure to cut her to the core with lacerating truth. But meeting her blazing eyes, I felt the words die in my breast, my anger shrivelling and flying away on the seaborne wind, replaced by a depth of pity and regret I knew had always lurked in my soul.

I gave her another formal bow. 'I am sorry to have caused you any distress, lady.' I turned and walked to where the Hope Killer sat, placing myself next to him, two guilty men awaiting sentence.

'I can stitch that if you like,' Al Sorna offered as I held a lace kerchief to the cut on my cheek. 'It'll scar otherwise.'

I shook my head, watching the Lady Emeren take her place at the far end of the first tier, her gaze studiously avoiding mine. 'I earned it.'

The Shield arrived shortly afterwards, leading a company of spear-bearing crewmen, who quickly moved to take up positions around the arena. No doubt he was keen that his moment of revenge should proceed without any assistance from the crowd now beginning to throng the seats. Their mood was tense rather than celebratory, many pairs of eyes bored into Al Sorna's back but there were no curses or catcalls, making me wonder if the Shield had made efforts to ensure the event at least bore some semblance of civilisation.

What absurd comedy this is, I thought. To pardon a man for a crime he did commit so he can face retribution for one he had no part in.

Last to arrive were the Ship Lords, eight men of middle or advanced years dressed in what I assumed passed for finery in the Isles. These were the wealthiest men in the Islands, elevated to the governing council by virtue of the number of ships they owned, a singular form of government that had survived surprisingly well for over four centuries. They took their places on the raised, long, marble dais at the far end of the arena, eight large oak-wood chairs having already been placed there for their comfort.

One of the Ship Lords remained standing, a wiry man, dressed more simply than his fellows, but with soft leather gloves on both hands. I sensed Al Sorna shift next to me. 'Carval Nurin,' he said.

'The captain of the Red Falcon,' I recalled.

He nodded. 'Bluestone buys a lot of ships it seems.'

Nurin waited for the hum of the crowd to die down, his expressionless gaze lingering on Al Sorna for a moment before he raised his voice to speak, 'We come to witness resolution of challenge to single combat. The Ship Lords Council formally recognises this challenge to be fair and lawful. There will be no punishment for any blood spilled this day. Who speaks for the challenger?'

One of the Shield's crew stepped forward, a large, bearded man with a blue scarf on his head denoting his rank as first mate. 'I do, my lords.'

Nurin's gaze turned to me. 'And for the challenged?'

I rose and walked to the centre of the arena. 'I do.'

Nurin's expression faltered a little at the lack of an honorific in my response but he continued smoothly. 'By law we are required to enquire of both parties if this matter can be resolved without bloodshed.'

The first mate spoke first, voice raised, addressing the crowd rather than the Ship Lords. 'My captain's dishonour is too great. Although he is a peaceful man by nature, the souls of his murdered kin cry out for justice!'

There was a growl of agreement from the audience, threatening to build into a cacophony of rage until a glare from Carval Nurin caused it to subside. He looked down at me. 'And does the challenged wish to resolve this matter peacefully?'

I glanced back at Al Sorna and found him looking up at the sky. Following his gaze, I saw a bird circling above, a sea eagle judging from the wingspan. It turned and wheeled in the cloudless sky, borne by the warm air rising from the cliff, above all this, above our sordid public murder. For I now knew this was murder, there was no justice here.

'My lord!' Carval Nurin prompted, his voice hard with annoyance.

I watched the eagle fold its wings and dive below the cliff face. Beautiful. 'Just get it over with,' I said, turning and walking back to my seat without a backward glance.

There was a curious expression on Al Sorna's face as I returned to my seat. Perhaps he was amused by my refusal to play along with this travesty. Later, in my more deluded moments, I wondered if there might have been some admiration there, some small measure of respect. But that, of course, is absurd.

'The combatants will take their place!' Carval Nurin announced.

Al Sorna stood, hefting his hateful sword. There was a brief hesitation as he placed his hand on the hilt, I noted the flex of his fingers before he drew the blade from the scabbard. His face was devoid of amusement now, dark eyes seeming to drink in the sight of the steel shining in the sun, his expression unreadable. After a second he placed the scabbard next to me and walked to the centre of the arena.

The Shield came forward, his sabre bared, blond hair tied back with a leather thong, clad simply in sailor's garb of plain cotton shirt, buckskin trews and sturdy leather boots. His clothes may have been simple but he wore them like a prince, easily outshining the finery of the assembled Ship Lords, exuding grave nobility and physical prowess, a lion in search of justice for its murdered pride. The good humour he had displayed at the harbour was gone now and he regarded Al Sorna with a cold, predatory judgement.

Al Sorna took his place opposite, meeting the Shield's gaze without demur, showing the same effortless inability to be outshone. He stood with his sword held low, legs parted in line with his shoulders, a slight crouch to his back.

Carval Nurin raised his voice again. 'Begin!'

It happened almost before Nurin's command had ended, so fast it was a moment before I, and the crowd, realised what had occurred. Al Sorna moved. He moved in a way I had never seen a man move before, like the eagle diving below the cliff edge, or the orcas swooping on the salmon when we left Linesh, a fluid blur of speed and a single, flickering slash of metal.

The Shield's sabre must have been fashioned of quality steel judging by the rich ringing sound it made as it skittered away across the arena, leaving him standing there unarmed and defenceless.

The silence was total.

Al Sorna straightened, offering the Shield a grim smile. 'You were holding it wrong.'

The Shield's face showed a brief spasm of either rage or fear, but he mastered it quickly. Saying nothing, awaiting death and refusing to beg.

'There was much laughter in your house,' Al Sorna told him. 'When your father returned from distant shores with presents and tales of adventure, you would gather around with your brothers and listen, hungering for manhood and rejoicing in his love. But he never told you of the murders he committed, honest sailors pitched to the sharks from the decks of their own ships, nor the women he raped when they raided the Realm's southern shore. You loved your father, but you loved a lie.'

The Shield bared his teeth in a feral grimace of hate. 'Just finish it!'

'It wasn't your fault,' Al Sorna went on. 'You were just a boy. There was nothing you could do. You were right to run . . .'

The Shield's composure shattered, an enraged roar erupting from his lips, charging forward, hands reaching for Al Sorna's throat. The Northman side-stepped the charge and slammed the palm of his hand into the Shield's temple, felling him to the arena floor, where he lay still and immobile.

Al Sorna turned and walked back to his seat, retrieving the scabbard and sheathing his sword. The crowd were beginning to react now, mostly in shock, but with a tinge of anger that I knew would only grow.

'This challenge is not concluded, Lord Vaelin!' Carval Nurin called above the rising tumult.

Al Sorna turned, walking to where Lady Emeren sat, shocked and staring at him in rigid frustration. 'My Lady, are you ready to depart this place?'

'This contest is to the death!' Nurin shouted. 'If you leave this man alive, you dishonour him in the eyes of the Isles for all time.'

Al Sorna turned away from the Lady Emeren with a gracious bow. 'Honour?' he asked Nurin. '"Honour" is just a word. You can't eat it or drink it and yet everywhere I go men talk of it endlessly, and they all tell a different tale of what it actually means. For the Alpirans it's all about duty, the Renfaelins think it's the same as courage. In these islands it appears it means killing a son for a crime committed by his father then slaughtering a helpless man when the pantomime fails to go to plan.'

It was strange, but the crowd fell silent as he spoke. Even though his voice wasn't particularly loud, the amphitheatre carried it effort-lessly to all those present, and somehow their anger and disappointed bloodlust abated.

'I offer no excuse for my father's actions. Nor can I offer any contrition. He burned a city on the orders of his king, it was wrong but I had no hand in it. In any case, spilling my blood will leave no mark on a man who died three years ago, peacefully in his bed with his wife and daughter at his side. There is no vengeance to be had on a corpse long since given to the fire. Now give me what I came for or kill me and have done.'

My gaze shifted to the spear-bearing guards, seeing hesitation as they exchanged glances and cast wary eyes at the crowd, now possessed of a rising murmur of confusion.

'KILL HIM!' It was the Lady Emeren, on her feet now, striding towards Al Sorna, finger pointed in accusation, snarling. 'KILL THE MURDERING SAVAGE!'

'You have no voice here, woman!' Nurin told her, voice hard in rebuke. 'This is the business of men.'

'Men?' Her laugh was harsh, near hysterical as she rounded on Nurin. 'The only man here lies unconscious and unavenged. Cowards, I call you. Faithless pirate scum! Where is the justice I was promised?'

'You were promised a challenge,' Nurin told her. He looked at Al Sorna for a long moment before lifting his gaze to the crowd, his voice rising. 'And it is concluded. We are pirates it is true, for the gods gave us all the oceans as our hunting grounds, but they also gave us the law with which we govern these Isles and the law holds true in all things or it means nothing. Vaelin Al Sorna stands as victor in this challenge under the terms of the law. He has committed no crime in the Isles and is therefore free to go.' He turned back to the Lady Emeren. 'Pirates we are, but scum we are not. And you, Lady, are also free to go.'

We were marched to the end of the mole and told to wait whilst they arranged passage for us with the few foreign vessels in port. A large detachment of spearmen stood guard across the quay to *discourage any last-minute vengeance from the townsfolk, although I judged the mood of the crowd at the conclusion of the challenge to be subdued, more disappointed than outraged. The guards ignored us and it was plain our departure would be marked with no ceremony. I have to say it was an awkward circumstance to linger there with the two of them, the Lady Emeren prowling the dock, arms tightly folded against her breast, Al Sorna sitting silently on a spice barrel, and me, praying for the turn of the tide and blessed release from this place.*

'This does not end here, Northman!' the Lady Emeren burst out after an hour of silent pacing. She approached to within a few feet of him, glaring, hating. 'Have no dream of escape from me. This earth is not broad enough to hide from . . .'

'It's a terrible thing,' Al Sorna cut in. 'When love turns to hate.'

Her baleful visage froze as if he had stabbed her.

'I knew a man once,' Al Sorna continued, 'who loved a woman very much. But he had a duty to perform, a duty he knew would cost him his life, and hers too if she stayed with him. And so he tricked her and had her taken far away. Sometimes that man tries to cast his thoughts across the ocean, to see if the love they shared has turned to hate, but he finds only distant echoes of her fierce compassion, a life saved here, a kindness done there, like smoke trailing after a blazing torch. And so he wonders, does she hate me? For she has much to forgive, and between lovers' – his gaze switched from her to me – 'betrayal is always the worst sin.'

The cut on my cheek burned, guilt and grief mingling in my breast amidst a torrent of memory. Seliesen when he first came to court, the way his smile always seemed to bring the sun, the Emperor giving the honour of his education in court matters to me, his early stumbling attempts at etiquette, listening to his latest poems far into the night, the fierce jealousy when Emeren made her feelings known, and the shameful triumph when he began to forsake her company for mine. And his death . . . The endless grief I thought would consume me.

Al Sorna had seen it all, I knew it. Somehow, there was nothing hidden from his jet eyes.

Al Sorna rose and stepped towards the Lady Emeren, making her flinch, not in hatred I knew, but fear. What else had he seen? What else would he say? Kneeling before her, he spoke in clear, formal tones, 'My lady, I offer my apology for taking your husband's life.'

It took her a moment to master her fear. 'And will you offer your own in recompense?'

'I cannot, my lady.'

'Then your apology is as empty as your heart, Northman. And my hatred is undimmed.'

They found a vessel from the Northern Reaches for Al Sorna, ships from the Unified Realm's northmost holdings apparently enjoyed rights of anchorage in Meldenean waters denied their countrymen. I had heard and read a little of the Reaches, how it was home to peoples of varied ancestry, and was therefore unsurprised to find the crew mostly dark-skinned with the broad features common in the Empire's southwestern provinces. I walked with Al Sorna to the ship's berth, leaving the Lady Emeren rigidly immobile at the end of the mole. She stared out to sea, refusing to grace the Northman with another word.

'You should heed her,' I told him as we neared the gangplank. 'Her vendetta won't end here.'

He glanced over at the still form of the Lady, sighing in regret. 'Then she is to be pitied.'

'We thought we were sending you here to your death, but all we have done is set you free. As you knew we would, I'm sure. Ell-Nestra never had a chance. Why didn't you kill him?'

His black eyes met mine with the piercing, questing gaze I knew saw far too much. 'At my trial Lord Velsus asked me how many lives I had taken, I honestly couldn't tell him. I've killed many times, the good, the bad, cowards and heroes, thieves and . . . poets.' His eyes became downcast and I wondered if this was my apology. 'Even friends. And I'm sick of it.' He looked down at the sheathed sword in his hand. 'I hope to never draw this again.'

He didn't linger, made no offer of his hand or any word of farewell, simply turning and making his way up the gangplank. The vessel's captain greeted him with a deep bow, his face lit with a naked awe shared by the surrounding crew. The Northman's legend had flown far it seemed. Even though these men hailed from a place long distant from the Realm's heartland, his name clearly carried a great meaning. What waits for him? I wondered. In a Realm where he is no longer merely a man.

The ship departed within the hour, leaving half its cargo unloaded on the docks, keen to be away with its prize. I stood at the end of the mole with the Lady Emeren, watching the Hope Killer sail away. I could see him for a time, a tall figure at the prow of the ship. I fancied he may have glanced back at us, just once, perhaps even have raised a hand in a wave, but he was too far away to be sure. Once free of the harbour the ship unfurled to full sail and was soon vanished beyond the headland, heading east with all speed.

'You should forget him,' I told the Lady Emeren. 'This obsession will be your ruin. Go home and raise your son. I beg you.'

I was appalled to see she was crying, tears streaming from her eyes, although her face was rigidly devoid of expression. Her voice was a whisper, but fierce as ever, 'Not until the gods claim me, and even then I'll find a way to send my vengeance through the veil.'

CHAPTER ONE

He took Spit and rode westwards, keeping to the shoreline, finding a campsite sheltered in the lee of a large grass-topped dune. He gathered driftwood for a fire and cut grass for kindling. The stems were dried by the sea breeze and lit at the first touch of the flint. The fire grew high and bright, embers rising like fireflies into the early-evening sky. In the distance the lights of Linesh seemed to burn brighter still and he could hear music mingled with the sound of many voices raised in celebration.

'After all we did for them,' he told Spit, holding a sugar lump up for the warhorse to chomp on. 'War, plague and months of fear. Hard to believe they're happy to see us go.'

If Spit cared anything for irony, it was expressed in a loud snort of annoyance as he jerked his head away. 'Wait.' Vaelin caught hold of the reins and unfastened the bridle before moving to lift the saddle from his back. Shorn of the encumbrance, Spit cantered away across the dunes, kicking through the sand and tossing his head. Vaelin watched him play in the surf as the sky dimmed and a bright full moon rose to paint the dunes a familiar silver blue. *Like snowdrifts in the height of winter.*

Spit came trotting back as the last glimmer of daylight faded, standing expectantly at the edge of the light cast by the fire, awaiting the nightly ritual of grooming and tethering. 'No,' Vaelin said. 'We're done. Time to go.'

Spit nickered uncertainly, forehoof kicking sand.

Vaelin went to him, slapped a hand on his flank, stepping back quickly to avoid the retaliatory kick as Spit reared, whinnying in anger, teeth bared. 'Go on, you hateful beast!' Vaelin shouted, gesticulating wildly. 'GO!'

And he was gone, galloping away in a blur of silver-blue sand, his parting whinny resounding in the night air. 'Go on, you bloody nag,' Vaelin whispered with a smile.

There was little else to occupy his time so he sat, feeding the fire, recalling that day atop the battlements at the High Keep when he watched Dentos approach the gate without Nortah and knew everything was about to change. *Nortah . . . Dentos . . . Two brothers lost and about to lose another.*

It was only a slight change in the wind bringing a faint scent of sweat and brine. He closed his eyes, hearing the soft scrape of feet on sand, approaching from the west, making no pretence of stealth. *And why would he? We are brothers after all.*

He opened his eyes to regard the figure standing opposite. 'Hello, Barkus.'

Barkus slumped down in front of the fire, raising his hands to the flames. His muscle-thick arms were bare as he wore only a cotton vest and trews, his feet shorn of boots and his hair matted with seawater. His only weapon was his axe, strapped across his back with leather thongs. 'Faith!' he grunted. 'Haven't been this cold since the Martishe.'

'Must've been a hard swim.'

'Right enough. We were three miles out before I realised you'd gulled me, brother. The ship's captain took some hard persuading before he'd sail his boat back to shore.' He shook his head, droplets flying from his long hair. 'Sailing off to the Far West with Sister Sherin. As if you'd pass up a chance to sacrifice yourself.'

Vaelin watched Barkus's hands, saw how they were free of any tremble although it was cold enough to make his breath steam.

'That was the deal, right?' Barkus went on. 'We get to live and they get you?'

'And Prince Malcius is returned to the Realm.'

Barkus frowned. 'He's alive?'

'I was sparing with the truth in getting you all out of the city without any fuss.'

The large brother grunted again. 'How long till they come for you?'

'First light.'

'Time enough to rest up then.' He unslung his axe from his back, setting it down close by. 'How many do you think they'll send?'

Vaelin shrugged. 'I didn't ask.'

'Against the two of us they better send a whole regiment.' He looked up at Vaelin, puzzled. 'Where's your sword, brother?'

'I gave it to Governor Aruan.'

'Not the brightest idea you've had. How do you intend to fight?'

'I don't. In accordance with the King's Word I will surrender myself to Alpiran custody.'

'They'll kill you.'

'I don't think so. According to the Fifth Book of the Cumbraelin god, I still have many more people to kill.'

'Pah!' Barkus spat into the fire. 'Prophecies are bullshit. Superstition for god worshippers. You took their Hope, they'll kill you right enough. Just a question of how long they take over it.' He met Vaelin's eyes. 'I can't stand by and watch them take you, brother.'

'Then leave.'

'You know I can't do that either. Don't you think I lost enough brothers already? Nortah, Frentis, Dentos—'

'Enough!' Vaelin's voice was sharp, cutting through the night. Barkus drew back in alarm and bemusement. 'Brother, I . . .'

'Just stop.' Vaelin studied the face of the man in front of him with all the scrutiny he could muster, searching for some crack in the mask, some flicker of lost composure. But it was perfect, impervious and infuriating. He fought to master the anger, knowing it would kill him. 'You've waited so long for this, why not show me your true face? Here at the end, what difference does it make?'

Barkus grimaced in a flawless display of embarrassed concern. 'Vaelin, are you quite well?'

'Captain Antesh told me something before he left. Would you like to hear it?'

Barkus spread his hands uncertainly. 'If you wish.'

'It seems Antesh isn't his real name. Hardly surprising, I'm sure many of the Cumbraelins we hired felt the need to use a false name, either through fear of a criminal past or shame at accepting our coin. What was surprising is that we've both heard his other name before.'

Still no slip in the mask. Still nothing beyond the concern of a true brother.

'Bren Antesh was once greatly in thrall to his god,' Vaelin told him. 'So great was his devotion it drove him to kill, to gather others who also thirsted to honour their god with the blood of heretics. In time he led them to the Martishe where most of them died at our hands, leading him to question his belief, to abandon his god, accepting the King's gold and giving it to the families of his fallen men, then seeking death in a foreign war, all the time trying to forget the name he had won in the Martishe: Black Arrow.

Bren Antesh was once named Black Arrow. And he assures me he was never in possession of any letters of free passage from his Fief Lord, nor were any of his men.'

Barkus remained still, all expression now vanished.

'You remember the letters, brother?' Vaelin asked. 'The letters you found on the body of the archer I killed. The letters that set us to war with Cumbrael.'

It was only a slight change in the angle of his head, a small shift in the set of his shoulders, a new curve to his lips, but suddenly Barkus was gone, like smoke in the wind. When he spoke Vaelin was unsurprised to hear a familiar voice, the voice of two dead men. 'Do you really think you're going to serve a Queen of Fire, brother?'

Vaelin's heart plummeted like a stone. He had been nurturing a withered hope that he might be wrong, that Antesh had been lying and his brother was still the noble warrior sailing away with the morning tide. Now it was gone and there were just the two of them, alone on the beach with death coming swiftly. 'I'm told there are other prophecies,' he replied.

'Prophecies?' The thing that had been Barkus grated a harsh, ugly laugh. 'You know so little. All of you, scribbling down your fumbling attempts at wisdom, calling it scripture when it's just the rantings of the mad and the power-hungry.'

'The Test of the Wild. Is that when you took him?'

The thing wearing Barkus's face grinned. 'He wanted to live so badly. Finding Jennis was a gift of life but his sense of brotherhood was so strong he couldn't bring himself to do what was necessary.'

'He found Jennis's body frozen, with no cloak.'

The thing laughed again, harsh, grating, enjoying its cruelty. 'His body and his soul. Jennis was still alive, half-dead with cold, but still breathing, whispering pleas for Barkus to save him. Of course there was nothing he could do, and he was so very hungry. Hunger does strange things to a man, reminds him he is just an animal, an animal that needs to feed, and flesh is just flesh. The temptation sickened him, the hunger driving him beyond the edge of madness, and so he wandered out into the snow and lay down to die.'

Hentes Mustor, One Eye, the carpenter who burned Ahm Lin's house, all once close to death. 'Death is your gateway.'

'They call to us, across the hateful void, the plaintive call of a soul near death, like a lost lamb drawing a wolf. Not all can be taken, only those with the seed of malice and the gift of power.'

'Barkus had no malice.'

Another venomous cackle. 'If there's a man without malice in his heart, I've yet to meet him. Barkus had hidden his so deep he barely knew it was there, festering like a maggot in his soul, waiting to be fed, waiting for me. It was his father you see, the father who had sent him away, who hated and envied his gift. He saw the wondrous things the boy could do with metal and hungered for the power. It is the way of things for those of us with gifts. Wouldn't you agree, brother?'

'Were you always him? Every word spoken since, every deed, every kindness. I can't believe it was all you.'

The thing shrugged. 'Believe what you wish. They come close to death, we take them, from that moment they are ours. We know what they know, makes it so easy to maintain the mask.'

The blood-song whispered, a faint but jarring note. 'You're lying. Hentes Mustor was not fully within your command, was he? That's why you killed him before he could tell me the lies you whispered to him in the voice of his god. And when you came for Aspect Elera you had three men under your yolk yet they attacked separately, no doubt your business with Aspect Corlin at the House of the Fourth Order taxed your abilities. I don't think you can fully control more than one mind at once, and I'll wager your grip can be broken.'

The thing inclined Barkus's head. 'Battle Sight is a powerful gift indeed. Soon you'll be close to death and one of us will come to claim it. Lyrna loves you, Malcius trusts you. Who better to guide them through the difficult years ahead? What malice lurks in your breast I wonder? Your Master Sollis perhaps? Janus and his endless schemes? Or is it the Order? After all, they sent you here to draw me out and in doing so robbed you of the woman you love. Tell me there is no malice there, brother.'

'If it's my song you want, why have you sought my death twice now? Sending hirelings into the Urlish to kill me during the Test of the Run, sending Sister Henna to my room the night of the Aspect massacre.'

'What use have we for hirelings? And Henna's mission was conceived in haste, so troublesome to find you at the House of the Fifth Order that night of all nights, before we knew what power you could offer us. She sends her regards, by the way. So sorry she couldn't be here.'

He searched for some guidance from the blood-song but found only silence. This thing was not lying. 'If not you, then who?' His voice faded as it came to him, borne on a despairing chord from the blood-song: Brother Harlick's fear in the fallen city. *Have you come to kill me?* 'The Seventh Order,' he murmured aloud.

'Did you really think they were just a bunch of harmless mystics labouring in service to your absurd faith? They have their own plans, their own agents. Do not delude yourself that they would hesitate to seek your death should you prove an obstacle.'

'Then why have they not attacked me since?'

The thing shifted Barkus's body in badly concealed unease. 'They are biding their time, waiting for their chance.'

Another lie, confirmed by the blood-song. *The wolf. The Seventh set its hirelings on me but the wolf killed them.* Had they seen it as evidence of some Dark blessing, protection afforded by a power they feared? Questions. As ever, there were always more questions.

'Were you once a man?' he asked it. 'Did you have a name?'

'Names mean much to the living but to those who've felt the depthless chill of the void they seem the conceit of children.'

'So you were alive once. You had a body of your own.'

'A body? Yes I had a body. Torn by the wilderness and wasted by hunger, pursued by hate at every turn. I had a body born of a raped mother they called a witch. We were driven out because her gift could turn the wind. The man who fathered me lied and said she had used the Dark to compel him to bed her. Lied that he refused to stay with her when the spell faded. Lied that she had used her gift to spoil the crops in revenge. With stones and rotting filth they drove us into the forest, where we lived like animals until the hunger and the cold took her from me. But I lived on, more a beast than a boy, forgetting language and custom, forgetting everything but revenge. And in time I took it, in full measure.'

'"He called forth the lightning,"' Vaelin quoted. '"And the village burned. The people fled to the river but he swelled it with rain until the banks burst and carried them away. Still his vengeance was not sated and he brought down a blast of wind from the far north to encase them in ice."'

The thing formed a smile, chilling in its complete lack of cruelty, a smile of fond remembrance. 'I can still see his face, my father, frozen in the ice, staring up at me from the depths of the river. I pissed on it.'

'The Witch's Bastard,' Vaelin whispered. 'The story must be three centuries old.'

'Time is as much a delusion as your faith, brother. To look

into the void is to see the vastness and smallness of everything at once, in an instant of terror and wonder.'

'What is it? This void you talk of?'

The thing's smile became cruel once more. 'Your faith calls it the Beyond.'

'You lie!' he spat, even though there was no sound from the blood-song. 'The Beyond is a place of endless peace, complete wisdom, sublime unity with the everlasting souls of the Departed.'

The thing's lips twitched for a moment and then it began to laugh, loud and hearty peals of amusement echoing across the beach and the sea. Vaelin felt his hand itch for the dagger in his boot as it continued to laugh, resisting the urge with difficulty. *Not yet* . . .

'Oh.' The thing shook its head, thumbing a tear from its eye. 'You utter fool, brother.' He leaned forward, the face of what had been his brother a red mask in the firelight, hissing, *'We are the Departed!'*

He waited for the blood-song's call but heard nothing beyond an icy silence. It was impossible, it was blasphemy but there was no lie in this thing's words. 'The Departed await us in the Beyond,' he recited, hating the desperation in his voice. 'Souls enriched by the fullness and goodness of their lives, they offer wisdom and compassion . . .'

The thing was laughing again, near helpless with mirth. 'Wisdom and compassion. There is no more wisdom and compassion amongst the souls in the void than there is in a pack of jackals. We hunger and we feed, and death is our meat.'

Vaelin closed his eyes tight, resuming his recitation, the words tumbling rapidly from his lips. 'What is death? Death is but a gateway to the Beyond and union with the Departed. It is both ending and beginning. Fear it and welcome it . . .'

'Death brings us fresh souls to command, more bodies to twist to our will, sate our lusts and serve his design . . .'

'What is the body without the soul? Corrupted flesh, nothing more. Mark the passing of loved ones by giving their shell to the fire . . .'

'The body is everything. A soul without a body is a wasted, wretched echo of a life—'

'I HEARD MY MOTHER'S VOICE!' He was on his feet, dagger in hand, crouched in a fighting stance, eyes now locked on the thing across the fire. 'I heard my mother's voice.'

The thing that had been Barkus got slowly to his feet, hefting the axe. 'It happens sometimes, amongst the Gifted, they can hear us, hear the souls calling in the void. Brief echoes of pain and fear mostly. That's how it all started, you know, your faith. Several centuries ago an unusually Gifted Volarian heard a babble of voices from the void, among them the unmistakable voice of his own dead wife. He took it upon himself to spread the word, the great and wondrous news that there is life beyond this daily punishment of grief and toil. People listened, the word spread and so began your faith, all built on the lie that there is a reward in the next life for servile obedience in this one.'

Vaelin fought to master his confusion, tried to stop himself willing the blood-song to speak, to give the lie to this thing's words. Wood cracked in the fire, the surf beat against the shore in a ceaseless rumble and Barkus regarded him with the cool, dispassionate gaze of a stranger.

'What design?' Vaelin demanded. 'You spoke of his design? Who is he?'

'You'll meet him soon enough.' The thing that had been Barkus clasped the haft of the axe with both hands, taking a firm grip, holding it up for the edge of the blade to catch the moonlight. 'I made this for you, brother, or rather I allowed Barkus to make it. He always hungered for the hammer and the anvil so, although he resisted manfully until I took away his reluctance. Beautiful, isn't it? I've killed so many times with so many different weapons, but I must say this is the finest. With this I can bring you to the brink of death as easily as if I were wielding a surgeon's knife. You'll bleed, you'll fade and your soul will reach out to the void. He'll be waiting for you there.' The smile the thing offered was grim now, almost regretful. 'You really shouldn't have given up your sword, brother.'

'If I hadn't, you wouldn't have been so willing to talk.'

The thing's smile vanished. 'Talking's over.'

He leapt over the fire, axe drawn back, teeth bared in a hateful snarl. Something large and black met him in midair, fastening its jaws on his arm, rending and tearing as they crashed together onto the fire, thrashing, scattering flame. Vaelin saw the hateful axe rise and fall once, then twice, heard the enraged howl of a slave-hound as the blade bit home, then the thing that had been Barkus was rising from the dregs of the fire, hair and clothes aflame, his left arm hanging ruined and useless, nearly severed by Scratch's bite. But the right arm was still whole, and he still held the axe.

'Asked the governor to set him loose at nightfall,' Vaelin told him.

The thing roared in pain and rage, the axe arching round in a silver blur. Vaelin ducked under the blade, lancing out with the dagger, piercing the thing's chest, seeking the heart. It roared again, swinging the axe with inhuman speed. Vaelin left the dagger embedded in its chest and caught hold of the haft of the axe as it swung round, backhanded a savage blow to the thing's face and followed with a kick to the groin. It barely staggered and delivered a stinging head-butt, sending Vaelin reeling across the sand, falling onto his back.

'Something I didn't tell you about Barkus, brother!' the thing said, leaping closer, axe raised. 'When you trained together, I always made him hold back.'

Vaelin rolled to the side as the axe bit down on the sand, twisted to send a kick into the thing's temple, surging to his feet as it shook off the pain and swung again, the blade meeting only air as Vaelin dived over the arc of the swing, ducked in close to snatch the dagger from its chest, stabbed again then stepped back to let the axe swing within an inch of his face.

The thing that had been Barkus stared at him, shocked, still, smoke rising from his burns, his ruined arm bleeding onto the sand. He dropped the axe and his good hand went to the rapidly spreading stain on his shirt. He stared at the thick slick of blood covering his palm for a second then slowly sank to his knees.

Vaelin moved past him and retrieved the axe from the sand, fighting revulsion at the feel of it in his hands. *Is this why I always hated it so? Because this was its final purpose?*

'Nicely done, brother.' The thing that had been Barkus showed bloodstained teeth in a grin of absolute malice. 'Perhaps the next time you kill me, I'll be wearing the face of someone you love even more.'

The axe was light, unnaturally so, making only the faintest whisper as he brought it up and round, slicing through skin and bone as easily as it did the air. The head of what had been his brother rolled on the sand and was still.

He tossed the axe aside and pulled Scratch from the dying remnants of the fire. Heaping sand onto the smouldering burns, tearing his shirt to press rags against the deep cuts in his side. The slave-hound whimpered, tongue lapping weakly at Vaelin's hand. 'I'm sorry, daft dog.' He found his vision blurred by tears and his voice caught by sobs. 'I'm sorry.'

He buried them separately. For some reason it seemed the right thing to do. He said no words for Barkus, knowing his brother had died years ago and in any case he was no longer sure if he could say them and not feel a liar. As the sun rose he took the axe and walked to the edge of the beach. The morning tide was coming in fast, the breakers roaring in from the headland. He hefted the axe, surprised to find the revulsion had gone, whatever Dark stain it had held seemed to have dissipated with the death of the man who had fashioned it. Now it was just metal. Finely crafted and gleaming in the sun, but still just metal. He hurled it into the sea with all the strength he could muster, watched it glitter as it turned end over end before dropping into the waves with a small splash.

He washed himself in the surf and returned to his makeshift camp, covering the bloodstains as best he could, then made for the road, walking back towards Linesh. It was an hour or so before he came to the agreed place and the desert heat was coming on swiftly. He chose a spot near a road marker and sat down to wait.

The blood-song rose as he sat there, a new tune, stronger and clearer than before. As his thoughts turned in his head he found the music changed, mournful as he recalled the final whimper from Scratch, bombastic as he replayed the fight with the thing that had been Barkus, and with the music came images, sounds, feelings he knew were not his own. He understood that for the first time he was truly in command of his song, he was finally singing.

Somewhere in a place that wasn't a place something was screaming, begging forgiveness from an unseen hand that dealt punishment of depthless pain, untroubled by mercy or malice.

In a palace far to the north a young woman composed the greeting she would offer her brother on his return, a carefully crafted speech combining grief, regret and loyalty with expert precision. Once satisfied, she laid down her quill, requested some refreshment from her maid and, when she was certain she was alone, put her perfect face in her hands and wept.

To the west another young woman gazed at a broad ocean and refused to weep. In her hand she held two wooden blocks wrapped in a finely embroidered silk scarf. Below her the sea beat against the ship's hull, scattering spume into the air. Her hand itched to throw the bundle to the waves, anger burning in her, a hard pain she couldn't escape, making her hate the thoughts it provoked. A desire for revenge was not something she understood, never having felt it before. From behind came a shout of pain and she turned, seeing a sailor collapsed on the deck having fallen from the rigging, clutching at a broken leg and swearing profusely in a language she didn't understand. 'Lie still!' she commanded, moving to his side, returning the blocks and the scarf to the folds of her cloak.

Aboard another ship sailing another ocean, a young man sat, silent and still, his face a blank mask. Despite his stillness, he provoked fear in those around him, their master's orders having made it clear that to awaken his interest invited the swiftest death. Although the young man was as unmoving as a statue, within his shirt the scars on his chest burned with a continual, fierce agony.

Vaelin focused the song to a single pure note, casting it forth across the deserts, jungles and ocean that separated them: *I will find you, brother.*

The young man stiffened momentarily, drawing fearful glances from those who guarded him, then returned to his previous immobile, expressionless state.

The vision and the song faded, leaving him sitting in the blazing sun, a dust cloud rising in the east, soon resolving through the haze into a troop of horsemen, the tall figure of Grand Prosecutor Velsus at their head, riding hard, eager to claim his prize.

Appendix I

Dramatis Personae

The Unified Realm

The Royal House of Al Nieren
Janus Al Nieren – King of the Realm
Malcius Al Nieren – son to Janus, Prince of the Realm, heir to the throne
Lyrna Al Nieren – daughter to Janus, Princess of the Realm

The Noble House of Sorna
Kralyk Al Sorna – First Sword of the Realm, former Battle Lord of the King's Host
Vaelin Al Sorna – son to Kralyk, brother of the Sixth Order
Alornis Dinal – illegitimate daughter to Kralyk

The Noble House of Myrna
Vanos Al Myrna – Sword of the Realm, Tower Lord of the Northern Reaches
Dahrena Al Myrna – Lonak foundling, adopted daughter of Vanos

The Noble House of Sendahl
Artis Al Sendahl – First Minister of the Council of Unity
Nortah Al Sendahl – brother of the Sixth Order, son to Artis, Vaelin's comrade

The Noble House of Hestian
Lakrhil Al Hestian – Lord Marshal of the King's Twenty-seventh Regiment of Horse, later Battle Lord of the King's Host
Linden Al Hestian – Lord Marshal of the King's Thirty-fifth Regiment of Foot, son to Lakrhil, friend to Vaelin
Alucius Al Hestian – poet and second son to Lakrhil

THE ORDERS OF THE FAITH

The Sixth Order of the Faith
Gainyl Arlyn – Aspect of the Sixth Order, Vaelin's superior
Sollis – sword-master and Brother Commander of the Sixth Order, Vaelin's master
Caenis Al Nysa – brother of the Sixth Order, third son of the House of Nysa, Vaelin's comrade
Barkus Jeshua – brother of the Sixth Order, son of a Nilsaelin blacksmith, Vaelin's comrade
Dentos – brother of the Sixth Order, Vaelin's comrade
Frentis – urchin and pickpocket, later brother of the Sixth Order, friend to Vaelin
Makril – brother of the Sixth Order, renowned tracker and later Brother Commander
Rensial – Master of Horse
Chekril – Master of Hounds
Hutril – Hunt Master
Jestin – Master of the Smithy

The Fifth Order of the Faith
Elera Al Mendah – Aspect of the Fifth Order

Sherin – sister of the Fifth Order, friend to Vaelin, later Mistress of Curatives

Gilma – sister of the Fifth Order, attached to the Thirty-fifth Regiment of Foot

Harin – Master of Bone Lore to the Fifth Order

Sellin – veteran brother of the Fifth Order, gatekeeper to the Order House

OTHERS

Scratch – Volarian slave-hound, friend to Vaelin

Spit – warhorse of foul temper, Vaelin's mount

Nirka Smolen – captain of the Third Company, King's Mounted Guard

Sentes Mustor – drunkard, heir to the Fief Lordship of Cumbrael

Hentes Mustor – younger brother to Sentes, called the Trueblade

Lartek Al Molnar – Finance Minister of the Council of Unity

Dendrish Hendrahl – Aspect of the Third Order

Tendris Al Forne – brother of the Fourth Order and servant of the Council for Heretical Transgressions, later Aspect of the Fourth Order

Liesa Ilnien – Aspect of the Second Order

Theros Linel – Fief Lord of Renfael, vassal to Janus

Darnel Linel – son to Theros, heir to the Fief Lordship of Renfael

Banders – knight and Baron of Renfael, bondsman to Theros

Gallis – climber, outlaw and later sergeant in the Thirty-fifth Regiment of Foot

Janril Norin – former apprentice minstrel, later standard-bearer in the Thirty-fifth Regiment of Foot

Bren Antesh – captain of Cumbraelin archers during the Alpiran war

Count Marven – captain of the Nilsaelin contingent during the Alpiran war

THE ALPIRAN EMPIRE

Aluran Maxtor Selsus – Emperor

Seliesen Maxtor Aluran (*Eruhin*, The Hope) – adopted son to Aluran, chosen heir to the Imperial throne

Emeren Nasur Ailers – wife of Seliesen

Verniers Alishe Someren – Imperial Chronicler

Neliesen Nester Hevren – captain in the Imperial Guard

Holus Nester Aruan – Governor of the City of Linesh

Merulin Nester Velsus – Imperial Grand Prosecutor

Ahm Lin – stonemason of Far Western origin

APPENDIX II

The Rules of *Keschet*

Keschet is played by two players on a board of one hundred squares. Each player begins the game with 1 Emperor, 1 General, 1 Scholar, 2 Merchants, 3 Thieves, 4 Lancers, 5 Archers and 8 Spearmen.

At the start of the game a player may place any piece in any square in the first three rows at the player's end of the board. The opposing player will then place a piece of the player's choosing in the first three rows at the player's end of the board. All pieces are then placed on the board in turn. The player who placed the first piece then makes the first move.

A piece is taken if the square it occupies is occupied by an opposing piece. The game is won if the Emperor is taken or if the Emperor is the only piece remaining to the losing player.

Any piece in an adjoining square to the Scholar is protected and cannot be taken.

The Scholar may move one or two squares in any direction.

The Emperor can move up to four squares in any direction.

The General can move up to ten squares in any direction.

The Archer can move up to six squares vertically or horizontally.

The Thief can move one square in any direction. A player has the use of any piece taken by the Thief.

The Spearman can move up to two squares vertically or horizontally.

The Lancer can move up to ten squares diagonally.

The Merchant can move either one square in any direction or to any vacant square adjoining the square occupied by the Emperor horizontally, vertically or diagonally, if the route is unobstructed by another piece.

ACKNOWLEDGMENTS

My profound thanks to my editor, Susan Allison, for taking a chance on a nobody, and to Paul Field, who wouldn't let me pay him for the work he did correcting the many errors with which I littered the original manuscript. Also, I'd like to acknowledge the considerable debt I owe the authors of all the fantasy works I've enjoyed over the years, none more so than the late great David Gemmell in whose mighty shadow I am happy to labour.

extras

about the author

Anthony Ryan lives in London and is a writer of fantasy, science fiction and non-fiction. He previously worked in a variety of roles for the UK government but now writes full time. Anthony maintains an active blog at www.anthonystuff.wordpress.com.

Find out more about Anthony Ryan and other Orbit authors by registering for the free monthly newsletter at www.orbitbooks.net.

interview

**Blood Song is an epic fantasy in every sense of the word –
particularly in that it took you six years to write! Why did it
take so long and what was the spark that started it all?**

Working a full-time job whilst studying part-time for a history
degree had a lot to do with the time taken to write *Blood Song*.
Also, although I had a one-page synopsis, I wasn't working to a
detailed plan, something I've subsequently learned is very useful
in speeding up the writing process. It's always difficult to pin down
the genesis of an idea but I recall the basis of *Blood Song* ger-
minating for a few years but not really coming together until I
started my history studies. The themes of religious conflict and
political intrigue were also at the forefront of my thinking in the
aftermath of 9/11 which probably had an influence.

**You were influenced initially by Lloyd Alexander's Prydain
Chronicles, and then later by legendary British fantasy author
David Gemmell. What was so special to you about the works
of these two writers, and how do you think they influenced your
own writing?**

Although I was aware of Tolkien as a kid, my first foray into fantasy
began with Lloyd Alexander, who was writing YA fantasy long

before it had a name. The Prydain Chronicles are essentially a coming of age tale mixing Welsh legend and epic fantasy, completely capturing my ten-year-old imagination from the moment I picked up *The Book of Three*. There are echoes of my main character Vaelin in Alexander's Taran, orphan and apprentice pig keeper continually beset with questions over his past and doubts about his future. Whilst Lloyd Alexander began my love of fantasy, David Gemmell ensured it continued into adulthood with the wonderful Wolf in *Shadow*, an action-packed but also sublimely sombre tale mixing the western with fantasy. Gemmell is primarily remembered for the pace and action of his books but I also think his characterisation is excellent; his characters are flawed, conflicted and, most importantly, consistent whilst also being capable of change, all elements I've tried to include in my own work.

What is it about epic fantasy as a genre that attracted you to it, from a writing perspective? Given that you studied medieval history, did you ever consider writing a purely historical novel?
I've read plenty of historical novels but not yet had the yen to write one – though I do have a germ of an idea for a historical detective story, so who knows? However, at the moment I think I would find it too restricting: you have to spend a long time on research and are stuck with recorded events that can't be changed. Epic fantasy gives the writer the room to create the history of their imaginary world allowing a great amount of scope for drama, spectacle and a combination of themes that would be denied the historical novelist.

You originally self-published *Blood Song* and achieved considerable success, so why did you decide to sign with a traditional publisher?
Simply put, I weighed up the pros and cons and decided it was the

best decision for me. Although I think self-publishing is a great thing, and continue to self-publish my Slab City Blues sci-fi novellas, I wanted the Raven's Shadow trilogy to have the widest possible audience, including foreign sales and access to bookshops. A traditional publishing deal still seems the best way of achieving that.

Blood Song eschews the multi-viewpoint format used by so many current epic fantasies, focusing instead on telling the story from Vaelin's point of view. What are the advantages and limitations of this more singular approach?

The primary advantage is that it enables a more thorough exploration of character over the course of a fairly lengthy narrative: we see Vaelin's journey into adulthood with all the many tribulations on the way, which hopefully adds a greater emotional resonance to the ending. Also, for a fantasy author, a single point of view begun in childhood enables a more narrative-driven approach to world-building; we learn about the politics and history of Vaelin's world as he does, avoiding the dreaded info dump in the process. The disadvantage is that a lot has to happen off-camera, which is why the sequel has four point of view characters instead of one, as the scope of the overall story has expanded greatly. If I ever got lucky enough to write the whole trilogy I had always intended to open out the narrative, a device I found particularly effective in David Eddings' Belgariad which features just one POV until halfway through the third book.

One of my favourite characters from the book is Master Sollis: grim and steely on the outside, but perhaps a *little* softer on the inside – if you can get past his stern façade. Was there any particular inspiration behind this character – an old school-teacher perhaps?

I had some great teachers as a kid (and some not so great), but I can't recall any even vaguely resembling Sollis. He's kind of the ultimate PE teacher meets the ultimate Sergeant Major. He came about because I needed Vaelin to have an unyielding mentor, someone even more single minded and devoted to the Order than he is, but also never needlessly cruel (at least in his own head).

You've made the jump to becoming a full-time writer – how has this changed your writing routine and lifestyle? Do you find you're a lot more productive, now that you don't have to fit the writing in around your work?

The main difference is that I'm a lot less tired these days. My decision to go full time was motivated by the experience of writing Book 2; producing two thousand words a day whilst commuting to a full-time job was not something I wanted to repeat. Oddly, my word count hasn't gone up all that much despite my heroic efforts to resist the lures of daytime telly (actually, that's pretty easy because it's uniformly awful).

You're a big film fan, so which actor would you like to see playing Vaelin in any film adaptation of *Blood Song*?

To be honest I've yet to see an actor that matches my vision of Vaelin. Also, he's never fully described in the book because I wanted the reader to conjure their own image of him, something I'm loath to spoil (at least until those nice Hollywood people cough up some option money). Writers are usually pretty bad at casting anyway; I read somewhere that Ian Fleming thought Cary Grant would make the perfect Bond, a good indication why casting directors are paid so much.

You've already finished the second novel in the Raven's Shadow trilogy, and are well into writing the third. Have you always had an overall plan in mind for how the trilogy would pan

out, or have you generally been making it up as you went along?

As I said earlier, I had only a one-page outline for the first book. The outlines for Books 2 and 3 are much more extensive, running to over four thousand words each. That being said, I do frequently deviate from them as I find actually writing the book the best way to develop plot and character. However, unlike the writers of *Lost*, I always had the general shape of the story in my head and know how it all ends.

if you enjoyed
BLOOD SONG

look out for

A DANCE OF CLOAKS
Shadowdance: Book 1

by

David Dalglish

CHAPTER

1

Aaron sat alone. The walls were bare wood. The floor had no carpet. There were no windows and only a single door, locked and barred from the outside. The silence was heavy, broken only by his occasional cough. In the far corner was a pail full of his waste. Thankfully, he had gotten used to the smell after the first day.

His new teacher had given him only one instruction: wait. He had been given a waterskin, but no food, no timetable, and worst of all, nothing to read. The boredom was far worse than his previous instructor's constant beatings and shouts. Gus the Gruff he had called himself. The other members of the guild whispered that Thren had lashed Gus thirty times after his son's training was finished. Aaron hoped his new teacher would be outright killed. Of all his teachers over the past five years, he was starting to think Robert Haern was the cruelest.

That was all he knew, the man's name. He was a wiry old man with a gray beard curled around his neck and tied behind his head. When he'd led Aaron to the room, he had walked with a cane. Aaron had never minded isolation, so at first the idea of a few hours in the dark sounded rather enjoyable. He had always stayed in corners and shadows, greatly preferring to watch people talk than take part in their conversation.

But now? After spending untold hours, perhaps even days, locked in darkness? Even with his love of isolation and quiet, this was . . .

And then Aaron felt certain of what was going on. Walking over to the door, he knelt before it and pushed his fingers into the crack beneath. For a little while light had crept in underneath the frame, but then someone had stuffed a rag across it, completing the darkness. Using his slender fingers he pushed the rag back, letting in a bit of light. He had not done so earlier for fear of angering his new master. Now he couldn't care less. They wanted him to speak. They wanted him to crave conversation with others. Whoever this Robert Haern was, his father had surely hired him for that purpose.

'Let me out.'

The words came out as a raspy whisper, yet the volume startled him. He had meant to boom the command at the top of his lungs. Was he really so timid?

'I said let me out,' he shouted, raising the volume tremendously.

The door opened. The light hurt his eyes, and during the brief blindness, his teacher slipped inside and shut the door. He held a torch in one hand and a book in the other. His smile was partially hidden behind his beard.

'Excellent,' Robert said. 'I've only had two students last longer, both with more muscle than sense.' His voice was firm but grainy, and it seemed to thunder in the small dark room.

'I know what you're doing,' Aaron said.

'Come now, what's that?' the old man asked. 'My ears haven't been youthful for thirty years. Speak up, lad!'

'I said I know what you're doing.'

Robert laughed.

'Is that so? Well, knowing and preventing are two different things. You may know a punch is coming, but does that mean you can stop it? Well, your father has told me of your training, so perhaps you could, yes, perhaps.'

As his eyes adjusted to the torchlight, Aaron slowly backed into a corner. With the darkness gone he felt naked. His eyes flicked to the pail in the corner, and he suddenly felt embarrassed. If the old man was bothered by the smell, he didn't seem to show it.

'Who are you?' Aaron asked after the silence had stretched longer than a minute.

'My name is Robert Haern. I told you that when I first brought you in here.'

'That tells me nothing,' Aaron said. 'Who are you?'

Robert smiled, just a flash of amusement on his wrinkled face, but Aaron caught it and wondered what it meant.

'Very well, Aaron. At one point I was the tutor of King Edwin Vaelor, but he has since gotten older and tired of my . . . corrections.'

'Corrections,' Aaron said, and it all confirmed what he'd guessed. 'Was this my correction for not talking enough?'

To Aaron's own surprise, Robert looked shocked.

'Correction? Dear lord, boy, no, no. I was told of your quiet nature, but that is not what your father has paid me for. This dark room is a lesson that I hope you will soon understand. You have learned how to wield a sword and sneak through shadows. I, however, walk with a cane and make loud popping noises. So tell me, what purpose might I have with you?'

Aaron shifted his arms tighter about himself. He had no idea whether it was day or night, but the room felt cold and he had nothing but his thin clothing for warmth.

'You're to teach me,' Aaron said.

'That's stating the bloody obvious. What is it I will teach you?'

He sat down in the middle of the room while still holding the torch aloft. He grunted, and true to his word his back popped when he stretched.

'I don't know,' the boy said.

'A good start,' Robert said. 'If you don't know an answer, just say so and save everyone the embarrassment. Uninformed guesses only stall the conversation. However, you should have known the answer. I tutored a king, remember? Mind my words. You will always know the answer to every question I ask you.'

'A tutor,' said Aaron. 'I can already read and write. What else can an old man teach me?'

Robert smiled in the flickering torchlight.

'There are men trying to kill you, Aaron. Did you know that?'

At first Aaron opened his mouth to deny it, then stopped. The look in his teacher's eye suggested Aaron think carefully before answering.

'Yes,' he finally said. 'Though I convinced myself otherwise. The Trifect want all the thief guilds destroyed, their members dead. I am no different.'

'Oh, but you are different,' Robert said as he put his book down and shifted the torch to his other hand. 'You're the heir to Thren Felhorn, one of the most feared men in all of Veldaren. Some say you'll find no finer a thief even if you searched every corner of Dezrel.'

Such worship of his father was hardly foreign to Aaron, and something he always took for granted. For once, he dared ask something he'd never had the courage to ask.

'Is he the finest?' Aaron asked.

'I don't know enough of such matters to have a worthwhile opinion,' Robert said. 'Though I know he has lived a long time, and the wealth he amassed in his younger years is legendary.'

Silence came over them. Aaron looked about the room, but it was bare and covered with shadows. He sensed his teacher waiting for him to speak, but he knew not what to say. His gaze lingered on the torchlight as Robert spat to the side.

'There are many questions you should ask, though one is the most obvious and most important. Think, boy.'

Aaron's eyes flitted from the torchlight to the old man.

'Who are the Trifect?' he asked.

'Who is what? Speak up, I'm a flea's jump away from deaf.'

'The Trifect,' Aaron nearly shouted. 'Who are they?'

'That is an excellent question,' Robert said. 'The lords of the Trifect have a saying: "After the gods, us." When the Gods' War ended, and Karak and Ashhur were banished by the goddess, the land was a devastated mess. Countries fractured, people rebelled, and pillagers marched up and down the coasts. Three wealthy men formed an alliance to protect their assets. Five hundred years ago they adopted their sigil, that of an eagle perched on a golden branch. They've been loyal to it ever since.'

He paused and rubbed his beard. The torch switched hands.

'A question for you, boy: why do they want the thief guilds dead?'

The question was not difficult. The sigil was the answer.

'They never let go of their gold,' Aaron said. 'Yet we take it from them.'

'Precisely,' Robert said. 'To be sure, they'll spend their gold, sometimes frivolously and without good reason. But even in giving away their coin, they are still master of it. But to have it taken? That is unacceptable to them. The Trifect tolerated the various thief guilds for many centuries while focusing on growing their power. And grow it did. Nearly the entire nation of Neldar is under their control in some way. For the longest of times they viewed the guilds as a nuisance, nothing more. That changed. Tell me why, boy; that is your next question.'

This one was tougher. Aaron went over the words of his master. His memory was sharp, and at last he remembered a comment that seemed appropriate.

'My father amassed a legendary amount of wealth,' he said. He smiled, proud of deducing the answer. 'He must have taken too much from the Trifect, and they no longer considered him a nuisance.'

'He was now a threat,' Robert agreed. 'And he was wealthy. Worse, though, was that his prestige was uniting the other guilds. Mostly your father tempted the stronger members and brought them into his fold, but about eight years ago he started making promises, threats, bribes, and even assassinations to bring about the leaders he needed. As a united presence, he thought even the Trifect would be reluctant to challenge their strength.'

The old man opened his book, which turned out to not be a book at all. The inside was hollow, containing some hard cheese and dried meat. It took all of Aaron's willpower to keep from lunging for the food. From his short time with his teacher, he knew such a rash, discourteous action would be rebuked.

'Take it,' Robert said. 'You have honored me well with your attention.'

Aaron didn't need to be told twice. The old man rose to his feet and walked to the door.

'I will return,' he said. His fingers brushed over a slot in the wall, too fast for Aaron to see. He heard a soft pop, and then a tiny jut of metal sprung outward. Robert slid the torch through the metal, fastening it to the wall.

'Thank you,' Aaron said, thrilled to know the torchlight would remain.

'Think on this,' Robert said. 'Eight years ago, your father united the guilds. Five years ago, war broke out between them and the Trifect. What caused your father's failure?'

The door opened, bright light flooded in, and then the old man was gone.

Thren was waiting for Robert not far from the door. They were inside a large and tastefully decorated home. Thren leaned against the wall, positioned so he could see both entrances to the living room.

'You told me the first session was the most important,' Thren said, his arms crossed over his chest. 'How did my son perform?'

'Admirably,' Robert said. 'And I do not say so out of fear. I've told kings their princes were brats with more snot than brains.'

'I can hurt you worse than any king,' Thren said, but his comment lacked teeth.

'You should see Vaelor's dungeon sometime,' Robert said. 'But yes, your son was intelligent and receptive, and most importantly, he let go of his anger for being subjected to the room's darkness once I told him it wasn't a punishment. A few more torches and I'll give him some books to read.'

'The smoke won't kill him, will it?' Thren asked as he glanced at the door.

'There are tiny vents in the ceiling,' Robert said as he hobbled toward a chair. 'I have done this a hundred times, guild-master, so do not worry. Due to the isolation, his mind will be craving knowledge. He'll learn to master his mind, which I'll hone sharper than any dagger of yours. Hopefully when his time with me is done, he will remember this level of focus and mimic it in more chaotic environments.'

Thren pulled his hood over his face and bowed.

'You were expensive,' he said. 'As the Trifect grows poorer, so do we.'

'Whether coin, gem, or food, a thief will always have something to steal.'

Thren's eyes seemed to twinkle at that.

'Well worth the coin,' he said.

The guildmaster bowed, turned, and then vanished into the dark streets of Veldaren. Robert tossed his cane aside and walked without a limp to the far side of the room. After pouring himself a drink, he sat down in his chair with a grunt of pleasure.

He expected more time to pass, but it seemed people had gotten more impatient as Robert grew older. Barely halfway into his glass, he heard two thumps against the outside of his door. They were his only warning before the plainly dressed man with only the barest hints of gray in his hair entered the living room. His simple face was marred by a scar curling from his left eye to his ear. He did his best to hide it with the hood of his cloak, but Robert had seen it many times before. The man was Gerand Crold, who had replaced Robert as the king's most trusted teacher and advisor.

'Did Thren leave pleased?' Gerand asked as he sat down opposite Robert.

'Indeed,' Robert said, letting a bit of his irritation bleed into his voice. 'Though I think that pleasure would have faded had he seen the king's advisor sneaking into my home.'

'I was not spotted,' the man said with an indignant sniff. 'Of that, I am certain.'

'With Thren Felhorn you can never be certain,' Robert said with a dismissive wave of his hand. 'Now what brings you here?'

The advisor nodded toward a door. Beyond it was the room Aaron remained within.

'He can't hear us, can he?' Gerand asked.

'Of course not. Now answer my question.'

Gerand wiped a hand over his clean-shaven face and let his tone harden.

'For a man living by the king's grace alone, you seem rather rude to his servants. Should I whisper in his ear how uncooperative you're being in this endeavor?'

'Whisper all you want,' Robert said. 'I am not afraid of that little whelp. He sees spooks in the shadows and jumps with every clap of thunder.'

Gerand's eyes narrowed.

'Dangerous words, old man. Your life won't last much longer carrying on with such recklessness.'

'My life is nearing its end whether I am reckless or not,' Robert said before finishing his drink. 'I whisper and plot behind Thren Felhorn's back. I may as well act like the dead man I am.'

Gerand let out a laugh.

'You put too much stock in that man's abilities. He's getting older, and he is far from the demigod the laymen whisper about when drunk. But if my presence here scares you so, then I will hurry along. Besides, my wife is waiting for me, and she promised a young redhead for us to play with to celebrate my thirtieth birthday.'

Robert rolled his eyes. The boorish advisor was always bragging about his exploits, a third of which were probably true. They were Gerand's favorite stalling tactic when he wanted to linger, observe, and distract his companions. What he was stalling for, Robert didn't have a clue.

'We Haerns have no carnal interests,' Robert said, rising from his chair with an exaggerated wince of pain. Gerand saw this and immediately took the cup, offering to fill it for him.

'We just pop right out of our mud fields,' Robert continued. 'Ever hear that slurp when your boot gets stuck and you have to force it out? That's us, making another Haern.'

'Amusing,' Gerand said as he handed Robert the glass. 'So did you come from a nobleman's cloak, or perhaps a wise man's discarded sock?'

'Neither,' Robert said. 'Someone pissed in a gopher hole, and out I came, wet and angry. Now tell me why you're here, or I'll go to King Vaelor myself and let him know how displeased I am with *your* cooperation in this endeavor.'

If Gerand was upset by the threat, he didn't show it.

'Love redheads,' he said. 'You know what they say about them? Oh, of course you don't, mud-birth and all. So feisty. But you want me to hurry, so hurry I shall. I've come for the boy.'

'Aaron?'

Gerand poured himself a glass of liquor and toasted the old man from the other side of the room.

'The king has decided so, and I agree with his brilliant wisdom. With the boy in hand, we can force Thren to end this annoying little war of his.'

'Have you lost your senses?' asked Robert. 'You want to take Aaron hostage? Thren is trying to end this war, not prolong it.'

He thought of Gerand's stalling, of the way his eyes had swept every corner of the room and peered through all the doorways. A stone dropped into his gut.

'You have troops surrounding my home,' Robert said.

'We watched Thren leave,' Gerand said. He downed his drink and licked his lips. 'Trust me when I say you're alone. You can play your little game all you want, Robert, but you're still a Haern, and lack any true understanding of these matters. You say Thren wants this war of his to end? You're wrong. He doesn't want to lose, and therefore he won't *let it* end. But the Trifect won't bow to him, not now, not ever. This will only end when one side is dead. Veldaren can live without the thief guilds. Can we live without the food, wealth, and pleasures of the Trifect?'

'I live off mud,' Robert said. 'Can you?'

He flung his cane. The flat bottom smacked through the glass and struck Gerand's forehead. The man slumped to the floor, blood dripping from his hand. The old man rushed through the doorway as shouts came from the entrance to his home, followed by a loud crack as the door smashed open.

Robert burst into Aaron's training room. The boy winced at the sudden invasion of light. He jumped to his feet, immediately quiet and attentive. The old man felt a bit of sadness, realizing he would never have a chance to continue training such a gifted student.

'You must run,' Robert said. 'The soldiers will kill you. There's a window out back, now go!'

No hesitation. No questions. Aaron did as he was told.

The floor was cold when Robert sat down in the center. He thought about grabbing the dying torch to use as a weapon, but against armored men, it would be a laughable ploy. A burly man stepped inside as others rushed past, no doubt searching for Aaron. He held manacles in one hand and a naked sword in the other.

'Does the king request my tutelage?' Robert asked, chuckling darkly.

Gerand stepped in beside him, hand wrapped in a cloth to soak up the blood. A bruise was already growing on his forehead.

'Stupid old man,' the advisor muttered, and he nodded to the soldier.

Robert closed his eyes, not wanting to see the butt of the sword as it came crashing down on his forehead, knocking him out cold.